THE
CITY

THE CITY

Stella Gemmell

ACE BOOKS, NEW YORK

THE BERKLEY PUBLISHING GROUP
Published by the Penguin Group
Penguin Group (USA) Inc.
375 Hudson Street, New York, New York 10014, USA

USA I Canada I UK I Ireland I Australia I New Zealand I India I South Africa I China

Penguin Books Ltd., Registered Offices: 80 Strand, London WC2R 0RL, England
For more information about the Penguin Group, visit penguin.com.

This book is an original publication of The Berkley Publishing Group.

Ace Books are published by The Berkley Publishing Group.
ACE and the "A" design are trademarks of Penguin Group (USA) Inc.

Library of Congress Cataloging-in-Publication Data

Gemmell, Stella.
The City / Stella Gemmell. — First edition.
pages   cm
ISBN 978-0-425-26418-8 (hardcover)
1. Imaginary wars and battles—Fiction.   2. Fantasy fiction.   3. Epic fiction.   I. Title.
PR6107.E45C58 2013
823'.92—dc23
2013000175

FIRST EDITION: June 2013

PRINTED IN THE UNITED STATES OF AMERICA

10   9   8   7   6   5   4   3   2   1

Cover art by Cliff Nielsen.
Cover design by Jason Gill.
Interior text design by Laura K. Corless.
Title page art © iStockphoto.com/ldeitman.

For Dave, of course.

PART ONE

The Deepest Dark

Chapter 1

First there was the darkness—heavy and choking, blue-black and tangible, filling the mouth and ears and mind. Then the smell—huge, as solid as rough stone beneath bare feet or a pillow over the face, suffocating thought. Finally, the sound of the sewer—the never-ending sigh of the stream, the drips and the splashes and gushing.

And the pitter-patter of sharp claws on wet brick.

The rat was big and old, and he was canny. He needed no light to follow the contours of the labyrinthine sewer in which he lived out his days. His paws detected the minute variations of texture on the bricks he raced along, high above the never-ending stream of life. The astonishing discrimination of his twitching nose told him how high the stream was flowing, the quality of its contents—a high, thin flood brought vegetation, small dead things, sometimes larger ones; a low thick turgid flow held its own treats for the discerning rodent—and the quality of the air, which was sometimes enough to make even a rat ill. He could tell by the air pressure on his sensitive ears whether he was running through a small tight tunnel, or where the ceiling opened high above him into one of the soaring vaults designed by a long-forgotten master architect, raised by a team of City builders, a wonder of mathematics, unseen for centuries, forgotten.

The rat could hear his friends pittering on the other side of the brick wall he followed, pattering in the next damp tunnel above him. But for a while he had outrun them all, following his nose's relentless demand.

The corpse was barely bloated, barely dead, the rigour of mortality only recently departed. It was naked save for a rag drifting round its neck, the skin pale and cold as winter sunrise. It had fetched up against the worn teeth of a broken metal grille, which for a short while resumed its long-abandoned role of stopping large objects from moving farther downstream into the deeper depths of the sewer.

A burgeoning of the stream would happen later that day, and the dead man would travel on alone—but for a while the rat kept him company.

The boy awoke with a start on the tiny ledge where he slept. He kicked out. The kick might have been an errant muscle or the deadend of a bad dream, but it was only a small movement. He'd been taking his rest on this ledge for long enough to know—even in sleep—he could not afford any sudden move, far less a sleepy roll, which would dump him into the stream of life unreeling endlessly below him. But when he went to his rest at night he was always dog-tired, dead to the world (dead, certainly, in the world's mind), and he lay unmoving, unconscious until it was time to wake.

Elija, who had been living in the sewer for four years, was ten years old.

He knew he held a privileged position. When he and his sister had first found sanctuary there their protector, an older boy, a redhead called Rubin, had to fight for their right to stay in that place of warmth and safety. Then for nights without number one of them had to stay on guard lest they be dumped into the stream by those jealous of their territory. But that was a long time ago; his little sister Em couldn't remember back that far. They had been in the sewers for longer than most of the Dwellers, and their status was, for the time, secure.

Elija shifted carefully, his bare foot detecting the variations of texture on the bricks until it hit an outcrop of broken cement, its contours better-known to him than the palm of his hand. He levered up to sitting. Watery light was filtering through broken stonework high in the roof above him. It wasn't light enough to see by, but it thinned the air and gave it a texture of motes Elija felt he could trap in his hand and keep for later in the day, deeper in the sewer, where it might be needed.

His memories were mostly of a crying woman and a hard-handed man, fist constantly raised, face red. Then there was the time of being alone with Em, running and hiding, always frightened. His dreams often contained blood, although he remembered none. The fear still lay on the edge of his consciousness, but he had no memory of it; he was glad to be safe.

Rubin explained to them about the stream. It was a small river which rose high above the City in the south, in a place of blue hills and silver trees under constant sun. It was called the Sheepwash there. It dived underground to take on its new guise as a sewer many leagues from the City. Goats dipped their feet in it in final tribute before it left the daylight forever.

The light was stronger now. Elija had been aware of the presence of his sister since he woke, but now he turned carefully and could see the curve of her dark head above the huddled lump of her body.

"Wake up, slugabed," he said quietly, with no real intention of waking her. She needed more sleep than he did. She didn't stir, although he could hear other movement around him as the Dwellers roused themselves for another day of darkness. There were stirring sounds, the occasional muttered exchange, a sudden echoing shout or imprecation to the gods of the Halls.

Elija stood and relieved himself into the stream, which now ran the height of a man below his ledge. He walked confidently along the narrow shelf and picked up the small bag of belongings which lay between him and Em at night. He sat down and opened it, taking out the piece of valuable sapphire moss they had found beyond the Eating Gate. The moss still smelled fresh and he tore a piece off and rubbed it into his face and hands, relishing the fast-fading sweetness, the tang Rubin had told him was called lemon. He was supposed to use it on his feet, he knew, to ward off foot-rot, which claimed so many of the Dwellers. But they only had a little left and he didn't want to waste it on his feet. He would see that Em did, though.

His hands clean, he foraged in the bag again and came up with strips of dried meat he'd bought from Old Hal. He chewed them slowly and thoroughly, coping stoically with the familiar cramps in his middle which flowed then ebbed.

He called again. "Wake up Em. Time to eat."

He kicked her gently and knew she was awake though she didn't move. From the sack he used for a pillow he took out the rags for his feet and spent the next few moments carefully winding them and rewinding them round ankles, heels, paying special care to the ankle bones, insteps, toes. In his years in the Halls he had got to know many people who were now dead, many of them from sicknesses arising in the feet.

Em was moving at last, going sleepily through her own morning rituals. Her brother did not speak to her and he focussed his eyes on far walls and the movements of distant Dwellers, giving her privacy.

It was as light now as it would get. Above him the vaulted dome was filled with a shining silver mist which never entirely went away but sometimes thinned and drifted in clouds. Hundreds of ledges ran along the curved walls, mostly above the height of Elija's shelf, mostly inaccessible and untenanted. The Dwellers called it the Hall of Blue Light. Elija and Emly called it home.

Rivers flowed in from three brick arches at the base of the dome, met in a maelstrom of water at the centre, then exited through a pitch-black maw towards the perils of the Eating Gate, the little Hellespont, Dark Water and, finally, to the ocean itself uncounted leagues away.

A harsh voice behind him brought Elija quickly to his feet.

"Lije. Em. Let's march."

And the new day began.

The leader of today's foraging party was called Malvenny. He was tall—a disadvantage in the Halls—and his face was long and thin, his nose hooked and bent sideways. Em said his eyes were green. She had the disconcerting habit of looking straight into peoples' faces, whereas Elija always addressed Malvenny at chest-level.

He followed the tall man closely, Em to his right, well within the sputtering light of Malvenny's torch. There were seven in the party, and only the dog-tail had a torch too. They carried plenty with them, of course, but used them sparingly in well-travelled Halls.

It was more than an hour's march to the Eating Gate, then more than that to their foraging-ground today. Malvenny had not told them where they were going—he was the leader, it was his privilege and he had the food—but Elija knew there would be poor pickings any closer. He had confidence in Malvenny. Elija walked briskly through the dark, watching Em's small feet and feeling her hot hand in his.

They reached the Malefactors' Cross, a sturdy bridge built of tarred rope and planks which led to the main highway. They crossed it—as Rubin used to say—with respect.

As he always did, Elija stopped in the middle for a moment to lean on the thick ropes and to look down into the Whithergo, a diversion from the main stream which, everyone knew, shortly plunged down a great hole deep into the fastnesses of the earth. Nobody went into the Whithergo tunnel. It led to only darkness and death.

"Get on there, boy," a gruff voice said behind him.

Elija watched his feet as he walked, and he thought about food, as he usually did if his brain wasn't busy elsewhere. He guessed what Malvenny was carrying—mealy cakes and dried meat, maybe some dried fruit if they were lucky. Once the tall man had given them some eggs, rock-hard and pickled in spicy vinegar, which they had all fallen on, delighted by something different to eat. Today Malvenny's sack looked sadly thin.

They stopped to rest at the Last Talking Point, beyond which the paralysing roar of the Eating Gate would make conversation impossible. They all sat, and Malvenny took the sack from his back and handed out fresh water and thin oatcakes. These were eaten ferociously and in silence. Elija felt his stomach grip them and he rubbed Em's back gently as she ate hers.

Malvenny returned his cup to his sack, cleared his throat and spat into the stream. "We're going to the Westering Shores." The others took the news without comment, except the man with the gruff voice, a newcomer whose name Elija didn't know.

"Where's that, man? How far?"

"It's a long way, there's good pickings, treasure sometimes."

"How far is far?"

"We cross the Eating Gate," Malvenny explained, "then take the rising Hall farthest on the far side. It's a long haul, but it's dry." He burrowed again in his sack as if to discourage more questions.

All he said was true. The shores rose for a long way, then plunged down again. As a result it was often drier than other places and pickings were found more easily. Even treasure, as Malvenny said. Em had found a silver and a piece of citrine glass there on the same day. But it was also true that it was more dangerous. If there was a flood, from a heavy storm in the distant outside, then the Westering Shores became a trap. By the time any Dwellers there realised the water was rising, it would be too late.

The gruff man, who now called himself Bartellus, had many names in the world above. The world had called him Shuskara. It had called him father, and son, and husband, and general. It had called him criminal and traitor. Now it called him deceased.

He thought the world was probably right as he followed two grimy children along a narrow slippery ledge through the darkness of the sewers deep beneath the City. The boy held tightly to the girl's hand, yet she walked on the side of the ledge nearest the sewer and Bartellus watched anxiously as her steps veered toward the stream then away to safety again. He was not sure the thin little boy had the strength to hold her if she slipped and fell. He wondered if *he* had.

The attrition rate among the City's soldiers, in their never-ending war with the world beyond the walls, was so high that the birth rate was plummeting. Children were becoming an increasingly rare sight. So each child should be precious, the old man thought, kept safe like a jewel, hoarded and nurtured. Not discarded, flushed into the sewers, or left as prey for evil men. He brought his hand to his chest in reflex invocation, praying to the Gods of Ice and Fire to overlook two such small children in this terrible place.

Elija didn't *like* the Eating Gate—it was dangerous to cross, it was so noisy your brain went dead, and the stench here was worse, if possible, than anywhere in the Halls—but he found it reassuring. It was a fixed point in his world. From the monstrous structure were measured the distances to all the other places under the City. Wherever he had been in his time as a Dweller, he could hear its cacophony, and know how far he was from home. Elija knew he would never get lost in the Halls, because of the Gate. He never went anywhere except as part of a foraging party, so he was unlikely to get lost anyway. Drowned, yes, caught by a trap-tide, crushed in a roof fall, murdered for pickings by a gang of reivers, killed by the emperor's patrols, but not simply lost. Expeditions never got lost, certainly not those led by Malvenny.

The Eating Gate was a high weir, built of timber and metal, dripping with water, slick with slippery weed. It rose taller than three tall men above the walking ledge, and measured the width of the stream, which at this point was more than thirty spans. He could barely make out the other side. The stream was running high today and Elija could not see the twenty great rolling barrels which formed the gate's machinery, but they were not far below the surface; the water was churning violently, heaving and rolling. They sucked in the stream high on the south side, pulverised anything floating in it between the turning barrels, then spat it out lower down. High on either side of the gate simple filters allowed the stream to flow continuously, should the tide be very full.

In the torchlight Elija could see the new man had his hands over his ears. Elija said, "You get used to it." He knew the man couldn't hear him, but he knew what he'd said. It was something you heard daily in the Halls. *You get used to it.*

Getting across the Eating Gate was no more dangerous than most exploits in the Halls. A wooden ledge crossed the structure a man's height below the top. It was reached on each side by spiral steps. It was slippery with water and rat droppings and the pale sinister plantlife that mysteriously flourished in the darkness and damp. You had to step carefully. Elija had seen a woman fall from the top of the Eating Gate once. A nasty death, but a quick one, crushed between the barrels in moments. Elija had no intention of falling.

A small hand pulled at his sleeve and he turned to see Em gazing at the top of the Gate, a rare smile on her heart-shaped face. Elija saw what she was staring at.

It was a gulon, a rare sight this deep into the Halls. The creature was walking casually along the top of the gate, stopping to look down at them, sniffing its way, then walking on, tail high. The company watched as it reached the end of the gate then padded lithely down the steps. It was a big thing, big as a pig, dark as the Halls themselves, with a sharp whiskery snout, crumpled ears and golden eyes. Its face was sharp, like a fox, but its body had feline grace. It sat and wrapped its bushy tail neatly round its paws and stared at them.

Em ran forward and crouched down in front of it, one grubby hand outstretched. The gulon stood and stepped back two deliberate paces, then stretched out its neck and hissed, showing strong yellow teeth. Elija was going to tell her not to get too close—you could die from a scratch down here. But the grey-haired newcomer strode forward and snatched up the little girl and put her down again next to Elija. Startled, Em looked about to cry, but then the familiar look of tired resignation came over her face. She held on to her brother's hand as the company passed wide of the watching creature and started up the winding stairs.

The gulon sat down again in a puddle of filth and started delicately washing its paws.

The company was more than a league's march beyond the Eating Gate before the noise of its machinery was sufficiently muffled to allow speech. The way was uphill and Malvenny signalled a halt, raising his torch. They stopped gratefully and were about to sit when Emly stepped forward to the edge of the ledge and stared across the stream. She turned to her brother and pulled at his sleeve, pointing to the other side.

Bartellus was holding a torch and, as he squinted through the thick air, he thought he could see a pale blur upstream. He lowered the torch and blinked and shifted his gaze back and forth slightly to focus his eyes.

"A corpus," commented a stooped old Dweller, not without relish. "Ay, that's a corpus." He nodded and looked around the company, seeking agreement.

Bartellus squinted again and could barely see what Em's sharp young eyes and the veteran's ancient ones had picked out. On the other side of the stream another, smaller, waterway joined it through a pitch-black tunnel, and at the junction there was a broken grille. The grille was broken in two halves, one fallen outward. Between the two halves a body had lodged. Bartellus could make out nothing of it, except an arm, or possibly a leg, stretched out, appearing and disappearing in the flow of the stream.

"Good," said Malvenny, "there'll be pickings."

He glanced around his team, then said, "You, new man, with me." He jerked his head. "Rest of you stay here." He set off without looking back.

Bartellus started up after him then, realising they had both the torches, turned back and thrust his burning brand into Anny-Mae's hand. When he turned again Malvenny was far ahead, just a bobbing point of light in the darkness. Bartellus caught up with him with effort and they continued on until the newcomer started to wonder if the leader knew where he was going. He had no doubt of the possible value of a corpse in the Halls. Where a copper pente could lead to a fight to the death, the chance of finding a gold tooth—perhaps several—was worth considerable risk.

They came to a break in the stream, where a mighty shifting of the land had broken the tunnel, moving it sideways, so the near side came close to the far side. A man could easily jump the gap, he thought. A man could easily jump the gap—if it wasn't dark, wet and slippery. And a slip of the foot didn't mean a hideous death.

Malvenny handed him the torch, took three steps back, then forward, and jumped lightly, landing rock-solid, his weight perfectly balanced. He turned back to Bartellus and gestured for him to throw the torch. Bartellus threw it carefully and the leader caught it nonchalantly. He stepped back.

Bartellus dismissed the image of the river of sewage beneath his feet, replacing it in his mind with a lush greensward. He jumped the stream easily, and by the time he landed Malvenny had turned and was already returning along the stream.

The corpse was that of a man. The body was bloated, so it was hard to judge if he was once fat or thin. His head was shaved and his skin decorated with the pale blue and green lines of tattoos. He was naked. A sad rag of clothing remained round his neck. Rats had been at him, Bartellus saw.

Malvenny squeezed through the broken grille and hunkered waist-deep at the man's head. He pulled open the mouth and peered quickly around, then stood up. "Tongue's cut out. No gold." He spat in the stream with venom. "Let's go."

Bartellus gazed at the corpse. It was an arm, lighter than the rest, that waved in the flowing water, waved in the direction of their little group which Bartellus could now see huddled on the opposite side of the main stream. The chest and back were covered with tattoos, lines that had faded, just as the colours of the skin had faded, until they looked like the lines on a map, a plan of campaign, thought the old campaigner.

Just as Malvenny was about to return through the gap in the grille, Bartellus stepped forward and squeezed through, forcing the leader to make room for him.

Tattoos were common enough, especially among the soldiery. Some carried pictures of spiders or panthers. That was the mark of the tribe. This man was a walking picturebook, his torso closely tattooed with birds and beasts and obscure signs. He even had tattoos on his scalp. Bartellus saw the man's hair had started to grow again in a dense stubble.

"Give me the torch." He held his hand up, but Malvenny said, "Time to move on."

Bartellus looked up. "Give me the torch!"

Malvenny paused. A Dweller for more years than he could count, he knew the movements of the stream and the times of the tides better than any man or woman. Without any compass he could calculate the trip to the Westering Shores and back precisely. When he said it was time to move on, it was.

But he realised the quiet-voiced newcomer could well break his neck if he refused. A long-time student of the practical, he handed over the torch, and watched as the older man bent again to the corpse.

There was an old scar, thick and white, high on the man's right shoulder, an S-shape which stirred a memory in Bartellus' mind. He studied it, frowning.

"Time to move on," said the voice behind him.

It was a brand, Bartellus realised. The memory stirred again, then disappeared, ungrasped. His memory was full of lacunae now. It worried him that whole episodes of his past had vanished into those gaps. The old soldier foraged in the pouch at his waist and took out a small sharp knife.

He looked up. "Do we come back this way?"

"Gods willing."

Bartellus paused, uncertain, then put his knife away and stood up. He looked down at the fading tattoos again, trying to commit them to his unreliable memory. Then he bent at the last moment and snatched the piece of cloth drifting round the corpse's neck. Malvenny looked at him oddly, but Bartellus nodded to the leader and they both climbed back through the ironwork grille. Malvenny waved to the waiting group on the other side of the stream, then set off uphill again. Bartellus paced thoughtfully behind him, the piece of cloth squeezed dripping in his fist.

Chapter 2

The long length of a season had passed since Bartellus was forced to retreat into the sewers, and he marvelled at the resilience of the Dwellers who had lived there for months, even years. He trudged along at the centre of their party, the two children in front of him, the little woman Anny-Mae at his side. The tunnel was high there, with vertical walls, and the foul stream ran in a deep channel. Even after a few days Bartellus found the smell endurable, and the nausea that at first had constantly cramped his stomach had faded.

Anny-Mae paused and beckoned, and he courteously bent his ear to her. "Nearly there," she told him cheerfully, beaming as if she were personally responsible for the proximity of their goal. And before long Bartellus felt the air around him lighten and the tunnel opened out, soaring high above their heads and widening on all sides. The light of the torches thinned and was lost in the deep expanses of gloom. Bartellus saw they were at the edge of a wide flat basin, where the main watercourse ran down the middle, leaving rolling banks of sludge on either side. The old soldier looked straight upwards, and for a moment found himself gripped with terror at the thought of the massive weight of the great City, bearing down on this shell of a sewer.

He heard a high thin squealing and saw a pack of huge rats flowing across the mudbanks, fleeing the unaccustomed light. He saw rats every day, they were constant companions in the Halls, but he had never seen such giant ones, or so many. "They're half blind," he had been told. "They can only tell light and dark, and they always flee the light." Somehow blind rats seemed more sinister.

He turned an ear to what Malvenny was saying. "Move quick as you like. We've got little time." The leader glanced meaningfully at Bartellus. "New man, stick with Anny-Mae. She'll tell you where you can't go. Stay away from the shallow vaults."

He waved a hand towards the darkest corner of the shores, dismissing them.

"What are the shallow vaults?" Bartellus asked the woman.

Her eyes were already fixed on the mud at her feet. "Over there," she explained, pointing, "the vaults beneath are crumbling like sweetcake. You'd fall through in a trice." She beamed up at him.

He glanced at where she was gesturing. "But, the children . . ." He could see the brother and sister already darting across the mudbanks searching for "pickings." An image of another world flashed across his mind of two other children, golden-haired, on a beach at sunrise, searching for crabs and shrimps in rock pools.

"Lije knows what he's doing," said the little woman. "They're lighter than

us, they can go safe. Everyone's afeard of it so there's good pickings." Her
sharp black eyes picked out the pain in his face and, misunderstanding, she
repeated kindly, "Young Lije knows what he's up to."

Bartellus found there was little for him to do. He held the torch, moving
it where she pointed, while the woman used a small rake, combing through
the sludge which lay in smooth undulating banks around them. She un-
hitched a flat sieve from the paraphernalia at her waist and sifted the mud,
picking over small objects unearthed.

Once she put up her hand and showed him a coin. He held the torch
flame close to it, but could make nothing of it. Her experienced fingers ran
over the dull surface. "Third Empire," she told him triumphantly, handing
it to him. "It's gold!" Then she was back to work, bent over, and he placed the
precious piece in a pouch. He wondered how they would divide their spoils.

Anny-Mae moved quickly, stopping occasionally to prod the handle of
the rake in the mudbank in front of her, testing the depth, the firmness of
the sludge. She pounced with pleasure on small things Bartellus would never
have spotted. She found several coins, though no more gold, half a broken
hinge, which she told him to pocket, and a knife handle. She found a metal
box, empty, which she discarded, and the leather cover to a book. She handed
that to Bartellus, perhaps thinking him a man of letters.

There were dead rats, and cats, and the half-eaten bodies of dogs washed
up on the shores. But they saw no more human corpses. Bartellus guessed
the layers of grilles stopped large bodies floating this way. He thought back
to the corpse and its tattoos. A memory nudged again at his brain, but he
failed to catch it and it fled away.

His thoughts were idling in the past when he realised the Dwellers all
stood listening. He could hear little above the sound of rushing water. Then
he heard it too—a far-distant banging as of a hundred saucepans being
struck like gongs.

"Rain!" shouted Malvenny, and the Dwellers started to hurry back the
way they had come, discarding precious sieves, rakes and trowels, carrying
only torches in their haste to get away.

Anny-Mae grabbed Bartellus' arm. Her face was anxious. "This shore
will flood in a trice," she told him. "We must scurry."

Bartellus saw the children were in front of them as they streamed back along the crumbling path, hurrying with care on the treacherous footing. "What was the noise?" he asked Anny-Mae's back.

"Dwellers high above," the woman told him, watching her steps, struggling as fast as she could on tiny feet. "They bang the drain covers when it rains. Warn us all."

Bartellus realised the stream they were following was rising as he watched. When they had travelled this way earlier it had been far below them. Now it was swirling just below the lip of the path, its surface foaming and roiling with grey froth and big bubbles which burst slowly and stickily. And he became aware they were still travelling down.

"This is downwards!" he cried, but Anny-Mae was too busy hurrying and watching her feet to answer him.

The children were quickly losing ground from the rest of the party, whose torches were flickering far ahead. The little girl suddenly slithered as her feet hit a slimy patch of pathway, and her legs went out from under her. She slid feet first towards the stream. Elija grabbed at her, but he was hampered by the torch he carried, and he missed and fell too. In the last moment, as she slipped helplessly to the edge, Bartellus snatched the girl's stick-like arm and pulled her up and into his chest. She was tiny, weighing less than a good sword. He looked into her white face. Her eyes were wide and unseeing, beyond terror and exhaustion.

The boy climbed to his feet and stopped in front of them, forcing Bartellus to halt. Anny-Mae pushed past, chasing the rest of the group, now gone from view. Elija glared up at Bartellus. The old soldier gazed down at him calmly, then said, "I will carry her. Let me help." Elija didn't move, and his face was set. Bartellus nodded his head the way they were going. "Move along, boy," he growled.

Elija turned and ran on, more quickly, and Bartellus raced to catch up with him, for the boy still held the torch.

When they caught up with the group, Bartellus' heart sprang into his mouth. They had arrived at the convergence of two mighty tunnels. Fresh water—he could smell it—thundered down a second drain, carrying lightly its burden of branches and other debris. It joined their rising sewer in a crash of tormented water roiling with debris.

A flimsy rope-and-plank bridge spanned the maelstrom. It was the only way. By the hectic torchlight Bart could see the water was foaming round the bridge, the drooping centre under water. Yet the first man was already making his way across, clinging to the ropes, dragging himself along, half drowned by the floodwater. The others were ready to follow him.

As Elija ran up, Malvenny thrust the boy onto the bridge, taking his torch. "Go, boy!" he shouted. Elija looked to his sister and hesitated, and another man thrust himself in front of him and jumped on the bridge, discarding his torch. Anny-Mae pushed the boy onto the bridge, then followed him, smacking him in the back. Elija cast a glance at his sister then grabbed the submerged ropes and started dragging himself across.

Malvenny, holding the last torch, yelled in Bartellus' ear. "The bridge'll go any moment!" he shouted. "When it does hold on to rope or wood. Don't let go!"

Bartellus stepped onto the bridge, which bucked and reared like a maddened cavalry horse. He felt the little girl's arms creep round his neck and tighten, and he grasped the ropes with both hands. Then he was submerged in the foaming water. In an instant all feeling left him. He could not breathe, could not tell which was up or down. He could not feel anything beneath his feet, or the girl's body against his chest, only rough rope under his hands.

Then the bridge gave way and he felt himself swept into darkness, a piece of flotsam in the turbulent water. He gripped rope and plank, then he squeezed his eyes shut and prayed for the life of the little girl.

In his dreams he often found himself in a lush green valley. On the faraway horizon grey mountains were capped with sparkling snow. He was on his knees in thick wet grass, each blade fat with drops of dew, and he ran his hands through its coolness. Then he would raise wet hands to his face and clean away the sweat and blood and the pain. He would stand then, and look around. There was no one to be seen, no beasts, no birds. The air was fresh, as if it had never been used. He wondered if it was the dawn of the world.

He had asked a fortune teller once whether the dream had meaning. The wizened old man, small as a child, had pitched his tent at the rear of an army as they waited to do battle, although Bartellus could not remember which army or which battle. The man did steady business throughout the night as frightened soldiers sought comfort before facing the new day.

"The valley is where you were born, general," the old man had said to him, grinning with ruined teeth. "The meaning is clear. Green speaks of fertility, and the valley represents a woman. Your birth was blessed by the gods. You will live long, have many sons and return to the valley before you die." He glanced over Bartellus' shoulder, already seeking the next customer's copper.

But the general stayed seated and scowled. "Your words are not clear to me, old one," he said. "Is the valley my mother, or is it where I was born?"

"Both," the oldster replied smoothly. "The green valley . . ."

"For," Bartellus cut across his words, "I was born on the desolate plain of Garan-Tse, in the midst of the Third Battle of the Vorago. My mother's cries were echoed by the screams of dying men and there was only blood and mud for leagues in every direction."

The old man squinted at him irritably. "It is a representational valley," he explained. "All men are born in blood and pain. But you are surrounded by fertility. You have sons?" Bartellus nodded. "And you are wealthy?"

When Bartellus nodded again, the old man shrugged. "Then you are a lucky man."

"Most men would not call me lucky," Bartellus growled.

"You are a general, general," the fortune teller argued mildly. "And you are alive. Most men would not call you *un*lucky."

A million drains sucked the rain down, channeling it through the ancient system of pipes and ducts, culverts and channels, drawing it deep beneath the City. Most of the water made it through the wide drains into the great river Menander which drove through the City's bowels. A weight of rain filtered through layers of the City's history, deep down to where the sewers were crushed and broken, squeezed flat by the weight of time. A thousand branches, washed into culverts and through broken grilles, scoured the walls of the sewers, washing away the dirt and debris of years, and for a while, a few days, the Halls were cleansed of filth and the smell was of grass and good earth.

On its perch on top of the Eating Gate, the gulon stretched its paws and laid its scrawny length along a piece of timber. Through slitted eyes it watched as scores of Dwellers were swept under the rolling barrels of the gate and pulverised. It closed its eyes and slept.

The boy Elija was dragging himself step by step across the thrashing bridge when it was torn apart by the stormwaters. His only fears were for his sister. I cannot rescue her if I die, he thought, and he clung desperately to a wooden plank and tried to survive. For a long time he was battered and flung about by the water, then at last he stopped moving and he realised he could breathe. He gratefully took a painful lungful of air, his thin chest sore and bruised. Opening his eyes, he found he was in total darkness. He was upside down and entangled in ropes, perhaps the ropes of the bridge. He could still hear the crash of water close by. Anxiously he tried to move his arms and legs. Everything ached, but nothing appeared broken. He could move, but he could not free himself. And if I *do* get free, he thought, where will I go in the dark?

Trussed like a goat for sacrifice, hanging helpless from the wall of a sewer in total darkness deep in the bowels of the City, the little boy started to cry.

When Bartellus rose to consciousness he realised instantly that the atmosphere had changed. Gone was the stifling foetid odour that had pressed on his senses for wretched days beyond counting. Now the air was lighter, and smelled of wet hay, rotten fruit, smoke and, faintly, flowers. He lay on his back, his body an old wooden raft barely floating in a sea of pain. There was a weight on his chest and, when he opened his eyes and stretched his neck, he saw it was the little girl, motionless. He thought she was dead, but when he tried to sit up his involuntary groan woke her and she scrambled away from him, eyes huge in her pinched white face.

Then the girl gazed up and around her, and for the first time it occurred to Bartellus that he could see. They were in a round stone chamber. All around torches in brackets cast moving shadows on the dripping walls. There were black and white pictures on those walls, faint and faded, of soaring birds and flying feathers. Bartellus and the girl were on a sturdy ledge high above the stream, which glided in a deep channel through the centre of the chamber. Bartellus laid his head back and rested for a while, watching the birds as they flickered eerily in the torchlight. He could do no more.

Then he heard a whisper of sound and lifted his head again. Floating like a mirage in the deserts of the south, a cloaked and hooded figure walked towards them through the yellow light. All his soldier's instincts deadened, Bartellus lay vulnerable as the figure approached and stopped before them. The old man saw the tip of a sword blade below the lower edge of the cloak. He thought he ought to move, to defend himself and the child, but he had no power.

"You are not dead," said a woman's impassive voice, echoing a little off the wet stone. Bartellus was uncertain if this was intended to reassure or was merely a statement of fact.

"We were caught by the stormwaters," he explained, noting as he said it that an explanation was scarcely necessary. Understandably, the woman did not reply. She loomed over him silently. Her presence was unsettling. He sat up with difficulty. His whole body seemed bruised and his back screamed with pain.

"This girl needs dry clothes, food in her belly and fresh water to drink," he told the woman.

She took a moment to answer. Then she said coolly, "I am sure you are right. But why are you telling me?"

Frustration overcame his exhaustion, and a rare spark ignited in his chest.

"The wretches who live here are the dregs of the City," he said. "Yet in my experience, young woman, none of them needs it explained why a half-drowned child needs food and drink and comfort! If you can't give this girl the help she needs, lead us to whoever can."

His words sounded pompous, even to him, and the child started to cry. Bartellus realised helplessly that he had frightened her.

The woman gazed at him unmoved. "This is not a market stall, or an orphanage, or a hospital, *old man*."

This time he held his temper. "No," he told her reasonably, "but you are well enough fed, by the look of you, and there is clearly organisation here. I cannot believe you cannot bring this child and a plate of food together. Is this so much to ask?"

"Why do you think there is organisation here?" the woman asked.

He nodded to the torches. "Elsewhere in the Halls any unguarded torch would be stolen within moments. There is authority in this place, and one that is respected."

She nodded in the darkness of her hood. "Very well. Come, child," she said, turning away and walking back across the bird-haunted chamber.

The little girl looked to Bartellus, who smiled reassuringly, and she trailed after the woman, glancing back often to see the old man was still there.

When the two had disappeared Bartellus raised himself up with an effort, marvelling that he had no broken bones. He walked to the edge of the stream, where he relieved himself long and luxuriously. Feeling remarkably cheered by this simple act, he followed the woman and child.

As he passed through the circle of torches darkness closed in again, and he blinked the grime out of his eyes until he saw a faint glow. Light was filtering through an archway to his right. There was a barred gate, open, and he passed through it, following the glow until he came to a round chamber lit not by the acrid light of torches but by soft candles, dozens of them. He squinted. All around were stone pillars, their capitals carved in the shapes of perched and watching birds. The room was very old and the stone stares of the carvings weighed down on him.

There was no sign of the girl, but the woman sat on the edge of a wide wooden table. She had thrown her hood back, and her hair was dark red in the torchlight. He saw her face was young, but lines of experience were already gathering at the corners of her eyes, which were the violet of flowers. An unsheathed sword lay across her thighs.

"Where is this place?" he asked her.

"The Dwellers call it the Hall of Watchers. They fear to come here. They fear my colleagues and me." She laid her hand idly on the sword's hilt.

His dislike of her rose quickly again, and he told her, "If your colleagues are anything like yourself, they probably fear sharp tongues more than they fear sharp swords."

She scowled at him. "First you ask for our hospitality, then you insult me?"

He glanced around the room, as if uncaring of her words or sword. On another table lay a jug of water and a platter of meat and biscuits. His stomach lurched with craving. He let his eyes pass casually over the food. He would starve to death before showing his need to this odious girl.

"You are thin-skinned and quick to anger," he commented mildly, as if it was of no consequence. "If you were one of my soldiers I would not let you bear a fruit knife, far less a sword."

The woman leaped from the table, blade in hand, but a soft voice said, "Indaro."

Bartellus looked round. A newcomer stood in a narrow archway half concealed by a wall hanging. Her long hair was white as ice, and her face was lined. Like the girl Indaro, she wore a close-fitting leather tunic. But while the younger woman wore leather leggings, like a cavalry officer, the elder wore a long midnight blue skirt above shiny boots. Round her shoulders was draped a brown greatcoat. On her breast silver gleamed.

"He is right, girl. You are too eager to take offence," she said. Indaro made no reply, but at a nod from the woman she stalked out of the room.

"If she were one of your soldiers, general, she would be dead long since," the woman said when Indaro had gone.

Bartellus felt his chest tighten. For all the horrors and deprivations of the Halls, he had become used to being an anonymous old man, no longer harried and chased.

She walked across to the table and poured a glass of water. She handed it to him. She was tall and graceful and he wondered who, in the name of the Gods of Ice and Fire, she could be.

"Do I know you?" he asked.

She looked at him curiously. "Do you not?" she answered. Then, "I am Archange Vincerus. What do you call yourself?"

He hesitated. "Bartellus," he said finally.

"A good name. And common enough. Particularly among our men at arms." She turned and picked up the platter of food and handed it to him. He took a biscuit and crunched into it. The surge of flavour and sweetness in his mouth made his head spin, and he slowly took a sip of water.

"Archange. I know that name." He cursed his treacherous memory, in which his experiences swirled and drifted, ebbed and flowed like mist over ice. "Who are you, lady, and why are you living in this sewer?"

"I do not live here. I merely visit," she said sharply.

Bartellus was suddenly tired of these women and their haughty ways. Why did he care what they thought of him? He took the platter of food and, sitting at the table, started to eat with unashamed need. She sat too and there was silence for some time as he devoured the meat and more of the biscuits. He drank two tall glasses of fresh water. It tasted like morning dew on grass.

Then, ignoring his companion, he closed his eyes and leaned his head back against the high-backed chair. He found his mind was clearer. He allowed himself to think of those other two children, his sons, he had seen waving goodbye in a sunlit garden as he left them for the last time. Joron, the elder, was waving above his head a wooden sword his father had made him just that day. The toddler, Karel, was waving excitedly too, following his brother's lead, but he was too young to understand what was happening. He stopped waving when he spotted one of the new puppies. He toddled over to it, and Snowy the white hound wandered across the garden to guard her pup. Bartellus' last sight of his smallest son was with his chubby arms round the patient hound's neck, his father forgotten.

Tears coursed down his face.

His wife, Marta, had not been outside to see him off. She lay in bed, exhausted in the last stages of a hard pregnancy. He had kissed her goodbye, and promised to be home for winter. He had no real fears for her; her two previous labours had been difficult, but their sons were born healthy, and she had regained her strength within days. He was sorry he would not be there to see his daughter born. He was sure it would be a daughter this time.

He could not remember kissing Marta goodbye. He was certain he had done so, for he always did. But he had been distracted by the coming campaign, and he had kissed her without thinking, a casual buss on the cheek. The last kiss.

Then he had ridden away with his old friend Astinor Redfall, who had come to summon him. He did not know, on that shining morning, that he was being taken to his brief trial and awful punishment. He did not know then, or for more than a year afterwards, that within the hour his family all lay dead, his longed-for daughter spilling from a great gash in Marta's belly.

Chapter 3

When Bartellus opened his eyes again, the woman was sitting at the table with him, a glass of water to hand, her gaze unfocussed. She had seen his tears but he found he did not care. He wondered how much time had passed.

"Have we met before?" he asked.

"Just once. A long time ago."

"Why did you rescue us?" he asked.

"Perhaps you were swept here by the floodwaters."

"The floodwaters which considerately left us together, the child safely beside me, in your antechamber?"

She sighed. "It is a sad reflection on your life that you ask why someone should save another from drowning."

He knew she was familiar to him. He racked his mind but nothing came to him. So much of his history had been washed away in blood and pain. Memory was a sly and fickle friend to him now. There were times when he could not bear the visions of his wife smiling up at him, his boys waving goodbye in the sunlight, but *that* memory pursued him relentlessly and remained crystal clear. Yet his days of glory, times he wanted to savour for they were never-changing, would never change whatever happened in the future, these shimmered and shifted, shifting sands in his tired brain.

"Are there others here like Indaro?" he asked Archange.

"Why?"

"Because she is fit and strong and claims to be a warrior. Why is she not in the army? Is that what this place is, a sanctuary for cowards who do not want to fight for their City?"

"People escape to the sewers for many reasons—they are not all cowards," she replied pointedly. "But there are easier ways for women to avoid military service. They can become pregnant. No woman carrying a precious child is allowed to serve, as you know, general."

He could not allow that to pass twice. "I am not a general."

She shook her head in a gesture of impatience. "Then you should not speak so casually of *your* soldiers. No one would take you for a scribe or an innkeeper.

"Besides," she added, smiling, "you *look* like a general." The years fell from her face.

For the first time in many days he realised he probably stank. Yet he felt comfortable, sitting in a chair with a full belly and, he had to admit, a pleasant companion. The air was warm and his clothes had dried for the first time in days. He sat back and looked around. The room was of cold stone, and the tables and chairs simple, but they were made of rich woods, and the wall hanging was heavily embroidered with fierce beasts and strange flowers. In the bottom corner a gulon stared balefully out at him.

"We are still in the sewers here, in the Halls," he said, "but you do not come and go through the tunnels. So there must be an exit to fresh air?"

She shook her head. "This is called the Hall of Watchers," she volunteered. "Centuries ago, perhaps hundreds of centuries, it was part of a great palace. Then the palace fell, or there was an invasion or an earthquake, I don't remember, and the ancient palace disappeared under a new one. And then another. There are many layers of old cities, most of them destroyed. But some buildings remain intact, like this, deep in the ground. We are very far below the present City."

"That is the first of my questions you have answered."

"I am not here to answer your questions."

"Why *are* you here?"

He caught her eye and they both smiled.

"We are both too old for such prevarications," she told him. She sighed again and shrugged the greatcoat off her shoulders. It was a silver crescent moon glimmering on her breast. "I can do nothing more to you than the world has already done."

They were silent for a while, then she offered, "You ask about my friend Indaro. She was at the First Battle of Araz."

Vile memories danced in his mind. "So were thousands of others," he replied. "Tens of thousands." Including me, he could have told her.

"Just a child really, gently raised." She looked at him. "Many people believe women should not be fighting this war."

"I am not one of them," he told her, not entirely truthfully. "The City would have been lost long since without its women warriors."

She shook her head sadly. "The men guard our City's past," she quoted. "The women guard our future."

It was a familiar argument. "If the City is lost then no amount of children and babies will help us," he retorted.

"The City *is* lost. It has been lost long since."

"Not while our armies defend it still."

In his heart he knew the City was reaching a vital crossway. The enemy cities were subjugated, their armies conquered, fortresses taken, yet still they fought on. The City was besieged, albeit from a distance. And it was casting its women into the war machine in a last desperate throw to win the war, at the risk of future population catastrophe.

"The City is great," he said stoutly. Although he knew it was not true and his words echoed emptily in the stone chamber.

"The City is dying, Bartellus. How can you spend a single day down in the Halls with the other Dwellers and see lives lived in absolute wretchedness, then claim that the City is great?" Her tone was calm, her face grave.

"The City is *all* its people, including the Dwellers," he argued. "How can *you* spend time with them, if indeed you do, lady, and not see their strength, their toughness, the uncompromising spirit that has helped the City survive centuries of war?"

"I cannot believe," Archange said, "that you are using the Dwellers as an argument for the City's greatness. No great city, by definition, should have people living in its *sewers*. Any city should be judged, at least in part, on how it looks after its poor, its frail, its dispossessed."

As so often in the past, he found he was arguing something he did not entirely believe. They were circling around a subject which was never spoken aloud by the wary. Yet in this hidden place he could bring himself to say the words, "The Immortal is pursuing this war. It will end only if the emperor wills it."

She eyed him gravely. "People who have told him that have been cruelly punished."

She took a sip of water, then said, "We are talking about two different things. If the City is great it is due to the courage and resilience of its people. But the war has brought it to the brink of ruin. As you say, it is the emperor who is responsible for that war. But he will never end it."

"How can you be so sure of that? And if Araeon himself will not end the war then Marcellus could."

She frowned at him. "Marcellus is loyal. He would never act against his emperor."

He did not pursue it, conscious that their words were beyond treason-ous. But it was good to have a conversation again, to think about something other than where his next food was coming from, or how badly his skin itched from the lice-bites, or how he could exist for one more day without falling into madness and throwing himself into the river of death.

Eventually she said, "When my daughter was small I told her the story of the gulon and the mouse. Do you know it?"

"Of course. A child's tale."

"The gulon and the mouse go on a long journey together. When they reach a far city the mouse says to the gulon, 'Let me sit on your shoulder so I can see this city and not be trampled underfoot by its people.' So the gulon picks him up and puts him on his shoulder. But then the people of the city think the mouse is the master and the gulon only the servant, and they point at them and laugh. The gulon is angry and plucks the mouse from his shoul-der and puts him down and the mouse is immediately squashed under someone's heavy foot. And the gulon has lost his best friend for the sake of his pride.

"And do you know what my seven-year-old daughter asked me when she heard this story?"

"Tell me."

"She asked, 'What is a far city?' When I told her it was another city a long way away she was baffled, for she believed this city is the whole world."

"Your daughter was not alone. Many people believe this. You have to see the City from outside to fully understand. Few people do, except its soldiers."

"Yet everyone knows we are at war."

He shrugged. "The enemy, the Blues, have been demonised, necessarily. People cannot fight a war, suffer its deprivations for so long, if they believe the enemy are human beings just like them. They think they are subhuman, incapable of building cities."

She shook her head but did not reply, and at last he asked, "How old is your daughter now?"

But she did not answer him, merely stared at the glass in her hand.

He said, "We saw a gulon in the Halls, not long before the storm broke."

"Where?"

"At what they call the Eating Gate. Do you know of it?"

"Certainly. It is an important cog in the underground machine. It is a long time since a gulon has been seen that deep in the Halls. It is a symbol of the City to some. They consider it a good omen to see one."

He snorted. "Someone should tell that to the gulon. It was an omen of death and despair for many Dwellers this day."

He thought of their doomed hunting party crossing the high weir, and his mind moved on to the corpse they had found. Biscuit crumbs lay thick on the table in front of him and he gathered them together, then spread them into a smooth layer. He drew a sign in the crumbs. "Do you know this mark?" he asked the woman.

She looked at him curiously. "An *S*? What of it?"

"A backwards *S*. I saw it on the shoulder of a corpse earlier."

"A soldier? Tattoos are common among the soldiery."

"Yes. He was covered in pictures. Like a child's storybook." She smiled, and Bartellus added, "It was not a tattoo, but a brand, burned deeply into the skin."

"Foreign slaves are sometimes branded."

"But there are few slaves left in the City now. And they are mostly young women from the east. This was a man, pale and middle-aged. Well-fed."

"Floating corpses always look well-fed," she replied. "Is it important?"

"Probably not. A part of my mind thinks it is. My memory is not what it was. But I have seen it somewhere before." He added, "Even his scalp was tattooed."

"With pictures?"

"No. They were small marks. Hundreds of them. They looked foreign. Perhaps you are right. I could make nothing of them."

"Where did you find him?"

Bartellus shrugged. "I've no idea. I was in a hunting party led by other people. I didn't know where I was then. I don't know where I am now."

He sighed. A few moments previously he felt he could stay there forever, but his mind, his soldier's mind, was returning as ever to his duty. Its weight was creeping back onto his old shoulders.

"If the child has been fed I will take her and go," he told the woman. "We must look for her brother. If we survived the floods he might still be alive too."

The little girl was spooning food into her mouth as quickly as her hand would move. Her dark eyes darted back and forth from the doorway to the plate. She was afraid someone would come in and take it away from her.

After a while she noticed the taste. It was sticky and sweet. There were hard bits in it. She spat some out into her palm and, putting the spoon down, poked her finger into the mess. The hard bits were dark and wrinkly. She put one in her mouth. It was so sweet it made her teeth hurt. It tasted like the smell of rotten pears.

She was about to put the rest of the food back in her mouth, when a memory came back to her of the last time she ate at a table with a spoon. A sharp voice had told her to wash her hands before she sat down. She looked at her grubby palm and rubbed her hand on her dress—it used to be her best pink dress, she thought sadly. Her palm looked a bit cleaner, but bits of food now lay on the floor. She slid off the chair and pushed the mess under the edge of the rug. Then she rubbed both palms on her dress again, until they were fairly clean.

Emly climbed back on the chair and ate some more food, now savouring its taste and texture. She was very thirsty. The red woman had placed a glass and a big pitcher of fresh water in front of her, and she looked at it longingly. But she knew she was not strong enough to pour water out of the pitcher without spilling it all over the clean table.

The cramps in her tummy came harder than usual and she rocked and moaned a little until they passed. Then she ate some more.

At last she looked around her. She was in a huge room which stretched off into the dark. On the stone floor were coloured rugs. She eased herself down off the chair and squinched her bare toes in the blue rug beneath her. It was soft as kittens' fur.

Looking at the door again uncertainly, she trotted over to the nearest wall. There were lots of wooden shelves rising up to the ceiling. A strong smell came to her nose, like the scent of smoke. She put out her hand and found smooth warmth under her fingers. Something toppled over with a flat thud, and she jumped, then she realised they were the backs of books, lots of them on every shelf. She had seen books before, though she had never seen so many. She ran her fingers over the bumpy gold lettering. She could not read, though Lije could. Thinking of her brother made her tummy feel empty again. Tears squeezed out under her eyelids.

"Don't touch them, girl!"

She spun round and saw the red woman in the doorway. Her face was stern, and sparks seemed to fly off her. Emly rubbed her hands on her dress again and remembered the food under the rug. She wondered guiltily if the woman knew it was there.

"Put these on," she woman ordered. She held some dark garments. Emly obediently went over to her. Without hesitation the woman pulled the little girl's dress off over her head. Rigid with embarrassment, Emly stood there under her chilly gaze. She had lost her drawers a long time ago, but she had not told anyone for fear of getting into trouble. Now this woman would tell her off.

But the sparks seemed to die down a little, and the woman said more kindly, "These are too big for you, but put them on and I'll cut them to size."

Emly scrambled into the long tunic, which came down below her knees, and the trousers, which flopped in folds round her ankles. The woman had a pair of scissors and she cut the trouser legs. Then she deftly plaited the remains into a belt to hold the trousers up. The girl wriggled around in her new clothes. The fabric felt warm and dry against her skin. She looked regretfully at her pink dress discarded on the floor. She saw it was dark grey now.

Kneeling, the woman looked up into the girl's face. Emly saw her eyes were like flowers.

"That's better," the woman said gently.

Then she stood, and the briskness came back in her voice. "Have you eaten enough?" She glanced at the full pitcher of water. "Not thirsty?"

Emly stared at her dumbly, then the woman shrugged and took her by the hand and led her out of the book room. They went down a wide flight of high stairs, Emly jumping down one at a time, then the woman opened a narrow wooden door and they went down another long flight of stairs, winding round and round until Emly felt dizzy. Finally they came out in a corridor lit by torches. At the end of it was the room where the old man was talking with another woman. Emly wondered if it was his wife. She was glad to see him again. Perhaps he would take her back to Elija.

"If the child has been fed I will take her and go," he was saying. "We must look for her brother. If we survived the floods then he might still be alive too." Then he turned to her. Emly thought he looked older than she had ever seen him. He smiled, but his face was pained as if his tummy hurt too.

The old woman said, "We are not, as Indaro said, an orphanage. But perhaps you should leave the child with me rather than take her back into the sewer."

"Why would I? I know nothing about you. You have answered few of my questions. Why would I trust you?"

"Are you the child's father, or her grandfather perhaps?"

"No. But I saved her life. In the army, if you save a brother's life, then you take responsibility for it. It is like that with this child. And I owe it to her to find her brother."

"You are not in the army and she is not a soldier." The old woman turned to her. "Would you like to stay with us, child, or go with this man?" she asked. Em immediately trotted over to Bartellus and thrust her small hand into his huge one.

"First we will find her brother," the old man said, "then we will leave this place, all three of us."

Then together they left the room and went back into the dark.

Chapter 4

The boy's dreams were of darkness and fear. No green valleys or blue skies for Elija—he dreamed of the world he knew, and he whimpered in his sleep.

When he awoke he was still in the nightmare. The darkness was complete. He opened and closed his eyelids a few times but could see no difference. One leg, caught underneath him in the tangle of ropes and wood, had gone dead. He dragged on the rope above to raise himself and free the limb. The ropes creaked and he heard wood cracking, but he did not care. Death in the stream rolling unseen beneath him would end his pain and terror. But the bridge held and he eased his leg into a new position where, after a while, it started to throb as blood flowed back through it.

He felt around with one foot until it found a loop of rope which felt secure. He tried to put his full weight on it, but it lurched sideways. It was only then he realised he was lying with his head down in the net of ropes. His tormented body had lost track of which way was up. He reached around and his hand found a piece of rough wood. He pulled on it and it came away. He heard it plunge into the stream. Carelessly he reached out and found another piece. He rested his weight on it and it stayed in place. His spirits lifted a little and he tried to pull himself up. But his body was fixed in place and, hard as he tried, he could not move. He could feel his heart beating wildly in his chest. Moving his hand he found a thick hawser pressed across his body. It was firmly fixed in place by the tangle of ropes and, much as the boy wriggled and struggled, nothing would shift it.

Elija cried for a while, then dozed.

He remembered when he was very young he slept in a warm bed in a room next to a chicken run. A woman with red eyes and rough hands would sing to him, a song with words he did not understand, but which made him think of sunlight and warm breezes. The chickens would wake him each morning with their chucking and grumbling.

He thought of Emly and wondered where she was. He knew she was safe somewhere, hiding until he found her. She was good at hiding. When they were small she would find nooks to hide in where even he could not find her. But she hated to be alone, and would always give herself away. "Here I am!" she'd cry, and come running out to show Elija the clever place she'd found. Later she learned to stay quiet and not give them away. Later still she stayed quiet all the time, and she had not spoken to Elija for more than a year. Although he had thought and thought about it, he could not remember the last words she said to him.

He wondered where Rubin was. In his mind's eye he imagined Rubin finding him, rescuing him as he had before, giving him food and fresh water, telling Elija of all his adventures since they last met.

They had first met in the Pedlar's Hall, a wide crowded place where the two small children had wandered in the hope of finding food in their early days. It was a dangerous place, Elija later discovered, where children were bought and sold, or often just snatched away.

A stout man with fat arms and only one eye had approached the children in the semi-darkness. "You want food, children?" he asked, and the dead weight of his voice made Elija clutch Emly close and move away, not speaking, not looking at the man.

"They are taken, good sir," said a new voice. Elija looked round and saw an older boy walking quickly towards them, his bushy hair flaming red in the torchlight.

The stout man scowled. "You've got their papers?"

"Certainly, sir. See." The lad thrust a fat wad of paper at the man, and whispered to Elija, "Do not go with him, friend. He is an evil man. Come with me."

Before Elija could decide, the red-haired boy picked Em up and ran with her across the Hall, dodging and weaving through the crowds. Elija ran after them. Too late, the man threw down the useless paper and yelled. He started to chase them, but they were quick and he was too fat.

Rubin took them through a maze of tunnels to a smaller well-lit Hall where there was food laid out on tables. No one sought payment, or shouted if they helped themselves, and they could eat as much as they liked. After Rubin disappeared Elija was never able to find the Hall again, and when he told other Dwellers of it they laughed at him, or called him mad.

Rubin watched with patient amusement as they ate their fill. Finally, when the youngsters had had enough, "I am called Rubin and I come from Paradise."

Elija munched and swallowed, reluctant to let the taste of the food leave his mouth, although he had eaten all he could manage and more.

The red-haired boy grinned. "And now, you see, you tell me your names and we can be friends."

"I am Elija, and this is Em. Emly." Feeling this was inadequate, Elija added, "I do not know where we come from." When Rubin nodded sympathetically, he asked, "Where is Paradise?"

"In the far east of the City," Rubin told him. "It is a place of great beauty. All the men are tall and the women kind, and they live in high golden towers. The sun always shines there, even at night, and every boy owns a dog. It is the law."

Elija looked at him suspiciously, fearing he was being laughed at. "Then why are you here?" he asked.

"To save you from the man."

Elija frowned. The food filling his belly was making his brain weary.

The older boy said, "I see what you are thinking, Elija, and you are clearly a person of intelligence. You are asking yourself why you should trust me. You do not know me, any more than you know the one-eyed man with the very short arms. I might be planning to sell you to reivers."

But he did not sell them to evil men. He showed them where to find food and fresh water, and the sapphire moss, whom to approach to find work, and whom to avoid, the safest places to sleep and the parts of the Halls to stay clear of. At last they found the prized ledge in the Hall of Blue Light. And, for a while, they were safe.

But Rubin vanished one day. Elija liked to think his friend had returned to the fabled land of Paradise, and he hoped to follow. He remembered only that it was in the east of the City. But he was told the Halls and shores to the east were the most dangerous, and only the despairing and those hunting the death gods went there.

In the darkness of the sewer Elija came awake again. He could hear only the sighing of the stream, the creak of ropes and his own breathing. Then he held his breath and listened. At last, over the sound of his own heart pumping noisily in his ears, he heard voices; the rumbling of a man speaking, the shriller voice of a woman. Then a third chimed in, gruff and harsh. They were far-off, and Elija could barely hear them, but he was certain. Casting away his terrors, he took an eager breath.

"Help!" he yelled. "Help me! I'm down here! Please help me!"

There was silence for a moment, then the voices came closer. His eyes detected a faint blur of light.

It seemed an eternity until the remains of the bridge were hauled up, and for a while he feared he would slip from his prison of rope and wood and fall. He held on tightly and cried out as the jolting hurt his bruised side.

"It's a boy," a woman said. "Half dead."

Elija felt a hard hand grip his arm and he was dragged upwards and dumped on the path above. His legs had no strength and he collapsed like a string puppet. His unaccustomed eyes smarted at bright torchlight, but he squinted and could make out several faces looking down at him.

"Thank you," he said. "I feared I was going to die."

The faces glanced at one another, then the woman said, "What a little gentleman. Your ma taught you to say thank you." She laughed and the others grinned. "Come on, lad," she went on, picking him up and setting him on his feet. "We're not staying here. You can come with us."

Elija tried to tell them he was too tired to walk, but they ignored him, and he awkwardly fell into step with the woman as they carried on. "My name is Elija," he told them, but no one replied.

They walked for a long time, through tunnels large and small. Mostly they travelled downwards, with the stream, keeping the water to their right, the rough, dripping wall to their left. Elija could recognise none of it, although at one time he heard a sound in the distance he thought might be the Eating Gate, but it was too far away to be sure. They climbed for a while then went down a long flight of crumbling stairs, slick and treacherous, a dark chasm to their right. They kept going down, and Elija thought he had never been so deep in the Halls before. After a while, his brain foggy and his legs weak, he wondered if they were still in the Halls, or in some foreign country he knew nothing of. He tried to remember what Rubin had told him of distant Halls, for Rubin was a mine of information, a gushing never-ending fount of it, and the little boy had only kept a few cupfuls of what he had been told in the long days while Rubin talked.

The woman, carrying a torch, and Elija were at the head of the party. He glanced at her from time to time. She was wrapped in many layers of ragged clothes, like all other Dwellers. But her feet were encased in heavy boots, a prized rarity in the Halls, and Elija thought she must be an important person. He tried to look round from time to time to see how many people were following. He could glimpse many torches and thought there were maybe twenty. Once in a while he heard a child's high cry or a groan, then the woman would turn to him and grin at him. He had no idea what the grin meant.

At last, when he felt he could not move another step, the woman stopped and told him he could rest. They were in a narrow corridor, rough-hewn and dry, and the boy fell to the floor, exhausted. He dozed for a while and when he opened his eyes again several people were sitting around him eating. His stomach growled painfully.

He licked dry lips. "Please. Can I have some food?"

They all glanced at the woman, who nodded, and a man gave Elija a flat round of grey bread. He ate it eagerly, looking round at his companions. The woman was tall and stout, and her hair was long and grey, her face red and stern. Her name was Badger. The man with the deep rumbling voice was a giant, taller than any Elija had seen in the Halls, with shoulders and arms like slabs of meat. He kept looking at Elija and smiling at him, revealing a few grey teeth.

"Please," the boy offered nervously, "I would like to go back to the Hall of Blue Light. I want to find my sister. She was lost in the storm."

There was a long pause and he thought they would ignore him again. Then Badger leaned towards him and bared her teeth. Elija thought of the gulon and its wide yellow smile.

"The Hall of Blue Light, eh?" she said. "It just so happens we're going there. In a couple of days. We have business there. We will take you back to your sister, boy."

As she spoke Elija saw a fat louse run out of her hairline and down her face and dive into the plait of grey hair. He imagined the plait was teeming, heaving, crawling with insects. But he tried to smile at her, grateful for her kindness.

He wondered if the old gruff man and Anny-Mae had got home safely. And if Em was with them. For the first time since the storm he slept peacefully.

When he awoke he was being dragged to his feet and they were on the move again. He wondered how far they would go this time, but the food in his stomach had given him some strength, and he marched alongside Badger, looking up at her occasionally, thankful that he had found a friend. Again they travelled without stopping for many hours. At one time they all had to squeeze through a low narrow tunnel, half filled with water, which turned and cornered until Elija thought it would never end. It was much easier for him than for the adults, and he wondered how it was possible the giant could make it through. But he did, for the boy heard his voice rumbling behind as they pressed on.

At the end of this long march, when they had stopped only once to eat and rest, they clambered through a narrow cleft in the rock and came out onto a wide highway. Elija gazed around. The roof of the tunnel was so lofty the torchlight could not reach it. A small stream trickled down the centre of the way, which was otherwise bone dry and dusty. Downstream Elija could just make out what looked like an enormous bridge spanning the way. Upstream there was only darkness.

Badger ordered a halt and her companions slumped to the ground. Some rummaged in their rags for food or drink, others fell asleep instantly. Elija was hungry and he looked around hopefully, but they all turned away, even Badger, and, stomach grumbling, he fell deeply asleep.

B oy! Wake up. Boy!"
      He felt hot breath wet in his ear, tickling, and he squirmed away in his sleep.

"Boy!" Sharp fingers pinched his earlobe and he awoke with a start. He tried to yell, but found a hand hard over his mouth, mashing his lips against his teeth. Panicking, his eyes flew open and searched around in the gloom. Someone's matted hair was over his face and he could barely see. He struggled to get away.

"Boy, listen to me. You must be quiet," the voice hissed. "Will you be quiet?"

He nodded, then drew in a breath to yell as soon as the grip on his mouth relaxed. But his captor was not fooled.

"We must escape," he heard, and it slowly filtered into his brain that his captor was a child too. The hair in his face withdrew a little and he looked around. The others still lay where they had fallen, like piles of discarded clothes, and the noise of snoring rose and fell, echoing in the high tunnel. Elija's captor leaned back, still holding his mouth, and he could see it was a girl, older than him, with long hair thick and dirty and a pale square face.

She leaned forward and spoke urgently in his ear. "We must escape before we reach their camp. They are reivers and will kill us and eat us."

He shook his head. She was wrong. These people had rescued him. They were looking after him. He had heard of reivers, but he thought they were like wraiths—something evil heard of but never seen. He tried to speak and she leaned her head close to his and cautiously released the grip on his mouth.

"They rescued me," he whispered.

"Why did they do that?" she hissed. "For kindness?"

Elija knew there *were* kind people down in the Halls, people like Rubin and the gruff old man he had last seen with Em. But deep in his gut he guessed these people he had fallen in with were not like that.

He looked around again, uncertain. The cavern was totally still; everyone slept the sleep of the dead. Just one torch glowed and the watchman was asleep beneath it, his mouth gaping open. It would be easy to creep away. But the thought of fleeing into the dark terrified him more than the risk of death at the hands of these people.

He shook his head. "I'm staying."

The girl scowled. "Then they will kill you."

"We will die in the dark."

"We will die if we stay here."

Elija felt tears crawling down his face. The girl looked at him with a *V*-shaped frown between her brows. How can she be so fearless? he thought.

"This is a well-travelled way," she explained to him. "I've been watching out for rats. We hadn't seen any for hours, but there are lots of them here. You only find rats when there are people. That means there are people nearby. We can hide in the dark until someone else passes by, someone with a torch."

"But they might be evil men."

"*These* are evil men." She shrugged and looked around her, as if already dismissing him from her plans. "We will die if we stay," she repeated.

"I'm staying," Elija told her, and turned his back on the girl and curled up. He closed his eyes tight. He guessed she was still sitting beside him, watching, and he tried to sleep. Fears skittered through his head. Was she right? Did Badger and her friends plan to kill them? Finally, brain and body exhausted, he fell into a doze.

Moments later, it seemed, he was startled awake by an angry shout and a high-pitched squeal.

"Bitch bit me!" a voice snorted. There was a thwack of flesh on flesh and another cry of pain. Elija closed his eyes tighter and curled up into a ball. He felt the stir of rank air around him as sleepers rolled over and sat up. Then a strangled yell rang out, and Elija opened his eyes.

In the torchlight he could see the watchman was holding the girl. Her feet were off the ground, but she was kicking with all her might and flailing with the other arm. Her face was growing red and she was weakening. Elija watched, eyes wide.

The others were laughing at the entertainment, and Badger stood up, straightening her rags and patting them down in a leisurely way, then went over to the struggling pair. The girl raised one bare foot and kicked the woman in the chest. The blow hardly rocked her, but she growled.

"Shall I bind her?" the watchman asked Badger, who rubbed her chest, wincing.

"Too much trouble to carry her," the woman told him. "Kill her."

She turned and looked down at Elija. He cowered to the hard floor, and her gaze passed over him.

The girl had stopped struggling. Her eyelids were fluttering and when the watchman set her back on her feet she slumped forward. He held her up with one hand and with the other dragged a rusty knife from the sheath at his side.

Elija took a deep breath, drove off his heels and ran, head down, straight at the watchman. The top of his head punched into a leather jerkin clothing slack flesh. He heard a breathless grunt and felt the man fall back. Elijah plunged forward onto the big rolling body and slithered over it, then lost his footing as he tried to rise. He looked around. All he could see was the flaring torchlight, and dark incoherent movement. A hand grabbed his arm and dragged him to his feet.

"Got you, brat," Badger's voice said. "Hold still!" she ordered, but Elija, in the madness of panic, flailed about in her arms until he slipped free. He ran in the direction he thought he heard the girl's voice—straight into a rock wall. He fell over again, then, seeing a tunnel opening, struggled to his knees and shuffled through it into empty darkness. He scrambled to his feet and walked quickly with his hands out in front of him. His fingers brushed a wall and he followed it, trying to hurry, trying not to fall over. The ground plunged away suddenly and he fell again, rolling down a short slope and fetching up in a shallow puddle. Something hurt in his side, but he got up and carried on. The shouting was drifting away behind him.

He heard a whisper of sound and had no chance to run before a hand grabbed his arm. Mewling in fear he tried to run away, but the hand held him like stone.

"It's me!" the girl said.

Elija felt his heart racing wildly. He could scarcely breathe.

"It's all right, it's me," she repeated. "My name's Amita."

He calmed down a little and felt the wild drumming in his chest slow. "I'm Elija," he muttered. "How did you find me in the dark?"

"I could hear your feet on the rock. You were shuffling like an old man."

"What do we do now?" he whined. "Where do we go?" The fear of being lost was rising again inexorably.

"We go back," she told him.

"Go back?"

"We go back and get the torch. You were right. We cannot stay in the dark."

"But what if they catch us?"

"They won't be expecting us. They'll think us too frightened."

Elija *was* too frightened, but his belief in Amita was growing and he didn't argue with her.

"It'll be easy," she said, nodding as if keen to convince him and, perhaps, herself. "They'll probably sleep again and we can just walk in and take the torch."

Elija thought about it, his brow furrowed. "But what if they decide not to sleep? Badger might want to carry on."

"Even better. We can follow them at a safe distance. They won't be able to see us in the dark and they won't hear us above all the noise they make. When they get to where they are going—well, then we'll decide what to do."

Elija could find no argument with this plan, but he said, "We need food and water."

"I know," she said.

In the end it was as easy as Amita predicted. The reivers had not slept again—they were pressing on to their unknown destination. The children heard the clamour of their progress from far away, and they slid into a deep niche in the rock wall to let them pass. The band carried two torches now, one at the front of the party and one at the dog-end. They were easy to follow, and one of them even dropped a half-empty waterskin which the children snatched up eagerly.

They walked for what seemed like hours. At last they guessed they were near their destination for the reivers started to hurry. Elija, footsore and lurching with exhaustion, found it hard to keep up. He could hear shouts and laughter and the sound gave him a little energy. The reivers stopped and Elija and Amita edged forward, careful to stay outside the reach of the torches.

The band had halted at a high narrow crack in a rock wall. They were jostling to get through and were pushing and shoving each other in their haste. The children heard Badger's voice cursing them all. Slowly the group diminished, then vanished completely like water down a pipe, leaving silence and darkness behind them.

The children moved forward, waited for a while, then stepped through the crack into the largest Hall Elija had ever seen. The cavern rose high above their heads to a hidden roof, from where daylight filtered thinly down through high shafts. The air was lighter here; it weighed less heavily on the senses. Elija was astonished to realise he could see.

Far ahead a wide river meandered through the centre of the Hall. Between them and the river was a broad shore crossed by plank paths, and spanning the river was a bridge of rusted metal and timber, which Badger and her band were hurrying over. They were elated now, for they were coming home, and Elija could hear them singing and laughing. Only then did he see that there were children in the centre of the group, small drooping figures being pushed and prodded across the bridge. On the far side he could make out a settlement of tents and shacks. Even in the gloomy light he could see it was a big community. In a square in the centre, illuminated by the shafts of light, dozens of people were gathering, perhaps to welcome the reivers home to their village.

Elija and Amita looked at one another, wondering what the fate of the other children was. "Where do we go now?" Elija asked.

"That way," Amita said with certainty, pointing to their right. "The river flows that way and if we follow it we will eventually come outside."

Elija quailed at the prospect. "I don't want to go outside," he told her. "I want to go that way." He pointed upriver.

"We'd just be going backwards, back into the sewers." She sounded tired and out of patience.

"We'd be going home!"

She flared at him. "*Your* home is in a sewer! Mine isn't!"

"I want to find my sister," he whined, suddenly squatting down and hugging his knees.

"Your sister was swept away in the storm. She's probably dead," Amita told him brutally. Then she sighed and knelt beside him and put her warm arm around his shoulders. "I'm just trying to get us to safety."

"I want to go home," he cried.

"It's not your home," she repeated. "A sewer isn't home. Home is a place with warm beds and food in the kitchen, and there's daylight. And people to care for you. We must find our way back to daylight. We can't stay in the dark."

"It's not dark here," Elija argued, hugging himself tighter. Hideous memories prowled the recesses of his mind. Daylight meant pain and despair and humiliation. For Elija and Em there was shelter in dark corners, in cellars and cupboards. Night was a time of safety.

Amita blew out her breath and stood up. She looked to the right, then set off in that direction without looking back. Elija hesitated for a few moments then jumped up and hurried after her.

That night they slept curled together in the lee of a stone pillar sunk deep into the shores. They were asleep long before day's end, and they were unseeing when from the west a red light slowly emerged from the gloom. As the world turned its fingers flickered towards them, then found them, and for a while they lay in a pool of light the colour of blood.

Chapter 5

The City had once been holy.

Long ago, when suns spun and worlds turned in a different place, a band of seafarers arrived on a sandy beach on the westernmost coast of a new land. According to the demands of their gods, on a hilltop they founded a settlement, which became a trading port then, in the course of a millennium, a city. When the city fell to the cruel swords of invaders it was built again, new buildings and roads covering the blood-soaked earth of the old.

In the new city the roads were crafted from white stone, the high towers enrobed with gold, and the temples decorated with carvings of heroes, gods and animals. Men and women walked the streets in rich clothes encrusted with gold and silver and pearl. They wore feathers and beads in their hair and, in time, they painted their faces to look like their gods. The gods saw their arrogance and laughed, and the city was destroyed in a heartbeat. An earthquake brought down the towers and high palaces, and the people all died and their blood soaked into the land. Only one survived; a child, of course, an innocent girl.

The city lay abandoned for a thousand years . . .

Elija interrupted Rubin's story. "What happened to the child?" he asked.

Rubin thought for a moment. "She wandered through the land for a long time. She was barefoot, and her only friends were the birds and the animals. She slept with her head resting on the warm fur of a fox, and sparrows covered her with their feathers. At last she travelled to a high mountain range. Friendly eagles flew down and plucked her up and she flew off over the mountains and was never seen again."

Elija screwed up his face in disappointment and Rubin laughed. "Now, back to my tale."

The city lay abandoned for a thousand years and grass grew over the mounds of the dead, and rats ran in the corridors. Then new invaders came marching in with shiny swords and shields. They revered the songs of the heroes of the past and they started building again. They built temples to their own gods. They even built temples to the old gods of the city. They were a reverent people, and in their day the city saw peace for the longest time in its history. Libraries were built, and theatres, and hospitals and schools. There were green parks in the city's heart, with fountains and lawns. Then news of distant wars reached the city and the people started to leave. First its soldiers marched away, with their camp followers, then their families. The news from afar became very grave and the politicians and administrators were the next to go, quickly followed by the traders and merchants. Only the poor people and the elderly were left. They stayed on; they had no choice. They lost all contact with the rest of their world and, without trade, they had barely enough to survive on. For many generations their lives were wretched. The parks and meadows ran to wilderness. The stone buildings fell to ruin, and the people lived on the rats with which they shared their meagre homes. But the human heart is strong and the population grew, and slowly the city came alive again. Men took up tools and started scratching in the wilderness, sowing the thin soil with seed and praying for rain. Small herds of sheep and goats and pigs flourished on the green grass at the edge of the city, and a primitive trading community was reborn.

And at last these people too started to build. And on the ancient layers of buildings, flattened by earthquake, toppled by invaders, crumbled by time and neglect, soaked in the blood of millennia, the present City slowly began to rise.

It spread as never before, devouring the shabby settlements on its borders, eating up the rivers and hills and layering them first in timber then in stone. There were no towers of gold, no carvings of rich woods, just stone upon stone and an implacable march to north, south and east. Factories and forges spat smoke into the air, and all the birds and animals fled. Except of course for the rats. Great walls were built around the City. Then, barely as the labourers were finished and the shiny bronze gates were closed, new, higher walls were erected farther out. The circles of gates would open from time to time to let out armies of soldiers, sent to pacify and pillage outlying lands.

Seven great families arose to rule the City, seven houses named Guillaume and Gaeta, Sarkoy . . .

"I know this story!" Elija interrupted Rubin again. "It's the tale of the Immortal and his brothers."

"Then," Rubin replied, folding his arms and sitting back, "I can tell you no more. You know everything I can tell you about the history of the City."

There was silence for a moment, and Emly nudged Elija in the ribs, then her brother said sheepishly, "Tell me anyway. It might be a different story."

"Are you sure?"

"Yes. Please."

"Their names were Guillaume and Gaeta, Sarkoy, Vincerus . . ."

"Broglanh, Khan and Kerr," Elija finished triumphantly.

"And," said Rubin, drawing breath, "they came to the City thousands of years ago. No one knows where they came from . . ."

"But they are very important."

"They *were* very important, Elija, yet some of the Families dwindled or died out, or perhaps they hid themselves away from their more powerful brothers."

"*Were* they brothers?"

"Perhaps. But they lived a very long time and had many offspring and it's said that even the gods can't remember if they were once brothers or not."

"*Are* they gods, Rubin?"

Rubin shook his head. "I don't know. I was told this by my father, who knew them all. And I asked him the same thing. So he asked me what I thought a god was. I said a god was a being apart, one unlimited by the laws of nature. He said in that case, yes, they were gods. And together they were called the Serafim."

Elija stared at his friend. His words were incomprehensible, but he nodded.

"My father said they came to the City to bring peace and justice and knowledge. And in the end they gave us none of those things. They became steeped in greed and vice; they sucked in wealth and breathed out only corruption. And the emperor, who we call the Immortal but whose real name is Araeon, is the worst of them all . . ."

Elija put his hands to his ears, frightened at these perilous words.

Rubin patted him on the shoulder. "Don't worry, Elija. We are safe here in the Halls. We could die any day, drowned by a flash flood or killed and eaten by reivers, lost in the Whithergo, executed by patrols. But at least the emperor can't hear our words. We are safe from him down here."

W*e're lost!"*
Elija's comfortable reverie about his days with Rubin had given way to present-day reality. "We're lost," he repeated to Amita.

They had been trudging forever. But the river meandered in great loops and they were making slow progress. They could not stick to the main path, along the riverbank, for it was too steep and slippery, but struck out towards an outcrop of white rock they could see in the distance. Once there, Amita said, they could use the rock as a reference point, heading towards the source of daylight. But the light was fading and Elija could barely see Amita's shape ahead of him. Within moments it would be pitch-dark again and they would be lost.

"We should have gone back to the tunnels," he complained, not for the first time. He was on the verge of tears.

Amita came to a halt, knee-deep in sticky mud.

"We're not lost," she told him with her usual confidence, "but I think we're going the wrong way."

"I can see the rock right there," Elijah replied, pointing to its gleam to their left.

The girl shook her head. "I mean, by the time we get there we won't be able to see."

"And we have no food or water."

So they sat there, defeated and out of choices, until the mysterious rosy light they had seen before appeared far to their right.

"That's where we should go," Amita told Elija, pointing.

Elija looked at it and felt only fear. He shook his head.

"It's a fire," he said. "It must mean danger."

"If it's a fire then there will be food," Amita told him persuasively.

Reminded of food, Elija felt his stomach cramp painfully. They had found water the previous day, running in a torrent from high above them. It tasted earthy, but they had kept it down and it had given them energy for a while. But it was two days or more since they'd eaten. He shook his head again. "I'm frightened."

"The river goes that way, I'm sure. We just have to cut across there." She pointed straight across the mudbanks.

Elija had walked shores like these many times before and he could tell by the sheen on the mud that it was perilous. "We'll be walking on shores," he told her. "It's too dangerous. There might be shallow vaults. We could fall in and die."

"I don't know what shores or shallow vaults are. It will be hard going. But there might be paths."

But there were no paths. The two children found themselves struggling through mud again, and after a while their legs ached and their chests hurt. There was a new enemy too, swarms of flying insects which buzzed around them, biting their skin and getting into their eyes and mouths. Neither of them had suffered these in the tunnels, and the constant persecution was almost more than they could bear.

The red light had vanished again when Elija realised he could no longer see the girl ahead of him.

"Amita!" he cried in panic. "Where are you?"

"Here!"

He felt her hand grab his arm and she pulled him towards her.

"Here. Hold on to this." He felt a wooden post sunk deep into the mud, and clung to it.

"It's a piece of fence," the girl said in his ear.

As the last light dwindled and vanished all he could hear was a distant squealing, like the sounds of a hundred crying babies, and his heart froze with fear.

Elija felt strangely comfortable when he awoke. He was knee-deep in mud, but it was solid enough to support his thighs and back, and he felt almost rested. He could hear the mewing sound again, but louder. He opened his eyes and was surprised to see daylight. It was a thick, soupy sort of daylight, but he could see better than he had in a long time. For all his fears, it was good to see again, and his spirits lifted a little. He raised his head. Amita was beside him. She was fast asleep. She had tied herself to the wooden post so she would not slip into the river in the night. Elija could see now that she was fair, and her thick blonde lashes rested on her cheek as she slept. He relaxed back against the mudbank, wondering how to extricate his legs from the sludge.

Then he heard muffled voices. He tensed and, raising his head, he looked about him, alarmed. At first he could see nothing but mudbanks rolling back in the half-light. Then the twin sparks of two torches, coming towards him down the river. Stretching over he shoved Amita sharply, then put his mouth to her ear.

"Stay still. There's someone coming."

He felt her start awake, then her head lifted and she looked at him, eyes wide. He nodded his head upriver and she looked past him.

"A boat," she said. "Be quiet. They won't see us."

So *that* was a boat. Elija had never seen a boat. There were no boats on the rivers of sewage in the Halls. He laid his head back down as Amita scooped mud over him, and over herself. They were filthy enough already and Elija had no fear they would be noticed, two muddy lumps in a sea of mud.

He heard a gentle lapping, and the creak of leather, getting louder.

"We're wasting our time," complained a rough voice, echoing weirdly in the great open space.

Another croaked, "Your time so valuable, Leel? What'll you do else this fine morning? Join the emperor in his palace for breakfast?"

A woman cackled, and Leel, whining, replied, "I'm just saying. Every morning we come this way, rowing all morning, just to see the same sight. Blockade's been there a year or more. I'm just saying."

"And *I'm* saying," the other man told him, "you do what I tell you, boy, and one day you'll be thanking me. There'll be pickings aplenty when our boys take them on. Dead sailors are easy pickings. Live ones too. Gold rings aplenty when we slice their ears off. Wouldn't want to miss it, would you?"

Elija lifted his head slowly and saw a wide flat shape floating on the river. Paddles on either side moved gently up and down. The boat was getting smaller as it headed towards the light. The light was so bright now it hurt Elija's eyes. A new ripple of fear coursed through him.

Chapter 6

Bartellus and the child wandered in the Halls for a long time before they saw anyone, anyone alive. At first the way they were following went down and down. The Halls became narrower and smaller, until they were merely tunnels. Bartellus was starting to believe they could go no deeper in the bowels of the City before feeling the flaming heat of the earth's core, when the Halls started soaring away again, high above the light of his torch. He wondered how deep they were, and how long ago these great chambers were built. He remembered what Archange said about city built above city.

"Do you know where we are?" he asked the girl, though he guessed the answer. She shook her head.

The hall was dry and dusty, as if water had not touched the floors for centuries. Yet they were well below the level of the stormwater tunnels. How could a lower level be this dry? Shrugging to himself, Bartellus dismissed the problem from his mind. He was no architect, no engineer. Just a soldier.

They pressed on, the girl still holding to his hand, and before long one end of a lofty stone bridge loomed ahead of them. It seemed to span a wide dry way, perhaps a river once, Bartellus thought. Surely not a road? Though he raised his torch, he could not see how high it went, nor the length of its span. The huge steps started well above their heads. It seemed a bridge made for giants.

"Shall we cross?" he asked the girl. He had convinced himself that the child had an instinct for where they were going in relation to where they had been. She seemed confident, although Bartellus guessed that she too had never travelled as deep as this before. He was happy for her to make their decisions for them. It was their only communication.

She looked around her gravely, then nodded.

He bent down and picked her up, placing her on the first of the giant steps. Then he motioned her back and, as she retreated, he threw the blazing torch onto the step beside her. She jumped forward and picked it up and held it for him.

He looked around. There was a pile of broken wood and large chunks of timber in one dusty corner, as if swept there by the giant bridgebuilder's broom. He dragged two of the bigger blocks to the base of the bridge, then several sturdy chunks of wood on top, making two makeshift steps. If they were forced to come back this way they would be able to get down again.

The steps of the bridge were too high for the child to climb, so Bartellus lifted her onto each one, then scrambled up himself. It was hard going, and when they had reached the top he felt no sense of progress. They stood together in the echoing darkness. There was no sound, not even of rats. Since the storm Bartellus had had half an ear cocked all the time, listening for the sound of water. He imagined it now, a tidal wave rushing at them out of the gloom, scouring them off the bridge like motes of dust.

But there was no water, no sound. Gathering his energy to go on, Bart took a last look around and glimpsed a white blur below them. His old eyes strained to see what it was, and he realised it was the shape of a woman, clad in pale robes, standing at the base of the bridge they had recently left. He opened his mouth to call out, but his heart suddenly withered in his breast. The figure carried no torch. No one could survive deep in the Halls without light. Into his mind came the tales, told by Dwellers with fear and sometimes relish, of creatures in the depths they called wraiths. He shook his head at such nonsense.

"Wait," he told the girl.

But when he looked again the pale figure was gone. He looked about, peering into the silent gloom. The child watched him curiously. "Nothing," he said.

They sat for a while, drinking the water Archange had given them, then they went on, climbing down the other end of the bridge. After that the way quickly started to rise, and it was their downward journey in reverse; first they travelled through high halls, then the tunnels became mean and cramped, and damp. Soon they were walking along the side of a stream again, just as they had done before the storm came. The tunnel was unfamiliar to Bartellus, but the girl seemed to know where they were. He was amazed she still had the strength to walk when he felt his legs would give out at any moment. He watched obsessively the torch he had taken from the Hall of Watchers. When it failed they would probably die.

He was considering calling a short halt when they heard voices and stopped. Coming towards them out of the mirk were four people with one torch. They stopped abruptly when they saw Bartellus and the girl.

The leader, a small elderly man with a grey beard, had fear and suspicion etched across his face as he approached them. He moved crab-wise, as if ready to run at the least threat.

"Where you going?" he asked roughly, peering up at Bartellus short-sightedly.

Bartellus wondered that an old man without weapons and a small girl could concern them so. Then he realised all four were elderly, that some carried injuries, and all looked battered by the storm. They no doubt feared reivers, or anyone who was stronger than them. An unfamiliar bubble of amusement welled up inside him. He felt as weak as a sick mouse. Yet these poor people were afraid of him.

He held out empty hands and told them, "We are survivors of the storm. We are seeking our way back to the Hall of Blue Light."

"We are all survivors of the storm," grunted the man sourly. "We would not be here if we were not." He spat on the ground, making his point.

Bartellus asked, "Can you tell us if we are near our destination?"

"I do not know your Hall of Blue Light. Is it beyond the Eating Gate?"

Bartellus glanced at the girl, who nodded with confidence.

"Then you are farsiders. We do not go beyond the Gate. It is too perilous. The patrols come from there. And the storms."

"Where are you going?" Bartellus asked him.

The man peered at him suspiciously. "Why would you want to know?"

Bartellus shrugged. "Perhaps you are travelling to a place of safety. Perhaps we could come with you."

"Perhaps it would not be a place of safety if we prattled about it to any stranger who asked," the man said, glaring at them sideways.

The other three started to shuffle along nervously, eyes down. The old man shook his head. "We want nothing of you farsiders. You bring only trouble. Leave us alone!"

He scuttled off and the four returned to the gloom. Bart looked down at the girl and shrugged. She pointed the way they had been going, and they moved along.

Once they detected the sound of the Eating Gate they knew they had reached known territory. Relieved, sure now that their torch would last the journey, Bartellus gave them another short rest. Sitting with his back against a dry wall, his eyes closed, he wondered again about the long and meandering path they had travelled. He could never find his way back to the Hall of Watchers. Although he thought the child might be able to. He was certain now, had been sure for some time, that they had not been swept helplessly into that stone chamber where he had met the warrior Indaro. They had been rescued from the stormwater and carried to safety. But for what purpose? His conversation with Archange had revealed nothing, at least to him. But he was sure she knew who he was. He was too tired to concentrate on the problem. Instead his mind idled back over the events of the last day.

Remembering suddenly, he delved in the pouch at his side and from the bottom brought out the piece of cloth he had snatched from the neck of the corpse. It was half dried, damp and wadded into a solid lump. Carefully he teased and stretched it out, as the little girl watched, her dark eyes serious.

He had thought it a kerchief or a scarf, but it was neither. It was a circle made from fine gauze, delicately embroidered at the edges with thread which had once been coloured. There were two tiny pieces of metal attached to its edges. He took one in his stubby tortured fingers and peered at it, moving closer to the torchlight, squinting. But his ageing eyes could make nothing of it. He looked enquiringly at the girl, who held out her hand. He gave it to her and she looked at it. Then she took the other piece of metal and held them together.

She looked up at Bartellus, realisation in her gaze. She put the two close to the ground and trotted them along. He took them from her and peered again. Yes, they were animals, a dog and a horse, perhaps. Or a donkey. Each cunningly crafted in gold.

"Is this a donkey?" he asked.

Her lips curved a little and he recognised the hint of a smile.

"Or a horse?" She nodded. She raised her hands over her head, and brought them down gracefully to her shoulders. Then she lowered her head and batted her eyelashes at him, a gesture so arch and comical that he laughed.

A veil. A woman's veil, weighted at the edges with gold animals. Most of the little weights had been washed away, leaving only the dog and the horse. Bartellus smiled at the child and handed it back to her. For a while she sat contentedly stroking the tiny beasts, following their tiny backs and tails with a small finger.

Bartellus wondered why the tattooed corpse was wearing a woman's veil round his neck. A love token perhaps or, twisted, a murderer's noose? He thought again of the brand on the man's arm. He picked up a piece of stick and traced the *S* in the dust.

"Do you know what this is?" he asked the child. She looked at it, frowning a little, then shook her head.

"Neither do I," he told her. "But it looks familiar. It was . . . drawn on the arm of the dead man we found."

Her heart-shaped face clouded over again, and he cursed himself. What was the point of reminding her of her brother? Of a time when her brother still lived.

Bartellus sighed. "Time to be moving," he said. She tied the veil neatly round her neck, patting the little animals. Then she jumped up, taking his hand.

It took them nearly half a day to get back to the Hall of Blue Light, with its familiar ledges and meeting maelstrom of waters. The storm had wrought many changes. They saw few people they knew there, and there were many newcomers. Bartellus was relieved to find Old Hal still in residence. The skinny old man, guarded by his four strapping sons, was the main conduit for food and fresh water in the upper Halls. Bartellus approached him, digging in his pouch again. He found the gold coin Anny-Mae had dug up in the shoals. He showed it to one of Old Hal's sons, who stood aside and let him through to the father's ledge.

The old man squatted on the floor surrounded by his hoard of food bags, pots of water and beer, and baskets of bread and roots. He looked up and cackled with enjoyment. "Bartellus, we thought you dead! Many of us dead these last days." He shook his head in sorrow, whether for lost lives or lost profits Bartellus could not guess.

"I have brought the girl back." Bartellus realised for the first time that he didn't know her name. "Elija's sister."

"Little Emly?" said Old Hal. "And Lije?"

Bartellus shook his head.

Old Hal frowned and gestured to one of his sons, who gave Bartellus two fresh loaves of bread, some dried meat, and a large jug of water. Bartellus handed him the gold coin. Old Hal rummaged in a wooden box and gave him five silver imperials in return. Bartellus looked at them. A gold imperial equalled five silvers. He was wondering if the old trader had made a mistake, and whether to mention it, when the man told him, "A gold is worth more than five silvers down here in the Halls." He shrugged. "That's the way it is."

Bartellus put the coins away, grabbed the food and made his way back to Emly.

It was many days before the old soldier found it necessary to join another hunting party. He and Em had fed well, and rested, and he still had four silvers left after he had bought them both clean clothes and himself a curved dagger. The silvers would last them a long time, but he had already received offers to work, and he could not go on refusing them. Turn down work when you can do without it, and the Gods of Ice and Fire will take notice, and there will be no work when it's needed. That was his philosophy.

The hard decision was whether to take the child with him. There would be danger for her wherever they went, but danger for her alone here too. An old midwife had offered to care for the child, but she could afford her no protection if the patrols came or, if the gods cursed them, reivers. Bartellus had asked Old Hal if he would take Emly under his protection but the old man had laughed and shaken his head. And the girl had skills that a hunting party could use: her eyes were sharp and she was low to the ground so she could spot things others could not; she was light and could go where others could not.

So one morning, as the dark light filtered down through the lofty roof of the Hall of Blue Light, Bartellus and Emly set off again. There were four others, and they were heading towards the Wideawake Sluice. This was a major floodgate which filtered off surplus river water. An expedition went there most days when the streams were high. It was fresh stormwater and the pickings were easy. It was also a place where Dwellers congregated, trading news and gossip.

The party of six made good time and they only paused once, at the

Eating Gate. The leader, a skinny leathery woman called Ysold, pointed down into the gate's mechanism and Bartellus saw one of the great rolling barrels which chewed up passing debris was now missing.

When they reached a place where they could talk again, Ysold edged up to him as they walked.

She winked up at him. "Information," she said craftily.

Bartellus frowned.

"There is money in information," she told him. When he continued to look baffled, she went on irritably, "The Eating Gate is breaking up, man. It is weakened. Next time there is a storm perhaps another barrel will break free. Soon there will be nothing to stop all the rubbish in the City being swept down through the Halls. The lower tunnels will start to block up, then the upper levels, then the Halls themselves. Soon the entire City will be flooded."

"Does no one maintain the Gate?"

She shook her head. "Time was when they sent regular teams down to repair it. Then, many years ago, they stopped. I don't know why."

Bartellus looked at her wonderingly, this tough old woman with beady eyes, wrapped in an old blanket with holes for her arms. How long had she lived here? He knew there was no point in asking. She would say what they all said: "Time out of mind."

"But someone would pay for information like that. Someone in power," she said.

She nodded at him, emphasising her point, but he shrugged. When *he* was someone in power, he had no interest in what went on beneath the streets of the City. If someone had crawled out of a drain and told him of a missing barrel in a mechanism which chewed sewage he would have sent them on their way with a flea in their ear and perhaps a hard kick to the backside.

But, "It is important information," he told her pleasantly. "Yet I would not know who to tell."

It was true. The emperor's palaces were awash with administrators. The armies could not move without teams of scribes creating wagonloads of paperwork. New roads and bridges were built only after a thousand counsellors had made work, and wealth, for themselves. The long, and increasingly fragile, supply lines which brought food and supplies into the City were the subject of continuous debate for counsellors, palace officials, administrators and, of course, the generals.

But who considered what went on beneath the streets of the City? In that other City, which continued to give its own vital service daily—unseen, unconsidered, essential.

Ysold frowned at him. "The emperor, of course," she told him eagerly. "Someone should tell the Immortal."

Then, seeing the party was dawdling along, she snapped at them to pick up the pace and she hurried to the front, holding her torch high.

Bartellus remembered the last time he had seen the emperor. It was the worst day of his life. He hoped fervently he would never see the man again.

Up ahead Ysold marched along, setting a cracking pace, on a wide stone path bordering a low-running stream on their right. The six Dwellers had become strung out, with Em and Bartellus, holding a torch, as the dog-end.

Suddenly Ysold cried out, and in the instant Bartellus saw swift movement to his left. He ducked and twisted, and a club swished past his cheek. He lashed out with his torch, catching someone a glancing blow. He glimpsed black shapes against the moving torchlight. The man who had attacked him was big and broad. He was also slow. As he lashed at Bartellus again with a club, the old soldier drew his dagger and, twisting, slashed the man's forearm. The attacker dropped the club, his arm nerveless. He snarled and ran at Bartellus, head down. Bart, his back to the stream, threw himself sideways, letting go the torch. He hit the ground hard, and groaned as his knee shrieked in pain. He forced himself up. His attacker had fallen on the edge of the stream, and was levering himself up on all fours. Bartellus kicked him hard in the ribs and the man plunged into the flowing sewage and disappeared without a cry.

Bartellus turned to find Emly. He could not see her, and hoped she had scurried into the dark. He could hear shouts and blows and scuffling, but only one torch was alight, and it was lying on the ground at the far end of their party. He could see a man with a sword raised, menacing a huddled shape on the ground. Bartellus reversed his dagger and threw it, with practised accuracy, into the man's head. He dropped like a stone. Bartellus ran to the fallen woman, but she was still.

Another of their party, a fair woman, was being dragged away by a man armed with a knife. Bartellus retrieved his dagger and ran towards them, but the man saw him coming, and with a single sweep, slashed the woman's throat and dropped her, disappearing into a tunnel at his back.

Cursing, Bartellus turned to a youngster who was defending desperately against a man with a sword. The boy held a quarterstaff inexpertly, and was being forced back to the stream. He was wounded, and was stooping painfully.

Bartellus shouted and the attacker turned, his blood-drenched sword raised. Bartellus leaped at him, fury fuelling his old bones, and sliced at the man's head. The man backed away from the blow and swept his sword up towards Bartellus' belly. Bartellus twisted away awkwardly.

"My sword against your knife, old man," grunted the black-bearded attacker, grinning.

Bartellus said nothing. He took deep breaths, rallying long-unused skills. The two circled and the black-bearded man risked a glance around, seeking his companions.

"No one can help you," Bartellus snarled, and for the first time in eons he felt the thrill of battle rising in his chest. Strength coursed through him. Then time started to slow. He could feel the hilt of the dagger, comfortable and familiar in his palm, the texture of the rocky floor firm beneath his bare feet, and the strength in his shoulders and legs as he circled, balanced and ready.

The bearded man lunged towards him, his sword thrusting for Bartellus' throat. He was so slow that the old soldier almost laughed. He had all the time in the world to sway sideways, all the time in the universe to choose his spot and to ram the dagger accurately under the man's armpit, seeking the heart.

The man fell in the dust and was still as only the dead can be. Bartellus picked up the lone torch and thrust it into a cleft in the rock.

"Emly!" he cried, all strength suddenly gone, familiar fear returning. There was only silence, and he found it hard to breathe through the pain in his chest. He looked around. The boy had succumbed to his wounds. Ysold was gone, perhaps into the stream. Only one woman lived and she was gravely injured. Bartellus sighed, his heart cramped with regret.

Then he forgot his pain as the little girl came running out of the darkness. She ran straight to him, cannoning into him, and he bent down and picked her up. He held her close, relief flooding through him. He felt faint and he leaned against the tunnel wall, the girl still in his arms.

"Are you all right?" he asked her. "Not hurt?"

She stared at him, and he said again, "You're not hurt?" She shook her head reassuringly. After a while he put her down and walked over to the semi-conscious woman. He sat with her for a long while until she died.

He thought back to that sunlit day when he rode from home for the last time. Companionably, it had seemed, the two men travelled slowly, talking occasionally. Astinor Redfall seemed subdued, Bartellus now believed with the unreliable clarity of hindsight. What was he thinking, this old comrade of his, as he escorted him unknowing to his trial?

The general's home was in the far eastern outskirts of the city, in the farming country of Salaba. As they rode, most of the land they traversed belonged to him. Who owns that land now? he wondered to the darkness. My old friend, as payment for treachery? Even as he thought it, despite everything that had happened, he could not believe it.

It took them most of the day to reach the palace, riding through bustling Burman Far, the ratruns of Lindo, wealthy Otaro and finally the palace precincts. They had been in no hurry, and even now he liked to think the man was reluctant to bring him speedily to his fate. When they reached the broad avenue called Clarion, he paused, as he always did, to gaze up at the palace. He had first seen it as a child, yet he never failed to be awed by its beauty. Carved from rosy red rock, its source now unknown, the emperor's palace entranced the eye and dazzled the comprehension. Men argued about how many spires and turrets there were. There was no answer. A man could walk round the palace and count them, of course, but that would be merely the number seen from outside. Within the palace, each window looked out on minarets, each internal courtyard was surrounded by spires, each narrow stairway climbed another tower. There was no internal plan anyone knew of. A man would go mad trying to make one. There were sixty-seven domes, he had been told. He had no reason to think this was true or untrue. He was not a man with a mathematical bent. Mathematicians and philosophers, astronomers and prophecers attended the emperor in droves. They were learned men, each in their way. They could speak on the harmony of the stars, the movement of the planets, the wisdom of the seasons and the majesty of the tides. Yet only the uncaring birds knew how many towers there were in the emperor's palace.

And deep within the vast building were the emperor's quarters, a fortress within a fortress, for the Red Palace was nothing if not a stronghold. For all its beauty, for all its flowered courtyards and gardens and fishponds and carvings, it was designed to keep out an invading enemy. The Immortal's residence was walled with green marble, cladding the ancient stone of the mighty fort built on the site more than a thousand years before. It was called simply the Keep. There were few portals between the Red Palace and the Keep at its heart, and even the general had never set foot in there.

The riders trotted their mounts into the outer courtyard at the Gate of Peace. Here wide shade trees welcomed the tired traveller, and there were cool fountains to slake his thirst. The palace guards, knowing them well, stood aside, letting them through to an inner courtyard, called Northmen, its alabaster walls covered with carvings of wolves and the fierce werewomen who were their companions.

"I must leave you here, my friend," said Astinor Redfall, black-bearded and powerful, as they climbed from their mounts. "I have supply business with a lord lieutenant."

The general grasped his friend by the hand. "I will see you later," he said warmly.

"Yes you will," replied Astinor, looking into his eyes.

The general walked the familiar corridors through the new wing. It was said that three entire palaces of minor Families had to be demolished to make way for this addition to the Red Palace. The corridors were higher than in the old part, and wider, the windows larger and the way lighter. He passed a dozen courtyards, some buzzing with life, some quiet and sombre even on this sunny afternoon.

Then the pale marble walls around them gave way suddenly to richly decorated gold-encrusted alabaster of the public rooms. A wide shallow flight of stairs rose up to huge golden doors. The staircase was flanked by members of the emperor's bodyguard, the Thousand, in their black and silver livery. The high doors opened.

The Immortal was seated in the public throneroom, surrounded by the usual generals, handmaidens, counsellors, lickspittles and toadies. Bartellus later remembered feeling flattered to have an emperor wait on him. He bowed deeply. When he lifted his head he was surprised his lord had not risen from his throne, embraced him, called him brother, as was his usual habit. Rather, the emperor frowned. The general's stomach lurched.

Araeon was tall and fair, of late middle years, with a blond beard closely following the line of his chin. Only his eyes were black, a peculiar absolute blackness which contrasted with his pale countenance. Shuskara knew one of them was glass, but at times both eyes seemed to be deep wells brimming with painful experience. At others, as on that day, they were dead as the eyes of a butchered deer, reflecting dully the flickering torchlight.

The Immortal frowned and asked, "Are you really Shuskara?"

Shuskara smiled faintly, hoping for a joke. "Lord?"

The emperor twisted his face as if having difficulty remembering. "You look like the Shuskara I have known and loved for a lifetime, a well-made man of elder years, his eye clear and his brow free of the stratagems of compromise." He looked around at his subjects, his face a mask of bafflement.

Stratagems of compromise? Shuskara had heard these elliptical ominous speeches from his lord many times before, but never as their target. He was unarmed, of course, in the emperor's presence, but his general's mind started evaluating tactics, seeking ways of escape. His eyes flickered over those present, seeking friends. He saw the Vincerii—Marcellus, First Lord of the City, and his brother Rafael—his fellow generals Boaz and Flavius Randell Kerr, these two making no attempt to hide their satisfaction. No help there.

"Have you nothing to say, soldier?"

I will not argue, Shuskara thought. *They always argue, and the words always sound like pleas for their lives. And it never makes any difference.*

"You have and always will have all my loyalty, lord."

The emperor gazed at him for a long while. "Loyalty is an odd beast," he said finally, musing. "Men speak of loyalty as if it were a simple constant, solid as that statue"—he waved a hand at something behind Shuskara—"reliable as the sunrise. Then we discover that loyalty can mean something else; it is dependent on changing conditions, perhaps passing seasons. It can mean compromise, appeasement, concession. Astonishingly," he went on, his voice grave and entirely free of astonishment, "it can mean betrayal."

Betrayal? As Shuskara's world fell apart his first agonised thoughts were for his family. He forced out the words, "You have and always will have all my loyalty, lord."

He drilled those words into his brain, determined they would be the only words he would speak that day and in the brutal, pain-filled days to come as the emperor's inquisitors tried to force from him information he did not have about events of which he knew nothing.

He was used to pain. As a soldier he had endured the agony of wounds great and small, and he had stoically endured other men's torture. He could deal with pain. What he could not tolerate, what sapped his strength and dignity more quickly than he believed possible, was the constant torment of thirst, hunger and sleeplessness. He was given sips of water, barely enough to keep him alive. After a few days he was lapping the dank walls of his cell like a dog. He chewed his own lips to make the blood flow. When the torturers came for him it was almost a relief, for the pain of their work distracted his suffering mind from his thirst. It seemed that whenever he fell asleep he was woken to be dragged off to torture, so in a while his brain refused to rest at all. He felt his mind slipping, sliding, breaking under the unrelenting horror, leaving cracks into which the torturers slipped their implements. Within only a few days he was begging for relief. The disinterested torturers watched him cry and plead, using their long experience to mine nuggets of useful facts from the indiscriminate mountains of information he tried to give them. He did not know what they wanted, but had he known he would have told them in a heartbeat.

The hideous days crept slowly by, and he was brought before the emperor again. Araeon was not in his throneroom this time, but a quiet parlour. Shuskara, his body battered and filthy, was stood on trembling legs on rich thick carpets between two tall impassive soldiers. He watched the emperor drink a goblet of water, cool droplets splashing and running down his chest.

"We were discussing loyalty, soldier," Araeon said pleasantly.

Remembering the long-broken promise to himself, Shuskara croaked, "You have and always will have all my loyalty, lord."

The emperor picked up a black plum, shiny with dew, and bit into it. Juice gushed from it and spurted down his chest. A servant leaped forward and patted it away with a blindingly white cloth.

"Why is it traitors always speak of loyalty?" the emperor asked, apparently to himself. "A hero of battle does not boast of his cowardice. A blind man does not brag about his eyesight. Yet for traitors this is a topsy-turvy world indeed." He smiled, pleased with his words, as he so often was. He waved his hand in dismissal.

In those endless days in his cell, Shuskara was often visited by a demon of the darkness. The demon told him what to say when he was brought before the emperor again. It knew the exact words that would halt this inevitable process of torture, slow dismemberment and death, words that would make the emperor reveal to him his supposed act of treachery, reveal the misunderstanding which had led to this wretched fate. In the bloodstained cell he saw the emperor apologise to him, fall on his neck with bitter tears of remorse. The demon showed him this, and for a while he allowed himself to revel in the fantasy.

And the demon showed him another story, one he clung to and depended on, as he depended on the few drops of dirty water he was allowed each day. It was of Astinor, somehow still free, racing for his home, stealing Marta and the boys away, delivering them to a safe place where the emperor would never find them. Shuskara stayed true to this story, even in his weakest moments never allowing himself to think of any other alternative for his family.

One night he heard the door of his cell whisper open. He rose suddenly to painful consciousness, panic flooding his body, terror bursting easily from the weak restraints he had bound it in. A hooded figure loomed over him and he cringed. A soft hand found his and pulled at him. He stood up clumsily, pain from his injuries forcing out a groan. The figure tugged him towards the cell door and he stumbled after. Quietly, in the almost-darkness, he was led through empty corridors. They walked for leagues, it seemed. Shuskara tried to speak to the figure but there was no reply.

Many emotions fought for supremacy in Shuskara's breast. Hope tried to force itself through, but he pushed it down ruthlessly. He told himself this was an amusing ruse by the emperor, to have him led in a circle round the dungeons of Gath, hoping for deliverance, but returning him at last to his cell and his torturers. After a long while, though, he knew he was not travelling in a circle. The extensive maze of tunnels, chambers and cells which made up the emperor's dungeons was well known to him. They had moved beyond them, and were still walking in a roughly straight line, to the east, his soldier's senses told him. Where were they going? He had no idea, but he allowed hope to raise its head.

They reached an old door, the last of many. His silent companion opened it with a key and, as it creaked open, pushed Shuskara through. It was slammed closed behind him and he found himself alone in a smoky alley at daybreak, surrounded by piles of rotting vegetables, the stinking debris of a food market. The door he had come through was small and rusty, half-hidden in a dark corner. It looked as though it had not opened in a hundred years.

Was he free? Were soldiers waiting round the corner to take him back to his cell, laughing? Shuskara walked to the end of the alley and found himself in a street he recognised in the eastern quarter they called the Armoury. He looked down at himself. He was filthy and in rags, but he was a free man.

Elation rising in his heart, his first thought was to find his family.

Bartellus' heart was still labouring from the battle underground. But he had killed three men. For the first time since that fateful sunlit day he had confronted his enemy and prevailed. His eyes were clearer. His mind sharper. He had protected the child, as he could not protect those other children. He looked at her. Em was sitting with her back to a rocky wall, playing with the animals on the veil she always wore. The new clothes were filthy already, the trousers frayed and ragged.

Wheels and cogs clicked slowly in his mind and the old man made a fateful decision. *I will stop running and hiding. I will return to the world, for good or evil, and take the child with me. I will find my enemies and kill them.*

His mind turned to Fell, the one comrade who had never let him down. He smiled in reminiscence. Fell was the finest warrior he had ever known. He could kill the unkillable. Yet he was racked with guilt, burdened with his need to save the unsaveable. *I will seek him out, see if he still lives.* Then in a flash of memory Bartellus remembered where he had seen the S-shaped brand before.

Filled with the strength of resolution he levered himself to his feet. "Emly," he said, and the girl jumped up.

Bartellus had no idea what to do with the three bodies. He could not bear to roll them into the stream, so in the end he left them where they lay, two young women and a boy lying in the darkness far beneath an uncaring City. He spoke a few words to the Gods of Ice and Fire, the soldiers' gods, asking that they be received as warriors in the Gardens of Stone. He had little hope of this. In many years of soldiering he had come to believe that his gods were giants of vice and cruelty, and that compassion was unknown to them.

Then he took up the torch again and, holding Em's hand, set off back through the tunnels towards the Eating Gate. The route was straightforward and he had no need of the girl's help.

When he and Em reached the Gate he swept the girl up, to her surprise, and cradled her in his arms. He climbed the treacherous winding steps to the top and crossed more carefully than he had ever done. He paused for a moment at the top and glanced down into the mechanism. There were nineteen rolling barrels now and the gap in them stood out like a missing front tooth. From high above he could see large pieces of debris—branches, crates and shapeless masses that could be dead dogs, empty sacks, or discarded clothes—spilling through the gate. He descended again on the far side of the Gate and walked on, past the point where they could hear and speak again, then on past the way that led to the Hall of Blue Light. At last he put the girl down. He looked at her and she pulled at his hand, thinking he had mistaken the way.

He crouched down and put his hands on her scrawny shoulders, her bones like chicken legs, easily broken.

"You know, don't you, Emly, that we will probably never find your brother?"

Her mouth turned down and her heart-shaped face creased into a silent wail at his harsh words.

"I was at fault," Bartellus went on ruthlessly. "I told you we would find him. But that was before we returned from the Hall of Watchers, before I realised how deep and wide and complex the Halls are. We could search for him down here for years.

"And we can't do that. You need safety, and light, and good water, and warm shelter. I cannot give you those things down here."

She cried silently, her thin frame racked by sobs. He hugged her to his chest and held her for a while. Then he pushed her from him and looked at her downcast face. "Every day we spend here puts us in mortal danger. I came here to escape the woes of the world of daylight, as I expect you and Elija did. I thought the world had nothing more for me, nothing even to fight for. But now I have you.

"I never thought I would ever have another friend I could trust. But I trust you, Em. And I think you're the bravest person I have ever known. You have a soldier's heart, and I trust you with my life."

She raised her tear-stained face and stared at him gravely. He wondered if she understood a word.

"We must go back to the world now, little soldier. We will go back to the world together."

He watched her until, tears still squeezing from her eyes, she nodded. Her courage tore at his soul. He stood up and took her hand in his, and together the old man and the little girl walked back towards the daylight.

Chapter 7

Elija and Amita waited until the rowboat was long gone before they pulled themselves free of the sucking mud and started to follow its passage. After only a short while struggling through the mudbanks they came to firmer land. There was hard rock under their feet and they made speedy progress. The light was so bright they could see all around them. The river was flowing towards a low, wide opening, through which the daylight gushed like water from a pump. The eerie shrieking sounds were getting louder.

Amita nudged Elija and pointed. A narrow waterfall was flowing down the rocky cliffside far to their left. They hurried over to it and Amita put her hand under the sparkling water. She tasted it, and her face lit up in a smile.

She rinsed the mud off her hands then cupped them and took a gulp. Elija followed her. The taste of fresh water, from a stream and not from an old barrel used a thousand times, was intoxicating. Elija felt his thoughts clear, as if the deadening fog of years was being washed away. He laughed.

He looked at Amita, his unseen companion through so many trials. She was taller than him, big-boned and strong, despite long-endured deprivation. Her hair, though mud-caked, was thick and pale and it was plastered to her body as far as her waist. There was a deep cleft in her chin. The light was so bright he could see her eyes were blue, and they stared at him critically as he watched her. He suddenly felt himself redden, and dropped his eyes under her gaze. He ducked under the gushing water and Amita joined him. The caked mud of years slowly sloughed off their bodies, and they stood there for a long time, occasionally glancing shyly at one another.

When they stepped out again, shaking themselves like dogs, the screaming sound was louder and more frequent, and it pressed on Elija's ears. It sounded like a soul in torment.

"What's that noise?" he asked, looking around him. He could see nothing but light ahead of them, dark where they had come from, and the rocky ceiling above.

"Just birds," she told him. "You must have heard birds before."

Not like that, he thought, thinking of the little dusty brown birds that ran around the rubbish heaps of his childhood.

"Come on," she said. "We're nearly there."

She grabbed his hand, as she had done so many times before. But it felt strange to Elija now they could see each other; to both of them apparently, for she let go and walked in front of him into the light. He followed her more slowly, scrambling at times over the uneven rock.

His senses started to spin. There was a heavy sound, crashing like a thousand trees at once on his ears. And a smell, which made his nose itch. It was quite unlike the smell of the sewers. It was clean and sharp and it went through his head like a knife-blade. He followed Amita, climbing on hands and knees, the bright light pressing down on him like a blanket.

Then at last they were out of the darkness and Amita stopped. Elija bumped into her, then he stood upright and looked around, squinting through his lashes. What he saw made him cry out in fear and he fell to the ground, hiding his head, drawing his legs up, trying to make himself small. The crashing sound and the screaming of the birds battered on his ears and his mind went blank with terror.

Through his fear he heard a laugh. Amita knelt down and put her arm round him. "It's all right, Elija," she whispered. "You're not used to daylight. It's the sun. It's so bright! And look at the fleet out there in the sunlight!"

Elija put his hand over his face and peered through his fingers, then slowly got to his knees.

It was the end of the world. They were on a rocky outcrop at the edge of a great hole in the land. In front of them there was nothingness, just silvery water, sparkling in the daylight, stretching away into the distance until it met the sky and disappeared. Floating on the water, dangerously close to the edge of the world, were high wooden buildings, dozens of them, with tall posts festooned with ropes. Elija wondered what stopped the buildings floating off the edge into the sky. In the air around them enormous white birds wheeled and flew, screeching their frightening sounds.

"What is this terrible place?" he asked the girl, his voice trembling.

She stared at him, half smiling as if suspecting she was being teased.

"It is the sea," she said, amazed. "Have you never seen the sea before, boy?"

She took his hand and together they stumbled towards the water, treading awkwardly on the sharp rocks. The sun was so bright they could only keep their eyes open for moments and Elija felt tears streaming down his face.

Then, above the screams of the birds, they suddenly heard boots scraping on the rocks. Elija spun round, nearly falling, and saw two men approaching wearing swords and light armour.

"Reivers!" he cried and they tried to run, but the jagged rocks cut into their bare feet and they both fell painfully. Elija tried to crawl away, back into the cave, but the pain in his hands and knees was agonising. They were streaming blood.

"Stop! Please stop. We won't hurt you!" one man said. "You're injuring yourselves."

"They're just children. No use to us," the other said.

Elija stared wildly at the two men, who had stopped a few paces away.

One was tall and dark, with strangely brown skin and a narrow face. The other was stocky and pale, and shorter than his colleague.

"Are you from the mud village?" the dark man asked them.

Elija had no idea what he meant and he glanced at Amita, who said nothing.

"The settlement in the cave?" the man asked, pointing to the opening the children had emerged from.

Elija shook his head.

"Do you understand the City tongue, boy?"

"Yes," Elija answered in a small voice.

"Where have you come from?"

He wondered what the words meant. Where *had* he come from? He remembered his first meeting with Rubin.

"I am Elija, from the Hall of Blue Light," he said.

The men looked at each other and grinned.

"And where is the Hall of Blue Light?" the dark man asked. His speech was strange, and limping, as if he was using unfamiliar words. When Elija made no answer he squatted down and said, "I am Gil. This is Mason. We mean you no harm, Elija."

"Wasting your time," the other man told him, looking around as if eager to be away.

"Is the Hall of Blue Light in there?" Gil asked, pointing to the cavern.

Elija nodded.

"Do you live in there?"

Elija looked at Amita again. He wanted to trust these men, but he had wanted to trust the reivers too. Amita said nothing. For once she gave him no lead.

He nodded doubtfully, unsure what they wanted him to say.

Gil glanced at his friend again, then asked, "Do you know your way through the sewers?"

Elija was suddenly distracted by the smell of roasting meat, greasy succulence wafting to them on the salt sea breeze. His nose twitched and his stomach cramped. Would these men feed them if he gave them the right answer?

"We call them the Halls," he volunteered, trying to give himself time to think.

Gil nodded. "Do you know how to find your way through the Halls, Elija?"

He seemed eager for an answer, and now the other man, Mason, was watching with interest.

"Yes," he told them.

That seemed to be right, for Gil smiled and asked, "And do you know the way to the palace?"

"Yes," Elija said more confidently, although he had no idea what a palace was.

"Are you hungry, both of you?"

Gil held out his hand, and after a moment Elija took it and slowly stood. He looked around. Now his eyes had adjusted he could see beyond the rocks to a sandy beach where two boats had been drawn up. There were others, dark-skinned men, and there was a campfire from where the savoury smells were drifting. Gil shouted to the men and one of them lifted a hand in acknowledgement. The words were strange and Elija did not understand them.

Turning to Mason, Gil said, in the City tongue, "This might be just what we need. Children would know their way through the sewers better than any adult."

Mason nodded. "Saroyan should have thought of that. Looking for Hall-walkers was her idea, after all."

Gil frowned. "Don't mention her name, even here," he warned. Then he added, "And we could trust them better than"—he nodded towards the opening to the caves—"those scum."

He gazed down at Amita, who still sat on the rocks watching them suspiciously. "Are you Elija's sister?"

"Yes," she said promptly.

He helped her up, then asked them both, "Would you like to go aboard a great ship?"

First the children were fed by the friendly men on the beach, then they were taken on a rowboat to the ship which, in time, took them far away. And it was not until a lot later that Elija realised it was not a City ship, but one of the enemy's.

PART TWO

The Plain of Blood

Chapter 8

Indaro swayed to avoid a sword-thrust, then with a grunt brought her blade down two-handed on the enemy's neck. Bone cracked like old wood. She dragged the weapon clear in time to parry a slashing cut from the right. A thrown lance bounced off the edge of her shield, missing her face by a hair's-breadth. The blow unbalanced her. She twisted and her sword lunged to the right, disembowelling the attacker, who fell screaming. She threw up her shield to block a murderous cut from the left, then her blade slashed high, braining a warrior without a helm.

Beside her Doon leaped on the back of a dead man and with swift cuts slashed the throats of two attackers. She paused for a moment and grinned at Indaro before stepping back down.

Indaro moved back from the soldier writhing in agony at her feet and pierced his heart with her sword.

She took the moment to glance around and feel the rhythm of the battle. The City's warriors had been moving forward steadily throughout the morning, pace by pace pushing back the enemy attack. The sun's warmth was creeping under the blood-red armour at her neck. They had been fighting since dawn and it was nearly noon. And they were still strong. As she paused two comrades ran past her, heading towards the enemy, plunging shouting into the melee.

Ahead of them an enemy soldier shook himself free and charged towards them. Doon sang out her battle cry, a shrill scream which made enemies' bones shiver in their flesh, and ran at the man. She ducked beneath a wild sweep and slashed her sword through his knee. Three more enemy warriors ran towards them. Indaro hurdled a fallen man and raced to meet them. She blocked the lunge of the first, nearly decapitating him with a reverse cut. The second warrior's sword sliced into Indaro's side, the third aimed a blow at her face. It was blocked by an upraised sword, and Doon smashed the soldier from his feet.

Doon turned to her, worry on her face. "How bad is it?"

Indaro shrugged. "Flesh wound." She had no idea how bad it was. The wound was numb, but she felt blood trickling down her hip under the leather kilt. Or perhaps it was sweat.

Looking round her, she stepped across a body and, wincing as she bent, picked up a discarded Blueskin shield. She hefted it and dropped the old cracked one. She settled the new shield on her left arm, protecting her injured side. She wondered how many shields she had got through that morning. Maybe six, she thought, seven. The Blues' were the best.

To her right a soldier in red armour staggered, dazed by a sword blow. Indaro turned to help, but the enemy swordsman hacked into the soldier's neck. Blood sprayed and the Blueskin turned to Indaro, scowling. There was bright blood in his blond beard.

Indaro attacked. The enemy parried, and Indaro barely avoided a murderous riposte which sliced her leather jerkin. This is a skilled swordsman, she thought, gathering her strength. The Blue came at her again with blistering speed and she found herself battling for her life. She parried and blocked with desperation, and was forced back step by step. The man was fighting fluidly. Looking into his calm face, she recognised he was toying with her; he could kill her in a heartbeat.

Stepping back, her foot hit a body in the dust. She was unbalanced, and the Blue sent a lightning thrust at her heart. She swayed gracelessly and fell to one knee. She swung her shield up. The enemy stood over her. She saw eyes watching her assessingly.

Then the trumpet screamed, ordering the enemy retreat. The swordsman paused, then backed away. He and his fellows were retreating in good order, protecting their wounded. From the ground Indaro watched him go, her shield still up. Then she dragged herself to her feet, suddenly overcome with weariness, and stood dumbly waiting for orders. In moments the word came, echoing along the ragged ranks, "Back to the earthwork."

She looked around for Doon, her servant and comrade, and saw her helping an injured Wildcat. Then, glancing often at the retreating Blueskin army, she returned slowly to the earthwork they had left at dawn that morning. She looked right and left. On every side all she could see was grey dust, corpses and blood. No plants left standing, no trees, no hills or landmarks. She had probably fought over this few hundred paces of land a dozen times. There was nothing to distinguish it from all the other battlegrounds. Each time she felt the need to make some mark, to show where brave men and women had fallen, a gift of lifeblood for the City. She understood why the ancients had built stone cairns to commemorate the places of battle. She smiled ruefully to herself. This grey dusty plain would be littered with cairns, each marking a daily engagement in a battle that had lasted half a year. She remembered fighting over this plain in winter, arms and legs encased in wool, both armies hampered by the need to avoid frostbite. Now it was summer and the sweat was pouring off her. Soon it would be so hot that soldiers would die in their hundreds from thirst and heatstroke.

"Indaro!"

She looked round and realised she had wandered away from her company. An officer was trotting over to her.

"Are you wounded?" he asked.

She remembered the injury to her side and struggled to free her armour. She pulled aside the jerkin. The officer peered short-sightedly at the flesh wound. "Lucky," he said. "Get it stitched."

He pointed her towards the field hospital, but as soon as he turned his back she sat down in the dust. The wound was bleeding, but not much, and she had no wish to join the badly injured, whose groans and screams echoed across the plain as the surgeons went about their grisly work.

Time passed as she sat there, then Doon was squatting down beside her, handing her a water jug. "You all right?"

"I'll get stitched when the rush is over." Indaro gulped down half the water then lay on her back in the dust and sighed. "Tired," she explained.

She felt Doon ease the sword from her hand. It was welded to the skin, sticky with blood. She heard the sword slide into its sheath. Doon pulled off her body armour for her, and the freedom in her chest made Indaro greedily suck in air, bloodstained and foetid though it was. Doon gently lifted her head and placed something soft under it.

Then Indaro drifted off to sleep, and the distant cries of the wounded became the screams of seabirds as she dreamed of home.

* * *

*H*ome *was soft grey stone atop sheer grey cliffs, a place where the gulls wheeled and cried in the sunlight.*

"Stay away from the cliffs," they always told her. "Don't go near the edge."

But she was only three and she had no idea what cliffs were. She toddled up to the edge and watched the great white birds soaring in blue light. She flapped her arms to mimic them and jumped about on the grass. When she looked down she could not understand what she saw. There was no more land, nothing in front of her toes but white sparkles far away.

"Daro, don't move! Stay still, baby!"

Hearing her daddy's voice she twisted round so fast she nearly fell over. Then rough arms grabbed her so hard it hurt and warm tears fell on her face.

Indaro shifted in her sleep and tried to roll over. The pain in her side woke her, and she turned to her back and stared at the darkening sky.

After that the little girl was confined to the grey house and its manicured gardens with their well-bred flowers and polite paths. When, years later, she walked up to the cliff edge again and looked down at the surf far below, the screams of the gulls calmed the pain in her heart. Her mother had died in the night. Her father sat at his desk staring unseeing at the wall. Indaro turned sixteen that day, and a new life was beginning.

The grey house was far above the City, facing the setting sun. For much of her young life Indaro heard no word of the City, and when she did she had no idea that she was part of it, she belonged to it.

So on her sixteenth birthday two soldiers came to the house and took her away, past the silent guards and watching servants, as her mother still lay in her deathbed and her father sat helpless with grief. Indaro was taken to a training camp in the south where she stayed for twenty days. She was taught how to kill Blueskins and was put in some dead warrior's uniform and given an old sword and sent to the desolate plain of Araz to fight a battle. It was later known as the Retreat from Araz, a low point in the history of the City and a shame on those who survived it.

When she was ten and was given everything she wanted in the world, Indaro had been introduced to a fencing master, a thin elderly man with scars on his face, who taught her the subtle art of the blade. She had natural grace and balance, she was told by the courteous old man, and her mother smiled and her father nearly burst with pride to see how she quickly acquired the skills of a champion swordswoman.

These skills were of little use on the plain of Araz where, overwhelmed
by one of the greatest armies the world had ever seen, the City's forces were
destroyed in two days of unspeakable carnage. Each moment was spent desperately hacking at flesh and metal and bone until it stopped moving. It was
a battle with no survivors; at least, no one still alive admitted having been
there. Indaro remembered those days only in brilliant blood-soaked flashes.
One of them was being hauled up the outside of the Wall of Victory in a
flimsy willow basket. Nothing she had experienced in those two days of
battle compared with the terror she felt in the last few moments; the terror
that hope—unlooked-for hope after despair and hopelessness—would be
snatched away in the final moment by an enemy missile. She was one of the
last to be dragged up the high wall to safety. The rest of the willow baskets
were destroyed by the enemy and the last hopeful survivors who, against all
odds, made it to the base of the wall were butchered, trapped and helpless
within a hand's-reach of rescue.

"Time to get your wound stitched," Doon's voice said. Indaro turned her
head wearily and nodded. There was always a time after a battle when those
who were going to die died, and those who were expected to live were treated
and routine prayers of hope sent up for them. Then the surgeons could turn
their tired attention to the less-badly injured. Indaro stood and slowly made
her way to the surgeons' tents.

Half a year after the Retreat from Araz the City's dishonour was partly
relieved when, in an audacious advance at night and in the depth of winter,
the legendary general Shuskara took back the land that had been lost, and
destroyed an entire Blueskin army with just two thousand hand-picked soldiers. The Second Battle of Araz established the City's eastern defence at the
river Kercheval, where it remained to this day.

The surgeon, a grey-haired woman with empty eyes, stitched the wound
in Indaro's side and bandaged it gently. Then she and Doon went to get some
food.

At the crowded mess tent they took two plates of fish, lentils and cornbread then walked over to an empty table. Around them men and women
sat or slumped, too tired to talk, many too tired to eat. Indaro felt her
bones sink into the wooden seat and she stared at the plate of food without
enthusiasm.

Then a hard hand smacked her on the shoulder and, as she cursed the jolt of pain in her side, a rangy, tow-haired warrior sat down next to her, slinging a heaped plate in front of him. With him were three other members of their company, the Wildcats, laughing and talking as if, Indaro thought, they had all been to a wedding.

"Still alive then, Indaro?" Broglanh asked her, stuffing bread into his mouth and talking round it. "That Blue swordsman nearly had you." He swallowed. "Could have had you, if he'd wanted."

"You were watching?" Doon asked venomously.

"I was busy," Broglanh defended himself. "I wasn't sitting around with my feet up. He was something special. Don't want to meet too many of them." Indaro privately thought he was right. They had become used to killing enemy soldiers swiftly. They all joked about the frailty of the Blues, how easily they died.

"Indaro can take anybody with a sword," Doon said loyally.

"You didn't see him," retorted blond Garret, and Doon glared at him too.

"Are you all right, Red?" Broglanh turned his head and looked closely into Indaro's face.

She nodded curtly. She hated being called Red, and he was the only one she allowed the discourtesy. Annoying though he could be, Broglanh always raised the energy levels wherever he went. Today though she saw deep bruises under his pale eyes, and she could smell the defeat on him. She picked up a piece of cornbread and chewed at it. The fish smelled bad too.

"Did you see old Bearfoot?" asked Broglanh generally. "He took out two at once with that bloody dangerous sword of his. Straight through both necks." He made a cutting motion at his throat and laughed, a sharp sound without humour.

"I saw," said Indaro. Bearfoot's broadsword was half a foot longer than regulation and he honed it to perfect sharpness every night. It was a legend in the company that it killed more of his friends than his foes.

"Did he make it back?" Doon asked.

Broglanh sniffed. "Of course he did. They wish. Reckon there's a price on his head."

"He's a menace." Indaro had seen the veteran fall in a melee, before rising again swinging the broadsword, City and Blueskin warriors alike ducking away from its threat. "And he must be wounded."

Broglanh shrugged. Just as they scoffed at their own wounds, so they minimised others. However black the day, however appalling the slaughter, no mention was made of the dead, only those who had survived. Indaro had seen the deaths of two warriors she had fought beside all season, six or so gravely wounded. But the talk was not of them, only of old Bearfoot, who had risen to fight another day.

"They say there'll be more recruits arriving in a couple of days," offered Garret, who kept his ear to the ground.

A groan echoed round the table. It was the most dangerous time for them all, when youngsters fresh from training camp were put on the front lines. They were either so terrified they were paralysed into uselessness, or so full of unjustified zeal that they put everyone else in peril with their antics.

"We were all recruits once," added Garret piously.

Broglanh snorted. "I wasn't," he muttered into his plate. "I was born a veteran."

There were nods all round the table. Indaro looked at her food. For the rest of them it was hard to remember a time when they weren't fighting. But after the Araz Retreat there were five years when Indaro had escaped the battles. She was invalided home, then her father's influence kept her in administration for a year, sending other soldiers to the front lines. Then she had dropped out of sight and for three years led an underground life which finally took her underground—into the sewers. She was a deserter, although she never permitted the word to enter her head those days, or these. She believed she was doing valuable work, and that losing her life in the carnage of battle would be a waste of her talents, a waste to the City.

Then she had met the old man Bartellus in the Hall of Watchers. And she had seen the look in his eyes—something between contempt and, even harsher, pity—and within a few weeks she had emerged from the tunnels and rejoined the Maritime Army, which was then fighting near her home, defending the coast of the Salient. That was eight years ago . . .

"This fish stinks," Doon said, wrinkling her nose. She spat chewed grey flesh on her plate and picked up the cornbread instead.

"Tastes all right to me," Broglanh said round a mouthful.

"Is there anything you won't eat?" Doon asked him.

Broglanh shrugged. "Eat while you can." He swallowed, "Somebody once said an army marches on its stomach."

"Thank the gods we haven't got any marching to do."

They all ate in silence. Even Broglanh was beyond conversation. Indaro, drooping over her plate, was thinking of the walk back to their camp, and it seemed an unimaginably long journey on leaden legs. It was taking all her energy to sit upright.

Suddenly she realised the atmosphere had changed and there was a tension in the air. She looked up and saw a tall dark-haired warrior making his way among the tables, a plate in one hand. All the soldiers had fallen silent. He was coming her way. She willed him to carry on past. He stopped and placed his plate on the table. He looked around at them. Nobody caught his eye, even Broglanh. The dark-haired man sat down and started to eat. Conversation resumed at the tables around them, though it was muted and Indaro could feel eyes resting on them.

Fell Aron Lee was their company commander and a legend. A twenty-five-year veteran, he was worshipped by his troops. Usually, in Indaro's experience, a soldier's reputation plummeted as fast his rank rose. Platoon leaders were held to be ambitious fools. The generals—with a few noble exceptions—were loathed with a perfect hatred as cruel, cowardly and stupid. Among the many and complicated ranks in between, the company commander was considered a simpleton or a coward, usually both. But Fell Aron Lee was simply a hero to them all. He had risen to fame during the Second Battle of the Salient, when he had masterminded an ingenious expedition which had taken back the beaches of that vital stronghold with the loss of only three soldiers, one of whom died when he was startled by a goat and fell off a cliff. Only the jealousy of senior officers stopped the man being a general, they all agreed, although there was the rumour that he was the bastard son of their lost hero Shuskara. There were always rumours.

Indaro had only spoken to him once, when she had returned to the army, gripped by doubt. On that day she still believed she might be executed for her three-year absence. She was brought into the tent of a dark-haired man of middle years dressed in regular uniform. He was sitting behind a desk leafing through papers, and the first thing she noticed about him was a deep dent the size of a man's thumb in the right side of his forehead. The skin of it was pale and stretched and it seemed to pulse. He looked up at her. His eyes were startling blue.

"Indaro Kerr Guillaume," said the guard with her, stumbling over the last.

"I knew your father," the officer told her, though his face remained stone.

The tension in her chest lightened a little. Then he added, "I never believed them when they said he raised a family of deserters."

Indaro's voice came out dry and wooden. "He knew nothing of my . . . absence. He has disowned me, sir."

It was a lie and the man knew it. He nodded though.

"My job is to win battles," he told her after a pause. "I need all the resources I can get. I'm told you are an excellent swordswoman. I cannot afford to waste you."

He gestured to the guard then returned to his work.

Sitting at the mess table Indaro covertly watched him eat. After a moment she realised he could not possibly recognise her among the hundreds of soldiers under his command. And what did it matter if he did? She sat back and flicked the dark red hair off her face. As she did so he raised his head from his food, a piece of bread halfway to his mouth. He gazed at her and nodded his head slightly before eating.

He turned to her servant. "Something wrong with the fish, Doon?"

"It's bad, sir."

"Here." He held out his hand. Doon stared at it like an idiot, then quickly passed him the plate. He sniffed it and cursed. "Garvy." He barely raised his voice, but in seconds his aide appeared from nowhere.

"Take this." Their leader gave him the plate. "Whoever's responsible for today's food. Is it Bazala?" The aide looked blank; he clearly had no idea. "Whoever. I want him in my tent by the time I get back. In chains."

The aide nodded and turned away, holding the plate of fish.

Fell Aron Lee looked around the table. "You know who I am," he said. It was not a question. "I'm looking for volunteers."

Indaro had spent all her adult years escaping one intolerable situation only to run towards another. She had fled active service to escape the bowel-clenching horror of daily death and mutilation. She had walked away from her post in administration because she despaired of the pointless paperwork which tangled the armies in a net of impotent ineptitude. And it was self-loathing that had made her, finally and reluctantly, turn away from Archange and return to the war. And now she was walking towards a new, unknown challenge, a new test.

They had all volunteered for the mission, though they had no idea what it was. Fell Aron Lee wanted two soldiers. He had picked Indaro and Broglanh. He told her to leave Doon behind, and as Indaro left the table with the commander she turned back and smiled at her, but Doon merely stared at her, caught, perhaps, between envy and concern.

The two soldiers followed their commander across the darkening land. They passed glittering campfires and rows of sleeping soldiers, dark lumps on the monochrome moonlit earth. It was late and the camp was quiet. There was no carousing, no laughter, only the sounds of muffled snores and the whine of distant machinery. As she followed her commander through the darkness, Indaro's legs felt no longer like lead. She was no longer bothered by the wound in her side. She could feel the blood thrilling through her veins at the prospect of a new challenge. Even a suicide mission would be better than another day of dreary slaughter.

"You're quiet," Broglanh muttered.

"I'm quiet?" she replied irritably. "I'm *always* quiet. You're the one who never stops talking."

"What do you think it'll be?"

"Let's wait and find out," she told him, as if indifferent. But in her mind's eye she was seeing a covert dash behind enemy lines dressed in a Blue uniform, the silent death of an enemy commander, an emperor's praise, redemption.

"They want spies," he hazarded.

"They've got spies." Then she asked, smiling, "Who'd make you a spy? You can't keep quiet about anything." Broglanh grinned.

When they came to the commander's tent they were told to wait outside, and in a few moments one of the cooks came out. It was not Bazala, and he was not in chains, but his face was white as his apron was intended to be. He stumbled away in the dark, flanked by guards.

Inside Indaro glanced around curiously. A narrow bed. An oak chest. A flimsy desk with three straight chairs. Boxes of papers. The only thing that stood out was a suit of dress armour on a rack, gold and silver glittering on red leather. Indaro imagined herself in such armour. Then she imagined Fell Aron Lee garbed in it, and she felt suddenly warm in the midnight tent.

"Sit down," their commander told them, gesturing at chairs, barely looking at them. "You are carrying a wound, Indaro."

How did he know? "A scratch, sir."

"Show me."

With only a second's hesitation, she lifted her jerkin. He stood and moved quickly to her side, peered, then nodded, satisfied.

Fell announced, "You will leave immediately to join the Thousand."

Indaro kept her face impassive, but inside she exulted. The Thousand were the emperor's personal bodyguard. Only veterans were hand-picked for that role, usually after some dazzling act of bravery.

"This is not a promotion," he added, watching their faces. "There has been some . . . wastage in the ranks of the bodyguard recently. You will join troops from other companies to buttress them on this one mission."

Indaro didn't care. This was a chance to get noticed, to have her name remembered for something, other than desertion. She could feel Broglanh crackling with excitement beside her. She wondered how much it was costing him to keep from blurting out something stupid.

"The emperor is presently at the Fourth Eastern Gate," their commander told them. "He is to travel with the sunrise. He will go north-east to the Narrows. The Third Imperial is there, battling an Odrysian army twice its size. Reinforcements are being sent this winter, cavalry and some infantry from the Maritime, and the emperor is on a morale-boosting trip, I'm told." He turned to his desk and rolled out a hard-used map. Indaro stepped forward eagerly. It was the first time, since she was in training, that anyone in command had bothered to explain anything to her.

She squinted at the map in the gloom of the tent. The dark bulk of the City filled it on the left. Fell indicated the Little Sea at the top and the Narrows stretching out beyond. Indaro could make out the line of the City wall snaking down the length of the map. She looked for the Salient, her home, but it was not there. Too far west.

"Where are we?" she demanded. The commander gazed at her without expression, then indicated a large space in the middle, blank but for some cross-hatching.

"Are these forests?" she asked, pointing to dark patches on the right.

"No," Fell replied, "they are the enemy, soldier." His finger moved down the parchment. "Odrysians, Fkeni here, some Petrassi, there are two armies of . . ."

"All just Blues to us grunts, sir," Broglanh said. He grinned at Fell, and his commander looked at him reflectively. Indaro thought something passed between them. Men and their bonding, she thought. Then Fell indicated a tiny drawing of a tower on the City wall.

"This is the Fourth Eastern," he said briskly. "You will have to ride hard to get there by dawn." He took one hand off the map and it rolled up with a snap. He told them, "It is unusual for the Immortal to make such a journey. The situation must be dire. You will ride to the gate and join his bodyguard immediately. My aide has your papers. He will go with you."

The he sat back down at his desk. "Good luck," he told them and, though she did not know the man, Indaro heard satisfaction in his voice.

As the men filed out Broglanh lingered, and asked, "Why us, sir? I mean, I know we volunteered, but you came to *our* table."

Indaro could have kicked him. She kept moving towards the tent flap, willing Broglanh to follow her.

Fell said coldly, "Because your commanding officer tells you, Broglanh."

"Yes, sir. And I see why Indaro would be wanted," Broglanh went on, and Indaro heard an unfamiliar note of slyness in his voice. "She's a sword master and you'd want that in the bodyguard. But me, I'm . . ."

"Should I regret my decision, soldier?"

"No, sir."

Broglanh turned and was trailing Indaro out of the tent when their commander volunteered calmly, "It should be obvious."

They turned and stared at him.

"What do you both share?" he asked them.

Indaro's brain had gone numb. When they said nothing he shook his head. "You both bear Family names," he said. "This increases your chances of being admitted to the Thousand. It is not just, perhaps, but it is so. Is that what you wanted to hear, Evan Quin Broglanh, that you have been chosen for this mission not for your bravery, or your keen intelligence, but for an accident of birth?"

Broglanh said nothing, but he smiled and nodded.

"Good luck," Fell Aron Lee repeated, and turned away.

Chapter 9

They were given mounts and, with Garvy in the lead, they rode out into the quiet night. It was a long ride, following the City wall, always in sight on their left. Sometimes they rode in its moon-shadow; at others it was a dark ribbon in the distance. They rode through silent army camps and past settlements of the lost and desperate, people prepared to live on the front line, or to die, to clean up the mountains of debris an army left in its wake.

Much of the time they journeyed across an empty land, where the great wall resembled the ruins of an old house left untenanted among green lawns. Sheep and goats cropped the grass in its lee, and the occasional tired nag turned to stare, as if in envy, as the warhorses cantered past.

At one point in the night Garvy led them through a gate in the wall. Indaro looked up as the high timber doors opened for them. She had never travelled in these parts and had no idea where they were. They had seen not a soul for an hour. There were ancient runes carved deep into the stones above the gate. Garvy spoke to guards in an echoing stone courtyard, lit by flickering torches, presenting papers and quietly answering questions. The soldiers protecting this distant outpost seemed watchful and efficient, but as they rode on through Indaro looked down and saw eyes staring at them as if in envy.

The three followed the wall inside the line of ancient stones until the next gate where, with the guards' permission again, they crossed back to the outside. Indaro turned in her saddle and looked back, wondering at their diversion, but there was nothing to see, only innocent grassland and the moonlit wall snaking towards the horizon.

It was close to dawn when they reached the emperor's encampment. Their first warning was a cry in the darkness, then a troop of lightly ar-moured riders appeared in the gloom. Garvy called a halt and they waited tensely, surrounded by silent horsemen, the creak of leather and clump of hooves and snort of horses' breath welcome in their ears after so many quiet leagues. Again papers were presented and questions asked, then the troop rode into the camp.

"About time," a gravelly voice said irritably. The speaker was a bushy-bearded warrior wearing the black and silver livery of the Thousand.

"I'm Fortance," he grunted at them. "We're ready to leave. Fresh horses. Lively!"

They swiftly remounted. Indaro saw Garvy turn away and ride off without a word. Then the Wildcats were ordered to the column and took their place behind a dark featureless carriage. Black and silver helms turned to watch them.

Within a short while a group of dark figures hurried from a nearby building to the high carriage. There was a flurry of movement. Some climbed into the imperial vehicle and some out again, servants perhaps, she thought. Then one figure came out and paused, looking round at the waiting riders and fidgeting horses. He was tall, caped, with light hair which gleamed in the torchlight. He raised a pale hand and light flashed off a jewelled ring. Indaro could barely see through the helms and feathered plumes nodding in front of her, but she felt a thrill through her spine as she craned to glimpse him. The emperor dipped his head and disappeared into the carriage. Then the armoured door swung shut, and the troop moved off.

Indaro realised the emperor's bodyguard were flanked by many more regular troopers, maybe hundreds. She had often been accused of arrogance, but she could not help wonder what difference two Wildcats would make in this moving sea of armour and weapons. She glanced at Broglanh and caught his eye. He grinned at her, clearly delighted. She knew how he felt. They were moving forward, they had a clearly defined task, and were free, if only for one day, from the carnage of the battlefield.

They rode at a trot, in close formation, through the dawn light. They were heading north. Indaro saw her moon-shadow bobbing on the armoured back of the trooper in front of her. Close on her left were hooded riders. She felt hemmed in, as if she were under escort herself, and she wondered how far they had to go, whether the ranks would ease out as they travelled. She felt a sensation of unreality, that she was riding just a few horse-lengths behind the emperor, the Immortal. She wondered idly if he was facing front, or sitting looking back towards her through the windowless walls of the carriage. The conveyance was pulled by a team of twelve. Indaro guessed it was heavily armoured. Despite that, she would have given a year's pay not to travel in such a vehicle, a sitting duck for enemy action. If I were in charge, she thought, the emperor would travel by horse, with merely two or three protectors, while a decoy was sent by carriage with hundreds of guards.

The company was opening out, and there was a horse's length between her and the rider in front. Indaro felt she could breathe more easily. It was more than half a year since she had ridden, and it was good to feel the saddle under her thighs, the familiar movement, the noise of leather and the heavy breath of the horse. Her mind drifted to the riding lessons when she was small, the grey pony she called Mousey . . .

Her eyes on the shiny armour in front of her, her mind in the past, she saw one of the horses immediately behind the carriage rear up as a sound like thunder exploded in her ears. The horse plunged screaming on its side, blood spraying from its neck, then another blast to her right threw horses and riders like rag dolls.

The mount in front of her faltered, perhaps injured, and Indaro dragged out her sword, standing up in her stirrups to find the enemy. The emperor's carriage was speeding away from the threat, the team of horses leaning into the traces, the bodyguard closing around from the front to compensate for the casualties at the rear.

Then another, more thunderous, explosion in front of the conveyance flung riders and their mounts into the air. Panicked horses tried to run from the noise and the tall carriage slowed, lurched and stopped then, with infinite slowness, toppled over.

For a moment there was empty ground between Indaro and the emperor's carriage and she kicked her horse towards it. Then the earth rose up in front of her and an armed warrior appeared magically at her mount's hooves. He thrust his sword at the horse's belly and Indaro dragged on the reins, leaned down and chopped his arm off. He staggered, his mouth wide open in a scream. Indaro could hear nothing. She was deafened by the explosions.

More enemy soldiers erupted from the ground, from hidden dugouts. Stiff from crouching in holes, they were unequal to an armed rider, and Indaro slashed and cut her way through sluggish heads and necks, trying to reach the emperor. Beside her she was aware Broglanh had been unhorsed and she glimpsed him fighting grimly, beset by enemy soldiers, one arm hanging uselessly.

Through the swirling dust she saw someone crawling weakly from the broken door of the carriage, a beardless boy, injured but still moving. An enemy lanced a sword into her horse's chest and it fell. She slid to the ground, sword still in hand, killed the enemy soldier, then ran towards the carriage. She helped the wounded youngster, thrusting a shoulder under his arm, wincing as his weight dragged on her injured side. She pulled him away and helped him to the ground in the inadequate shelter of a dead horse. She saw he was barely in his teens, his eyes dark and wide. He was dressed all in green silk and there was a random piece of wood stuck in his chest. She was surprised he was still alive.

She turned back to the carriage, and spotted movement, someone struggling under the shattered frame. Then she saw an enemy soldier running towards it, fast as an athlete. Indaro slid her knife from its sheath and threw it at his head. It stuck in his neck and he staggered, but he managed to throw the missile in his hand before he fell. It missed the carriage and rolled under the hooves of one of the struggling horses. Indaro dragged air into her lungs, and raced towards it, but she had moved hardly three paces when there was a huge explosion and, in deathly silence, the black carriage was torn to pieces in front of her eyes.

Indaro was hit by the soundless blast and was thrown to the ground, rolling, protecting face and eyes. Then she was up again and running to the wreckage. But there was nothing left there, just two twisted bloodied torsos, charred and broken. Her breath caught in her chest, and her heart felt pierced. The emperor. Her emperor. Dead.

Through the whirling dust she saw Fortance. He was staring at the bodies. He had a head injury and the tears pouring down his face made tracks in the blood. Then he saw her and shouted soundlessly. He pointed to the east, where she could see enemy soldiers fleeing towards the sunrise, their work done. Fortance held his wrists together in front of him, nodding urgently at her. She understood. "Take prisoners."

Through the dust, among the dead and dying warriors and beasts, she saw an uninjured horse, a grey mare, wandering, trailing her reins. Indaro ran to the mount and grabbed the reins and took a second to stroke the mare's nose, looking into her eyes, then she leaped on her back. She kicked the flanks and, well-trained, the horse chased towards the escaping enemy.

On a small rise a group of enemy warriors were making a stand, surrounded by City soldiers. Swords thrust and hacked and clanged, but Indaro could hear nothing. Neither could the Blues. She cantered up behind them and slashed a warrior's head from his shoulders with one cut. She saw her fellows shout out in triumph. She killed two more, one with a thrust to the chest, one skewered under the arm. The City soldiers, heartened, tore into the enemy with renewed strength. Indaro remembered Fortance's order. When there were just seven enemy left standing, she gestured to her comrades, wrists together, until they nodded their understanding. As they bound their prisoners' hands, she trotted the horse slowly back to the wreckage. The last few enemy, all injured, were being herded together for questioning later, when they had regained their hearing. But discipline had reasserted itself among the City ranks, and they did not need to hear orders as they set about tending the wounded, despatching the injured horses. A screen had been set up around the wreckage of the carriage and men of the Thousand solemnly stood guard. Too little, too late, Indaro thought.

She found Broglanh sitting among the wounded, waiting patiently for someone to tend his broken arm. His face was grey with pain, and she helped him get comfortable, leaning against a tree stump. He was talking to her, as if she could hear what he said, but she thought he was rambling. She spoke to him too, words of reassurance unheard. She spotted a canteen on a wandering horse, took it to Broglanh and helped him drink. He said something to her and grinned and she knew he was joking. He had not realised the emperor was dead. She smiled.

At last there was a buzzing in her ears, she swallowed several times, and her hearing came back, tinny and faint.

"Can you hear me now?" she asked Broglanh. But he had passed out, his broken right arm cradled in his left hand.

Indaro stood and looked around her. Warriors trained in the surgeons' craft were treating the most badly wounded soldiers. The prisoners had disappeared, taken away for interrogation. She searched for a while for the boy dressed in green, but could not see him. She guessed he had died. Then she spotted Fortance shouting orders at a group of riders, sending out scouts to look for other enemy soldiers. She walked over to him.

"Your orders, sir."

Fortance looked at her. His face was still bloody, but his tears had been wiped away. She guessed his days as an officer of the Thousand were numbered. Only death and dishonour awaited him.

"Indaro, yes?" he asked.

"Yes, sir."

"The company will divide. One group will go post-haste to the City with the emperor. You will go ahead with that group."

Conflicting emotions battled in her breast. She knew she had acquitted herself well, and was glad Fortance had noticed her. Yet Fell Aron Lee had charged her with protecting her lord, and she had failed to do so. If she had been faster, quicker on the uptake, quicker on her feet, she could have stopped the assassin. She had assisted an unknown lad before she helped her emperor.

"Yes, sir." Then she said formally, "I'm sorry, sir, I couldn't stop him."

Fortance nodded. "You did well, soldier. You probably saved the emperor's life."

For a moment the words meant nothing. Then, "Saved?" she repeated.

Fortance said, "The Immortal was injured. But he will recover, thanks be to the gods."

Indaro stared at him, speechless. It was impossible that anyone had survived the Blues' sorcerous explosion. And she was certain, as sure as she was of anything, that when she had seen Fortance after the blast, the man had thought his emperor dead. She opened her mouth, then thought better of it, and turned away.

She spent the next hour walking among the wounded, giving them water and stitching the most superficial of wounds. Finally they were ordered to mount and she ran to the waiting grey and climbed into the saddle. The emperor had been removed to a baggage-cart and a canvas screen erected around him. It was an undignified conveyance, but experienced surgeons were a long way away and it was necessary to get the Immortal back to the City as soon as possible. Fast riders had already been sent back for help.

As they made their way across the wastelands of Salaba, Indaro was riding in the rear with the ordinary cavalry, perhaps forty riders. The remains of the Thousand, fewer than twenty in all, rode ahead. She called to mind

Fortance's face, and tried to guess if he was lying to her. But she did not know the man, and shock and grief made liars of us all, she thought. She realised she was dog-tired and wondered how long it had been since she had slept, or eaten.

They were heading for the ancient Paradise Gate, to the south of the gate they had left the day before, and closer to the centre of the City. Even so, it would take them the rest of the day to get there.

There was a cry from up ahead and the company came to a halt, riders putting hands to swords and looking around. As the dust settled Indaro saw horsemen riding towards them across the flat meadows from the west, bright with silver and gold glittering in the sunshine. There were more than a hundred riders, she thought, in lines of four, and they stayed rigidly in formation as they drew near and reined in. Behind them trailed an empty carriage of plain wood.

The troop's leader was a woman with grey hair cropped like a man's, slim and straight, dressed in ordinary riding clothes, with nothing to indicate rank. She slid off her horse and spoke to Fortance, then disappeared into the baggage-cart.

"Who is that?" Indaro asked the tall rider alongside her, but he shook his head. She wished she were with the Thousand, whose members would certainly know, being closer to the emperor and the mighty.

But the tall rider had asked the man next to him, who had asked also, and eventually the answer came back down the line.

"She is Saroyan, Lord Lieutenant of the East," the rider told her. She nodded, and he grinned at her.

Lord lieutenants held a compromised position in the ranks of the nobles, she remembered Archange telling her. Chosen by the emperor, their powers were potentially sweeping, yet they held no position in relation to the emperor's armies. Thus it took a powerful personality to stamp his or her authority on the post. Mostly, she had heard, they coasted along in a ceremonial role, enjoying the pleasures of rank without engaging with any of the responsibilities.

But this Saroyan acted like a soldier, ordering the troops with brisk authority. She ducked out of the carriage and mounted again. Fortance trotted his horse over and she asked him questions, and listened to him closely, her eyes on his. He turned and cast a look over the troops, then they both gazed at Indaro. Fortance beckoned to her and Indaro heeled the grey forward. Up close she could see the woman was older than she at first seemed. Her eyes were very light, almost yellow—a colour Indaro had never before seen in a living being. She wore a ring in her right ear with a light grey stone.

"This is Indaro Kerr Guillaume," the veteran warrior said, "of the Wildcats. She stopped the assassin reaching the Immortal's carriage."

Saroyan stared at her coolly, her protuberant eyes pale as ice under winter sun.

"Guillaume," she said. "Reeve's get?"

Indaro nodded, fearing the woman would say something about deserters, but the lord lieutenant merely blinked, then turned away. She ordered the company to divide again. The ordinary troopers, including Indaro, were to ride on into the City with the baggage-cart. The rest of the Thousand, perhaps in disgrace, would return to the site of the ambush and help the wounded. Two surgeons from the City would go with them. Saroyan remounted her horse and turned back towards the City, riding in front of the cortege. The rest of the riders fell in behind.

Their progress was slow, and the steady movement of the mare was conducive to sleep. Indaro was so tired she kept drifting off in the saddle, waking suddenly from time to time, her knees gripping the horse with a start. The tall rider, who had chosen to ride next to her again, tried to make conversation, but she was too exhausted to be polite.

The City came in sight. First a brown smudge appeared in the distant west, between the grey mare's ears. Indaro felt the thrill run through many of the troopers as they saw the first sight of their home. She guessed they had been fighting far away too. They were riders of the First Adamantine Cavalry, and they called themselves the Nighthawks.

"How long since you were last in the City?" she asked the tall rider.

He turned cold eyes on her, perhaps reluctant to speak to someone who had largely ignored him.

"Three years," he told her, biting off the words.

She nodded, impressed. Armies had been in the field longer than that, but not often. It seemed the assassination attempt was good news for these soldiers.

"You?" he asked civilly.

"A year, slightly less."

The stain on the horizon resolved itself into a tall grey slab of mountain, surrounded by low green foothills. In front of them Indaro could now make out the line of the wall. They were perhaps an hour away at this pace, and she allowed herself to start thinking of food and, best of all, sleep. And she wondered what would happen to her now. Fortance had her papers. Had he passed them on to the lord lieutenant? Or had she, an odd duck in this flight of hawks, been forgotten?

Indaro had never been to the Paradise Gate; she had never entered that part of the City, and she was pleased when the cortege sped up slightly, as if even Saroyan was eager to get home. They were riding now through green pasture, horse meadows and sheep fields, divided by lively springs. The highway was of flat stone. Elderly field workers stopped to stare as the cortege passed. Indaro saw a group of young girls relieved, if only for moments, from some dreary task, jumping up and down and waving with delight as the riders passed by. Some of the men at the rear of the procession waved back.

As they drew closer, Indaro looked up at the grey-green mountain which rose abruptly before them. It was called the Shield of Freedom and was said to be riddled with caves and tunnels, the last sanctuary of the emperor and his Family if ever this part of the City were invaded. At its foot were rolling green hills where the palaces of the mighty nestled in fabulous gardens.

The high bronzed doors of the Paradise Gate opened for them. Indaro glanced at the runes carved on the gate posts as the riders thundered through.

The barracks of the Nighthawks lay hard against the inner wall. The massive stones of the wall, worn smooth and rounded by the bitter rains of millennia, formed one side of the troopers' mess where Indaro found herself that evening. So hungry and tired she was beyond making decisions, she would have eaten or slept, whichever opportunity presented itself first. She found the stables, where she saw the mare fed and watered. Then she followed the Nighthawks to their mess. She was sat at a table slumped over a thick tasteless stew when the tall rider found her.

"You do not belong here," he commented, sitting down.

She raised her eyes to him wearily. He was clean-shaven, like Fell, and his eyes were grey.

"I am with the Third Maritime, under Randell Kerr," she volunteered.

"Ah, the Maniac."

She nodded her head. "Some call him that." The general was well-named, but she would not admit that to a grey.

She volunteered, "My papers were given to Fortance . . ."

"A dead man."

He is full of observations, she thought. ". . . so I will eat and sleep, then I will seek new orders."

He nodded, then smiled. "They call me Riis."

"Indaro."

"Will you have sex with me, Indaro?"

She almost laughed, but instead she told him gravely, "I have not eaten for three days and I cannot remember when I last slept. Perhaps four days. And I have been in two battles since then."

"So is that a yes?"

She smiled. He *was* very handsome. "No, Riis," she said.

After she had eaten he pointed her in the direction of the sleeping quarters, where she found a narrow bed among snoring soldiers and drifted off to sleep, her sword clutched to her, her brain too tired to try and make sense of the day. When she awoke again it was dark still, or again? The troopers sleeping around her seemed to be different ones. Did I sleep for a full day? she wondered. She felt refreshed, and she got up and retrieved her helm and breastplate from under the bed then, shrugging, thrust them back again. A grey would scarcely lower himself to steal red armour. She would return for them. She strapped on her sword and made her way out, seeking someone in authority.

The barracks were silent, and the only soldiers she saw, drinking outside an inn across the street, were staring gloomily into their mugs. She glanced up at the quarter moon and saw the dawn was chasing the night. The night air felt cool and clean on her face, and she was entranced by the City around her. The great wall dominated her vision. It was higher here than she had ever seen, and it sloped away from her as it rose. She wondered how thick it was at the base. She must have crossed through it, but she could not remember entering the gates the previous day. She turned away from the wall, looking towards the great bulk of the Shield of Freedom which filled her vision in the other direction. It stood like a sentry in the moonlight. She recalled her father telling her it was also called the Serafia, though she did not know what that meant. Lights flickered and gleamed from the top of it, and from the base a line of lights—a pathway perhaps—rose in a wavering line weaving back and forth up the massive silvery rock

She followed narrow alleys and twittens between high buildings. This was the design close inside all the City's gates, a second line of defence against invasion. This was the quarter they called Paradise, and she saw it was well named. She passed shops and craftshouses, but even at night warm lights gleamed behind barred windows. All around her she saw the jewelled glow of stained glass, and the gleam of polished woods. Among the shops high wooden doors guarded the homes of the wealthy. Once she paused to see a company of young women, guarded by private militia, descend from a rich carriage and flutter into a courtyard. Inside she glimpsed a playing fountain and flowers gleaming startling white in the moonlight. The guardians of the fluttering moths turned to stare at her as she passed, suspicious of a lone soldier in the night. She glared back at them, contemptuous of warriors who chose to guard the daughters of the rich, and contemptuous too of the girls whose fathers' influence kept them out of the armies. She thought of her home on the grey cliffs and wondered if her father still lived, and where her brother was.

At last she came out into a moonlit square where stood a white temple to the god of virtue, Themistos, the philosophers' god. From here she could see the Shield, the Serafia, again. She was surprised that her long walk had brought it no closer. The air must be very clear, she thought, sniffing the light breeze. It smelled of flowers and morning bread. From where she stood the land sloped downwards to a sluggish river, crossed by three bridges. On this side of the river must be the homes of the wealthy, facing west, with the Shield in front of them.

The emperor's home, the Red Palace, was far away, on low land many leagues to the west. The palaces of other Families were said to be on the Shield. She idly wondered if a Guillaume palace was up there somewhere, unused, untenanted.

She realised the night around her was changing. She could hear the chirping of early birds and the morning braying of donkeys. Soon there would be people around. Reluctantly she turned back towards the wall. It would not do, she thought, to be charged with desertion twice in one lifetime.

When she got back to the barracks a soldier told her Fortance was looking for her. She followed the man's directions and, after a few missteps in the warren around the Paradise Gate, turned a corner onto a stone parade ground. She spotted the old warrior talking to the lord lieutenant again. And she paused, just out of view, watching them.

Indaro seldom disliked a person on sight, but she found herself repelled by the woman. Saroyan was thin and tall. Plain as a scorpion. Cold as ice. She became suddenly convinced the two were talking about her. Saroyan's head slowly turned towards her, and she flinched, backing into the protection of the wall. When she peered out again Fortance was walking away into the distance and Saroyan still stood in the same spot.

Indaro decided that if she had no orders it was her duty to return to her company. All thoughts of ambition, recognition, promotion, had vanished, and she was eager to get back to her comrades. She retrieved her armour from the sleeping quarters and found the mare fed and rested at the stables. As the sun cleared the horizon in a glory of pink and gold she slipped out through the Paradise Gate and headed the horse towards it.

Chapter 10

The waves of colour formed a pattern under the heat of the noon sun. At the start of the battle the lines of blue and red were straight and wide, strong and firm. Outlying patches of grey and black were solid, fast-moving. The craftsmen who created these patterns had no doubts about their abilities and deployed them with a confident hand. They had done it so often before. The lines clashed, blending their colours, bleeding blue into red, red into blue. As the long day wore on the colours lost definition and clouds of dust further confused the patterns. By the last stages of the battle, when the surviving troops returned to their defences, everything on that plain would be grey tinged with red.

The battlefield was flat and so deep that high wooden towers had been built at its rear so the architects of the battle could watch. The generals were gathered on a tower with their aides and servants. Some were eating and drinking, food laboriously winched up to them, for they might be there some time. Others forebore to indulge themselves while their troops were being slaughtered, but they chatted and sometimes laughed and only once in a while turned their attention to the carnage sprawling beneath them. A few stood quietly watching every move, every valiant push, each bitter blow.

Fell stood with these men, impotent fury swirling in his heart. For one hundred and fourteen consecutive days he had stood, armed and armoured, at the front line of his warriors and endured every triumph, every reverse with them. But this morning Flavius Randell Kerr, general of the Third Maritime, had ordered him to stay back and watch from the tower.

"City can't afford to lose you," the mad old man had told him as they walked the lines at break of dawn.

"I lead my troops into battle," he told his general between gritted teeth. "I have no other useful function."

The general shook his head. "Got to keep good men in reserve. We'll be needing new generals one day, boy."

Fell Aron Lee gazed at the elderly fools quaffing morning wine and telling war stories. I'd rather kill myself, he thought.

He looked around desperately, hoping to see the City's first lord. Marcellus was the one warrior Fell admired, for he was the only one of the mighty ever seen in the first line of battle, and was always the last to leave the field. Fell had never fought alongside him but, as much as he had any ambition in this war, it was to stand shoulder to shoulder with Marcellus Vincerus. He could not see the man on the tower. He did not really expect to. He would be somewhere in the battle below, or fighting the enemy in a far distant conflict. He spotted Rafe Vincerus, Marcellus' younger brother, but he knew little about the man and could scarcely appeal to him.

Fell took a deep breath. To Randell Kerr he commented, forcing calm into his voice, "I can't remember when last a general died. Was it Victorinus

Rae Khan who had an apoplectic fit while being serviced by three whores? Or Jay Garnay, who fell off his horse and injured his leg and insisted on treating the wound with rats' droppings until he died of gangrene?"

Kerr grunted. "Doesn't matter how they die, boy. Fact is, you could be the first general to lead his troops into battle since Shuskara. If that's what you want."

"Marcellus leads his troops."

"Man's First Lord of the City. Can do what he wants."

Fell knew the general had never changed his mind in forty years. Yet he went on arguing, "I have no talent for strategy."

Kerr waved a hand dismissively at the other old men. "There are more than a hundred generals in this City, boy, and only two of them know anything about strategy. And I'm not one of them. Like everything else, this is about politics."

"I have less talent for politics. The only thing I know is fighting."

Randell Kerr was a tall man, though stooped by age, with the face of a tired hound, and jug ears. His big ears waggled as he shook his head.

"There are ten thousand men and women out there who know about fighting," he said, pointing towards the battle, where the City troops were slowly giving way to the Blues. "One more won't make any difference today."

Fell wanted to grab him by the ears and shout, *Yes, one warrior can make a difference! The strength and courage of one soldier can turn a battle.* Just as an act of cowardice can. But he could not say that to the man, for if he did not understand it now, then he never would. Not for the first time, Fell wondered how a man like Randell Kerr had survived a long life in the army.

As they watched, trying to make out the tactics of each side through the roiling dust, a bulge appeared in the blue line far distant. Slowly it swelled and pushed forward into the red line, which gave way reluctantly. Fell could see from their vantage point that a patch of black was forcing its way in from the right. Enemy cavalry intent on joining up with the Blue infantry and cutting off the red wing. Fell's breathing was shallow. He knew with complete certainty that the red troops in peril were his own company.

Behind him he heard two generals discussing a wager over a dog race.

Black rage gathered in his heart and, resisting the temptation to charge at the old boys and tip their carcases off the tower, he ran to the steep wooden steps and began to climb down. On the ground he snatched a horse's reins from a startled groom and leaped into the saddle. Belatedly he realised he had no armour, or arms apart from a thin-bladed knife. He could pick up a shield and sword on the battlefield.

The horse was strong and fast, a beautiful black stallion, probably wasted carrying a general from palace to mess to inn and back, he thought, leaning forward, urging the beast on. He rode round the rear of the field, his blood thrilling with the speed of the stallion and the prospect of the battle to come. He passed lines of dead and wounded soldiers dragged away from the battle by harried, courageous stretcher bearers. Lame and injured horses wandered in his path and his fine mount eased past them scornfully. Down here on the ground it was hard to work out where he was in relation to the action he had seen from the tower. Fell Aron Lee had never arrived at a battle from the rear before. And the dust obscured everything. Only the sounds were familiar, the heart-stopping shriek of metal on metal, the sickening thunk of metal on flesh, awful cries of the wounded, and the screaming of horses.

He rode, more slowly now, through ranks of infantry. Men and women turned and looked at him, amazed, as he passed. Some were heading towards the front line, some leaving it. It was chaos in the choking dust, and Fell needed the high sun to tell him which way to ride. Then at last he could glimpse riders, black riders, the glint of metal and the swirl of horses' manes and tails through the veil of dust. He guessed, he hoped, they were the cavalry company he had seen bearing down on his soldiers. Too much time had passed. They could all be dead.

He had little experience fighting from a horse, but he slowed his mount and leaned from the saddle to grasp a sword sticking out of a corpse. Then he heeled the eager stallion forward again and plunged it straight into a group of three black-clad riders.

They weren't expecting an attack from the rear. One died instantly, Fell's sword slicing his neck. The two others turned. One got his shield up as Fell's sword came stabbing towards him. The other cut at Fell's head. He ducked and stretched forward, snatching a shield from the dead cavalryman. He brought it up in time to deflect a second blow. A sword lanced for his head but clanged off the shield and he stabbed with his own sword deep into the enemy's belly. The third man raised his sword to hack at Fell's head and died with the knife in his eye. Fell snatched up a new sword and a long Missian spear.

"Wildcats!" Fell bellowed into the dust. "Wildcats to me!"

He had no idea if any of his warriors could hear him, but more and more of the enemy riders were turning their horses to face this threat from behind. Officers yelled new orders, thinking ranks of fresh fighters were attacking their rear.

A Blueskin rider galloped towards him, screaming his battle cry. Fell's spear glanced off his breastplate and plunged up through his jaw and into his brain. The trooper was lifted off his horse's back and the spear snapped under his weight. Fell dropped the weapon and drew the new sword, looking round. The Blue cavalry was forming a fighting circle, quite needlessly, to defend itself from the attack from the rear. He grinned.

A cavalryman came from nowhere and a sword slashed at Fell's head. Fell swayed away from the cut and plunged his own sword in the rider's armpit.

At last he spotted a red blur through the roiling dust. Red-armoured infantrymen were hacking their way through the riders.

"To me, Wildcats!" he roared again.

Two Blue riders came at him side by side, spears levelled. He slid off the horse and ducked under its belly, then came up behind one rider and slid his sword under the man's armour at the waist. Feet on firm ground again he felt battle lust surge through him. He snatched a second sword from the dead rider.

"Wildcats!" he bellowed, looking around for someone else to kill.

Then he recognised his own warriors with him, tearing into the remaining black riders. One soldier was bearing a spare breastplate, which he thrust on his commander's chest. Automatically Fell strapped it on.

The soldier's eyes widened and Fell turned like lightning, his sword coming up to deflect a spear-thrust from horseback. He grabbed the spear and dragged it from the rider's grasp. The trooper unsheathed his sword, but as he brought it up Fell smacked the horse on the nose with the flat of his sword. The horse shied violently and the rider missed his mark. Fell spun the spear and plunged it through the man's neck.

The riders were retreating, and the red warriors followed them, enthusiastically picking off the stragglers.

"Wildcats group four!" Fell and the company started forming a fighting square.

Then the enemy trumpeter caught up with events and the retreat order rang out. Fell waited silently, breathing heavily, leaning on a battered sword, until they heard the City orders.

"Stand down. Hold your position."

He breathed a deep sigh. Ordered back to their lines, Fell would have to face Randell Kerr. Unpredictable at the best of times, when crossed the man they called the Maniac was capable of any atrocity. Fell had seen him order a soldier crucified because he hesitated when told to kill a stray Blueskin child.

But they were holding, and now Randell Kerr's wrath would have to wait.

It took Indaro two days to return to her company. She crossed the open country known as Limbis, once known for its vineyards, now a wilderness of dry scrub dotted with poor villages and broken-down farms. Battles had raged back and forth across Limbis for more than five years and, though the area was now considered secure, it was useless for vines. The former vineyard workers, those that had survived, or returned, scraped a meagre living growing hemp and grain and grazing goats. It took Indaro half a day to ride the length of Limbis, and when she smelled the fumes of the northland furnaces in her nostrils she crossed by a minor gate and rode outside the wall, now heading south-east.

After a night spent in the lee of the wall, she set off again towards the battleground she had left two days before. Alone in the flat grassy landscape, she pushed her horse to a canter.

Once again she thought there was something strange about the ambush incident. No living being could have survived that final blast in the carriage. And who was the boy she had rescued? Why did she not see him again? Half her brain thought she had imagined him, in the shock of the explosions. And why did she fear Saroyan, for fear her she certainly did? Her father's enemies were all long dead. And she was just a common soldier.

She put it out of her mind as the grey raced across the short grassland of the eastern plain, heading towards the battlefield of Salaba. The wall was well behind her, and there was nothing on the horizon but a distant line of grey hills.

She could smell the battlefield long before she saw it. The sun was sinking rapidly behind her and the armies would be preparing for rest. She could smell roasting meat and smoke, and the metal tang of shed blood, and the other bodily smells that hang over an army that has been occupying the same benighted place for nearly a year.

At last she saw the red glow of campfires in the gathering dusk. They stretched from one end of the horizon to the other. Reining her horse in she paused, then dragged on the reins and kicked the grey to the south. The Wildcats would likely still be on the right flank. She could tell there had been no fighting that day, for the noises that came to her across the plain were subdued; the soft snorting of a thousand horses, and the quiet sounds made by a hundred thousand warriors preparing for rest. No screams, no cries, no pleas for death.

She came to supply wagons first, some of them heavily guarded, and the camps of the old whores, who were getting ready for the night's business. Some called out to her as she passed, and she waved and smiled, but walked her horse on. When she came to the horse lines her mount snuffled in recognition, and she slid down from her back, patted her for thanks, and handed her to one of the boys, with instructions that she be well fed for her long journey. She asked where the Wildcats were, but the horse boy had no clue, so she carried on walking south.

At last she was stopped by a sentry she recognised, and asked the way to Fell Aron Lee's tent. When she reached it it was near midnight and she hesitated to enter. Then the tent flap moved and suddenly he was beside her.

"Indaro?" She heard the frown in his voice. How had she annoyed him already?

"Sir, I've just got back." She could barely see him, but she could smell blood and sweat. She was tall, but he loomed over her and she could feel the heat coming off him.

"Broglanh was injured," she volunteered. "Broken arm."

"What happened?"

"We were attacked."

He nodded impatiently.

"There was an enemy attack on the emperor's carriage. One of their magical explosions. The emperor was injured."

Fell said nothing for a moment, then tightly, "Will he live?"

"I'm told yes." She blurted out, "But I saw the injuries! No one could have survived that. Yet they're saying he will recover."

The commander nodded, as if expectations were fulfilled. "The injured man you saw was probably a proxy," he explained. "They say the Immortal never leaves his palace these days. He uses substitutes who look a little like him. I thought the mission a strange one."

Irritable beyond discretion, she blurted out, "So you guessed you were sending us on a fool's errand?"

Fell stood in the darkness feeling helpless and frustrated. Whenever he met this annoying woman it was after a battle or, as now, at the end of a long day. He could feel ill-temper rising from her like mist. He was repelled by her arrogance—who else would have the gall to stand and criticise him as she did?—yet drawn to the vulnerability he guessed it cloaked.

So he found himself explaining, "The emperor's proxies have to have a bodyguard, else it would be clear to the enemy that they are substitutes. And he may sometimes leave the City." He admitted, "I am just repeating gossip."

She was silent, then she said, "The carriage was torn apart. I saw the mutilated bodies."

"Some brave soul gave his life for his lord."

She argued, "But if that is true, what was the point of continuing with the pretense? Yet the commander behaved as though the emperor was gravely injured and escorted him back to the City."

"Then perhaps it *was* the emperor and he was less badly hurt than you thought." But as Fell said it he was doubtful, and he found himself being drawn into her reasoning. "Or perhaps a proxy was in the carriage and the emperor rode among his men. *I* would. But," he argued with himself, "their commander must know who is emperor, who is decoy.

"Who was in charge?" he asked her.

"Fortance. He seemed grief-stricken."

"Fortance is a veteran of the Thousand. He served with the Gulons, the elite century. He knows the emperor if any man does. Did he accompany the emperor back?"

"No. On our return we were met by an escort from the City."

"The Thousand went back to the City?"

"No. The bodyguard stayed at the attack site. I thought it was a punishment. The emperor went back to the City with the First Adamantine."

"The Nighthawks. Who was their commander?"

"I don't know. But we were met by Saroyan, the Lord . . ."

"Yes, I know who Saroyan is," he told her.

"Um. Fortance told her who I was. I mean, my family name."

"Why?"

She hung her head in the moonlight. For once in her life she seemed reluctant to speak. "I tried to stop the assassin. I didn't succeed, but perhaps I hampered his aim."

Conflicting emotions vied in his heart. "You saved the emperor's life?"

She shrugged. "Perhaps."

"And Fortance pointed you out to Saroyan for praise?"

"Mmm."

Suddenly Fell realised they were speaking openly. He lowered his voice. "This is no business of yours, soldier. Go back to your unit. Say nothing."

"But, sir . . ."

He leaned towards her, feeling her warmth. "Just for once, Indaro, shut your mouth. Rejoin your colleagues and forget about the last few days."

He waited to see if she would argue again, but she bowed her head, exhaustion taking over. Without another word she disappeared into the night.

Chapter 11

The storm of the century began over waters very far from the City. Sailors on foreign galleys looked to the sky with dread, and their captains made haste for shore and harbour. The winds picked up quickly and soon the skies were filled with roiling, boiling clouds like octopus ink. The air was sharp with the tang of metal. Thunder grumbled just below the horizon. The winds rose and started to howl. By the time the first lightning flashed most ships were safely harboured, hatches battened, lines tied, the sly gusts plucking at loose stays and poorly furled sails. Those boats still racing for safety were picked up by the ferocious winds and flung about, mere flotsam in the grip of the gale.

The storm headed east, taking its time, moving relentlessly across the waters towards the City. The seagulls forecast it first, and they fled before the storm long before human senses could detect it. As the great white birds crossed the City's coastline old salts looked up and heard their eerie cry, and they knew a blow was coming, though the horizon was clear and the sun still shone blandly down. The birds continued eastward, and men and women far inland watched them pass with unease. Seabirds were seldom seen in those easterly parts, and hasty invocations were made to many gods, especially the gods of sun and rain, and the east wind, and the cruel god of the north wind known as Cernunnos.

The white birds streamed over the tall turrets of the Red Palace of the emperor. The passed across the slate and tile roofs of the rich and power-ful and the tarpaper shanties of the poor, caring nothing for any of them. They looked down on the great eastern walls of the city and the only thoughts in their small sleek heads were of sanctuary.

The battlefield of Salaba was more than a hundred leagues from the coast and the gulls paused there and started wheeling and circling, thoughts of safety giving way to thoughts of food. Beneath them was the wide, slug-gish brown ribbon of the river Kercheval crossing a flat plain that had once been rich with grain and horse meadows. On its western side the armies lay entrenched, six leagues distant from each other, indistinguishable to a seagull.

Had the birds passed over a year before they would have seen much the same sight, although the armies were lying six leagues farther north. Were they to pass over a year in the future they would spy an empty plain, empty at least of people, the first flush of green tinting the blood-soaked soil, the wild beasts returning once the savage warriors had gone.

Indaro was lying on her back in the sunshine staring at the sky, her head resting on her folded red jerkin. She rejoiced at the sight of the gulls. Living on the coast for most of her life, she knew they fled before a storm. And bad weather, despite drenched clothes and sodden bedding, was better than the four days of inactivity they had endured under the relentless sun. She was hot and deeply bored, and even a torrent of rain would be welcome.

"There's a storm coming," someone behind her said.

Doon snorted derisively, and pointedly stared at the blue sky. Blond Garret, who always seemed to be within Indaro's eyeline, argued, "There's not a cloud in the sky." Now Broglanh was no longer with them, Indaro seemed to have inherited Garret, an unwanted bequest.

The first speaker, whom Indaro identified from his voice as a stone grey northlander called Malachi, explained, "Seabirds are flying inland. If they've come this far, it'll be an earth-shaker."

Garret asked, "What's an earth-shaker?"

It was a question Indaro wanted the answer to, although she would have never asked it herself. She was torn between admiration for people like Garret, who had no concerns about displaying his ignorance, and contempt.

"In our northland forests it's a giant tree, which if it's felled, makes a crash you can hear around the world."

Apparently convinced, Doon scrambled up and started packing Indaro's belongings in canvas sacks and covering their armour and weapons. Indaro knew the woman was glad to have something to do, and it made no difference to her if Malachi's prediction was true or not. For four interminable days they had stayed rooted to the same spot. The enemy army had not moved either. She could not see them, but she knew it. When twenty thousand warriors started donning armour and preparing weapons, they could not do it quietly. Even from six leagues you could hear the sound like waves on gravel.

"Perhaps they'll attack during the storm," offered Garret. His conversation was mostly speculation about when the enemy would attack, or when they would attack the enemy. He had the startling ability to be almost always wrong.

"Do you think so, Garret?" Doon asked slyly, rubbing a layer of grease on Indaro's helm.

"*I* would," he said stoutly. "Catch us by surprise."

"We five won't be surprised then, thanks to you," came a new voice, deep and hollow, and full of amusement.

Indaro lifted her head and craned round. Malachi, who was lean with cropped grey hair, crouched over a tiny fire which apparently produced no heat and only a wisp of smoke. Beside him was another northlander, barrel-chested, with bright ginger hair and beard in many braids. He returned her look, and winked.

"What are you doing here?" she asked the pair, sitting up and swinging round, glad of someone new to talk to.

Malachi coughed and spat into the frail fire. "Our company was slaughtered by horsemen in the last attack," he explained. "Including our leaders. There's only twenty of us left. We've been divvied up into other companies."

"Welcome to the Wildcats," she said pleasantly. "I'm Indaro. This is Doon."

"Your body servant," the ginger man commented, watching Doon go about her chores.

Indaro nodded. She had no intention of explaining that Doon was more friend than servant, that they had known each other since they were children and had grown up together, that she would give her life for Doon as readily as her friend would give hers for Indaro. And she was used to the sneers, and the tedious ribald jokes about the two women. They slid off her as though buttered.

"I'm Garret," volunteered the blond soldier, unaware as usual of any nuance in the conversation. "You northlanders are said to be very fine warriors," he added generously.

Both men glared at him, but Garret smiled in his friendly way. In that moment there was a faint, almost imperceptible, roll of thunder, far in the western distances. Malachi cocked his head and nodded at his colleague, vindicated.

"It'll be an earth-shaker," he repeated.

It began with huge widely spaced drops of water, "as big as Marcellus' breastplate," said Doon, falling on them, sounding on armour like distant gongs. She and Indaro scrambled into their poor tent, which was hardly big enough for two, and they peered out and watched the fat drops hit the dust, making it ripple. The thunder rolled towards them and when they saw the first lightning flash they glanced at each other, as excited as schoolgirls by the relief from the tedium.

The sky darkened and took on a weird greenish tinge, then the rain started falling in earnest, drumming on the canvas above their heads, quickly weighing it down. Thunder cracked overhead and a flash of lightning speared the earth right in front of them. They heard men shouting and the terrified whinnies of horses, then the sound of running hooves. They grinned at each other.

"Who'd be a horse boy?" Doon said without sympathy.

A sudden rivulet of water ran into their tent and Indaro felt it soaking greedily into her bone dry clothes. In their year in this embattled place they had seen all the weather there was to see, she thought, and rain wasn't the worst of it. She peered out to check on how the others were faring, but she could make out little through the grey wall of torrential rain. The air became colder and darker; the thunder was almost continuous and the lightning made the air smell salty and metallic.

It darkened further and the rain came down even harder. Both women were soaked now, from rain dripping through the canvas above and rising round their ankles. The sound was deafening. They clung together, all excitement, all amusement, washed away. They just waited for it to end.

But it did not end. The rain clouds seemed anchored above them, the thunder and lightning yoked in place. After a while the rising water forced them to stand. They threw aside the useless tent and merely stood there in the wall of rain. It was hard to breathe without sucking in water. They felt they were swimming without sight of shore, disorientated. Indaro took up her helm and put it on to protect her from the rain, to help her breathe, then snatched it off again, for the sound inside was horrendous.

They seemed to be standing thigh-high in a river. The debris of the army camp—sticks and wood of campfires, straw and grain from the horse tethers, bits of food, clothing and tents—were swirling around their legs. The latrines had flooded and their contents had emptied themselves into the camp. The water was still rising, and Indaro started to feel fearful. She had never seen rain like this. Would it ever stop, or would they soon be swimming for their lives? She could no longer see Doon, only feel a firm hand on her wrist. She remembered Doon could not swim.

There had never been a storm like it, in all the City's ten-thousand-year history. It swept in from the north-east one bright sunny morning and by the evening, when the deluge mercifully stopped, thousands had been drowned by the waters and tens of thousands were homeless. Homes were destroyed, those of the poor already barely clinging to life were swept away by the force of the floods, those of the wealthy toppled as their foundations collapsed. The rainwaters poured into the sewers, drowning everything that lived. Most of the City's crops, vital to see the beleaguered citizens through the winter, were wiped out and entire herds of farm animals died.

At Salaba the river Kercheval broke its banks and flooded both armies. For decades the wide river had been fought over, sometimes one side taking it, sometimes the other. Often the armies were camped on opposing banks, staring at each other across the lazy brown waters. But at the time of the Great Flood both armies were camped on the south-east of the river.

The enemy had the slightly higher land, farthest from the river, at a place they called Barren Heights. The "heights" were barely six feet above the floodplain on which the City warriors were camped. But those few feet made a world of difference, an ocean. The City army was inundated, several feet deep, by the floodwaters. The soldiers had to swim for their lives, and those who could not swim, or had been so imprudent as to wear their armour, drowned in their thousands. The Blueskin army was flooded too, and drenched from above, and many of their soldiers drowned.

But maybe it was the superior position of the Blueskins, or their greater distance from the river, or perhaps their generals were just quicker to recover. But when the rain slowed and the Reds were still floundering half dead in the water . . .

The Blues attacked.

Doon had never felt such fear. One moment she was ankle-deep in rain, the next, rushing water was up to her chest. The river, which she had last seen lying placidly half a league from the army, surged through the centre of their camp, flushing them all off their feet like rats down a gulley.

Her head plunged under the muddy brown water, which flowed into her mouth and nose. She flailed her arms, spluttered as she found air, then panicked as she sank once more, weighed down by her heavy cotton trousers, leather jerkin and boots. She felt a strong grip on the collar of the jerkin and she was dragged up through the water. Her face came out into air and she sucked in a shallow lungful. She grabbed the arm holding her and breathed again, her feet kicking around, trying to find something to stand on. But then she and her rescuer were both hit by an armoured body, alive or dead, at hip level. She was knocked sideways, down into the water again, and she felt the reassuring hand on her collar ripped away.

Thick muddy water was all around her and she had no idea which way was up. Greyness entered her head and she felt consciousness leaving. In a way it was a relief. Better than drowning, she thought . . .

Then the last conscious spark deep inside her felt hands grip her shoulders and she was dragged out of the water again. A voice close to her ear screamed, "Breathe, Doon, keep breathing!" Her chest hurt and she was too tired to breathe. The calm cool darkness was captivating. Weakly she tried to pull away from the hot nagging voice.

Time passed sluggishly, and she found herself on her back, hard arms gripping her from behind. Her head was out of the water, her lungs open and free. She breathed luxuriously. A wave of water washed across her face and down her throat and she struggled feebly. But the arms held her tight and one hand shifted to support her chin, holding it out of the water as she was carried securely above the floodwaters.

Then she felt firm ground under her boot heels, and she scrabbled for purchase. The person holding her let go and she fell on her behind in shallow water. She stood up, limbs shaking, and looked around. She had been carried to a small rise in the land, topped by two flat grey boulders. It was under water, but the flood was only knee-high and the tops of the boulders stuck out. She was surrounded by scores of half-drowned bedraggled warriors, stripped of their armour, their weapons and strength.

"All right?" someone asked.

She looked round. It was the red-braided northlander who sneered at her for being a servant.

"Did you rescue me?" she asked, frowning.

"I saw Indaro drag you out of the water, but you both went under again. I saw you couldn't swim."

She found she still didn't like him, though he had saved her life.

"Thank you," she said, trying to sound heartfelt. She looked round. "Where's Indaro?"

"She's all right. She's over there." He pointed to the west and Doon saw Indaro kneeling beside an injured warrior. When Doon waved she nodded.

The northlander was turning away. Doon asked him, "Where's your friend?"

"I don't know. I'm going to look for him."

She realised his arm was bleeding. "You're injured," she said.

He glanced down and shrugged.

"I'll help you find your friend," she offered, anxious to help him now.

He shrugged again, then nodded. "He answers to Malachi."

"What's your name?"

"Stalker."

The rain had stopped and the water was receding as she watched. She guessed the river was going back into its bed. As far as the eye could see there were huddled, dead and half-dead warriors, many wounded, most disorientated by the strength and ferocity of the flood. Corpses of men, women and horses floated in the deeper waters, all slowly making their way back to the river. Floundering among them were soldiers trying to make their way to safety. The higher ground where Doon stood was rapidly becoming crowded. Some had climbed up on the flat boulders and lay there as if drowned. Everyone alive was covered with mud, and most of them were injured. It was as bad as the aftermath of any battle she'd seen.

Doon started picking her way among the living and the dead, staring into faces, trying to find the northlander Malachi. It was hard to recognise anyone under the layers of mud. She wondered if she would know Malachi if she saw him. She remembered he had short grey hair and was wearing a northlander's variation on the red City uniform, embellished with a beaded belt and fur-edged waistcoat.

She found a woman she knew well, half conscious and in danger of drowning. She dragged her higher, then found the woman's legs were crushed. She held her hand until she died, then stood and went on. The air was getting lighter and she could see better. She found she was walking on firm ground again. At last she found him. Malachi seemed uninjured, and he was binding another man's leg in a splint. The injured soldier, a youngster, barely sixteen, was unconscious.

"Is he alive?" she asked, squatting down beside them.

Malachi glanced at her. "He passed out. It was a nasty break." He sat back and sighed. "Infection'll probably kill him."

"Stalker's looking for you."

"That old woman." Malachi grinned. "So you're *his* servant now, are you?" He stood up and looked around, as if searching for more wounded.

Doon flushed. She knew he was joking, but she was still irritated. She knew she had a reputation for humourlessness, so she managed a thin smile.

At that moment there was a sudden silence. The dull, mud-muffled sounds around her all stopped. Everything slowed. She saw Malachi stop and turn. He looked straight at her, his mouth moving. For a second more she could hear nothing. Then his words reached her, hollow and unreal.

"They're coming!"

She turned to the south and saw a line of warriors bearing down on them. They were charging through muddy water, which was slowing them, but they were still coming on. Doon stared for a moment, unwilling to believe her eyes. How could they be attacking? They'd been hit by the flood too. Then she cast around for a sword. All their weapons lay deep in mud and water. All she had on her was the knife at her waist.

A Blue far in front of the line came charging at her, shouting his battle chant, a spear aimed at her midriff. But he was sluggish, hampered by the slippery mud, and she swayed easily away from the spearpoint. He cannoned into her and she drove the knife in under his breastplate, then ripped sideways with all her strength. As he fell she grabbed his sword from its sheath.

It was a broadsword, too heavy for her, too long, but she held it steadily with both hands and advanced on the enemy. She sucked in her breath, then screamed her high ululating battle song. Malachi turned to her briefly and grinned, a sword ready in each hand. Then the wave of warriors hit them.

It was a battle such as she had never known before, a battle in slow motion. Both sides were handicapped by the water and thick sticky mud, but the Blues had somehow managed to get themselves armed and organised with astounding speed. The City warriors were groping around in the knee-deep water, trying to find swords, breastplates, spears and helms. Meanwhile they were being attacked by waves of Blueskin soldiers.

Doon found that the plain they'd been fighting on for a year, apparently flat as a griddle cake, was in fact ridged and pitted and under the churning water it was pocked with holes ready to trip and trap boots.

She saw two enemy warriors coming her way and lurched towards them, the heavy sword raised. The first Blue had not adapted to this slow battle and he tried to swing his sword at her head. His feet slithered in the treacherous mud and he stumbled to one knee. The other soldier planted his feet first then lanced his sword at Doon. She parried clumsily then took one hand off her broadsword, grabbed her knife and thrust for his eyes. She missed and pierced his neck instead. Blood fountained and he fell, clasping the gaping wound. The first soldier was on his feet again. Doon lunged at him, but he sidestepped and parried the broadsword, sending a riposte which slammed into Doon's jerkin, glancing off the heavy leather and missing her hip by a hair's-breadth. But the force of his blow unbalanced him and as he fought to get his feet under him she raised the big sword and brought it down on his unprotected head, shattering his skull.

Doon looked round for some idea of which direction the battle was going. It was impossible. Everyone was plastered with mud, and she could not tell if someone was an enemy or friend until they were close up. She had lost all sense of direction and had no idea whether her friends were in front of her or behind her. On top of that, the sun had come out again and a warm mist was rising all around.

Then relief flooded through her as she heard the familiar bellow, "Wildcats to me! Reds to me!" Her heart soared. Fell Aron Lee was alive and rallying his troops!

Pausing only to pick up the two spare swords, she started making her way towards her commander's voice.

Fell lay on his back in the darkness, hands clasped behind his head, legs crossed at the ankles, waiting for dawn. It was the height of summer, and he calculated he was facing due east, so when the sun rose it would appear between his boots. Not that he would still be resting by then. As soon as the sky started to lighten the Wildcats would prepare for the next enemy attack.

The sky was moonless, the air around him hot and black as pitch. His uniform was still damp against his skin, although half a day had passed since the deluge. Earlier in the night they had seen the pale blur of enemy campfires, but they had made no fires themselves. They were too exhausted to stand, to think, to do other than lie down where they were and sleep the sleep of the half dead.

Fell stared ahead of him, hardly blinking, waiting for the first faint blue-ing of the black. He was trying to rest his body, for he had not slept. His mind was filled with strategies for surviving the day.

He had no idea what happened to the rest of the Maritime Army. All dead, maybe. Or fled. Perhaps other small groups had survived, defending themselves in a tight formation, like the hundred and four men and women lying around him in the night.

They had not stood a chance. The Blues had been on higher ground when the flood hit. And their commander, their general, whoever it was, had ordered an attack so quickly that the Reds had been swamped as thoroughly as the water had overwhelmed them moments before. Thousands died in the first hour. Thousands turned and fled back towards the City, chased by the triumphant enemy. Fell's Wildcats had stood their ground on the small em-inence of land with the poor defence of two low boulders. They had fought grimly, waiting out the day. By the time the sun fell and the enemy returned to their lines there were one hundred and four Wildcats left: sixteen were not expected to survive the night, thirty-four were beyond fighting, forty-three walking wounded. Just eleven soldiers unhurt.

For the first hour or so of the short night he had considered retreating into the darkness, trying to put a few leagues between them and the enemy. But they were all too exhausted, too shocked by the total disintegration in one day of an army of twenty thousand warriors. And there were too many wounded. So he decided to hold the ground, relying on the boulders to give them limited cover, and see what another day would bring: perhaps reinforce-ments from the City, perhaps word that another company lay close by, ready to link up with them. Fell realised bleakly that his decision had probably condemned them all to death. But he could not leave so many wounded.

He thought he detected a slight lifting of the blackness. He blinked the grit out of his eyes and peered. Yes, he thought, another day is dawning.

"Garvy."

"Sir." The voice was close, a little pained. Garvy had a dislocated shoul-der. It had been wrenched back in place and the arm strapped securely against his chest, but he was unlikely to have had any sleep.

"How's that shoulder?"

"Fine, sir."

"Give me the numbers."

He heard Garvy carefully stand. And as if permission had been given, there were suddenly sounds all around, shifting bodies, coughing, spitting and groans as his soldiers awoke and faced the new day. There were some moans and cries of pain. It was a bad day to be already wounded. Only eleven unhurt, he thought. May the Gods of Ice and Fire help us today.

"Sir?"

"Yes." He couldn't recognise the voice.

"Jonas J is dead, sir."

"Tell Garvy. He's making a count."

Soon he could make out shapes against the lightening horizon. The sky was velvety blue and he could see lines of pink and red low in the east. He groped around and found the waterskin beside him and took a deep swallow. He found his breastplate, then he stood up, brushing down his mud-caked uniform. Garvy moved alongside him. He could see the white bandage.

"Fourteen died in the night."

"Move the bodies into the enemy's path."

"Sir?"

"The first wave might stumble over them in the dark. Move the remaining wounded close together between the boulders. Any deserters?"

"No, sir."

Despite everything, pride rose in Fell's breast. Not one deserter. Every soldier had elected to stay and fight, fight for his friends, rather than slip away into the night.

He nodded curtly, not trusting himself to speak, and Garvy moved away. Soon there was a sense of purpose in the camp as bodies were carried out into the line the enemy would take, and the surviving wounded were moved closer together behind the wall of remaining fighters.

Fell cleared the dust from his throat. "Wildcats. Eat and drink when you can. They'll be on us soon."

He had no orders to give them. Survive if you can. Fight to the death if you can't. No use telling anyone that. He picked up his sword and felt the edge with his thumb. Blunt and chipped.

He heard a woman's cry behind them, among the wounded, and thought of Indaro. Fell had last seen her defending two wounded soldiers, faithful Doon at her side. She was unhelmed and her red hair shone like molten copper in the sunlight. Her face was calm, focussed, no fear, no doubt. He thought her the most beautiful woman he had ever seen. If I survive this, he thought, I will . . .

"They're coming!" cried a voice, tight with fear. And the new day began.

There were no cavalry, at least. Fell was grateful for that. Perhaps the Blueskins lost all their horses or riders in the flood. Or, more likely, the cavalry were busy on a more important mission than wiping out a small band of Red stragglers. Did that mean the rest of the army was still fighting somewhere? Fell hoped so. If the Third Maritime were destroyed the City would be vulnerable to the south and east.

They wasted no time on light infantry either. Now the ground was dry again and hardening quickly under the sun, they sent in heavy infantry, headed by the huge dark-skinned men from the forests of Mulan, armoured in thick metal from head to knees. The Reds knew them well, and called them beetles. The only way to kill them was to hamstring them first, or to get a blade between the two sheets of armour that met under the arm, or slide it down under the high collar. If you could get in close enough and avoid their axes and broadswords. Though they were heavy, they were still fast.

Fell, at the head of his warriors, ran at the first beetle, dodged the flying axe and, with a yell, leaped in the air and slammed his blunt sword on the top of the man's helm. The sword broke, but the sound inside the metal helm must have been prodigious, and the beetle paused. In that second Fell rammed his knife into the gap at the armpit. He twisted it, seeking the heart. The beetle fell, stone dead, and the Reds cheered.

Someone threw him a new sword, and the battle started.

Fell had killed three more beetles and the sun had risen in the sky before he realised he was injured. It was his left arm, not his sword-arm. He dropped back for a few moments to check the wound, to make sure he was not going to bleed to death. Two Reds stepped forward to cover him. He pulled cotton wadding out of the pouch at his side and stuffed it in the wound, pulling his sleeve down over it to hold it in place.

He looked around, gauging the battle. The enemy were still attacking from front and left. If they had circled Fell's little army the Wildcats would all be dead by now. Either their commander was stupid, or they were short of soldiers themselves. Nothing he had seen in the last day or so indicated they were led by stupid men, and a small spark of hope ignited in his chest. They were undermanned too.

For one glorious insane moment he considered ordering his troop to attack.

No, he thought. Defend, defend, defend. They had to try and save the wounded. But he needed to know the Blues' strength. He ran to the nearest of the two boulders and leaped on top. But the rock was too flat to give him a view. He looked around. "Queza."

"Sir." She was a short stocky woman, well-muscled but graceful, and agile as a monkey. And lighter than any man. She jogged over to him, eager for an order.

He turned to one of the northlanders, an iron wolf of a man, who was picking through a pile of swords, trying to find a good one. "You."

"Malachi," the man said flatly.

"Queza. This soldier and I are going to lift you up. I need to know how many are coming against us."

"Yes, sir."

Malachi climbed on the rock and stood beside him. Fell flexed one knee and patted his leg. "Thigh and shoulder."

Queza swarmed up him, and he felt her balance on his shoulder shift as she put half her weight on Malachi. Her hand on his head slowly released as she stood up. He and Malachi held on to her lower legs.

The moments went by with painful slowness and he wondered how long it would take the enemy to notice such an open target. He heard a missile of some kind swish overhead, then Queza cried, "Let me down!"

She clambered down with less grace than she'd climbed up, but she was grinning from ear to ear.

"A hundred, sir, hundred and twenty at best."

"Riders?"

"Half a dozen horses in the rear. Messengers, I expect. No cavalry."

Fell was grinning too. He nodded and clapped her on the shoulder and Queza ran back to her place. Let's call it a hundred, he thought. We've got forty-five, with four unhurt. All we have to do is kill two more each and we'll walk away from here.

Chapter 12

Night descended with terrible slowness, and still the enemy came on.
Indaro stole a look to the west, where the sun had fallen in splendour, leaving a sky streaked in yellow and purple like an old bruise. Her body felt like that bruise, sore and aching all over. Her right shoulder was numb and her sword-arm had all the strength and agility of a week-old piece of meat. She wondered how long she could keep on defending. The enemy were suffering too; her opponent was moving like a zombie, and their encounter was merely a dull exchange of blows, each weary beyond words.

Indaro had little time for prayer, but this day she prayed to the Gods of Ice and Fire to intercede with Vashta, the guardian of night, to bring darkness soon. If they survived one more night, maybe reinforcements would come with the dawn. Maybe.

"Daro!" The word crept slowly into her tired brain. She moved back two steps to give herself space and glanced at the speaker.

"We're retreating to the rocks," Garret told her. He was covered in blood and looked ready to drop.

She nodded and gazed at her opponent, who had made no attempt to follow her, but just stood there, exhausted, his sword barely raised in defence. She summoned all her remembered strength and speed and darted forward, skewering him in the throat, before backing away.

She had not heard the enemy order to retreat, but after a few moments they started fading back into darkness. She took a deep breath, then walked over to a wounded enemy soldier, lying twitching, his entrails lying in a bloody rope at his side. His eyes were open but unseeing as she stood over him. She slashed his throat, then wiped the blade on his leg. It was a good blade, she thought, the best she'd had in days.

She found the man's waterskin, and slung it on her shoulder, then turned back to her colleagues, where the wounded were gathered between the rocks.

The two flat boulders were a poor defence, but on that empty plain they were the only cover to be had. The most badly wounded lay in lines between them, and Fell had placed less injured soldiers on the tops of the rocks to deter attacks from the flanks.

There were few without wounds now. She looked down at herself. She was covered with blood, but her only injury was grazed knuckles. She thought she should help with the wounded, but there were so many of them and she was so tired. She took a deep breath then walked over to help.

Fell saw her and stepped towards her. His face was grey and his cheeks sunken. His blue eyes were dull. He gazed at her expressionlessly. "I'll take that water," he grunted. Then, pointing at the rock where Doon lay, "See to your servant."

She nodded and clambered up onto the flat boulder. Doon was sitting with six others, most with broken legs or ankles. She was splinting the leg of a friend of hers called Marchetta. It was a bad break and Marchetta had fainted. Indaro helped Doon quickly wrench the bones back in position, and bandage them to a broken sword blade. They both knew it would be impossible to walk on for several weeks, and would probably never heal, even if the enemy were suddenly to vanish away in the night.

When they had finished, Doon rolled over on one side to try and get comfortable, and Indaro saw her face tense as her wound pulled.

"Let me see that," she said.

"It's all right. Leave it alone," the woman replied irritably, moving the leg away.

"You don't want to survive this, then die of gangrene."

"If it's going bad, there's nothing you can do. You just gave our clean water away."

"I've still got some salve left." Indaro groped in the pouch at her side and came out with a small corked pot which had survived the flood.

Doon sneered. "You're the only person who thinks that stuff does any good. I think it's poison."

Indaro could not blame her. She'd bought the salve from an old woman in the southern frontier town of Saris, where they'd been camped for more than a year. She was told it was made of oak moss and willow bark, both rare plants in the hot dry southlands. She'd smeared the green stuff on many minor wounds, to some effect she'd thought. Then she used it to try and save the life of Maccus Odarin, a comrade and a great fighter for the Wildcats, who'd suffered a trivial leg injury which turned rotten. She'd used almost all of it, daily applying it to his wound as he grew sicker and the leg blackened. They had to cut the leg off in the end, and he died anyway. Since then no one else would touch the stuff and avoided it as if it were cursed.

"All right. I won't use it. Just let me see the wound. Remember you're my servant." Indaro managed to smile.

Reluctantly Doon let her unbandage the wound, which was deep and wide across the back of her left thigh near the buttock. Indaro could see slashed muscle, but the blade had missed major blood vessels. Nevertheless, it had taken an age to stop bleeding and the previous night Indaro had feared it never would. It was still leaking blood and pale fluid. But, as far as Indaro could tell by the dying light, it looked clean.

Doon, who couldn't see properly, twisting round, asked, "Well?" There was fear in her eyes. There were many kinds of death, and none of them wanted Maccus Odarin's.

"It's good," Indaro told her. "Better not let Fell Aron Lee see it. He'll have you back on the front line tomorrow." She lay back on the warm stone, groaning with painful pleasure as her shoulder muscles started to ease.

"How many are we left?" she asked, knowing Doon would be watching every sword blow, counting every fallen comrade.

"Eighteen on their feet. I don't know if anyone's unwounded, except you. And Fell." She shrugged. Of course Fell was unhurt, she was saying. He was invulnerable. In more than one hundred days of battle he had remained unhurt. He was charmed, they said.

Indaro looked down to where their commander was moving among his battered troops, squatting down to speak to each of the wounded. She knew he would not be telling them how courageous they were, or speak of living to fight another day. It was not his way. Fell's fighters knew they were the best. He did not need to tell them. No, Fell would be assessing each man or woman, judging if they would live or die, and if they would live, if they could fight again tomorrow.

He looked up and saw her watching him, and she thought she saw some emotion pass across his face. Then she realised she was imagining it. She had never met anyone as guarded as Fell Aron Lee.

And besides, it was getting dark. She looked to the west, where the remaining light was an eerie greenish grey. There were heavy layers of clouds in the sky, and she detected for the first time the slight chill of coming autumn in the air.

"Look!" Doon said. Indaro turned to look where she was pointing.

A figure was jogging towards the besieged camp out of the north. Indaro saw it was one of their own and called down, "Incoming scout."

Fell stood and walked to meet the woman and the two had a brief discussion. Then he looked around him and said, "Listen." He had hardly raised his voice, but everyone heard him and silence fell on the camp.

"They've pulled back to the river. With no moon, it's unlikely there'll be an attack this night. Now, we're short of water and I want everyone to hand in their waterskins. Garvy will ration it out in the morning, first to the . . . wounded, then the rest."

The pause was barely perceptible, but Indaro caught it. She knew what he was saying, as did everyone. Water would be given to those of the wounded expected to survive. Those already in the shadow of death would get no comfort, not the smallest sip of water, as they came to their cruel end. It was hard, but it was understood.

Fell said, "The Blues are no better off than we are. They have no more water or food. They have many dead and injured. And they are using up more energy attacking than we are defending. I'll not lie to you, our future is in the lap of the gods. The side which gets reinforcements first will win the day. We are only forty leagues from safety and I have sent out a messenger. We could be relieved tonight. If not, and if we receive no aid tomorrow, then we hold on."

He paused as if finished, then he suddenly spoke again. "We are all veterans here. We have all been through this before and survived." Indaro saw men and women looking at each other and nodding agreement. "Tomorrow we will be called to fight again. We will answer that call as we always have. There will be blood and there will be death. But that will not stop us. It never stopped us before, and it will not stop us tomorrow. So rest now, and know that tomorrow we will step up again, for the City and for our comrades in arms. We are the Wildcats and we never give in!"

He turned away. There were no cheers from the tired fighters, but Indaro felt the wave of warmth, of unity, sweep through the camp, and men and women went to their rest with their souls burnished by Fell's words. She knew she was probably destined to die the next day, but she wasn't afraid. She looked at Doon, who nodded at her. They were both thinking the same.

Garret scrambled up on the boulder beside them. He flopped onto his back and lay breathing heavily. Then he rolled over, and asked Doon, "How's the leg?"

Doon scowled. "Staying away from the wounded, Garret?"

"*You're* injured," he retorted.

She shrugged. "We're all injured. That doesn't make me one of the wounded."

He rolled over again and sighed. "Do you think they'll attack in the night?"

Indaro found the fragile feeling of calm inspired by Fell's words drifting away. "Tonight. Tomorrow. What's the difference?" she snapped. We won't last one more attack, she was thinking. And few of them believed reinforcements were on the way.

"Fell sent Keema on the last horse. She'll get through," Garret told them with his relentless good cheer.

For some reason, his use of Fell Aron Lee's given name annoyed her. "Are you an idiot, Garret?" she replied, her temper flaring. "She'll get through— and then what? There's probably an entire Blue army between us and the City, and if she gets through, as you say, do you really think the generals will pull a detachment away from fighting them to send to rescue our little unit? When has that ever happened?" She glared at him as if he were responsible. "Can you think of a single time when that has happened?"

Garret avoided her gaze, looking down to where Fell Aron Lee was moving about, talking to his fighters, sending guards out to the perimeter. He mused, "I wonder where old Brog is now. Lucky to have missed all this."

Indaro shook her head. It was pointless railing at Garret. He was not a fool, but there was something missing in his character. She had never seen him lose his temper, or get downhearted. If she had been asked a year ago she would have said he was not an exceptional fighter, yet here he was, still alive when many exceptional fighters were dead. As far as she was aware, he had never even been seriously wounded. She shook her head. They called Fell invincible. Yet Garret had been through everything their commander had, and no one called him invincible.

"I expect he'll catch up with us sometime," she told him more calmly. "Time to get some rest."

She didn't expect sleep to visit her, lying on a rock in the heat of the summer night, the heavy stench of blood in her nostrils, her hands and face sticky with it. But exhaustion proved more powerful than discomfort, and within moments she was deeply unconscious. When the sound they all dreaded came, she was oblivious, and it took a sharp kick on the leg to wake her up.

"They're coming," Garret yelled in her ear. "Cavalry!" She reached for her sword and rolled up onto her feet, appalled. The sound of thunder echoed through her head as horses galloped into their camp, their riders armed with torches and spears.

Cavalry, she thought. Reinforcements have arrived—for the enemy!

There was howling chaos in the darkness as the injured warriors lying between the boulders were trampled by metal-shod hooves. The remainder of the Reds were on their feet, defending desperately, but riders were all around them, streaming through the gap in the rocks and round their sanctuary. There seemed to be hundreds of them. From her high position all Indaro could see was the flare of torch flames and a frenzy of moving black shapes. She chose her moment and leaped on the back of a rider passing the rocks. The weight of her pushed them both off the horse and they fell and rolled, Indaro losing her grip. She curled up in a ball as horses swept by on either side of her, then she jumped up, grabbing the torch off the ground, looking round. In the flaring light it was impossible to tell which of the fighters on the ground was the enemy. She saw a horseman coming towards her and assumed it was a Blue and she thrust the torch in the horse's face. It reared, veering away from her. Its rider hung on grimly, then Indaro stepped up and thrust her sword deep under the enemy's breastplate. As the rider tumbled from the saddle Indaro leaped on and grabbed the reins. She held the torch up, trying to make sense of what she was seeing, acutely aware she could now be taken for a Blue. There were no orders. Where was Fell?

A horse appeared before her in the darkness. "Wildcats!" she screamed— and the rider lowered his spear and charged. Indaro's mount skittered sideways and Indaro swayed at the same time, and the spear missed her. She sliced her sword across the enemy's neck as he passed. She felt the clang of metal, then the give of flesh and the rider slumped in the saddle, though he stayed on the horse, which trotted off into the gloom.

Indaro saw two Reds backed against a rock, one of them badly wounded, clutching his side. They were under attack by three enemy foot soldiers. She charged her horse towards them just as the injured man slumped to the ground, a knife in his neck. The other Wildcat killed an enemy soldier with a sword-thrust to the groin. Then his eyes flickered to Indaro as she rode up. The moment cost him his life as he was cut down. Indaro screamed and sliced her sword across one head, then impaled the last Blue, thrusting deeply down through neck and chest. She dragged the blade out.

"Indaro!" She turned the horse and saw Doon calling to her from the boulder. She rode over. "We're retreating!" her friend cried, pointing towards the west. She was standing awkwardly, a bloody knife in her hand and an enemy dying at her feet.

Indaro gazed around and nodded. There were too many of them, and most of the City's wounded soldiers were dead. The torches had been lost in the fighting, and darkness was now their only defence.

"Where's Fell?"

Doon shrugged. "I don't know where anyone is, but I saw some of ours going that way." She pointed again to the west.

"Get on," Indaro ordered her, turning the horse so its rump bumped against the rock. Doon got on awkwardly, her breathing sharp and agonised in Indaro's ear.

"Your right!" she cried, and Indaro twisted to see two horsemen bearing down on them, spears lowered.

One of them aimed at her body, the other for the horse. Indaro deflected the first spear with her sword, but the blade broke, and the second spear struck their mount in the belly. It screamed and its back legs collapsed, throwing the two women to the ground. Indaro hit her head on a rock as she fell and, dazed, struggled to get up. The two horsemen dismounted and came at them and Doon, limping heavily, stepped in front of her, her sword raised. The two riders looked at each other, grinning. Easy meat, the look said.

They attacked Doon together, as Indaro rose shakily to her feet. She shook her head, trying to clear it, but the world was blurred and her eyes could not focus. Nevertheless, she ran at the two soldiers, waving her blade like a child, and one turned to counter her. Taking a breath she dived and rolled clumsily at the first man's legs, slashing wildly at his inner thigh with her broken blade. The second man, wrong-footed, turned and Doon flung her sword at him. The throw was poor and he was hit on the shoulder by the pommel. But he staggered, then Indaro was up and sprang at him and buried the broken blade into his side.

She grabbed his sword and, her head clearing, looked around. There was darkness all around, except in the east, where they could hear shouts of triumph from the enemy troops. The injured horse was writhing and screaming, blood pouring from its belly. She knelt and cut its throat and its blood poured over her.

She looked at Doon, who was sitting in the dust, her face white in the dim moonlight.

"Which way?" she asked. Which way do we run, she was asking. Now we have lost.

Doon shrugged. "I saw some of ours going west. But they'll chase us that way, back towards the City. We could go north or south. It might be safer."

Indaro shook her head. "If there are other Reds out there, we'll join with them."

She helped Doon stand and, her shoulder under her friend's arm, struggled off into the night.

The sea was jewel-dark green and blue. It felt warm against his naked body like a bed of soft velvet under moonlight. The man lay resting deep in its depths, cocooned by thick, viscous water stroking his naked skin. Bubbles slid past his body, rising upwards towards watery sunlight which shone down hazily as if through glass. Big bubbles rose slowly, lingering against his chest and flanks, while small bubbles fizzed between his toes and fingers. He was lying on his stomach and the weight of water felt heavy on him.

He suddenly remembered he could not breathe, and struggled to lift his head. The smell in his nostrils was of earth and blood . . .

Fell tried to open his eyes but they were glued shut. He could barely move. His chest felt crushed and he could not breathe properly. It was so hot. His right hand was stretched out ahead of him and, with an effort, he pulled it in under his shoulder and tried to lift himself. His head was pounding in time with his heartbeat and the sudden movement made it spin. The entire earth and his body lying upon it lurched hideously and he clung on and rode it out. Then he sucked in another muddy breath and tried again. There was something lying on his back, on his legs. With an effort that made him groan he pulled his head and right shoulder free of the weight upon him. When the world stopped lurching again, he prised his eyes open and looked around.

It was bright daylight, and he was lying by a pile of corpses, carelessly thrown in a heap. Face to face with him was Malachi, the northlander who had served in his company for a few doomed days. Half his head had been hacked away. Fell looked around sadly, seeing faces he had known for months, for years, eyes dusty in death.

He remembered the alert in the night, the galloping riders, a rearing horse, a kick in the head. The Wildcats hadn't stood a chance. Where were the guards? Was he the only survivor? Fell groaned and sank back down in pain.

But after a moment he thought, they have piled the corpses. To burn them? Energised by fear, he lifted himself up again and dragged his battered body from under the dead soldiers. He lay for a while, exhausted, then stirred himself and got to his feet. He found it hard to stand upright, for the pain in his head made him dizzy and weak. He looked around, squinting against the sunlight which pierced his head like blades.

He could see no movement, no survivors. Most of the dead had already been injured when the night attack came. They had no defence against the cavalry. Raising his sights he could see no sign of the enemy. But that did not mean they were not coming back. They hadn't gone to the trouble of piling the corpses for nothing. They were probably chasing survivors. Fell would, if the positions were reversed. He had to be well away from this place when they returned.

He searched for a waterskin but they had all been taken or used up. Finally he found one with a little water in the bottom, and he sucked it down, feeling the pain in his head recede slightly. He found a sword which was blunted but not broken, and a dagger with the point missing. He sat down and eased off his right boot and took out the slender knife he kept there as a spare. He stuck both knives in his belt, and the sword in the scabbard. He checked the pouch at his side. Luckily they had been in too much of a hurry to loot the corpses and it was still intact. There was some dried beef wrapped in paper and he munched it down stolidly. It was hard to swallow, the dry

tasteless meat clinging to his tongue and teeth. He wished there were more
water.

Only then did he consider which way to go. The enemy were between
him and the City, but safety lay that way. Yet any horses that had run from
the battle would have gone north, towards the river, for horses could always
smell water. He decided to head north in the hope of finding a stray mount.

The sun was at its height as he set off, a piece of crimson cloth wrapped
around his head to shield his eyes. He walked in the heat of the afternoon
without seeing any enemy soldiers, or lost Wildcats, or horses. To the east
and north he could see nothing but flat plain disappearing into the dusty
distance. He walked through low scrub and the going was easy, but the pain
in his head grew more violent. He stopped once to vomit up the beef, then
set out again. His steps became shorter and more uncertain as his head spun
and his vision blurred. The headache was becoming unbearable and he
moaned as he walked and the movement jolted his head. Finally his legs gave
way and he collapsed on the ground, knocking himself out for a moment.

He came to and retched again, although there was nothing left in his
belly. He looked around him, the brown landscape jumping and swooping
sickeningly in his vision. Weak as a lamb, he crawled over to a small depression in the land guarded by a low rock. There were dry grass and twigs
within his grasp and he quickly built a small fire, his hand shaking as he
struck the flint. Then, on the verge of unconsciousness, he took out the small
packet of herbs he always kept with him and threw them on the fire. There
was little left, and he prayed to the healing gods of Ascelus that there would
be enough. His head in his hands, he breathed in the acrid fumes, holding
down the nausea, concentrating on staying awake. He took another deep
breath and felt the opiates reaching into his system. The pain racked up a
notch and he moaned. Then he carefully laid his head on the earth and fell
into blackness.

When he came to again the pain had gone and he lay there for a while
luxuriating in its absence. Since a spear had pierced the bone of his head in
a battle ten years before he had been victim to ferocious headaches. The
herbs had been given to him, not by a healer but by a maidservant at an inn
in Otaro two years before. The girl had found him helpless on the floor of his
room, deep in the throes of a disabling headache. She had offered him the
herbs but he had refused them, suspecting witchcraft, and she had nursed

him for the four days it took for the pain to pass. When he left she pressed the packet of herbs upon him and he had taken them, grateful for her kindness but intending to throw them away. Forced by desperation to use them a few weeks later, he had discovered their power. He took the first opportunity to return to the inn to reward her, but she was long gone, pressed into the army, the landlord said, her small child left in the care of a blacksmith's old mother. Fell, another fatherless child, had left a year's wages with the crone, who had first been delighted and grateful, then had tried to prise more from him, thinking him the child's sire.

Now the last of the healing herbs was gone, and he feared future attacks.

Dismissing the problem from his mind, he stood up and looked around him. It was getting towards dusk and he was standing at the edge of a sea of long grass. The breeze from the north ruffled it like waves on water. Above him a white hawk circled effortlessly, seeking prey on the ground. He sniffed the cool evening air. The smell of the grass was exhilarating, but it was the smell of water that lifted his spirits. The river was nearby. There he could drink his fill and find new strength. He might find a horse to ride and, even better, he might find an enemy corpse.

Chapter 13

Simios Highnorth was a young warrior of the Tanaree. The thin fuzz on his cheeks could not yet be called a beard, yet he was already a two-year veteran.

He had been born to an unwed shepherd girl who left the care of her flocks one night to deliver the child in fear and pain as the world slept. When her small village awoke the next morning the squalling dark-haired babe proved her shame for all to see. The villagers stoned her, of course, and she fled, the babe still bloody in her arms. Her elderly parents, dazed and bewildered by this sudden and hideous turn of events, had no choice but to follow her, and the four refugees found sanctuary in a village twenty leagues on, where the child turned out to be the son of a hero, a brave cavalryman lost in the endless war.

Simios grew to be tall and strong, red-cheeked and curly-headed, but he was a quiet young man who sat at the edges of conversations and never joined in the heated barroom debates of the loud, opinionated soldiers who were his comrades. He was the one who was always content to steer his drunken friends home after a night of excess, and if he slept badly it was because he worried about his mother and not about the next day's battle.

In his last visit home the previous autumn he had become joyfully engaged to the daughter of the village dyer, but he had not yet told his friends for he feared the coarse raillery he would endure, and he hid her keepsake, a piece of fine cotton embroidered with the lovers' names, away from sneering eyes.

Fell Aron Lee found the young man's body, his throat hacked out, his brown eyes filled with sand, and he celebrated. The Blues were usually scrupulous about clearing away their dead, but this soldier must have been killed before the flood, his body washed down the river where it joined in unwilling companionship with scores of City soldiers, their corpses already bloating in the fierce heat.

Fell stripped off his battered red uniform and packed it away in an abandoned knapsack, knowing he would need it again if he escaped enemy territory. He was reluctant to leave his breastplate, which had served him well, saving his life again and again throughout the last five years. But he could hardly wear it, or cram it into the bag. The dead man's clothes were well looked after, cuts and tears finely stitched, he noticed as he pulled them on.

He was debating whether to take the boots or not, trying to judge their size, it being difficult to prise the boots off a dead man, when he heard the sound of distant voices, and he lay flat on the sandy bank. It was a platoon of enemy soldiers, with a cart, collecting bodies from all along the river. It took them some time to load the wooden cart and then they were off towards the east. They never came near Fell, and once they had disappeared he stood and set off in the opposite direction. He decided against changing his boots. It was hardly uncommon, after all, for a City soldier to be wearing Blue boots or vice versa.

As he walked he tried to visualise where he was on his drowned campaign maps. He was now well north-east of the battlefield of Salaba, and if he travelled directly east he would, he thought, see the City walls by midday tomorrow. He had plenty of water and was uninjured, and he felt remarkably cheerful as he strode across the barren land. He wondered, as he had done before, if the healing herbs had a secondary effect of buoying his spirits. Deep in his mind he knew he should be feeling remorseful at the loss of so many troops, guilty that he chose to defend an indefensible place rather than make a night run for the City.

He had heard the soldiers' whispers that he was invulnerable, that he suffered scarcely a scratch while those who had marched beside him down the years were gutted, poisoned, beheaded, drowned and, in one hideous case, burned to death. It hadn't stopped his warriors, men and women, being drawn to him, hoping perhaps that some of his fortune would spill onto them. He could hardly complain about his good luck. But gliding through the war as a survivor while his friends and comrades died one by one had provoked in him an overpowering sense of guilt.

It was a cliche of war that the man who feared to lose would always fall victim to the man with the will to win. But Fell's calculated approach to each battle, factoring in the potential survival of his troops, made him a rarity among commanders, popular among his men and unpopular with rivals. Although he had now outlived any rivals, he guessed.

He thought again about Indaro and wondered if she survived.

Constantly on alert as he walked, he found it easy to avoid the small groups of enemy soldiers he encountered. Once he lay flat on his stomach in the poor shelter of a prickly bush as a troop of Blues, cheerful in victory, marched straight past him. He slept deeply that night in the lee of a low outcrop of rock, and in the morning light he started refreshed, though his stomach complained from lack of food.

He was starting to believe he would soon see the City walls, and wondering if he should ditch the Blue uniform, when he heard the sound of boots marching hard from the south. Suddenly, over a low rise, he saw a small band of soldiers heading straight towards him. He readied himself to prove his identity as a loyal soldier of the City if necessary.

But it was a Blueskin platoon of seven, with an officer on horseback. As they approached he put a pleased expression on his face and walked briskly towards them. The officer was a sour-faced man, probably Fkeni, his leathery face marked by deep tribal scars, his ears notched.

"Where have you strayed from, soldier?" the officer asked him, scowling down.

"The 10th," Fell grunted. After a year at Salaba he knew the enemy companies almost as well as his own. These were infantrymen and would have no knowledge of cavalry personnel. He was not sure about the officer, though.

"I thought the 10th were lost in the flood?"

The rider's long dark face gave nothing away, but this was a test.

"No, sir!" Fell frowned as if puzzled by the comment. "We lost a few horses, but the men survived. No, we were chasing the City Rats and walked into an ambush. I got hit by a sword hilt, I think, and when I came to I was alone. Good to see you. I thought for a moment you were poxy Rats."

"Who was your commander?"

"Marloe."

"Your name, soldier?"

"Peiter Edo, sir."

The officer nodded and gestured him to join the company. Fell took his place at the rear of the group, nodding to the man next to him.

But the officer turned in his saddle to question him again. "Do you know Aldous Edo, your namesake?"

"No sir."

"But he's second-in-command of your company, man."

"No sir," Fell replied stolidly, "not in my time."

He had no clue if his answer had satisfied. He knew the names of several officers of the 10th, which is why he'd chosen the company, but he had not heard of an Aldous Edo. The officer gazed at him for a long moment, then he turned back in his saddle and walked his horse on. Was he fooled or not? Fell had no idea.

"Good boots?" asked the man next to him, a tall young soldier with old eyes and a bandaged neck. He was looking down at Fell's feet.

Fell confided in a low voice, "Ten times better than ours. Always get the best pair of boots you can. Others, they look for gold teeth. I look for boots. I can march twelve hours a day on these."

"Friend of mine lost both feet because of bad boots," the other man told him. His eyes were red-rimmed and he blinked constantly.

"Quartermaster's in the pay of the enemy," Fell asserted, nodding.

The man looked at him, surprised. "You think so too?"

"Stands to reason," Fell said.

The man in front, hearing their conversation, chipped in with a complaint about the fit of his helm, and Fell grinned to himself. Soldiers are the same the world over, he thought.

"What's this officer like?" he asked his new comrade, nodding at the man on the horse.

The red-eyed soldier hawked and spat in the dust. "Don't know him," he said finally. "Not even sure he's an officer," he confided. "He's just the one with the horse."

They were marching towards the south-east and once again Fell wondered what had become of the bulk of the City army. His troops had been at the far right flank, so when they were hit by the flood they were cut off. But the rest of the army must still be intact. He had walked north then east and now south-east, and he was starting to wonder if he had walked all the way round it.

He was reluctant to call attention to his ignorance, but at last he asked, "What are our orders?"

The red-eyed man looked at him curiously. "Mop up survivors," he answered slowly, as if speaking to a child.

Fell shook his head. "I must have been out longer than I thought," he said, coldness creeping through his body. "Survivors from the flood?"

"No, lackbrain," the soldier said, grinning. "Survivors from the battle. Salaba, the greatest victory the world has ever known. Twenty thousand Rats dead in one day."

The stalemate at Salaba, which had endured for more than a year, had been broken, Fell learned, by the devastating flood. It was not just his company that was cut off and destroyed; the entire Maritime Army had been overwhelmed. Even some of the generals had been killed, forced, perhaps for the first time in decades, to take up the sword in defence of themselves and the City. Many had been captured, it was said, and tortured to give up the secrets of the City's defences. Fell wondered if Randell Kerr had been compelled to fight for his life. He remembered the tall tower with the generals gulping wine on top and visualised it surrounded by enemy soldiers, on fire perhaps. He found no sympathy for them.

He thought of Indaro again. He had not seen her body among the corpses. He hoped she was dead rather than captive. It was said the Blues would torment women soldiers before killing them, although he had never seen evidence of it.

It was twenty years before when, the City running dangerously low on manpower after so many years of war, it had been decided to press women to fight. Fell was a young infantryman himself then and he cheerfully joined in the sneering contempt for the frightened girls sent to the front line. The generals, forced into a plan they had no faith in, acted typically. They made the girls fight but did not train them or equip them properly. So they died in their thousands, fulfilling the men's predictions. But it was the male soldiers, many of them with wives and sisters and sweethearts at home, who found compassion in their hearts and took it on themselves to train the women, to equip them in dead men's breastplates and helms. But an entire generation of City women had been wiped out before the generals conceded that if they were to fight they had to receive the same training and equipment as men.

Indaro was part of the third wave of women warriors. By then the sixteen-year-old girls were treated as well—or badly—as the boys were. When Fell first met the woman, in his tent on that golden night, he knew well who she was—the daughter of a suspect politician, sister of a renegade, and a deserter herself, working with the woman Archange, traitor to the City. When she walked into his tent at midnight he had not decided what to do with her.

She was tall and painfully thin, her cheekbones like blades stretching the skin of her face. She was dirty and clearly exhausted, yet she held herself with a grace that instantly excited him. Her dark red hair was the glory of the sunset after a storm, and her violet eyes, on a level with his, were flecked with grey under dark brows. He found himself lost for words.

The silence lengthened, and all he could think of to say was, "I knew your father."

She stared at him, her eyes widening a little. He realised she thought he was challenging her with her father's past, so he amended, "I never believed them when they said he raised a family of deserters." *A family of deserters?* What was he saying? Could he *be* more insulting?

Indaro's voice was dry and distant as she stared over his head. "He knew nothing of my . . . absence. He has disowned me, sir."

It was a lie and Fell knew it. But she was not defending herself; she was defending her father.

"My job is to win battles," he told her, wondering as he spoke why he was explaining himself to her. "I need all the resources I can get. I'm told you are an excellent swordswoman. I cannot afford to waste you."

After that he kept her in his sights. He agreed to her petition to have her servant with her. The request amused him. Indaro clearly found no need to fit in with her comrades. While the rest of the troops, himself included, wore old leather jerkins, once red, faded to pink or grey by the sun and rain, Indaro was always clad in bright red body armour, supplied regularly from the gods knew where. Word came back to him that she was arrogant and unpopular. Fell was not surprised.

Then came the battle of Copper Creek when, wounded herself and armed with two swords, she had held back a platoon of enemy soldiers so her injured comrade Maccus Odarin could escape to safety. Maccus *was* popular, and after that Fell heard no more criticisms of Indaro.

He found himself watching her obsessively, and after each engagement he assured himself she was still alive. He was constantly pushing her from his thoughts, yet at the most awkward moments he could smell the scent of her hair, visualise the fluid graceful line of her back as she turned away from him.

But he had barely spoken to her again until, entrenched at Salaba, he had received orders to despatch a troop of veterans to serve with the emperor's bodyguard. He chose to misunderstand the message. He could not afford to lose the warriors. But he had been waiting for a chance to send Indaro away. And Evan Broglanh. The situation at Salaba had deteriorated steadily over the last six months, and Fell feared the eventual outcome. Still, he was reluctant, torn between the desire to send Indaro to comparative safety and the wish to keep her close. When he made his decision it was, at least in part, because he would have an excuse to speak to her again.

When he found her and Broglanh together at the mess hall, it seemed like a gods-given opportunity. She had volunteered instantly, as he had known she would. So did the others at the table—Doon, Broglanh, the young blond lad whose name he could never remember. He had returned to his tent satisfied, believing he was sending them to safety, not into an ambush. Yet somehow she survived it, as she always did.

The barren land to the east of the City was formally named the Plain of Defiant Endeavour, but people called it the Treeless Plain. And it was not a plain at all, but a series of steppes, rising from the bed of the great river Kercheval to the City. It was arid and at first glance appeared lifeless, but in fact it teemed with small creatures. Lying at the lip of a small hollow, Indaro had been watching the east for hours, feeling dusty and dry as the land in front of her. No enemy soldiers had marched into sight, but battalions of rabbits had entertained her as they scurried around the unpromising scrub seeking food. She wondered how so many beasts could survive on sparse windswept scraps of grass and brushwood. Indaro was on her stomach, chin resting on folded arms, head covered with a ragged piece of cloth to guard her from the sun. The rabbits would come closer and closer to her, big eyes watchful, until one would spot her and suddenly bolt. Then scores of them would run, their white scuts bobbing, until they all suddenly stopped again and sat up on their haunches. She wondered what they were so fearful of: what predators fed on rabbits in this unwelcoming land? She glanced at the bright white sky, but there was nothing up there, wheeling and watching, ready to take a skinny coney for its young.

The comical creatures took her mind off the ache in her stomach and the incessant, tormenting thirst. It also took her mind off the injured soldiers lying in the dip behind her. After the massacre, she and Doon had limped to the west, moving through the night until at dawn they had come across a small group of Reds who had also escaped the carnage. Two were mortally injured and had died on the first night. On the second night another died. Now they were five. She and Doon, whose wound was healing well, and Garret, who was unhurt of course. Stalker, the red-braided northlander, had a shallow wound in his side and a broken ankle but he could move on a make-shift crutch. It was Queza who was the problem. The small woman had a stomach wound, probably from a spear. It had stopped bleeding but was leaking pale fluid and it stank, and Queza was now semi-conscious, muttering feverishly. They expected her to die on the first night, but she was holding on, and Indaro could not bring herself to leave her. Queza could survive if she was brought to the City, and she could be brought to the City if relief came. So Indaro watched the east, for the enemy, while Garret watched the west for City troops.

It was the middle of the afternoon and Indaro was close to dropping off to sleep when she heard a sound of scrambling and Stalker lay down awkwardly beside her.

"We should try and make a move tonight," he said. His face was grey with pain.

Indaro knew he was right, but she said nothing.

"That girl of yours is going to die. There's no point us dying with her." It was an argument he'd made before.

"We can make a litter. Garret and I will carry her."

"You can scarcely carry yourself, woman. We're all as weak as one-day pups."

"She's tiny. She weighs no more than a knapsack."

He shrugged. "Suit yourself. Garret's a fool for you. He'll do anything you say."

With an effort, Indaro sat up and swung her knees round, ready to stand. The movement made her head spin. They had to get water soon or they would all be dead.

"Don't worry about us," she told the northlander. "Try and keep up."

He grinned and started to shuffle on his backside back towards the others. Indaro glanced once more to the east—and saw movement. She shielded her eyes and squinted. A distinct moving dark blur.

"Incoming," she said quietly.

Yantou Tesserian, the Fkeni rider, felt the newcomer's eyes boring into his back, piercing his leather armour and tickling his backbone. He didn't like the man. He didn't like him and he didn't trust him. The Tenth?

He didn't believe a word. Yantou knew this tall man with his blue eyes and arrogant walk was either a deserter or a dunghill Rat. Probably a Rat, probably an officer. But for the moment the man was walking unknowing towards the 17th Eastern, Yantou's own company which, by the Fkeni's reckoning, was less than a half-day's hike to the south. The newcomer was saving them the bother of tying him up and dragging him along. Officers were always kept for interrogation, although most of them were ignorant bastards, kept in the dark by their generals, even in battle.

In the village where Yantou was born, in the foothills of the beautiful and perfidious Mountains of the Moon, tall men were pitied. They made poor soldiers. Like high trees, they were vulnerable to the axe, ready to topple in a strong wind. Short men, brawny and strong like Yantou, were low down, ready to strike for the vital parts, the genitals and the belly. Tall soldiers waved their swords at your head and neck, the most effectively defended part of the body. And these tall trees, these high waving fronds, made easy targets.

But they were treacherous. Their heads were so high, you never knew what they were thinking. Yantou pulled his horse to a halt and, turning in the saddle, waved his men on in front of him. The tall newcomer passed him without a glance. Yantou stood in his stirrups. He turned this way and that, scanning the dead plain. Nothing.

Far away to his right rabbits were feeding. They were too distant from Yantou to pay him any heed, but suddenly they ran. Away to the west, their white tails flashing the alarm. They were not running from him. What were they running from? Rabbits were stupid creatures. Sometimes they would flee from a tumbling leaf. He stared hard to see a threat they might be escaping. Nothing.

He debated with himself, then pulled his mount to the right and signalled the men to fan out. The platoon loped in the direction he indicated, spears and swords at the ready. Yantou trotted his horse beside them, unsheathing a spear as he guided the beast with his knees. Rabbits scattered on either side of the running men.

There was a rise in the land fifty paces ahead. Forty. He saw a furtive movement beyond it and grinned, imagined fear. He held the spear aloft. A red figure rose up then darted to his right. It was a woman, fleeing. A female Rat. He turned the horse towards her. It was a foolish mistake for the dunghill to arm its women.

He chased her. She was fast. But he was faster. He readied himself to launch his spear, hesitated, reluctant to end the hunt. Suddenly she bowled over, rolling, out of sight beneath his horse. He dragged on the reins, hauling the beast round, then saw a moving blur at his right stirrup. She came up in a heartbeat and lanced her sword into his side. It veered off the armour, then sliced through his hip, burning. He brought the butt of the spear down at her head but she was already gone. The horse, caught by surprise, whinnied and reared as something hit him on the nose. Her sword. Yantou, disabled by the wound to his hip, hung on grimly, then felt another blow to his back. He slid off the horse, sword in hand, and landed on one knee, looking around. The woman was already racing back to her comrades, Yantou forgotten.

He put one hand awkwardly to his back and it came back sticky with blood. It improved the grip on his sword. He followed the woman. He saw she was battling with two of his men, her sword red, coated with his life-blood. Two others of his platoon were dead, and the tall newcomer was fighting with Alva, his best fighter, a doughty swordsman, and small. Yantou stumbled towards them to help Alva. Over a low lip of land he saw another battle, a big red-braided man and a blonde woman both defending a wounded warrior. A nest of Rats.

His legs were weakening and he wondered how grave his wounds were. He made towards Alva, then somehow he was on his knees, staring down at the dry dust, where his blood was soaking in as fast as it could flow. He looked up. Alva was lying dead now, his head half severed. The tall man was running to aid the woman.

Now Yantou was lying staring at the sky. It was white and bright and hurt his eyes. So he closed them and darkness gathered around him, comforting. After a long while he opened them again and saw the face of the tall man above him. His eyes were blue as the skies of Yantou's home. They watched Yantou with a terrible compassion.

Chapter 14

Is he dead?"

Fell nodded.

"Did he tell you anything?"

He shook his head. "Not that one. All I know is the 17th are south of here. They were marching to meet them. We must keep moving west."

Indaro watched him bend to feel Queza's pulse. If she never saw him again, that was how she would remember him, marking the living and the dead, mustering his resources, his face stone. She took another long swallow from a liberated waterskin.

She had thought them all doomed when the Blues came straight for them, the officer on his horse, six men running. All she could think of was to take out the rider first, leaving six fit men against Garret and two soldiers who could barely stand. She could scarcely believe it when, having downed the officer, she returned, expecting to see her friends all dead, to find Fell battling alongside them. Where had he come from? Her bruised and battered mind believed he had risen from the earth, a fighting pit demon, or fallen from the sky, a vengeful angel. Then she realised he had been delivered by the enemy and, for the first time in that season and in many before, she offered thanks to the Gods of Ice and Fire.

Now the Blues were all dead, and they were all alive. And they had water aplenty. The only problem was that the officer's pony had bolted. Fell had sent Garret to look for it, but so far he had not returned.

"Horse or no horse," Fell told them, "we must make for the City tonight. We can fashion a good litter from their spears and carry Queza."

Indaro glanced at Stalker, but his face was expressionless as he tended a cut on Doon's shoulder. The northlander said, "You're wounded." He pointed at Fell's chest.

Fell looked down. "So I am."

Indaro said stupidly, "Where's your breastplate?" When he ignored her, she said, "Let me see to it."

He sat down obediently, tearing off the bloodstained rags of his shirt. She sloshed water over the wound, a wide shallow cut high above his heart.

"Careful with water," he grunted. "We've a way to go yet."

Then he sat back and closed his eyes as she prepared needle and thread. She worked right to left, knotting the stitches separately lest the wound be torn open again. There was an old scar on his chest, above the right nipple, and the sword had sliced through it. It was like the letter S, with a scant tail. It wasn't a sword cut. She realised it was a burn, like a brand. She remembered Broglanh had one like it. Leaning in close, squinting slightly in the gathering gloom, Indaro felt breath brush her hair and glanced up. Fell was looking down at her, his face close to hers. Then he shut his eyes again and leaned back. There was a tattoo on his right shoulder, an eagle clutching a sword.

"Is that Fourth Adamantine?" she asked him.

At first he said nothing, then, "Yes."

"And the scar? Is it a brand?"

But he said nothing, and she wondered why he was still so cool to her. Did he even now think of her as a deserter, just a necessary resource? What could she do to redeem herself? Then she realised the eyes were unfocussed. He was listening. She raised her head.

Doon, who was sitting high on the lip of rock watching the land, sang out, "Incoming!"

They all reached wearily for their swords, then Doon added, "It's Garret. What's he carrying?"

It was a long branch, dry but sturdy, with a wide fork at one end. The soldier handed it to Stalker, then turned to Fell and said, "Sorry, sir. I couldn't find the pony."

Fell nodded. "Any enemy?"

"No. I saw birds circling a long way to the south. But nothing nearby, alive or dead."

Stalker padded the fork of wood with rags and settled his arm over it. The branch was just the right length for a crutch. Stalker grinned and slapped Garret on the back. It was the first time Indaro had seen the man smile. His ankle had been broken again in the battle and his foot was at an unnatural angle. Indaro was surprised the man could smile. She was surprised he could do anything other than lie down and cry.

Fell asked him, "Do you want me to straighten that foot again?"

The northlander glared at him. "No."

"Very well. Then prepare to march."

They walked through the night. It was moonless, but so starry Indaro could see their shadows on the dusty ground, ghostly in the semi-darkness. She looked up at the dead stars and they looked down on her, mocking their attempts to keep their fragile bodies alive for a few more heartbeats. Fell and Garret carried Queza's litter while Indaro trudged alongside with a knapsack packed with the Blues' food and medical supplies. Stalker struggled as best he could, while Doon watched the rear. Every now and then they stopped for these last to catch up. It was slow.

As the first faint light touched the eastern horizon Fell called a halt and they all sat and drank water, Garret keeping watch. Indaro felt Queza's neck, as she had done countless times before. Each time she expected to feel nothing, but she closed her eyes and concentrated, and after a while she felt the weak pulse of life, an irregular pitter-pat, pat-pitter. She looked up to see Fell watching her and she nodded, and Fell shook his head in wonder. She trickled some water into the woman's mouth. On a whim she took Queza's hand and squeezed it, trying to send some of her own strength into her. Still holding the hand she dozed off.

She awoke to the dawn, a wonderful clash of coral and deep blue heralding the long days of autumn, her own time of the year. As a child she always looked to the ending of things. She glanced around. Everyone slept, except for Fell, who was sitting guard, dressed in his own uniform again. She wondered if he ever slept. Again she checked Queza's pulse, then went over and sat with her commander.

"How is your wound?"

He shrugged; it was not worth mentioning.

"Will we reach the City today?" she asked.

"Barring enemy action, yes." He held his gaze to the east.

"Queza could survive."

"Maybe."

"She is small and light. Perhaps the blow from the spear did not penetrate so far if her body was pushed back by it."

At last he turned and looked at her questioningly.

"I mean," she explained, "a big solid man would have withstood the blow and the spear would have penetrated farther."

"An interesting idea," he replied. "However, do not hope for Queza. Belly wounds are the worst."

They both knew it well enough, but this was a comfort zone for conversation. They were both experts in wounds and death, and the many agonising stages of dying.

Keen to keep him talking, she offered, "My father told me that wounds often go bad because dirt on the weapon and pieces of dirty clothing are pushed into the body and left there to rot." She added, warmed by the memory, "He told me to always wear a clean shift under my armour."

For the first time ever she saw amusement written across his face. The new lines followed unfamiliar pathways, and he looked like a stranger, one who was not necessarily a man of war.

"When did you last have a clean shift under your armour?" he asked with a smile.

She smiled too. Cleanliness was a foreign concept to her, as unfamiliar as cheesemaking or necromancy.

"Last year, perhaps, when we were at that place with the orange trees and thatched houses."

"Copperburn."

"Yes. It was lovely there. The fallen leaves made the land look as if it was on fire."

He said, "Autumn is my favourite time of year."

He swallowed from his waterskin then handed it to her. She took a deep draught. She was going to make a comment about water, to keep him talking, but as she opened her mouth, what came out was, "Do you dislike all women warriors, or is it just me?"

He frowned, his face becoming more familiar. "I do not dislike you. And I respect our women. They have proved their worth time and again. They do not have the brute strength of the men, but they are quicker, more agile, and often more ruthless."

It was said that women were quicker to go for the groin. They would slice the genitals off an enemy with no compunction. Sometimes they seemed to enjoy it.

He went on, "They suffer more wounds than the men, but the wounds tend to be less grave and they survive them better."

Indaro knew this. She guessed he was thinking out loud, and had the sense to keep quiet.

"But I do not think women should be fighting this war. The enemy doesn't use them. They despise us for doing so."

"The enemy don't have to. And why do we care what the enemy think?"

"We don't care. But we should be aware. This is called intelligence," he answered.

"You were a soldier already when women joined the army?"

"Long before. I remember when they first arrived. Most of them frightened, untrained. They were slaughtered in the thousands." He looked down at his hands and she noticed for the first time that two fingers were missing from his left. She wondered what he was remembering. "It was pitiable," he said. "Some of us swore it would never happen again, but it took a long time for the generals to realise women were worth more than to be used for the enemy to practise on before they met real soldiers."

She sat quietly, conscious of violent emotions as he recalled the past.

"A woman should be a safe harbour for a man," he said quietly, "a bowl of grain, a jug of water, a soft blanket before an open fire."

She felt anger rising, but she kept it to herself, and despite the insult of his words she was astonished he would speak so intimately to her.

They sat together in something like companionship for a while, then she said, "My father was not a traitor."

"Your words are valueless. You would defend him if he were a traitor or not."

"He is my father. His blood runs in my veins. So you are right. But you would defend your own father. Sir."

He was silent for a while, staring to the east. Then he offered, "My veins run only with the blood of strangers."

He pointed in the direction he had been watching. "Look. Garret saw birds circling. I thought that was a cloud, but it is a cloud of birds. A big one. And they are coming this way. Carrion birds keep vigil over corpses."

"But corpses do not move."

"They also stalk the injured. Injured prisoners, perhaps, a lot of them."

"The Maritime, returning with enemy wounded?"

He looked at her again, and his eyes were bleak as winter seas. "There is no Maritime, Indaro. The army was destroyed. We might be all that survives."

She sat there, dumbfounded, as he roused the others, and within moments they were walking once more through the new morning.

They were within sight of the City walls when Queza died. Indaro was walking beside the litter when the woman gave a little sigh as if a hard decision had been made. Heart full of dread, Indaro stopped the two bearers and they stood, patient as dray horses, as she felt for a pulse. But the faint flicker had departed. The flesh was dead, though the body was still warm with the memory of life. The men set the litter down and they walked on, leaving Queza for the carrion birds.

The rhythm of thundering hooves behind them was the last sound Doon wanted to hear.

She was walking with Stalker, with Fell and Indaro ahead and Garret bringing up the rear. From time to time Fell would stop to allow Stalker to catch up. Doon wondered how long the northlander could keep going; it was taking all his strength to keep propelling himself forward on the crutch. And she marvelled that Fell could not see it would be better to let the injured man lead, setting the pace, rather than striding ahead then waiting for him with scarcely concealed impatience. He and Indaro make a fine pair, she thought. The woman can wait for nothing either.

"I wonder what they're talking about," she mused to Stalker, not really expecting an answer.

But after a few more laboured steps he asked her, "Is your commander a sword master?"

"You've seen him fight."

"That's not what I meant."

She shrugged. "I don't know. There are always rumours. Believe them or not. He is said to have a woman and child somewhere."

"We all have a woman and child somewhere."

"Speak for yourself. But he has no interest in Indaro. I think he dislikes her."

The man stopped and stared at her in disbelief. "That blow to your arse has addled your brains," he snorted, then he moved on.

She had no more time to think on it, for the sound of galloping hooves ended it all. In the last few hours Doon had allowed herself to hope: that they would survive and reach the City; that they all, even Stalker, would live to fight again. The hope washed away in a heartbeat as she turned and saw the silver pennant of an enemy cavalry detachment racing towards them across the darkening land. Thirty riders, maybe more. They would overtake them in moments.

Garret had drawn his sword and was backing towards her. His face was white and she heard him mutter, "One more hour. Just one more hour."

It was hard to bear. Doon had feared she would die in the flood, then, as the Wildcats were slaughtered one by one, she had suffered an injury which could easily have killed her but which was mending day by day. Now, to be so close. But she knew the end when she saw it and she drew her sword and prepared to die. She had heard tales of what they did to women captives. She would not surrender and she would not lie down while blood still ran in her body. In a way it was a relief. The last years had been so hard . . .

Fell Aron Lee, his face expressionless, ordered them to stand in line abreast, with Stalker in the centre, and he and Indaro on the flanks. Doon and Indaro looked at each other, and Doon saw acceptance in the other woman's eyes. Doon grinned, then threw back her head and sang out the high ululating screech of her people. Fell glanced at her. He smiled grimly. She saw him reach into the breast of his battered jerkin and pull out the insignia of his rank, a silver square with four gold bars.

The grey troopers rode around them, whipping up dust. At a word from Fell, the five backed into a tight circle. Doon watched the horses striding past her, circling, leather creaking, horses snorting, bridles jangling, the smell of the animals tickling her nose. She hefted her sword, feeling the dampness in her palm, her dry mouth. At an order the riders stopped and turned towards the five. Spears were levelled and they stood in the centre of a ring of metal points. Doon took a deep breath.

Fell raised his insignia aloft. The gold gleamed in the sunlight.

He called, "I am Fell Aron Lee, commander of the 2nd company of the

14th regiment of the Maritime Army of the West. I demand honourable treatment for these warriors of the City."

The enemy leader sat high in the saddle on a great warhorse. He and his mount both wore grey armour, and his helm was silver and graceful, with a grey plume atop. He reached up and took it off to reveal a long dark-skinned face.

"We have been looking for you," he told Fell.

I ndaro stared in surprise as the grey leader beckoned to one of his riders. They conferred for a moment and the other dropped back. Moments later they saw a messenger galloping, not east to where they had come from, but west towards the City. Indaro watched his dust-trail, baffled. Then, at a word, most of the riders dismounted, easing their backs, stretching their legs, swigging from water bottles and talking in low voices. The leader climbed down, leaving ten riders still mounted, lances and swords at the ready.

Fell ordered his warriors to sheathe their weapons and rest, and they all sat, uneasily at first then, despite themselves, relishing the idleness. Time crept by and night drew on. Fires were lit and a grey trooper asked them if they needed water, but Fell shook his head.

"What's going on?" Doon asked impatiently. Indaro knew she hated uncertainty, was always happiest when there was a plan to follow.

"I don't know," Fell replied.

He leaned back on his elbows, and Indaro saw a flicker of pain cross his face.

"Let me dress your wound," she said softly.

He nodded, and she dragged over the bag of medical supplies they had taken from the dead platoon and pulled out a fresh dressing. He took off his jerkin and opened the borrowed shirt.

"Lie down," she ordered, and he lay back and stared at the stars. Sky blue eyes, she thought and, despite their hopeless situation, she felt a warm glow in the pit of her stomach. Her traitor body, offered this unaccustomed rest, told her what she needed was the release of sex. Wonderful, she thought. Good timing.

"Why did you join Archange?" he asked her, taking up their previous conversation as if nothing had happened in the meantime.

She concentrated on cleaning the wound, aware his eyes were on her. At last she explained, "My brother Rubin disappeared into the sewers. He was younger than me. He despised the war. He refused to fight and said he would rather side with the Blues."

Fell raised his eyebrows, and she added, "I know what you're thinking, but he was no coward. That is what everyone said, but it is not true. But he felt the war was wrong and, like you, that women should not be serving. When I last saw him, when I was home on leave, he told me what he was planning to do. I tried to dissuade him, for his own sake, and for our father's, and mine I suppose. But he would not listen and when he disappeared I knew where he had gone. So I followed him. It was not the best decision I ever made." She smiled ruefully. "I had no idea what the sewers were like, how many hundreds of leagues of darkness and terror, the thousands of desperate people living down there. It was a nightmare. And there was so little chance of finding him in the dark. Then I met Archange."

"A traitor to the City."

"Archange is no traitor. She is more loyal to the City than . . . any of us."

"The only reason she has lived this long is because she is Marcellus' sister."

Indaro hid her surprise. Then, realising it scarcely mattered, she said, "I didn't know that. Have you ever met her?"

"Just the once." Then, reverting to their previous subject, he asked, "Was your brother ever found?"

She shook her head. "I like to think he survived and is now living in safety somewhere, and my father knows and is content to conceal him. And I know that these thoughts are treasonous. But, if we are to die . . . Anyway"— she shrugged—"I don't suppose it matters now."

She asked him, "Why has the messenger gone towards the City? To arrange your ransom?"

"I'm not important enough to ransom."

"But they were looking for you? Why would the enemy be looking for you?"

"I don't know. But I expect it is a matter of politics. Our general, our *late* general, I suspect and fervently hope, used to say everything is about politics."

"I despise Randell Kerr. And I despise his sentiments. The man's a fool, a dangerous fool, yet you're quoting him."

Fell grinned at her, and the anger in her chest drifted away and she laughed. She realised she was enjoying herself. Here, at the end of the world, she felt happy for the first time in years. She saw the others looking at them curiously.

"Can we survive this?" she asked him softly.

"I have asked myself that every day of the last seven. We are still here."

She had finished the dressing, noting that the wound was healing slowly. She packed away the bandages. Then she leaned forward and kissed Fell on the mouth. He tensed, then she felt his lips soften and his tongue touch briefly against hers, and she pulled away again. A promise, she thought. If we survive this.

"The messenger's coming back," announced Garret.

The mounted man galloped up and flung himself from his horse to speak to the grey leader. Then he disappeared into the darkness with the rest of the riders.

Yet more time passed and nothing happened once more, until a tinge of pink appeared in the eastern sky and Indaro could make out the shapes of friends and enemies around her.

Doon stood and stretched. "What's going on?" she asked irritably. "Why don't they just kill us and get it over with?"

But Indaro wasn't listening. "Can you hear that?" she replied, cocking her head.

They all looked to the west. Under the lightening sky they could see a troop of cavalry issuing from the distant City. Indaro's heart lifted. Relief, at last. She swung back, raising her sword. But the grey riders were casually packing their saddlebags, getting ready to leave.

"What are they doing? What's going on?" she asked, looking to Fell.

He shook his head. "I've no idea."

Within moments the City troop arrived. They drew to a halt many paces distant. There were just seven riders—a woman leader and six warriors in black and silver. The leader stepped her mount forward. Indaro recognised the short grey hair, the skinny, ungainly frame. She frowned. That woman Saroyan again. Was this unlikeable woman dogging her steps? Why did she appear each time there was a mystery? She and the grey leader walked their mounts to one side and talked quietly together. The two teams of riders stared at each other across the heads of the five bemused captives.

Time passed and voices were raised, then lowered. Bargaining for our lives, Indaro thought. What will the bargain be? What are our lives worth? Finally the man and the woman trotted their mounts back to their respective lines. The woman nodded her head in a valedictory gesture to the greys' commander. The City riders were about to leave again.

Fell stepped forward. "Saroyan!"

The lord lieutenant looked at him as if seeing him for the first time.

"I am Fell Aron Lee," he announced. "I was decorated by the emperor for valour after the Battle of Coulden Moor, and I hold two gold suns for twenty years' service. With me are four faithful warriors of the City who have courageously offered their lives in its service every day for more than four years."

He lifted his voice again to a bellow. "Would you turn us over to the enemy to die like dogs in the dust?"

Indaro waited, tensed. For a long moment there was no sound but the sighing of the breeze past their ears and the breathing of horses, and the only movement Saroyan's mount turning. It was a young beast, and skittish, but the woman paid it no mind as it trotted lightly in a circle. Then she gripped it with her thighs and said a soft word and it shook its mane and settled down.

"Your orders are to go with these troops," she told Fell coldly. "They will not kill your warriors if you go quietly."

Fell said, "We will not surrender to the enemy at the word of a traitor."

The woman appeared not to be offended, only impatient. She walked her horse over to Fell. Indaro stepped up to Fell's shoulder. Saroyan glanced at her with dislike, then she leaned from her saddle. The moonstone earring gleamed in the rays of the rising sun.

"You can keep your team alive or condemn them to death," Saroyan said. "You can go with these soldiers trussed like a deer and laid across a saddle or riding like a free man. Your choice. Either way you *will* go, Fell Aron Lee."

Then she dropped her voice. "This is about Arish," she said, "and a promise made long ago, which you now have a chance to honour."

What's Arish? Indaro thought. She watched Fell's face tighten and his eyes narrow. There was a long moment when he seemed turned to stone then, stiffly, he nodded.

Saroyan spoke two words in a foreign tongue to the grey leader. Then the City cavalry turned and rode back towards the distant wall, leaving their soldiers in the dust.

At an order the greys mounted, and five riderless horses were brought round from the rear. The leader told the City soldiers to surrender their weapons and mount up. At Fell's word they gave up their swords. They helped Stalker onto a horse then each took a mount.

The leader rode up to Fell. "Your four soldiers," he said in his strange accent, "are a guarantee of your good behaviour. Do I have to bind your hands behind you?"

Fell shook his head. He stayed at the head of the company, with the leader, as Indaro and the others were guided back to the centre. Indaro heard Fell ask, "Where are we going?"

The leader replied, "To Old Mountain."

PART THREE

The House of Glass

Chapter 15

The tall, crooked building loomed like a stooping heron over Blue Duck Alley. Its layers of cellars had been laid down in the unremembered past and now the deepest level was always under water. The ground floor of the house was a centuries-old squat, square stone building, its windows boarded against the prying eyes of neighbours and the thieving fingers of their children. Above that rose four storeys of crumbling bricks and mortar, each slightly smaller than the one beneath, the arched windows painted gaily in different colours. And on top, comically, apparently an afterthought, riding like the crow's nest atop a ship's mast, was an overlarge structure of timber and red tile, an attic, a workroom, and the heart of the house. The whole building, supported by its neighbours only to the first three floors, leaned forward vertiginously, overburdened by the weight on top. Indeed some former resident, perhaps worried by the way the house shifted ominously in the strong northerlies, had built a latticework of timber which reached out from the front wall of the workroom and grasped the pitched roof of the high lodging house on the other side of the alley. Now the two tall buildings leaned against each other comfortably, held together and apart by the sky highway. Only the pure white cats—the ghost cats—which made the quarter their home deftly trod this wooden path high above the stones of the alley.

The dank chambers on the ground floor of the House of Glass housed the furnace, a workroom and storage space. At the rear was a small courtyard, the home of brown rats and the white cats which preyed on them. The first floor housed storage and a small kitchen, scarcely used. Above that was a parlour and study, and above that a jumble of bedrooms on two floors, also mostly unlived-in.

The workroom at the top of the house was reached by a sturdy wooden ladder, cursed daily by those obliged to climb it. The dark-haired young woman who worked up there didn't care. The room was bright and airy, and she loved it, and no amount of grumbling by her father, or by lame Frayling who worked for them, or by the parade of servants and housekeepers drafted in to clean the house, made any difference.

The girl sat in the wide west window, her bare feet up on the sill, looking out over the bustling City, across the jumble and tumble of roofs. Lindo was a poor quarter, bounded to the north by Burman Far and to the west by the Old Wall. Far below her was a maze of alleys and squalid streets, thousands of shanties built of richer people's refuse. Dotted about were big dark ruined buildings, once the homes of the wealthy, now rookeries for the poorest of the poor. There were few houses as tall as the House of Glass, so her view stretched over squalid Lindo, towards far Otaro and its turrets and grey forests, to the Red Palace in the misty distance. The mist had been lying heavily on the City since the Great Flood a month before; in the early mornings it looked like the sea, grey and troubled, from which tall buildings poked like outcrops of rock.

She turned back to the workroom and her work. The attic room was alive with light and colour. Sheets of stained glass leaned against walls and low-set windows, refracting the sunlight in a thousand sparkling patches of crimson and ochre and leaf green splashing across the plaster walls. On a big oak table in the centre lay the sections of glass for the window she was working on. It was a tall narrow panel commissioned for the home of a fat merchant in Otaro. She gazed at it critically but with pride. At the top of the panel a silver leviathan basked on sunlit waters, spume blowing from his head. At the base of the window a green-skinned giant of the deep crept across golden sand, its tentacles oozing ahead of it. Between the two monsters was a seething stew of fishes in every colour of the spectrum, framed by waving fronds of flowering plants.

"Where did you see such coloured fish?" her father had asked, believing she had never seen the sea, nor knew anyone who had.

She had shrugged. She had seen enough fish on the fishmonger's stall, their scales shining in delicate shades of pink and green and brown. She imagined that they lost their colours in death, as people did, and that in life they had shimmered with the brightest colours available to the gods' palette. So now she fashioned green fish with gold stripes, and red fish with blue heads, and herds of tiny fish in every shade of yellow she could create, each with a crest of black. The leviathan had golden teeth, the squid blue eyes. The sea itself was dappled silver, but it was lost beneath the swirling collage of movement and colour.

The panel was nearly finished. Most of the panes of glass were laid in place on the wide central table. She had two more sections to complete, important ones near the base, which would lie at eye level on the merchant's wall. There were the tips of the monster's tentacles—green on yellow. And her own sign. Then, when the final panes had been baked in the kiln, fixing the paint to the glass surface, Frayling would join her to help cut and solder the lead calms which would bind the whole work into one piece.

She walked over to the original watercolour painting of the panel, now well-worn and ragged, which she had first pinned to the wall more than half a year before. She looked at it for a while, then returned to the table of glass. She closed her eyes and relaxed her shoulders, letting her thoughts calm and settle into the creatures on the panel. She imagined the tentacles, their sinewy rubbery strength. She saw them touch the sand, then reach forward, groping.

Then there was a step on the ladder, a stumble and an oath. She frowned a little and allowed her mind to drift back to the workroom.

"This year, by all the cursed gods, I will have a staircase built!" Her father's head, grey-haired and tousled, appeared in sight, and he struggled up the rest of the steps into the room.

She smiled and raised her eyebrows at him. He saw her look and admitted, "I know, I say that every year. But next summer I'll do it, I swear. Frayling will leave us if he has to carry many more sheets of glass up here."

She watched him fondly. There was no red left in his hair, and his face was heavily lined with age and sad experience. He avoided her gaze and looked down at the floor. When he spoke it was with reluctance. She guessed what he was going to say.

"The merchant's servant has been here. He wants you to go to his house to see the fitting of the window."

A wave of panic trembled across her stomach, and she shook her head. "You," she whispered, pleading.

"I know I can do it," he replied gravely, "and I will go with you, but it is a matter of courtesy. This is your most important commission. He is a good client. And he is a good man. He does not deserve your disrespect."

There was metal in his voice she seldom heard, and her heart sank, for she knew she could not refuse him. She hated meeting people, and feared to speak to them. Many people thought she could not speak, and called her "dummy" behind her back, and sometimes to her face. The fact was that she used her words sparingly, as if she had merely a cupful which she offered to people a drop at a time. Her windows spoke for her, she believed.

She did not need words to tell her father how she felt about visiting the merchant.

"How long?" he asked her, glancing at the oak table.

She held up four fingers.

"Then I will tell him we will deliver on the last day of the month." He walked over to the south window. Outside a sturdy pulley had been fixed to the wooden beams jutting out over the alley.

"This is the biggest work you have ever fashioned," he said. "It will be very heavy. I think it should be lowered down in two, maybe three, parts. And reassembled at the merchant's house."

He saw the unwillingness in her face, and added, "It is very heavy, and very fragile, and it is worth half a year's work to you. It is a long way to Otaro. If there were an accident, it would be best to lose only a third of your work, rather than all of it."

He was right of course, but she could not explain to him, if she even had the words, how important it was to her to finish the whole work in one piece and see it leave the House of Glass complete. The last half year had been blissful. Her heart had raced with excitement each morning as she awoke and thought of her work for the day. These last few days would be sad, for the sea window she had laboured all her skill and love on would be gone. If it were to leave this place in pieces, unfinished, it would leave an empty place in her heart.

But, she thought, the days would be spoiled now anyway, with the prospect of meeting the fat-faced merchant, and the friends and hangers-on who would no doubt be invited to see the window put into place. They would all glance at her from the corners of their eyes and, when they thought she was not watching, speak to each other in hushed tones, smirking or sympathetic, according to their natures.

Her father looked at her levelly, awaiting her reaction, so she forced a smile and nodded. He knew it was forced, and loved her for her bravery. And she loved him for not mentioning it.

"Thank you, little soldier," he said.

Bartellus climbed back down the steps, stopping from time to time to ease his aching knee. When he and Em had first taken the house in Blue Duck Alley he had looked doubtfully at the steep stairways, and the ladder up to the workroom, but thought to himself he would seldom have reason to go there. In fact, he now spent part of each day up there with Emly. He loved to watch her work. He had always admired her grace and strength, even as a child. Now, aged just sixteen, she had added to that a skill beyond his comprehension. He saw the delicate paintings she made of her planned work, and marvelled as she turned thin paper and delicate brushwork into superb stained glass windows which delighted the eye and warmed the soul. She would take panes of plain glass fashioned by Frayling in his workroom on the ground floor, and transform them, reshaping them by nibbling away at the edges with a tool called a grozing iron, then painting them with black paint, creating faces, and muscles, and, in this panel, waving sea fronds, the spots on the monster's tentacles, and fishy frills.

Emly loved her work, and she loved the home where, he hoped, she had been happy for the first time in her life. But she knew, just as he did, although they had never discussed it, that they would have to move on soon. They did not lead the life of fugitives, but that was what they were.

Bartellus slipped out of the side door and turned into Blue Duck Alley, following its meandering length away from the Old Wall. They were in the part of the City called Lindo. It had once been a place of wealth and privilege, but that was many centuries before. Most older people called it the Armoury, because for generations the forges of the emperor's armourers were situated there, benefiting from the brisk north wind that blew perpetually along its sloping streets. But the City grew, and the armourers and their forges were relocated farther south and east, towards the edges of the City and closer to the armies they supplied.

Now the Armoury's high houses of the rich, those that still stood, were grim rookeries for the elderly. In a City permanently at war, those who survived their years of armed service had nothing to look forward to in old age except a half-life crippled by injury and by the dementia that was a curse on all the aged. The rookeries housed the dregs of the City, maimed or demented old men and women, packed into verminous apartments, dozens to a room, barely living, barely alive. In his short time in the sewers they called the Halls Bartellus had never seen such squalor as dwelt in the rookeries of Lindo.

Between the rookeries were the smoking shacks and shanties of the working poor, those who struggled to maintain a craft when materials often could not be had, and the workers in the houses of the rich in wealthy Otaro and Gervain. The jumble of huts, built of timber and tin and cardboard and debris, moved constantly, and the maze of alleys between them shifted daily. It was easy to get lost in their depths, and careful folk went nowhere near them.

The whole quarter had been scoured clean of these patchwork homes in the devastating flood two months before. Bartellus, riding out the storm with Emly and Frayling in the House of Glass, saw them swept away and thought them gone for good. Yet within days the surviving inhabitants had returned and started rebuilding.

Since the Great Flood and the destruction of the Maritime Army the City's situation had become dire. Supply routes were interrupted and supplies dried up. Fewer citizens could make an honest living. Crime was soaring. The poor people of Lindo had to steal to feed their children and themselves. Only four years ago it had been unsafe to go out at night. Now it was perilous in the hours of daylight too, and Bartellus always went armed. Under his old greatcoat, slung over his shoulders to keep his arms free, he strapped a large knife, honed to perfect sharpness, in a sturdy leather scabbard. He had used it several times, and his hand was ready on the haft as he strode down Blue Duck Alley.

He crossed Parting Street, the main thoroughfare leading north out of the City, and the border between Lindo and neighbouring Burman Far. The stench of tanneries and slaughterhouses, which had been in his nostrils since he stepped out of his home, started to fade. Here in Burman, a place of markets and bakeries and grain houses, the streets were patrolled by militias employed by the powerful so they could walk unmolested in daylight.

Bartellus walked through the People's Market, his destination most days. He passed the half-empty stalls, sad old women with their small offerings of sesame seeds or cobnuts who wailed at him to buy as he passed, small boys from beleaguered farms in the north trying to sell small bags of potatoes for a single pente each. The winesellers had gone, and the meat-vendors. In a small pen malnourished flyblown cattle were being sold off as a last resort by a desperate smallholder.

The People's Market was a place of information. Not just gossip, although there was plenty of that, but over the years Bartellus had learned to judge the progress of the wars by the foodstuffs available on the stalls. Today, he saw that the only fish available was river fish, which meant the sea routes were blocked, or the military had commandeered fishing boats for some doomed enterprise. Either way, there was a crisis on the eastern, seaward, side of the City. But there were plenty of spices—corima, fellseed and red ghurr—which indicated a boat had arrived from the far south and east, perhaps two or three days ago. So the crisis which had deprived the City of sea fish had only happened in the last day or so.

The information was of more than passing interest to him, and he wondered about the state of the armies and of the City, beleaguered as it was by enemies on every side. He could not ask. Since he and Em emerged from the Halls eight years earlier he had kept his head low. To the poor folk of the Armoury he was Old Bart, the glassmaker's father. No one questioned his history. As an old man he was invisible, and that was the way he planned to keep it.

He bought two loaves, warm from the oven. The price was higher than ever, which meant grain was harder to come by. The bakery was guarded by men with cudgels. Bartellus chewed on one loaf as he wandered around the market stalls, hiding the other under his coat. He bought a bag of dried figs and one of red rice, then negotiated with a burly Garamund farmer for a basket of green apples. These were rare and costly, but he knew Em loved them. He paid an urchin a pente to take the food back to the House of Glass, promising Frayling would pay him the same on receipt.

The boy ran off, the basket under one arm, the rest of the food clutched to his thin chest. Bartellus had no doubt he would help himself to an apple or two, but he did not mind. In the world's terms Bart was a rich man, although he was at pains to conceal it.

He thought again about their impending visit to the merchant's house, and he frowned. He had believed what he said. He thought it right for Emly to attend on the merchant, and he would have to go with her. He was proud of his adopted daughter and wanted her talent recognised. He believed that in ten years, perhaps five, she would be creating glass windows for the emperor's palace. He had told her that. But he had not told her he would not be with her. If he lived that long, he could never again show his face in the Red Palace.

There was another, more urgent, reason he wanted his daughter's talent recognised by powerful men. She was fifteen, she guessed, perhaps already sixteen. She needed a powerful patron to keep her out of the army. The fat wine merchant wasn't such a man, but commendation by him might lead to more influential connections.

And the merchant he had no concerns about. He seemed a pleasant enough fellow, not well-endowed with brains. It was his son that worried Bartellus—a sly, skulking youth with a mean eye. Bart had disliked him on sight, but he recognised this was at least partly because such a young man should be in the military, serving his City, rather than still lolling at his father's table. The way the boy had watched him made him cautious. He could not have recognised him. He had been a babe when Bartellus was commanding the armies of the east and north. And no portrait of the general existed that he knew of. Nevertheless, he was suspicious of the boy, and hoped he would be absent when the glass window was delivered.

Bartellus was aware of the irony: he despised the merchant's son for evading armed service, while himself plotting to keep Emly from the war. But he had come a long way from that dark day in a sewer when he had argued with an old woman that girls should be drafted to serve their City with their lives and deaths.

He was comfortable with his about-turn, and if someone had accused him of hypocrisy he would have shrugged, and explained, "She is my daughter."

It was a long walk and the thin autumn sun was making him sweat under his greatcoat by the time he arrived, limping slightly, at the Shining Stars Inn. The old, sprawling brick building had once been a monastery. But the holy men had long since met their gods, and now it served as a hostelry for visitors from other parts of the City and, rarely now, foreigners. Bartellus seldom entered the inn, but ducked under a low arch into the wide, well-planted courtyard. A career soldier himself, he enjoyed the company of veterans, and his heart relaxed as he walked among the patterned tables where other old boys idled away their mornings playing knucklebones, checkers and urquat. In the corner of a cobbled wall in the shade of a fig tree he spotted Creggan and Dol Salida as they set out the urquat table. He smiled and walked over to them.

The two boys, brothers, who had followed him from Blue Duck Alley, watched Bartellus go into the inn's garden.

Scowling, the younger boy grumbled, "I told you he'd come here. Walking all morning for nothing."

"We'll still be paid, stupid," his brother told him. "It's where he goes after this they'll want to know."

"He'll be there for hours. He always is. Let's go home and come back later."

"You go. It doesn't need two of us."

But the younger boy sighed and sat down in the shadow of a low wall. His brother grinned and sat with him in the dust. The sun rose over the inn and their patch of shade slowly disappeared as they waited.

About time," grumbled Dol Salida, as Bart sat down at the five-sided table, arranging the coloured counters and dice in front of him. "We nearly started without you."

Bartellus nodded gravely. His friend always said that, but the only game they played was urquat—and that was a three- or a five-handed game. It required both luck and skill, and Dol Salida was a master; perhaps the best in the City. But after three years as his students, Bartellus and Creggan had acquired skill enough to make the game interesting for him, the master told them smugly.

After agreeing on the day's small wager, Creggan started the play by throwing the dice. The rattle of the bone pyramids on the wooden table was infinitely comfortable to Bartellus and he settled back in his chair with the prospect of enjoyable hours ahead. A servant quietly put a jug of ale at his elbow, for he was well known at the Shining Stars, and his credit was good.

"How's that daughter of yours, Bart?" asked Creggan after a while, sitting back and taking a sip of ale.

"Well, thank you," Bartellus replied, staring at the counters in front of him.

"That window will soon be finished, eh? The fish one."

"Very soon."

"I'd like to see one of the windows some day."

Bartellus grunted agreeably. Although he liked the two men, he had no intention of inviting them to his house. He believed in keeping the different parts of his life separate; in that way one could not compromise another. Emly would not meet Creggan and Dol Salida, and none of them would know of the whore's attic in Gervain he visited. None of them would learn of his visits to the Great Library, and long evenings studying ancient manuscripts on the history of the City. If people found him secretive, well, so be it. He had reason to be.

Dol Salida won the first three games briskly. Creggan sighed and complained, as he so often did, "There is no point playing you. We're wasting our time."

The master grinned, and set out the board again. "You have beaten me before, Creggan. Let me see, last spring wasn't it? And Bart beat us both only a few days ago. Consider my feelings, man, how dull it must be for me to win all the time. Would you like to increase our wager?"

"No," both men said with feeling, and Dol Salida laughed.

He was a gregarious man, with an easy smile. Though his head was bald and brown he affected a wide white moustache which he stroked absently as he played. Bart had long ago learned that the master's moustache-stroking, though apparently involuntary, gave no indication as to his game strategies. When Dol left the Shining Stars, Bartellus had discovered, he would go back to a wife and many grandchildren in a crowded house close by the Red Palace. A former cavalry officer, he had been invalided out with a shattered leg a decade before. He leaned heavily on a stick now, but if the limb pained him he never let on.

Creggan, by contrast, was a widower. He had no children, and he lodged with a blacksmith's family in Gervain. He seldom spoke about himself, and Bartellus knew only that he was an infantryman and had served in the forces of Grantus, victorious commander of the southernmost armies, some twenty years before.

Unlike most of the old soldiers around them in the courtyard, who spoke of nothing else, the three men seldom discussed the war, and rarely referred to their fighting years. They came together to play urquat and their conversation was limited. Bartellus spoke of Emly's work, Dol Salida of his family, and Creggan of the birds of the City which were his passion.

So it was rare for Creggan to comment, "I hear we lost a naval battle two days ago."

Bartellus said nothing, and there was a pause before Dol Salida laid down two counters then muttered, "Half-truths and speculation. Where do you get your information from, Creggan? These old gossips?" He gestured to the grey veterans hunched over tables around them.

Creggan shrugged. Finally Bartellus volunteered, "There was no sea fish in the market today. Only river bream and reedfish, that I could find." The two men glanced at him and nodded.

Bartellus thought that was the end of it, but after a while Creggan offered, "I heard it from a soldier. Infantryman. In there." He gestured towards the inn.

"Oh, not a gossip then," Dol Salida replied sarcastically. "Just a drunken grunt." He chuckled.

"Was he seeking information, or selling it?" asked Bartellus. "In exchange for ale?"

Creggan shook his head, threw the dice and groaned. "No luck today," he complained. "No, he paid his way. He was talking to Fat Lanny. I just overheard."

Bartellus smiled to himself. Fat Lanny had served ale at the Shining Stars for time out of mind. He spent his days with old men telling war stories and showing their scars. He always nodded and smiled, and went on wiping glasses. Bartellus doubted he listened any more.

Their game went on and the sun rose high above them, sparkling down through the leaves and dappling the table.

"Funny thing about him," Creggan said.

"About who?" Dol Salida asked irritably.

"The man in the inn yesterday."

The master sat back and stared at him. "By the gods, man, you think as slowly as you play. Are you still on about that barfly? Did you fall in love with him?"

Unruffled, Creggan repeated pedantically, "Funny thing. He had a tattoo on his bicep the same as the inn sign. Seven stars. I pointed it out to him and we laughed about it."

"The Shining Stars refers to the Seven Sisters," Bartellus told him. "It's one of the pictures placed there by the sky god."

"I know that, man," Creggan said, irritated himself now. "I'm not a simpleton. It's a regimental tattoo, Second Adamantine. I just thought it was funny, a man with seven stars on his bicep drinking ale at the Shining Stars Inn."

"Hilarious," grunted Dol. "Are you going to play or not?"

Creggan threw his dice, then went on, "And he had an odd mark on his forearm. A brand, like it was burned into the skin. Like an S."

"A burn?"

"No, I mean he was branded. Like a horse."

Memory flashed in Bart's mind. A dark-haired soldier with sky blue eyes. "What did he look like?" Bartellus asked, trying not to sound too interested.

Creggan shrugged. "Like a soldier. Shabby. I don't know. Fair hair."

"How do you know he was a soldier?"

Creggan gave him a pitying look. "The tattoo. Anyway, you can tell."

"Tall?"

"He was sitting down. Why do you care?"

With a satisfied grunt, Dol Salida turned over the red counter to reveal a white disc on a blue background. "Moon and two," he said grinning. The other men sat back, defeated.

Bartellus asked his friend, "Do you know of this brand, Dol?"

The master shrugged. "Slave mark, I expect. Why, are you interested?" he asked, his penetrating dark gaze flicking at Bart.

Bartellus kept his voice casual. "How could a man have both the honourable tattoo of the Second Adamantine and a slave mark?" he asked, gathering the counters together.

Dol shrugged. "I couldn't care less."

Then, perhaps lulled into complacency by the warm sun and the ale, Bartellus volunteered, "I saw its fellow a long time ago. On a corpse."

"Blueskin?"

"No. At least, I don't think so. He had many tattoos on his body and head. This single burn mark was on his shoulder.

"It is strange," he pondered. "I have thought it over and over and can make no sense of it."

"Sense of what?" Dol asked.

Bartellus explained. "Tattoos are common among soldiery. Men carry the mark of their regiment, the symbol of their unit. Even members of a platoon sometimes carry the same tattoo—it welds them together, shows their pride in their unity."

The two men nodded, and Dol rolled up his sleeve to show a striking serpent, symbol, Bartellus knew, of the First Imperial cavalry. A mark of great honour.

"And this man had such a tattoo . . . ?" the master asked.

"He carried what looked like a regimental tattoo on his back. A rampant goat with a serpent's tongue."

The two others laughed. "A goat?"

Bartellus shrugged. "It is not unusual," he said. "It is false modesty. In fact, they think of themselves as lions, or eagles, but they use the sign of the lustful goat to show they are careless of such boastfulness, that they are more interested in rutting. It is false modesty," he repeated, "and not very subtle. But then soldiers are not known for their subtlety."

"So you know this tattoo?"

"No. I have seen similar pictures, but not this rearing goat with a flickering forked tongue."

"But you think he was a soldier?"

"Had been a soldier at some time, I'm sure. I recognised his battle tattoos. But his tongue had been cut out."

"Informer," said Dol heavily, nodding to himself.

"Maybe," Bartellus replied. "But here is the conundrum. Some soldiers wear a simple sign on a bicep or shoulder. But most of their tattoos are covered under clothing or armour, not on arms or legs. In a soldier's code, it is considered vulgar, fit only for slaves or women or foreigners, to have limbs covered with tattoos."

"But this man did?"

"No, his arms and legs were clean of marks. But his scalp was shaven and covered in small tattoos, from high on his forehead to the nape of his neck.

"And why would anyone have unblemished arms and legs and neck, then cover his head with tattoos?"

Chapter 16

The Great Library was a city in itself. Built over millennia, it sprawled across several acres, and included living quarters for labourers and custodians, eating houses, kitchens, stables and a blacksmith's forge, gardens, orchards, two lakes and an entire wing for foreign visitors, now largely untenanted. And storage rooms, thousands of them, piled with millions of books in many stages of preservation or decay. The history of the library was a lifetime's study, and it was said that down the years many old men, invalided out of the army and with time on their hands, had spent their declining years labouring on the matter, many of them producing their own texts to add to the millions of words already existing on the subject, mostly unread and unregarded.

In the long afternoon Bartellus made his way, as always, to the central reading room, a huge chamber of light and shadow, its ancient roof supported by hundreds of soaring stone pillars. The green glass roof was centuries old and in a constant state of repair. Instead of a quiet refuge for scholars, the Chamber of Pillars was often a place of bustle and noise, and danger. Workmen laboured high above, talking and arguing and occasionally shouting a warning below of a dropped tool or piece of fumbled glass. On the floor there was the continual movement of the custodians, men and women dressed in sage green, who trundled small wooden carts piled with books. The cart wheels made a clickety-click percussion over the stone flags. The high windows either side of the hall were of green and yellow glass and the light in the chamber had a queasy underwater quality. When it rained there was the constant drizzle and plop of water into the hundreds of rusty vessels placed in every aisle and corner.

The hall was cold as charity in winter, and hot beyond bearing in summer, but Bartellus found the atmosphere enlivening, and it was with a light step that he strode to his usual table, deep in the centre of the hall, flanked by two carved pillars. Carvelho was already there, as Bartellus knew he would be.

"Bartellus!" his assistant said, looking up and seeing him. "This is a fine day!"

Carvelho was a former infantryman of the Maritime, invalided out ten years before. He was in his forties, lean and muscular, and looked more like a street fighter than an academic, until you noticed one arm had been amputated above the elbow. He relied on the small fee Bartellus paid him to supplement his army pension and keep a wife and three children somewhere in the Library quarter. Carvelho was enthusiastic about his work, and if he guessed that the old man's main interest was not what he pretended, then he never let on.

"How so?"

"I have come across a reference in this"—Carvelho waved a manuscript Bartellus knew to be the working journal of a courtier in the far eastern Dravidian empire two thousand years before—"to the third Dravidian emperor . . ."

"Argipelus."

"Yes, Argipelus, writing a letter to Mohastidies . . ."

An early emperor of the City, Bartellus remembered, frowning with the effort.

"Asking for green marble for his palace." He grinned his lopsided grin, and Bartellus smiled in response. Carvelho believed his own ancestors originally travelled from the outskirts of the Dravidian empire far across the Little Sea. He was fascinated with the history of the civilisation and delighted when he discovered any long-ago link with the City. "If we could find that letter—what a breakthrough that would be!"

"Indeed." Bartellus sat down at the table. "Now, I have narrowed down some subjects for you." These were his invariable words. He handed Carvelho a piece of paper. The younger man looked at it and nodded and set off happily towards the huge central stack of drawers, protected by tarpaulins, where lay the thousands of catalogues of books, their subjects and location. Eventually, before the end of the day, he would come back with a list of twenty or thirty books, and between them they would winnow them down to a dozen or so to order from the custodians. They would arrive in the wheeled carts the next day. This work would take Carvelho most of the afternoon, leaving Bartellus to study in privacy the volumes already heaped in front of him. Six out of seven of those books were of no interest to the old man; they were merely a diversion to disguise from Carvelho, and from anyone who showed more than a passing interest, Bartellus' real pursuit.

When he and Em had emerged from the dark of the sewers eight years before he had not guessed he would ever think again of the Halls and their wretched Dwellers. Yet the words of the long-dead Ysold pursued him. The woman, in the last hour of her life, had told him the Eating Gate was breaking down, that it was no longer repaired, and that eventually the entire City would flood as a result. Bartellus wondered, despite himself, why a job, once deemed important enough to justify teams of engineers descending regularly into the peril of the deeper Halls, had been abandoned. He had been a bureaucrat himself, of sorts, and he knew it was probably just an oversight, a lost piece of paper, or a few thousand talents saved on someone's budget.

Yet, without occupation one day, he had wandered into the Great Library to see if he could find any reference to the Gate—and had become hopelessly trapped. After a few months of floundering in the enticing pathways of history, he had found the journal of an engineer called Miletos, an engaging character, whose humour and intellect shone out from the dusty parchment and faded inks. The man never mentioned the Eating Gate—indeed, after nearly eight years, Bartellus had yet to find the official name of the structure—but his musings on the architecture of the long-ago City, and his knife-sharp comments on the personalities of his day, fired Bartellus' imagination for the first time in decades. Indeed, Miletos' journal was the only work the old soldier had ever stolen from the library. He had spirited it past the beady eyes of the crones who watched the exits, split into three parts and tied round his stomach. That was six years before and he still felt guilty about it.

Since then he had been drawn as deeply into a study of the City's architecture as he had once been lost in the Halls themselves. It was almost impossible to link the murky tunnels, caverns and bridges he had encountered in his brief sojourn in the Halls with the dry descriptions by dry-as-dust engineers of triple-bore drains, intercepting sewers, catchpits and overflow weirs. It was a maze, perhaps a hopeless one, but Bartellus loved the challenge, and he revelled in the work.

Then one winter's day a green-clad custodian had lingered at his table, the clicking wheels of his laden cart slowing then falling silent. The man, small and thin-featured with red hair and a humped shoulder, asked him genially about his interests, commenting on the pile of volumes stacked around Bartellus, all on the subjects of engineering, architecture and the history of the City's construction. The custodian had questioned him keenly, his bright pale eyes fixed on him with a scholarly fervour. Bartellus, appalled at the thought he was being watched, abandoned his studies at the library that very day, and it was more than half a year before he ventured there again. Then he started to conceal his real interest in a welter of other subjects. And he employed Carvelho as his proxy. He saw the red-headed custodian from time to time, but the little man seemed to have forgotten him.

With a sigh of contentment Bartellus pulled a familiar volume towards him, bound in cracked leather, entitled *The First Life of Marshall Creed*. In his younger days Creed was a ship owner from the isle of Iastos, a trader in obsidian and mother-of-pearl and something of a rogue and a chancer. He had fallen on hard times after a hurricane wrecked half his ships, and he fetched up, after many escapades, most of which Bartellus considered pure fantasy, resident in Otaro. In those days, more than four hundred years before, the City was open to all foreigners, and it was a central hub of commerce, its port thronged with ships of all nations. Creed, with his long-suffering wife and five daughters, rented a house from which he conducted a variety of businesses on the farthest fringes of legality.

It was the last three chapters of his *Life* which interested Bartellus. Creed was an old man by then, and the autobiography took on a melancholy tone. The author abandoned the boastfulness and arrogance of the previous pages, and spoke instead like a man with a last mission before the end, which he could see coming with sad clarity. He took to wandering the City, marvelling at its beauty and cruelty. He spoke with awe of the Rainbow Gardens, which in those days spread out from the palace in great arcs more than ten leagues long, each planted with flowers in just one colour of the spectrum. He talked with mathematicians and astronomers, who explained to the old man the complex formulae used to build the twenty-seven crystal towers of the Red Palace through which the sun would shine in succession on midsummer's morn. He described the glass birdhouses on the Shield, where the brightest birds from all over the world were brought to breed and flourish, to be released over the rooftops, filling the sky with colour on feast days and to honour the gods. He wrote of the Cages, metal prisons in which the most despised criminals, men and women, were hauled up the outside of the City's walls, some of them already half dead from torture, some fit and still struggling, to die a lingering and hideous death from shock and thirst as an entertainment for all to watch.

And he described, in the finicky detail of an old man who can no longer judge the attention span of his readers, a trip down into the sewers beneath the palace, to the Dark Water, the name he gave to the great river Menander as it dove beneath the City, and to the Magisterium Gate, a construction intended to break up and pulverise large objects which found their way into the high sewers before they could cause obstruction farther down in the narrower tunnels.

The Magisterium Gate was not the Eating Gate, of that Bartellus was sure, for it had only sixteen "rotating engines," as Creed described them, whereas Bartellus was certain the Eating Gate had twenty barrels—nineteen when he last had sight of it. But the mechanism appeared the same, and Creed joined a party of engineers who went down to the Gate to maintain it one day in midsummer when water levels were low and dangers at a minimum. The author spoke of the long walk down through leagues of stinking tunnels, the ghostly inhabitants who disappeared into darkness whenever anyone approached them, and one curious incident.

After a detailed description of the Gate, the party made its way back up towards the light. Not a moment too soon for the old man. He wrote: *"Woefully I trudged, my spirits cloaked in darkness as my boots were encrusted with ordure. I felt I would never be liberated from this mournful place although, indeed, I had been in its depths for not half a day. My young companions laughed and shouted and joked, but their sounds of desperate cheer echoed hollowly from the dripping walls. Our return journey was painfully longer*

than the outward walk for, I was informed, unforecast rainfall in the distant
world outside rendered that way impassable. I admit to a stomach full of ter-
rors at the news. I can imagine no more frightful place to be lost than in the
bowels of those awful eternal tunnels.

"Poor old man that I am, I found myself lagging behind the strong young-
sters who were my companions. Too proud, old fool, to cry out to them to wait
for me, I struggled on, falling farther and farther behind. Their torches began
to fade out of sight and only then did I cast aside self-conceit and call to them,
but by then it was too late and they did not hear me.

"As I was fearing I had been lost to the darkness, my legs weakening with
fear and fatigue, the welcome light of a torch flickered on the far side of the
stream I was following. I turned with relief towards it, for I thought one of
my companions had returned for me, unaccountably taking the wrong side
of the water. But I was astonished beyond words to see it was a woman, hold-
ing aloft the flame and watching me with calm interest."

Bartellus shifted in his hard seat, leaning forward to peer at this intently.

"She raised the torch higher, and I could see she was garbed in long pale
robes, hooded, like an angel or a spirit of the Domanii. Then my senses reas-
serted themselves, and I realised she was but a real woman, for her robes had
been snipped off immodestly above the ankle bones and her feet were clad in
strong thick-soled boots, sensible footwear for a walking in the drear sewers.
She threw back her hood and I saw she was not young, yet not old. Her hair
was the silver of moonlight and her face that of a stern angel.

"I roused myself to call out to her for aid, but a cry from farther down the
tunnel indicated my companions had registered my loss. I saw their torches
hurriedly making their way back to rescue me, and the woman faded away
into the darkness."

He and the sewer workers carried on climbing more slowly, and Creed,
diligent still despite his fear, described the many tunnels they travelled
through.

"It seemed like a lifetime before we saw the happy sight of daylight filtering
through ornate metal grilles above our heads. Within an hour I was back in
the bosom of my family, and I spent many days recovering from my ordeal.
Indeed, for weeks afterwards the coming of night would put me in an anxious
torment, for I feared the walls were closing in and I slept with a night light in
my chamber for a season."

But come the autumn of that year he had recovered his spirits enough to meet one of the workers who had accompanied him on his underground journey. The man, dour and grizzled, had been working in the sewers for the emperor for more than a decade.

"'You should have told us, sir,'" said the man solemnly when I had finished my strange story. 'The gullible call them wraiths, but I believe they are enemies of the City, burrowing up through the drains.'

"I thought about the tall, graceful figure I had seen. The good man's theory that this was an enemy tunneler seemed unlikely but I had no wish to offend him. So I said, 'Wraiths? Do the gullible say why these spirits inhabit the depths?'

"The older man looked away. 'It is not known,' he answered curtly, 'if they live there or descend there to seek their victims. Some say they live there in an enchanted place called the Hall of Watchers.'

"'Enchanted?' I could not help smiling as I repeated this unlikely word. 'Are they wraiths or witches?'"

But the man did not answer him and Creed, after questioning others of the sewer workers, dismissed this talk of the Hall of Watchers as a myth similar to so many others, such as the spirits of dead children which inhabited the palaces of the Shield, or the angels said to descend on battlefields to suck out the souls of dying soldiers. By the time of his death, he came to dismiss his own vision as phantasmagoria conjured by a mind disordered by exhaustion and the fumes of the sewer.

Bartellus sat back. He had read these passages a dozen times, infuriated by the lack of information. He stared at the pages in frustration, hoping meaning would drift off them if he glared at them for long enough.

The Hall of Watchers was the only link with the world he knew. He often thought about the warrior Indaro. He cursed himself for paying so little attention to his surroundings at the time and retaining so little memory subsequently. He remembered the torch-filled hall with its carvings of birds, the small quiet white room where he had supped in strange companionship with the old woman. It had all seemed like a dream, a brief respite for his mind from the hellish endurance of his life. He and Emly had not spoken of those times for some years, and when he had last questioned her, the girl's memory of the events was murky.

As he sat, musing on the past, Carvelho returned. He pushed Bartellus' piece of paper back across the table to him, and added his own list of books. He was smiling.

"I remembered what you said some time ago," the man told Bart eagerly. "About your interest in military tattoos. You told me not to trouble myself with them at the time, but I saw this volume."

He hefted a large tome and read, *"Cryptic Codes: Formal and Informal Insignia among Armed Men.* It is by a soldier called Anabathic Marcellus."

Bart shrugged, trying to show lack of interest, though he was caught between apprehension and curiosity. He frowned and told his friend, "It was a whim, that's all. I do not want to read it. Return it with these." He had piled up books to return to the custodians. Carvelho looked disappointed and turned away, back to his work.

But in a moment of weakness Bartellus ran his hand over the embossed cover. Despite himself, he slid it over to him and smelled the odour of rich leather. Sighing, he turned the heavy pages with their shiny plates. An expensive book, he guessed. He closed it and looked at the cover again. "Anabathic," he thought, *"one who marches uphill."* He wondered who hid under that pen name. There were many Marcelluses. Marcellus Vincerus, First Lord of the City, was writer and historian. Did he call himself Anabathic for the purposes of publishing this obscure book?

The shiny pages slid pleasingly under his fingers as he leafed through them. The bright colours of the pictures leaped out at him: running horses, rampant lions, tigers at bay, soaring eagles and slithering serpents rioting across the pages. As he had said to Dol Salida and Creggan, the soldiery favoured animals of pride and power.

As he looked through the book memories, warm and comforting, rose from the pages, not of blood and death and pain, but the companionship of other warriors, the certainty of shared goals and shared enemies, the sure knowledge of respect and continuity and friendship.

And, inevitably, he thought of Fell, his friend and most loyal aide. And for the first time since his imprisonment doorways started opening in his mind, one after another swinging smoothly on their hinges, revealing worlds of colour and change, and pain. He remembered Fell by his side as they galloped their horses towards the first line of infantry in the victorious Battle of Black Creek. He saw him years later, laughing with his comrades of the 19th Imperial, as they drank yet another inn dry in the long summer of '47.

Then old Bart walked through a darker, older, door and saw again Fell's trial before the emperor, anonymous faces, for so long the blank straw dolls of the quintain, resolving themselves into flesh and blood men—the Vincerii of course, and Flavius Randell Kerr, the old goat, and tall Boaz. All watching with interest and calculation and without one hint of compassion.

And, standing before them all, the woman who had appeared in his life in the darkest of days. Archange.

It was coming up to sunset, and the library was closing its doors, when Bartellus slipped out into the lengthening shadows. He set off towards Gervain and the attic of the whore Callista, his greatcoat wrapped around him against the cool summer night.

The two boys levered themselves up gratefully from the lee of a low wall and trotted down an alley beside the building, where a crooked red-haired man met them at a side door. He thrust a piece of paper into the bigger boy's hand before stepping back through the high narrow doorway.

In the darkness the younger brother yawned. The hour was getting late and the day was cooling fast. But there was still a task to do. Before they reached the comfort of home and their mother's cooking, they first had to visit their paymaster.

Emly raised her head and untied the frayed piece of string at her neck. She pulled back stray strands of dark hair that had fallen over her face and retied the string. Then she bent again to the last piece of the panel. By tradition, the paint on stained glass was black, to complement and contrast with the clear colours of the glass. But Emly's signature, the mark which was her own and which was becoming recognised in the homes of the wealthy, was the one spot of coloured paint to adorn the window.

She took a narrow brush and dipped it into a pot the colour of damp earth. In the bottom right-hand corner of a piece of clear glass she deftly sketched the shape of a gulon. Then with tiny brush and black paint she highlighted its foxy tail, wrapped around its body, and its sharp pricked ears. She stood and went to a corner cupboard and took out a small precious pot of gold paint, made specially for her by a friendly goldsmith in the Avenue of Mercy. With it she drew in two golden eyes. The gulon looked out at her from the glass, and immediately she felt the hostility of its stare.

She was so accustomed to making the mark that she seldom any longer thought of its significance. The gulon she had seen in the sewers was the first and only one she had ever encountered, and it had been on the day her brother Elija disappeared. She remembered little of that awful day, only the big ugly gulon and the way it hissed at her, baring long yellow teeth. And her last sight of her brother on the bridge in the failing torchlight seconds before it was swept away. No day passed when she did not think of Elija, but she no longer thought of him with hope in her heart, only sad regret.

She put the brush down and her hand dropped to her side. The panel was far from finished. It was now a jigsaw of bright shards of glass, shaped and painted but separate. It was ready to be joined together into a work of art with strips of lead called calms. The work still to be done involved skill and craftsmanship, and she and Frayling would work many more hours to complete it. But her creative work was finished and, as always, she felt more sadness than satisfaction.

The previous piece she had painted, with the tentacles of the monster, had dried, and she placed it on a wooden tray. She laid a piece of felt over it, then put the gulon piece on top. Grasping the tray under one arm, she hoisted the hem of her skirt and tucked it into her waistband before climbing carefully down the ladder. At the bottom she covered her legs again and descended the flights of stairs to the ground-floor furnace room where Frayling worked.

Frayling must have heard her coming, for he opened the workroom door and took the heavy tray from her arms. He was a tall young man, thin and stooping, with mouse-coloured hair that flopped over his face. He was still shy with Emly though he had worked for her father for more than two years. He was more outgoing with Bartellus, who claimed the man had a dry wit, though Em had never seen any evidence of it. Frayling got around nimbly enough on a single crutch. His right leg had been cruelly crushed, and was useless to him except as a prop. He was unmarried and had no relatives. His room was a tiny cell on the first floor, and he seldom left the house.

"So," he said to her, nodding nervously, "the gulon."

She gazed at him. A fine pair, she thought, a shy man and a speechless woman.

"Did you tell Bartellus," he asked, blinking nervously, "about the watcher?"

When she said nothing, he added reprovingly, "You said you would."

Em had been trying not to think about the man she had seen loitering in Blue Duck Alley. It was four days before and she was in her attic workroom, sitting on the wide sill overlooking the alley, feeding crumbs to the birds, when she leaned out and looked down to the cobbles. She could see the tops of people's heads and she was tempted to drop pieces of bread and see if they hit anyone. One head stood out from the usual slowly milling crowd of workers and street vendors. It was topped with fair hair which caught the sunlight. The man was strolling down the alley as if he had all the time in the world. As he moved farther away she could judge he was a tall man. A soldier, she thought. He walked with a swagger, in contrast with the shuffling, apologetic gait of the poor people of Lindo.

She thought no more about it until she spotted him again later that day. He was leaning against a corner, half hidden in deep shadow. She was sure it was the same man, and he seemed to be watching the House of Glass. Emly jumped up and ran down the stairs all the way from the attic to the ground floor. She went into the front room at street level, a room never used for it was musty and damp. There was a window onto the alley, boarded up but with gaps between the boards. It was thick with grime. She breathed on the glass and rubbed at the spot with her fist. The man had vanished from the corner, and she was disappointed. But moments later she saw him coming towards her, strolling like a man who owns the world, she thought. He was certainly a soldier, for he wore military boots and a faded red jerkin which might once have been part of a uniform. And he was armed, with a sword sheathed on his left hip, and a long knife at his waist on the right.

He was coming close, looking up and down at the House of Glass, glancing with interest along the narrow alley beside it. He had very pale eyes, she saw. Emly ducked away from his gaze, though there was little chance he would spot her behind the dusty glass. When she looked again he was gone.

She shook her head at Frayling. She wished she had never told him, for he would be at it like a dog on a bone until she told Bartellus.

"If you don't tell him, I will," said the servant, then he blushed for his forwardness.

Chapter 17

Bartellus' bad knee was aching by the time he reached the quiet twittens of Gervain. The quarter was in the north-west, nestled comfortably between the luxury of Otaro and the imperial precincts of the Red Palace. It was perhaps the safest area of the City for an old man to walk alone at night, and Bart's grip on his dagger loosened for the first time since he left the Great Library.

As he neared his destination he trod more quietly, alert for footfalls behind him, for shadows slinking into darkness. But the quarter was still and silent, the only sounds the distant chatter from a small inn, brought on the night air, and his own laboured grunting.

He slid into a narrow lane then into a shadowed doorway. Climbing the steep stairs to Callista's garret he wondered as always if this was a wise thing to do. Aside from his love for Emly, this was the only part of his life which made him vulnerable. He knew it but he could not abandon it.

He knocked twice on the mean door at the top of the steps and it opened immediately, releasing a gust of rank air.

"About time," a voice grunted. "We're not here for your convenience, man."

"Convenience scarcely comes into it," Bart barked. Not for the first time he wondered why he was trusting his life, and perhaps Em's, to this disaffected soldier, one-eyed, sarcastic, bitter. Vitellus he called himself, a former member of the Thousand, the elite bodyguard of the emperor. As such he was a deep well of information on the Immortal and his ways, and on the geography of the inner palace, called the Keep. He considered himself the chief of this motley chain of conspirators, but Bart saw him as the rattling link which put them all at hazard.

He looked around the group. Seven today. I trust none of you, he thought.

"Welcome," said the man who called himself Sully. Small and slim, an ex-soldier as they all were, he worked as a servant in a palace on the Shield. He was sharp of mind and Bart put more faith in the man's opinions than any of them. "We were saying there was a naval battle two days ago."

"I heard."

"You heard what?" demanded Vitellus. Always ready to argue, to confront.

"Only that there *was* one."

"South of the Salient. Two of our ships sunk. We don't know how many of theirs. The blockade was broken for a day."

"There was fresh fish in the market," said Bart.

Sully smiled. "Fishermen only need a few hours to bring in fish by the netful. For many of them it is the difference between life and death."

"What do *you* have for us, old man?" Vitellus asked Bart.

Bartellus shrugged. *Nothing.* Vitellus sniffed, as if this confirmed his expectations. Bart offered them valuable information on the Halls and secret pathways under the City, although it was of little use to these soldiers in their obsession with politics and personalities.

Jonto, a serving cavalryman, growled, "We're not interested in fish, man. Vitellus and I have heard talk of a coup attempt."

There's *always* talk of a coup attempt, Bart thought. But he nodded encouragingly.

"The Emperor's Hounds," Jonto said. The Hounds were a century of the Thousand, led by a thirty-year veteran called Fortance, Bart recalled.

"What about them?" he asked.

"They fouled up a bodyguard detail. Their leader was demoted and moved to another century . . ."

"He's lucky he's not dead," put in Sully.

"And there's been a shake-up. Reassignment to and from other centuries. It's made a lot of people unhappy."

Sully said what Bart was thinking. "Soldiers are always unhappy. They always have something to moan about."

"The Hounds are blaming Rafe Vincerus for the defeat of the Maritime."

"Why not blame Flavius Randell Kerr? He was the army's general," asked Sully. But Bart knew the answer—Flavius was dead and Rafael alive. No sport in blaming a dead man.

"And there's something else," said Vitellus. He glanced at Jonto. "Talk among the Leopards. Against Marcellus. And his doxy."

Marcellus Vincerus was once wed to Giulia, sister to Marcus Rae Khan, head of the Family Khan. Marcus was popular enough among the soldiery, but less so than his sister, the only woman to have ridden with a cavalry unit a decade ago in the Family's army. When Giulia left her husband's embrace to return to the Khan palace on the Shield, it was rumoured to be because of Marcellus' dalliance with a famous courtesan.

They fell to discussing the whore, who was much despised. It was a favourite subject. Bart looked at them with contempt. Pride and ambition fed these men. They saw themselves heading an army, leading their peers, cheered by the people, brutally crushing enemies. Meanwhile, they gossiped like fishwives, swilling too much ale, and peppering their largely invented yarns with salacious detail.

For him, no one would shout his name in triumph. If Bartellus found a way to revenge himself on the emperor for the brutal killing of his family he knew nothing more waited for him than death, torturous and lingering, or sudden. His ambition was to thrust a knife deep into the man's heart, or slit his throat, whichever proved practical at the time. To avenge the four innocents who had died at Araeon's hands—four out of millions. And if he found a chance to punish the others who had conspired against him, or who had stood by and watched the entertainment of his betrayal and torment, then so much the better.

He would do his best to first detach himself from Em, to put her in a place of safety but, much as he loved her, he knew he might condemn her with himself.

So the old general drifted from one little band of plotters to the next, never staying long enough to risk identification, always watching and waiting for the one man who could help him penetrate the palace, then the Keep and reach Araeon. To get into the palace you needed the right papers, the right face. The Keep was next to impossible to infiltrate, and the Immortal was said seldom to leave it these days.

He caught Sully's eye, and the small man smiled slightly. He was the only one Bart had any time for, for the man listened to the bluster and idle threats of the soldiers and took them all in, revealing little. He wondered if Sully was a spy. In case he was being watched, Bart always took a roundabout route home and, if he was in any doubt, stayed at an inn overnight and returned in the plain light of day.

After listening to hours of pointless gossip, fuelled by ale brought by the whore's ancient mother from downstairs, Bartellus resolved to abandon this group, but try to stay in contact with Sully. He would not attend the next meeting, but he would wait outside and follow Sully home afterwards. He had not the energy for midnight skulking this night.

Halfway through a meandering yarn by Vitellus he suddenly walked to the door and left without a word. He heard them sneering at him as he went down the stairs.

In the Great Storm the rains had come down too hard and fast for the sewers and storm drains to cope, and the narrow streets of the Armoury had become raging rivers. Many hundreds, perhaps thousands, of people had died in the flash floods, drowned in the seething streets or trapped helpless in their homes. It was rumoured that the City's gravediggers could not respectfully lay to rest all the corpses, and that after dark for weeks afterwards carts rumbled through the night carrying the dead out to the Salient to be dropped in the sea. Since then the quarter of Lindo seemed to lie lower, sinking into sodden foundations. Cellars previously dry lay underwater, and residents whose homes already stood in the wet had been forced to move to the upper rooms, despairing of keeping their goods and furnishings dry.

The white cats of Lindo did not like to get their paws wet and had migrated to the upper levels—the roofs and upper storeys, the bridges and buttresses which supported the crumbling buildings. They abandoned the damp streets and waterlogged cellars to the black rats, only coming down at night to feed.

Many of the cats were still pure white. Over the centuries they had often mated with lower feline orders, but their bloodline was strong, and when a deviation occurred—brown paws or a ginger mask—it would disappear again in later generations. They mated often amongst themselves, and raised their kits in the nooks and crevices of the crumbling chimney stacks and rotting eaves on the north side of Blue Duck Alley.

The sky bridge between the House of Glass and the lodging house opposite was a highway for the cats. They would hunt at night among the hovels of the shack and shanty village south of the alley. Then, when daylight threatened, they would make their way to the glassmaker's house, ascending its wedding cake of storeys with ease, and cross the wooden sky bridge to their nests.

Far below them Bartellus, returning home after midnight, gazed up and saw the white shapes gliding across the sky. He sniffed the air. The cobbled stones of Blue Duck Alley were cooling quickly, radiating their stored warmth into the night. And they told their own story in the smells they released. Bart guessed a barrel had broken when Doro's ale house had received a delivery, for good wood was hard to come by these days. The contents had sloshed down the alley and the stones were still sticky under his boots. There was the faint scent of herbs as well. Bartellus sniffed again. Perhaps cooking smells from Meggy's lodging house, for the woman used cheap herbs to disguise the unwholesome whiff of cheaper meat. Or a whore had passed by recently, her skin rubbed with herbs to make up for lack of soap. And laid over all there was the familiar and sharp stench of blood and shit which signalled a death somewhere near the alley on this warm summer's day.

Bartellus noted this with interest but without revulsion. In fact, his stomach was grumbling. He had eaten a good rich stew at the Shining Stars, but that was long hours before, and he looked forward to a hunk of the bread he had purchased that morning, with cheese from the dairy in Parting Street, and onion relish he had bought from Meggy, but which he guessed was made by the whore who rented her attic. Meggy's food had improved considerably since the young woman had moved in with her two boys in the summer.

Bart glanced up at the attic window, where a faint light shone. He wondered if she plied her trade in the same room where she lived with her two boys. It was of no more than passing interest. She was scarcely more than a child herself, and thin as a sword.

He left the alley, ducking into the narrow passageway beside the House of Glass and dragging out the big iron key which opened the side door. The door was always locked. They had two keys—one was always on Bartellus' person, the other hung on a hook inside the door. If Bart was out he locked the door from the outside. If Frayling needed to go out too, Emly used the second key to lock the door from the inside. Then Frayling had to knock to be let back in. There had never been a day in the last two years when all three of them had left the house at the same time.

He was expecting to be greeted by midnight silence, to slip quietly into his bed and permit thoughts of plotters and conspiracies to drift from his mind. But he was scarcely through the door when he was waylaid by both Emly, clattering down the stairs, and Frayling, looming suddenly from his ground-floor workroom.

"There was a watcher," Frayling told him, glancing at Emly, who nodded. "A soldier. Miss Emly saw him. I think he means us ill."

This amounted to garrulousness from the young workman, but worry was etched across his face, so Bartellus hid his amusement. He looked at Emly, whose face was anxious too.

"When was this?"

Frayling burst out, "Four days ago, then again today. He was watching the house." He looked to Emly again. She nodded. "A soldier," she whispered.

They both watched him, looking for reassurance. He shook his head. "Why do you say he was watching the house, Em?"

"He *was*," she answered. "Fair and tall," she added. "Red uniform."

She was never a child to panic about trifles, so Bart knew she was probably right about what she saw. He remembered Creggan's words about a soldier asking questions, and a muscle in his heart cramped.

"How old?"

She shrugged. She could not guess the ages of men.

Bartellus, his brow furrowed, threw off his greatcoat and climbed the stairs to the candlelit parlour followed by the two youngsters. He crossed the stifling room and poured himself a glass of wine from the jug. He sat down in the comfortable chair he always used, and he sighed.

Emly and Frayling stood waiting for him to speak.

"This is not good news," he admitted. "This might be about my past—my past before I became Bartellus." He looked at Frayling, but if the youngster found his words surprising he gave no sign of it. "If this soldier is watching us it might be he knows who I am. Then others may also know, and we are in danger and will have to leave here."

And, he did not have to add, Emly could no longer pursue her vocation, and they would have to disappear, perhaps travel overseas, for Bartellus could now afford the life of a rich man if not his reputation.

Emly's face fell and his heart was cut by the pain in her eyes.

"But," he said, cursing himself, for tiredness had made him careless, "it might have nothing to do with me. Perhaps he is merely planning to rob the House of Glass." He smiled at Em, seeking to calm her fears, but she stared back at him with big eyes and he remembered the little girl he had first met, eyes wide, blank with terror and dread. And he vowed to himself at that moment that if this watcher had truly found him, found Shuskara the lost general, then he would kill him, and kill whoever he acted for, and he would bury his past forever.

He smiled broadly at Em and told her, putting confidence in his voice, "It won't come to that. I'll see that everything will be all right."

He felt the warm solidity of certainty in his chest, and his spirits soared at his own words. He almost felt like laughing. In truth, he would kill a thousand men if it would put a smile back on his daughter's face.

In the days that followed Em was consumed with worry about the threat of the watcher, despite her father's words. But eventually fear of the unknown soldier had been replaced in her heart by fear of the trip to the merchant's house.

Now the day had arrived, the warmest of the year so far, and Emly sat in a jolting carriage, her father beside her, followed by three carts holding the precious cargo as they made their way through the dusty City. At the last moment, leaving the House of Glass, Emly had snatched up her old veil to protect her from the sun and the hot swirling dust. Now she was glad she had it, for their little cortege was accompanied by an armed guard, employed by the merchant, of more than thirty soldiers. She and Bartellus sat in the open carriage facing backwards, watching over their valuable cargo. Bart was quite at ease among so many soldiers, and they joked and laughed with him as they marched alongside, but Em found it hard to bear the covert looks of the men, and she ducked her head and looked down at her best blue dress. As ever, she stroked the tiny horse and dog attached to the veil. Over the years five more animals had joined their strength to weigh down the veil. But it was still the horse and the dog she loved, and she galloped them across her blue lap, exercising them on this sunny morning.

She had kept the veil after they escaped the Halls, for it was her only possession apart from the ragged clothes the warrior woman had given her. In times of fear, and there were many in their first days out in daylight, she would clutch the wadded, dirty cloth in her fists, and gaze at the horse and the dog and pretend that she lived in a safe place and the two animals were her best friends. It was some time before Bart found them their first home, and a great deal longer before she started to feel secure there. Then she washed the veil over and over, cleaning out the last remnants of the sewer, laying it out in the cleansing sun to dry. Spread out, she could see it was cunningly made of a shiny thread that was fine but tough. It was a long time before she realised there was a pattern in the lace. The pattern had probably been clearer, she thought, when the veil still held its tints. There were animals concealed in the stitchwork, following each other in a circle. Once she found one, the others were easier to see. There was a dog and a horse, a strange misshapen creature she discovered was called a wyvern, a seahorse, a rabbit and a dolphin. And in the centre was a gulon, its bushy tail curled around the shape of a heart. Delighted, she had shown the animals to her father, but his eyes were too weak to discern them among the intricate threadwork and, besides, he wasn't really interested.

The going was very slow and there was a long way to travel in the jolting carriage. They descended the winding length of Blue Duck Alley until they reached the wall of the temple of Ascarides. Then they followed the wall, with its sturdy lean-to shops and merchants' houses, and passed the barracks of the Maritime Army, now empty and echoing, a dark place under the summer sun. They crossed the edge of Burman Far, Bartellus pointed out to her, with its temples and bathhouses, and on to Otaro. They had travelled nearly half a day before they reached the Avenue of Victory.

"Look," her father said, nudging Em. "You can see the Red Palace from here."

Emly pushed back her veil and peered in the direction he was pointing. In the sun she could see distant towers gleaming.

"Green?" she asked, frowning.

"Some of the towers are covered with gold, they say, more probably copper. But the old part of the palace is built of pink marble imported from the western continents many hundreds of years ago."

She smiled politely, but Emly only wanted to learn about things that lived, that ran and swam and flew. Not old buildings.

The carriage and its following carts turned sharply away from the avenue into a narrower street lined with high buildings. It was cooler here, where the sun could not reach them. The walls were high and looked damp, and green moss crawled up them, clinging to the dank brick.

"We're nearly there," said Bartellus quietly, and Em's stomach clenched with anxiety.

They drew up outside a tall house, standing alone on one side of a quiet square. The square was six-sided, paved with warm golden stone, with a fountain in the middle. Em looked up at the house, of the same soft stone and decorated with carvings. There were many windows, and above each was a carved beast, an animal or bird or fish. Above the main door in front of them were two porpoises, leaping side by side. Em smiled to herself and her stomach relaxed a little. Perhaps this merchant had commissioned her sea window because he liked creatures of the sea.

As the carriage pulled up the main door opened and a flurry of servants rushed out. Two brought wooden steps to the carriage, for Emly and Bartellus to climb down. The same two then accompanied them up the three wide shallow steps to the door, hovering as if to catch them if they suddenly tumbled down. Inside the porch more servants offered Em and her father cool water in crystal glasses. Meanwhile, the rest were busy unloading the glass panels as the soldiers stood by. Em could hear Frayling's high anxious voice offering diffident orders.

They were shown through to the courtyard of the house which, Em was charmed to see, was a replica of the square outside, six-sided, with a pool full of colourful fish in the centre. Here the merchant met them, florid and sweating, effusive and kind. As Em gazed round the courtyard, taking in the windows and carvings, sidling towards the pool to look at the fish, he smiled and asked, "Do you like my house, Miss Emly?"

She nodded and whispered politely, "It is . . . pretty."

The merchant smiled broadly at the first words he had heard from her. "It is indeed. It was built more than five hundred years ago for a companion of the emperor. She loved all beasts and birds and creatures of the sea, and you will see many throughout the house. It is called the House of the Creatures of the Earth."

Em was delighted by the name, and the merchant, pleased, led them through another doorway guarded by porpoises into an inner courtyard replicating the outer one, then through a third porpoise door into a hexagonal parlour lit by lamps. It was dark in there, and cool. The merchant glanced upwards then looked quizzically at Emly. She craned her neck. The roof of the parlour was of glass, she was surprised to see, obscured by a riot of greenery and white flowers.

"In the summer we permit plants to grow across the roof to keep the room cool," the merchant explained. "In winter they are cut back to allow the sun in."

There was no one else in the room. Em sat in a corner of a comfortable upholstered sofa with running cats carved into the wooden arms, and Bartellus and the merchant discussed the news of the City. Em was quite at ease, her father at her side, until the room started to fill with guests.

Then Bartellus arose. "I must go and help Frayling," he told her. "Stay here and I will find you when I can."

He ignored her pleading eyes and vanished out through the door, struggling a little against the crowd pressing in. The merchant was greeting people and laughing, and Em sat back in her seat and tried not to be noticed.

For a while she was ignored and she sat, head down, tracing the lines of the carved cats with her fingers, wondering how long it would take for the craftsmen to fix the marine window in place, how long she would have to stay there.

"Miss. May I get you some more water?"

She looked up and saw a servant standing respectfully at a distance, his head bowed. She shook her head.

To her relief he went away, but he shortly came back with a plate of food—pink shrimp on small pieces of bread. She shuddered at the sight, thinking of the living shrimps frolicking on the ocean floor in her window.

The servant bent his head to her and whispered confidentially, "They are serving squid and leviathan next."

She looked up at him, appalled, but he was smiling and she realised he was teasing her and smiled back nervously.

"May I sit down?" he asked.

She looked about her, for she was afraid he would get into trouble, then she realised the servants moving among the guests bearing trays of food and drink were all dressed in cotton smocks. This young man was wearing handsome silk clothes and shiny leather boots. She felt foolish, and before she could react he had sat down beside her, one arm at her back, saying, "I am Tolemy, and this house belongs to my father."

His face was close to hers, and she ducked her head and tried to lean a little away from him, but he only leaned in, and she could smell wine warm on his breath. His features were even, handsome even, but his eyes were bright with drink and his speech was slightly slurred.

"I have just seen your sea window," he said. "It is a marvel that such a girl could make so fine a work. Your hands must be very cunning." He slid his hand across one of hers. It was hot and damp and, repelled, she moved her hand away.

"My father told me you were a girl of few words, Emly," he said. "He also told me you were a beauty, but it is hard to tell underneath that pretty veil. Will you not take it off for me?"

She shook her head, looking round, wishing her father would come back. The guests standing around them in groups all had their backs to Em, making a wall in front of her, and she felt she and this man were alone. She decided to go and search for her father, or the merchant, but when she tried to stand she found Tolemy was sitting on her skirt which had spread across the sofa. As she struggled to get away he laughed.

"Take your veil off and I will let you go," he whispered, pressing in towards her, one hand creeping around her waist, then up to her breast, cupping the softness, then pinching the nipple hard.

She tore the veil off and thrust it at him, and he sat back and laughed out loud, releasing her skirt. She jumped up, just as the merchant came into view, staring suspiciously at the flustered girl and his laughing son.

"Are you all right, my dear?" he asked her, glowering at Tolemy.

She nodded, aware she was flushed and dishevelled. "Father?" she asked.

"They are nearly ready. Would you like to come and see your window?" He held out one hand to guide her way. She nodded gratefully.

She took no pleasure in the presentation of the sea window. Its placing, in a high wall where the morning sun would shine through it, was well-judged. The guests in their silks and rich jewellery, applauded and praised the workmanship, and the merchant made a speech, congratulating both Emly's work and his own fine judgement. But she could still feel Tolemy's hand crawling on her, and inside she railed at herself for being such an innocent. Bartellus stood beside her, his head high, proud of her and her work, but he quickly saw the anxiety in her eyes. Mistaking its cause, he said quietly, "It looks wonderful, little soldier. Don't you think so?"

She nodded and raised a smile for him, for it was true, it did, and he told her, "In a few moments we can go home. Away from all these people. I'm so proud of you."

He patted her shoulder and she wanted to throw herself into his arms. But she knew she could not tell him about the merchant's son, for he would be angry and feel the need to protect her. And that reminded her of the watcher again, and she was afraid.

It was only when they were safely in the carriage, and well on their way back to their home in Lindo, that she realised she had left her precious veil behind.

Chapter 18

Dawn was just a faint pink light in the east of the City when Bartellus let himself out of the House of Glass into the new morn. He locked the door and put the great iron key in his pocket. Limping slightly on his painful knee, he walked up to Blue Duck Alley and sniffed the air. There must have been a fall of rain in the night, after they returned from the merchant's, and the morning felt newly washed.

He headed off briskly towards the library. Bartellus wanted to put distance between himself and the House of Glass before the world awoke. He had left instructions to Emly and Frayling not to open the door to anyone.

The Great Library was just opening as he arrived, its east doors groaning open to let in the low rays of the sun. Bartellus made his way through the yellow-green light to his habitual table. He sat down and wondered what he was going to do all day. He was surprised Carvelho had not returned the latest pile of documents.

A docent, a thin old woman with a shuffling walk, came slowly over and handed him a message, resentment on her face. "This has been waiting for you for three days," she told him. It was from Carvelho, to say his wife was ill and he would not be at Bartellus' service. Bart frowned. His ordered life was being disrupted on all sides. He crumpled the note up and threw it on the table, and stared at the pile of documents in front of him: old books, their leather bindings hanging off, rolls of dry ancient paper, each with a dangling name tag, and sheaves of documents in brown folders. He realised he had no interest in reading about the City's architecture that day.

Instead he pulled towards him the book *Cryptic Codes: Formal and Informal Insignia among Armed Men*. He turned to the back, then the front, for an indication of how they were arranged, but there was no index. He sighed and started at the beginning.

Almost immediately he found one of his own tattoos—the green serpent with a rat in its coils, symbol of the 14th Imperial Infantry, the Ratcatchers, long since disbanded. Fell would have the same tattoo, he reflected, and Astinor Redfall, if he lived.

Another custodian came by, and raised his eyebrows at Bartellus, perhaps commenting on his early arrival. Bart gave him a stern look: none of your business, and the man went on his way.

Over the course of the morning the old man tracked down three of the smaller tattoos he had remembered on the corpse's body, and found that the soldier had served with the 24th Vincerii, and the Emperor's Rangers, two decades before, who then called themselves the Lepers, and he had fought at the Second Battle of Edyw. A distinguished service, indeed, although there was little to stop any fool of an impostor having the tattoos inscribed. But Bartellus remembered the many old wounds on the man and believed his tattooed friend was an authentic soldier. He uncrumpled Carvelho's message and wrote the names down on the paper, confident he would not remember them the next day.

At last, flipping idly through the pages, he came to the one he was seeking near the back of the book: the rampant goat with flickering red tongue. He sat back in surprise, then looked again. It was surely the same tattoo; it could not be mistaken for any other. He turned to the start of the chapter; it was called *Allies and Tributaries*. Then he turned back to the tattoo and the inscription beside it: *Royal bodyguard, under Matthus III, last ruler of Odrysia, king of the Little Sea.*

Bartellus looked again at his *aide memoire*. The Second Battle of Edyw. He had marked it in the book with a fragment of paper. He turned to it, then sat back again, his mind returning to slaughter. The first battle of Edyw had been a triumph, Shuskara's armies of the east outnumbering and outmanouevring the Blueskin tribesmen. The City companies had settled down in the invaded lands and achieved a measure of security. This lasted a season, a long, warm spring. But their inevitable reward for success was to be given a more difficult task. Shuskara was ordered to push north and east towards the Little Sea, up the Edyw valley. There were mountain ranges to left and right, peaks confidently held by tribesmen who were on their home territory and eager to take revenge. They sat back in their mountain holes and waited until the City's supply lines were stretched to the breaking-point, then they attacked. Thousands of City soldiers died in the first two days. The generals were ordered to retreat, and the ones at the rear were able to. Shuskara had the hideous choice of pulling his forces back to safety, or staying and trying to back up the beleaguered forces in the front line. His troops dug in.

The Second Battle of Edyw, he knew but had since forgotten, was the only time in the history of the City's armies when veterans of both sides in a battle had adopted the same tattoo. It was a grudging tribute to the other side, a recognition that in a battle in which both armies had fought each other to a standstill, losing more than nine in ten of their men, there was more that united the common soldiers of the two armies than separated them.

So his tattooed friend had fought *for* the City, in infantry regiments, and *against* it, in the bodyguard of the Odrysian king. And he had fought at Edyw, but on which side? The book had raised as many questions as it had answered.

Inevitably his mind turned down well-worn tracks to the veil he had snatched from the man's neck, the veil which, for some reason, Emly cherished and which she had worn only the previous day. It was a piece of fine threadwork. Had it also come from Odrysia? He resolved to look at it again when he got home. Bartellus was concerned about Emly. He had hoped the previous day would leave her proud, with her head high. Instead she had been anxious and upset when they returned from the merchant's house. The day took more out of her than he had expected.

His thoughts were idling when he suddenly realised he was being watched. He looked around. Far across the library a man stood leaning against a desk. He did not appear to be looking at Bartellus, but the old soldier knew in his bones that moments before the man's eyes had been on him. In the watery light Bart could not see the man well, except that he was tall and rangy, with light hair. A soldier, almost certainly.

He rubbed his tired eyes and when he looked again the man was gone.

Bartellus closed the book and thrust it to the bottom of the pile of documents. Then he grabbed his coat and followed the stranger's steps. When he reached the spot where the man had been standing he looked around. Ahead of him was the main corridor to the front doors of the library. On either side were several smaller doors, leading he knew not where. Shrugging to himself, he hurried down the corridor. Reaching the high dark atrium, clad with stained and dirty glass, he paused again. There was no one in sight. But the heavy front door was just closing, settling with a soft sound on its familiar iron latch.

Outside he was rewarded with the sight of his quarry disappearing into a side street across the square. Bartellus hurried, almost ran, across the busy square to catch up.

In the shadowy side streets he found it easier to follow, for his prey clearly had no thought he was being pursued. The man stopped and dawdled at a street stall, choosing something to eat. Bartellus closed the distance between them cautiously, ducking behind a wall as the man turned and casually glanced behind him. He was chewing on a piece of fruit, tasting it. Through a broken piece of brickwork, Bart could see him clearly. He was tall and lean, with tow-coloured hair, and he was older than he had first appeared. The man bought a handful of fruit, then carried rapidly onwards.

Before long it became clear that he was heading for Lindo. He was taking the route Bartellus himself took most days: through the north of Burman, across the river at the Serpentine Bridge, then following the winding length of Parting Street and approaching the Armoury from the north-east. It was the quickest way. Perhaps the stranger knew the City as well as he did. Perhaps he had followed Bart before.

Striding along, a little out of breath, he racked his brain to work out who this man was, or whom he acted for. Bartellus' heart laboured. They would have to leave sooner rather than later. The next day, if possible. He would lose a lot of money selling the house quickly. There was little demand for property in the Armoury. And Emly would be distraught to have to walk away from the House of Glass.

They had reached Blue Duck Alley, and Bart allowed the man to move ahead of him, confident he knew where he was going. Em and Frayling would let no one in. The house would appear empty. But the man paused and looked around, then suddenly turned into a twitten. Bart turned off too, following a dank narrow way between two houses. Peering round the corner, he saw the man reemerge in a small lane running parallel to Blue Duck Alley. There was no one else in sight, and Bart stood in the shadows, craning his neck to see the man. The soldier looked round again, then stepped into a dark doorway opposite a pile of empty crates. Bart knew it well. It was the rear of Meggy's lodging house.

H ours after Bartellus left the House of Glass, Frayling went out too. He waited until he heard Emly lock the door behind him, and set off on the long walk to Otaro.

When he had got up that morning, rising from his cot bed after a rare night of deep slumber, he had felt all was well in his world. The previous day he had seen his work praised by important men. Even though his name was never mentioned he knew, and Emly and Old Bart knew, how much he contributed to the marine window. His chest had swelled with pride as both of them turned to him and smiled. Emly looked pale, but after the merchant's speech she came over to him and took his arm, leaning into him and whispering, "Thank you." She had thanked him before, often enough, when he handed her a prepared calm, or opened a door for her. But this was heartfelt, and he found he had no voice himself as his throat closed up with emotion. What a pair we are, he thought.

The very thought of them as a pair made him tremble and sweat. He adored Emly. His days were only complete when she was within his sight. Mostly he was content, though, working in his ground-floor room, to know she was several floors above him in the attic workroom. If she was not in the house, he could feel its emptiness.

That morning he knew Bartellus would be out. The old man had told him, before he went to his rest, that he would be away all day, from sunrise to sunset. He told them not to open the door to anyone. Frayling respected and liked the old man, who had been kind to him, and he was concerned that Bart was deeply worried. He knew nothing about the man's past, except that he had one. He wished he could help. He daydreamed as he worked on his glass that one day Bart and Emly would need him, that he would help them in some way and they would thank him as they had both thanked him the previous day. "Frayling, I owe you my life!" Emly would say, throwing herself at his chest, and he would stroke her hair and tell her he loved her.

But he was surprised to see, when he came out of his chamber, that Emly was also dressed to go out, and she was waiting for him impatiently, a pretty frown on her face.

"Where are you going?" Frayling blurted. It was not his place to ask, but she rarely went out, certainly not on two days running.

"The merchant," she told him firmly, though her eyes were downcast and she bit her lip with anxiety.

He asked her why and, reluctantly, in her abbreviated way, she told him she had left her veil there, that the merchant's son had it. She did not want Bartellus to know, for he had worries enough already, and he would insist on going. Frayling knew how she valued her old veil; he had helped her create its tiny ornaments. He did not understand why the merchant's son should have it, but he did not hesitate.

"I will go," he said, the metal in his voice startling him. It surprised Emly too, for she looked up at him, her dark eyes searching his face in a way that made him blush.

"With me," she whispered.

Frayling shook his head. "I will go," he said again. "You cannot go on that long walk. Not after yesterday. And," he realised, "you do not know the way on your own."

He thought he saw relief on her face, but she said, "Your leg?"

"My leg needs a good walk sometimes," he lied. "Stretch it out."

Frayling had never seen service in the armies. He was a small child, living with his mother and sisters in Gervain, when a badly laden cart had shed its load of building stone, crushing the little boy's leg as he played in the street. His life was saved, and his leg knitted together, but it was a wadded mass of shattered bone and muscle. It pained him constantly, and was of little use. He limped around the House of Glass as best he could, and dreaded the steep steps up to the attic room. He often thought he would be better off without the leg, and he wished he had the courage to have it chopped off. When he went out he took a sturdy wooden crutch with him. Its padded leather cushion nestled comfortably under his right arm, and he could swing speedily through the streets.

It was a long walk, although much shorter than their ride the previous day, for Frayling had lived in the City all his life and knew its alleys and twittens. Nevertheless, before he was halfway his injured leg pained him more than it had in weeks. And he was hungry. Yet he was buoyed by the thought of Emly's gratitude when he returned bearing her veil in triumph.

As he stalked the streets he rehearsed his words to the merchant over and over. "Good sir, I am the servant to Bartellus, the glassmaker's father. He has commanded me to come to you to ask for the veil which his daughter, Miss Emly, left here yesterday by mistake." It was polite and to the point. The fat merchant could hardly refuse.

When he arrived at his destination the sun was past its peak and the heat at its worst. The stone house looked closed, shuttered against the noon heat. There was no one in the square, and the streets around it seemed deserted. Muttering his speech to himself, Frayling limped up the steps to the front door and rapped on it.

There was a long wait, but eventually the door groaned open and a servant stepped out. He was thin and old and dressed in black. He looked the visitor up and down. Frayling nervously made his speech, stumbling a little over "glassmaker's." The servant stared at him moments longer, then went back in and shut the door in his face.

Frayling did not know what to do. He stood there, wondering if the man would come back, or if he had been dismissed. At last he steeled himself and rapped on the door again. He waited but the door remained shut. Desolate, he sat down on the steps, relieving his right shoulder, which also ached from the long walk. He waited a while, looking up at the door from time to time.

Finally thirst overcame him and he levered himself up and limped towards the fountain in the square. He was halfway there when he heard the door open again behind him. He turned and hurried back to where the old servant stood impassively.

"Yes?" Frayling asked nervously. "Yes?"

"The master of the house tells me you are mistaken," the man told him in cold tones. "There is no lady's veil here."

The door swung shut again. Despairing, wondering what else he could do, Frayling stepped back and stared up at the house. From a first-floor window, unshuttered, a young man was watching him, young, ruddy faced. Frayling remembered seeing him the previous day. The man gazed at him until Frayling turned away.

B artellus was angry with himself. It seemed he had been living in a fog for the last few years. He had worried about the library custodian who had shown interest in him, whereas the man was probably harmless. After all, it was his business to show interest in the library users' work. Yet Bart had allowed himself to fall into carelessness, regularly visiting the Shining Stars, an inn patronised by veterans. He had allowed himself to believe none would recognise him because that was what he wanted, for he enjoyed his games of urquat. And, more seriously, he had chosen the company of clandestine plotters, however inept.

He had taken his coat off and poured himself a glass of wine when he heard a knock at the side door. He froze. What now? He went downstairs, wine cup in hand, and heard Emly clattering down from the workroom.

Once again he cursed his idleness, for not having a spyhole in the door. He stared at it undecidedly, then went into the kitchen and came back with a knife. He placed one foot close to the door so it would not open far, then unlocked it and peered round.

A hooded figure stood there.

"Identify yourself," he barked.

"Do you *still* not know me, Bartellus?" a woman's voice asked. She pushed her hood back. In the unforgiving light of late afternoon she looked older, though softer, her bundle of white hair pinned randomly on her head. Silver shone on her breast.

Bartellus stood there in shock, letting the knife fall to his side.

"Would you leave me standing in the filthy streets of Lindo?" Archange asked.

He stood aside and she swept in, pushing the door shut behind her, as he seemed unable to. She glanced at Emly and nodded.

"Well, general," she barked, "do you usually lock that door? You should, you know."

Bartellus pulled himself together and turned the key, then he said, "Forgive me, Archange. I am surprised to see you. How did you find me?"

"It was not difficult. You are leaving great bootprints all over the City. Now, do you have somewhere I can sit?"

Bart took her up to the parlour and settled her in his own chair, while he perched on a wooden stool. Emly followed and lingered in the doorway.

Archange looked at her. "Fetch me some watered wine, child."

Bart added, "And some lights. It will be dark soon.

"You were lucky to find me here," he told Archange. "I only came back early because I was being watched."

"Luck had nothing to do with it. You were following my man. He was charged with leading you home so I could speak with you at my convenience."

Bart sat open-mouthed. "I was lured here? Lured to my own home?"

Archange shrugged. "I have no wish to linger in the streets of Lindo in the dark."

"Lindo is not so bad," he told her mildly. "When we last spoke you were living in a sewer."

"I was not living there," she told him briskly. "I was merely visiting."

She smiled then and he smiled back and remembered how much he liked her.

"I see you have recovered your memory," Archange commented, arranging her skirts around her and settling into the upholstered chair as if for the night.

Bartellus shook his head. "There is a miasma in the Halls that dulls thought. I think the mind tries to block out the stench of the sewers, but it also blocks out normal reasoning."

"Nonsense," she answered impatiently. "You had suffered many shocks. Your best friend betrayed you, you were tried, punished and tortured, and then, when you escaped, you discovered your family had been butchered. You were forced to survive in the sewers of a City you had served with courage and grace for all your life. That is what your mind was trying to block, general."

Bartellus could only nod. He felt foolish, as he always seemed to in her presence.

Emly came into the room with wine for Archange, then lit the lanterns.

Smoky fumes filled the room and she cracked a window open. Faint voices and a cool breeze filtered in from the alley below.

The woman gazed up at the girl and asked, "Do you remember me, child?"

Em glanced at her father, then said, "Yes, my lady." She bobbed a little in a curtsey.

"How old are you now?"

"Fifteen," Em whispered. It was what her father had told her to say.

"And for how many years have you been fifteen?"

Em looked to Bartellus again, for she did not know what to say.

"Leave us for a while, please," Bart asked his daughter gently.

But she did not move and stood blushing furiously at her own defiance. Inwardly he sighed. He knew this time had to come eventually, when she found out about his past and the uncertainty of any future security. He nodded and Em sat on the floor.

"This has been a strange day," Bartellus said to the old woman. "I was thinking about you earlier, about the trial and Arish."

"That was why you chose the book on military tattoos, rather than your usual choice of history and architecture."

"Do you know everything about me?"

"I know about the library, of course, and the inn you go to. The Shining Stars. And the house in the Street of Bright Dancers. It is foolish for a man on the run to get into fixed routines, although difficult for an old man not to."

He spread his hands. "We have been in this house for four years now. We have always felt secure. I have become complacent," he confessed.

"Yes, complacency can easily be mistaken for safety." She leaned forward and said urgently, "You must leave here, Shuskara. You have attracted unwanted attention."

"Attention from whom? Your brother?" he replied sharply.

"Marcellus?" She shook her head. "I have no idea what Marcellus knows. He does not confide in me. Your name has not passed between us in twenty years. But I know there are rumours that Shuskara is alive and living in the Armoury. It did not take me long to find you, and it will not take others long. You must leave here as soon as you can, general. Take your daughter and flee, tonight if possible."

He felt the wisdom of her words deep in his bones and it was all he could
do not to take Em's hand and walk straight out the door into the night. He
forced himself to stay calm and try to think. "Where did your information
come from?"

"Here and there. Rumours and gossip and speculation. I have met many
people in my long life and many of them still owe me favours."

Frustrated, he asked, "Who are you warning me against, specifically?"

"*Specifically?*" she mimicked. "You will know that better than I. Who
still wants you dead? You are an old man now. Tell me who you are a threat
to, and I will tell you who your enemy is."

She paused, then asked, "Do you know what your crime was? Why the
emperor turned on you?"

Bartellus had had a great deal of time to think on it, and he had come to
many different conclusions over the years, but he said, "I don't know. He
spoke of disloyalty, betrayal, the usual words. I should have seen the signs. I
had seen it so often before, with other men. First he would stop calling them
'my old friend.' Then there were cool looks where there had once been warm
embraces. Before my friends came for me I heard there was a meeting of the
generals I was not told about. Astinor said it was nothing, a supply problem.
I chose to believe him."

"We all choose what to believe," she commented. "When I returned to
the City I was told you had been executed. It was said you were plotting with
the Gaeta pretender. I forget his name now. He had a brief run of glory before
being caught and butchered. Others said the Immortal was taking his revenge on you for the trial of the hostages."

Bart frowned. That had not occurred to him. "But that was so long ago.
More than twenty years."

"Twenty-seven," she corrected him briskly. "Who knows what goes on
in his mind? We know he has a long memory for slights."

"Then he would have more likely blamed you."

She said haughtily, "He does not dare. Marcellus is perhaps the only one
he still fears." She shook her head. "He would not dare move against me."

"Marcellus is loyal?"

"Scrupulously."

Bart sat back and sipped his wine. He glanced out the small window and
saw the sun had set and night was gathering round the house.

"It is getting dark," he said.

"Then I will have to rely on my warriors to get me safely home."

He remembered the long-ago day in the sewers, and the obnoxious red-haired woman in the Hall of Watchers. "Is Indaro still one of those warriors?"

Irritably, Archange replied, "No, thanks to you, I lost Indaro shortly after our last meeting. You shamed her into returning to the army. She rejoined the Maritime. She is almost certainly dead now."

The total obliteration of the Third Maritime the previous summer was something Bartellus still found hard to comprehend. "What happened?" he asked, "How did the Blues destroy an entire army?"

She shook her head. "I know nothing of military matters."

"And . . ." For a moment he could not remember the name. Yes, of course. Astinor. "Astinor Redfall? What became of him?"

"The man who betrayed you. Astinor died five years ago. Of a cancer of the belly. It was a long, hard death. He had little time to enjoy the fruits of his treachery." She gazed at Bartellus. "Does that give you satisfaction?"

He shook his head. It didn't. They sat in silence for a while. Then he asked, "Why did you come here, Archange? You could have easily sent me a message, considering how little information you have given me."

"I did not come here to give you information," she said tartly. "A scrap of paper crosses the City much more easily than I do."

He waited, and eventually she said, "When we met last, you asked me about a brand you found on a tattooed corpse. Did you ever discover its significance?"

He was surprised and wondered that she should remember that after so long. He shook his head. "No, but only today I came across the meaning of some of his tattoos. That was why I was looking at that book." He thought of Fell and the fact that he bore a brand too, but decided not to mention it. "I could follow the soldier's career, in part, from the pictures on his body. Anyone with access to army records might be able to find out who he was."

She appeared to be half listening. Absently, she said, "Tell me."

"He served with the 24th Vincerii, and the Emperor's Rangers when they called themselves the Lepers. Now, that was for a very short time about eighteen years ago, when I was serving at the Salient." She nodded. "And," Bartellus added, "he had fought at the Second Battle of Edyw."

She nodded. "The survivors from that are a small, select company. Quite easy to trace, I'd have thought."

A peevish part of him felt like saying, "I thought you weren't interested in military matters?" but instead he told her, "Of course, it does not mean he fought on our side. We don't know how many Blues still walk around bearing that tattoo."

"You think your dead man could have been an enemy?"

He watched her face as he answered, "He also bore on his back the symbol of the royal bodyguard of Odrysia. Under Matthus."

"An intriguing corpse indeed," she commented drily.

There was a long silence, and Bartellus watched the woman. She seemed to be thinking, staring sightlessly at one of the lamps. He wondered again how old she was. How much could he trust what she said? Could he trust her at all? He looked away, out at the darkness resting against the windowpane. This meeting felt like a conspiracy, but what poor conspirators they were, two old folk, both with failing memories.

At last Archange said, in an apparent change of subject, "Indaro's name was Indaro Kerr Guillaume."

Bartellus had a sudden image of a slender, ascetic man, with dark, hooded eyes, staring at him across a dinner table, subdued anger, then a sudden burst of laughter.

"I knew her father," he said. "Does he still live?"

"I believe so."

He shook his head. "That is a miracle. They bear the name of two Families, twice the threat to the emperor."

"The Immortal valued his advice. Still does, perhaps," she said. "And Indaro was just a common soldier. And a woman. Twice *un*threatening. There was also a son, who disappeared."

She looked at him. "That was why Indaro was in the Halls. She was seeking her brother."

"Tell me about the Hall of Watchers."

Her hand went to the silver at her neck. The hand was brown and wrinkled and looked as if it had been dried in the sun. "It was as you guessed. It was a lifeline for young women who did not want to fight in the war. And did not want to get pregnant to avoid it. A way station before I could smuggle them away to safety. You disapproved at the time, I remember," she added pointedly, flicking her gaze to Emly, who was watching them both, drinking in their words.

He was not going to defend himself. "I changed my mind," he said simply. "What happened to them?"

"They went mostly to non-aligned lands, and sometimes to our enemies."

"I read a book recently, it was hundreds of years old, but it spoke of wraiths living in the sewers of the City."

She frowned. "I saw no wraiths or ghosts or spirits."

"Does that work still go on in the Hall of Watchers?"

She shook her head. "It is under many feet of water now. The Great Storm wrought untold damage to the sewers. I'm told"—she shrugged as if to take no responsibility for the news—"one of the engines that filters the water was destroyed."

"The Eating Gate?"

She looked at him blankly, clearly not remembering their previous conversation. "Possibly. I only know what I was told. Debris, pieces of houses and tree branches, corpses, were swept farther down into the sewers, breaking existing dams and creating new ones elsewhere. The geography of the Halls is completely changed. Where once it was dry it is now underwater. And some tunnels which were raging torrents are now dry. I am told. I have not been there for years. And it changes all the time. It is unstable. It was once a dangerous place to be. Now it is deadly.

"And," she added, "the water level is rising throughout the City. Many levels below the Red Palace, in the ruins of palaces long forgotten, the water rises daily."

Then she offered, "The Hall of Watchers was under the emperor's palace, deep down, far beneath the dungeons even. It once was a palace itself, thousands of years ago."

"How did you get to it?"

But she looked out into the night. "I must be gone," she said. She struggled to get up, impatiently waving away Bart's proffered hand, leaning on the arms of the chair. When standing she gazed at Em. Archange asked, "Did you know your father was a great general, child?"

Em, eyes huge, shook her head.

"Did you know he is not your father?"

Bartellus felt dread clutch his stomach, for it was something they had never discussed, and he had no idea how much Em remembered.

But Emly nodded her head calmly.

"And do you remember your brother?"

Another nod.

"You don't say much, do you?"

The girl lowered her eyes.

"She has gotten out of the habit of talking," Bartellus said.

Archange looked at him, and her face was grave. "I will make you the same offer I made eight years ago. Give the girl to me. I will see she is safe. She will be educated, well-treated. She may even, after a while, somewhere, take up glassmaking again. Can you do any of that for her?"

Bart glanced at Emly, who was watching them both warily.

He said, "I will give you the same answer I gave then. I will leave that up to Emly."

The woman replied, "Your danger now is greater than it was then. Then you merely faced death by drowning. Now you face imprisonment and torture, both of you."

A bolt of fear shot through Bart's chest, but he nodded calmly. "I will think on it, Archange. Truly. Thank you. How can I contact you?"

She thought. "You cannot. But I will find you."

He asked, "One more thing. Was it you who freed me from the dungeons?"

He thought she was going to give one of her annoying elliptical replies, but she said, "Yes. Not personally. But it was one of my women."

"Thank you. You must have thought I was mad when I did not know you in the Halls."

She reached out and patted his hand. "No. I saw a man grievously wounded. I am glad you are healing. Be safe. Get away from here."

He opened the door and stepped out into the side alley, looking both ways. He could see no one. Then she stepped out with him, and he saw a shadow, two shadows detach themselves from a wall farther up. She gave Bart one last glance then hurried away. He watched as the three turned into Blue Duck Alley. He went back in and closed the door, locking it. Em was watching him.

"Who is she?" she whispered.

She had been born into the nobility, Bartellus told Emly. Into the great imperial Family of Vincerus. She was sister to Marcellus and Rafael, considerably older than the brothers. But, or at least this was how the story was told, when their father died Archange became completely dependent on the boys, then just children, and she a woman of mature years and independent nature.

She was a great beauty, Bartellus explained, with many suitors among the rich and powerful, and among those seeking to be rich and powerful. Yet she chose to marry a soldier, and not a common soldier, but a foreigner many years younger than herself. The marriage did not please the two boys who controlled Archange's life, and they opposed the liaison and shortly afterwards the young foreign soldier disappeared, killed, paid off, fled—no one knew.

Archange vanished from the pages of the City's history for many years. When she reappeared again it seemed she was still determined to embarrass the Vincerii. She chose to call herself an advocate, interpreting the City's labyrinthine and frequently contradictory laws before the emperor's counsellors on behalf of supplicants. This was clearly no suitable task for a woman, and the Vincerii, it is said, tried to dissuade her with promises and with threats, but she already had gained the permission of the emperor, who clearly had his own agenda, and Marcellus and Rafe had no means to rein in their sister.

At first Archange was outstandingly unsuccessful as an advocate. She represented mainly women left destitute by the death of a father or husband or elder brother, falling calamitously from a life of ease to one of hardship and shame. Archange tried to wrestle the City's serpentine laws into a shape which benefited them. And mostly she failed. But after a while she had some small success, and her causes became, for a while, fashionable.

Then Archange overstepped herself. She agreed to speak at a criminal trial, a sensational one, one which Bartellus could never forget, a trial which the woman won, in a way. Afterwards she disappeared for a second time, and eventually the uncaring world forgot her name again.

"You can pack one bag," he told Emly. "We will leave at dawn."

Then he frowned, remembering their servant. "Where is Frayling?"

Chapter 19

Emly was packing her bag in her tiny candlelit bedroom. She folded into it her two spare dresses, and added stout winter shoes, thick stockings and drawers. There was also her warm coat, but she would wear that for it would be cold at dawn. Into the cloth bag she threw a handful of the cheap jewellery she had bought at market stalls, wooden bangles and beads of painted clay. She took a deep breath and tried to be practical. What would they need? Then she went downstairs to the kitchen and found candles and soap.

Trudging back up to her bedroom she realised tears were running down her cheeks. She hurried into her room and closed the door. She did not want Bartellus to see her crying.

She lay on her bed in her old brown dress and stared at the ceiling. There was no chance of sleeping, so she would lie there until dawn. She wondered where they would sleep tomorrow. Her mind was full of the words she had heard, and she sorted through them, trying to make sense of them.

Despite what her father thought, she had no regrets about leaving the House of Glass. She had allowed herself to become happy, but deep down she had known that happiness would be short-lived. Her life had been a story of flight, and she was grateful for their four years there. The most important thing, the only important thing, was to keep Bartellus safe. Although the old woman Archange had called him Shuskara. Was that his real name?

She got off the bed and went upstairs, paying a last visit to her work-room, to see if anything there might be useful on their flight. She picked up the heavy pliers used to cut the calms, and a narrow scalpel for slicing paper. Both could be used as weapons, she thought. She wandered over to the north window, opening it and peering down to the alley. Below was a pit of darkness. No one moved. She heard distant sounds, muffled laughter, the hoot of an owl, the rumble of carts. She remembered it was the middle of the night, for Archange's visit had kept her up far beyond her normal bedtime, and most of Lindo would be fast asleep.

The only lights were farther up the alley, where a few low windows shed patches of light onto the cobbles. Early shift workers, she thought, or whores. Then in the distance she saw a shadowed figure appear briefly in a patch of light, then vanish again into darkness. Her heart beat faster and she watched as the figure appeared again in the next light and, before it vanished again, she saw it was a man with a crutch, coming slowly towards the House of Glass. There was a long gap before the next light, and Em waited impatiently. Finally the figure crept into the light and then there was no doubt, for he stopped and leaned against the wall as though he could go no farther, beaten and bowed.

It was Frayling.

Hours before, Frayling stood leaning on his crutch, looking up at the merchant's house, determined not to leave empty-handed after such a long struggle to get there. He knew he had barely the energy to get back to the House of Glass this day, and he feared crossing the City at night. But he could not admit to himself that he was beaten.

He drank some water from the fountain, then sat down on the far side of it, where he could not be seen, his back against its warm stone wall.

He tried to concentrate on the problem at hand, but his thoughts kept drifting to Emly. The day he had first seen her had been the first day of his life. Among the wretched and downtrodden, the halt and the lame of Lindo she had seemed to him like the girl who lived on the moon, in the stories he was told as a child, who stepped down from her home in the sky at night, to walk among the poor giving gifts to children. Emly was dark and quick as a bird, graceful and strong as the ghost cats that patrolled the rooftops. Her small fingers were nimble, and his favourite days were those when he was asked up to her workroom to help her bind the glass pieces with lead calms. She was the kindest person he had ever met, for he had met very few in his difficult life.

He had been working at a stonemason's, helping shift the heavy stones for the master carvers to make their marks on. It was hard work, but it was all he could get, and when he was finished for the day he could do no more than sleep until it was time to work again. His leg pained him constantly, and he was paid barely enough to keep body and soul together. He was limping home to his hovel late one day when he heard the new occupant of the house opposite Meggy's was looking for a servant. By the time he got to Blue Duck Alley there were thirty or more men outside the tall crooked house, and arguments and scuffles were breaking out. Frayling stood at the back of the crowd, leaning on his crutch, cursing himself for wasting sleeping time on a fool's errand. Then an old man stepped out of the house and surveyed them all. He was a tough old boy, Frayling thought, with hair gone grey, and light green eyes.

"I want an honest man," the old man announced, looking around him, "a veteran who will serve me as he once served the City. In return I will pay a fair wage and meals."

It turned out that every man there had served in the army, even Frayling, who didn't know a broadsword from a branding iron. The old man started moving among the group, asking questions, his speech sharp, his pale eyes quick to seek out dishonesty. At last he came to Frayling.

"Your name?"

"Frayling, lord."

"What regiment?"

Frayling blushed and looked at his feet. "The 42nd, lord."

The old man frowned. "42nd what?"

Frayling tried desperately to remember anything that sounded military, but his mind remained empty, and he stared hopelessly at the ground.

"Are you honest, Frayling?"

"Yes, lord," he replied wonderingly, having just been caught in a lie.

"How did you injure your leg?" the old man asked.

"A childhood accident," Frayling confessed with shame.

"Can you manage stairs? This house is built mainly of stairs," the man said.

"Yes, lord," Frayling answered, his heart leaping. "I can do anything as well as a man with two good legs."

"Come with me and prove it," the old man told him. "And don't call me lord."

The sun was going down on the warm quiet square when Frayling scrambled clumsily to his feet. He had decided to have one more try, one last hope of earning a look of gratitude and admiration on Emly's face. He limped across the square and, pushing down his fears, rapped firmly on the door again. After a very long time the same servant opened it.

Frayling cleared his throat and spoke his rehearsed words. "I wish to speak to your master." And, in an inspiration which sealed all their fates, he added, "The veil I am seeking is priceless, and if it is not returned to my lord's house he will seek redress in the court of the Immortal."

Emly took her work shoes off and, holding them in one hand, flew down the stairs to the hall. She did not want Bartellus to hear, and add to his worries. She quietly eased open the door. Although she was in a hurry, her years of hardship had made her cautious, and she locked the door behind her and pocketed the key before running up the pitch-black side alley. She heard pitter-pattering sounds in the lane at her feet and imagined rats running alongside her, keeping pace with her. She had not been out in the hours of darkness for several years: the cool night air was stimulating and she felt her spirits lifting.

She found Frayling still in the same spot, the wall holding him in a sitting position, although he seemed to be asleep.

"Frayling," she whispered, and he stirred. Recognising her, he gathered his crutch under him and tried to stand. Then she saw the blood on his face and body. She tried to help him to his feet. She was too small to put her shoulder under his, but she supported him with her arm around his waist as they slowly limped homeward.

"What happened?" she asked. One side of his face was a bloody mess, the eye closed. There was blood on his jerkin, but she did not know if it was from the face injuries or other wounds.

"Merchant's men," he whispered, eyes downcast, "two of them, beat me. I asked for the veil." He groaned, from pain or frustration.

In her mind's eye Em saw herself going to the merchant's house, perhaps with militia hired by her father, and demanding the veil and redress for Frayling's injuries. Then she remembered they were to disappear that dawn, and she realised they could not take Frayling with them, for it would be too dangerous for the crippled man. She knew he adored her, this tall shambling man with his useless leg and kind heart. He wanted to be her protector, and she wished that he could. She had seen too much of men's savagery, and understood something of the hideous lives suffered by many women, the poor and the unprotected. All her short life she had relied on others to keep her safe, first her brother, then Bartellus. It frightened her that just one old man's life stood between her and a possible future of pain and misery.

When they reached the House of Glass she unlocked the door and let them in. In her head she had rehearsed a little drama to conceal from Bartellus the fact that she had been out in the night. She put a finger to her lips. Frayling frowned and nodded. Then she rapped hard on the inside of the door, and waited until she heard her father moving about upstairs. Then she flung open the door, grinning back at the servant.

"Frayling!" she cried dramatically, more loudly than was necessary.

Then she fell back in terror, trying to close the heavy door again. But the three big men looming in the darkness merely pushed her to one side and walked in. Two had swords drawn, the third, a stout ruffian with a grey beard, had a nail-studded wooden club. He pushed the door closed behind them.

The leader, a dark-faced man with an eyepatch, grabbed Em by the arm. "Where is the old man?" he asked. He glanced up the stairs. "Up there?"

She shook her head, and he threw her down. She fell hard against the door and her head bounced off the oak. The world went dark for a moment and her limbs lost their strength. The one-eyed man turned his back, while the second swordsman raised his weapon to stab her. Then the swordsman fell as, with a shout, Frayling hit him round the head with his crutch. The one with the cudgel laughed briefly as his friend went down, then he casually swung the club at Frayling. The crippled man tried to get out of the way, for the club moved slowly, and it hit him a glancing blow on his bad hip. Frayling gave a scream of agony and collapsed at the foot of the stairs. Em shook her head clear and scrambled across the floor to him. The servant's eyes were open but he seemed paralysed by the pain.

Then there was a shout from above and everyone looked up. Bartellus had appeared at the top of the stairs. He took two steps downwards. Em watched him take in the scene below, then the old man retreated back to his room.

*   *   *

The one-eyed leader, known as the Wolf, did not call himself an assassin, although he could not argue with anyone who did. He simply followed the orders of his protector, and if he was told to kill, well, he did so as efficiently as possible, without hatred or cruelty. He had no idea why he had been ordered to kill this old man who scurried up the stairs away from them, but he doubted it would take all three of them.

The Wolf was once known as Casmir, an infantryman of the 18th Serpentine, who fought loyally for his City for more than fifteen years, first under the legendary Grantus, then his successor Victorinus Rae Khan. His final battle was a trivial skirmish in a small tribal village south of the Plakos. Afterwards the City warriors moved on, leaving at their backs a village of corpses. They also left Casmir, for he had taken a deep wound to the stomach and a blow to the head and he lay as if dead in his own blood. There he suffered for two days or more, dying slowly, though not slowly enough not to be aware when an impatient carrion crow took out his eye. Casmir was at last discovered by another troop of City fighters and, against all probability, survived. When he had recovered from his wounds, which took many weeks, he took time to hunt down all the former comrades who left him to die, those whose names he could remember. There were still some left to find, but he suspected they were dead already from other causes and his rage was less potent now, quenched by blood.

His protector's orders had been clear. "Kill the old man . . . and make sure he is dead!" This last was something of a joke between them. "And anyone else in the house, if you see fit."

The Wolf did not see fit to kill the girl. He did not kill girls without good reason. He was annoyed that Derian had stabbed at her, and amused that the cripple had downed the swordsman with his crutch. But he could not blame him when Derian leaped up and stabbed the cripple in the chest. The girl squealed like a rabbit on a stick.

"Let's see if there are any more mice in this hole," the Wolf ordered. And, pointing at the girl, he said, "Bring her along."

Leading the way, sword raised, he stepped lightly up the stairs to the landing where he had seen the old man. He looked swiftly left and right. There was no movement. He could hear the stair treads creaking and the sound of Ragtail's laboured breathing. He turned and put his finger to his lips. The girl opened her mouth to shout, and Ragtail dropped his grip on her arm and grabbed her round the head, muffling her mouth with his great hand. There was silence. The Wolf gestured to Derian to go to the left, while he slid into the right-hand room. A narrow bed, a chest and a threadbare rug. No one hiding.

He stepped out onto the landing again and looked up the next flight of stairs. How many were there?

He cleared his throat and, pitching his voice at a conversational level, said, "Come down, old man. We have already killed the cripple. We will slit the girl's throat if you don't appear." He had no idea of the relationship between the old man and the girl. She could be a serving maid and her slit throat a matter of indifference to her master. Still, it was worth a try.

Then the darkness on the landing above them thickened, and the old man was standing there. He held a sword in one hand and a dagger in the other. By his stance the Wolf guessed he knew how to use them. But it would make no difference. They had the girl, and it now seemed that she was the old man's weak point. So it was all over, really.

Looking back, it was not clear quite what happened then. One moment the old boy was standing, defiant but already defeated, at the top of the stairs. The next there was a whirl of movement. Ragtail went down, a knife in his throat. The pommel of the thrown sword, spinning end over end, hit the Wolf on the side of the head and he staggered and went down on one knee, dazed for a moment.

"Run, Em!" the old man shouted, and the girl leaped up the stairs, racing past the Wolf, kicking him in the face with a flying heel. He stood up, shaking clear his head, and picked up his sword.

The girl had disappeared into the darkness of the upper floors. The old man still stood in the same spot, only now he was unarmed.

But then he charged.

He took several running steps down the stairs, reckless as a child, and launched himself at Derian and the Wolf. Both men had their swords up, but the staircase was narrow and Derian was behind. With a jolt the Wolf realised the old man was going to hit him with the force of a runaway cart. He put both hands on the sword, bracing himself. At the last moment he saw the old man had padded his forearms with a coat, and he hit the upraised sword arms first, head down. Then he cannoned into the Wolf, and the three men crashed down the stairs to the lower landing, the old boy on top.

Angry now, the Wolf scrambled from under the melee and leaped to his feet. His sword was lost, but Derian was up too and he was still armed. The old man lay on the wooden floor, winded by his fall, helpless.

"Kill him!" snarled the Wolf.

Derian grinned. "A pleasure," he said. He stepped forward, then fell to his knees, howling in pain.

The Wolf realised the cripple was not dead, and had crawled up the stairs and grabbed his lost sword. He had hacked it across the back of Derian's leg, drawing blood, perhaps severing something. The Wolf shook his head. What a shambles! After his joke about making sure the enemy was dead. He almost laughed. He took out his dagger and, grabbing him by the hair, cut the cripple's throat. Then he turned to the old man.

"He was harder to kill than I thought," he commented pleasantly.

The old man watched him from the floor. He was pale and breathing heavily. He had found a dagger from somewhere, Ragtail's perhaps, and held it by its hilt. A tough old soldier, the Wolf thought. Despite the shambles, it was a shame to kill him.

Taking his time, keeping an eye on the dagger, in case the man reversed it for another throw, he retrieved his sword from the cripple's dead grasp, glancing sourly at Derian, who was moaning and clutching at his injured leg.

"I should have come alone," he commented.

"Who sent you?" asked the old soldier.

The Wolf frowned. He would have liked to oblige the old boy with an answer, but loyalty meant discretion, and he had vowed never to tell his protector's name, even to a dead man.

Instead, in a bid to be pleasant, he offered, "I will not molest the girl."

The man said nothing, just watched him with his pale eyes. Then he slowly levered himself to his feet. The Wolf let him. He had no wish to kill this man as he lay on the ground. The old boy took a knife-fighter's stance and circled cautiously. The Wolf was thirty years younger than him, and armed with a short sword, but he treated the man with respect. If the events of this night had taught him anything it was never to take anything for granted.

They were both right-handed, although the assassin could use his left hand with deadly accuracy. The Wolf thrust experimentally at the old man's throat. The man weaved to the right, his knife leaping forward and nearly cutting the Wolf's shoulder. He is game, thought the Wolf, and he is working on an old soldier's memories. He smiled inwardly. If he were fifty years younger, he might give me problems. Out of politeness he turned his stance to minimise his profile.

The old man's knife flickered forward and the Wolf instantly took his chance, weaving and thrusting for the man's chest. But the old man's blade slid against his, deflecting it, and in that moment the old man stepped in and threw a ferocious punch with his left fist which rocked the Wolf backwards to the edge of the down staircase. He teetered, getting his balance, and the old man moved forward. The Wolf recovered and stepped back down two steps to give himself room.

In that second he saw the old man reverse the knife and pull his arm back to throw it. Good, thought the Wolf, as he swayed easily to the right. The knife thunked into the sloping ceiling beside his head. The Wolf, short sword in one hand, grinned and looked the old boy in the eyes as he dragged the knife out of the ceiling. Then he leaped forward with his sword. The old man raised an arm to defend himself and the Wolf thrust the dagger into his side. He felt it ram home through flesh and muscle and the old man sagged against him. Carefully, the Wolf helped him down to the floor, leaving the knife lodged in his body.

He ran back down the stairs to Derian, who was dragging himself to his feet.

"Go find the girl!" he commanded. "Or do I have to do everything?" Derian was pale and could barely use his right leg but he nodded and swallowed, and started limping up the stairs to the upper storeys. The Wolf looked around the shabby rooms on the ground floor. There was a work-room, with pots of paint and foul-smelling potions. He piled several of them in a haphazard heap, then emptied one pot over the others. He had no idea if it was flammable, but it smelled as though it ought to be.

He glanced through a gap in the boarded-up window. Dawn was break-ing. He could see the buildings on the other side of the alley and the early birds were beginning their song. It was a good time to be out in the City, walking through the waking streets to the sound of birdsong, he thought. Then he remembered Derian and scowled.

He ran up the stairs, flight after flight, glancing left and right as he went. He found his man on the top floor. He had discovered the girl and was laboriously tying her to a heavy chair with a rope he had found. She was crying and struggling, and Derian cuffed her round the head as the Wolf arrived.

"What are you doing?" the leader asked, amazed.

"I thought you'd want to ask her questions," Derian replied sulkily.

"Questions? About what?" Derian shrugged, staring at the floor. The Wolf shook his head in wonder at the stupidity. The gods defend me from imbeciles, he thought.

"It is nearly dawn," he said. "We can't be seen here."

He returned to the hatch in the floor. Derian asked, "What about her?"

The Wolf shrugged. "What about her? I told the old man I would not molest her," he said. "I keep my promises."

They went back down through the building, stepping over the body of the old man on the first landing. On the ground floor the Wolf grabbed a candle and threw it on the pile of paint pots. Disappointingly, nothing happened for a moment. Then he saw a thin blue line of light surge across the floor. There was a small explosion of flame, then quickly the whole pile caught alight.

He opened the side door and together they stepped out into the fresh new morning.

Chapter 20

The pool of blood was widening, and soon it would start to sizzle.

Bartellus lay on his side watching with interest as reflected flames flickered on the shining slick surface of the blood pool.

He was curled up, hands clutched protectively round the dagger embedded in his side, trying not to move, trying not to breathe. When his chest moved he could feel the blade rasp against a rib. *That broken sword is the only thing keeping you alive, sir.* Bartellus could still see the officer's white anxious face bobbing above him as he was carried off the battlefield. He had wanted to pull the weapon out, to ease the pain. He had known his lifeblood would gush out with it, but it seemed not to matter. The young officer had restrained him, holding gently on to his hands.

Now the old man was lying on the landing below the second staircase, and from the sounds below him, roaring and crackling, he knew the ground floor of the House of Glass was well alight. The flames were crawling up the wooden walls of the stairwell. Pulling the blade out would mean a quick death. A better choice than burning alive. Emly would understand. She would not blame him.

He pictured his daughter's face. Then he realised he could not remember when he had last seen her. He tried to concentrate, but his thoughts were swirling like water in his head. He could not stay focussed on Emly. He kept seeing the young officer. What was his name? Gilliar? Gellan?

There was an explosion in a room below him, and a blast of hot air warmed his face. Paint, perhaps, or the chemicals Em used on the glass. He opened his eyes. He had to think of Emly. Where was she? Why was he thinking about her? Her bare feet. Her bare feet running up the stairs. Suddenly he remembered the attack in the night, the two men, the fight, the blade in his side. Emly fleeing.

With a groan he lifted his head and saw flames all around him. He slowly rolled over and onto his knees. The agony in his side made the world lurch and he paused while it righted itself again. Then, on all fours, flames reaching for his clothes and grasping at his hair, he slowly crawled up the stairs.

There were thirteen stairs. On the next landing he rested, still on hands and knees. He could not let himself lie down, for he knew he could never get up again. He peered around him, looking into the bedrooms on either side. No sign of Em.

"Emly!" he cried, but there was little breath in his lungs and it came out as a whisper. He pressed on up the next flight, inching his way, outpacing the fire only by moments.

Finally, after eons, he reached the bottom of the wooden ladder which led to Em's attic. He looked up and tried calling her name again, but the effort made him cough wretchedly. Agony surged through his body and darkness covered his eyes. He could not climb up there. It was impossible.

Then he heard something above him, a regular rasping sound like someone scouring a pan. He listened hard. There was silence for a while, then the sound started again. It gave him hope, and a little strength, and he forced himself up the steps, one agonising rung after another, clinging on with bloody hands, his feet dragging as if weights were tied to them. After an age he reached the top and peered over into the attic.

Emly was roped to a heavy wooden chair, which was lying on its side. She was gagged and her hands and feet were tied. She was rubbing the ropes around her wrists against the sharp corner of a metal chest. She was facing him and when she saw him her eyes widened above the filthy paint cloth they had used for a gag. The old man forced his feet up the last few rungs, then slid across the wooden floor towards her, his pain for a moment forgotten. He fumbled at the back of her head to unknot the gag then, angered by his weakness, wrenched it roughly off over her head.

"Hands! Hands!" she whispered, terrified, and her eyes looked beyond him and he saw the flames reflected in them.

His thick clumsy fingers worked at the knots in the rope. His blood gave them grip, but he was weakened by his wound and rendered incompetent by his fear for her, and it took precious moments to untie her. When she felt the rope loosen she tore her hands free and unwound the rope at her waist, then bent to free her feet. Bartellus looked behind him. Flames were roaring up from the stairwell, setting fire to the wooden rafters above and crawling across the ceiling. Smoke was pouring across the floor.

Emly was free. She bent down to him and grabbed his arm, his shoulder, on his uninjured side.

"The window!" she whispered.

He shook his head. The thought was preposterous. "I cannot," he told her, his voice muffled and rasping from the smoke.

She grabbed his face and pulled in close to him. "I will not go without you!" she said, her words firm and uncompromising.

He sighed and, resting on her thin shoulder, he stood and struggled across the workroom to the window. She threw it open and helped him onto the wide sill. He gazed down. Blue Duck Alley was far below them, and down there he could see excited faces looking up. In front of them the latticework bridge stretched in the darkness to the opposite building. Impossible.

"I cannot," he told her. "This is a path for cats, and deliverance for you. But not for me."

"I will not go without you," she repeated, and he heard the iron in her words. She started pushing him out of the window, beating at his back with her fists, shoving with her shoulder. He tried to hold her, to thrust her in front of him onto the bridge, but even her frail strength was too much for him.

He could feel himself dying, but he could not take her with him.

With a huge effort he reached up with his left arm and caught hold of a wooden beam. He felt her lift his boot up onto a secure foothold, then, with a groan, he swung himself up onto the bridge. He clung on, riding out the pain, forcing back the darkness in his head. Emly was right behind him, placing his right hand then his right foot on the beams of the bridge. He moved his weight to his right side, and she immediately took his left hand, guiding it forward again. They were high above the alley now, with nothing but dark air between them and the cobbled stones. His head felt a bit clearer, and the night air cooled his burning side. He stretched forwards and took one more shuffled pace. On the far side of the bridge he could see two young boys watching him from an open window. He could hear thin cries, like the mewing of gulls. They were shouting at him, their eyes wide with excitement. He guessed they were egging him forward.

He shifted his grip and moved his feet to a lower beam, so he could rest for a moment against the latticework. There was an explosion of glass and a blast of hot air as the window behind him was blown out. He heard glass crashing on the street below and the excited shouts of spectators as they fled the falling shards. He quickly stepped another pace forward, conscious that Em was behind him and closest to the inferno. His right hand slipped on the smooth wood and he half fell, landing hard on his hip, grabbing on again at the last moment, tearing the wound in his side. Pain stabbed through him and his vision blurred.

That broken sword is the only thing keeping you alive, sir. What did that damn fool know? That sword was keeping him from the battle. His men needed him now and he would not let them down.

*   *   *

Emly saw her father reach purposefully for the dagger embedded in his side. She knew what he was about to do and she grabbed his hand to stop him. He struggled weakly for a moment, then let go and his body relaxed against her. She guessed he had passed out. He was half sitting against a diagonal beam and she was squatting behind him, holding on with one hand, the other arm wrapped tightly around his chest, her bare toes digging into the timber.

"Father! Father!" she called in his ear, trying to bring him round. Behind her she could feel the heat of the inferno, and she knew the flames were licking along the lattice bridge towards them.

"Bartellus!"

Weak with exhaustion and fear, she looked ahead at the attic window of the lodging house opposite. It was a few paces away, but might as well be a hundred. She was not strong enough to move him. She could barely hold on herself. Before long her grip would fail and they would both plummet to the cobbles.

She spoke into Bartellus' ear again, leaning her head against his, and for the first time in a long time her words came clear and fluid. She did not know if she was speaking out loud or the words were still trapped inside her head.

"Remember, Father, the great stone bridge in the Halls," she told him. "You said it was a bridge made for giants. We had no idea where we were or where it lead. I was so small you had to pick me up and place me on each step then clamber up after me. You did not leave me in the darkness, in all the long darkness of the Halls, you did not leave me and save yourself. Now I will not leave you on this bridge. I would rather die here or on the stones below than go on without you. Now you must wake up and we will climb to safety together."

But Bartellus did not hear her words. Despairing, she looked ahead to the window again. There were three anxious faces, a woman and two boys. As she watched the bigger boy climbed out of the casement. The woman clutched at him, her face contorted, imploring, and Em saw them frowning, arguing, although all she could hear was the roar of the fire so close behind her. The boy shook the woman's hand off his arm and he launched himself out onto the bridge, climbing swiftly and with confidence towards her. In moments he was at her side, clinging on easily to the latticework of beams. Disappointed, Emly realised he was only young, perhaps ten or twelve.

"What's wrong with him?" he shouted at her over the roar of the flames.

She indicated the knife buried in Bartellus' side and the boy's eyes grew large.

"Help me," she told him.

Each took one of the old man's arms, and between them they tried to lift him but, holding on grimly to the wooden beams, they had not the strength between them to shift the dead weight. Emly cried in frustration and looked fearfully behind her. The farthest beams of the bridge were blackening in the heat, and smoke was rising off them, whipping away into the night.

The boy stared at her helplessly and glanced past her. His face was yellow in the light of the fire. She guessed he regretted his decision to try to help.

"Back!" she told him.

He shook his head and tried again to lift the old man. One of Bartellus' feet slipped from the beam and his leg dangled over the drop. Emly wrapped her arms around her father and told the boy fiercely, "Back! You're in the way!"

His face fell and reluctantly he turned and made his way back to the window. But before he got there a new figure appeared, dark against the light. It was a man and, as he too started to climb out of the window, Em saw it was the tall, pale-eyed man she had seen watching the house. He eased past the boy and made his way along the bridge towards her. She was suddenly conscious that her arms were trembling with the effort of holding on to the old man, her knees cramped from squatting on the beam. She glanced down, and the oval faces of the spectators, turned up towards her, lurched and doubled under her vision. She dragged her eyes away, back to the soldier.

He reached out and grabbed Bartellus by the upper arm.

"Let go," he ordered her. "I will take him."

She just stared at him in fear, unwilling to release Bartellus into his grip. But she had no choice. This man was either her saviour or her killer. She did not know which, but in either case she was helpless.

He glanced beyond her. "You have only moments," he told her flatly.

She nodded, and relaxed her grip a little. The man knelt carefully beside them. "Tie his wrists together," he told her.

She stared at him for a second, then understood what he meant and tore off the cloth belt at her waist and twisted it. As the soldier held Bartellus she

tied the belt around each of the old man's thick wrists, then round both together, knotting it as tightly as she could.

The tall man turned round carefully on the beam, holding on with both
hands. "Put his arms over my head," he ordered.

She did as she was told and, as she did so, Bartellus seemed to rise towards consciousness and he gripped the man's neck with his arms.

"You cannot lift him!" Em whispered, and he looked at her curiously.

"Have you a better idea?" he asked, and she saw a trace of humour in his
pale eyes.

He did not wait for her answer but took a deep breath and straightened
his knees, lifting Bartellus off the beam. But the old man's weight shifted and
the tall man's foot slipped. He came down hard on one knee, his left arm
raking across a diagonal beam, tearing his sleeve and the flesh beneath it. In
a long slow moment of fear Em saw him grab hold of a lower beam and saw
the muscles on his arm bulge as he shifted the weight of his burden back to
centre. And she saw, on his forearm, the familiar mark of the S, white against
pale skin. The brand Bartellus had asked her about, the mark he had made
in the dirt so long ago in the Halls, the mark she had seen him draw in idle
moments, always wondering. Who was this stranger with the mysterious
brand?

Then, with a convulsive jerk and a deep groan, the soldier straightened his legs and lifted the old man clear of the bridge. Bartellus moaned
and seemed to cling more tightly to his back. Slowly, placing each foot and
hand with care, the man carried his burden towards the safety of the opposite window. Emly, casting nervous looks behind, followed as closely as
she could, lifting Bartellus by the belt when she could, trying to ease the
burden.

As they came close to the window the older boy and the woman climbed
out, and between them they helped carry Bartellus over the low sill. As soon
as they took his weight, the rescuer ducked out from under the tied hands
and reached backwards, grabbing Em by the arm.

Behind her there was an explosion of flame, a blast of hot air on her back
and shrill cries from the street below. In the moment the bridge dropped
away beneath her she placed her foot on the windowsill. The tall man stead-
ied her and, as if she had all the time in the world, she smiled up at him,

stepping lightly down into the room as if she were being handed down from a rich man's carriage.

They both dropped on their knees beside Bartellus.

"We must take the knife out," the soldier said. He looked up at the boys' mother. "I need some clean towels, rags, anything to staunch the bleeding."

Between them they got Bartellus onto a low pallet bed, then the man drew out the knife. He carefully examined the wound before wadding cloth into it. The padding became instantly red, and Emly's heart lurched. He pressed more cloths against the wound, and bound them roughly with bandages.

The soldier stood. "Keep him still," he told the woman, "and give him water if he will take it."

He turned to Emly. "He's a tough old boy," he said. "He's survived worse than this."

"Thank you," she croaked, her voice rendered even more reluctant by the smoke and fumes. Then, feeling her words were inadequate, she smiled and nodded.

He stared at her. His face was dirty with soot and his pale eyes and lashes were startlingly bright. She remembered that this was a man she had been fearing and, nonplussed, she found herself reddening. She whispered, "Who are you?"

He coughed smoke from his chest. "My name is Evan Broglanh," he told her, "and many years ago your father saved my life." When she made no reply, he said, "And you are Emly?"

She nodded.

"Tell me, Emly," he said, "have you heard your father speak of Fell Aron Lee?"

PART FOUR

The Good Son

Chapter 21

As a small boy Fell had been sent to live among strangers.

In the barracks and encampments where he had lived his life he had listened to men tell of their mothers, of saints and angels, sweet smiling women, warm and comforting. He thought of himself as unsentimental, and he found the mawkish sentimentality of brutal men hard to understand and, at times, difficult to stomach. He had witnessed the rape and mutilation of women, and turned away, his heart a stone in his chest, and seen the same men in their cups with tears in their eyes speak of their virtuous mothers and cherished, virginal, sisters.

He remembered no mother, although in fragments of dreams he sometimes saw a girl's face, a child really, looking down on him, soft lips on his forehead and the smell of warm milk and clean linen. But his earliest clear memory was of a long frightening journey, of being passed hand to hand in darkness lit by flaming torches, of the smell of burning and of horses and blood.

He had been raised in a foreign barracks with other boys, outlanders all. They had been taught to compete, and encouraged to fight, rewarded for strength and fitness, and skills with sword and fist. But these children were not permitted to kill each other, for they were valuable. And if friendships developed the boys were split up and moved to a different barracks. They were all taught the same language and, as they grew towards manhood, they learned anatomy and battlefield surgery, strategy and logistics, some mathematics and a little philosophy. It was a good education for a soldier, and Fell was near puberty before he understood that all boys were not raised in the same way.

And he was very much older before he learned that not all children were unhappy and that, for some, childhood was blessed.

He was no older than six when he was roughly roused from his bed one night and told to dress. It was winter and the boys' dormitory, an echoing stone hall whose walls soaked up all warmth, was icy, the floor slippery. Fearfully, the child pulled on woollen trousers and a padded jacket as two tall soldiers watched him impatiently. His numb fingers started to fumble with the belt which held the short sword he was ordered to carry with him everywhere, but one of the men stopped his hand.

"You won't want that, boy," he growled and, grabbing him round the wrist, he strode off.

The boy had trouble keeping up as he was half lead, half dragged through the midnight palace. They crossed the starlit square where the boys exercised each day, then through the great stables, which seemed to stretch for ever. The boy saw the benevolent heads of the horses gaze out at him as he passed, their dark eyes kind and curious. The boy wondered if Lancer, the little pony he had been learning to ride, was there, but he could not see her. Then they hurried through a wide carved doorway and he was in the Red Palace proper where, he thought, he had never been before. Here the halls were high, and the torches the two men carried gleamed off pale stone and carved faces but did not touch the yawning ceilings. It was warmer than the barracks and the child stopped shivering. His nose detected the warm smell of roasted meat and his stomach rumbled painfully.

"Come on, boy. Do you want me to carry you?" his captor growled down at him as the boy's shorter legs began to fail and he stumbled, his arm aching where the man held it so tightly in his hard hand.

"He's a child, Flavius," the other soldier said mildly. "The emperor can wait another moment or two. The Lion of the East isn't going anywhere."

The man called Flavius grinned, and slowed his pace a little, allowing the boy to keep up. He glanced up gratefully at the second man, who had red hair, and who returned his look sternly.

Finally they reached a place where the halls were as wide as they were tall and the carvings of faces on the walls shone like the sun. The boy felt very small as he padded alongside the tall men, across shiny green floors like ice on a wintry lake. Then there were two great glowing doors, flanked by armed men, doors which seemed to open on their own as the three approached. They entered a huge room, much larger than any the boy had ever seen. It was thronged with people, men and women, who turned and looked at them as they entered. The buzz of conversation faltered and stilled. The two men paused then, at some unseen gesture, stepped forward. The little boy could see nothing but bodies clothed with bright fabrics, swords in shining scabbards, hands bearing heavy rings and jewelled bracelets, ankles cuffed in gold. People stepped out of their way as they passed through the throng in silence.

Then they moved out from the crowd into an empty space and the two soldiers stopped, the boy between them. The red-haired one leaned down and whispered briefly in his ear, "Try not to cry."

Frightened and confused by the night's sudden events, the boy felt his eyes start to prickle at the sliver of compassion in the words, and he gulped and forced back the tears. He stared ahead of him and saw a big dark chair, as wide as his bed was long, with thick cushions and pillows, amid which sat a man with fair hair and a fair beard. The fair man was drinking from a shiny cup and talking to a very tall man standing at his side. Fell could not hear what they said, but they spoke for a long time. Meantime there was silence in the hall. The boy wondered if would be all right for him to sit down, for his legs felt sleepy. But then the fair-haired man turned to him and all the child's tiredness was forgotten, for the man had an empty socket where one eye should be and the gaping hole was crusted with dry black blood.

"So this is the cub?" the man said, sitting forward in the chair, and some people in the room laughed.

"His name is Arish," the red-headed man told him. "He has been with us for two years."

The fair man stood and he seemed to sway for a heartbeat, and several of the people around him stepped forward, but he waved them away. He walked over to Arish and crouched down in front of him, putting the horror of his ruined eye in front of the child's face.

"And are you a good boy?" the man asked him.

Arish felt tears start to form again but, recalling the redhead's words, he concentrated on the good eye, which was black and cold, like the water in a deep well. He announced, "Yes, sir."

"I am your emperor. You must call me sire, boy." The eye stared at him unblinking.

Confused and anxious, the boy did not know what he meant. Then he suddenly understood. "Yes, *sire*," he said loudly, and the people behind him laughed again.

The emperor stood. "What shall we do with him? Flavius?"

The growling soldier said, "The family is all dead. He must die too. Or he could bring us trouble in days to come."

The emperor nodded and asked the red-haired man, "Shuskara, my friend?"

The man shrugged. "Flavius is right. The family is all dead. Every cousin and distant aunt. And in ten years' time no one will care. We have put the best resources of the City into training him. By the time he is of fighting age he will be its loyal son."

The boy looked from one to the other, wondering whose family was dead.

The emperor clapped the redhead on the back. "Very well, my friend. Let us hope we do not live to regret your advice. Galliard!"

An armoured soldier, huge and bearded, appeared from the back of the room. At the sight of him the murmur of conversation started again in the hall. There was some laughter, and a few shouts, although the boy did not understand what was said. As the bearded soldier came closer Fell saw he was carrying something round on a big stick. The shouts and cheers increased, and the emperor grinned. He gestured to the warrior, who slammed the stick down in front of the little boy. Stuck on top of it was a shaggy thing, stinking and green. It looked like one of the plaster heads the boy had seen in the palace's portico, only this one was badly made or someone had damaged it. He wondered why the soldier was showing it to him. Uncomprehending, he looked up at the emperor for explanation.

"This is your father, boy," the emperor said, pointing at the green thing. "Do you not know your own father?"

But the words meant nothing to the small boy, and his mind was calm and he no longer felt the threat of tears. He thought the emperor wanted something of him, but he did not know what it was, and he could do nothing about it.

The emperor looked around the great room. "From now on the City will be your father, boy," he announced, "and you will be a good son."

His given name was Arish, but for many years the people of the Red Palace called him Cub, until long after the reason for it was forgotten.

He told his comrades he had met the emperor, and called him sire, and most of them sneered, for it seemed that most of the boys had met the emperor at some time, and those who had not would not admit it. He watched the faces of the tall, bearded armed men he saw each day and occasionally he saw his friend Shuskara or the man called Flavius. Shuskara never spoke, but he winked at him once, and the little boy treasured that moment as he endured the hard physical training, the gruelling endless hours of sword practice, and the lessons which he found difficult when his belly was often empty and his body cold. All the boys soon learned to steal food from the palace kitchens and Arish, always watchful and cautious, was surprised to discover that their tutors and trainers and even the kitchen staff turned a blind eye. If the thieves were caught redhanded, though, they were severely punished, beaten only short of permanent injury.

He was smaller and younger than the other boys in his dormitory, and his first lesson, hard-learned, was to keep his head low and not be noticed. He made friends, necessary allies, with two other boys, brothers called Sander and Tomi. They banded together to defend themselves from the casual assaults of the older boys. But one morning he awoke in the dormitory to find the brothers no longer there, their beds empty. He plucked up the courage to ask one of the sword masters where they had gone.

The man was old and brown-skinned, a veteran of many battles, with a shaven scalp that bore the deep cleft of an old scar. He glared at the boy and Arish flinched, fearing the man would knock him down, as he had done before.

But the sword master sighed suddenly, as if he was very tired, and said, "They have gone home, Arish. They have gone back home."

Encouraged by the man's reply, Arish asked in a small voice, "When will I go home, sir?"

The sword master squatted down beside him and put his hand on his shoulder. "If you work hard at your lessons," he told the boy, "and practise hard in the field, the emperor will let you go home one day."

For a long time that promise kept the boy strong. He did as he was told, worked long hours at his books, and was dauntless in practice, running faster than other boys, climbing higher, fearless in the ring, and unbeatable with sword and knife. And he taught himself to take his mind to another place when the older boys bullied him, and beat him and abused him. And after a long time the hope in his heart slowly disappeared, and was replaced with a stony endurance.

And the years went by, and he did not go home, and at last *he* was an older boy. He was about thirteen, a watchful, solitary boy, when the day of his manhood arrived.

It was a welcome diversion in their training when, two or three times a year, a group of boys was taken to the forests beyond the southern edge of the City, and abandoned there to make their way on their own back to a given point—a watchtower, a hilltop, or outcrop—in a set number of days. These were called "wildings," perhaps because the boys had an unaccustomed chance to run wild, away from the hard stone walls and harder discipline. They were often given more than enough time to find their way to their destination, and the wildings were considered something of a holiday, although not for the smaller, younger boys who anticipated them only with fear.

But Arish was no longer smaller or younger. He was not the oldest of the group of eight, but he was no longer threatened by any boy, and the others, even those who were now young men, walked around him carefully.

They had ridden from the barracks at daybreak, and by midafternoon were deep in the forests of sweet oak and grey alder. Arish knew he had never been in this place before, for the trees were more open than he had seen on previous wildings, the undergrowth less entangling. They passed a high deadfall of trees, toppled by storms or quakes, which he had never seen before. He knew there was no point trying to remember the backtrail, for they had been brought by a meandering route. Following the two silent soldiers guiding them, they had left the main forest way some time before and their mounts were picking their way along a deer path. It was autumn and the nights were chill and the leaves had fallen. The sun was starting on its way downwards towards the horizon when the soldiers broke their silence to bid them dismount, and collected the horses, then left, returning the way they had come leaving eight boys standing in a wide glade knee-deep in rustling leaves.

The two oldest, a stout bully called Ranul, and a dark-faced quiet boy called Sami, chose the way to go and Arish could not disagree with their decision. Ranul declared they should travel as far north as possible before dark, and the boys set off. But almost immediately they came to a deep ravine, clothed in dry scrub and dead trees, across their way. Ranul decided, sensibly, that they could not risk the climb down with darkness nearly upon them, so they camped for the night.

They lit a fire and Ranul and the others entertained themselves by teasing and threatening the two smallest boys. But it was early days, there was plenty of time, and they were tired after the long ride. So, leaving the youngsters with the promise of horrors to come, they settled down to sleep. Arish watched it all but said nothing. Ranul was two years older than him, but Arish had seen him bullied himself when young, and he understood the need to take revenge, even on the innocent. He did not despise Ranul for his weakness, only his willingness to show it. He slept well that night, awaking once to hear distant howling.

At dawn the next day they set off again. Ranul had chosen to find his way round the ravine, for they had plenty of time, and he led them eastwards. Arish would have gone west, for the rivers flowed to the west in these parts, but he went along, saying nothing. The older boys were in high spirits, for this freedom from the grind of training and lessons was intoxicating and the air was like wine. They ran through the sunlit woods, kicking the piles of fallen leaves, shouting and baying, and rolling on the red and gold ground like pups. The two youngest trudged along miserably, trying to make themselves look smaller, and Arish brought up the rear, as always.

One of the older boys, a thin whey-faced lad called Jan who had been bullied ruthlessly when younger, at last turned his attention to the youngsters. Overexcited by the fun they were having, but suddenly bored by it, he stood up and brushed leaves off himself, then looked around for the two little boys who were trying to make themselves invisible against a tree.

Jan shouted to them, "You two, come here!"

The two watched him with frightened eyes as he slowly strolled towards them. Then, predicting their fate, they both turned and set off into the woods as fast as their short legs could take them. Jan laughed and ran after them. He caught one of them easily and the other disappeared into the trees.

"He'll have to come back sometime." Jan grinned to Ranul, returning with the skinny fair-haired child struggling in his grip.

Ranul looked down at the youngster. "What are you going to do with him?" he asked, the light of anticipation in his eye.

"They've been standing there watching us like a couple of straw dummies," Jan said, "so we can make dummies of them."

Ranul grinned, and between them they stripped the little boy's clothes off as the others cheered and jeered. The child was cast aside, and the two set about stuffing his clothes with fallen leaves, making a fat dummy which they leaned against a tree.

"Set fire to it!" one of the others cried.

Arish looked at the naked child, his face pinched and white. He knew the boy feared not just the inevitable spiral of violence, but ultimately being forced to return to the barracks without his clothes. He would be punished harshly for that. As one of the boys brought out phosphorus sticks to set the fire, Arish considered intervening. He had no doubt he could beat any of these boys, but any fistfight would rapidly escalate to knives and swords, and it was likely at least one would die. They would all be punished if they returned to the barracks one short. He kicked at the leaves at his feet. They were bone dry, for it had not rained for weeks. Any blaze would quickly spread.

He was about to speak when there was an anguished cry from the woods, in the direction the other child had run, and the sound of frenzied barking. The cries rose to screams which made Arish's blood run cold, and they all hesitated a moment, glancing at each other for courage, before setting off towards the sound.

They breasted a small rise in the wooded land and came to a sudden halt. A pack of twenty or more dogs was savaging the body of the little boy. He was dead by now, and his carcase was being easily dismembered by the growling, snapping pack. One of the dogs, a huge black, compact beast with heavy jaws dripping blood and gobs of meat, turned and glared at them, his small eyes ferocious, a low threatening growl rising from deep in his massive chest.

The boys backed away from the hideous sight. One of them vomited helplessly, and he was left standing as the group turned and ran. The boys pelted back to the glade, where the fair-haired child had dismantled the dummy and was nervously pulling his clothes back on.

"What happened?" he asked Arish, terror in his eyes.

"He's dead," Arish replied shortly, and he grabbed the child's arm and ran with him after the other fleeing boys.

They ran and ran, devouring the leagues through the open country, kicking up leaves around them as they chased through sunlit trees. There was silence behind them for a time then, with stomach-clenching terror, they heard the baying of the chasing pack.

His initial panic under control, Arish had been thinking as he loped along. The pack was following, but the dogs were no longer hungry and were not running very hard, for they could have outpaced their prey long before now. The boys could not run in darkness, so they must find sanctuary before sunset. The trees around them were all thin and spindly and could not be climbed. The only thing the dogs would respect was fire. As he ran he watched out for somewhere they could defend.

The trees had thinned out and now they were running in harsher, more uneven land, down a wide shallow trail which was funnelling them between rocky hillsides. When he spotted a likely place Arish called out to Ranul, who hesitated, a look of anger on his reddening face. Arish pointed to a shallow depression on an outcropping of rock.

"We can defend that!"

Ranul slowed, panting, glancing behind them in a picture of indecision.

"The sun is going down! Do you want them to catch us in the dark?" Arish shouted.

Ranul looked up at the hillside, then again at the trail behind them. He nodded, and they both diverted off the trail and up to the area of open ground in front of the cave-like depression. The other boys turned and followed them. At Ranul's orders they started collecting twigs and brush and dry branches. Soon they had a big pile and Sami set light to it, his hands trembling. The blaze caught instantly, and they all stood back as the flames roared up above their heads. Then they ran about, collecting piles of wood, as much as they could find.

It was getting dark before the dogs trotted into view below them. There were fifteen of them, Arish counted. Most were big and grey and wolf-like, but the black beast seemed to be their leader.

"They are hardly panting," said one of the boys, who was still struggling to get his wind.

"They are wolves," Sami told them authoritatively. "They could run for days."

"We will need a lot of wood to last the night," Arish said, looking around them. "Here." He took up a burning leafy branch and handed one each to Ranul and Sami. Then he charged the dogs with his own blazing brand and they scattered. Encouraged, the two followed him and drove the pack away so the other boys could gather more wood. By the time night fell they had a ring of three fires in front of the rockface and a huge pile of wood with which to feed them. They settled down against the wood pile, watching the darkness beyond the fires. They could not see or hear the beasts, but they knew they were out there.

When dawn broke the pack was not to be seen, and some of the boys started chattering with nervous relief, convincing themselves the dogs had gone for good. Arish knew they were wrong, and that they needed a new plan for them all to survive the day.

"They will be hungry again today," he said quietly to Ranul and Sami as they broke their fast with a little of the remaining water and some cornbread. "And they will catch us and kill us, one or two of us, if they get the chance." He nodded his head at the little fair-haired boy who sat frozen and silent, staring out at the woods, hardly blinking, not eating.

"Leave him for them," Ranul said callously. "That could give us another day. We can get to safety in that time."

Arish looked at him, wondering if he meant it.

"We cannot stay here and we cannot outrun them," he went on, as if nothing had been said. "We have little water and less food. We need to find a sturdy tree for us all to climb."

"The trees we've seen are too small," said Sami, "otherwise we would be having this conversation in one of them."

"Over there"—Arish pointed to the north—"those high woods look thicker, and older. We might find a tree which will support us all, above the dogs."

From the corner of his eye Arish had been watching Jan, the thin, pale bully, who had walked away from the safety of the fires to piss. Though there was no sign of the pack, there was an unnatural silence which Arish found threatening.

Then, in the moment he saw a blur of movement and opened his mouth to yell, two dogs, running with amazing speed, attacked the boy. As if in a planned manouevre, one hit him in the legs, grabbing him by one ankle, while the other leaped from the other side, grabbing the boy by the throat. Jan gave one hysterical shriek before his throat was ripped out. He was dead before his body hit the earth. The rest of the pack arrived within moments, the big black dog among them, and they set about tearing pieces of meat off the carcase.

The horror had happened so quickly that the other boys were running to help, unaware that Jan was dead before they had even moved. Two boys, their swords out, reached the corpse at the same time as the other dogs arrived. One ran his sword through the dog which had Jan's leg in its jaws. The thrust was sure and the dog died instantly. Another, a grey animal with heavy, dripping jaws, leaped at the boy, then collapsed, whining, as Arish's sword hacked at its neck.

Arish shouted, "Back! Back!"

"We can take them!" Ranul cried, turning towards the black beast that was crouched at the corpse's shoulder, chewing, his tiny black eyes never leaving the boys.

"We can't, Ranul! If they attack as a pack we can't survive."

As Ranul approached the black leader, his eyes fixed to the dog's, his sword up, a second animal ran in suddenly from the side and leaped at the boy. Too late Ranul brought his arm up, but the beast missed its target and instead caught the boy by the upper arm. The two fell in a writhing, struggling heap and the other boys ran forward. A blow from the hilt of Ranul's sword forced the dog to let go and retreat. Ranul, his face white, blood pouring from bites in his arm, was helped back to the safety of the fires. Arish and Sami stood with swords raised, ready to spear any dog which followed, but the pack were only interested in dismembering Jan's body. The two boys backed away behind the fires.

Ranul tore off his sleeve and looked at the jagged wounds. His face was white as he wiped off the saliva and blood.

"We were lucky," he confessed. "By rights they could have had us all. Jan was stupid," he added. Arish thought he had been stupid too, but he said nothing.

When his wounds had been dressed, Ranul looked up at Arish. "Climbing a tree seems a good plan," he agreed. "But then what? We are still without water and food. Our people will not come looking for us for days. Then they will find only starved corpses hanging from a tree."

"One of us can run for rescue," Arish told him. "The dogs will not chase running meat if it is hanging in a tree just out of reach."

"One of us?"

"I will go."

"So you run to safety, Cub, while the rest of us act as bait?"

Masking his irritation, Arish shrugged. "You run then. Or Riis. Or Parr."

"It's a good plan," admitted Sami quietly. "And Arish is the fastest runner. He should go."

Eventually the dogs finished their meal and trotted away from the mess of red and white bones, no doubt seeking somewhere to rest. The boys all rested too, until the sun was high in the sky. Then they set off, burning brands in hand, each of them trying to look all ways at once, towards the treeline. At last they found a tree that was perfect. It had no branches lower down and the boys had to boost each other up. But the lowest branches, on which they perched, were heavy and thick, and ran parallel to the ground. When they were all safely up there, out of the pack's reach, they relaxed for the first time in two days. Except for Arish, who was busy packing all their remaining water into his backpack, with Sami's firesticks and a little dried meat. He glanced at the sun and saw he had several hours before it set. If he did not reach safety by then, he would have to find another tree to roost in.

The dogs were not in sight, which meant nothing, but even if they could see him he thought it was unlikely they would follow, with rich boy-meat in their bellies. His brain told him this, but his stomach was uncertain. Trying to think only of the map he held in his head, he slithered down the tree and without hesitation set off for the north-west.

For the first few leagues the boy ran with his heart in his throat, spooked by every sound. At times he was convinced he heard padding paws behind him, but when he looked round there was nothing. After a while he began to relax, his breathing became even and his stride lengthened. He ran with the falling sun at his left shoulder, and he rested that night in the branches of a giant oak.

When the sun reappeared the next morning, he realised he could see the blue roof of the Adamantine temple gleaming through the trees. He was only a short walk away from their target. He reached the building shortly after dawn and blurted out his story to the waiting soldiers. A detachment of riders, with spare horses, set off the way he described, and by sundown the five other boys had been brought back in safety. They were all, even

Ranul, laughing and joking about the close shave they'd had, preening themselves in front of the seasoned soldiers who had rescued them.

The next day the six boys were arrested and charged with killing the emperor's dogs, for which the penalty was death.

Chapter 22

It was just before dawn at Old Mountain and the sun still lingered below the jagged horizon. The sky above was the colour of opals but the land was dark. The mountains all around were painted in various shades of black, crowned or capped in wet grey mist. Between them the deep valleys, clothed in lush rainforest, lay waiting for the sun to adorn them in shining droplets of diamond and pearl.

Indaro was dressed in leathers and furs, but the moisture from the low-hanging clouds had seeped through the gaps in her clothing, dripping from her hair down under her collar, trickling into her boots. Her feet were bare in the fur-lined boots, because she liked to feel the soft rabbit pelt between her toes, but she had been standing on the mountain for more than an hour and the coney was starting to feel clammy against her skin.

She cleared her mind of thoughts of discomfort and closed her eyes. She could feel the sun's growing light on her face and soon she would feel its warmth. This was the fifth morning in a row she had made the long climb in semi-darkness up to the top of the mountain, hoping to see the sunrise. Sheeting rain and heavy cloud had been her reward on four occasions. Mason had predicted she would be lucky today, and it appeared he was right. Indaro stretched her spine, lifting her face, ready for the touch of the sun's rays. Nudged by the movement, a cold trickle of cloudwater ran down her back and she shuddered. She cleared her mind again and waited for the sun.

She waited and waited then, rising impatience bursting through her practised calm, she opened her eyes. Out of nowhere the mist to the east had thickened. Ahead of her the Gate of the Sun—the deep cleft between the mountains where the new sun should appear—had completely vanished under a blanket of cold dark cloud. There would be no sunrise today. Again.

Behind Indaro the two girls giggled and she turned and frowned down at them.

"I don't know why you think this is funny," she said grumpily. "It means you'll both have to climb up here again tomorrow."

They laughed out loud then, as though they could guess what she said. They both jumped up and, gesturing for her to follow, started bounding back down the mountain, confident and sure-footed in their hide boots despite the poor light. She trailed down more slowly, watching her feet, knowing they would have to wait for her to catch up. They were supposed to be her guards, after all.

This morning marked the end of her hundredth day of captivity.

At first she had tried to escape. In her small white cell there was a window, open and unbarred, high above her head, and she spent fruitless hours plotting how to reach it and wasted all her energy trying to do so. There was no furniture in the little room, only a clean mattress to sleep on and a bucket. Try as she might, she could find no way of fashioning an escape device with a soft mattress and a wooden bucket. But frustration led her to throw herself at the wall, leaping over and over again to reach the high sill. Twice she knocked herself out, and in compassion or perhaps irritation her captors finally moved her to a cell with no windows.

She had spent the first days in the prison at Old Mountain fearing the horrors of torture and slow death, then, as these fears slowly faded, they were replaced by anxiety for Doon and Fell and the others. But it was more than a month before she was able to ask after her friends, for none of her captors spoke her tongue. The women were small and neat, with dark skin and eyes, dressed uniformly in wool shirts and skirts, and they smiled at her when they brought her food and emptied the bucket. After a while she started talking to them, telling them about her father and the grey house on the Salient, and her brother Rubin, and her friendship with Doon, but she did not speak of the war or the battles she had endured. They listened to her politely, and she watched their eyes as she spoke, occasionally saying something to shock or surprise, but their faces stayed polite but bland and she truly believed they did not understand her.

On the first chill morning of autumn she had spent a sleepless night trying to keep warm under thin blankets when there was a knock at her cell door and, after a courteous delay, a man walked in carrying a pile of blankets and a second mattress.

He placed them on the bed, saying, "You'll need these. The nights will get colder."

Backed against the wall, she watched him, afraid for the first time in weeks. A man who spoke her language, and could understand her words. Would the interrogation start now? Was he what they were waiting for?

He looked around. "I meant to bring a stool to sit on," he told her, then shrugged and sat on the floor, his back to the closed door. He was beyond middle-age, burly, clean-shaven, with grey hair and a lantern jaw.

"My name is Mason," he said.

She was silent, and he added, "And you are Indaro Kerr Guillaume."

A thousand times she had contemplated her interrogation, particularly in the dark hours at dead of night, and she had resolved to say nothing, ask nothing. But, lulled by her treatment thus far, she found herself asking, "What of my friends? Are they alive?"

Mason nodded. "They are very much alive. Stalker had surgery on his ankle. He may be walking again soon, though he will always carry a limp, the surgeon tells me."

He watched her, waiting for another question, a comment, but she was silent and she remained wordless for many days.

Climbing back down the mountain in the dawn light she broke out from the jumble of thick vegetation onto the lip of a path where her two guards waited for her before plunging down the final stretch to their mountain home. Indaro paused, as she always did. Old Mountain sat on a sloping saddle of rock slung between two mountain peaks. At the highest end of the saddle were low grey buildings huddled around a massive stone keep. Lower down, to the west, the land sloped more steeply and had been terraced to offer flat terrain for crops. Sheep and goats were brown and white dots. On either side of the saddle, the cliffs dropped vertically to deep green river valleys far below. There was only one way up to Old Mountain, she had been told, which is why it had never been conquered. Taken by treachery, besieged and starved out, but never conquered.

Indaro looked around her at the jagged green and grey peaks stretching off into the distance on all sides. She could hear nothing but a distant bleating. She took a deep draught of morning air. Its cleanness and clarity fizzed through her veins like wine, and she wanted to laugh out loud. The two girls looked up at her.

"Let's go," she told them, and together they walked back down to her prison.

After that first visit Mason came to see her most days. She refused to speak to him and he seemed not to mind. He was happy to listen to his own voice, telling her stories of Old Mountain, tales of his childhood, musing on philosophy and history and the music of the stars. He seldom asked her questions, but when he did and she did not answer he would nod to himself, as if she had said something insightful, then carry on talking. She wondered who he was and why he was devoting so much time to a common soldier. He had been a warrior himself, she was sure, by the way he held himself and by his vocabulary. He spoke with no accent, and could have blended easily with the residents in the City. He was not dark-skinned like her little guards or the leader of the riders who had brought them here. But the enemy came in many skin shades. Mason was not a cruel man, she decided, but neither was he her friend.

One day he stopped coming, and she missed his visits more than she would have expected. The subsequent days crept by with appalling slowness until one morning a guard, whom she called Gala, entered the cell with a pile of books in her arms. She squatted and placed them neatly in the corner of the cell and, gesturing to them, said, "Mase." She tipped her head and Indaro nodded. "Mason," she said. "From Mason."

They were all on the subject she had listened to him talk about so many times—the history of Old Mountain and its people. But their range was wider and deeper, and the books dealt with not only far-ago history but more recent days, their allied neighbours, and politics. Reading for hours each day she absorbed the stories uncritically. And when she first read about the City she did not recognise it immediately, for it had another name. When she realised what she was reading about she threw the book down in disgust.

On Gala's next visit Indaro pressed the books into her arms and gestured for her to take them away. She was offended that Mason believed her so naïve, such an easy dupe.

The next day he arrived at her cell at the usual time, the wooden stool in one hand.

"You didn't want the books I sent you?" he asked, seating himself against the door.

"I am not a fool, Mason," she said, although she knew it was pride talking and he had used it against her to make her speak.

"I was not aware I had treated you like one."

She convinced herself she was justified in speaking in defence of the City.

"I am not a child to be influenced by . . . fantasies of the tyrannical City and the peace-loving Blues."

He shrugged and spread his hands. "I thought you must be bored and I found some books for you. This is a fortress, not your Great Library. There were few books to be had, particularly in your tongue. I'm sure you are familiar with all the arguments for and against the war, and whether it can be prolonged without the deaths of all of us. I'm sure these are common currency among both our peoples, in inns and homes throughout the City as they are in our own. I did not seek to offend you by offering you such familiar arguments."

She thought he was mocking her, and she looked at him narrowly and did not reply. She resolved to speak no more.

As if he knew what was in her mind he stood and picked up the stool. "We have started off badly today. I shall go away and come back tomorrow."

As a soldier she had cursed the City daily, as was her right, but she would not listen to an enemy criticise her home or belittle the sacrifice of so many of her comrades. She grew angry thinking about it, yet when Mason next visited she found it impossible to harness that anger to her cause.

When he had settled himself on his wooden stool, he said, "You call your enemy Blues, or Blueskins, yet in fact there are a dozen nations and cities allied against the City. The Odrysian alliance alone includes Buldekki, Fkeni, Panjali, even some remaining Garians."

She said, "The first great battle we fought was against the Tanaree tribesmen who painted their faces with blue dye. When others joined their fight we just kept calling them Blueskins. You call us Rats. It is a convenient way to speak of the enemy. It has no significance."

"Dunghill Rats. Yes, we do call you that. Do you know when that first battle was?"

"Long ago. Before the City came under siege."

"It was many centuries ago. The City had encroached on tribal lands over the centuries, arrogantly taking minerals for its furnaces, and livestock for the citizens' bellies. The Tanaree were a harsh people with unforgiving ways. They practised vendetta even among themselves. Then they chose a leader who declared that for each tribesman killed they would kill ten City warriors. So the City poured more soldiers into the area. The Tanaree are all dead now, long since wiped out."

"It is a foolish thing, to take on the City," said Indaro proudly.

Mason shook his head. "A millennium ago the City lived in harmony with its neighbours. Now it is a great bloated spider which has killed most of them and sits in the midst of a wasteland. For hundreds of leagues around it the land has been fought over so many times that the land is barren, home only to the dead and dying. This is what you are fighting for, Indaro."

"The City wants peace, but peace with honour." It was a well-worn phrase. But she thought of the generals, and the contempt in which they were held by the common soldier, for the way they threw thousands of troops away on hare-brained schemes and doomed ventures. And she knew it was a lie.

"There can never be peace while Araeon is emperor," Mason replied.

Indaro was offended by an enemy's casual use of the emperor's name. "You speak of peace yet you attack us on all sides. Most of my friends and comrades, most of the people I have ever known, have died at your hands. You will only be content when the City has fallen and all its people are dead."

He shook his head again. "We do not want that. Many of us respect the City and its history. But Araeon places himself behind the walls of the Keep, in the centre of the Red Palace, deep in the heart of the City. He hides behind his people. They die for him in their thousands. And we will not rest until *he* is dead."

"We?" she repeated. "Who is 'we'? Do you claim to represent the Blues, Mason? Here in this abandoned fortress at the arse-end of nowhere? Are you speaking for the allied Blueskin armies?" she asked mockingly.

He answered her gravely. "Yes, I do represent the Blues, some of them anyway, some men who still have power and influence. And this old fort was chosen deliberately. It might not look impressive now, but it was once the centre of a great kingdom. Perhaps it will be again. If our plans to end the war are successful."

What plans, she wanted to ask. But she would not give him the satisfaction. Instead she said, "The Immortal craves peace, but not on his enemy's terms."

He laughed. "Have you met the Immortal?" he asked. "You are so certain you know what is in his mind." He leaned forward. "Would you even know the emperor if you saw him?"

Indaro thought back to the ill-fated day when she and Broglanh had joined the Thousand. It seemed like years ago. She remembered a fair man, bearded, tall. A man who was certainly dead now, whoever he was.

"I saw him recently," she said.

Mason looked at her thoughtfully. He was quiet for a while. Then he said, "I know people, people who are now very old," he said slowly, as if choosing his words carefully, "who told me of the City when it was at its peak, a beacon of civilisation in a barbaric time. All its people were literate and its schools and libraries educated the world. The City's parks were legendary, stocked with rare and endangered animals. Its buildings were roofed with bronze and copper. The great river flowed through the centre, not underground as a sewer, as it is now. It was a thoroughfare for great ships from cities beyond the seas."

She shook her head. "You are speaking of a place which never existed, except in children's storybooks, or in someone's hopes and dreams."

He shrugged. "Perhaps you are right," he admitted. "But it *is* in decline. You cannot deny that. And all the while Araeon lives the City will continue that decline."

She leaned forward and spat out, "*You* are the reason for the City's decline, our enemy, the Blueskins. The Immortal wants only peace for his people."

Mason smiled thinly. "Then why did he start the war?"

"The war had been going on for centuries. You cannot blame the emperor for that."

"How long *has* he ruled, Indaro?"

"I don't know. A very long time. He was emperor when I was small. I saw him once at my father's house."

"How old was he then?"

She thought about it. "Perhaps in his thirties, forties. I was a child and my mind's eye is probably unreliable."

"And when you saw him recently?"

"A man in his fifties," she said, remembering the Immortal climbing into the black carriage, his hair golden, or was it silver? "Sixty maybe."

"Yet you told me this emperor is the only ruler your father has ever known. How old is your father?"

Had she said that? Her father was very old, by far the oldest man she knew. She didn't like to admit she didn't know.

Mason said, "He is an old man. He had a wife before your mother?"

"Yes."

"More than one?"

"Yes."

"And children?"

"Yes."

"Do you know them, these children of former wives?"

"They are all dead, I believe."

She was uncertain. The emperor must be older than her father, yet the man she saw was only half his age. She remembered a phrase used by the old wives who gossiped in the kitchens of the Salient—"back when the Immortal was a boy." It always meant time out of mind, unknown ages ago. But it was just an expression.

She recalled a conversation with Fell. She said to Mason, trying to sound authoritative, "The emperor has decoys, proxies, maybe many of them. The chances are the man I saw was *not* the emperor."

"You are missing the point. Your father is, what, eighty or more? So the emperor must be older than that. Yet these decoys are younger men. A baffling royal policy."

"Perhaps the emperor is vain and he prefers to wear a younger public face. It would be surprising if he did not. Men have their vanities."

"But by that thinking he can never afford to be seen in public, if he is in his dotage and his proxies are men in their prime."

"Perhaps that is the case," she replied, feeling uneasy. She wondered again why Mason came to the cell every day, spending time with her, trying to change her perception of the City and its emperor. What did it matter to him what she believed?

"What is your argument?" she asked him. "That the Immortal has been emperor for longer than the ages of men? Perhaps," she smiled, joking, "he *is* immortal?"

When he made no reply, simply raising his eyebrows, she said impatiently, "Only the weak-minded and superstitious believe he cannot die. It is merely a title. He is a man, like you."

"No, Indaro, I'm not saying the emperor is immortal. But he is *not* a man like me."

Fell's cell was built of cold stone, and its small barred window looked out onto the central courtyard of the keep at ground level. When it rained hard, and it rained a lot in Old Mountain, water ran in through the window, flowed across the floor and out under the heavy wooden door. The room was too small for the three soldiers, and it was cold, and the damp sank into their bones as the days cooled further. Garret had developed a racking cough. Stalker had not recovered as well after his surgery as Fell had hoped, and the northlander spent most of his days lying on his bed staring at the low ceiling. Each of them had a thin mattress, raised on a pallet above the damp floor, and they were fed regularly if frugally.

No one spoke to them, and their food came in and their bucket went out through a sliding grille contraption in the metal door. On one chill day in autumn several blankets were pushed in. Handing them out, Fell decided it would be a long winter.

It was the next day when the cell door was thrown open and two armed guards walked in. One of them pointed to Fell and gestured with his head. Fell glanced past them at other armed men outside, then he went with them. The other two prisoners watched him wordlessly.

As he walked in the centre of the group of armed men, a mixture of feelings swirled in his chest. He was glad the long wait was over, and he hoped to find out what had happened to Indaro, and why they were being kept there. He did not fear interrogation. A captive for more than three months, he could tell the enemy nothing about troop deployments or strategies—not that he could have revealed much before. But he was a cautious man, and it was with concern that he contemplated his future at the hands of a group of armed men who were his enemy.

He was led across the wide stone square in front of the keep. He looked up at it. It was built of massive stones carved precisely to fit together without mortar. They were green with lichen and moss, and he guessed the keep was very old. There were no windows on the side he could see, just a featureless wall with a single door, high but narrow, up a steep flight of steps.

As he was about to enter the door, guards in front of him and behind, he paused as if to look round. The guard at his back bumped into him, cursed in his own tongue and shoved Fell through the doorway. Poorly trained, Fell realised with interest. Big bearded men bristling with weaponry, but without the basic knowledge to keep clear of their prisoner. I could have killed him then, and one or two others, he thought. His spirits rose, and for the first time in weeks he started to plan.

He was taken up several flights into a bare room furnished with just a table and two hard chairs. A clean-shaven man was seated at the desk.

"Please sit down," he said politely. "My name is Mason."

Fell nodded with equal politeness. "I am Fell Aron Lee."

Mason offered, "And you command, I should say commanded, the company of the Third Maritime who called themselves the Wildcats."

Fell nodded.

"Under general Flavius Randell Kerr."

"Yes."

"What is your opinion of Randell Kerr, as a soldier?"

"He is a general, not a soldier."

Fell had decided not to restrict himself only to name and rank. If he escaped, *when* he escaped, he wanted it to be with as much information as possible. He could not win information by staying silent.

Mason smiled. "I am not interrogating you."

"You are asking me questions."

Mason spread his hands. "I am merely making small talk."

"I am sure you have more interesting things to do than make small talk. I know I have. The lice won't pick themselves from my clothes."

Mason wrote something on the paper in front of him and looked up.

"I have an obsession with the past, I admit it," he told Fell confidingly.

"When I first arrived at Old Mountain, more than a year ago, I had always dreamed of coming to this place. I had an important role here and outwardly, I hope, I appeared confident and efficient. But in my heart was the glee of a five-year-old opening a birthday gift. Each day I listened to the silence, for there is a great deal of silence here, you will have noticed it. It must be very different from the life you are used to, in battle and in the confines of the City, which we call the dunghill, or the Rats' nest, I'm sure you know. Each day I revelled in the silence of this fortress and thought that I could hear in its depths the footfalls of the people who built it, thousands of years before."

He gazed at Fell, who watched him expressionlessly.

"They were great builders and mathematicians," Mason went on, "and they have left us many marvels carved in the eternal rock. They worshipped the stars, and believed the sun and the moon were also stars, whose eternal paths happened to pass close by our world. They communicated with each other in a language that has been lost to us, but we have thousands of examples of their script, which is elegant and beautiful, and which our scholars still struggle to decipher. People throughout the world admire the Tuomi. Except the people of the City, for they have not heard of them. They know of nothing beyond their walls. Do they?" Fell made no reply.

"It is my hope," Mason added pleasantly, "that when this war is over, or perhaps if it is still continuing, I will visit your City and walk in its streets and hear the footsteps of its past. Perhaps you will join me."

Fell smiled to himself. Better and better, he thought. A man who likes to hear himself talk. I have already won two valuable pieces of information today.

When Doon came awake on the third morning after her escape from Old Mountain, it was long after sunrise. She opened her eyes to see watery daylight filtering through the gaps between the mouldy planks of her shelter. She sat up, groaning at the ache in her back, then she shuddered as she felt the scuttling of insects which had worked their way into her clothes as she slept. She leaped up and brushed herself down convulsively, then, feeling something crawling across her back, she dragged off Indaro's red jerkin and shook it out. A centipede as fat as her finger fell and scuttled away. She took the rest of her clothes off and shook each piece out, then put them back on swiftly as the cold damp air started soaking into her bones. Last of all Doon shook out her boots. She glanced with concern at the soles before she put them on. They were badly worn and would not last her much longer. She could not survive in this unforgiving country without boots.

The hut she had sheltered in the previous night was barely standing. Its wooden walls were wet with damp. Great blooms of fungus clung to the planks like living creatures, and writhing vines had invaded the rotting roof. It was only slightly better than sleeping out in the forest, which had been her only other option.

She lifted down a red-stained parcel hung on a roof beam and unwrapped the cloth in which she had reserved some berries from the previous day. When she had discovered them, big and crimson and succulent, she had hesitantly eaten a few, waited for a while to see if they poisoned her then, reassured, ate them hungrily. When her belly could handle no more she had picked several handfuls and taken them with her to break her fast the next day. But when she opened the cloth she found the berries had already started to rot and were covered with a thin grey film like a spider's web. Disgusted, her stomach rebelling, she threw them down. She gathered up her two knives and stepped out into the light, glad to be leaving the miserable night shelter.

She sat on the edge of the cliff, listening to the ever-present ear-piercing shriek of birds and the chattering and shuffling sounds from the lush dense undergrowth. She was feeling tired and defeated. Since she had escaped from the mountain fortress she had travelled ever west, towards the setting sun, believing that if she journeyed for long enough she would eventually reach the City. She felt that if she took a north-south route—though many had presented themselves to her for she had crossed several rivers—then she would soon be lost. But the terrain in her path, to the west, always seemed to be the most difficult, as she climbed high hillsides and struggled down their far slopes, wrestling always with the impenetrable cloudforest in her path. Although she had plenty of water and enough food, she was feeling weaker by the day. For the first time she let herself wonder if she would die in this ghastly place, her body swiftly eaten by the running, slithering and creeping creatures she saw all the time. As a soldier she had spent more of her life sleeping on the ground than in a bed, and she was used to sharing her blanket with insects and small animals. But she had never experienced the rich, and terrifying, abundance of life in this forest. In her long-ago in-fanthood, before her life at the Salient with Indaro, she had lived on a farm in the far south of the City, where her people struggled from sunrise to dusk to persuade thin rocky soil to bring forth green plants. Here, she thought, in this fertile greenery, she could throw a seed on the soil and watch it instantly throw down its roots and climb for the skies.

She hated it, and part of her yearned for the harsh battle plain they had left months before, where the bones of their comrades would now be drying cleanly.

She was not used to being alone, yet she had been on her own for nearly a hundred days now. After their capture and their betrayal by Saroyan the five prisoners, surrounded by enemy cavalry, had ridden towards the distant eastern peaks. It had taken them days to get there, then half their party had peeled off, riding for the north, while Doon and Indaro and the others had been taken across the foothills then through a high pass in the mountains, then on again ever east. They had travelled across wide rivers and a cool high plain before coming to these highlands and, eventually, this lush forest with its roaring waters.

They had been fed, not well, but enough to keep them strong enough to ride. Stalker had lapsed into unconsciousness and slid off his horse as they reached the high plain. Doon had feared they would simply leave him there to die, but they slung the northlander across a horse and, a grey rider on either side of him, moved on.

The other four were separated during the day and at night they were too tired to talk, slumping off their horses and into blessed sleep, their aching bodies given only the hours of darkness to recuperate. Doon fell victim to ague, shivering and sweating alternately, and found it hard to stay in the saddle. Indaro hovered anxiously, checking the wound to her thigh time after time, fearing an infection. She gave Doon her bright red jacket to wear, perhaps to keep her warm, perhaps to give comfort.

Fell stayed silent day after day. He had no orders to offer.

Then, as they were riding higher and higher one day, dusk started to gather, but the troopers did not stop. Still they went on, riding in darkness with only the stars to light them. Finally they saw lights ahead and their horses' hooves were clattering on echoing stones. Walls loomed above them. Throughout the ride Doon had assumed that when they reached their prison she and Indaro would be gaoled together. It had never occurred to her that she would be alone. That, more than anything, fuelled her need to escape.

For the long days of her captivity she had waited for the first interrogation, ignoring the small women who brought her food each day, lying on her bed staring at the ceiling. Then the day had come and she acted. A big bearded guard had followed the small woman into the room. He gestured to her to come with him. Doon had swung her legs slowly off the bed, as if tired or sluggish, then she punched the big man in the jaw. As he went down she knocked the frightened woman unconscious before grabbing the soldier's knife and gutting him with it. She darted to the door and peered round, expecting more guards. But there were none. Quickly she dragged the guard's clothes off and put them on, including the heavy helm. She knew she would not pass even a casual inspection, but night was falling. She locked the door of the cell behind her and walked self-consciously towards the main gate of the fortress. She had watched from her window often enough to know the way. Then she waited in the shadows, watching the gate, watching for her chance, fearing every moment the alarm would be raised. Finally the gates opened to let in a convoy of carts bearing food. Doon merely walked across the courtyard and out the gates. It was one of the easiest things she had ever done.

Now, sitting on the cliff, staring down at the river, she knew what she had to do. She could not keep on moving west. The going was too hard. She could not find enough sustaining food, and her boots were giving out. The only chance was to climb down to the river then follow its course, maybe find a boat and see where the waters took her.

Her mind made up, she stood, her heart lighter, and started to search for a way down.

Chapter 23

In later years Shuskara had never mentioned their first meeting, when Fell was the child Arish, son of the Lion of the East, a man recently deceased. The second meeting between general and boy was very different.

Arish and the other boys were taken down to the deepest dungeons of the Red Palace. Fearing what would be done to them, at first they dreaded reaching their destination but, after trudging through leagues of tunnels, leading ever downwards, Arish for one started to yearn for rest. After the voyage of emotions of the last few days, the terrified flight from the dogs, then elation, then fear again, the boys—the eldest barely into manhood, the youngest only a child—were exhausted.

The fair-haired boy was stumbling along silently when suddenly he fell as if poleaxed and lay still in a pool of filth. The rest straggled to a halt, bumping into one another, hampered by heavy chains. One of the guards kicked the child, but he remained motionless. The other prisoners stared at one another for a long moment and it was Sami who said, with some reluctance, "I will carry him." It was a difficult manouevre, with shackles around his waist and wrists, but he managed to get the boy into his arms. The guards watched him indifferently. Then they set off again, shuffling because of the shortened chains.

At last the boys were herded into a cell and left, still chained together. There was barely room for them and they found, in the pitch-black, that along one wall ran a channel with pungent water which flowed in one side of the cell and out the other. The small chamber stank of damp, excrement and fear, and the sweet rotten smell of decaying bodies. Once the door was opened and they were given a jug of water. That was all they lived on for three days.

Then, when they were certain they had been left to die, the door opened to a blinding flare of torches and a voice demanded, "Who is your leader?"

They all feared what might be done to a leader and there was silence in the cell.

The voice said, "Sharpish! Or I'll take the first I grab to speak for you all."

"I am the leader," Arish announced as he stepped forward. No one argued.

The way up was much shorter than the way down, but it involved many stone steps, and Arish, racked by hunger and thirst, moved in a haze of pain and misery. He wondered if he was to be killed that day, and the thought was not unwelcome.

He was brought to a small square room where the stench of the sewers was partly masked by the smoke of torches and scent of herbs crushed underfoot. The walls had been whitewashed recently, for the smell of paint lingered. There was a wooden table and two chairs. A man sat waiting. He looked up as Arish entered, and said, with satisfaction in his voice, "I thought it would be you, boy."

The wave of relief which flowed through Arish was so powerful that his legs nearly gave way under him. It was Shuskara, his friend and hero from childhood, now the greatest general in the City. This man would not see him tortured to death for killing dogs.

"Sit," the general ordered. Arish slumped gratefully onto the wooden seat. Shuskara gazed at him. "Have you been fed?" he asked. Arish shook his head.

"Food and water," the general ordered a guard, who saluted sketchily and left.

Shuskara waited until the boy had drunk his fill, and eaten the meat and bread brought for him. Occasionally he stood and paced around the room. As the food took effect, Arish felt his mind clearing, and he noticed the general was greyer, his face more lined with care, than when he had last seen him. He was dressed in civilian clothes, comfortable soft shirt and trousers in shades of grey. The brawny old man could have passed for a farmer or a blacksmith.

Finally Shuskara sat down again and spoke. Arish heard his voice was gruff with some unexpressed emotion.

"I saved your life when you were a child," he started abruptly. Arish nodded and opened his mouth to thank him, but the general cut him off. "But I do not know if I can save you this time, boy."

Arish frowned. He could not comprehend the words. Shuskara was the highest general in the land. Surely he could do anything? Save a man's life, or condemn him.

"They were just dogs," he muttered, aware that he sounded sulky.

"They were not just dogs, boy. They were the emperor's dogs."

"But how could we know that?"

"You were on the emperor's land. Therefore they were the emperor's dogs."

Arish opened his mouth to argue, but common sense cut in. He had not reached his majority without learning something of how the City worked. They were the emperor's dogs because the emperor said they were. There was no point debating it.

"Will you speak for us?" he asked his friend.

Shuskara lowered his greying head, and Arish thought a great burden must be on the man's back.

"No," the general said, shaking his head. "You must understand, Arish, that to speak for you is to speak against the emperor, and that means certain death. The only one who can argue for you is an advocate, who is considered immune from a charge of treason for the purposes of a trial." He shook his head again. "At least, that is the theory."

"Do you know of such an advocate?"

Instead of answering, the general asked, "Do you not wonder, boy, why I helped you when you were a child, why I try to help you now?"

In truth, Arish had not. When he was a child he was too young to question other people's motives. Now he was too scared and miserable to wonder why a great warrior like Shuskara should descend into this hell to help him. He felt ashamed.

"Why do you, sir?" he asked meekly.

"Because I owe a life to your father."

"I did not know my father."

"Yes, you did, Arish. You just do not remember him."

"He sent me to a foreign city to be a hostage, a slave, when I was four years old. I do not try to remember him."

Shuskara shrugged. "It was the convention in the old days, when there was still peace, of sorts, between the City and some of its neighbours. The tributary kings sent their sons to the emperor's court to be educated and trained in the arts of war."

"They call us guests, but in truth we are hostages," Arish said bitterly.

"Yes, hostages for the good behaviour of the king. Yet your father rebelled and you are still alive. As are the others. You are the last. All your fathers are dead, most of them under the swords of the City's warriors. Yet the emperor has not had you killed. Do you never wonder why, the six of you, when you talk at night?"

"Perhaps that is the purpose of this trial."

Shuskara looked annoyed. "Nonsense, boy! You have a better head than that. If the emperor decided to kill you you would be dead in a heartbeat. He does not need reasons."

"Then why?"

The general leaned forward again, resting his elbows on the table. "I do not know. The Immortal does not confide in me. But I believe he is conflicted. He sees you as a potential threat, yet he still yearns for the days when the world paid him tribute and sent its sons to him to be educated, when his court was the hub of culture and commerce for the known world." He shook his head. "This has not been the case in my lifetime. But you are the last reminders of the days before the darkness fell and the City stood alone against the rest of the world."

"Then he should treat us with honour."

"Perhaps he has plans for the six of you."

"There were eight of us. Two were ripped apart by the dogs. Some plan."

Shuskara sat back and sighed wearily. "Perhaps he just wants you dead."

"Perhaps he is insane," Arish whispered.

"Do not say that to anyone, boy, even to your friends."

They sat in silence for a while. Shuskara called for more water and some wine. He offered wine to the boy, who had never before taken wine and turned it down.

"How did you know my father?" Arish asked at last.

"I was raised in his court."

"You are my countryman?"

The general smiled. "No. My father was a mercenary. He came from the City originally, but he fought for the highest bidder for his services throughout the world. His name was famous in those days, although I doubt anyone alive has ever heard it.

"His name was Adrakian. There came a time when he needed somewhere safe to settle his wife and children. Your grandfather, who was then Lion of the East, offered him sanctuary in return for his services. I lived at the Lion's Palace for ten years."

"What happened to Adrakian?"

The general sighed. "Few mercenaries make old bones. He was killed in an ambush while escorting a convoy of silk intended for the palace bedchambers. It was an easy little job. The attackers were common criminals. Adrakian was hit on the temple by a thrown club. He died half a year later, paralysed and drooling."

"No end for a soldier," Arish responded formally. In the silence he asked, "Why do you owe my father a life?"

Whenever he was taken to see Mason, Fell schooled himself not to ask about Arish, or react to any mention of the name. He knew his former life had a bearing on his imprisonment, but if he seemed uninterested they could not use it as leverage.

He nodded to Mason, then sat down in his chair, took the glass of wine offered, and asked affably, "What are we to talk about today?"

Mason stared at the ceiling as if he had not thought of the matter until that moment. "Your peculiar allegiance to the City and its emperor," he said finally, "despite everything it has done to you."

"I am the City's loyal son," Fell repeated, as he had done a dozen times.

"Yet you are not of the City."

Fell nodded.

"It seems to me, Fell," Mason said, "that you hold more resentment for your father, for sending you to the City, than you do for the emperor, for killing your father."

Fell shrugged. He genuinely didn't care.

"The early resentment," Mason went on, "the child's emotion, is still stronger for you than that of the man."

Fell stared at the ceiling. "I am not given to self-examination," he said. "And I have no interest in your attempts to get inside my mind. It is unnecessary. I am hiding nothing. If you want to know anything about me, just ask."

"I already know everything about you."

Fell thought that unlikely, but he said, "Then you know I am a soldier. I have spent my life in the service of the City. I am its loyal son. But if I wanted to raise a rebellion, if that is what you hope of me, then I could not. My army is gone, my company is dead, except for four souls. I could no more lead an army against the emperor than could a beggar in the streets of Lindo."

Mason nodded thoughtfully. "You are right. But you misunderstand me. There is only one man alive who can turn the armies against Araeon and it is not you, Fell."

Fell stayed silent, waiting.

"A soldier of genius and charisma, a general all the warriors of the City would follow if he were to ask them, a man who, I believe, would be glad to see the emperor die for all the wrongs committed against him, and against the people of the City."

Fell shook his head. "If you are speaking of Shuskara, then he is dead."

"No, he is not."

"He lives?" For the first time Fell wanted to believe this man.

"My agents have seen him. His resentment against the emperor is great. With a few good men at his side he could lead a rebellion which would destroy Araeon and the ruling Families."

"Then he doesn't need me."

"But he is slow to trust, obviously."

Fell found sarcasm rising irresistibly. "He doesn't trust enemy plotters who ask him to conspire with them against the emperor. You amaze me."

Mason smiled thinly. "He trusts only his daughter—and you."

"He has no daughter."

"When did you last see him?"

Fell did not have to think about it. "Fifteen years ago, the Battle of Trassic Fields. We destroyed the Blues, an army of Buldekki tribesmen financed by the Odrysians."

"And afterwards Shuskara dismissed you as his aide, after ten years at his side."

The memory still burned. "Yes."

"You were given command of the company they now call the Pit Wolves. Shuskara said you were as a son to him and it was time to further your own career, that one day you would be a general."

How can he know this? Fell wondered. No one else knew of the conversation.

Mason smiled. "It is not hard to guess," he confessed. "And soldiers gossip like old wives. Everyone knew Shuskara and Fell Aron Lee were as father and son. Everyone knew he wanted to keep you close, like a son, but knew you had to make your own path. He saw you as a future general. Everyone did. In those days.

"My point, Fell, is that a lot of blood has passed under the bridge since you last saw him. The general was tried, tortured, imprisoned, his family slaughtered. Now he lives quietly under a new name out of the gaze of the emperor. His daughter is adopted. But Shuskara trusts you, and he has his own reasons to want the emperor to fall."

"You have spoken to him?"

"No. It is impossible for a foreigner to enter the City these days. It is a place of dread and mistrust. But messages can pass in and out, with effort."

Fell stood to stretch his shoulders and back, and paced around the small room. He had no reason to believe this man, and every reason not to. Despite himself, he was intrigued. He walked behind Mason, who did not turn to face him, or tense.

"Let me be sure I understand," Fell said. "You want me to return to the City, find Shuskara, and tell him we should turn the armies and take the City, killing the emperor—because our enemy wants us to? This is your plan?" He laughed, feeling some of the stress falling from his shoulders.

"You pledged once to kill the emperor."

"I was a child."

"You were thirteen, almost a man, and had just watched a friend suffer a hideous death."

Fell felt the brand on his chest itching, and resisted the urge to touch it.

"There were five of you, and you all endured the pain of the brand, even the youngest, because you believed the emperor was evil and should die. Are your convictions less strong now than they were then?"

He didn't wait for an answer. "Of course they are. We all make compromise with age. You forgot that pledge and got on with your life. For you were privileged, aide to the famous Shuskara, friend to the greatest man in the land. Why would you remember a child's vow when you had so much to lose?"

Fell sat down again but he said nothing.

"Do you think they all forgot, Fell?"

"Apparently, for thirty years have passed and the Immortal still lives."

He looked into Mason's eyes and thought he saw contempt there, but he reminded himself that this man was trying to manipulate him.

"Would you like to know what happened to them? Ranul and Evan and Riis and Parr?"

"Not really," Fell replied. "I would like to return to my cell. You are mistaken if you think I have anything to offer you, or you me."

F ell."

The wall was plastered and had once been painted white. But it was damp and much of the paint had bubbled and fallen off, leaving the dark grey plaster wall with leprous pale patches. Fell had looked at that same small piece of wall every day for more than a hundred days. He knew its islands and oceans and voyaging chips of paint better than he knew his own face. It was home to him, somewhere to retreat to away from the sounds and smells of the two men in the cell with him. He stared at the wall map and in it travelled in his mind to past glories, battles won, women known, friends remembered.

"Fell!"

They had stopped calling him "Sir." Had he told them to? He couldn't remember. There had been so many conversations. For the first few weeks in the cell they had talked all the time to relieve the boredom and to help Stalker deal with the pain of his shattered ankle. They talked first about the battles they had come through, then about their families and homelands and the women they had known. Then Garret and, eventually, Stalker started to tell of their fears and hopes, the familiar plans so many soldiers cherish, for a farm, a few horses, a family of their own.

"Fell!"

He rolled over. "Yes."

The cell was barely big enough for the three narrow pallets. There was one along each wall, leaving a rectangular space where the inward-swinging door opened. In that space each of them exercised diligently in turn every day to keep their muscles strong. But the beds were not long enough for Fell or Stalker, and the ceiling was too low for them to stand upright. Each time Fell was taken from the cell he revelled in the chance to walk tall, to stretch his back and shoulders. Neither Stalker nor Garret had left the cell in weeks, and the confinement was bearing down on Stalker particularly. He had been restricted to his pallet while his bones healed, and now he was able to move about, but could not, his leg muscles twitched and crawled as he tried to sleep, and he was subject to agonising cramps, waking his cell mates nightly with yelps of pain. Stalker's torture was affecting them all, and Fell knew he would have to do something about it.

He had made two escape attempts. The first time he was being marched to see Mason and he waited until a guard was close behind him then spun on his heel, crushing the man's throat with his elbow before making a break for the northern wall of the fortress. He had eventually been cornered by six men at swordpoint. After that, before he was allowed out of his cell he had to thrust his hands through the hole in the door to be chained. Nevertheless, with hands chained in front of him he had clubbed down two guards and snatched a sword before holing up in a corner of a small sunlit courtyard. It was two days before they winkled him out, weak from thirst. Now he was chained with his hands behind him until they reached Mason's interrogation room, when he was shackled by the legs to a metal ring in the floor before his hands were released. He had toyed with the plan of capturing Mason and holding him for ransom, but suspected the door guards would merely leave the man to die.

When he rolled over to look at Stalker he guessed the northlander was going to complain again about his confinement.

"What?" he asked discouragingly.

But the man surprised him. "I've got an escape plan," Stalker said.

Fell sat up. "Let's hear it." Garret sat up too, ever eager.

"Well." Stalker carefully swung his feet to the floor. "The next time you go to see your friend Mason. To take a glass of wine with him." He paused to underline his point and Fell nodded impatiently. "Ask the man if we can have an urquat board and counters and dice. He'd hardly deny you that."

"If they have such a thing. Why?" Fell asked.

"Oh, and a dead cat," Stalker added.

Fell sighed and leaned back, closing his eyes.

"Then," Stalker went on without a trace of humour, "we can use the cat gut and bones to make a slingshot, and kill the guards by shooting the dice at them. Then we use the board to make wings and one of us can fly away from here and come back with an army to rescue the others."

Fell twitched his face muscles into a mirthless smile. But Garret leaped to his defence. "Don't you think Fell would get us out of here if he could?"

Stalker glared at him, and Fell felt irritated too. Over the months it was hard to know which was more annoying, Stalker's constant griping or Garret's good cheer. He turned over to stare at the wall again, but Stalker would not leave it.

"Mason's given you a chance, man," he said urgently to Fell's back. "He wants something of you. It means you have leverage."

Fell sat up again. Reining in his anger, he asked calmly, "Are you out of your mind? Assuming I agree to his scheme and convince him that *he* has convinced *me* to kill the emperor, and he lets me go back to the City, do you think he will free you too? Why would he? You would be hostages for my good behaviour. When I returned to the City and it became clear the emperor had *not* been assassinated, then he would kill you and the women in a heartbeat."

Stalker shrugged. "Then at least we'd be out of this pigging cell."

Chapter 24

When the gods first walked upon this land, when the stars were young and the world was new, they stepped out of their ships in the great harbour and strode up to the hilltop. As was their custom, they captured an animal, a man, and roasted him alive until his screams stopped, then divided him up among them and ate the sweet meat. They agreed that the meat was good and the land was fertile, and they elected to stay.

At first the people of the land feared them, as well they might, and ran from them. But over time they found the gods had much to teach them, they had much to learn, and they could profit from learning. So they were taught to trap and snare the wild beasts, to herd and domesticate the meek ones, to grow crops and to make wine and ale. Then they learned the wonders of mathematics, the pleasures of philosophy, and the beauty of art. And the gods taught them to wage war on their neighbours more efficiently.

So the people worshipped their gods and everyone was happy.

Eons passed; the City rose and fell and rose again.

As the people learned to be more like gods, so some of the gods became more like people, and forgot they were gods and bred with the men and women of the City. Their descendants were not immortal, but they lived very long lives and they bred among themselves to strengthen this gift. Some of these started to call themselves gods and were killed by the true gods for their arrogance. The others remained arrogant, but kept their thoughts to themselves.

Over time the people's devotion to their deities started to fail. Some even declared they did not exist. These were killed and eaten, but the world was a very fierce place and the non-believers declared it just a coincidence. Belief in the gods continued to founder and some of the temples fell into ruin and, one by one, the gods returned to their ships and left the land to seek somewhere new where they would be honoured and loved and feared.

The only gods left were those too old and tired to move on (for even the gods become old, given enough time), or those who most loved the people of the City, or those who still perceived a profit in staying. These were the weakest of them and in time their names were forgotten, their existence forgotten.

Their descendants, who had banded together and bred together to strengthen their bloodlines, formed seven Families, and these Families ruled the City for millennia. In a very long life you could accumulate a great deal of power, and many descendants to support you and, sometimes even, wisdom.

Of the seven Families, two died out centuries ago, Kerr and Broglanh.

"But I know people called Kerr." Arish interrupted Shuskara's narrative as they sat in the whitewashed room above the palace dungeons. "There is Flavius Randell Kerr, your friend."

"Flavius is not my friend," replied Shuskara. "But yes, there are many

Kerrs, including Reeve Kerr Guillaume, once one of the emperor's closest advisors. But they are long-ago scions of the Kerr family tree and they are careful to make no claims to belong to a ruling Family.

"The others," he went on, "are of course, Araeon of the Family Sarkoy, and Guillaume, Vincerus, Gaeta, and Khan. Of these Sarkoy and Vincerus are the most powerful. You know these names well, of course."

"And there is a delicate balance of power," said Arish eagerly, keen to show he understood the City's politics. "They furnish the City's armies. More than two-thirds of the armed forces are supplied by the emperor and the Vincerii, including the Maritime, a Sarkoy army, and the Adamantine, a Vincerus army."

Shuskara nodded. "And I have finally come to my point," he told the boy. "Your advocate is of the Family Vincerus. She is . . ."

"She!" cried Arish, appalled. "A woman? What use is a woman to us?"

Shuskara's face darkened and his voice became grave. "It seems to me, boy, that you should be grateful for any help you can get. Few people would speak against a decision by the Immortal. An advocate who is also a member of the Families has a better chance than anyone. And Archange is very wise. If she agrees to do this, though I am not sure she will, you should consider yourselves very lucky."

"Then will you speak to her for us?"

Shuskara nodded. "That is why I am here. I am to see her this evening. I will send a message to you. I doubt you will see me again. It does me no good to be connected with you."

He stood and knocked on the door and the guard opened it.

Reluctant to return to the squalid cell, Arish said hastily, "You never told me why you owe my father a life."

Shuskara shook his head and frowned. "My memory," he said gruffly, and he waved away the guard and sat down again.

He said nothing for a while and Arish thought he had forgotten the question again, but at last the general said, "I was sixteen when your father became Lion of the East, and he was eighteen. We were the closest of friends, closer than brothers. I mourned his father's death more than I was to mourn my own father's a year later. Since we were young your father told me he would make me his first general when he was king, and I never doubted that.

He was always a boy of his word, and when he became a man that did not change.

"Your country was always at war with somebody," Shuskara continued. "Later it went to war with the City, but at the time they were allies, and the Lion's main enemy was Tanares. The country no longer exists, but at the time it stretched along the tree-lined valley of the lower Arceton, called the Shining River, to the east, in the foothills of the Mountains of the Moon. There were constant skirmishes and the border constantly changed. The people of the valley suffered grievously in those days, for the Lion's soldiers often took them for Tanaree, and the Tanaree believed they supported the Lion.

"It is commonplace during wartime to think that all death and horror that falls on us is a result of the conflict, so when reports came to the Lion's Palace that the people of the valley, men, women and children, simple peasants, were being crucified in their hundreds, we condemned the Tanaree for their cruel practices. Perhaps they in their turn blamed us, and it was a long while before our intelligence told us that the atrocities were the responsibility of a band of Garian warriors from the north. These Garians believed, perhaps they still believe if any survive, that those who do not share their religion should suffer torment and death. The more exquisite the torture the more honour to their blood-drenched gods."

Arish saw his jaw clench and his eyes harden as he thought back down the years.

"I was sent with a small army to the valley to track down these Garians. You know, Arish, I have been a soldier for more years than I care to remember and I have seen some terrible deaths. I have inflicted them myself. But at the time I was hardly more than a boy, and the sights I saw stained my soul forever."

He stood and paced the white room. Arish saw he favoured his right knee. The older Fell, battle-hardened, would have noticed other injuries suffered by the general and adapted to over the many years.

"We did not hunt down all the Garian bandits," explained Shuskara, "but our army's presence stopped the killings, and I returned to the Lion's Palace older and wiser, but with a dark place in my soul.

"By the end of the summer the Garians had been wiped out or had fled, and at the turn of the year we heard that their leader had been captured. His name was Malkus Tesserian.

"Now Malkus Tesserian was my sword master when I was a child living in Odrysia. He was huge and bearded, and a devout Garian, and I found it amusing as a child to see him worshipping what looked to me like children's dolls. He was a stern man, and humourless, but a good teacher and he treated me and the other children fairly enough. I found it hard to imagine the sword master I knew inflicting the horrors I had seen, but I knew terrible things were done in the name of religion.

"I thought about it for several days—the time it took for Tesserian to be delivered to the palace by our troops. Finally, when our victorious army was in sight I went to your father and asked him to spare the life of the captured leader. Looking back I can only guess what I was thinking. Your father was surrounded by his advisors, the old counsellors his father relied on, and the young men who fawned upon him, hoping for a place in his inner circle. I cannot remember, but I imagine that I hoped to demonstrate to them the power I wielded over the new king, my influence as his good friend. I don't know.

"He had already been advised by those around him to kill Tesserian justly, in the way he had killed others. But your father listened to me. I told him the man had been a good teacher to me, that any skill I had with a sword was down to his early tutelage. This was false modesty. I knew I could wield the blade better than anyone there, including your father.

"The counsellors were all angered by my request and they argued with me that the man should die, but your father said nothing, although his eyes grew cold.

"At last he nodded and said, 'Very well, Shuskara. And what should we do with him? Let him go?'

"I hadn't really thought that far. I said, 'He should be returned to his stronghold and told that if he ever crosses the Shining River again he will be executed.'

"Your father looked at me hard. 'It will be as you say, my friend.' It was the last time he was to call me friend. 'But now you owe me a life.'

"You have probably guessed already that the man brought before us was not my old tutor. It was his son, of the same name, a man touched by the gods of chaos, a killer who delighted in the torment of others and who felt no remorse, no pity, no mercy. He was released and sent back to his home, where he continued to kill and torture until he was executed by the soldiers of Randell Kerr a year later.

"I left the Lion's Palace the next day, and never returned. I believe it lies abandoned now."

The trial of the six boys was not held in the emperor's Great Hall, or in the Court of Law, where most criminals were brought for a show of justice. The day after Arish met Shuskara the captives were taken from their grim cell, sluiced down with icy water to take some of the stink off them, fed some watery gruel, and led back through the tunnels. When they were brought, blinking, into the light they found themselves in the Circle of Combat, an ancient stone amphitheatre in the south of the City, once used for gladiatorial displays, now abandoned to the rats and red ants.

It was early morning and the pale sun had barely cleared the crumbling walls of the arena, and the boys were left in the middle of the sand still chained together. But they were now in the custody of soldiers, not dungeon guards. Arish asked for water and it was brought to them. Then he asked for food and they were given good fresh bread and a little meat and some fruit. So it was that by noon, when spectators started to gather, that the boys felt stronger than they had in days.

Arish had not told them a woman was to speak for them, for he had received no message from the general, and he did not want to discourage the others with news which might prove false. He only told them the general was finding an advocate.

So when a woman walked across the sand towards them they only stared at her. Even Arish did not realise who she was, for he had little experience of women beyond the old servants who dished out their meals in barracks and the skinny whores they eyed hungrily on street corners. This woman was tall, taller than most men, and with the bearing of a general. She wore long robes in shades of blue, and her snowy hair lay in a thick plait on her shoulder. Despite the whiteness of her hair her face was unlined, grave, and with a beauty that stopped the heart. Arish and the others shied away a little as she walked up to them, for this was a creature as strange to them as the white panther of the Mountains of the Moon or the speckled phoenix of the Wester Isles.

She did not appear to notice, and she smiled and said, "I am Archange Vincerus. I am your advocate. I will speak for you today." She looked assessingly at the silent boys. "You must tell me exactly what happened on the wilding."

At first they all blurted out the story in an incoherent jumble, and she listened, black eyes flickering from one to another, until she held up a hand and they fell silent. She pointed to Sami.

"You tell," she commanded, and Sami told their story carefully, leaving nothing out, and she listened. She asked the boy a few questions. Then she said, "You will not be allowed to speak at your trial. Is there anything else you wish to tell me, or ask me, before it starts?"

The smallest boy, Evan, piped up, "The dogs ate my brother."

Archange looked down at him for a long moment. "What is your name?" she asked gently.

"Evan Quin," the child said, stumbling over the last name as if he was not used to saying the word. "Conor was my big brother. The dogs killed him and ate him up." His pale eyes welled up, and he said, "They were bad dogs."

Archange nodded, and she asked them all their names, and their fathers' names, looking at each one gravely and with concentration. Then she turned and walked back across the arena to where the nobles were filling the imperial stand. Arish saw her talking to someone, and realised it was Shuskara. He wanted to wave, to attract the man's attention, but the general had his eyes averted from the sand. He nodded as Archange spoke. His face was very sad. Arish felt hope draining away.

The emperor was joined on his gold balcony by the two men chosen to decide the boys' fate with him. Arish later found out that these were Goldinus Vara, the wealthy owner of a fleet of trading ships, who had been given this entertaining role in lieu of payment of an imperial shipping contract, and Bal Carissa, an ancient seer and long-standing advisor to the king, who was so far into his dotage that he was unlikely to understand what was taking place in front of his nose. Arish squinted to make out the emperor, but all he could see was a fair, bearded man.

The air was hot and dry. The sand seemed to suck all moisture from it, and the water they had drunk hours before was just a memory. The arena was a bowl of sunlight. Arish felt light-headed, and when at last the prosecutor walked out in front of the eager crowd he had to concentrate hard to understand his words.

It was a soldier, in the uniform of a senior general, with a sword at his hip. Arish felt his spirits lift a little. A soldier would understand the need to kill the dogs. A soldier would not lie down and let himself be killed, by man or by dog.

But as the general addressed the emperor Arish listened in rising disbelief.

"My lord emperor," the man cried, "you have done me a great service today. Few people are lucky enough to win the chance to speak on behalf of the emperor, for the Immortal needs no one to represent him. His word is law, his smallest whim a command, his every command writ in the stones of eternity."

Arish heard Sami give a small discouraged sigh, and he turned his head a fraction and they exchanged glances.

"But this day," the general went on, "the emperor has shown his generosity, his magnanimity, his imperial munificence and, rather than simply have these young thugs executed, as all sane men know they deserve, he has granted them the mercy of a trial.

"Now"—the man was striding about as he spoke—"the facts of this case are simple. These boys are all foreigners who have been generously granted sanctuary here. Sons of renegade kings and enemy rulers, they are potential traitors in the heart of our beloved City. Nevertheless, the Immortal, in all his"—the man struggled for another word—"munificence, sheltered them in his palace and gave them the best of educations, both in the arts of war and the pursuits of peace. They were treated as honoured guests. Even when their parent kings betrayed the emperor and took up arms against him, still these boys were granted refuge here."

The general clutched his chin as if marshalling complex thoughts.

"Now, it is the custom, as you all know, to allow our young trainee soldiers a great deal of freedom. Other lands, other cities, might look at us and wonder why this is. It is because"—he paused and raised one hand theatrically—"our emperor, in all his . . . wisdom, believes that a life, a heart, given to the City freely, is a life worthy of the name." He fell silent as if dumbstruck by the grandeur of this thought.

Despite everything, Arish felt a bubble of hilarity rise up through him. The man was clearly a fool, possibly drunk. As an opponent, the boys could ask for no worse.

The prancing idiot told the audience of the day of the wilding as if it was a festival. Arish thought back to the youngsters running through the trees, rolling in the leaves like pups, and thought the man was not entirely wrong.

"Then," the general went on, "these boys realised they were hungry. They had eaten when they left the palace, but the generous fare they were given was not enough for them. So they conspired to kill some of the imperial hounds which run free in the woods, to kill and to eat them."

Ranul was growing red in the face, a volcano about to erupt in steam and fire. Arish whispered fiercely, "Shut your mouth, Ranul." Ranul gave him a venomous glance. Arish added, "This fool can say what he likes. Our advocate will tell the true story. Give her the chance." Ranul scowled, but said nothing.

The general told the spectators that three dogs had been killed, and he ended his story with the boys returning home, drunk with freedom and replete with dog-meat in their stomachs. He bowed elaborately to the emperor and his fellow judges, then to the lady Archange as she stood and walked out to the sand. There was a sudden cacophony of jeering and catcalls, and Arish wondered whether it was for the prancing general or their woman advocate.

The day was warm and Archange took off her long outer robe and folded it and laid it neatly on the sand beside her. She was now wearing a straight pale blue tunic over a white dress. There were silver chains round her neck and on her breast. She seemed as relaxed as if she were in her own chamber.

The heckling rose to deafening levels. The spectators, all of them men, content for their sisters and daughters to die on the field of combat, resented a woman daring to speak in public. Clay bottles and pebbles were thrown, and once Archange stood back swiftly as a thrown knife pierced the sand near her feet. Arish saw even some of the soldiers were shouting abuse.

The woman stood and waited patiently, hands folded. She looked as though she could stand there for hours. At last the noise began to die down. Archange stirred and looked around.

She raised her chin. "Warriors," she cried.

This aroused more abuse, but it quickly died down this time.

"Warriors," she repeated more quietly, and the remaining hecklers were quieted by others wishing to listen.

"Warriors are trained first to defend our City, and to defend themselves, then to attack our enemy. That is why they are given shields and swords. The shield to defend, the sword to attack. They do not lie down and let themselves be killed.

"These young warriors before you have spent years in training to defend the City. Some of them have already fought at the side of seasoned soldiers. Some are still too young." She gestured to little Evan.

She raised her voice. "And I echo the words of my friend General Galada. The emperor has also done *me* a great service today. He has permitted me to speak on behalf of his warriors. There can be no greater honour.

"It is true these young men are the sons of foreign leaders, foreign kings. They are the sons of men who were once our allies. They came here in good faith to learn the City's ways, and to fight for its honour. If their fathers have since turned away and betrayed the City, then they are not to blame.

"General Galada here," she gestured to the old soldier, "was the son of a Fkeni chieftain killed in the battle of Edyw. Yet he has spent forty years serving the Immortal with honour and integrity. No one would throw back in his face the fact that he is the son of a traitor."

The old boy flushed and Arish smiled. There were some shouts from the spectators, at the expense of the general.

"Now the dogs," Archange went on. "I have spoken to the imperial huntsmen, and to the foresters whose job it is to patrol the woodland where these boys were sent on their wilding. They tell me wild dogs in this part of the City are a menace. Hundreds of people, most of them children, are savaged to death each year, and each year the packs grow larger. None of the foresters will go unhorsed for fear of dog attack. Yet these six young men were sent there, on foot, unwarned, on a training exercise.

"They were attacked by a dozen or more hungry, savage dogs. They did not choose to kill them for meat. As the general himself told us, the boys had recently had food, and even in this City, in the dire straits we now suffer, we are not reduced to feeding our soldiers dog-meat." There was a ripple of amusement through the arena, and Arish felt his hopes rise. What the woman said was unarguable.

"They defended themselves," she went on. "They defended themselves against attack, as they were trained to do. As any warrior would."

She swung round. "What would you have done, general?"

The general shook his head and said something unintelligible. Then he raised his voice to the crowd. "The dogs belong to the emperor," he cried. "It is against the laws of the City. Even the emperor cannot break the laws of the City."

Archange spoke towards the imperial balcony. "We are not talking about puppy dogs, general. Nor the faithful hounds which accompany the Immortal on his hunts. These were wild dogs which wandered into the imperial domain. Rabbits which roam the City's meadows are snared and killed by citizens for food, and the stream and rivers are fished for their bounty. We do not bring to trial the rabbit-hunters and fishermen."

Some people in the audience shouted agreement.

"Let me remind you, these dogs would have presented such a peril to anyone coming across them—innocent workman, traveller or child. In past years the emperor has organised hunting parties to run down and kill wild dogs in his domain. We of the City should be grateful to these young soldiers for freeing us of them."

She paused, then she repeated the concept she wanted the crowd, and the judges, to understand and remember.

"We should be grateful to these soldiers as we are to all our brave troops. We should be applauding them not putting them on trial!"

Archange bowed to the balcony and walked away to a spattering of applause.

The six boys stood waiting while the emperor and his two judges talked. Arish squinted at them in the sunlight. The emperor seemed to say little. It was the merchant, Goldinus Vara, who did most of the talking and, by his gestures, Arish guessed he was debating with the emperor. The old academic seemed to be asleep.

Arish felt a hollow place in his stomach where fear gripped him. Debate or not, he had no doubt what the verdict would be. They would all die here on the sand, in front of a happy, cheering crowd who would then go home to tell their wives and children that they had seen enemies of the City executed this day. His life would end here. The idea was not so bad. What he had seen of life he had not enjoyed. It had been full of brutality, terror, need and loneliness. The fear gripping him dissolved a little and he felt calmer. He hoped the method of execution would be quick. To one side of the imperial balcony he could see the emperor's executioner, Galliard, who had served the Immortal as long as anyone could remember, standing waiting for the verdict, his hands on the haft of a huge axe.

Arish looked at the other boys. Evan was leaning against Sami, who had his arm round the youngster's shoulder. In the last few days Arish had discovered that Sami was essentially a kind boy, now the false bravado had been stripped away from them all. Sami had looked after Evan when the others ignored him, and it was Sami who always made sure the small amounts of food and drink they had been given were equally divided.

Sami saw Arish watching him and gave a rueful smile. He patted Evan on the shoulder and the small boy looked up at him trustingly. Arish thought that no one had ever looked to him like that. He resolved that if he survived the day then he would also become worthy of trust.

The murmuring of the crowd softened as the merchant Goldinus stood up and stepped to the front of the balcony. He held up a hand for quiet.

"The verdict of the judges is that the case is proved," he announced. "The six boys before us are guilty of killing imperial hounds, for which the penalty is death!"

There was a roar of excited approval from the crowd and sighs of fear from the boys. Arish felt a wonderful sense of calm overcome him. This was the end. There were no more decisions to be made. No more struggle. No more dreading what each day would bring. He looked up at the blue sky and told himself he would not see it again. But instead of regret he felt only relief.

Goldinus was still standing, and after letting the crowd have its celebration, he held his hand up again and the noise quieted.

"But the emperor is magnanimous and, above all, fair," he cried. "He concedes that the Lady Archange made a valid point in her argument. Therefore, generously, he has decided that just one boy will die to satisfy the requirements of the law. The rest will live. They must decide between themselves which these will be. They have until the sun touches the top of the Shield to choose."

There was a murmur of resentment from the crowd for the spectacle they had been denied. The boys stared at each other in confusion and shock, then turned to look at the falling sun.

"No, no," stuttered Sami, "they cannot make us choose. It is not fair."

Arish said, "Nothing about this is fair."

He wondered at his own reaction. He had felt only relief when he heard they were all to die, but now there was a chance of life, and a good chance, he was reluctant to volunteer to be the one to die under Galliard's axe. He opened his mouth to speak, but nothing came out. He heard them arguing among themselves, yet no one stepped forward. They all hoped someone else would.

"We must draw straws," said Sami. "It is the only way."

He looked at their pale faces, one by one. Reluctantly they all agreed. Arish said, "Don't include Evan. He's not to blame for any of this."

"No one's to blame," Ranul muttered, but the little boy said stoutly, "I want a straw."

"You understand what it means?" Arish asked him.

"Let him have a straw if he wants," argued Ranul, and Arish gave him a cold stare. But the child nodded his head. He was old enough to know what he was doing.

Riis ripped the sleeve off his tunic and carefully tore it into six strips. He handed them to Ranul who, his back turned, tore the end off one strip and hid them in his fat fist, leaving the ends sticking out. Arish glanced at the sun, plummeting towards the mountain. "It is nearly time," he said, his stomach churning with fear again.

"Ready?" Ranul asked, turning round. Arish saw his face was grey and he was blinking rapidly.

Evan was given the first choice and he chose a long strip. Then Arish, Riis and his brother Parr all picked long strips. Only Sami was left to choose from the remaining two. He glanced into Ranul's face, then picked one of the strips. It was short.

Ranul blew out his breath in relief. The rest stared at Sami. They had no idea what to say. Arish touched his shoulder in a gesture of comradeship, then the others did the same. Sami nodded to each of them. Then he stepped forward. There was a cheer from the crowd. Galliard walked across the sand, accompanied by two soldiers, who took Sami by the arms.

Then there was quiet from the spectators again as the merchant Goldinus stood to speak. His voice was thinner, more distant now, and Arish thought he looked smaller. Arish frowned. Dread gathered in the pit of his stomach.

Goldinus cried, "The emperor, in his great wisdom, has decreed that the criminal shall be put to death in the way the ancient gods decreed. He will be roasted to death."

In the stunned silence Arish heard a thin, inhuman screaming. He saw Sami struggling in the hands of his captors, saw the boy turn and stare back at his friends, his mouth open, his face contorted with terror, his eyes panic-stricken.

And the crowd burst into delighted cheers.

Chapter 25

Fell Aron Lee was a patient man. It was a patience won by necessity and practice. The life of a soldier consists of long days of mind-numbing boredom interrupted by moments of gut-wrenching terror. Fell had learned to harness the long days, sometimes weeks, occasionally months, of inactivity. When he was young he had found that by closing his eyes and clearing his mind he could reach a place of calm, a sanctuary from the sights and sounds around him. It took a great deal of practice, for it was easy to be distracted by laughter, a loud conversation, or by the itching in his clothes, or the pleasant fantasies of intimacy that any young man enjoys. But then he had had a great deal of time.

Fell had been a soldier for more than thirty years. The state of calm still did not come easily to him, particularly in the cramped cell with two other prisoners, but when he achieved it it sometimes rewarded him with revelation.

After weeks of captivity he realised he no longer wanted to be a soldier. He had spent his life killing other men, and some women, even a few children. He rarely met anyone who was not either a soldier or the men and women who serviced them. But Mason was not a soldier, or at least not one on active duty. Fell enjoyed their conversations more than he could say, for they roamed across the world, encompassing religion and history, astronomy, music, and agriculture and animal husbandry. Mason was knowledge-able and well read. Fell had not read a book in his life, but he had spent his years of service listening to the conversations of other men, many of whom were, in other lifetimes, farmers or blacksmiths or scholars, or who had trained in the priesthood, before the war enveloped them all. He was surprised how much information he had retained. Each day he looked forward to meeting Mason and afterwards, back in his cell, he would ponder their discussions.

It came to him as a shocking realisation that he preferred this life in a cold cramped cell with two other men than to be back on the battlefield, but it was the truth. And he wondered how impoverished his former life had been for this to be the case.

When he returned to the City, he resolved, he would leave this war to others. He had no idea what he would do with the rest of his life, but he hoped it would include Indaro.

He had known many women, from the grimiest whores who patrolled the harbour-front to ladies of wealth and leisure, and once, deliciously, a general's daughter. He had become attached to none of them. They were just a resource to him. He used their bodies in the same way as he used the female soldiers he sent to their deaths daily. He did not despise them, as he knew many men did. He liked some of them and disliked more than a few. He only had one rule, one ethic, as Mason would put it, although Fell saw it as a practical rule like keeping your sword honed, or sleeping when you had the chance. His rule was never to have sex with female soldiers in his company. So he had watched Indaro hungrily, covertly. His eyes dwelled on the long line of her thigh, the curve of her hip. At a distance he burned for her. But when they spoke up close he was always drenched by the icy water of her arrogance, her argumentative nature, her inability not to answer back. He always walked away from her frustrated in body and mind.

Frustration had been the overwhelming emotion of his time in captivity. Indaro strode into his thoughts at all times, as arrogantly as she had done in his life. The thought that she might be in the next cell, separated from him only by a stone wall, was disturbing and tantalising.

The kiss she had given him shortly before they were captured had been cool and perfunctory. He had no idea what it meant. When they got free of the fortress he would be sure to find out.

But first he had to escape. Outside the walls he would find somewhere to hole up, waiting for the search teams to leave in his pursuit, assuming he would be running for the far City. Then he would find a way back in and free the other men, and Doon, and Indaro.

So he waited patiently for the right time. He knew his guards would eventually become sloppy. More than two months had passed since he made his last escape bid. In the meantime, he had practised calm submission. When they came for him he took on a shambling gait, fixing his eyes down to the stones. He occasionally muttered to himself or stared wildly at the sky. He knew experienced guards would not be fooled by this, indeed, would tighten the security around him. But these men were not experienced. He was convinced now they were a group of peasants dressed in uniforms and given cheap swords. They even looked alike, so he guessed they came from the same village, perhaps one raided by the Blues, their men taken captive and pressed into soldiering.

Occasionally they sent only five guards rather than the usual six. Fell took no advantage of this when the weather was bright. He was waiting for a time of rain and mist, of which there was plenty in Old Mountain. At last a day came, a day when the low wet cloud seemed to touch the ground, and when there were only five guards at the door of the cell. Fell meekly allowed himself to be chained, his hands behind his back, and they set off.

The route was always the same. They marched along the corridor and up steps to the outer courtyard. This they crossed, two guards in front of Fell, usually four behind. Today there were just three guards behind him.

The keep was fronted by a wide ditch, and the steps up to the oak door rose high above the ditch, which now had a foot or so of water lying in it. As they marched towards the steps Fell raised his head slightly and squinted at them. The uneven stone was puddled with rain and muddy from the boots of many soldiers going to and fro.

As they climbed the steps Fell lagged slightly until he sensed the first of the rear guards closing on him. Then he stumbled on an uneven stone and, as the guard came up to him, stuck out his boot and deftly tripped him up. The guard fell against him and the two of them tumbled off the stairway into the ditch.

They landed in soft mud and neither was injured, but both were winded and Fell still had his hands chained behind him, his body trapped beneath the weight of the guard in his heavy rain-soaked uniform. Before the guard could scramble up Fell pulled hard and twisted and, with an agonising crunch, his left arm came out of its shoulder socket.

Fell gave an anguished yell, only partly exaggerated. The shoulder had been dislocated so many times over the years that it popped out and in again quite easily. It was painful, but tolerable. He yelled again, as the guard got to his feet and gave him a couple of kicks in the ribs. The other men came pounding down into the ditch.

"My shoulder!" Fell gasped, as they grabbed him and hauled him to his feet. "My shoulder!" Knowing they couldn't understand him, he indicated with his head until the platoon leader tore off his shirt and looked at the crooked limb. The man glared at him, clearly suspecting a trick. Fell knew the man was in a quandary. To put the shoulder back in place meant extending the arm first, which they could not do with Fell's arms chained. The man almost certainly had orders not to unchain the prisoner on any account. On the other hand, he believed Fell to be incapacitated by pain, and there were five of them. He drew his sword and ordered his men to remove the chains.

They were deployed all around him. The leader faced him, sword unsheathed but point downwards in a relaxed grip. One man held Fell's right bicep with both hands. One held his left arm, about to raise it to pop it back into the socket. This one had a knife in his belt and Fell concentrated on its exact position, its angle in the belt. He hoped it was sharp. Fell was uncertain of the two guards behind him. Under the sound of the drumming rain he had heard one other sword being unsheathed, but he did not know on which side of him the man stood. The other could well have his sword out already, or a knife. He had to assume they were both armed.

He calmed his mind, relaxing his body, letting his knees unlock, loosening his shoulders. He took a deep breath, sucking it in sharply as if preparing for anticipated pain.

Time slowed. He felt the man's calloused hand grip his wrist, place the other firmly against his torso. There was an endless pause, then he twisted it. The shoulder went back into place with an audible crunch and Fell shouted out and leaned towards the guard at his right. When the guard on the left dropped his arm he was tensing it already. He threw his weight against the man on his right, who automatically braced to support him. With his left hand Fell grabbed the knife from the belt. He swept it round, arcing down and up again. It slashed down through the great artery in the inner thigh of the leader, and up into the throat of the man holding him. As the leader raised his sword, shock slowing him, Fell spun out of the grasp of the right-hand guard, reversed the knife and threw himself backwards against the leader, the knife plunging into the man's belly. Two down.

The guard who had popped his shoulder, now on his right, was still struggling to get his sword out. The two unknowns were in front of him. One had a sword raised, and was bringing it down towards his neck. Fell rolled off the leader's body and the sword thudded into the corpse. Fell sprang to his feet. In one smooth move, he snatched up the leader's sword and leaped over his body, plunging the sword into the chest of the man who had fixed his arm. He dragged it out again. Three down.

The two remaining guards hesitated as Fell faced them, sword in hand. Then they both turned and ran, clambering up the bank of the ditch and disappearing into the mist.

Fell laughed shortly, then bent and grabbed the leader's sword-belt and knife. He sprinted up the side of the ditch and ran in the opposite direction to the two fleeing guards.

That, he knew, was the easy part. He had come this far before. Getting out of the fortress, when he had only the haziest idea of its geography, was another thing. He had spent hundreds of hours standing by the high window of the cell, watching the traffic of troops, and the small female servants, their routines and the movements which were not routine. Unless they had spent months creating an elaborate hoax for him, which he thought was quite possible of Mason, the entrance to the fortress was in the south. So, keeping close under walls, hidden by the mist and heavy rain, he made his way to the west, towards a low tower he had seen and marked in his mind. Like the other squat stone towers within view of his cell, this one had narrow unshuttered windows. And the tower appeared unused, for he had never seen movement there. He needed some height, so he could see the layout of the fort.

He made his way to the tower with little difficulty. It was not only unused, but long-abandoned. The door was padlocked, but the wood of the frame had crumbled in the damp air. Fell spent a few precious moments digging around the hinges with the knife. Then, having dug some finger-holds, he pulled hard and the door came easily off its hinges. He squeezed through the gap and pulled the door back into place as best he could. A casual glance would see only an unbroken padlock. He felt his way up slimy stone steps in the gloom then, as thin daylight started to reach him, raced up to the highest floor. Cautiously he peered out of a narrow window.

He grinned. As he had calculated, from this vantage point he could clearly see the south wall of the fortress and the main gate. He watched for a long time, until darkness fell.

D awn was just a possibility in the eastern sky when Fell was awoken from an uneasy sleep by the rumble of cart wheels. He rolled to his feet and looked out of the tower's narrow window. The main gates were lit by just two torches, but in their dim flicker he could make out three pony carts crossing the courtyard towards them, bound for outside. Fell snatched up the sword-belt and raced down the steps, reckless of falling in the pitch-black. This might be his best, his only, chance.

He took a moment to pull the broken door neatly shut behind him, in case he had to retreat there again. Then he ran to a low building on the corner of the courtyard and peered round. The first cart had reached the gates, and he could hear the murmur of conversation between the gate guards—a dozen or more—and the carter. Laughter came to him on the night breeze. He ran lightly, silently as he could, across the cobbles to the rear of the third cart. Before he got there the gates groaned open, just wide enough to permit the exit of the carts, and the first went through. The other two rumbled forward, then stopped again as the second carter reached the gate. The third lagged behind a little, leaving its load still in darkness.

Fell was baffled for a moment, for it seemed the carts seemed empty. Then he saw the low, long shape lying on the cart bed, and realised it carried a corpse wrapped in a shroud. The carts were taking three corpses outside the rocky fortress for burial. He took no more than a heartbeat to wonder at the reverence for the dead implied by three carts for three corpses. Then he dragged the body off the rear of the cart and ripped off the shroud. He left the dead man lying in the dust, then climbed on the cart and wrapped the fabric around him as best he could, hoping darkness would cover its meagre fit.

Almost immediately the cart jolted forward a few paces and stopped again. The carter and guards spoke to each other in their alien tongue and Fell, who could now see the glimmer of the torches through the rough weaving of the shroud, held his breath, gripping the sword to his side. After a moment the cart moved forward, then someone yelled out and immediately the cart lurched to a stop. The shroud was snatched from Fell's face and he found himself staring into the angry face of a guard.

Instantly he rolled off the cart on the other side from the man, then rolled back under it, catching out the guards who were running the wrong way. Fell leaped up, speared two men, one in the chest and one in the throat, then jumped back up onto the cart. The sudden commotion startled the pony, which started forward, blocking the gates from closing. Swords slashing at his legs, Fell leaped up onto the carter's seat and held his sword down at the man's throat. The frightened carter dropped the reins and threw himself from the seat. Fell leaped on the back of the pony, reaching behind to cut the traces. Then he kicked the pony and it set off as fast as it could out of the gates and into the night.

It was a thin, poor beast which could barely take Fell's weight, and as soon as they were in darkness he slipped from its back and slapped its rump. It trotted off, following the main road. Fell dropped off the side of the road and headed west.

It didn't take him long to realise why Mason had claimed Old Mountain was impregnable. Once off the only road, winding narrowly up to the fortress, the land was steeply sloped, almost vertical in parts. Fell scrambled across the slope, forced downwards all the time. At first there was plant growth clinging precariously to the rock, and he clambered from bush to bush. Then the undergrowth dwindled and vanished, leaving Fell on the exposed side of a mountain, with no way back up and few handholds. The prospect of going down was grim, but he had no choice. It was starting to grow light and far below he could see a shining river, its banks clothed with trees. There had clearly been a recent landslip and the vertiginous mountainside beneath him was covered with shifting shale.

He sat for a moment to get his breath. He was not built to be a rock climber; too heavy and with a high centre of gravity. And his boots gave him no purchase on the scree. But he took a deep breath, then launched himself onto the slope, trying to cling on with all four limbs. He immediately started sliding and slithering, stabbing his knife into the shale at intervals to slow his progress. At one point he slid for twenty paces, picking up speed fast until his foot knocked against a protruding rock. He tried to get his boot to it but it slipped off. Sliding farther, he reached out with one hand and grabbed the rock, gripping hard and tensing his body and slowing his slide to a stop. The shale carried on roaring past him and he feared he had caused another landslip, but at last it too came to a halt. He was sweating heavily and his heart was racing, and he stayed there for a while, clinging to the side of the mountain, until his heart slowed. Then he let go of the rock and continued down.

At last he made it to the point where the landslip ended, and he could climb down the rest of the way. He was far from the fortress now, at least in altitude, and he thought it unlikely they could find him. But his original plan, to hole up somewhere then find a way to sneak in and free the prisoners, had to be abandoned.

He decided to head west. The river, still far below, ran north to south, and it was tempting to take the easy way. But if he went along it he would soon be lost, whereas if he followed the setting sun he would eventually reach the City, or lands he recognised.

He started to regret his decision almost immediately. The way down was as steep as ever but was now clothed in thick undergrowth. His knife, rendered useless by its hard treatment on the scree, could barely chop a twig. So he ended up hacking his way through near-impenetrable undergrowth with the sword. He knew it left him effectively unarmed, both weapons blunted, but he could see no other choice.

The forest was so lush, so rich with life, that it seemed to thicken in front of him as he watched. Even the air smelled green. After a while it began to rain and he held his head back, opening his mouth to the welcome water. When he had crossed the river he rested for a long while, then with a sigh set off up the opposite hillside. By nightfall he had travelled only a short distance; behind him he could still see the scree slope he had slid down and he thought he could make out the square towers of the fortress far above in the east. He spent the night in the branches of a small spreading tree. He had no idea what predatory animals there were in these parts, but he did not care; he was anxious to gain some height above the crawling, squirming life on the ground.

By the third day he had reached more open land. The hills were lower and the going easier. He no longer had to struggle for each pace covered, and he began to enjoy walking, feeling the muscles in his legs tiring, then strengthening again. He started looking around him with interest. He had seen few animals apart from a sort of hairless squirrel and some small striped rodents with flat snouts. Once he heard what sounded like a lion's roar in the distance, but he had seen nothing bigger than a lone grey badger. There were many birds, small brightly coloured creatures which flitted from plant to plant, more like big insects than birds.

He started to make plans again. When he returned to the lands of the City he would identify himself to the first army troop he found and raise a company to return to Old Mountain. He had got out, so he would find his way in again; no one would expect him to break in. Then he would free the other prisoners and between them they would open the main gates. In his heart of hearts, though, he knew there was little chance of a rescue mission for four common soldiers, and the treacherous part of his mind considered Stalker and Garret, Indaro and Doon were better off as captives of Old Mountain than as warriors of the City. When he won Indaro's freedom, however it happened, he would do his best to ensure she would never have to fight again.

At last he came to a high, cool plain. He hiked across it, moving quickly, ever westward. By the end of the day there was a thick haze clouding the setting sun, and he thought he could see distant hills. Was it the City? He chose to believe so, and he stepped out eagerly, although he knew it would still be several days' walk until he got there. He slept on warm dry ground in the lee of a rock, and woke only once, to hear a distant cry.

In the morning he started walking across land which shelved away slowly in front of him. Suddenly a familiar stench came to his nostrils. He stopped, senses on high alert. He drew his useless sword, looking around. All he could see was flat, dry plain, empty of life. He stepped forward. Breasting a small rise he found himself above a wide hollow in the rocky land. In its centre were staked out two bodies, naked. They were small dark women, similar to the ones he had seen at the fortress. They had been dead for a while and the corpses were partly eaten by animals and insects. He checked the perimeter and found lots of bootprints, arriving and leaving, but many hours old.

At last he walked down into the hollow. Then his footsteps faltered.

Under an overhang of rock he could see a splash of colour, bright red clothing a third body. His heart jerked like a jackrabbit on a snare. He stumbled down the slope and ran to the woman. She was still alive. It was Doon.

Fell sawed through her bindings with his knife, then looked to her injuries. Blood was leaking from everywhere; there were minor stab wounds and bruises all over her body. Her face was grey and her eyes closed. She didn't seem to notice when he freed her arms and legs.

"Doon!" he said crisply. But she did not answer and he thought she was near death. He placed his hand on her neck and felt her life force, thin and thready.

Carefully, aware that she must have internal injuries, he took off Indaro's jerkin, then stripped off his tattered overshirt and wrapped it round her before covering her with the jerkin again. He sat against the rock, leaning her body against him, his arms wrapped around her. He had no water to give her, no food, no salve for her wounds, only the comfort of another soldier's company in her dying time.

The morning went by slowly as he listened to her faltering breathing and tried not to think about what might have happened to Indaro. He cursed himself, thinking that if only he had water Doon's life might be saved. But he had nothing to carry it in, and he last drank from a muddy brook more than a day ago, before he reached this dry plain.

When he felt a slight movement in his arms he realised she was trying feebly to struggle against him.

"Doon," he whispered, "it's Fell Aron Lee. You're safe."

She stopped resisting. "Indaro?"

"She's not here," he said cautiously.

"You escaped together?"

"Yes," he lied. "Indaro has returned to the City. She asked me to look for you." He was ashamed as he said it. Although he would have personally petitioned the gods themselves to save Indaro, he had scarcely given her servant a thought. All he could think was *It could have been Indaro.*

"Who did this to you?" he asked.

She was quiet and still and he thought she'd drifted away. But then she whispered, "I walked into them. City soldiers. I thanked the gods for my luck." She bit her lower lip, already ragged and bloody. "They didn't believe I was one of them. Even though I had Indaro's jacket."

He had nothing to say. He knew how enemy women were used.

"I told them all I knew of the Maritime, names of my comrades, details of troop movements, nicknames of the generals. They said they didn't believe me. They didn't want to believe. They chained me with two enemy women. We had to follow their horses. Sometimes they kicked into a gallop and dragged us a short while for fun. One woman died that way. They were angry she died so easily. They wanted us alive. When we stopped for the night . . ." Her face was expressionless but a tear welled up under one bruised lid.

"I'm dying," she whispered.

When he said nothing in reply, she roused a little. "Am I dying, sir?" she asked.

Fell looked at the blood pool, growing wider and darker. Above them he sensed the flight of carrion birds.

"Yes, soldier," he said softly.

"Have you a knife?"

He took out the blunt blade and showed it to her. She craned her neck to look up at him. Holding his eyes she nodded slightly.

Fell had seen many a mutilated warrior go gratefully to his death, mercifully released by the severing of the great blood vessel in the inner thigh. Without hesitation he leaned forward and nicked the artery and watched the blood pump sluggishly out. She had not much left to give.

"Tell Indaro . . ." Doon whispered.

"What?" He bent closer.

But she said no more and after a while he closed her eyelids against the dust from the plain. Then he closed his own eyes and bowed his head.

Arish sat with his eyes closed, hands over his ears, like a small boy again, trying to block out the horror. Days had passed but the appalling scene played itself again and again in his mind's eye.

"Arish, it's time," a voice said.

He looked up. It was Riis, tall for his age, grey-eyed and serious. "You said you'd be there," the younger boy said.

Numbly, Arish nodded and levered himself up. With Riis at his heels he walked out of the barracks and across the litter-strewn yard at the back to a small copse of scrubby trees where he had agreed to meet the other boys after dark. He had avoided them since they had been freed. But he said he'd be there that night. He would likely never see them again. Earlier that day he had been called to meet Shuskara, and the general had told him he was to be his new junior aide. Arish was to have a new name, his past erased from the history of the City. They were to leave the next day for the Salient.

The last five boys were gathered round a campfire, and Arish wondered how they could sit there so calmly when all he could see in the flames was a writhing, screaming horror.

"About time," commented Ranul, with some of his old ill-temper. Ranul had been most changed by their experience, Arish thought. The bully had vanished, and in his place was a sadder, more thoughtful young man who no longer caused pain and fear for the pleasure of it.

"Parr made it," he told Arish. "We all agreed. You were too busy." The words were petulant, but they came from memory and habit, not from feeling.

Arish looked at the long metal thing Ranul was holding, its curling end in the fire, white with heat. "A brand!" Arish felt his flesh crawl.

"We've all agreed to take the vow, and be branded with this—an S—so we never forget, however long it takes."

"The vow?"

"To kill the emperor."

Fell sat for a long time with Doon's cooling corpse in his arms. At last he laid the body down gently then stood and looked around him. He had no way to bury her in this hard land. He made a heartfelt prayer to the Gods of Ice and Fire to receive her as a warrior in the Gardens of Stone. Then he stripped off the red leather jerkin, folded it and tucked it under his arm. He strode back up to the lip of the hollow.

In the silence of the high plain he could no longer ignore the compelling whisper which had been speaking to him for so long. He looked to the west, where lay his duty as a son of the City. There the sun shone high and bright in an azure sky.

It could have been Indaro, he thought.

He turned to the east, where clouds hung over the highlands, and he set off back towards Old Mountain.

Chapter 26

Indaro threw aside the book she was trying to read and stared out of the cell's window, bored beyond sanity. The view was startlingly beautiful—gleaming green cloudforest topped by crystal sky—but she was sick of it.

She had been transferred to this chamber from her old prison cell when ice started to form on her water bucket at night. She was considered an honoured guest, so Mason told her, and she now had a bed with blankets, and was fed twice a day, though frugally. But the door to the room was still locked.

Mason had suggested she awake before dawn to witness the new day appearing at the Gate of the Sun, a rite which was important to the old ones of the Tuomi. She had no real interest in such pointless practices, but she played along, hoping to find advantage in the ploy. Five mornings in a row she had risen in darkness to make her way up the mountain to watch this event. Five times she had returned disappointed. Today she and Mason were to walk up to the Gate of the Sun together, so she could see it in daylight.

The mornings and evenings were cooling fast, but here at the start of autumn the days were still warm. She could not conceal a weapon easily. She had hidden a chicken leg a week or more ago and honed the bone to sharpness on the stone floor of her room. It made a poor weapon but, deftly wielded, it could pierce a vital blood vessel. She dressed in a skirt and loose tunic, trusting it would hide the bone stuck in the waist of her skirt against her belly. She hoped her guards were well-armed—the more weapons the more chance of snatching one. With a sword in hand she would take on the entire garrison.

Yet when her cell door opened Mason was not there. Instead guards escorted her through the dark halls of the fortress to a place she had never seen before, where huge carved stones looming above her dripped with wet and the smell of time. Oak doors, carved heavily with monstrous beasts, opened ponderously and she was shown into a great chamber. It was very high, the ceiling lost in darkness, and the stone floor stretched before her like a City avenue. It was illuminated by lights in glass boxes which gave a steady light. She had heard the enemy had such magical knowledge unseen in the City. At the far end of the room a fire blazed in an enormous hearth. It was the first fire she had seen for weeks and she was drawn to its comfort. In front of the hearth was a wide table, and at the table were five people. On one side were Mason and an olive-skinned rider dressed in grey. Next to them sat a pale young man with dark curly hair. On the other side were, to her astonishment, Saroyan, Lord Lieutenant of the East—and Fell Aron Lee.

Fell gazed up at her coolly, his eyes piercing her as if trying to penetrate her with meaning. She nodded and sat down beside him, folding her hands on her lap.

"Where are the others?" she asked him.

"They are not needed here," Saroyan answered, as if she were in charge of the meeting. She was dressed in worn riding clothes and there was a hurried, sweaty air about her as if she had ridden post-haste to this rendezvous. Indaro already knew she was in league with the enemy, yet it was still a shock to see her here, in his heartland.

The grey-clad rider spoke. "My name is Gil Rayado. My father was Tuomi." Indaro noticed he spoke the language of the City with an accent, and a slight lisp. He was very good-looking, she thought, his long black hair held back at his neck, his beard shaped and trimmed. "There are perhaps fifty Tuomi warriors left," he explained, "and about two hundred women. So, like you, Fell, I am one of the last of my people. In a hundred years their names will probably be forgotten."

Indaro was careful not to show it, but she was surprised. Fell, the last of his people? What did that mean? At her side, Fell made no response.

Gil Rayado went on, "Mason here is the product of many races, but he was born and raised in Petrus. He calls himself a Petrassi scholar." There was a hint of amusement in the man's voice, and Indaro guessed this was a joke between the two.

"Saroyan . . ."

"We know what Saroyan is," Fell interrupted.

"But," said Gil mildly, unperturbed, "this introduction is not only for your benefit. It is also for my young friend Elija." He indicated the curly-haired boy, who blushed under their scrutiny. Indaro wondered how he had earned his place at this table.

"Saroyan," Gil went on, "is a Lord Lieutenant of the City. She is not a soldier. She is an administrator."

"What does that mean?" asked Elija, his voice barely audible.

All eyes turned to Saroyan. She stared at the table, as if unused to having to explain herself, but eventually she said tightly, "There are forty administrators in the City under four lord lieutenants. They deal with matters such as food distribution, building works, internal laws. Everything which is not to do with the military's actions in the field. Over the years I have become responsible, among other things, for troop rotations inside the palace."

"Fell Aron Lee," Gil continued in his slight, delicate accent, "is a warrior of the City. But he is also the son of a king, the last king of the ancient cities of Llor, who called himself the Lion of the East."

Indaro stared at her commander, not trying to hide her surprise.

"Yet you fought for the City?" Elija asked Fell.

Fell ignored him, and Mason said reprovingly, "We all have much to learn today, boy."

Gil continued, "Elija, on the other hand, is a son of the City who has sought sanctuary among its enemies. He spent many years living in the tunnels under the City," he explained. "He knows his way around them better than anyone."

Indaro wondered if anyone gathered around the table knew she too had lived there, that she also knew her way around. Then Gil spoke her name.

"Indaro Kerr Guillaume is also a warrior of the City. She is of two ancient lines. Indaro's father was formerly counsel to the emperor.

"Now," Gil said, looking around at them all, "events are suddenly moving quickly within the City and we find time is pressing. But it is important we all understand why I have brought you here. Mason will tell you some history."

Mason leaned forward on his elbows. His face was grey and lined and Indaro thought he looked exhausted, as if he had not slept for a long time.

"The City is thousands of years old," Mason began. "But there was, of course, a time when it did not exist. Its own histories say it was just a barren hilltop surrounded by lush green pastureland to the east, thick forests of oak in the mountains to the south, cliffs looking over the ocean to the west, and the shores of the Little Sea in the north. The people were primitive, their lives short and brutal. They probably prayed to some simple weather gods, but we know nothing of that.

"The mysterious travellers, those who founded the City, were entirely different. We do not know who they were, or where they came from. But we know they were called, or called themselves, Serafim. They were taller and stronger than the natives, much longer-lived. They knew about mechanics and mathematics, medicine and, fortunately for us, they had a written language."

"*Un*fortunately for us," Gil put in, "we cannot read it."

Mason glanced at him and went on, "It has been my work of the last twenty years to try to decipher some of the earliest texts that have been found, scrolls that date back more than a thousand years."

"Where did these documents come from?" asked Indaro.

"We are straying from our path," Gil put in mildly.

Mason looked at him. "So the travellers, much more advanced than the natives, were considered to be gods. They taught the people how to hunt wild beasts, to herd and domesticate sheep and cattle, and to grow crops so they would not have to rely on the hunt. The travellers gave them skills to build homes and eventually palaces, and the talents to create works of art and learning. So the people built the City and the travellers were their gods and their teachers and guardians. Under their tutelage the City became a centre of learning for the known world, a hub of commerce, rich and powerful. The people of the surrounding nations gathered there to learn, to enrich themselves by trade and by learning."

Indaro shuffled her feet. Ancient history was of no interest to her. She was regretting sitting beside Fell, for she could not look at him without being obvious. With her face turned politely towards Mason, she could only see, from the corner of her eye, Fell's left knee, and his hand on it, drumming impatiently out of sight under the table. She could feel the warmth of his body, feel the tension in him, as if he wanted to jump out of his skin. She wearily returned her attention to Mason's lesson.

"Then came the time of the Families, those who were said to carry the blood of the travellers in their veins. They were taller and stronger and longer-lived than the common folk, and they ruled by might and by right. Sarkoy, Khan, Kerr, Vincerus, Gaeta, Guillaume and Broglanh. Every child of the City knows these names. They fought among themselves from time to time, but they also bred among themselves to keep their bloodlines strong. So they were mutually dependent and, however one Family might loathe another, it was in all their interests not to let feuds become a war.

"But the richest blood does thin over the years. Broglanh and Kerr are still honourable names but none of them makes any claim to be descendants of the gods. Indaro carries the Kerr name, but makes no claim to rule in the City.

"Five Families are still in contention, of course. Araeon, your emperor, of the Family Sarkoy. The Vincerii, the brothers who control the armed forces. Khan, controllers of the treasury. Gaeta, a minor Family interested more in scholarship than in warfare. And Guillaume. This Family has never ruled. Their palace on the Shield remains untenanted. Taxes on their lands remain unclaimed. Meanwhile many eyes turn on Reeve Guillaume."

"My father never made claim to power," Indaro said. "He is an old man who tends his garden."

"There is your brother," said Mason.

"Rubin is probably dead," Indaro said bleakly. "I have not heard of him in years."

The boy Elija lifted his head. He stared at her, and she looked at him curiously.

Suddenly Fell stood up, as if he could stay still no longer. His chair crashed to the floor behind him. "Why exactly are we here?" he asked, restrained anger making his voice rough. "You say time is pressing, but you give us a . . . history lesson."

"There is one factor which binds us—all here wish to see the end of the war," Gil told him. "Even now thousands of City soldiers are facing thousands of Blueskins, as you call us. The Second Adamantine is fighting an incursion of Fkeni in the north. These are people who have only recently been pulled into the war, yet already they have lost a generation of their young men. In the east the remainder of the Fourth Maritime is engaging the infantry phalanxes of the Petrassi, probably your greatest foe. Thousands may die today, and tomorrow, and the next day. Meanwhile we are all short of food, and some of us are starving."

Indaro felt a surge of pride. Some of the Maritime were still alive, still fighting! She caught the eye of Saroyan, who regarded her thoughtfully.

"Perhaps there are some here who don't want the war to end," the woman commented.

Eyes turned to Indaro. "I want to see the end to this war," she said quietly. "But I do not want to see the City defeated. I have fought for many years, in winter and summer, on plain and mountain, and I have lost comrades, friends. I cannot see their sacrifice wasted."

"It is a familiar argument," replied Saroyan, "but a sterile one, for if everyone feels that way then the war will be endless."

"Until the entire continent is barren of life, our cities mere ruins stalked by shadows," added Gil. "Most of us are soldiers here, but even for soldiers there comes a time when we put down our arms and say, 'No more.' Even if the war ended today it might take the land centuries to recover. And the war will not end today."

"So what is your plan?" Fell was pacing in front of the hearth.

Gil said briskly, "There are three parts to it—emperor, palace and City. The emperor must die, the palace taken and the City pacified. These three need to be executed within a narrow timescale for success."

Indaro had discussed the Immortal with Mason many times. He had told her he believed Araeon's death would end the war. He had almost convinced her, sitting in comfortable conversation in this distant fortress. But now her stomach churned at the thought that she had become part of a plot to assassinate the emperor. She wanted to look at Fell, to see his reaction, but feared that if she did so their thoughts would be plain for all to see. There must be some reason he was pretending to go along with these conspirators. So she kept her eyes meekly on the tabletop and listened.

"Shuskara is the linchpin to our plan," explained Gil. "He is the man Elija and Indaro know as Bartellus." Indaro remembered the old man in the Hall of Watchers, who had treated her with contempt, who had prompted her return to the battlefield. He was the legendary general? She looked at Elija, wondering how he knew the old boy.

Gil went on. "The revelation to the armies within the City that their lost general has returned must come on the day of the emperor's death. Only the most traditional of the armies will be in the City that day—the Second Adamantine, and the Fourth Imperial. Shuskara, their hero, will bring them behind the new emperor."

"Does Shuskara know of his part in this plot?" Fell asked, his voice loaded with scepticism.

Mason nodded. "That is why this summer has been so long. The general was grievously injured by his enemies, and it has taken him time to recover. But he is well now and is ready to act. He knows of your part, Fell, just as you know of his."

"You are in contact with him?"

"Indirectly."

Fell blew out his breath in frustration. "This is . . ." he spat out, "a day-dream! Here we are, six of us, with no power or authority, in an abandoned fortress far from the action, yet we are plotting to conquer a city and assassinate an emperor. It is nonsense!"

Mason started, "Trust me, Fell . . ."

But Fell turned on him, his voice dark with anger. "Why? Why should I trust you? Or him!" He pointed at Gil. "I certainly do not trust her!" He indicated Saroyan. "And she does not trust us."

He turned on Indaro. "Do you have a weapon?" he demanded. Dumb-struck, she hesitated then nodded.

"You see?" he said to the others. "You can't trust Indaro and she doesn't trust you!"

There was angry silence in the room, in which Fell walked over to In-daro and, looming over her, held out his hand. She reached beneath her tunic and pulled free the sharpened bone. She handed it to him and he threw it on the table. It looked pathetic.

Mason said mildly, "Sit down. I know this is new to *you*, but I assure you it is not a scheme recently hatched. Many people are involved and the planning has been going on since it became clear Shuskara is still alive. Now, to continue . . ."

But Gil interrupted him. "We have no reason to conquer the City, Fell, if that is what you fear. We could not if we wanted to. We do not have the numbers, or the supplies. We no longer have the heart. We just want an end to war, so all of us can lay down our swords and return to our homes. We will try to build our countries again, restore the land, although some say it is too late now."

"What is stopping you going home?" asked Fell.

"You are, Fell, and Indaro. And your comrades. Araeon would send you and all his remaining armies to chase us down and destroy us in our homelands, no matter the cost to the City. So he must die. It is the only way."

Indaro wondered if she could believe him.

Gil went on smoothly. "But we *do* plan to capture the palace and winkle the emperor out from his Keep, whatever the cost to *us*. Saroyan will see to it that mercenaries are rotated to guard the palace on the given day, along with units of the Thousand. This is the only part of the plan in which our troops will be involved and we do not want them killing regular City soldiers at this time. The invading company, around two hundred men, hand-picked, will attack the palace through the sewers, guided by Elija. Indaro will join that group, if she so chooses."

Indaro frowned. "Through the Halls? The Great Flood will have damaged the tunnels and gates. They will be more treacherous than ever. When were you last there?" she asked Elija.

The young man flushed again. "A long time ago," he admitted. "I know the Halls are much changed but I have studied them and I think I can find a way through."

"Have you sent scouts?" she asked Gil.

"Of course," he said. "But with limited success."

"When is all this to happen?" Fell asked, resuming his seat next to Indaro.

"Before the autumn rains," answered Gil, "to give the invading army its best hope." He glanced at Mason. "At the Feast of Summoning, we have decided. That is in twenty days' time."

"So Shuskara will turn the armies to his side. And your invading force will take the palace," Fell said. "And the third part of your plot, to kill the emperor?"

"That is where you come in," Gil replied.

Chapter 27

Fell's return to Old Mountain had taken less time than he had calculated, for he was sure of his destination and he could see the old fort from way off. He half expected to be found by a search party, but met no one.

It was dusk on the sixth day since he left. He paused on the road looking up at the great gates, his heart still undecided. If he re-entered the fortress now he would be throwing in his lot with the enemy. He would be a traitor to the City, as certainly as if he had already taken arms against it.

As he stood, holding on to the moment, his gaze drifted upwards. Above the massive stone lintel two dark figures were barely visible in the twilight. They were carved creatures of stone, facing each other, guardians of the gate. His breath caught in his throat as he realised where he was. He had looked up at those two beasts a hundred times as a child. The Lions' Gate. He had been brought to his own home, the centre of his father's kingdom. He had not recognised it. He shook his head in wonder. Why had Mason not told him?

His mind finally made up, he hammered on the high oak doors to be let in. The guards who opened them seemed surprised to see him.

Fell had been a soldier for thirty years, and for all that time his mind had been filled with strategies for the battle he was fighting or plans for the next one. In the brief periods of rest he had blurred his thoughts with alcohol and willing women. Memories of Sami's hideous death, and the vow he had taken, had been buried in the back of his brain. These last weeks of enforced idleness and reflection had returned to him a perspective he had mislaid for three decades.

He had taken the vow with the other boys, had submitted to the agony of the brand. Even the smallest, Evan, had suffered the ordeal. At the time, in the immediate aftermath of the horror in the arena, Fell had believed his vow. He believed that one day, when the time was right, he would kill the emperor. But the very next day, as he rode out at Shuskara's side, suddenly plunged into an exciting new life, it was easy to set aside that childish pledge.

Yet he had never forgotten it. And when Evan Quin had reported for duty with the Wildcats the previous autumn Fell had known him instantly, although he had gained the new name Broglanh. But the younger man had not recognised him.

Doon's death at the hands of the emperor's men had been the final affirmation that the vow he had made so long ago was one he was fated to fulfil. And the thought kept running through his brain—*it could have been Indaro*. It could have been Indaro, captured, raped, tortured and killed by soldiers of the City.

He had never felt this way about any woman. When she was out of his sight all he could think of was her. When he was with her he wanted to touch her, hold her, and protect her. She was sitting next to him at the table of the high council and it was all he could do not to reach out and take her hand.

He had asked Gil Rayado, "Why me?" but it was Mason who took a breath and replied, "To return briefly to the travellers." Fell sighed inside. He had had more of the history of the City than he could stomach.

Perhaps Mason was aware of the frustration among his audience for he paused for a moment, then he went on, "It is said that the crimson eagles that live in the Mountains of the Moon live for a thousand years, for they have no predators and even man the hunter cannot reach them in the high peaks where they make their nests. To the rabbit or stoat that fears the great bird and whose lifespan lasts only years, then the eagle must seem immortal."

Mason seemed to be choosing his words carefully. "So," he went on, "a man whose life is many times longer than the generations of those around him will also be called Immortal. We do not know how long the travellers—the Serafim—lived, but it must have been a very long time, for their descendants, those products of unions between City folk and their gods, those with only half, or a quarter or less of Serafim blood in them, their lives still spanned many generations of normal men and women. We do not know how old the Vincerii are, for instance, but they might be only one or two generations from the travellers."

"You are saying that Marcellus and Rafe are a thousand years old?" Fell asked, his voice rich with disbelief.

Mason nodded. "Possibly."

Fell smiled and shook his head. "You are an intelligent man, Mason, but you are speaking of children's nightmares or the midnight tales of old men. How can men live for a thousand years?"

"They have abilities we don't fully understand."

"And you believe the emperor is the same age?"

"No, Fell. I believe he is much older."

Fell leaned back and folded his arms. He could see Indaro better from that angle. She turned to him, her face serene. What on earth was she thinking? He could never guess.

"Listen, Fell." Gil took up the argument, knowing Mason had lost credibility. "We believe Araeon is one of the original Serafim. One of the first. And the only one, perhaps, with no descendants of his own."

"He has no sons?"

Gil looked at Saroyan to answer. She said nothing for a long while, as if reluctant to give away information.

Then, "Among the descendants of the Serafim it is said he kept himself pure," she said reticently.

Fell snorted. As a soldier he had little time for concepts of male purity.

Indaro said suddenly, "You told me he is not a man." She was addressing Mason. "What did you mean? What is he?"

"I said he is not a man *like me*. But he *is* a man."

Indaro frowned, and Fell remembered what she had told him about the man who had survived, impossibly, when the emperor's carriage was destroyed by an explosion. "Is he a sorcerer?" she asked in a small voice, as if embarrassed to be asking the question.

Mason seemed unwilling to speak. He looked at Gil, who shrugged, and at Saroyan, but she was staring at the table.

"The word is meaningless," he said finally. "He has skills, abilities, which seem like sorcery to some. But all that matters to us is that he is a living man made of flesh and blood who can be killed."

"Why do you want Fell to kill him?" asked Indaro. "I mean, why Fell?"

"You must understand," replied Gil, "that Araeon is very difficult to get to. He is guarded by the Thousand, and hidden behind layers of . . . proxies, you call them. It is uncertain even what he looks like. There are many pictures of him, imperial portraits, but they are all of a fair bearded man of middle years with no distinguishing marks. You and Fell have both seen him, but could you pick him out in a crowded room?" He looked at them both in turn. "No?

"So the only way to get to him is to draw him out. He has lived a very long life, much of it in the confines of the Keep. He is the emperor. He has complete power. Anything he wants or needs or commands, it is instantly obeyed. Our sources suggest that the only time he lets down his guard is if his curiosity is piqued. We hope to offer him something that he cannot resist."

"And what is that?"

"A son."

Fell gave a bark of laughter. Elija, eyes wide, asked, "Fell is the emperor's son?"

Gil exchanged glances with Saroyan. "No," he said. "He is not. But the emperor believes he could be."

"You said he kept himself pure," commented Indaro, puzzled.

"Purity is a matter of interpretation," replied Mason. "For Araeon it means not spreading his seed, not mingling it among the common folk. It does not mean celibacy."

"Then how . . . ?" asked Indaro.

Mason turned to her. "We believe he kills any woman he has sex with." He glanced at Fell. "We have the testimony of witnesses who say he visited the Lion's Palace, seduced, or raped your mother, Fell, but for some reason he did not kill her.

"Years later his forces attacked the palace. Both your parents died there. It is said that he killed your mother himself, although she took his eye out first."

Fell was silent for a while, remembering the child Arish and the one-eyed man. He asked, "Why did he not kill me?"

"Perhaps he was conflicted. Perhaps after so long a life he was curious to know what a son was like. You were no threat to him. He could have had you killed any time. So perhaps he let you live, day to day, year to year. Watching and waiting.

"Until suddenly you disappeared after the trial. He could not find you for many years. You were thought to be dead. Finally, we believe, he, or someone in the palace, connected the boy Arish with the general's aide Fell Aron Lee. Shuskara was grievously punished for his part in that deception."

Fell shook his head. "That was years ago. If he has known about me since then, why am I still alive?"

Mason spread his hands in an admission of ignorance. "We do not know. What we do know is that the emperor ordered Flavius Randell Kerr to keep watch on you, to pull you out of the fighting and keep you safe. But you disobeyed orders and disappeared again, this time into a battle from which there were few survivors."

Fell thought it through. The only sound he could hear was his own heart, and a distant dripping from the damp walls of the hall. Despite himself, he was excited. He could feel the charge building in his blood.

But he shook his head. "It was mere coincidence that your riders came across us," he said, looking at Gil.

"We had been searching for you for a time," replied Gil. "Both we and the City had roving bands seeking survivors from the battle, seeking you. It was no coincidence that we found you, merely luck that you survived to be found."

"Why do you need Fell?" Indaro asked. "Why not have someone impersonate him? The emperor would not know."

"Because Fell is the son of his mother, and it may be that the emperor is able to see that. Also, Fell is a consummate warrior, and if anyone can fulfil this mission, it is him," Gil said. "We do not know when they will meet, in the imperial chambers, which is unlikely, or in a hall crowded with bodyguards, which is probably the case. Fell might well have to kill a dozen or more highly trained men to get to the emperor."

He gazed at the table in front of him and when he spoke Fell detected the taste of deceit. "Also he can kill without weapons."

"So can I," Fell said grimly.

Mason nodded bleakly. "We will discuss this later, you and I," he said.

"It is suicide," said Indaro.

"Yes," agreed Mason, "of course."

Indaro looked at Fell. For the first time in that long afternoon he was again the man she knew. Nothing that had gone before was important—who his father was, whether the emperor was immortal or not. Now there was a battle to be fought and Fell was himself again.

"So the invasion through the sewers is merely a distraction?" He addressed Gil, the other military commander there.

"A diversion, yes, but also a fallback," the man replied. "If you fail in your mission then the invasion force will attempt to kill Araeon. That is why we want you with them, Indaro."

She nodded, but she was wondering why they all thought she was going along with the plan. No one had asked her if *she* wanted to kill her emperor.

"Two hundred invaders against the Thousand. Poor odds," Fell commented, glancing at her. She shrugged, as if uncaring, or confident. Inside, she agreed with him.

"That is why we have chosen the Day of Summoning," Saroyan told him. "At least three centuries of the Thousand will be elsewhere."

"We have chosen two hundred warriors because we must use small boats to smuggle them to the coast beneath the Salient, into the maze of caverns there. Anything larger will be noticed," Gil explained. "Surprise will be our best weapon. Better than a hundred extra warriors."

Indaro thought she would rather have surprise *plus* a hundred warriors, but she held her tongue. Despite herself, now they were speaking of battle, like Fell, she was lifted by the prospect of action.

"Who will the invasion force be?" she asked Gil.

"Odrysians and Petrassi mostly. I will lead."

Fell said, "Good. Add Stalker and Garret. They are worth two men apiece."

"You will order them?" asked Mason.

"No. I will ask them to volunteer. And we will need plans of the palace, of the Keep."

"We have a friend in the palace who is charged with finding them for us. And maps of the sewers. We have only days before we ride. We must use the time well."

They all sat back and there was silence. Indaro knew they were all deferring to Fell.

"This cannot be the first plan to assassinate the emperor," he commented. "Others must have failed before. We need to know why."

Saroyan answered him. "There have been several that we know of and, I'm sure, many that we don't. The last was some eight years ago. The assassin came within moments of killing him." They watched her and eventually she went on, "He must have planned for some considerable time. He dressed as a Panjali messenger." She explained, "These men are used by the Odrysian kings to send vital messages to their counterparts in other lands. The man's head is shaved, a message is tattooed on the scalp and the hair allowed to grow back. The foreign leader then has the head shaved again to reveal the message. The messengers elect to have their tongues cut out as a token of their discretion. He was a very brave man."

Indaro saw the reflection of memory in her face. "You were there?"

Saroyan nodded, glancing at her.

"You know the emperor?"

The woman nodded.

"Then why," Indaro burst out angrily, "don't *you* kill him?"

Saroyan's face went pale and her lips tightened.

"It is not that simple," replied Mason.

"Why?" Indaro asked. "You are asking us to risk our lives on this half-baked conspiracy, when all she has to do is walk up to the emperor and stick a knife in his gut."

"Indaro is right," said Fell. "You are asking us to die for this cause. At least you could tell us the full truth."

"Everything we have told you is the truth," Mason answered.

"We have been rotting for weeks in your gaol," growled Fell. "Fed lies and half-truths. Now you present us with this ramshackle plan and tell us we must execute it within days. It is doomed to failure without the luck of the gods. Indaro and I, and Stalker and Garret, are lucky soldiers. We would not be here if we weren't. But luck can only achieve so much. It is not enough that everything you tell us is true. That is a politician's answer. We need complete honesty. We need to know everything you know. We do not want any unpleasant surprises when it is too late."

In the silence that followed, Indaro realised he had not named Doon, and a cold numbness reached into her heart.

Then a voice asked, "Who will be emperor?"

They turned to look at Elija. Reddening, he lowered his gaze. "When the emperor is dead, who will be emperor?" he asked again. "One of you?"

"No," Gil replied, sitting down. "Marcellus Vincerus."

"Is he in on this conspiracy?" Fell asked. "Does he know he is fated to be emperor? Is it *his* plan? And are you just his agents?"

Gil shook his head. "He knows nothing of this. He is loyal to the emperor. But with Araeon dead, Marcellus will take the throne. He is First Lord of the City. It will be his duty."

"Do you know him so well?" Fell asked.

"No, but I do," Saroyan put in. "He will do his duty. And he will end the war."

Indaro wondered at the woman's motives. Gil she believed. Even if he had concealed intentions, she believed he was in this to end the carnage. Mason she was not sure of. But Saroyan, with her reticence and half-explanations, reeked of deceit. Indaro looked at Fell, who clearly agreed with her; he was scowling at the lord lieutenant.

"If he is so keen to end the war, why does he not kill the emperor himself and take command? With the Thousand behind him, he would be invulnerable."

An unfamiliar expression crossed Saroyan's face. Indaro realised it was disgust. Was this cold-faced woman offended at the suggestion that Vincerus kill his emperor?

Mason rubbed his face with his hands and sighed. "You do not understand the relationship between these people. They are not like us, Fell. They have known each other for centuries, longer. They have fought together, and against each other, betrayed each other and conspired together down the generations. Marcellus is younger than Araeon, and he sees the emperor as his father, grandfather, teacher and rival, as well as his emperor. Araeon is the last of his kind. When he is gone Marcellus and a very few others will be adrift in a world of mayflies, short-lived creatures who can achieve nothing before they die.

"But I believe Marcellus *will* end the war. That is what this plan rests on. He knows it is destroying the City and the lands about it. Araeon does not care any more how many die, as long as he can win. He can no longer see it is not a winnable war. Marcellus has more clarity. I believe he will be a good emperor, as emperors go." He added, "All our futures depend on that belief."

He called to the guards for wine and food. "We have much more to discuss today. In ten days you will ride for the Paradise Gate. From there Indaro, Elija and Gil will set out to join the invasion boats at Adrastto. Fell will enter the City and join Shuskara. The City is hard to get into now, more so since the mutiny in the Little Opera House. It takes special papers, which will be supplied by Saroyan."

The lord lieutenant stood suddenly and gazed impatiently at Mason. "Saroyan must return to the Red Palace," he told them. "She has a long ride and the sun is falling. We will not see her again."

The last words seemed heavy with fate. As the woman turned to leave, wearing weariness like a cloak, Indaro asked her, "Why do you dislike me?"

The lord lieutenant walked round the table to her and looked into her eyes. Indaro saw real antipathy there. Saroyan said coldly, "Because I do not trust you, Indaro Kerr Guillaume. I know your father and he loves the City, for all its faults, and he would never betray the emperor, for all *his*. I believe that deep down you are the same, and therefore at the end you will betray us all."

And she stalked out, leaving Indaro shocked by her words and the depth of her loathing. Fell rested his hand on her shoulder. It burned like fire. She looked at him.

"Pay no attention," he said gently. "She does not know you. Now, come with me. I have grave news."

PART FIVE

Lords of Blood

Chapter 28

In a far-flung wing of the Red Palace, distant from the public clamour and from the insistent smell of horses and cavalrymen, was a suite of rooms clustered around a pretty flower-filled courtyard. In the warm days of autumn all the windows were flung open to take in the scent of the late-blooming roses clambering up white-painted walls and spilling fragrantly into casements.

A small slender woman, her fair ringlets tied above her head with ribbon, slipped out of a silken robe and stepped into an enamelled bath. She sat down gracefully and, with a sigh, slid luxuriously under the petal-strewn water.

"Ow!" she cried, sitting up again quickly and feeling around in the bathwater.

"What's wrong, my lady?" asked her new maid, hovering anxiously.

The woman pouted. "Did you throw thorns in with the rose petals?" she asked plaintively, showing the maid a tiny piece of twig she had found in the depths of the perfumed water.

The maid took it from her. "I'm sorry, my lady," she said, her face creased with worry.

The woman's face cleared and she chuckled. "Don't be a fool, Amita. I'm only teasing. You haven't been here long, but you will find me a considerate employer, as long as you are sensible. Now, please soap my back. Use that bottle there, with the lavender floating in it."

Amita poured a little of the soap onto a soft cotton cloth and gently washed the woman's back, from her hairline where tiny fair tendrils escaped their ties down to the cleft of her buttocks. The back was perfect, pale as moonstone, unblemished as moonlight itself. Afterwards the woman leaned back in the water, eyes closed. Amita took the chance to look at her face critically. The afternoon light, shining directly in the casement, cruelly betrayed her age. There were young crow's feet at the corners of her eyes and the skin under her chin was a little loose. The Lady Petalina behaved like a girl of sixteen, but she had seen more than forty summers, Amita guessed.

Petalina sighed again and brushed wet flowers from her thighs. "I think I'll wear the blue and cream cotton this afternoon," she mused.

Amita was unsure what to do. Was she supposed to fetch the dress now? This was not a simple thing. There were hundreds of dresses, and Amita had no idea which one was meant. Or should she continue to attend her mistress in the bath and get the dress later? She was wondering whether to ask when she realised Petalina had opened her big blue eyes and was regarding her.

"When I have bathed you will dry me and powder me," she explained. "Then I will put on a clean silk robe and lie down for a nap. That will give you time to fetch the dress. Call one of the under-maids to empty the bath and put it away and to help you clean this room and take the towels to the laundry." Then she closed her eyes again languorously.

Amita had been told Petalina had once been a serving maid herself. The woman had been kind to her, so far, but was said to have a fiery temper. Amita had seen no sign of that. But then, she had been in her employ less than a day.

"Remind me," Petalina asked, her eyes still closed, "where did you come to me from?"

"From the house of general Kerr, my lady. I served his granddaughter."

"Ah yes, the poor child who died of a lung infection."

"Yes, my lady, it was very sad."

Petalina opened her eyes again and gazed at Amita. Amita looked innocently back, then dropped her eyes, hoping her assumed grief for a child she had never known would conceal her lies. Pretending to have served a fourteen-year-old girl would cover her deficiencies as a lady's maid, she hoped.

"The general's wife is a woman of great beauty," Petalina commented. "A rare beauty. And are there other grandchildren?"

"There are five sons, I believe," Amita replied. "Most of them grown. They all have children. Her Ladyship . . ."

"Yes?" The blue gaze was penetrating.

"She . . . has very fine eyes, my lady." Truth to tell, the general's wife was a horse-faced woman with pox-marked skin and a nose like a marble. She had loyally produced sons for a family which specialised in generals in quantity rather than quality. Or so Amita had been told.

Petalina continued to gaze at her maid, then the corner of her mouth twitched and she gave a little chuckle. Then, to Amita's surprise, she slowly sank under the water, until only the topknot of curls could be seen. There was a gurgle and an explosion of bubbles, then her head came out of the water again and, dripping, she smiled at her maid with glee.

"I think we are going to get on very well, Amita," she said.

Once Petalina was out of her bath, dried and powdered like a babe, and settled on her day couch in a white silk robe, Amita found her way to the wardrobe rooms, where Petalina's hundreds of dresses were to be found. This meant going outside and across a private garden in the shadow of the palace wall, then through a passage which brought her out to the back of the suite of rooms. She had been shown the way by one of the under-maids, who had complained about the inconvenience. Amita had agreed with the girl, but in fact it was perfect for her, as it gave her an excuse to slip into the garden whenever she wanted.

There were three large wardrobe rooms, one for day dresses, one for evening gowns and one for cloaks and shawls. Shoes and gloves, muffs and hats were in a fourth room filled with cupboards and shelves and drawers. Only Petalina's linen and her silk day gowns were close to hand.

At last Amita found a flimsy cotton dress striped in blue and green and, hoping it was the right one, draped it with a linen cover and carried it round to the front of the building, holding it high above the ground. When she let herself into the vestibule she heard the deep tones of a man's voice coming from Petalina's parlour. She hesitated. Should she take the dress into the bedroom? If the door from bedroom to parlour was open she would see and be seen. She had been taught that personal servants were blind and deaf to the activities of their employers, and invisible to their eyes. Biting her lip, she pushed through the door into the bedroom. She crossed the pink-and-cream-painted room and, her back to the parlour door, hung the dress up, taking off the cover then brushing it down lightly with her palm.

"Amita!" Petalina's voice was commanding, and Amita went through obediently to the parlour. A lean weather-beaten man with a bald brown head and a wide white moustache was leaning on a stick by the open window. He was watching his hostess, who was dressed only in flimsy silk, and he no more than glanced at Amita.

"You may go now," Petalina told her crisply. "Attend me an hour before sunset. In the meantime, go to Assaios and ask her to fit you for three new shifts. Do you know where to eat?"

Amita nodded, and Petalina dismissed her with a flick of her perfumed fingers. The girl left the room and quietly closed the door behind her. Then she paused and listened. The voices were soft but clear in the still afternoon.

The visitor said, "He returns from the east tomorrow. I needed to speak to you first."

Petalina's voice was more serious than Amita had heard before. She told the man, "He sent me a message to tell me he would be here with the dawn. I wasn't expecting to see him again before winter."

"Why is he here?"

"Some sort of crisis." Petalina's voice was careless. "Something lost. Or something found. There's always something. But you should not come here in daylight, Dol Salida. You're too easily recognised. What happened to our midnight tryst?"

The man grunted. "To be seen coming to your rooms at night is too perilous. Marcellus would have me killed. My presence here in daylight can have an innocent explanation."

Petalina laughed. "There are no innocent explanations in this palace," she told him.

Then they lowered their voices, or moved farther into the apartments, for Amita could hear no more.

Amita, daydreaming, gazed at herself in the sheet of polished tin decorating the main door of Petalina's rooms. She knew she was not pretty. She had been told so often enough as a child. Her best point was her shining fair hair and usually she hid behind its curtain. Now, though, the hair was pulled back out of sight under a modest grey scarf, and her dark brows dominated her thin bony face with its anxious eyes.

She was twelve when she and Elija fled the City. She was now twenty, and Elija eighteen. And Emly would be sixteen. She always included Emly in any thoughts about herself and Elija, because Elija always did, and because she knew that if his sister still lived Elija would discover her one day and then she, Amita, would have to leave him. In her mind pictures she imagined Emly looking like her brother, dark and sparrow-boned, with kind eyes and a sweet smile. She wondered where he was, and a trickle of fear ran through her.

After several weeks on board ship Amita and Elija had been taken to a distant island, a place of green hills and grey sandy beaches, where they were housed with the family of a ship owner. They were still frightened then, for everything in their lives in the City had taught them to be frightened. The ship owner's wife instructed them in the language of the island's people, and she showed them how to read, and for a while they even went to a school there. They were happy days.

Then one day a ship had come for them. They feared they were to be returned to the City and they said a sad farewell to the kind wife and the islands. But they were taken across the sea again, then by land for many days to a small farming community. There they met the man called Gil who was to be their guide and mentor. And there they were set to learning the arcane and difficult script of the old City, a language long ago abandoned except in some imperial documents.

Amita left Petalina's rooms and turned left down a long corridor which led deeper into the palace. After a few wrong turnings she found Assaios, the grim-faced housekeeper of the south wing, and tried to be patient while the woman slowly and methodically had her measured for clothes more suitable to a palace servant, then lectured her on her duties. She had already been told by Petalina that she need pay no attention to this old woman, but Amita saw no reason to make enemies and she stood with head lowered submissively as Assaios told her where she was forbidden to go, how not to address her betters, not to look at anyone even if they addressed her, and about the restrictions on water, food and fuel, where and what she could not eat, and about her clothes, her manners and her status, which was non-existent.

Amita spent the time deciding what to do with the unexpected gift of an afternoon's liberty. With only thirty days to go before the Day of Summoning she needed to know her way round this wing of the palace and to find a route to the Library of Silence, as she had been ordered. She had studied meagre plans of the palace before she was brought here, but she could not recognise much of what she saw. Those maps dated from when this wing was the women's quarters of the palace, more than a hundred years before. Now it housed sets of apartments for guests of the emperor and the other lords and their friends. Much of it was empty for much of the time. But, still, it was guarded, she had seen armed men in the corridors, and to wander round haphazardly during daylight hours would call attention to her.

So, reluctantly released by Assaios, she decided to make her way back to Petalina's rooms, making a mental note of all side corridors, staircases up and down and doorways she saw on her way. She would memorise them, for she had an excellent memory, then investigate them one at a time as the days passed. If it came to it, she could always ask where the Library of Silence was, but she would only do that as a last resort. It had been drummed into her over and over that she must not be noticed.

"Girl!"

She had reached the long corridor leading back to her employer's rooms, and was lingering beside a staircase decorated with gilt carvings of fruit and flowers which curled upwards into the light and downwards into darkness. She started nervously, glanced at the man who had called her, then dropped her head. It was the man with the moustache who had been visiting Petalina. Her heartbeat quickened.

"Sir?"

He limped over to her, leaning on his stick.

"You are the Lady Petalina's new girl?"

"Yes, sir," she mumbled, staring at her feet.

"Where were you employed before?"

"At the palace of the general Kerr, sir."

"Who brought you here?"

She glanced up quickly. His keen, deep-set eyes probed her face and she looked away, trying to show fear, which was not difficult, and bafflement.

"I don't know, sir. A servant, sir."

The man said nothing for a moment. Then, "What is your name?"

"Amita, sir."

"How old are you?"

"Fifteen, sir."

"Where are you from?"

"Sir?"

"Where were you born?"

They had prepared her for this. "In Gervain, sir."

"Who are your parents?"

"My father was a soldier, sir."

"In one of the Kerr regiments?"

She stared at him, etching confusion across her face. "I don't know, sir," she wailed, then she added tearfully, "I'm a good girl, sir." The man's face, which had been friendly, became tight with annoyance at her tears, and he grunted, "Get along, girl."

She ducked her head and scurried off.

D ol Salida had learned the game of urquat in an Odrysian prison camp east of the Fkeni city of Palim. Looking at himself now, old and bald and with a game leg, it was hard to believe he was once a reckless young cavalryman, as all cavalrymen must be if they are to face the eastern tribes, particularly the Fkeni, whose subtle and creative ways with execution are the stuff of nightmare. He was lucky to be captured by the small band of Odrysians in the fight, although after four years in their camp he would have argued with the word *lucky*. But he was released, in a rare exchange of prisoners with the City, with all his limbs and his genitals intact and he thanked the Gods of Ice and Fire for that.

He had learned patience in those four years, a hard lesson for a young rider whose opiate was speed and self-believed invulnerability. And he had learned the art of urquat, for art he considered it, requiring as it does a fusion of memory, focus, luck and cunning. An urquat set comprises one hundred and twenty two-sided counters with fifty-six different symbols on them. Sets of urquat counters were manufactured in various colours, to make memorising them even more of a feat. In his friendly games at the Shining Stars Inn with Creggan and Bart they always used the same set, in red, blue and white. But for the Blue Moon Challenge, in which Dol Salida played annually, a new set of different-coloured counters was opened for each game. It was a challenge which had once attracted more than a hundred masters from lands near and far. Now it was played out each year among the dozen or so who still lived in the City and it was a lacklustre affair, which Dol nevertheless attended without fail.

As the prison had taught him patience and urquat, so, in its turn, the game had taught Dol focus. And those two qualities, patience and focus, practised now over many decades, had contrived to create the foremost qualification for his present assignment—vigilance.

He was especially vigilant when he saw a new face. He had a prodigious memory for faces and names and had never before seen this whey-faced maid Amita. Which in itself was suspicious. He limped the streets of the City each day, watching faces, particularly those of girls of an age to be in the army. This was his official employment, the one the City paid him to do. And he had attended the Kerr palace on occasions, as part of the work the City didn't pay him for and knew nothing of. But he had never seen this bony face before. Hardly remarkable, for there must be hundreds of girls hidden away in laundries and taverns, brothels and barns, working in fields and factories, who rarely saw the light of day. Yet his vigilance was heightened in matters concerning Petalina.

He had known the woman, and her younger sister Fiorentina, since they were maidens in their father's home and he was a distant cousin of some sort. He had ridden away to serve the City when they were mere children and beneath his interest, but he had noticed them with painful clarity when he returned to his home some years later, on the death of his father. Petalina had always assured Dol he was the one to receive the precious flower of her virginity. He had never believed it, and he was amused when that fragile bloom proved robust enough for a second blossoming when Petalina met Marcellus. In the decades that followed Dol Salida had always stayed in touch with her. She was his first love, and when her association with Marcellus eventually proved valuable to him, well, all the better.

He smiled to himself. The young cavalryman he once was would have sneered at the maxim "You can never be too careful." But these were the words the older man lived by and they had kept him safe in an increasingly unsafe City.

He was making his slow way towards the administration offices of the Red Palace in the west wing of the new building. It was his excuse for being there. He would raise the matter of Petalina's new maid with Dashoul, who was responsible for many mountains of paperwork in the name of security. He would ensure this girl was investigated and questioned.

Dol had five daughters himself. Three had died in the war, for they were blessed with his recklessness although not his luck. The other two had survived, and he now had eight grandchildren, two of whom were, in their turn, fighting for their City. Each night at his unremarkable home adjoining the palace precincts he prayed to the gods to deliver the pair from evil and bring them safe home. He had never been tempted to use his influence, his many contacts, to steer the youngsters in his family away from the worst of the fighting, despite the frequent tearful nagging of his wife, Gerta. He despised those who spoke in support of the City but subverted it by bending its rules for their own purposes.

So he was disappointed, but not surprised, when he noticed that the daughter of his urquat partner Bartellus was not growing any older. Three years before, when Dol and the old soldier had first met, the girl was fourteen, but now she was only fifteen. He was not crass enough to question Bart about it. He had primed Creggan, musing about the girl when the two were alone at the urquat table, waiting for Bart to appear. Once Bartellus arrived Dol changed the subject, knowing that eventually Creggan who, once faced with an unanswered question, hung on to it like a flea on a dog, would eventually come round to asking.

Dol Salida then approached the dogged Dashoul, not to inform him of Emly's status, but to enquire about Old Bart himself. He discovered Bartellus was a man of the City, born and bred in Gervain, who had served his emperor loyally over two decades in the 14th Imperial and later the infantry company they called Ballatye's End. He had been invalided out fifteen years before at the rank of sergeant, had dropped off the map for a while, then reappeared living in Lindo with the daughter. All this Dashoul could validate. Except that the Bartellus in his records had three sons, all now dead serving their City. And not a daughter in sight.

Dol kept the discrepancy to himself, for it could be a stumble by the City's bureaucracy, as the name Bartellus was scarcely unusual, and he had decided to set a man to following Bart when he heard the old man had been knifed in an attack on his home. The House of Glass had been destroyed by fire, along with the neighbouring houses. Bartellus was gravely wounded, but he survived and was nursed back to health by the alleged daughter. Dol

Salida was not a cruel man, and he had better things to do than press an injured old man's only daughter into the army. There would be plenty of time when he was back on his feet again.

But then the old man, whoever he was, disappeared, the girl with him. This had piqued Dol's interest further and he had set out with renewed vigour to find out who the old soldier was, and what had become of him.

Dol had wandered by the gutted house in Blue Duck Alley, had idly chatted with its neighbours, bought ale in local inns, and quietly met some of his army of informants. He found out little he did not already know. The House of Glass had been torched certainly, perhaps by assailants unknown, perhaps by Old Bart himself, they said. But the man had been stabbed, and had been rescued from the burning building by his daughter and a heroic passer-by who had carried him across the wooden bridge which joined the attics of the glassmaker's house to those of the lodging house opposite. Afterwards the old man and his daughter, the passing hero, and the woman and two children living in the top floor of the lodging house had all disappeared into the teeming City.

Dol had exerted all his considerable charm on the lodging house owner, to no avail. The woman, Meggy, thin and tired and frightened by anyone asking questions, however charming, had made it her business not to know anything of the business of others. She sat on the front step of her building, feeding noxious scraps to a smelly dog, and refused to discuss any of her residents or even look Dol in the face. She could tell him nothing about Bartellus or Emly, except their names, and knew less about the mysterious rescuer.

Dol had thanked her extravagantly for her non-existent help and turned to set off on the long walk back to Burman Far. As he did so he caught the eye of a thin, dirty child who scuttled away from him round a corner, then peered back around it, eyeing him calculatingly. He limped over to the boy, who skittered away down the street, pausing at the next corner. Dol had not the time or energy for this game, so he slipped a silver double-pente into his palm and flashed it at the urchin. The boy gestured for Dol to follow, and ran down a side-alley. Sighing, Dol followed, taking out the curved knife he always wore at his side.

The boy led him to the rear of a stable, where bales of hay were guarded by a fat man who lay against one, snoring loudly.

The urchin sneered, "Don't need that pig-sticker," nodding at the knife in Dol's hand.

"I'll be the judge of that," Dol replied gruffly.

The child rubbed his grubby nose with a grubbier hand. "I saw it," he said proudly. "I saw the fire."

"Tell me something I don't already know and this coin is yours," Dol told him, pocketing the double-pente and resting his rear against a bale of hay.

"I dunno what you know," the boy said sullenly.

He had a point. Dol shrugged. "Try me."

"I saw it go on fire. There was flames all up it . . ."

"Do you know Old Bart and Emly?"

The boy nodded.

"Do you know where they are now?"

"They went to the 'firmary."

This was not true. The infirmaries were the first places Dol checked. He heaved himself back up on his feet.

The boy said hastily, "I dunno where they gone now. But I seen the soldier."

"What soldier?"

"Soldier what climbed up the bridge."

"The man who rescued them?" All he had heard was that the man was tall and blond.

The urchin nodded. "I seen 'im in the alley."

"Since the fire?"

The boy shook his head impatiently at his slowness. "Nah. Before. 'E was watching."

"Watching what?"

"Watching Ol' Bart and the girl. I seen 'im. Down side of Meggy's."

"Was he now?" Dol flicked the coin at the boy, who caught it deftly and dropped it into a pocket inside his filthy trousers. "Tell me everything you can remember about him."

"'E was tall . . ."

"Taller than me?"

The boy grunted derisively, "Yer. An' younger."

"How old?"

The boy put his head on one side in a pantomime of thought. "Young as 'im." He pointed at the snoring man, who Dol reckoned to be about thirty.

"'Is hair was fair. 'E 'ad on a sort of soldier's coat wiv no arms. Red."

"Red uniform jerkin. Any marks? Stripes or buttons? Did the soldier have tattoos?"

The boy closed his eyes in thought. "Nah," he said eventually.

Dol sighed. To find an anonymous soldier in a city full of soldiers was a challenge worthy of his skills.

"He 'ad a mark on 'is arm," the boy volunteered.

"A tattoo?"

"Nah. Like he got burned by the fire, only"—the boy screwed up his face—"only it was old."

"An old burn?" A memory was jolted free deep in Dol's memory. "Was it like an *S*?"

The boy stared at him uncomprehendingly.

"Like this," Dol bent down and drew an *S* in the dirt. "An *S*."

"Yer. Sssss."

Dol had the memory complete now—Creggan talking about a soldier in the Shining Stars Inn, and Bart asking questions. A soldier with a military tattoo of seven stars, tall with blond hair, and a brand on his arm.

"Ssss," repeated the boy, pleased with the sound. "Might be fer 'is name."

"His name, yes it might be," Dol said absently, thinking of the urquat game.

"It was Sami," volunteered the boy.

"What was?"

"'Is name. It was Sami."

Dol barely stopped himself from grabbing the annoying child by the throat.

"You know his name, boy?" he roared.

"Yer," said the urchin defensively, stepping back. "I 'eard it. When they was leavin' Meggy's. Nex' day or the nex'. She liked 'im, Meggy did. I saw. 'E was kind to 'er ole dog. I 'eard 'er. She said to 'im, 'Take care, Sami,' she said."

Chapter 29

It was a palace of intrigue, a place of secrets. Its deepest layers had been laid down in the unremembered past when the river Menander flowed innocently in sunlight past newly built stone halls and mud-brick homes. The river had been spanned by bridges, and more bridges. Then the bridges themselves were built upon and as the centuries marched past the great river sank altogether under the rising City, to become merely part of the sewers. Men had forgotten its name.

But the river did not go away. Millions of tons of water poured each day from the south and, in the rainy season, from the high plains to the east. It flowed under the City, through the lowest levels, crushed and flattened by history. It seeped through cracks in old stone and forced the stone to crumble. It penetrated prehistoric oak pilings. Then it exited the City through a multitude of tunnels and caves, sieves and conduits, drains and ditches, eventually running to the sea.

But antique mechanisms, built long ago by wiser men, no longer worked, and some of the water had no place to go. As the deepest layers of the City's buildings slowly collapsed, so the flood levels rose.

In the crucial years when the gates and weirs beneath the City started to fail, the palace engineers had not the will or the courage to do anything about it, leaving it to later generations, for whom it was then too late. Mechanisms which could have been repaired now lay drowned. As the lowest levels of the Red Palace collapsed, great cracks appeared in its stone walls, and in the nights people could hear a wretched groaning as the fabric of the palace was tortured by the rising water. Walls and ceilings were shored up by huge timbers, but this often made the problem worse, for the pressures built without balance and the palace twisted and writhed like a great animal struggling in a trap.

The engineers, in a bid to relieve the problem, built three dams outside the walls to the south, to store rain and snow-melt from the mountains and leach it into the City under man's control. For a decade or so the scheme worked and water levels stabilised. But two of the dams were on land lost to the Petrassi. Until now they had been left intact by their new lords, but more than one engineer's dreams were haunted by fear of what would happen if the enemy decided to destroy them and unleash their waters on the sinking City.

The Hall of Watchers, where Bartellus had first met Indaro, and near where the historian Marshall Creed had glimpsed an angel in the darkness, had been part of an early palace built centuries before. Then a new building was erected on its carcase, and somehow it had disappeared from the plans of today's engineers and the entrance to it was known to only a few. The stone carvings of birds perched in black water now, their blind eyes watching the sluggish lapping and sucking as the water oozed in and out through what was once a portal into the sewers.

Two levels above the drowned hall was the Library of Silence. This too had been abandoned, thousands of its books moved up to drier levels, others left to rot.

Amita had been told to seek out the library for two reasons. Firstly to confirm the library entrance to the sewers was, as feared, now unuseable. There were few known portals from the sewers to the palace, and the changing geography of the tunnels made even those perilous or impossible. If the Hall of Watchers was impassable, another route must be found, and quickly. So Amita was also tasked to search the library for plans of the City which showed other portals, perhaps in the flooded dungeons.

Five days after she first arrived at the palace she made her way, cloaked and hooded, at dead of night to seek out the sewers again. Petalina had entertained her patron Marcellus until not long before, and now the man had left and Petalina slept. Amita guessed she had several hours to herself. Thin light filtered through the high windows of the corridors as she padded barefoot on stone. She hurried for she knew she had far to go and much to do. Even at night the palace was busy, and she stopped several times, sliding out of sight in doorways and round corners, and once behind a statue, to avoid troops of soldiers and others with a mysterious mission in the midnight palace. She could afford to be seen once, for she could claim she was new to the palace, and both lost and stupid. But a second time would call attention to her, and that would never do. So she moved from shadow to shadow and prayed to not meet anyone, least of all the man with the moustache and gimlet eyes.

It took her more time than she had hoped to find the gilded stairway, which she now knew was called the Pomegranate Stair. For a while she was uncertain she was in the right place, for the stairway was lit by torches and blazed with reflected light, whereas when she had seen it before it was in the thin grey shafts of late afternoon.

She hesitated, then ran lightly down to the next storey, looked around, then went down two more levels. Here the balusters were shabby and chipped, some were crooked and several missing. The blaze of lights ended here and another, grey stone, stairwell curved farther downwards into darkness. With nervous fingers she unhooked a torch from the wall and set off down.

The smell of dank decay in her nostrils reminded her of the stench of the sewers. At the bottom of the stairwell a corridor stretched both ways. Amita chose left. This lower part of the palace appeared abandoned, and she moved quickly. Once she heard the smart slap of boots on stone in the distance, but otherwise she was surrounded by stillness, broken only by the soft spluttering of the torch.

After a while she stopped, admitting to herself that she had come the wrong way. She turned and hurried back, running to make up lost time. But when she could just make out the glow of the Pomegranate Staircase again in the distance she paused. She could hear many bootsteps coming down the stairway. Her heart beat faster and she quietly bracketed the torch and slid into a shadow on the wall.

Two figures met in torchlight at the bottom of the stair. One was a dark-haired man, his beard neat and close-cut, dressed all in black. The second was only a boy, younger than herself, with fair hair and a thin gawky frame. He was clothed in green silk which glistened slickly in the flickering light. Amita shrank back, fearing they would somehow sense her presence.

The dark man was asking, "Why are we meeting in this dreary place, lord?"

"I like it down here," the boy told him. "It reminds of the old times. I had forgotten for a moment that you don't like to get your feet wet, Rafe. Or your hands dirty," he added slyly.

He glanced up, and Amita saw there were two armed soldiers in the darkness above them on the stair.

The boy sighed, as if bored with the conversation already. "I am seeking army records," he told the man called Rafe.

"Down here? I thought they were transferred to Dashoul in the south wing?"

"Not all of them. Anything older than twenty years still languishes in the Library of Silence."

"They will rot away if they are not rescued," said Rafe. "I will see to it. What are you seeking?"

"Nothing important," the boy told him evasively. Then he said, "I am told you are responsible for the repossession of the Gulon Veil."

"Yes, lord."

"You have the emperor's eternal gratitude. We thought it long gone from the City. Where was it?"

"A girl in Lindo. She gave it to a merchant's son, perhaps as a love token. He recognised it and reported it to the palace."

"How did this merchant's son know of the veil?" asked the boy. He sounded sulky, Amita thought, and she wondered who he was. "How many people knew it was lost, and of value?"

"Very few, lord," said Rafe mildly. "But we could scarcely hunt it down if no one knew it was lost. The merchant's son was tipped off by one of the girl's associates, who boasted that it was of great value to the emperor. So he sought out an agent of the palace. My network of contacts is legion. Eventually they always draw in the information we need."

"Eventually," the boy repeated. "How did this girl come to have the thing?"

"We don't know. My agents took it upon themselves to destroy any evidence of its existence." Rafe sighed, "The gods save me from servants with initiative."

"Nevertheless, Rafe, you have our gratitude. We've been eight years without its power, and the reflections were . . . increasingly difficult. Ask anything of your emperor."

"You are generous, lord." Rafe turned back towards the staircase, then the boy said, "The merchant's son. See to it that he is . . ."

"Rewarded, lord?"

"Killed."

Rafe bowed and said formally, "With your leave, lord . . ."

"You have always been anxious to seek the light, Rafe. It is unnatural."

Rafe glanced up the staircase. "Like you, lord, I do not sleep, but my lady does and sometimes I like to watch her."

Then he asked again, "What were you seeking in the records, lord?"

The boy hesitated then, as if anxious to prolong the conversation, said, "I am on the track of a soldier called Fell Aron Lee. It seems he is not who he says he is."

Rafe chuckled. "None of us are. Fell Aron Lee," he mused. "I have heard the name recently. When was it? Kantei?"

"Before the rout at Salaba, lord," one of his warriors replied. "He commanded the Wildcats. He left the tower to join the battle against his general's orders."

Rafe smiled. "Yes, of course. Flavius was beside himself. Fell was lucky to die in battle, for Flavius would have had him crucified if he'd lived. What did you find out about him?"

"A history of exemplary service to the City. But there is no record of where Fell came from—of his father and his early years there is nothing."

"There are many fatherless sons in the army."

"But he has no mother and no place of birth. It appears he sprang into existence as junior aide to Shuskara at the age of fourteen. This in itself makes him suspicious. You believe he died with the rest of the Maritime?"

"Chances are. Why do you seek him?"

"I have heard he has made a claim of me."

"A claim?"

The boy shrugged.

"Heard from whom?" Rafe persisted.

"The usual channels. Information passed through Dashoul's people, or through Saroyan." He shrugged again as if it was unimportant. Then he said petulantly, "It is not your concern. Rafael."

Rafe nodded and bowed again. "Good hunting then," he said and, flanked by his warriors, he stepped lightly up the stair. The sound of clattering armour faded until Amita was surrounded by oppressive silence again. The boy stood in the pool of torchlight for some time, apparently deep in thought. Amita waited, fearing he would come her way, ready to flee, but suddenly he started walking down the corridor in the opposite direction. After a few heartbeats Amita followed at a careful distance.

The boy passed several ornate doorways without pause for he seemed to know where he was going. Then he vanished from sight. Amita crept along the corridor to where he had disappeared, terrified that he would suddenly return and confront her. He had exited through a wide doorway which led to a round chamber in which another flight of stone stairs led farther down. Amita had left her torch behind, fearing he would see the glow. So she crept down the stairs in darkness, knowing she would be caught if he returned. Each time she was tempted to turn back and flee this wretched place she reminded herself that the days were passing quickly and Elija's life might depend on what she found.

She had been descending for some time, holding blindly to the stone wall, when her bare foot stepped into water. Its slimy cling brought back all the anxieties of life in the Halls. It was up to her knees and she felt forward carefully with the other foot, wondering if there was another step down. But there was not; she was at the bottom. There was a dim torch glow coming from her left. She crept towards it, testing each footfall lest she come to more stairs.

The water was icy cold, and the air around her felt thick with the smells of standing water and wet stone. She shivered, with cold and with dread.

She found the boy in a room to her right. The carved oak door was half open and reflected the flicker of his torch. She looked for a bolthole and found, a little farther along the corridor, a deep niche in the wall where she could hide if he came out. Then she returned to the carved door and watched through the crack.

The chamber was full of books. Some of the shelves were empty, but there were piles of books, apparently randomly laid on tables and stools. Some had been left on the flooded floor and were fat and pulpy. The boy had climbed onto a central table and seated himself there, his long legs folded under him like a spider's. He had a pile of books beside him and in the light of the torch he was opening each one and leafing through. Each volume was large and he balanced them with difficulty on his bony knees. Amita wondered why she was still watching. He could be there for hours, and if this was the Library of Silence, which she guessed it was, she must come back. She wondered what the time was, whether it was dawn. She had just determined to leave and return another night when the boy slipped down from his perch. He placed the book he had been reading open on the table and briskly tore out several pages. He closed the book and placed it on a shelf among similar volumes. Then he headed for the door.

Amita moved away, careful not to make a splashing noise. She slid into the niche she had found and saw the glow of the torch shine brightly on the grey water at her feet, then diminish as the boy sloshed back towards the staircase. She followed the torchlight and saw it go upwards as he climbed the stairs. Then, when all sounds had ceased, she grabbed a torch off the wall and headed back to the library.

Petalina rose slowly to wakefulness. She lay adrift in the tangled sheets, unwilling to move. Her throat was sore and her eyes gritty. Her limbs were leaden, like lumps of meat. She took a deep breath and coughed.

"Amita!" she croaked.

But no one came, and at last she pushed herself wearily on one elbow and looked around. It was still before dawn and weak light was filtering through the windows, which faced east, bathing the room in shades of grey. It showed upturned wine cups, empty bottles and discarded clothes. Still no one came. Petalina, exhausted by her effort, flopped back down again and lay like a starfish, staring at the ornate ceiling.

I'm getting too old for this, she thought.

She had known Marcellus Vincerus for nearly thirty years. She loved him deeply and she owed him everything: her wealth, her status as a palace courtesan—others who plied her trade were called whores—and even her life. He was a remarkable man and she missed him when he was away. When he walked into her room the air fizzed like sparkling wine, and when he left the wine became mere water.

But he was a bull. He was vigorous in everything he did, and he had as much passion and strength as he had decades before, when she first took him shyly to her bed. Perhaps more.

And I am just an old whore, she thought, and one day I'll admit that I can't keep up with my lover.

But it will not be today.

She sat up with determination, trying to ignore the ache in her lower back, the aches all over. Freeing her legs from the coiled sheets she slid out of bed and padded to the window, flinging it wide to let the morning in. She took a deep draught of cool air, smelling moist leaves and cut grass, and walked into the parlour. It was immaculate, cleaned and tidied by Amita after the lovers had moved to the bedroom. I am not such a lady, she thought, like Fiorentina, that I do not notice these things.

"Amita?" she said again, not really anticipating an answer. Her maid expected her to sleep until well into the forenoon, for she was young, and would have done that herself if she had the chance.

Petalina poured herself a glass of water and drank it greedily. Cleansing drops spilled down her naked breasts and belly. Still holding the glass, she stepped towards the vestibule, to the narrow wall bed where her maid slept. Then she thought, Why disturb the girl? She went back to bed and pulled the coverlet up to her nose, luxuriating in the lingering warmth.

A mita stared at the stubs of missing pages in the book. She had been taught the ancient script of the City, but this was in an unfamiliar, cramped hand and it took her a long while to work out what she was looking at. The thick damp yellowing pages, with their tiny precise writing, contained army lists, column after column of names of soldiers listed for each year in order of regiment and company, and including father's name and date and place of birth. Leafing backwards, she found the last regiment listed was the Second Adamantine Infantry. But so many pages had been torn out that it was impossible to see if the boy had been interested in that regiment, or a following one. Either he was very careless with these forgotten books or cautious to cover his tracks, Amita thought.

Realising she was wasting her time, she slid back into the icy water and brought her mind back to her quest. Clearly any hope of access to the Halls ended here in the knee-deep water. Nevertheless, anxious to complete her mission in full, she lifted the torch and started searching for the portal. In the rear of the library, deep in the mouldy stacks, she found a narrow panelled doorway, hinged on the inside. Amita stared at it reluctantly for a while, fearful that if she pulled it open she would unleash a wall of black water. Finally she realised the door was badly cracked and would never have held against a flood. She pulled it open a little and instantly smelled the foetid odour of the sewers. The water on the other side was also knee-deep. She dragged the door open with difficulty for it had rotted and warped. She thrust her torch through the gap, then her body. She stood in an empty round chamber, similar to one she had passed on her way down. Somewhere under the oily water lay steps leading down to the Hall of Watchers.

Her first task accomplished, she returned to the main library. She was worrying about the passage of time, and trying to guess if dawn had yet arrived. She resolved to investigate a small part of the chamber, then return another night. Bracketing the torch, she started methodically working her way along the shelves, using the frail wooden ladder when needed. Many of the books were covered with blooms of fungus, all were damp and decayed, and she dislodged armies of small beetles as she dragged each volume from its perch. She could hear the skittering of rats in the darkness of the stacks, and was conscious of the vulnerability of her bare ankles. From time to time she kicked out, thinking she felt movement against her skin, but the rats feared the torchlight and left her alone.

She avoided the many shelves of smaller books, deciding plans of the palace would either be in wide, flat volumes like the army lists, or in rolled documents. The big books were heavy and she had to clutch them to her to carry them to the central table to open and look at. She felt filthy, covered with dirt from the rotting books themselves and the fungus and mould clinging to them. Time weighed on her, but she kept picking out one more book, then one more, in the hope it would hold the information she sought.

Finally tiredness got the better of her and, climbing down the ladder manhandling a heavy book, she slipped and fell. She went down in the disgusting water, then jumped up quickly as a rat skittered close by.

Time to go, she resolved, abandoning the book to the water. As she reached up to take the torch from the bracket, she saw a pile of thin rolls of paper on the highest shelf above the doorway. Swamped by indecision, she stood for a long moment, then she dragged the ladder over and ran up the rungs, took the whole pile of papers down and took them to the central table.

They were plans! A quick look showed pale faded lines marking the outline of buildings or roads or perhaps sewers. She could not tell in the dim light in her tired state. She had no more time to waste, so she roughly folded the thin rolls in half and wrapped them in her shawl, then tied the shawl to her back and hurried away.

When she emerged at the Pomegranate Stair she saw dawn was already well broken. Conscious that in her filthy state she could not afford to be seen, she made her way cautiously back, hugging the dawn shadows. Several times she saw servants or soldiers coming her way, but they all had sleep in their eyes, and they did not see her standing statue-still in patches of gloom.

When she arrived, racked with nerves, back at Petalina's apartments, she peered into the bedroom, but her employer was still fast asleep. Breathing a deep sigh, Amita unwrapped the plans and stowed them in the base of her wall bed. She bit her lip anxiously. Though they were hidden, they stank, even to her, and she knew she would quickly have to move them away. There was no time now. She washed and re-dressed, then wrote a quick, carefully worded note. Checking on Petalina again, she left the apartments and went out in to the enclosed garden. There she slid the note into a crack in the garden wall in the shade of a fig tree.

A cavalry officer without a horse is a sad man indeed, thought Captain Riis.

The Nighthawks, the First Adamantine Cavalry, had become the victims of their own success and of the City's critical shortage of mounts.

The horsemen had still been in their Paradise Gate barracks when the Maritime Army had been hit first by the devastating flood then by the opportunistic Blueskin attack. They had mounted up and sallied out to aid their comrades, but the battlefield was far to the east and by the time the Nighthawks reached it, the infantry was routed, tens of thousands lying dead and dying on the plain. The riders, two thousand of them, engaged the enemy far to the south of the field, overwhelming and slaughtering, to a man, a Blues infantry company. Flushed with success, they eventually returned to the City, after a dozen skirmishes, forty men lighter but with more than one hundred and fifty extra horses found wandering riderless and half starved in the weeks after the rout.

The cavalry had been hard-hit over recent years by lack of new foals. The plains to the east of the City had been horse pastures for time out of mind. The light cavalry needed mounts that were of medium build, fast and agile yet with an enduring spirit, and many generations of such horses had flourished on the sweet grass of the plains. But the attrition rate among mounts was high, for broken legs accounted for huge losses in pitched battle. And as their pastures were threatened by the enemy the young horses were brought in closer to the City. Eventually there was nowhere left for them to graze and they could only be fed by importing grain from the City's allies far across the western seas. Still, the rate of horse deaths far outstripped the supply of feed, and the Nighthawks were celebrated for bringing in so many new mounts, a small bright spot in the gloomy aftermath of the battle.

That was in the winter. When spring came, and with it the threat of renewed campaigns by the enemy, the generals decided, in their wisdom, to form two new cavalry companies, made up of new young troopers on the rounded-up horses, and others borrowed from the Second Celestine and from the First Adamantine. Despite the outraged protests of the Nighthawks' commander, the company, deprived temporarily of its mounts, was put into the troop rotation of the palace guards, to the disgust of every rider.

So it was that Riis, now second in command of the horseless cavalry, came to be walking the wall of the south wing with two of his men.

"I'm hungry," complained Berlinger, a morose man, burly for a rider. "My stomach thinks my throat's been cut."

"That's your trouble, Berl," Riis replied, "you let your stomach do your thinking for you. If you get any fatter you'll never get on a horse again. Then you'll have something to complain about." The riders all moaned constantly about being out of the war, but Riis guessed many of them were glad of the respite from battle.

He gazed down into the pretty garden below. He could see the fig tree and a buttress.

"What's so interesting down there?" Berlinger asked.

"Women's quarters," said the third man, Chevia Half-hand, a veteran rider of Fkeni descent. "Whatever you're thinking, Riis, you could be put in irons for."

Ignoring him, Riis strode towards the steps leading down into the garden.

Berlinger said, "We're not allowed in the south wing. You know that."

"I'm not going in. I just need to piss," Riis answered, jogging down the steps.

"When did you get so pigging coy?" Berlinger called after him.

Riis had watched this garden over the last few days and he knew only two windows overlooked it, both high in a tower and both belonging to an ancient relative of the Vincerii. He ducked under the fig tree, out of sight of the two riders, and freed the loose brick in the buttress. He tucked the piece of paper he found into a pocket, relieved himself against the tree trunk, and jogged back up the steps.

Chapter 30

A few months previously Riis had been fighting on the north-eastern front against an allied army of Odrysians and Fkeni tribesmen at Cloud Ridge. The Nighthawks had then been in the field for more than three years and he saw no end to their ordeal, for the Blues had mountainous terrain to fall back to, a warren of narrow passes and box canyons and caves and tunnels, whereas the City forces had only the meagre protection of the shallow river Simios. One by one Riis had seen his comrades, including his brother Parr, die and there was still no sign that the First Adamantine and the infantry they supported would be relieved.

So it was with a dull sense of release that he heard he was among a hundred Nighthawks deployed to buttress a company of the Thousand guarding the emperor on a journey from the Fourth Eastern Gate on some unknown mission. He had mounted his horse and headed out, avoiding the looks of the men they were leaving in the midst of carnage.

He was under few illusions that the man they were to guard was really the emperor. He had watched the Immortal closely over the years, as closely as it is possible for a soldier in the field to watch an emperor who rarely leaves his palace. He had come to the conclusion that the man had several stand-ins. Riis' childhood ambition to kill the emperor had never been abandoned, but it receded further in his hopes and dreams the older he became. Still, he was glad to get away from the battle for a day or two, for he believed this diversion was just that, a harmless diversion.

He was riding some way behind the imperial carriage, behind a red-headed woman rider, a Wildcat, watching the way her buttocks spread pleasingly as they met her saddle, idly wishing he were that saddle and she astride him, warm and wet, when the imperial carriage suddenly rose like a rearing horse, and a sound like thunder battered his ears. He was wrestling with his panicking mount when a second bigger explosion hurled riders and horses around like dice.

Riis was thrown from the horse and for a moment he thought he was badly injured. He could feel nothing, hear nothing, see nothing in the flying dust. Then his vision cleared and he saw the redhead again. Somehow she was still mounted and as he watched, frozen in eerie silence, she leaned down and casually chopped the sword-arm off a warrior who lunged at her horse's belly.

Enemy soldiers were erupting from the ground. They were sluggish and hampered by the bodies of dead and dying horses and men, and the woman slashed and cut her way easily through heads and necks. The Blues were unequal to her, and Riis felt unequal as he watched.

He stumbled to his feet. He could hear nothing and he kept turning round, fearing he was being attacked from behind. He cast about for an uninjured mount, but there were none in sight. He saw a Blueskin warrior lying near the rubble of the black carriage, blood gouting from a half-severed leg. He walked over and cut the man's throat, and felt instantly better. A horse came trotting towards him through the swirling dust. He whistled, then realised it probably couldn't hear either, and signalled to it with the hand gestures all Nighthawk horses knew. To his surprise it obediently walked over. Riis leaped on its back and raced off in the direction he had seen the woman going.

When at last he spotted her she was crouched beside an injured man, a soldier with a badly broken arm. She had taken off her helm, and her thick coppery hair flowed freely. As he watched she pulled it back in her fist and tied it in a ragged knot at her neck. He stared at her stern profile and thought she looked like a goddess, albeit a dirty one, for her face was smudged with dust and smeared with sweat. As he watched she touched the injured man on his good shoulder in a friendly gesture. The man wore Wildcat armour too, and Riis wondered if they were lovers. The woman stood and looked around. Her gaze passed over him as if he were a tree stump, and she walked off. Riis looked back to where the injured man was leaning his head back, his eyes closed in pain. With a start Riis realised he knew him. He walked over.

"Evan?" he asked, crouching down.

The soldier's eyes opened wearily, but there was no recognition. His face was grey and sweating and he cradled his broken arm with his good hand. It was a bad break, the white bone sticking out through red meat.

"Evan, it's Riis."

They had run into each other several times over the years since the night of the branding. For a while they had served together.

Evan blinked dust from his eyes, then nodded. "Son of a bitch," he said, with some of his usual spirit. "Still alive, then, Riis? Joined the horse-shaggers now, I hear?"

Riis grinned at him. It was good to see Evan again.

"Where's Parr?" the injured man asked.

Riis was tired of the question. He and his brother had served together for more than twenty years. Since Parr was killed it was always the first thing he was asked.

"Dead," he said shortly.

Evan leaned his head back, closing his eyes. "Got any lorassium?" he asked.

"Some," Riis told him, digging in a pocket. Evan's eyes opened. "Good man," he said. "I'll need it before the bonesetter gets here."

Riis pulled out a lump of the dried leaf. He rolled it into a ball and put it in Evan's mouth. His friend chewed on it for a long time, then sighed.

"There are fewer of us now," he said blurrily. "Ranul's dead too."

"I hadn't heard."

"But I found Arish. The bastard."

Riis frowned, wondering if the pain was confusing his old friend. "Arish disappeared thirty years ago," he said. "Are you sure?"

"Changed his name. Bastard," Evan repeated. "Thought I didn't know him."

Rallying, he sat up and spoke in Riis' ear. "We've got to get 'em together," he said, with the intensity of a drunkard.

"Who? Get who together?"

"Arish. Calls himself Fell Aron Lee."

Riis stared at him in surprise. Everyone had heard of Fell Aron Lee.

"And Saroyan."

"Who?"

"Lord lieutenant."

"What's he got to do with this?"

"She. Cold bitch. We've got to do it soon. Or we'll all be dead. There's only three of us left."

"Does she . . ." Riis looked around. "Saroyan. Does she want *him* dead?"

Evan nodded. "More than any of us."

Riis could make no sense of it. His friend seemed to drift off, and he sat down beside him to await the surgeon. His thoughts wandered on familiar paths, and after a while he nudged the Wildcat gently and asked, "Evan, that woman you were talking to . . ."

Evan's eyes were closed but he smiled and said slurrily, "Same old Riis." He feebly grabbed Riis' arm. "Keep an eye on her for me," he asked urgently.

"I will," Riis told him. "If I get the chance. Is she your woman?"

But Evan had closed his eyes again. "Indaro," he said, before slumping into unconsciousness.

Weeks later, after the destruction of the Maritime and the Nighthawks' demotion to guard duty, a message reached Riis at the Paradise barracks. It said merely "Big-Bellied Pony, noon tomorrow" and was signed *Sami*. Riis stared at it for a long while. His long-ago vow to kill the emperor seemed naïve and childish at this distance. He shrugged and made no decision, but a foul-up in the rotas meant he was off-duty that day. He argued to himself that there was no harm going.

The Big-Bellied Pony tavern, in Burman Far under the Third Imperial Wall, was small and dark and smelled of rot and sweat and sour ale. Riis pushed his way in through the doorway and blinked as his eyes got used to the gloom. It was crowded with workers and whores, but no soldiers, he noticed. He looked around for Evan Broglanh.

A whore in a shabby red dress and headscarf brushed up against him, grabbing his belt. "Take me out back, darling?" she leered at him. Riis saw with distaste she was old enough to be his mother and that under the spangled scarf her hair was grey. He shook his head.

But when she nuzzled his ear her voice was metal. She said, "Follow me, you fool."

He trailed after her through a narrow corridor and out into a foetid passage.

"Evan told me about you," the woman said, turning. "He didn't tell me you're a simpleton." She was tall for a woman, middle-aged, mattock-faced and thin as a sword. Her eyes were pale and protuberant. He disliked her instantly.

"I didn't know who I was meeting," he answered feebly.

"You know now," she replied. "You do know, don't you?" She stared at him impatiently, like some disagreeable tutor, until he answered, "Yes, I know."

"You took an oath, as a young soldier, one you have not fulfilled," she said.

He was silent. He had never spoken of this to anyone except his brother.

"Yes, I know all about it," she said impatiently. "Five boys swore to kill the emperor thirty years ago. Now there are just three left and the task is within their reach. Arish and Evan have chosen their part. But we need someone already in the palace." And she outlined to him the plan of invasion and assassination.

"You want me as a doorman," he said, frowning, after she'd finished, "to let enemy troops in, and to stand by and applaud as Arish kills him. I'll do it myself."

"Fell is our best hope."

"Fell isn't here. I am. I'm a palace guard, remember?"

"And who do you think is responsible for that, idiot?"

Riis stared at her. After his conversation with Evan he'd asked around about Saroyan, and found that, among other things, the lord lieutenant was responsible for troop deployment within the palace. But he had not made the connection.

"We have infiltrated someone else into the Red Palace," the woman went on. "A girl. She is maidservant to Marcellus' whore. She will contact you with information and you will keep an eye on her."

"So you want me to be a doorman and a childminder? And if I find an opportunity to kill the . . . target, if for instance he's standing alone in a room with his back to me, do I have your permission?" he asked sarcastically.

She smiled thinly. "You don't like women, do you?"

I love women, he thought. I just don't like *you*.

She said, "The emperor is not a normal man. He will be hard to kill. Fell has the best hope. Probably none of us will survive this. You will have your chance to die for your City."

Riis scowled. "I don't want to die for the City. I want to kill the emperor and get away with it. And if I get a chance then I will take it."

"Fell wants to kill him too, remember. And Evan Broglanh. Of all of you, Evan is the one who kept in sight the vow you made as children. The rest of you were sidetracked—Fell with his mission to save his warriors, you with your women, Ranul . . . well, Ranul was perhaps the best of you," she said thoughtfully.

"What happened to him?"

Saroyan ignored the question. "I must go now. You will not see me again. Broglanh will stay in touch. If you must, you can leave messages for Sami at this inn."

And Riis did as he was asked. He shepherded the girl Amita to her new quarters with the whore Petalina. Though she had no idea who he was, he wanted to get a good look at her. She was pale and fair and looked no more than fifteen. She had shining hair and hid nervously behind its pale curtain. He wondered what sort of conspiracy it was that thought a girl like her would be useful.

He watched her sometimes at night as she scurried around the palace. He was amused by her dogged persistence, although he thought she was wasting her time. Once he had been forced to kill a guard he spotted stalking her through the darkened corridors. He suspected the man planned to violate the girl, rather than report her for snooping. Either way, it could not be permitted. Riis dragged the man's body down to a lower, drowned, level where it sank into the silent water.

Amita was a chore to him, a chore and a nuisance. But when he heard she was dead, he grieved for her more than he would have thought possible.

The sisters Petalina and Fiorentina, in a family not blessed by the gods with boys, had been raised by their father to hunt and ride to hounds, to swim and run, and to use a sword, as well as the more maidenly pursuits of singing and dancing. A later generation of girls was to be pressed into the army, to die in their thousands on battlefields in sight of the City, but in those days their father was seen as a harmless eccentric for the education he gave his daughters.

Petalina, sitting in the emperor's feasting hall before a board groaning beneath the weight of gold plate, ornate candlesticks and cutlery, startling sprays of exotic flowers decorated with stuffed hummingbirds and bright fish, not to mention mountains of food and gallons of wine, wondered what their father would think of them now.

She looked along the table at her sister, who was listening to her husband, Rafael Vincerus, as he spoke confidentially in her ear. Fiorentina must have felt her gaze for she looked up and saw Petalina and smiled. Rafe saw the look and turned and raised a glass to Petalina.

"Would you like some more little fishes?" asked the tedious foreigner at her side. He must have thought she was smiling at him, and he was presenting her a basket full of the dried fish which was a delicacy in his land. What a strange people, she thought. The Wester Isles are surrounded by living fish, yet its people value this dry chewy abomination which tastes like salted wood.

"No, thank you." Petalina smiled warmly, her eyes on his, and added apologetically, "I'm afraid I have only a tiny appetite."

He smiled condescendingly as if confirmed in his opinion that ladies rarely admitted to eating, if they ate at all. Petalina smiled at the thought of Marcellus and herself a few hours before, after a robust session of lovemaking, devouring a leg of mutton together and how he had laughed at her as she tore into it with her teeth.

She wished he was with her, for the empty chair on one side gave her no excuse not to talk to the ambassador. He had only one topic of conversation and, try as she might by asking him about his family, and the customs of his country, and his opinions on the war, he would not be diverted from his pet subject. Having heard all she ever wanted to about fish, Petalina had cast about for some diversion. But she could not talk to the guest opposite her, a dashing captain of the isles' navy, for a herd of flying fish, painted and pinned on sticks, were in her way. Fish all about me, she thought in despair, and despite herself she giggled, concealed it with a cough, then straightened her face.

"Are they very beautiful, the Wester Isles?" she asked the ambassador, sitting back in her chair and turning towards him so he could have a good view of her breasts. Our trade links are crucial, Marcellus had reminded her, as if she were unaware of it. Keep the man happy. See he has anything he wants. Anything? she had asked him archly.

The ambassador gazed fixedly at the twin mounds of pale soft satiny flesh presented to him, and replied, "Yes, very beautiful, my lady." He dragged his eyes back to her face and she rewarded him with a smile of such complicit warmth that she could see sweat popping out on his forehead.

"What is beautiful, sir?" asked a deep voice. "My lady Petalina?" She felt a strong hand on her shoulder, then sliding down her back, as Marcellus dropped gracefully into the empty seat beside her. As always, she felt the thrill of his presence and saw all eyes along the great table turn to her lover.

There was a moment's silence as Marcellus looked around him, acknowledging faces with a smile or a nod, then he raised a glass to Fiorentina, in an echo of his brother's gesture moments before.

"Indeed," replied the ambassador as Marcellus returned his enquiring gaze on him, "the lady Petalina is beyond beautiful. She is . . ." His ambassadorial skills, if he had any, deserted him and he laboured for a word. Petalina wondered if he was going to compare her with a fish. The entire company fell silent as the man struggled. "She has a beauty that is seen only once in a lifetime," he finished rather lamely.

Petalina smiled sweetly at him, wondering if he realised the insult he had offered to every other woman in the room. She glanced again at Fiorentina, who returned her look gravely, but her eyes were twinkling. She spoke to her husband and Rafe leaned across the table, pushing aside a bush-ful of roses, and attracted the ambassador's attention. The fish man apologised to Petalina then swung to speak to him.

I love you, my sister, thought Petalina.

"I trust you kept him entertained?" Marcellus asked her quietly.

She looked up into his eyes. The brothers were unalike, Marcellus the bigger, heavy-shouldered, fair, Rafael smaller and more graceful, and dark. But their eyes were the same, black as midnight—not the very dark brown often seen among eastern tribesmen or the people of the southern wastelands, but pure pitch-black, and shiny as wet pebbles. They scared her a little, the eyes.

"Like most men," she told him, "he is not difficult to entertain."

"I saw you were entertaining him with your breasts."

She shrugged. "I would have thrown off all my clothes and leaped astride him if it stopped him talking about fish."

Marcellus laughed. "Now you have met him," he asked her, "what choice of companion would you make to sweeten his night?"

"Easy," she answered. "A boy."

He raised his eyebrows. "But he was entranced by your womanly bosom."

She smiled at him, then said, lowering her voice, "All men are fascinated by breasts but there are those who want to sink into them, to wallow in them, to succumb to them, and those who are fearful of them. He was entranced as a snake fascinates a mouse. He is a man of deep uncertainties and seeks sexual comfort from what he knows. Trust me, the ambassador of fish will be well satisfied by a pretty boy, perhaps two, but it must seem to be very discreet for, like all important men, he is anxious to be well-thought-of."

"Like all important men?" he repeated, sitting back and gazing at her sternly.

"Yes, my love," she told him complacently. "Even you, when you were younger, judged yourself by the opinions of others, I'm sure. But it is so long ago that you have forgotten."

She wondered again how old he was. He had to be at least seventy, for she had first met him thirty years before and he was not young then. Yet there was still more gold in his hair than grey, and his clean-shaven face was unlined, except around the margins of the eyes. He was as strong as he had ever been, stronger. She feared for him, for more than half his year was spent campaigning, and each time he sallied out with his troops she was afraid she would never see him again. It was the one ambition of his life to see an end to the war. Or so he told her. Where, though, would he be without it? She feared that if the war ended, as he wished, and he went into retirement, then he would quickly age and die.

She realised Marcellus was looking at her and she wondered, not for the first time, if he could read her thoughts.

The servants were bringing another extravagant course of food the City could ill afford and which would probably be largely wasted. Marcellus, who was served first, poked with his knife at the folded package of red and green leaves, revealing a heap of pink shrimp. Petalina moaned quietly in revulsion.

"Eat it," he ordered her with mock severity. "These shrimp died so we might live."

"Ambassador," he said, leaning across her, and she gladly sat back to let him converse. It gave her an excuse not to eat.

"We will have a chance to speak at length tomorrow," Marcellus told the man, "but I was wondering if you and your colleagues would be interested in another trade agreement."

"What is that, my lord?" The ambassador's two colleagues, down the table, abandoned any pretence at conversation with lesser men and swivelled round to listen.

"The Wester Isles is famous for its timber. I believe you have forests of oak and beech still uncut."

"It is true," replied the ambassador smoothly, "yet our western allies take all our surplus trees, and crave more. They are building a new city and need all the building stone and timber they can buy. We have many binding agreements with them."

"Do these binding agreements dictate the length and span of the timber required?"

"Of course, my lord."

"Then there will probably be room for agreement between us. You supply your allies with timber for building. Any that falls short of their requirements we might buy for carriages and carts."

Petalina was wondering why her lover was claiming to be interested in timber. There was always a shortage, it was true, since the oak-clad mountains to the south fell into enemy hands, but it was not Marcellus, First Lord of the City, who dickered over supply contracts.

He smiled warmly at the ambassador. "Perhaps, if you have finished at table, you would join me in the Serpent Room to discuss it."

The man had clearly not finished, for he held his fork poised in readiness for another bite, but he put it down hastily and said, "It would be an honour, my lord."

They stood and Marcellus ushered the ambassador through the ornate doors at the end of the hall. The ambassador's colleagues, uninvited, looked at each other, then gladly returned to their meal.

Petalina smiled to herself. No one says no to Marcellus, she thought.

For thousands of years the Wester Isles had languished in happy obscurity, its natives devoting their lives to fishing, logging and boat-building. Their only contact with the outside world had been the trade in these vessels: small, clinker-built fishing boats and larger cargo ships. The ambassador himself had been a fisherman for thirty years. Then the isles had come under the eye of the beleaguered City, which had been willing to pay inflated prices for wood for its buildings and fish for its citizens' bellies. The City's gold flooded the islands, and with it came civilisation, closely followed by administration. Within a few years the isles had a bureaucracy and a government, ministers, bankers, commissioners and creditors. The simple fisherman, friend to a newly created minister, left his devoted wife and children, and was sent abroad to lie for his country in the most famous court in the world.

He missed his wife and their three growing children, and their golden oak home built on the dunes surrounded by tall grasses that sighed and shifted in the wind off the sea. He hated the City. With every footfall he felt farther from the natural world of seasons and tides he was used to. Here there was just stone upon unrelenting stone; he could feel the many genera-tions of cities beneath his feet, and they reeked of blood and death. Since he had been in the palace he had felt a low vibration of anxiety deep in his soul, and he became certain, as each hour passed, that he would not leave alive.

He was not a foolish man. He knew how others viewed him, and he saw the slyness behind the courtesan's smile. She had been told to entertain him, and she had done so, but her pride forced her to disclose to him her real feel-ings, almost concealed, of amused, indulgent scorn. He wondered if she had any clue how he really felt about *her*, the ageing whore with her doll-like face and her childish finery.

If the emperor's feasting hall was designed to impress, then the Serpent Room was intended to inspire unease. It was not a huge room, on the scale of the Red Palace. It was wide, but quite low. And everywhere, on ceilings, floors, walls and furniture, were snakes. Painted, carved, stuffed, and live slithering ones in glass tanks. The ambassador looked round nervously. He did not mind snakes. But then he had never seen thousands together at one time before.

"I hope you do not mind snakes?" Vincerus asked him. He had a mischievous smile on his face. "I imagine that its designers, whoever they were, hoped to arouse fear in visitors, to put them at a disadvantage. In fact, only a child would be frightened by these poor creatures. It is a fine example of more being less."

The ambassador relaxed a little. He had been daunted by the prospect of meeting the Vincerii, but the brothers had been nothing but courteous and appeared to be open and candid. Such powerful and charismatic men, he guessed, had no reason to be devious. Marcellus was tall and well built, with fair, shaggy hair and a boyishly handsome face. The ambassador estimated him to be about forty, maybe a little more. He had very dark eyes which contrasted strangely with his fair countenance.

"How do you like our City?" asked Vincerus affably, sitting on a snakeskin couch and gesturing that he do the same. The ambassador looked round at all the serpents' eyes on him and sat on the edge of his couch.

"It is remarkable," he replied honestly. "I have been here before, once when I was a child. I saw the emperor in a parade. It was the highlight of my young life. I'm sorry the emperor did not attend tonight."

"The Immortal does not go to feasts," Marcellus replied and, though the words were light, the atmosphere in the room cooled. The ambassador felt the low thrum of dread in his belly.

Nervously, he said, "Rumours of his death reached our islands last year. I am glad they proved untrue."

It was as if he had not spoken. The lord said, "You and your colleagues have a busy schedule, I'm sure," although nothing could be further from the truth. "I will get to the point. I have no interest in timber. We have battalions of supply officers to deal with that. I have a proposition for you, for your government." He leaned forward and the boyishness dropped away. "You may know that the greatness of our City is buttressed by the workers in the furnaces of the northern wastes. Their work is hard and the death rate high. The war has decimated the population of the City and that of our many tributary kingdoms. We need more workers to man the furnaces."

The ambassador was silent, baffled. But we are just a small country, he thought, of fisherman and loggers. We have no spare workers.

Marcellus went on. "To the west of you, weeks to the west, I understand, is a large land mass which has been so far uncivilised."

"Yes?" the ambassador said, wondering.

"There are thousands, tens of thousands of potential workers there. The City will pay generously for every man or woman brought here to work in the furnaces."

There was a moment of silence. Then, "Slaves?" the ambassador asked.

"Workers. We have found that slaves and convicted criminals die very quickly in the furnaces. Workers, however, are asked to sign a year's contract. This is a legal document which is binding on both the worker and the City. This gives them hope that at the end of their year, if they survive, they will return home with generous compensation. Hope keeps them alive. Some of them."

"How many of them?" the ambassador asked sceptically.

Vincerus frowned. "I'm sure some functionary in the palace offices can tell you the number if you really wish to know."

So this is why we are here, the ambassador thought. This is why we have been invited here, and wined and dined and flattered. He is asking us to become slave masters. He felt the ground underneath him shifting, and his sense of dread burgeoned.

Playing for time, he feigned naïvety and asked, "But why would they agree?"

"They will be handsomely paid."

"In their own terms?"

"In the City's terms."

"You want men of the Wester Isles to sail to their land, fill our ships with these people. By force?" Marcellus shrugged as if indifferent how the mission was fulfilled. "And bring them here to die in the service of the City. For which we will be paid."

"Handsomely."

The ambassador looked at the floor. "I cannot . . . in all conscience . . ." he started. Then he had an idea. "I must return and discuss this with my peers," he said, managing a thin smile which, he guessed, looked ingratiating. "It is not a decision I have authority to make myself. You will hear our decision very shortly."

He looked up again at Marcellus, and wished he hadn't. The man was not frowning, but his face had lost all expression. He looked suddenly older, like his own father. And his eyes, his eyes had lost all . . . life. They had disappeared. They were just two empty holes in his face. The ambassador blinked.

"You are lying," Marcellus said flatly, his voice as cold as winter seas. "You are lying because you are a weak man who does not dare to say no. You are right in that. It is best not to say no to me." Each word was heavy with meaning and with each one the ambassador felt the life and energy being sucked out of the room.

Marcellus was silent. His strange eyes held the ambassador.

"I . . . no . . . I," was all the man could manage.

He felt he was being sucked into the eyes; all the room was being drawn in. And the palace and City and the world. The eyes were dark dreadful holes filled with emptiness that would never be filled. He was being drawn in and he would never get out and he would spend eternity in the horror of the emptiness. Terror closed his throat and he started to panic and he felt his limbs were flailing about, although he knew he was really seated immobile on the couch. The sane part of his mind prayed for unconsciousness or the relief of a heart seizure. He was drowning in the blackness, gasping for his last breath forever, through an infinity of eternities until the world ended and the skies fell and still he would be struggling for one last breath and . . .

"Yes!" he gasped.

Then there was release.

He never lost consciousness, nor believed he was in a nightmare. For the next hour he lay curled on the snakeskin couch in the empty room shaking with fear, fear that was totally focussed. He was terrified of Marcellus, of what the man could do to him and his wife and children, terrified of the possibility of even seeing him again. At last his colleagues from the isles, wondering, came into the Serpent Room and helped him, trembling, to bed. The ambassador did not sleep that night. The next day he signed the pieces of paper placed in front of him. On the voyage home he had a seizure of the brain. He lingered, cared for by his loving wife, for half a year and never spoke again.

* * *

The Serpent Room had been built more than two hundred years before, and was once the Lord Chancellor's bedchamber. It was buried deep in the palace, and its single window looked out on one of the palace's myriad enclosed courtyards. Because the Chancellor was an important man, a water closet had been secreted in the wall in a corner of the courtyard, with doors both to the chamber and to the outside. At some time the inner door had been walled up and forgotten, but the small dark room still existed. Nothing could be seen from within it, but much could be heard of what happened in Marcellus Vincerus' favourite parlour.

After silence fell in the room there was a long pause, then the listener heard the door to the Serpent Room open and close and there was silence again. The listener wondered if the luckless ambassador was still alive, for it sounded as though the First Lord of the City was strangling him. The listener shrugged to himself, too concerned with his own safety to worry about a foreigner. He waited long anxious hours until it was pitch-dark before he let himself out into the courtyard and made his way to his room to write his report.

Chapter 31

Dol Salida read the listener's tiny, precisely written words early the next day, then he set a light to the paper and watched as it flared then became ash. He sat back and stroked his moustache absently.

The report told him little he did not already know. It was hardly a secret that they needed slaves. The City was fighting for its life. The population was dwindling; it was rare to see anyone of fighting age walking the streets, and the sight of children, playing or labouring, was increasingly rare. When Dol was a child he had had several years of schooling, even in the poor quarter of Barenna where he was raised. Now there were no schools, for there were few children to attend them and no one to man them. The City was filled with the old, the maimed, the forgetting and the forgotten. Workers were still needed, though, to mine metal and man the foundries which produced armour and weapons, and to build ships and the new defences.

Yes, the City certainly needed slaves, although, Dol thought, Marcellus must be getting desperate to insert himself into the problem. Did he coerce the ambassador to agree to his proposition? The spy's report was unsatisfactory. Marcellus was a ruthless man; he would not have the power and influence he had if he were not. But would he really half strangle a foreign ambassador to get him to comply? It seemed . . . well . . . crass. Marcellus was known to be even-tempered and, according to the bland words of the report, the ambassador said nothing to arouse the man's anger. Dol Salida had checked with the palace that morning and found the delegation had left at dawn, all present and correct.

Dol reached down a hefty file of papers from a shelf above him. The file was marked *Hallorus* and appeared to be a minute report, wearisome in its abundant detail, of the daily doings of an Otaro businessman with interests in the manufacture of body armour. The man existed, but he was of no concern to Dol Salida. The dossier was in code, one of the urquat master's own devising, another legacy of his time in the prison camp. It was about Marcellus. It contained every word Dol had heard spoken about the First Lord of the City, everything he had read, everything he had surmised from his daily interactions within the palace and outside with people who had met the man, or who knew people who had met him, his body servants, or their relatives. If Marcellus was mentioned in his hearing, the date and time of the conversation was noted, along with who did the speaking, and to whom, with cross references to their own files.

Dol's main employment was for Dashoul, the palace's head of intelligence, to use his wide network of friends, comrades and relatives to seek out and hunt down truanting girls, and some boys, who should be serving the City's armies. For this he was paid, though not handsomely. His brief to study Marcellus—in truth, to spy on him—was one which took little time but a great deal of his attention, and he received no pay. His patron had made it clear he would receive only her gratitude and the remote chance of future advancement.

There were files on all the senior members of the Families, though few had political or military influence any longer. Of them all the files on the Guillaumes and Khans were thickest. Neither Marcus Rae Khan nor Reeve Guillaume had been seen in the Red Palace for decades. Yet each was an important player, in his way. Marcus was of a similar age to the Vincerii, a senior general who took no part in the emperor's strategic plans, for he ruled his own army and went where he wished. He was indispensible though, a commander of brilliance, whose troops adored him, and the palace had to put up with his unorthodox tactics for it could not afford to lose him. Reeve Guillaume was a politician, one who had always stayed scrupulously loyal to the Immortal. Despite this he was under effective house arrest in his home on the Salient, and had been for twenty years.

The *Hallorus* file was one of many and Dol Salida perused them all regularly in the comfortable silence of the night, for he had long since given up sleeping in a bed because of the pain in his leg, and he very seldom slept at all, just dozing a little in his study. So he updated the dossier, in his fine, disciplined script, then the brief file on the Wester Isles ambassador.

Then he browsed through other references to the emperor's death, of which there were hundreds over the years. After an hour or two of this he sat back again and let the information percolate through his mind.

The Immortal had been emperor for as long as Dol remembered. Try as he might, he could not find any record of when he came to power. All emperors of the City are named Immortal which made it impossible to pin down the dates of their successions. He had to enquire tactfully, for it was considered disloyal, treacherous even, to suggest that the title Immortal was anything other than the literal truth.

Marcellus was another matter. He was a man of integrity, soldier, politician and historian. But he was not without weakness. Despite his vital role in the City and therefore the war, he would spend half a year on the front line, fighting with his troops, something which seemed reckless to Dol Salida, who knew as well as any that a stray missile or unlucky sword blow would kill the First Lord and cripple the City's ability to make war.

His other frailty was his liaison with Petalina. Marcellus was wed to Giulia Rae Khan, sister to Marcus, but the woman had long since returned to live with her family in their palace on the Shield, and Marcellus was free to dally with his courtesan. Dol had no moral objection to the affair, yet it showed a fallibility in Marcellus he found surprising. But it made his own job easier, and if Petalina had noticed that she saw more of Dol Salida when Marcellus was in the City, then she did not reveal it.

Again he wondered about the new maid Amita. A few questions in the right quarters had revealed that the one family who had *not* employed her was the Kerrs, so where was she from? It was possible she was retained by Marcellus himself, to keep an eye on Petalina. Or by persons unknown, to watch Marcellus. The possibility that she was employed by Marcellus was the only thing that was stopping Dol from taking her in for interrogation.

In a palace beset by intrigue, his loyalties were conflicted to say the least. The fact that he spied on Marcellus did not trouble him. Marcellus was de facto leader of the City, and as such was the focus of everyone's attention.

The old soldier suddenly felt his body stiffening from long hours in his chair, and he stood up with difficulty, stretching his useless leg, sweating as the pain clawed at him. If I were a braver man, he thought, I would have this old leg cut off and be done with it. He bent and peered out of the study window. Dawn was a pale promise in the east and the streets were still dark. Sniffing, he could smell baking bread. His spirits rose a little. Another long night over. In a few moments his servant would come in with food and drink and his day would begin.

Amita was growing increasingly anxious. The sheaf of plans she had stolen from the library weighed heavily on her. After the first night she had taken them from the hiding place in her spare clothing and secreted them in Petalina's dress rooms. She had written a brief note to her unknown contact, describing where the plans were, and left it in the gap in the buttress wall. But the next day the note was still there, damp from overnight rain, and there it had remained for two more mornings.

Early each day, after her first chores were complete and before Petalina awoke, Amita went to the wardrobes and took out the plans and pored over them. She traced her fingers along the faint lines, trying to interpret the tiny writing, and attempting to discover some correspondence with the corridors and chambers she passed through daily. Nightly, barefoot and shrouded in black, she roamed the palace, building up her knowledge of its geography, its vast, labyrinthine wings on many levels. And each morning she attempted to discover what she had seen in the stark lines on the plans. It was a while before she realised that the plans had originally been drawn in coloured inks, and that the different colours had faded at different speeds over the years. She guessed that the levels of the palace were each allocated a different colour. This helped her orientate herself.

When she found the first landmark she knew, the Pomegranate Stair, a pale spiral of ink, she took up her pencil and hesitantly drew a small square beside it on the plan. Then she repeated the square on a piece of blank paper and wrote Pomegranate Stair in the City script. That led her to the Library of Silence, and half a dozen other points in the part of the palace she recognised, and she became bolder, drawing them on her explanatory paper with a firmer hand. Each day she left the paper rolled up with the plans ready to be collected. But no one came for them.

On the third day, while Petalina took her afternoon nap, Amita wrapped up the plans with her notes inside, and pushed them under the shoe bags. She could not lock the rooms, for her contact had to get in, and her fear was that the under-maid, who cleaned them, would notice and report the unlocked room to Petalina. But she thought it unlikely, for she had made a point of being kind to the girl, and she hoped the maid would tell her about the unlocked rooms rather than go to her employer.

Biting her lip she hurried through the garden, glancing at the buttress wall. She wondered what she should do if the note were never collected. She had no other way of contacting her friends. The days were getting shorter and colder as the Day of Summoning loomed. She shivered as she let herself back into the warm apartments.

"Where have you been?"

Petalina was standing in her white silk shift looking out of the window. You could not see the buttress wall from there, but Amita felt a whisper of fear, as if her employer could guess what she'd been doing.

"I was brushing your gowns, lady," she said, a rehearsed excuse. "I do some every day, so I don't have to do them all at once."

"How very economical of you. Every afternoon, when I nap?"

"Yes."

"And at night, when I wake up and you are not here? Do you brush gowns then?" Petalina had an expression on her face Amita could not interpret. She decided to be as truthful as she could be.

"I sometimes walk the corridors, when I can't sleep." She lowered her head, contriving to look contrite.

"It is not safe out there at night. There are soldiers about, who would take advantage of a girl like you," Petalina told her sternly. Then her face softened and she smiled. "Or is that what you're hoping for?"

Amita was shocked. "No, lady!" she cried, dismayed that the woman would think that.

But Petalina, with a wave of her hand, had dismissed the matter. "Look at this!" she said, holding out a small bouquet of pink and yellow roses for Amita to admire.

"It is very pretty," the girl replied, taking it and sniffing it. The roses were fresh, but were interleaved with silk petals and linen leaves. It *was* pretty, but Amita wondered what it was for.

"It is a corsage," Petalina explained. "Marcellus wants me to go to the Little Opera House tonight and he sent this for me to wear."

"To wear?"

"Pinned to my gown."

Amita privately thought the weight of the thing would spoil the line of any dress, but she kept her thoughts to herself. At least Petalina, easily distracted by a few flowers, seemed to have forgotten her nightly excursions.

"If you are to meet the lord tonight there isn't much time," Amita offered. Getting Petalina bathed and powdered and dressed and decorated always took hours. She handed the flowers back, but Petalina cried, "Ouch!" dropping them. She sucked her finger then showed it to Amita, like a child. "It pricked me," she complained.

As she bathed Petalina talked guilelessly about Marcellus, and Amita listened with half an ear. The woman was a contradiction and a puzzle. Much of the time she behaved like a girl of sixteen, sometimes like a child of six. Yet Amita knew she was an intelligent woman and there were moments when she caught a look of cool calculation in the courtesan's eyes that was at odds with the words she spoke. She had no doubt Petalina had not simply forgotten her night adventures, and she resolved to be more cautious in future.

By twilight Petalina was more quietly elegant than usual, in a grey silk dress, with a row of moonstones at her throat. As she picked up the posy to pin on, Amita thought the garish roses would add nothing to her beauty. Then she saw a drop of blood marring the silken petals of the corsage.

Petalina was aghast. "It's ruined!" she cried, her eyes wide with the drama. "The blood will never come out!" She glanced at the doorway where two tall guards waited to escort her. "And I'm late already."

Amita bit her lip. "I will mend it," she said reassuringly. "I will cut out the damaged petals. There are so many of them it will never show."

Petalina stared helplessly from the flowers to Amita. With her wide brow and huge blue eyes, she looked like a worried kitten.

"But I'm late already," she repeated. "The Little Opera House is on the other side of the palace."

"Then go now, lady. I will mend this and run after you. It will only take me a few moments."

"Do you know where it is?"

"I'll find it. I'll catch up with you. I promise."

Petalina turned to the door, looking up trustingly at the two bodyguards in their black and silver armour. When they had gone Amita ran to her workbox and found a tiny pair of scissors. She carefully cut out the blood-stained petals, then looked at the result critically. It was lopsided. She turned the posy over and found hidden petals underneath. She snipped one out and with a needle and thread, sewed it in place of the damaged ones. She tweaked the roses a little to hide the stitches. It would have to do.

With the posy in one hand and her skirts raised in the other she ran out of the apartments and down the corridor.

She knew in theory where the Little Opera House was. It was in the middle of a lake to the west of the palace. This meant she had to follow the corridors straight ahead until she came to the green marble walls of the Keep, the heart of the palace, then bear left until she reached outdoors. Once outside, she hoped the lake would be obvious.

Heads turned and soldiers laughed coarsely as she sprinted down the marble and stone corridors, skirts raised, posy in hand. She ran through narrow corridors with low white ceilings and high halls with ornamented vaulting, up and down steps and stairs. She was out of breath when she saw the first of the sea green walls ahead of her. She ran round a left-hand corner and found herself at the top of another staircase. She plunged down it, then stopped suddenly at the bottom, frozen.

Walking sedately out from behind a marble pillar was a gulon.

Amita had seen such a creature once before, in the Halls, but this one was far bigger. It was the size of a large dog, and the top of its head came nearly to her chin. Its striped coat was tawny and grey and its eyes, though gold, were otherwise dauntingly human, the long dark curved lashes sprinkled with fat drops of moisture.

It stopped when it saw her and regarded her thoughtfully. It seemed that she barred its way, as it did hers. Amita backed up onto the staircase, and after a moment it walked past her, eyeing her all the time. As it passed she smelled the stink of its oily coat and heard its hissing breath. Then it slithered behind a wall hanging, its brushy tail lingering for a heartbeat, then gone. Amita grabbed her skirts again and dashed on.

It was only in her dying moments that she recalled the gulon was wearing a golden collar.

Chapter 32

The Little Opera House had been replicated in confectionery a hundred times on the tables of the emperor's feasting hall. It was round and white, and from the shore of the lake it seemed spun of sugar, its slender pillars apparently too brittle to hold up the ornate roof. It was approached by a white marble causeway, and as Petalina hurried across it, flanked by the two silent soldiers, she wondered, as she had done before, which came first, the building or the lake it graced. Beyond the lake was marshland dotted with sheep, pale humps just visible in the dwindling light.

She did not recognise her guards. Outside her rooms she was escorted constantly by members of Marcellus' personal bodyguard, many of whom she knew, but these two were strangers to her. She assumed her lover had made some personnel changes, for he often said that highly trained warriors had better things to do than trail around the palace after him. Or after her, she thought, although he did not say that.

The causeway was cool and windy, but inside the hall steps led down into a bowl-shaped chamber which was cosy once filled with people. Tonight there was an autumn chill in the air, and Petalina could make out the white ovals of swans through the twilight. The moon was full, its rounded shape echoing the drifting swans and grazing sheep.

When she stepped into the hall she was surprised to see that she was not late—or, at least, that others were later. Apart from the musicians, who were tuning their instruments in the usual cacophony, and the dozen or so guards, there were few other guests, mostly elderly counsellors. She looked around, but Marcellus was not there, although Rafe was. And there was no sign of her sister.

"Where is Fiorentina?" she asked Rafael as he walked up to her, smiling.

"She believes she has a chill," he answered her seriously.

Petalina scowled prettily. "Hmm," she commented.

"She asked me to remind you of the headache you had on the night of the talk by Bal Carissa on the netherworld of the early empires."

"Scarcely the same thing," she told him, glancing up at her brother-in-law and batting her eyelashes. "There's no one here to talk to," she complained, looking around.

"I am here, my lady," he replied genially.

She tucked her hand under his elbow. "Then you must be my escort for the night, for it seems Marcellus has abandoned me."

Petalina remembered Amita and the corsage. The wretched girl has got lost, she thought with irritation. She looked at the main door hopefully. At that moment Marcellus walked in, followed by four armed guards. There are more soldiers here than audience tonight, Petalina thought. With Marcellus now in attendance, the soldiers started to close the doors. At the last moment Petalina saw Amita slide through the gap. She was stopped by the soldiers briefly, then allowed through.

Amita spotted her and hurried down the steps. She was wearing the better of her two dresses, brown cotton with shell buttons and, with her fair hair down, she did not look totally out of place in the hall. She had a pin at the ready and she deftly attached the corsage, glancing at Petalina's face to see if she was angry. Petalina saw Marcellus watching them. He'll think I forgot it, she thought. He'll be annoyed with me.

"Go, quickly!" she whispered to Amita, who scurried back up the steps to the doorway, head down, trying to make herself small.

Marcellus and Rafe were talking together at the centre of the hall. As always, all eyes were on them, yet the soldiers, usually keen to stay close to their heroes, basking in their presence, seemed to have withdrawn from them and the Vincerii stood alone. Petalina smelled the scent of danger on the night air. She looked to Marcellus and saw he had noticed it too.

Then there was the familiar, sliding sound of a sword being unsheathed. All the warriors round the circumference of the hall were drawing their weapons.

There was a moment of stillness, in which the only person moving was Amita. She did not seem to notice the tension, and had reached the door and was struggling with the heavy iron handle. Petalina saw her appeal to one of the soldiers. The man lifted his sword and casually pierced the girl in the side. She fell like a bloody rag doll and lay still.

Petalina, appalled, brought her hand to her mouth. Then there was a flurry of action. Marcellus and Rafe, neither armed, backed together towards the centre of the hall. The musicians and guests, realising who were the targets, cringed away from them. Petalina was paralysed. She gazed appealingly to Marcellus, but he was not looking at her.

A soldier stepped forward, the first one to draw his sword.

"Your death is long overdue," he said to Marcellus. "Only with your death can the City live again."

Petalina, hand still to her mouth, saw Marcellus had relaxed, looking for all the world as if he was at a party. When he spoke, his voice was warm and seductive. Despite her fear, Petalina smiled, for she had heard this voice so many times before.

"You have always been a warrior above others, Mallet," Marcellus replied pleasantly. "Do not let your concern for your men blind you to the realities of this war."

Petalina saw the other guests and the musicians smile, and the atmosphere lightened. She could see the danger was averted, that Marcellus would convince the renegades of the error of their ways. She turned to Amita and, without fear, climbed the stairs to the girl and crouched down beside her.

There was a pulse in her throat, although blood still poured from the girl's side.

"The child needs aid," Marcellus said to the soldier Mallet. "Let us tend to her, then we will talk about your grievances like civilised men."

Mallet seemed unmoved by this reasonable offer and his men still stood, swords in hand, as if on the edge of battle.

Then Mallet spoke again. "I can see you are speaking," he told Marcellus. "But my men and I cannot hear you. We have filled our ears with cotton soaked in wax. The power of your voice has no effect on us. Now, traitor, prepare to die!"

R iis turned his back on the opera house doorway and started to walk back along the marble causeway, five men of the Thousand watching him go. He sighed and rolled his shoulders. He and his ten had only to wait until the end of the concert, and see the Vincerii and their guests safely off the premises in the custody of their bodyguards, then the Nighthawks would be finished for the day.

"Roll on midnight," grunted Berlinger at his side. "I'll sleep like the dead."

They had been on duty five nights in a row, "wall-sitting," Berl called it. Somebody had to walk the walls—the citizens expected it. In the unlikely event that a large enough contingent of the enemy could cross many leagues of no-man's land, dodge past the multiple guard posts, all without being seen, then launch a night attack on nigh-on-impregnable walls. But tonight they were on bodyguard duties, backing up the Thousand, which was short at least two centuries. One, they had heard, had got itself ambushed by a stray band of Blues, and the Gulon century were on some mysterious mission in the east.

The Nighthawks, riders of the First Adamantine, considered themselves the elite cavalry force and, now horseless, they had taken a lot of stick from other regiments, especially the Thousand, who considered *themselves* the elite. So Riis had expected the usual raillery from the bodyguards on duty at the opera house. But they had been strangely subdued.

Riis sniffed the air. It was a clear night, with a cool breeze coming from the west off the far-distant sea. He and his ten would wait at the end of the causeway, away from the jibes of the bodyguards, where they could relax until midnight. And afterwards, in the depths of the night, Riis would find a chance to slip from his bed and make his way round the walls to Petalina's garden to see if a message awaited him.

They were partway across the silent causeway, Riis walking ahead, when, on the following breeze, he heard the faint but unmistakable sound of a sword being unsheathed. He stopped and turned and held his hand up as Berl opened his mouth to speak. Yes, the sound of many swords being drawn came from the opera house. Riis drew his own weapon and raced back along the bridge, followed by his men.

The five men of the Thousand—from the century called Leopard—had closed the doors, and they turned to face them, their own blades raised.

"Leave it, Riis," cried their leader, a veteran well-known to them. "Turn away!"

Riis shook his head. "You know we can't do that, Kantei. Stand aside!"

Beyond the doors they could clearly hear the clash of metal on metal. Riis had no idea what was happening, but he knew if there was swordplay in the opera house, the Thousand should be in there, protecting their lords, not outside guarding the door against aid. He lowered his head as if debating with himself, then sprang forward, lancing the leader in the sweet spot in the neck, a hair's-breadth above his body armour. Kantei staggered, mortally wounded. But even as blood gouted from his throat he launched himself at Riis. Riis swayed back. Kantei's sword sliced through his leather jerkin and across his bicep. Then the man fell dying to one knee and Riis plunged his sword down through his neck into his heart.

He leaped back. "What are you doing?" he asked the remaining four, who were staring at Kantei's body. "Your duty is to Marcellus!"

"We're taking care of Marcellus," one told him grimly.

With a roar he leaped forward and Berlinger stepped to meet him, his sword deflecting his opponent's then clanging against the raised shield. Riis bent swiftly and grabbed Kantei's shield. The body was slumped at his feet, half on and half off the causeway. Riis kicked it into the water to give himself room.

Riis had ten men, and there were only four Leopards left. But the causeway was narrow, and they could only take on two at a time. And the

Thousand were in full armour, with shields, while Riis's men had only light leather protection.

Berlinger killed his man, then immediately fell to the sword of another bodyguard. As Riis battled he heard the splash of Berl's body hitting the water. The marble under their feet was already slippery with blood.

After the first two bodyguards fell, the Nighthawks could make no headway. The men of the Thousand battled as if possessed. Riis found he was fighting just to stay alive against the armed man in front of him. Next to him Chevia was stabbing and cutting. Riis' opponent snarled and lunged suddenly for his heart. Riis twisted and the man's sword scraped along his chest, ripping into the leather. Riis leaped to his left, his sword striking home. It was a poor blow, pounding into the armoured shoulder, but it knocked the man off-balance. Riis clouted him round the head with the shield and the man tipped into the water.

Immediately the last Leopard leaped at Riis, and the Nighthawk was thrown back on one knee. He lunged at his opponent, but his sword caught on the man's shield, breaking the tip. Riis reached backwards and felt another sword being slammed into his hand. But the bodyguard was on him, his sword stabbing towards his face. Riis could not swing his sword round in time. Then the man dropped suddenly, a knife in his eye, and disappeared into the black water.

Riis sprang up and helped his comrade despatch the last bodyguard. Then they ran to the opera house doors. They were closed and barred from the inside.

Inside the opera house Petalina knelt on the floor, tucking her shawl under the maid's head. Blood leaked from Amita's side, and Petalina knew it meant the girl still lived.

She stared in despair at the fight in the centre of the room. Marcellus and Rafe were backed against a wall, battling impossible odds. Both had acquired swords, but both carried injuries to arms and chests. Still they fought on against heavily armed men. Their swords moved with a speed that was uncanny, and four of the bodyguards already lay dead.

As she watched, Marcellus leaped forward and skewered a soldier in the narrow gap above the cheek-guard. The man stumbled backwards, crashing to the floor only feet from where Petalina crouched. His sword slithered across the floor towards her. She stared at it uncertainly, then made up her mind.

She grabbed it and jumped up. It was heavier than the swords she had practised with as a girl, but she hefted it and sprang at the nearest body-guard, who had his back to her. She thrust the sword at the gap under his arm, but the weight of the weapon misled her and it clanged against armour instead. The man turned, snarling.

Marcellus, though fighting for his life, somehow seemed to notice, and he cried, "Lady, no!"

Petalina backed away from the soldier, then her foot slipped in the blood on the floor and she went down hard on one hip. Pain shot through her. Angered by her own incompetence she forced herself back on her feet again, then ducked as the soldier swung his sword. She used both hands to thrust her weapon at his groin. It slid in easily and she dragged it out again. The man stopped in his tracks and fell to his knees. Then, to her horror, he slowly got up, pouring blood, and advanced on her. Backing away, she swung the sword back and forth, trying to fend him off. She caught the edge of his helm with its tip and wrenched his head round. He fell again, and she slammed the weapon down on the back of his neck. He lay still.

Panting, she looked around. Her effort had made little difference. Marcellus still had ten enemies surrounding him.

Suddenly he bellowed, "Enough!"

The sound was so loud it made Petalina's head ring, but it seemed to get through to the deafened soldiers, who faltered to a halt, bloody swords still at the ready.

Marcellus looked at her across the hall. "You are valiant, my lady," he said and, although the words were said quietly, they rang in her heart like a bell of celebration.

Then he turned to the bodyguards. "Let the women go," he said to them, pointing with his sword at Petalina and the injured girl, then at the door. His meaning had to be plain, even to deaf men.

But the leader of the rebels sneered at him. "Why would I spare your whore, Marcellus?"

Marcellus asked, "Why would you kill *me*, Mallet? We have fought side by side a score of times. Why do you betray your City?"

"*You* are the traitor," Mallet snarled. "Once you and the creature you call emperor are dead, we will make peace with the Blues. They want this war as little as we do."

"This is your philosophy, Mallet? Surrender and die for the cause of the enemy?" Marcellus asked.

But Mallet had not heard him. He was ordering his men using hand signs. Petalina guessed they all had only moments to live.

The Vincerii, injured and outnumbered, looked at each other for a long moment. Nothing was said, but Petalina guessed a decision had been made. Marcellus turned and gazed at Petalina across the bloodstained hall.

"I have always loved you, lady," he told her. The words were spoken without warmth, but they struck her heart and tears filled her eyes, for he had never said this thing to her. She tried to smile, for she knew he was telling her because he was about to die, and she with him. "I will never forget you and I will always honour you," he said.

Then both men lowered their swords and there was an uncertain silence in the chamber. Petalina felt a buzzing in the base of her skull and a headache sprang up. She shook her head, trying to dislodge it, and she saw one of the soldiers do the same. But it rapidly built up, and she felt a heavy sense of dread in her stomach. Fear and nausea rose up and swallowed her and within moments she was trembling. In front of her throbbing eyes the brothers seemed to have grown taller than the men around them. The headache was splitting her head in two and her stomach felt distended. She squeezed her eyes closed and held her hands to her head and screamed to try to release the awful pressure. When she opened her eyes she saw soldiers dropping their swords to the floor and gripping their heads. Only Mallet raised his weapon and tried to step forward to attack the brothers. It seemed he was trying to force himself through an invisible wall. Blood started pouring from his mouth and ears and eyes, but still he tried to advance. His mouth was open in a silent scream.

The last thing Petalina saw in this life was the soldier exploding in a fountain of blood, his limbs and head flying apart, his blood cascading over the floor and walls and the two men in front of him. Mouth wide, eyes huge in their sockets, Petalina felt the awful pressure building up inside her and she prayed for relief.

*   *   *

Outside Riis slammed his hands on the solid doors in frustration. He had sent three of his men to find something to use as a battering ram, and the other two climbing round the outside of the opera house, above the lake, to seek a way in. These two came back to report that the white walls were slippery and offered no purchase. Riis gazed up at the high filigree roof, wondering if he could get in that way.

Then, from inside, he heard the grate of the locking bar being raised and he stepped back as the doors were flung wide. The stench of bloody death blew out like a gale, and Riis felt a sickening dread deep in his stomach. Yet in a heartbeat the dread was replaced with elation as Marcellus calmly walked out, followed by Rafe. They looked strange and sinister, for the moonlight made it appear as if they were soaked in black paint. Then Riis realised they were both drenched in blood, as if they had been swimming in it. What has happened here? he wondered. He felt the hairs on his neck rise in the breeze across the water.

Marcellus was silent, looking around him. But Rafe said, "Captain Riis, isn't it?"

Riis, awed and flattered that his name had been remembered, replied, "Yes, lord."

"What happened here?"

"We heard the sounds of battle inside, lord. But the men of the Thousand refused us entry. We killed them," he said simply. He wanted to ask questions but was afraid to.

Marcellus seemed to rouse himself. "You did well," he said. "Give me your knife."

Riis swiftly unsheathed the dagger at his side, reversed it and handed it to his lord. "It is stained," he said apologetically, for he had wiped it roughly on the clothes of one of the dead bodyguards. Then he realised how foolish he sounded, for the hand he gave it to was drenched in blood already. Marcellus spun the knife, then turned and threw it into the lake. It thunked into the neck of a rebel soldier who was feebly trying to swim to the shore under cover of darkness.

"See that these bodies are cleared away, captain," Marcellus ordered.

"Your dead comrades will be treated with great honour. The bodies of the rebels will be burned."

"Yes, lord." Riis glanced into the silent darkness of the opera hall. "Are surgeons needed?" he asked uncertainly.

"No. They are all dead. Including the Lady Petalina."

Riis said nothing. It was not his place to commiserate with the man. What happened in there? he thought again.

"The rest of the Leopards must be rounded up," Marcellus went on. "It may be that they are innocent of this plot but we cannot risk that."

"Yes, lord."

"So," Marcellus looked directly at him for the first time. Riis resisted stepping back, compelled by the power of the man. "I find myself in need of a new century. Choose ninety-nine warriors of the First Adamantine, of any rank. You have full authority. You are now their commander. It will be known as the Nighthawk century. The name of the Leopards will be expunged from history."

Riis bowed his head and said, "It is an honour, lord."

He asked, "Do you want the Nighthawks to question the Leopards?"

"No. That will be done by others. We will find out who is responsible for this night."

Then the two men walked away, back along the white causeway, their bodies glistening with drying blood, their bloody bootprints stretching back after them.

Riis took a deep breath and stepped into the opera hall. He looked around, uncertain of what he was seeing. There were no bodies. Instead, every surface—the walls, the floor, even the high ceiling of the round hall—were drenched with blood. The air was thick with it. Riis breathed in through his mouth and felt, with a tremor of panic, that his lungs were filling with blood. As his eyes accustomed to the torchlit carnage, he started to see bits of bodies, gobs of brain and flesh, shards of bone, the occasional larger piece of flesh strewn across the hall. On one wall half a hand was slowly sliding downwards in the sticky blood. It stopped, then started again. Riis stared at it, mesmerised. Then he shook his head, looking away.

He turned to his two comrades, standing pale and silent beside him. "Get a clean-up crew," he ordered. "There is nothing left here to bury."

Chapter 33

The first snows arrived early that year, piling on the pain for the besieged City. It was said by the superstitious that if snow fell before the Feast of Summoning then a hard winter would follow, and old crones looked to the sky and shook their heads and forecast bitter days ahead. In the daytime the snow lay slushy in the streets and alleys, muffling the City in silence. It melted slowly on roof tiles and forced its way into attics and window frames. Then, as the thin sunlight dwindled away, it hardened to ice. The streets of the Armoury, and parts of Barenna and Burman Far, already dangerous at night, became impassable by ordinary folk in the hours of darkness.

The poorest of the City's people, those existing on the margin between life and death, already stalked by hunger and disease, and the human predators which fed off the unfortunate, died quietly in the hundreds each night. Those with a will to stay alive descended into the sewers, becoming Dwellers, for it was warmer underground. Ferocious winter weather had always been the Halls' best recruiting-sergeant. So the population of the City diminished further, and the demand on supplies slackened, and the administrators dealing with food distribution congratulated themselves on their skilful allocation of resources. Those same administrators had nominal responsibility for fuel distribution, but supplies of coal and oil had long since diminished to a point where only the palace, and only parts of the palace, could be warmed in winter.

It was five days before the Feast of Summoning, on the day marked for Lady Petalina's funeral, and Riis wrapped a greatcoat over his new uniform and hurried through the chilly corridors of the palace in the first light. He could see his breath in front of him and his hands were rammed into his pockets, his shoulders hunched against the cold. He was aware he looked nothing like a commander of the Thousand, and self-consciously straightened his posture as he neared the Keep. He glanced at his new aide and grinned. Darius shook his head. Riis had been told to attend a meeting of the Thousand's commanders in the Keep. He had never entered the Keep before. Today he would be walking into the emperor's lair, something that only a few weeks ago would have been impossible. He was anticipating it with trepidation and excitement, and he guessed Darius, though innocent of Riis' ambition, felt the same.

A veteran rider, Riis had found himself suddenly, unexpectedly, a commander of the Thousand, and he had no idea how such a creature carried himself, what his daily duties were, or how he treated his men. Like most soldiers before him, each time he had been promoted he had merely mimicked the behaviour of the man he had replaced until he had his feet under him and could make the role his own. Here he was adrift. He had never been a part of the imperial bodyguard, and his only dealings with them had been competitive, at best grudgingly cooperative. And he could get no help from his new peers, for the other century commanders clearly despised him for the route he had taken to promotion.

Darius, normally laconic to the point of terseness, had followed him without question until they reached the green walls of the Keep, when he asked, "Is this a briefing?"

Riis shrugged elaborately. "How would I know? I was told last night by an aide to general Boaz to be at the Keep today at dawn, on the orders of Marcellus."

Darius grunted.

Riis spread his hands. "I know. But what can I do? I can scarcely refuse to go."

"Watch your back."

"That's why you're here."

The two men walked up to the main entrance to the Keep. The bronze doors, deeply inset into curved walls of sage green, were decorated in relief with epic scenes from the Immortal's life. The doorway was flanked by soldiers in black and silver livery. Riis recognised they were of the Black-tailed Eagle century. He was about to identify himself when one soldier sprang to open a small door set in the great doors. Bristling with insecurity, Riis wondered if this was a studied insult. The soldiers did not salute him. Should they? Riis didn't know the etiquette of the Thousand yet.

He stepped into the Keep, Darius at his shoulder. They were in a broad foyer with a wide staircase winding up at each end, and several doorways in front of them. Riis had expected something remarkable, for he was at last in the emperor's territory. But this was just an empty room, cold as a widow's tit. Riis and his aide looked at each other.

Then a tall figure stepped from an open doorway and a rough voice demanded, "Commander Riis. In here."

"You were not told to bring an aide," general Boaz grunted, glaring at Darius, who coolly returned his stare.

"I was not told not to," Riis replied pleasantly, staring up into the man's eyes. It was rare for him to meet someone taller than himself. "I have yet to be informed of the protocols of the Thousand."

"The convention," a voice said as they stepped into the meeting room, "is that members of the Thousand, even the commanders, are just simple warriors serving their City, and as such it would be inappropriate for them to have aides. It is, of course, nonsense," said Marcellus, holding out a hand to beckon Riis into the room. "The commanders of the Thousand are important officers with many layers of responsibility. They have armies of servants in their homes, and many of them have several aides. They just do not normally bring them to commanders' briefings."

"I was not told this was a commanders' briefing," Riis answered. "I was merely told to be here." He was aware he sounded defensive.

The First Lord nodded. "Your aide can stay. Your name, soldier?"

"Darius Hex, lord."

Marcellus nodded. "Was your father also named Darius, although they called him Socks?"

Darius stared stolidly at a point on Marcellus' forehead, determined not to be awed. "Yes, lord." For the first time since Riis had known him, he felt annoyed by the man's taciturnity. He felt like saying, "It's all right to be impressed by Marcellus Vincerus. He is worthy of our respect." A vision of two men clothed in blood fluttered on the edge of his mind, but he pushed it away.

Riis looked around him. It was a round chamber, faced with white marble. Around the walls were carved the ten insignia of the bodyguard. One was covered over, and Riis felt pride in his heart to know the symbol of the Nighthawks was destined to appear there. There were more than a dozen soldiers in the room, seated and standing. Boaz, stooping like a heron, loomed over Rafe Vincerus, a slender figure dressed in black, who leaned idly against a wall.

"For those of you who have not been here before," Marcellus explained courteously, "this room is called the Black Room, not because it is black, but because it was built by the architect Tomas Black as an example for the emperor of a perfectly round room with a perfectly round dome. Architects tell me there is a word for such things, but I confess I cannot remember it. It is here that the commanders of the Thousand meet, and here that the emperor addresses us all when he sees fit." Riis felt his heart racing. If he kept his position as commander, if he lived long enough, then without doubt he would be face to face with the emperor in this room some time in the future.

Marcellus' face became grave. "Today we will mark the funeral of the Lady Petalina, killed by treachery. Her only living relative is the Lady Fiorentina, who has arranged the rites and interment. It will be a private affair. Because of the revolt of the Leopards, security will be higher than we would normally see at a funeral. You all have your orders."

He paused, then said, "It is easy to overstate the importance of events such as those in the opera house. Although innocent people died, the rebellion was a failure. Mallet's intent was to kill me and my brother. We will probably never know why, although we must assume the plot was hatched far from the City. But he did not succeed.

"He will have some success, however, if we lose our focus." He paused for emphasis. "The Thousand exists to protect the emperor, not the Vincerii. Increasing security around us inevitably risks compromising the guard on the Immortal. You need to all be aware of this and ensure it does not happen."

One soldier spoke up, his voice casual as if chatting with a friend. "It would make our task easier if you and Rafe presented separate targets. The fact that you are so often together is a problem for the Thousand. We have discussed this before." Riis looked with interest at the bushy-bearded, gravel-voiced man. He was clearly relaxed in the company of Marcellus to speak so openly to him.

"Are you suggesting we not attend the lady's funeral rites?"

The soldier seemed unperturbed by the edge in Marcellus' voice. "I would suggest it if I thought that would do any good, lord. No, I'm saying you should be more conscious about presenting an easy target."

"We are soldiers. We can take care of ourselves," said Rafe.

"No one doubts that, lord." Riis swung round. The speaker was a woman, seated on a couch behind him. She flicked a glance at him as he turned. She was of medium height and middle age, with unkempt ginger hair, and big breasts beneath the leather uniform. Is she a commander? he thought. He had no idea there were female commanders of the Thousand.

"But Fortance is right," the woman said. "We are only suggesting the two of you attend scheduled events separately."

Marcellus sighed. "All our lives are scheduled, Leona," he said. "But we will think on what you say." He waved a hand, and the warriors started filing out of the room. Riis glanced at Darius and they made for the door too.

"Riis." The word was said quietly. Riis turned back to Marcellus.

"Stay a moment," he said. Riis nodded to Darius, who followed the others.

Marcellus watched the door close. "I have a mission today for your Nighthawks, far from the funeral."

"Yes, lord."

"Do you know the lord lieutenant Saroyan?"

A great hollow opened up in Riis' chest and he found he had stopped breathing. Is this it? he thought. Does our plan to kill the emperor end here? And he wondered who had betrayed them.

Marcellus was looking at him enquiringly. Riis tried to think what the right answer would be. He furrowed his brow.

"I know her by sight," he admitted uncertainly.

"Saroyan is on her way back from the east, attended by six of her private guard. By noon they should be at the Paradise Gate. I want you to take a troop of your most trusted men and intercept them before they are within sight of the City. Kill them all."

Riis nodded and said, "Yes, lord." He turned towards the door, trying not to think.

"Do you want to know why?" Marcellus asked his back.

"I do not question your orders, lord."

"That is what this room is for, Riis, so the commanders can question my orders."

He explained, "We have information that Saroyan was involved with Mallet in his rebellion. I found it hard to believe; I have known her for a long time and would have waged my life on Saroyan's loyalty. It seems I very nearly did." He shook his head with regret. "I was fooled. Saroyan is unpopular with her peers and is something of a martinet, and I confused that with loyalty. It is always the wild cards we watch with suspicion.

"I could bring her in and put her on trial, but that would cause unrest in the palace, perhaps throughout the City. She is not popular, but she is respected. It is more practical to have her killed by marauding Blues, her body found in a few days' time. A tragedy for the City. Another funeral. Her fellow-conspirators, whoever they are, will know what caused her death."

Riis nodded. Dismissed, he wandered out of the Keep and found Darius waiting for him. His aide cocked an eyebrow. Riis shook his head repressively and they walked in silence back to the barracks.

As one of those fellow-conspirators, he had no idea what he was going to do.

Chapter 34

In the end, all eighty-one remaining warriors of the Leopard century were executed. It was considered impossible, Dol Salida was told, to distinguish between those who had actively plotted against the Vincerii, those who had known about the rebellion and done nothing, and those who were innocent, if any warrior can be called innocent. So they all had to die. Each was killed with a clean sword-thrust to the heart.

One of Dol's informants was in the execution squad, and when Dol questioned him days later his sword-arm was still weary and he was heartsick at the slaughter of veterans who had fought for the City without stinting, without hesitation, and now without honour. He told Dol that after the men were executed their bodies were stripped and examined for brand marks.

"Brand marks?" Dol asked, suddenly interested. "And did you find any?"

The soldier grinned mirthlessly. "Veterans, some of them in for over twenty years? What do you think? These men have scars on their scars, yes, and burns aplenty. No, we didn't find any S-shaped brands but then, between you and me sir, we weren't really looking very hard."

It was around eight years ago when the rumour came to Dol's ears that the Vincerii were interested in a man with a brand shaped like an S. This was all Dol could glean, despite discreetly targeted questions, and he tucked the information away for when it might become useful. So he was doubly interested when, one day that summer at the Shining Stars Inn, Creggan had told him of the man at the bar with a similar brand and Bartellus, remarkably, had pricked up his ears and asked Creggan about him.

Bartellus had asked, "Do you know of this brand, Dol?"

Dol shook his head. "Slave mark, I expect. Why are you interested?"

"How could a man have both the honourable tattoo of the Second Adamantine and a slave mark?" Bart asked.

Dol replied, "I couldn't care less."

Then, unusually for a man who generally kept his own counsel, Bartellus volunteered, "I saw its fellow a long time ago. On a corpse."

"Blueskin?" Dol asked him.

"No. At least, I don't think so. He had many tattoos on his body and head. This single burn mark was on his shoulder."

Bartellus was a mystery, an enigma far more significant than just a man hiding his daughter's age, Dol Salida had decided. An intelligent man, and one who was inclined to hide that intelligence, Dol had noticed, Bart kept his own counsel on most matters, but he could not hide his interest in the architecture of the City, a subject he could always be drawn on, particularly in respect to the tunnels and sewers and dungeons. This was hardly suspicious in itself. And having a truant daughter was disappointing but scarcely astonishing. But now someone had seen fit to burn down the House of Glass with Bartellus in it, and he and his daughter had disappeared. In the last weeks Dol had used all his network of contacts, informants, friends and colleagues to seek out the old soldier. The name Sami given to him by the urchin in Blue Duck Alley had proved a dead end; there were a thousand Samis in the army, it turned out.

The urquat master had decided the only way to find the old fox was through his cub. The man would hardly permit the girl to continue her profession, if they were being hunted, but the daughter could still give him away. Dol stumped the streets visiting the few remaining suppliers of materials for glassmaking, until he found the maker of dyes Emly had once patronised. The old woman, with long grey hair in several braids, badly crippled in both feet, was reluctant to talk about her customers until he mentioned his niece Emly, when the old girl's face brightened and she became positively garrulous about the talented child. She had not seen her recently, and had no idea where the girl dwelled now the House of Glass was gone. But she helpfully told Dol the name of a craftsman who made Emly a special gold paint. And it was that man who told Dol he had not seen the girl in his shop, but had only five days before spotted her in the marketplace in front of the temple of Ascarides, the god of widows and orphans, admiring her own small window on a side wall.

Of course! Bartellus betrayed by the vanity of his daughter. With some reluctance he had reported the girl to Dashoul, so he could set his hounds on her, with the order that the girl, once spotted, be left alone and followed, for the father who kept her out of the army for more than a year was as culpable under the emperor's law as the girl herself.

Dol sat in his study early one morning watching the shapes of chimneys and rooftops slowly emerge from the dark. The grey sky turned to silver and now he could see the roofs were covered with a thick layer of new snow. Ice-stars had formed in the corners of the window overnight.

The Feast of Summoning was only five days away. He shivered. Petalina, his first love, was to be interred today, her cold body embalmed with oils and unguents then placed in the imperial vaults, a signal honour for the child of a merchant. Dol would not be going to the rites. He had sent his excuses to Fiorentina, who understood his reasons better than anyone. Petalina's death at the hands of Mallet and his men had shocked and grieved him. Her liaison with Marcellus should have kept her safe, *had* kept her safe. And Dol's world, the City, would be a lacklustre place without Petalina in it.

He sighed and shifted his slippered feet, feeling a cool draught around his ankles. He listened, hearing the door to the side alley beneath him closing quietly. He could not hear footsteps, but he stood and limped over to the inner door. Seconds later there was a quiet triple-tap on the wood. He waited. After a few moments there were two more taps. Dol unbolted the door.

The visitor was called Sully. He was small, thin and clean-shaven, a precise man with the demeanour of a bookkeeper rather than a veteran warrior of thirty years. Dol had known him for that long. He had rare qualities for an old soldier, in that he listened and watched, and spoke only when he was certain of his words. He was quick-witted, and Dol valued him more highly than any of his associates.

Sully sat in his habitual chair. He rubbed his hands together to take the chill off them, and took a sip of the tisane Dol had ready. "It is said," he began without preamble, "that the emperor is planning a root-and-branch purge of the Thousand, that none of the centuries are safe, except perhaps the new one, the Nighthawks."

"Said by whom?"

Sully shrugged, as he always did when his source was only rumour and speculation, bar gossip and soldiers' tittle-tattle.

"But what do you think, my friend?"

The little man was silent for a while. Finally he said, "Despite the events of the last few days, the emperor and Marcellus rely on the loyalty of the bodyguard and history has shown they are right to do so. The warriors of the Thousand are well-rewarded. They have prestige, fame and wealth. After such a plot you have to look at who would benefit from Marcellus' death. It would not be the bodyguard."

"Who would benefit? Who were Mallet and his men acting for, if not for themselves?"

Who would take Marcellus' place if both Vincerii were dead? Who knew what the emperor would do? It was a subject the two men had discussed many times over the years. It was always the sticking-point. Who knew what a man would do when he kept himself secluded, spoke only to Boaz and the Vincerii, some servants, and a select few of his bodyguard. What went on in the Keep was the deepest of the City's secrets.

Dol sat back. "What is known of this new commander, the Nighthawk?"

"Riis, his name is. He and his brother were hostages of the palace, two of the last, sons of some northern lord. Otherwise nothing is known against him. He fought for three years in the Blue Ridge campaign, and he's still alive. A survivor."

"The brother?"

"Not a survivor. Riis is said to have a reputation with women."

"No women in the First Adamantine. Can't keep it in the company."

"Old values," said Sully approvingly. He added, "He is much hated."

"Inevitably," Dol replied. "Keep a close eye on him. Anyone new is a person of interest. There is . . . "—he searched for the words—"a pregnant atmosphere in the palace at the moment, a feeling of impending danger."

"No one seems to know why Mallet acted as he did," Sully offered. "It was quite out of character. He had served the Vincerii for more than twenty years. The Thousand have always been loyal to them. None more so. Perhaps that is why there is a feeling of uncertainty."

He drank his tisane in silence for a while, glancing at Dol over the edge. He had something more to say. Dol raised his eyebrows inquiringly.

"I have some good news for you," Sully told him.

"Oh?"

"You were right, the girl could not resist going to look at her own work. She was seen at the Old Observatory in Gervain, admiring her window. She was followed home to her bolthole. Bartellus was not there, so they plan to seize him this morning."

Dol rubbed his hands. "Excellent," he said. There was a twinkle in Sully's small dark eyes. "Something else?" Dol asked.

The little man nodded. "I waited out of sight until I saw him return late at night. To ensure his presence when the palace's men came calling."

"Yes?" said Dol.

"I have met him before," Sully told him.

The horses and riders pounded through the Araby Gate and out onto the snowy plain. The snow was almost hock-deep, covered with a night-time crust of ice, and the hooves threw up showers of crystals into the frozen sky. Riis heard whoops of delight from the men behind him, exhilarated to be released from the City and to be back on horseback. Despite the turmoil in his mind, his spirits lifted as he breathed in; the air was sharp as diamond. Ahead of them their path crossed virgin snow all the way to the distant crest of hills, and the sky above shone silver.

Leaving Marcellus and the Keep, Riis had chosen twenty troopers and hurried to the stables of the Thousand. For the first time he exercised his full authority as commander to requisition horses from the stablemaster, apparently the only man in the City who did not know, or chose not to believe, of the Leopards' demise. For himself Riis had picked a huge grey stallion which the stablemaster eventually conceded was called Sunder.

Sunder had clearly not been exercised for several days for he frisked and danced, also thrilled by the clear air and sparkling snow. Riis, who had been riding since he was at his mother's tit, allowed the big horse to have his way and when the beast suddenly set off at a gallop towards the rising sun he leaned low over his neck and let him go. Sunder was not a young horse, but he was game and powerful, and within moments they had pulled away from the rest of the troop. Riis tried to form a plan.

His promotion to commander of the Thousand had been a box of mixed gifts. It had hugely increased his chances as an assassin, but decreased his role as a conspirator. He could scarcely creep the halls of the palace at night; he was far too visible. Every member of the Thousand knew his face, and hated him.

So it was some time after the women's death before he took the risk of returning to Petalina's garden. Hooded and caped, he had climbed the palace wall once more on a bright moonlit night. He knew the rota of wall guards—who better?—and within an hour he was under the fig tree and groping in the darkness for a message hidden in the bricks. His fingers found a piece of paper but he could not read it in the shadowy garden. He climbed to the top of the wall again and in the light of the moon he could make out Amita's neat lettering, telling him how to find a package she had left for him. Frowning, he followed her words, letting himself into the room to the rear of Petalina's suite. He took the chance of lighting a phosphorus stick and held it up. He was surrounded by the soft grey shapes of crowded dresses hanging on the walls like corpses. The musty air, laced with stale perfume, smelled like death to him, and in the sputtering light he imagined Amita's narrow ghost moving across the room, a dead woman's dress draped over her arm.

He moved through into the second room. As instructed he looked under the piles of shoe bags and found an old leather satchel shoved out of sight. He pulled it out and glanced inside. It was full of folded papers. He left the rooms gratefully and went back out into the clean night.

That day he risked sending a message, via an illiterate soldier, to Sami at the Pony, and the following morning went there after sunrise, hoping Evan had got the note and would be there. He told Darius he was to meet an old friend, knowing his aide would guess he had a rendezvous with a prostitute.

The squalid inn was almost empty in the dismal light of morning. Its only customer lay on the floor in a dead drunk, a dog licking his face. The barkeep leaned stiffly against the stained counter, his face grey, his body motionless. Strangely, without its customers the place smelled even worse. Riis breathed through his mouth and peered around in the gloom for Evan. He saw him in the corner, slouched over a table, his fair hair tucked under a cap.

"Drink?" his friend asked as Riis slid into the seat opposite.

Riis looked at the scummy liquid in Evan's glass. "I'd rather hammer nails into my eyes," he said.

Evan grinned. "For a soldier you're a bit of a daisy, Riis."

Riis dumped the leather satchel on the table. He was not in the mood to be mocked. "The girl is dead," he said curtly. "She found these plans. I can't make head or tail of them, but it seems she could."

Evan nodded. "We heard she died in Mallet's rebellion. Who killed her?"

Riis shook his head. "I don't . . ." Then he said, admitting it to himself for the first time, "Marcellus, I think."

Evan stared at him. "Marcellus? Why?"

"I don't know. I mean, I don't know if he did. I got there too late. They were all dead. Except the Vincerii." Covered in blood, he thought. Drenched in it.

"Why would he kill her? Did he find out who she was?"

"I don't know. No, I don't think so. She was just in the opera house. Attending the whore. I don't even know if Marcellus knew her." He shook his head. "She was just unlucky."

Relieved, Evan clapped him on the back. "Not much of a spy, are you?"

Riis said, "She was just a girl."

"She was old enough," Evan said indifferently. Riis remembered from past battles that Evan Broglanh had few sympathies for the casualties of war. "She knew what she was getting into."

Riis shook his head. "No," he said with certainty, "she didn't."

And he added quietly, "None of you know what you're getting into."

Out on the snow-covered plain Riis pulled on Sunder's reins and the warhorse dropped into a trot. They were coming up to the line of foothills called the Araby Break, and Riis expected, if Marcellus' information was correct, to see their target soon. The Araby Gate was the easternmost of the City gates, lying north of the Paradise Gate but within distant sight of it. If Saroyan and her escort were heading for the Paradise Gate they could not have missed them. Riis waited for the other troopers to catch up, then stopped to address them.

"On the other side of the Break," he told them, his breath puffing out in the frozen air, "is a woman rider and her six guards heading for the City. It is our job to stop them and kill them. Take out the escort but leave the woman to me."

There were whispered comments from some of the men, and a few sniggers, but Riis chose not to hear them. Some of the riders pulled off the knitted caps and felt scarves they were wearing against the cold and replaced them with their new silver helms. Riis saw the pride in their faces and he looked at his own helm, still tied to his saddle horn. He had not even tried it on yet. He pulled his cap off but decided to leave the helm where it was. He was unlikely to need it.

They set off again, bunched in tight formation, and as they reached the crest of the Araby Break Riis could see, as predicted, the tiny dots of riders heading towards them across the flat land between hills and river.

"No prisoners!" he bellowed, and the troop thundered down the slope towards them.

Saroyan and her small escort spotted the attackers from far away and they turned and raced for the river Kercheval.

Riis, exhilarated by Sunder's speed and the frosty air in his face, urged the big horse on. Saroyan and her guard had been in the saddle for some time, and their horses had too little to give. He caught up with the fleeing mounts before they got to the river, and slashed the rear horse across the rump with his sword. The beast slowed, whinnying, and Sunder dodged round it and carried on chasing. It was as if he knew Riis' mind. He had to reach Saroyan before the others.

The Kercheval was in winter spate and could be crossed with care, not at full tilt. At a command from the lord lieutenant the bodyguards slowed and turned, spreading out to guard her retreat as she alone urged her mount back into the icy water.

Sunder thundered towards them, and two came forward to meet him, trying to cut him off. Riis felt the horse bunch his muscles to charge to the right and he leaned to his left, slashing his sword through one of the riders' reins then, on the rise, piercing the other rider's jaw. Within moments the other Nighthawks had caught up with them and Saroyan's protectors were fighting a hopeless battle for her life and their own.

Riis guided Sunder round the slaughter and plunged him into the river. He could see the woman was on the other side already, her horse clambering up the shallow bank. He had no real plan, just to reach her, protect her somehow. Then he heard the swish of a thrown weapon and saw a light spear thud into the fleeing woman's back, throwing her off the horse and into the snow. He reined in Sunder and turned, glaring back at the trooper who was grinning with pride at his accurate aim.

"Stay there!" he ordered.

Riis felt the icy water crawl up around his waist as Sunder swam across the deep-flowing river, and his teeth were chattering when they reached the other side. He threw himself off the horse and ran to the woman, who was trying to crawl away through the snow, leaving a bloody trail behind her.

"Saroyan, it's me! Riis!" he said, but she did not hear him and he put his hand on her shoulder, trying to stop her struggle. "It's me, Riis!"

Though the wound was deep and looked mortal, she writhed away from his touch. "Take your hand off me!" she spat, her face contorted with disgust.

Riis sighed. Even in death she was a disagreeable woman, he thought. He sat down in the snow a few paces away.

"I've been ordered to kill you," he told her.

"Who by?" she asked, turning painfully on her side, blood staining her mouth. "Who wants me dead?"

"The Vincerii."

"I don't believe you," she spat.

"Nevertheless," Riis said tiredly, "it is the truth. The Vincerii . . ."

"The Vincerii," she mimicked. He was amazed at the depths of her loathing. "You don't know what you're talking about, you fool. *I* am Vincerii," she said. "We do not kill one another in the Family Vincerus."

He just stared at her. He did not know what to say.

"You're a fool, Riis," she repeated. "I knew it from the start. You could have warned me and let me go."

Riis, who had thought through every option, said, "If I let you flee they would want to know why and eventually, under questioning, I would tell them everything, and our one chance would be gone. This way, I survive and maybe our plan survives too."

"You could have fled yourself, saved me and the plan."

He said nothing.

"You've killed my guards?"

"They were brave men and I regret their deaths." He looked up. The two mounts stood together companionably, blowing and puffing in the frigid air, their bodies screening Riis and Saroyan from the eyes of his men. He peered through their legs. The battle appeared to have ended.

"I don't have much time."

She glared at him still, but he could see the pain and exhaustion in her eyes, the look of failure he had seen so often in a defeated enemy.

She muttered to herself. "Who gave you the order?" she asked, still not wanting to believe it.

"Marcellus."

"Then we have all been betrayed," she whispered to herself.

Riis had no idea what to say, but he sat with her, casting covert glances across the river. Two of his men had started to cross.

"Lie down," he said finally. "Rest. I will say you are dead." He knew there was no chance of her surviving, wounded as she was, in icy wet clothes, without shelter.

Obediently, like a child, she laid her head down in the snow.

"I'm sorry," Riis said, and he mounted again, grabbed her horse's reins and trotted Sunder away. Glancing back, he saw a dark huddle of clothes against the whiteness. Then it started to snow.

On the ride back Riis felt anger rising inside him—anger for Amita and her pointless death, and anger at the conspiracy in which he had so little faith. Of the handful of plotters he knew of, two were already dead. Within five days a small army would invade the palace and his own men would fight to the death to repel them. He had little doubt that Saroyan was right in one thing—if anyone could kill the emperor then Arish could. But Arish knew nothing about the palace and, crucially, he knew nothing of the power of the Vincerii. The slaughter in the Little Opera House haunted his sleep. Did they cause all those people to be . . . pulverised? Even Marcellus' own lover? Each time Riis looked hard at it, it seemed insane. Yet in the crystal air he stared at it again and could see no other alternative. The human soup he had witnessed saturating the walls of the building had been real enough.

What is Arish getting into? he thought.

By the time they returned to the Araby Gate Riis had made his decision. He could not save Amita or Saroyan. But he could save Arish, and Evan Broglanh, and his own men, and perhaps hundreds of soldiers loyal to the City. The assassination attempt could not happen if the emperor was already dead.

So Riis had until the Day of Summoning to kill him.

PART SIX

The Day of Summoning

Chapter 35

The gods of winds and waters were many and various, and capricious in their moods. In the City the ancients had worshipped the deities of the four winds, although modern folk, of a less superstitious bent, prayed only to the god of the northerlies, whose ever-presence could scarcely be doubted. Simpler people worshipped the gods of the seas, the rivers, rain, snow, lightning and thunder. And the country folk, whose every activity was affected by the whims of the weather, prayed to the same gods, as well as the lesser deities of fog, frost and the kindly morning dew.

Elija lay in the bottom of the boat, helpless in the coils of seasickness, and prayed to them all. At times he hoped he could detect a change in the movement of the craft, a slight lessening of the swell, and he prayed more fervently, imagining his ordeal was coming to an end. But then the seas would surge again, and so would his stomach, empty now except for the small sips of water he had managed to force down.

He had spent the hours of daylight staring at the grey wood of the plank in front of his face. The vessel, once a fishing boat, now promoted to a military landing craft, stank of fish and he imagined he could see the pattern of scales imprinted into the timber. Often they looked like faces.

They had been in the boat for three days and three long nights. The convoy of four vessels travelled under cover of darkness, and in the daytime hid in the lee of islands and rocks, evading the ships of the City. The boat was wide and low, unlikely to be spotted except from up close, and it wallowed and lurched, and few of the fifty-odd soldiers packed aboard had not suffered. Elija doubted that, when he reached dry land, he would be able to stand, and he wondered how the warriors could possibly fight.

"Here, lad, have some water."

Elija shook his head miserably, then he felt a strong hand lift him by his collar, and a waterskin was thrust against his mouth.

"Drink." There was no refusing. Elija sipped some of the water, conscious that it tasted of old socks, and tried to hold it down.

"Good lad." Stalker set him back gently, and said, "Not much longer." It was what he always said. Elija had stopped believing him two days before.

The big northlander had taken it upon himself to look after the boy, urging him at times to take bread or pieces of dried meat. Stalker himself seemed unaffected by the movement of the boat, indeed he seemed to relish it, sitting looking out over the grey waves sniffing the air like an old dog. That morning, as the sun rose and while the boat still rocked at its night berth, Stalker had suddenly thrown off his clothes and clambered over the side and swam in the sea, for no reason. The other soldiers had jeered and shouted, and when the northlander had climbed back into the boat, his braids dripping, his white skin bright red in patches from the icy waves, he had muttered sheepishly, "Bit of a wash." But Elijah thought he had done it for the fun of it, and he was cheered for a while.

"Look," Stalker said, pointing to the east. "Land."

But Elija had seen land before and was not to be fooled.

He dozed for a while, dreaming he was climbing a high cliff. The cliff was made of cake and he had to keep stopping to eat some. Someone below was urging him onwards, but he had to eat the cake, even though his stomach was full, and the roll of plans under his arm kept slipping and slithering out of his grip.

When he awoke again it was pitch-dark. He felt a bit better, for the lurch of the boat had lessened. He guessed they had stopped somewhere sheltered for the night. The ship creaked and groaned, and he could hear water slapping on the other side of the planks by his head. It was icy cold. The light snow which had accompanied them when they set off from Adrastto had quickly turned to a steady penetrating rain. His clothes were soaked. Around him he heard the snores and smelled the smells of too many soldiers packed together in a small space. And he could hear murmured voices.

"How's the ankle?" the woman asked Stalker.

"All right." The man bit off the words, not wanting to talk about his crippled limb.

"When we go ashore in the morning you must hang behind," Indaro told him, for she was in charge of the boat. "Three days in this and your ankle will have stiffened up. If we meet opposition straight away I don't want you in the front ranks." The northlander made no reply and his silence spoke loudly. "You'll get your chance," Indaro added.

"You want me to babysit the boy?" Stalker asked gruffly.

Indaro hesitated. Elija knew that was not what she meant.

"No," she said. "I have assigned two bodyguards to Elija. I want you to stay to the rear because you would be a liability in the front ranks until your ankle has warmed up." She added briskly, "That's an order."

Elija had been a little frightened of Indaro when he first met her at Old Mountain. He had no experience of women warriors. The only women he met in the Halls were whores or crones, who smiled most of the time, to appeal or ingratiate. Indaro seldom smiled, and there were deep vertical frown lines between her dark brows. Elija had avoided her. But the day after they first met she had approached him and stiffly told him she had seen Emly with Bartellus after the flood. She told him every detail and nuance of the meeting, then patiently told him again when he asked. He had known for some time that Em was alive, but this was the first time he had met anyone who had spoken to her, even if it was eight years before, and he absorbed every word.

In turn he told her of his time with Rubin. She had known her brother was there, and that was why she had followed him. She had spent two years in the Halls but had not been able to find him. Elija wished he could tell her what happened to his friend.

Then news reached Old Mountain of Amita's death, followed, days later, by the crumbling roll of papers, the plans of the palace and sewers she had given her life for. No one could tell Elija how she had died, but he knew she was fearless and he guessed she had died bravely, determined to give him a chance of success. For many nights Elija wept over his loss, and for as many days he sat with Indaro as they pored over the captured plans, conjuring stone walls and tunnels and waterways from the faint cold lines on sheets of flimsy paper spread out in front of them.

He was impressed and daunted by Indaro's knowledge of the Halls, and he found it impossible to imagine such a woman living down there. She told him she knew only a small area—beneath the south wing of the palace which housed the Library of Silence and the Hall of Watchers and the city to the south of that. He, on his part, had kept to the main routes used by Dwellers to cross the vast network of tunnels, but knew no area well, except for that around the Hall of Blue Light which, they worked out, lay beneath the

Great Library and was therefore useless to them. Neither of them knew anything about the caverns below the Keep, nor anyone who had been there.

One morning the two were joined by a stocky, fair-haired soldier called
Garret, who had arrived with Indaro and Fell at Old Mountain and who,
unlike most soldiers, could read. After watching and listening silently for a
long while, Garret asked them, "What I don't understand is, if the Hall of
Watchers, which leads up to the palace, is flooded, you say, then surely the
whole of the Halls, everything we are looking at"—he gestured to the plans—
"is underwater too."

Indaro said curtly, "It's more complicated than that."

She said no more, so Elija explained, "Gil has put scouts in, from the
Salient caves, which is where I escaped from the Halls. They found someone
who still lives in the sewers, a Dweller, who says the flooding and the shifting
of debris over the last two years has blocked some tunnels and made areas
that were previously flooded now above the water, just as some areas that
were once dry are now flooded."

"Can't this Dweller show us the way up into the palace?" Garret asked.

"I don't think so. It is hard to explain what it is like down there." Elija
thought about it. "You see, every day is a struggle for life in the Halls. Everyone keeps their eyes on the ground, looking for treasure, as they call it, or at
their backs, fearing an attack. There are areas where Dwellers never go, because they are too dangerous, or because they are heavily patrolled. They . . .
there is no curiosity about the world above."

"But there must be escape routes, in case of flood."

"Each centre of population, like the Hall of Blue Light where my sister
and I lived, has its own escape route. But these are all out into the City, up
vertical drains with ladders, called high funnels, which the engineers used
to use to get to certain parts of the sewers. These supply air to the Halls. But
none come up in the palace, that I know of. There are none on the plans. And
the palace is too closely guarded. At least, it is now. Indaro says there used
to be a way from the palace to the Dungeons of Gath, and a path from the
dungeons out into the City, in Lindo."

"The Dungeons of Gath?" Garret asked.

"The oldest dungeons in the City," answered Indaro. "They lie under
the Shield. Although the palace dungeons are almost certainly underwater,
the Dungeons of Gath might not be."

"It is a long way from the Shield to the palace," Garret said.

"It is even longer underground," replied Indaro. "And there is a very good chance part of it is flooded."

Elija and Indaro looked at one another. "So we have dismissed that idea," explained Indaro. "We will seek an entry directly into the Keep. Gil's contact claims there is such a way, although there is no indication of it on any of the plans we hold."

"And if it is not there?"

"Then we will fail and Fell and Broglanh will have to manage without us," she said bleakly.

Elija was pulled from his reverie as a sudden flurry of movement rocked the boat. He sat up, feeling cold and stiff. The dim light of dawn was all around them, but all he could see to the east was the dark shape of a high cliff looming above. After three days of inactivity the soldiers were cheerfully repacking their packs, donning body armour, and chewing on last-minute rations. Elijah peered over the gunwale to the rocky shore where the first boat, the supply vessel, had already tied up. Supplies were being carried ashore—coils of rope, weapons, food and water, medical supplies, and boxes of the strange lanterns Gil had recently showed them.

Elija's boat was the next to disembark. Ropes were thrown to soldiers on the shore, and the boat was hauled towards the rocks, where mooring posts had been driven into cracks and crevices. Elija saw the first person leap ashore. It was Indaro, a light pack on her back, her sword-belt held high. Then the rest of the soldiers poured over the gunwales.

"Elija!" Garret, now one of his bodyguards, gestured for him to leave. Elija levered himself up.

"May your gods guard you, lad," said Stalker, and Elija turned and nodded to him, his heart full of fear. He never thought he would be reluctant to leave the boat.

But now he had to go back into the sewers.

Bartellus no longer prayed to the gods. He no longer believed, as he once had, not so long ago, that soldiers who had died with valour in their hearts would be received by the Gods of Ice and Fire in the Gardens of Stone.

Now he lay in a dungeon once again, with the terrible threat of torture and slow death hanging over him, and he grieved for the people he had betrayed. He tried to close his mind's eye, but it was lidless, remorseless. Over and over he imagined Em being dragged away, struggling and crying. And he saw again, with merciless inevitability, his small sons waving goodbye to him in the sunlit garden, his pregnant wife smiling tiredly as he left his family to pursue his shiny military ambitions. These old ghosts from the past clung to him with sticky fingers, and they would not let him go however much he begged their forgiveness.

His ancient body ached all over. Since the stabbing and fire he had never recovered his full strength, and the long walk through the tunnels to this cell had been a torment. Two fingers of his left hand had been broken in the struggle for his capture, and he had not the courage or will to straighten and bind them. His mind felt muddled, enmeshed in grief for the past and terror for the future. He was on his own in a large cell intended for many men. The floor of slimy stone sloped slightly and the lower half was flooded. He curled up in the driest corner, away from the water, cradling his broken hand, and tried to ignore the scurrying of rats' claws in the dark.

He was tormented by not knowing. He did not know why he was in prison. The gods alone knew there were many possible reasons. Had Fell Aron Lee's conspiracy, and Bart's part in it, been found out? Had someone discovered his real identity? Or both? Or was it simply that he had been imprisoned for concealing Emly's true age? When he had tried to speak to his silent guards, on the torturous walk to this cell, asking them why he had been imprisoned, offering them all his wealth in return for a chance to speak to an advocate, he had been at first ignored, then cuffed impatiently to the ground.

Worst of all, by far, he did not know what would happen to Em. Her best hope was that she would be treated as a deserter and sent to some training camp before going to war. The thought of gentle, sensitive Emly being forced into body armour, a sword thrust into her hand, and sent to kill enemy soldiers was a torment to him. But that was her best hope. Her worst was that they had guessed her part in the conspiracy against the emperor, or discovered she was the daughter of general Shuskara. Her future then was one he could not bear to contemplate. He kept telling himself, repeating the comfortable story to himself over and over, that Broglanh would hear of their capture, would go to her rescue as he had saved them both before. He was resourceful and courageous, and he had a network of friends. But Bart had not seen Evan Broglanh for many days before the dawn raid. He had no idea if he was even in the City.

Bartellus wondered if he had been left there to die, abandoned without food and water for a terrible, but comparatively brief, death, and some traitor part of his mind hoped that was the truth. He could not face torture again. But he knew this was not so. His captors would scarcely have gone to the trouble of bringing him all this way through the dungeons when they could have executed him at his home. He had been brought there for some dark purpose.

He cursed himself for his pride and his vanity, both teased out of him with small effort by the ambitions of Fell Aron Lee. He was told only he could save the City and, in his dotage, he chose to believe it. He had forgotten the vow he had first made deep in the Halls, to keep Emly safe, his first and most important task, had abandoned it when offered the chance of being Shuskara again, the victorious general at the head of his adoring troops.

Again his pitiless memory, like a cheap mummers' show, showed him his daughter being taken away. She was dressed only in her nightshift and they tied her hands and threw her into a cart like meat on a butcher's slab. He could not remember if that had really happened, or if it was a nightmare. His captors had hit him over the head and he thought the only thing left in his skull now was headaches. He recalled being forced into a carriage, black and closed. He squeezed his old eyes closed in pain, trying to close his mind's eye, yet the two small boys waved to him, and his wife smiled wearily. But now the boys' faces were wizened and contorted like those of malevolent imps and Marta's soft lips opened to reveal a flickering red tongue, and Bartellus moaned.

He felt something move against his foot and his leg twitched convulsively. He had heard of prisoners being eaten alive by rats, and his courage failed and he wept in the darkness.

Indaro leaped ashore. The rock felt wonderfully solid under her feet. She clasped her sword-belt around her hips and looked around. The cave mouth in front of them, across a terrain of sharp rocks, was low and very wide, a murky slash in the cliff from which a dark river poured. The stench of sewage made her nose wrinkle, and she smiled grimly to herself. She had thought that part of her life over.

Looking up she could see in the growing light the cliffs of the Salient rising above, dark grey against the lighter grey of the dawn. Her father's house was up there, just out of sight. She was closer to it than she had been in years. Yet she knew in that moment, a moment of sad clarity, that she would never see it again.

Putting aside the thought, she turned to see the last of her men climbing from the boat, Stalker in the rear moving awkwardly. There were fifty-five in her group, including Elija, Garret and Stalker. The rest were Petrassi and Odrysians, the Petrassi dark and slender like their leader Gil Rayado—silent, pitiless killers, she had been told; the Odrysians were fairer and with a boisterous temperament. They had joked and clowned around on the boat, apparently unaffected by nausea or fear. Indaro reminded herself that it was only days since she had thought of them all as Blueskins, the enemy. Now she was leading them into battle. They had no women warriors, and she had caught many curious glances in the days at sea. She had wondered, back at Old Mountain, if she should be put in charge of a team, but Fell had insisted and Gil had conceded graciously enough.

She had last seen Fell Aron Lee three days before at the Paradise Gate. His leave-taking to her was a dour nod, then he rode up to the gate alone, while she and the others had turned and skirted the wall and headed north to the port of Adrastto. They were to meet again, in the Keep of the palace, if that proved possible, at noon on the Day of Summoning. Tomorrow. Indaro knew their mission, and Fell's ambition, was to kill the emperor and end the war, but hers was to survive to see Fell again and to ensure his safe escape. If she had to kill the emperor to achieve that, then so be it. She would walk through the Gardens of Stone and take on every warrior who had ever lived if she could save Fell.

She could see the first scouts emerging again from the caves, clambering over the rocks on the north side of the river. They spoke to Gil Rayado and he nodded. He gestured to Indaro, and she jogged over to him.

"The way seems clear. There are no lights, no sign of habitation. No sign of guards."

"Elija said the way was not guarded when he was here."

"Nevertheless," replied Gil thoughtfully, "I am surprised. Security in the

City has tightened a great deal in the last months. I expected to find a welcome party."

"Perhaps we will, farther in," said Indaro and the leader nodded.

"We must consider this good news," he said. "Let's go."

They were both aware, though there seemed no point in saying it, that the cave might be unguarded because it was no longer possible to get into the City that way.

The supply master and his team had been breaking out crates full of the glass lanterns Indaro had been first shown back at Old Mountain. They were tall, with a narrow chimney, the base filled with flammable oil. Once lit they became very hot and each was mounted in a wood and metal cage which could be hung up or stood on a flat surface. In her years in the Halls Indaro was used to carrying flaming torches to see the way; they were dangerous and smelly and inclined to go out when it was most inconvenient. These were smaller and they shed more light, and they could be set down whenever there was a pause in their journey.

Better still, each lantern lasted a precise period of time, so they could be used to mark the passing of the hours underground. Some had been lit at dawn, and the supply master and two of his team had been designated timekeepers, so they would know how close they were to their scheduled time limit of noon the following day.

And, best of all, Indaro thought, in a battle the lanterns would make effective weapons.

She turned back to the daylight, to see Elija standing at the mouth of the cave, a picture of indecision. She walked back towards him over the sharp rocks. His eyes were huge in his ashen face and he scarcely seemed to see her. She wondered again if he could be relied upon or if at some point he would have to be carried, their guide, their light in the dark places.

"Elija," she said, peering down at him, caught between sympathy and impatience. "Are you all right?"

He nodded but did not move. She looked to Garret, jerking her head towards the depths of the cave. The soldier patted Elija on the back. "C'mon," he said in his cheery way. "You'll feel better when we get underway."

Thank the gods for Garret and his platitudes, Indaro thought, leaving them and turning to her troop. Her platoon was called Dawn and she was to take point, accompanied by Elija and his two bodyguards, Garret and a

Petrassi soldier called Nando. They were all lightly armoured, for there would be much climbing to do, and each carried, in addition to his weapons of choice, a waterproof pack. Every third soldier held a lantern, and as they moved into the darkness of the cave, Indaro was very aware that their presence would be quickly known about if there were still Dwellers living there.

Elija had copies of the plans in his pack, but they had spent so many hours poring over them that Indaro felt she could recall them all from memory. Their route would be dictated by what they found, but her hope was that they could follow the river upstream for the first few leagues, all the while it flowed due west, then, where it veered to the south, they would strike north, hoping to meet the great channel marked on one of the maps as the Fallowly Dike, on others as the Dark Water. This river passed, or had once passed, beneath the palace and was, she and Elija decided, their best chance of finding their way into the Keep. They had to assume all channels and tunnels were clear and negotiable. When they reached one that was barred by debris, or flooded, then they would divert their path and seek a new way.

They had over a day and a half to travel seven leagues underground, as the stormcrow flies. It was not long.

Gil, Mason and Fell had been dismayed when they heard the news that Bartellus had been captured. First Amita dead, then Saroyan, now this. The old man was not vital to their mission to kill the emperor. But Fell's hopes for the future of the City, one that could recover from the death of the emperor and move forward in peace, rested on the general Shuskara rallying his old regiments, the Second Adamantine and Fourth Imperial, rotated into the City by Saroyan in the days before her death.

Indaro privately thought the old man, if not suffering torture, would be safer in prison than he would have been in their original plan, entering the palace with Fell to confront the emperor. When—if—the mission succeeded and the Immortal was dead, then would be the time, she thought, to descend into the dungeons to find Shuskara and bring him out in honour.

Taking a last glance at the lightening sky, she stepped into the shade of the cave and reluctantly let the foul air flow into her chest. The boats had landed on the north side of the river, the left bank. It was a commitment made several days before, for they could not be sure of being able to cross the river farther up. Elija had told them of the bridge which served the settlement of reivers, but could not know if it was still there.

The north side of the river was the more difficult. The mudbanks to the south rolled out like a gentle plain as far as the eye could see in the gloom. Those on the north were steeper, and Indaro quickly abandoned any attempt to stay upright and, putting on gloves, clambered up the bank on all fours. She was painfully aware of the picture she presented to her men and thought it an inauspicious start to her command. They spoke together in their own tongue and she could only guess what they were saying.

After a while the terrain flattened a little and she was able to stand. She raised her light high and peered towards the east. She could see nothing. She put it down and blinked a few times, trying to find some night-sight. At last she saw what Elija had described—shafts of weak daylight shining from the unseen ceiling of the cave onto a distant huddle of huts on the far side of the river. She turned to Elija and he nodded.

The shafts of light were a mystery. They could not be cut through to the top of the cliff; it was too high. They must be cut diagonally into the cliff face. But by whom and for what purpose? Clearly not to illuminate this sad cluster of hovels. The shafts must have been there first, before the community grew up in their lukewarm light. The community was strange too. Since they lived so close to the sea, why not build outside, or in the shelter of the cave mouth, rather than deep in the dark, amid the shoals of sewage? Indaro shrugged to herself. It was not her problem.

There was no sign of movement among the dwellings. From Elija's report, the community was once bustling with activity. But now the shacks and huts looked empty and the only life that could be seen was the rats, a pack of which were even now streaming like water across the flats, and the ever-present flies.

Indaro picked up her lantern and moved on. The farther they walked into the dark the thicker the air became and it was harder to breathe normally. Their feet were sinking into the mud and each step became a struggle. She heard the men cursing behind her. Elija, smaller and lighter than them all, was managing best.

"Is it like this all along the bank?" she asked him.

He shrugged, a slight movement in the gloom. "Maybe the going is firmer the farther we get from the river."

It took another two hours, measured by the light of the lanterns, to reach the wooden bridge which served the settlement. Indaro raised her light.

"I'm glad we chose not to go that way," said Gil, who had come up behind her. She nodded. The bridge was broken in places, wooden planks hanging off it into the slow-flowing river, and rotten where it remained. It would be possible for rats or cats to cross, but Indaro thought the mouldy, slimy timbers could not bear a person's weight.

"Perhaps that's why the community was abandoned?" she offered. "It would not be easy to rebuild."

"Where is the entrance you used from the Halls?" Gil asked Elija.

The boy pointed. "Over there. It is directly east of the cave opening, for we could see the setting sun through it. This path leads to it." He looked across the river. "I wonder what happened to them all," he said.

"Drowned in the floods, or cleaned out by the City's patrols." Indaro shrugged. "They're all dead now." She glanced at Elija and thought she saw a faint smile on his face.

"I wish I could tell Amita," he said.

Chapter 36

Emly rose slowly to consciousness. She lay in a narrow bed, warm under her heavy winter coat. Below her, in the kitchen of the bakery which had been their sanctuary for three days, she could hear the rattle of pans and the sharp orders and complaints from the cook and her husband as they prepared the day's loaves. The sounds were comforting and Em fell asleep again.

When she awoke a second time the rain, which had thundered on the roof tiles all night, had stopped. She opened her eyes to see the pink fingers of sunrise creeping through the dirty window. The attic room was filled with rosy light. Emly sighed and put her nose out from under the covers. The City was deep in winter, but the kitchen below kept the tiny room warm as its ovens once day began. Despite all that had happened, Emly had not felt so safe for many weeks.

She lifted her head and craned her neck. Evan lay on the other bed, flat on his stomach, his face pressed into the pillow, one arm above his head, the other hand trailing on the floorboards. She could see the faded red of his jacket and the tow-coloured hair, spiking up all over his head. He slept, as always, like the dead.

He had told her once that a warrior could sleep anywhere, yet be instantly alert when needed. She rolled over and ran her hand across the dusty floor, scooping up a pebble she had dug out of her shoe. She threw it at the sleeping soldier. It hit him sharply on the top of his head. He did not stir. She smiled.

"Is it always your duty to rescue me?" she had asked him, when he had found her hiding among barrels at the rear of the Shining Stars Inn, their designated meeting place should some disaster occur.

He had said gruffly, "It is no duty," but she knew he was angry at himself for not being there to stop Bartellus being taken.

"There were six soldiers," she had assured him kindly. "You were outnumbered. It would do no good if you were captured too."

He had given her a long, unfathomable look, then said, "You haven't had much to do with warriors, have you, girl?"

She shook her head. He was the first she had ever met, apart from her father.

The palace soldiers had come for Bartellus before dawn.

They had been hiding in an abandoned stable, once the home of one of the cavalry units, now disused except by courting couples who coupled in the mouldy straw beneath them as the refugees waited silently above in the loft. Evan had furnished them with food and spare clothing. Em begged to be allowed out, although Bartellus showed no interest in leaving the loft. Since he was wounded he had aged and his memory had become poorer, and his legs were shaky underneath him. Emly saw him staring into the distance sometimes, his mouth moving as if he was talking to someone in his head. She knew he was once a great general, and he was a great man to her, but she could not believe he would ever lead troops again.

On the morning of their capture Emly had gotten up early and climbed down into the body of the barn, to have some privacy to change her clothes when, on the other side of the wooden plank wall, she heard the faint stealthy sound of a sword being drawn. Bartellus was still asleep upstairs.

She had screamed, "Father! They're coming!" and ran for the loft ladder, but before she could get there two men burst in through the barn door and raced towards her, swords raised. She turned and sprinted to the rear of the barn, but the small door there opened and four more men came filing in. Trapped between them, she circled round one of the horse stalls and scrambled through the gap left by a loose plank that Evan had shown her on their first day there. It was big enough for a small man to get through, but, looking back fearfully from the street outside, she saw they did not try. Emly knew they were not interested in her. It was Bartellus they wanted, or rather Shuskara, the famous general.

Evan had also shown them an escape route from the upper barn, down a rope attached to an ancient pulley which looked rusted and useless but which he had oiled in readiness for an escape. But Bartellus had had no chance to use it. He was probably still asleep when he felt a blade at his throat.

Terrified that the soldiers might just kill him in the hay, Em watched from a distant corner until she saw the old man—still living—bundled into a black carriage. She followed the carriage as it rumbled through the streets, but it went where she feared—to a side gate of the Red Palace. She had sat down and cried then, feeling more alone and bereft than she had since she was a child. Then she got up and dried her tears and made her way to the Shining Stars Inn, where Evan found her at last.

She lay on her side watching the soldier sleep. Tomorrow was the day he had been waiting for, the Day of Summoning, when he would join the rebel commander she had heard so much about, Fell Aron Lee, and enter the palace and kill the emperor. Bart was to have gone with them, and there was a small part of Em's heart that was grateful that he would not, for it was, he said, a suicide mission. Evan had agreed with him cheerfully, but that would not stop them.

She had noticed Evan's manner towards her and her father was very different. With Bartellus he was relaxed and often witty. He teased the old man, mocked him sometimes if he thought it would stir Bart to greater effort, although Em never doubted his respect for him. His conversation was often coarse, and he entertained Bartellus with stories about warriors they both knew, battles they had both fought in, and jokes which were often obscure to Em.

With her, though, especially if they were alone, he was grave and courteous, treating her with a respect she felt she had not earned. When she tried to tease him as she did Bartellus he would smile politely but otherwise not react. She had asked him once if he had children, and he had given her that long, impenetrable look and finally shook his head.

She found herself thinking about him a lot. When he was with her she felt safe, and despite her fears for her father, happy.

This was to be their last day together. That evening, after dark, he was to take her to the house of a man who would employ her as a servant. He was a kind old man, Evan told her, a librarian, who needed someone to cook and clean. She would be safe there under a new name.

She was aghast. Until then she had refused to take the words *suicide mission* to heart. "Will you not come back?" she asked him.

"If we survive," he told her, gazing into her eyes to see if she understood him, "I will return for you when I can, but it might not be for a while, so you must be patient. Yes, we might not come back at all. There is another soldier you can trust. His name is Riis. I have told him where you will be. If he lives, he will come to you and see you are safe."

He fell silent, and she stared at him. "If," he said at last, "no one comes for you after several days, then you must assume the mission has failed and we are all dead."

"And Father? What will happen to him now?"

"I expect they have taken him to the dungeons. I will find him."

"The dungeons?" A flicker of memory teased the back of Em's mind.

"He will not be killed immediately, or he would have been left dead in the barn. And from tomorrow the palace will be in too much of an uproar for anyone to bother with one old man. If we succeed I will get him out. I promise you."

"We owe you so much," she had said simply.

He had shrugged, as if he did not care what she thought. He was so brave. She wondered if there had ever been a time in his life when he was frightened, or apprehensive, as she always seemed to be. She thought it impossible.

So she lay in her bed and watched him sleep and willed the day to pass slowly. It had started raining again.

B art's belly was empty when he was captured at dawn, and it was not long before it began to cramp. He endured the pains stoically, trying to ignore them, trying to sleep on the cold wet prison stones, trying not to think. The cramps slowly drifted away, as he knew they would. It was not the first time he had been half starved.

But when the torment of thirst started to claw at him, the old soldier abandoned his plan to give in and die. He rolled slowly over and sat up. He dragged out a shirt tail and tore off a strip to use as a bandage. The pain of forcing his broken fingers back into place was almost more than he could bear. He sat sweating and nauseous for a long while. Then, using one hand, he crawled over to the door. He felt around in the dark. The door joined the floor snugly; he could not even get a finger under it. But the cell had clearly been flooded more than once. Firmly putting aside that thought, he found the wood was soft, almost spongy in places. He picked at it with stubby fingertips, trying to find some purchase, but he merely got splinters in his good hand. He needed a tool of some sort. He started methodically searching the floor of the cell, first the drier part then, reluctantly, the flooded area. He found debris aplenty, all of it rotted and slimy. And he found the end of a narrow pipe where clearly water flowed into the cell or out of it again, but it was firmly cemented in.

When he was close to giving up he found something hard under his searching fingertips. He held it, turning it round and round, feeling its contours. It was metal, thin as a pin but flaring at one end, about the length of his thumb. It felt frighteningly flimsy, but it was all he had. He dragged himself back to the door and started to pick at the wood.

As he worked he realised he was not in the Dungeons of Gath, as he had first believed. Those dreadful dungeons were for prisoners who were to be kept alive, for torture, or for some other purpose of the emperor. To be kept alive they had to be fed, however frugally, and the doors to the cells were all reinforced at the base with metal, and fitted with grilles which opened for food to be slid in.

This chamber, into which a hundred men could have been packed, was either an oubliette, where prisoners were locked away and simply forgotten, or a temporary holding cell. He had heard the main palace dungeons were underwater, but there were other prisons beneath the palace. He did not know them all. He briefly allowed himself a happy fantasy in which the invading soldiers of Fell's army would find his cell and release him, and he would join them, storming up the tunnels, bursting into the Keep, capturing the emperor and condemning him to death as he begged and wept.

Sitting in the pitch-dark, scraping at a stout wooden door with a tiny pin, his courage faltered suddenly and he sat in hopeless misery for a while. Then he roused himself and started again.

No sounds reached him in the cell, no distant crying or screaming, no shouted orders or whispered conversations, nothing but his own rasping breath and a sinister glugging from the pipe in the corner of the chamber. And the scuttling and scratching of rodents. So he heard the clump of boots at some distance and he stopped, waiting. The bootsteps became louder and he dragged himself away from the door.

The painful glare of light poured in and he put an arm across his eyes, cowering against expected violence. There was a soft thud of something being thrown on the floor, then the door slammed and the bootsteps marched away. Bartellus felt around and found a soft cloth with hard shapes in it—biscuits. He thrust them into his shirt before the rats could get them. And a waterskin. He drank gratefully, knowing now he was to be kept alive—for what?

When he went to work again it was with a fresh urgency.

It was after noon and Evan had been down to the bakery and returned with a fresh loaf. He and Em sat on their beds eating the warm, pungent bread, while he told her one of his stories about a battle he had been in with her father, although Bartellus had been general and Evan just a dirty grunt, he said. It was a tale full of heroism and humour and Emly drank in every word, her eyes wide, her lips parted in anticipation of his next words. She knew it was partly, possibly all, invention, but she loved to hear him talk and she knew he loved to see her so entertained.

He roared with laughter when he finished his story, and she laughed delightedly, although the punchline was baffling to her. Then he leaned back against the wall, finishing off the last crumbs of bread that had fallen down his tunic.

"Where do you come from, Evan?" she asked, keen to keep up the intimate atmosphere. But his good humour slipped away like water down a drain, and he narrowed his eyes. Then, as she watched him, he relaxed again. She guessed it was a reflex in him to be suspicious of questions.

"From a country far in the north-west. Its people call it Gallia, but in the City it is known as the Land of Mists."

"Is it beautiful there?" Em could not remember a time when she had not lived within walls of stone and brick. She glanced out of the grubby window to see rain sheeting down a brick wall an arm's-length away.

He shook his head. "I left when I was a child. I do not remember it. Sometimes"—he paused, his eyes gazing into the past—"sometimes I think I remember a blue lake and a waterfall. But perhaps it was something someone told me."

"Did you come here with your parents?" She was always eager for stories of mothers and fathers, of families living their lives together.

He picked more crumbs off his chest. "No. I was brought here as hostage. There were many of us boys, sons of distant kings and tribal leaders, all allies of the City. We were brought here to be trained in the ways of war, and as hostages for our lords' good behaviour."

He added, "I was the very last, the youngest of them. Me and my brother."

"Where is your brother?"

"Dead."

"What was his name?"

"Conor."

"I have a brother too. His name is Elija." Then she said, "Did you ever go home again, to your parents?"

"No."

"What happened to them?"

"They died."

His face was sad, but Em felt a selfish spark of satisfaction, for it was another thing that tied them together—they were both orphans.

She thought about what he had said, then wondered, "Why were you the last? Did the emperor decide it was cruel to treat little boys that way?" For it

certainly was, she thought, unconscious that as a child she had suffered in
ways that were unknown to him.

He grinned at her, his good humour restored.

"No, I don't think the emperor saw the error of his ways. There are no
more allies," he explained. "No more kings to pay tribute. They've all been
destroyed by the armies of the City."

"All of them?"

"There are lands far away, across the sea, where maybe they don't fear
the City. But everywhere we know, for hundreds of leagues around, there is
only desolation and death. The City has no allies left, only enemies, and soon
it will have destroyed them all."

She had never spoken of this with anyone before, because Bartellus refused to discuss politics, as he called it, and poor Frayling, the only other
constant in her recent life, knew nothing of events outside the walls. She felt
very grown-up, discussing these matters with a warrior of the City.

She hesitated, for she was reluctant to offend him, but she asked in a
small voice, "But you are a soldier. You have been part of this."

She thought he was not going to answer her, but at last he looked at her
and asked, "Have you seen those big flocks of birds? In the autumn. They fly
around in the sky, they look like smoke, twisting and turning all together,
like one big smoke-bird. Have you seen them?" He waited for her to nod,
then he said, "You have never seen one bird decide to go another way, have
you, for it would die on its own. Soldiers are like those birds. They do what
all the other soldiers do, or else they will die. And when you're fighting each
day, just trying to stay alive, and keep your friends alive, you don't think of
what you're doing, whether it's right."

She held her breath, not wanting to break his thread of thought. He said,
"It takes something . . . valuable to happen to make you see what you're doing
is wrong, to set you back on the right path."

"Did something valuable happen to you?"

"I met someone," he said absently, staring at his hands.

She waited, but he was not going to explain. She guessed he meant Fell
Aron Lee, the warrior hero whose fate would shape all their futures. Evan's
face was tender, reflective. He was drifting away from her, no longer thinking of her. His dirty blond hair, which was shaved short as any soldier's when
they first met, had grown over the months, and now it curled in tendrils at

his neck. He was clean-shaven and she could see more than one scar marking his face. She remembered the S-shaped brand on his arm, and felt a
movement in her loins that was painful in its intensity. She moved from her
bed and sat beside him. She put her arms around his chest and nuzzled her
face into his neck. He smelled of sweat and bread and an exotic male smell
which made her heart race.

She felt him tense, then he carefully disengaged her arms, picked her up
by the shoulders and placed her back on her own bed.

"We should have sex, Evan," she said, trying to sound matter-of-fact, as
if suggesting a walk in the rain.

"No. We shouldn't," he said.

"Why not?"

"You are too young."

Brought up in the Halls as she had been, Emly was very familiar with
human congress in all its forms. And she knew she was not too young. Her
body was shrieking to her that she was not.

"No, I'm not," she stated, and she smiled at him knowingly and thought
she saw a flicker of indecision in his eyes.

"And you are the daughter of Shuskara," he added. "He would cut off my
balls and string them up to make a necklace with my ears and toes." He
grinned at her, and she knew she would not sway him.

Then he suddenly stood. "I must go," he told her. "I'll be back before
nightfall." And he left the room before she could take a breath.

The rain was so heavy, the attic room so dark, that it was hard for Em to
tell when the long day came to an end. She waited, anxious and bored, playing over and over again in her mind her advance to the soldier and his reaction. She tried to think about her new life with the librarian, as housekeeper,
but she could not picture it, for if it came to pass it would mean that her
father and Evan were both dead.

When he came back the room was dark, lit only by the two oily candles.
He was carrying his worn leather sword-belt and a roll of cloth which he
dumped on the floor. It clattered, metal on metal, and she guessed it contained more weapons, knives perhaps. Evan was preparing for war, and she
could not go with him.

She was lying under her winter coat again, for the bakery had closed
hours before and the room was cooling quickly. Evan glanced at her, his face

expressionless. She wondered what he was thinking. Lifting her hands to her hair, she pulled out the ribbon and let it down, then sat up so it flowed over her shoulders. She looked into Evan's face and, holding him with her eyes, she threw off the coat and stepped out of the bed, naked. She walked up to him and stood up close, her nipples brushing his chest. He did not move. She reached up and put her hands round his neck, then stood on tiptoes and kissed him. He was much taller than her and she had to draw his head down. For a moment she thought he was going to reject her again, but then his mouth softened against hers. He kissed her for a long time, and she felt his body heat and his hardness.

He picked her up and laid her gently on his bed.

Chapter 37

R iis thought the booming beat of his heart must be audible to anyone as he crept through the corridors of the midnight Keep.

He had spent his soldiering career facing his enemies from horseback, bearing down on them with a scream, protected by his armour and a moving mountain of flesh and bone. He was unused to stealth in any area of life. And the profound silence all around oppressed him more than the dark and the atmosphere of dread in the emperor's redoubt.

The two guards at the doors to the Keep had presented him no problem. They had stood obediently to attention, staring ahead, as the new commander of the Thousand wandered by. He had placed himself between them, greeting them amiably. With two swift strokes of his long knife he slashed the throat of one and spun on the other, who only had time to get his sword half raised before the knife pinned him through the eye. Easy, Riis thought. Too long at their posts, bored beyond reason. When was the last time they had been attacked here in the heart of the palace? Never.

He had debated if it was worth disposing of the bodies. No guards at the door would raise the alarm as swiftly as dead ones. But in the end he dragged them to a dark spot under nearby stairs—it might give him a few moments.

Now he was hurrying through unknown corridors expecting the clang of the alarm at any moment. He had no idea where the emperor was, or how big the Keep was, or indeed if anyone else lived in there.

If I were an emperor, where would I be? he thought.

Upstairs, of course. No emperor would live in the depths of the palace, near the drains and sewers and rising floodwater. So each time Riis had a choice he went up. Yet he seldom *had* the choice—the Keep seemed to be leading him ever downward, corridors shelving away steeply, leading to blind alleys and more darkly downward steps. After an hour or so he guessed he was lower than where he started.

Sliding through double doors, unguarded, he came to a great empty chamber lit by many torches but still cold and dank. It was a round room, high and deep. A wide staircase travelled round the curved wall, spiralling down to the distant floor. He entered at the top, looked down and saw the only other way out was far below. A chilly miasma seemed to cling to the distant floor. He shook his head. He had no wish to go down there. He left again quietly, retracing his steps.

He had expected to dodge servants and soldiers, as he had when he shadowed Amita during her night walks. But in the Keep there was no one, and the only sound was his traitor heart and the sigh of his breath on the still air. He stopped often, listening for movement. After a while he found himself listening hopefully for a sign of life.

He was in a narrow, dank corridor, smelling of tainted meat and stagnant water. This is a place of the dead, he thought, and he realised he was terrified. Battling the urge to flee, he unsheathed his sword. The rasp of metal cheered him a little, and the firm feel of the leather grip in his palm.

Then he heard a sound, a sliding sound, soft and deliberate. It was coming from farther down the corridor where darkness pooled between torches.

Riis realised he was holding his breath, and he let it out silently, then stepped forward, sword raised.

In the gloom he could make out a still shape. With relief he realised it was a gulon. He took a deep breath and felt his chest ease. Just a gulon. Standing in his way. He had seen them in the streets of the City from time to time. This was a big one, though, far bigger than he had before seen, its snout almost up to his shoulder. Round its neck it wore a wide gold collar like a pampered lapdog.

It gazed at him with its eerily human eyes, and its long lashes seemed to tremble in the damp air. It made no move.

"Shoo!" he said, a bubble of laughter rising to his lips. He raised his sword and stepped forward, though he had no intention of harming the beast. "Out of the way, you dumb animal."

It stood its ground, unmoved by his bluster. Riis decided to push past it, then wondered if it would bite him. Do gulons have teeth, he asked himself? Perhaps it would be simpler to just kill the thing. But he was reluctant, as it stood there regarding him with its darkly human eyes.

It opened its mouth and made a small sound like a baby's cry. Its breath carried the stench of sewers. Riis shuddered. He lowered his blade, intending to barge past it. He stepped to one side and simultaneously it stepped that way too. Riis grinned. So you want to play, he thought.

Then, as if unleashed, the gulon lunged forward with unearthly speed and closed its jaws round his throat.

In the caverns far beneath the Keep those other creatures that lived and died in the Halls, the rats, paused briefly in their perpetual search for food to watch the invading army pass by. It was making slow progress. Though the going was now flatter and firmer, they were still ankle-deep in slippery mud, and the soldiers watched their step, mindful of the moving river of sludge to their right. The stench was appalling and some of those whose stomachs had happily endured the choppy seas and who had laughed at their weaker colleagues now suffered in turn, vomiting regularly beside the path as they marched. They all carried plenty of water, for Indaro had made them aware that dehydration could be a problem by the time they reached their destination.

She was trudging along at the back of the group when there was a sudden hush and the army faltered to a halt. Like the rest of them, she gazed ahead and her heart sank.

The river curved towards the south here, and a mountainous pile of debris had built up on the outer side of the curve at some time when the flow was at its highest. It was impossible to say how long it had been like that—an hour, a year. It was completely impassable.

Indaro looked across to the other side of the river, now unreachable, where the path was clear and flat. We should have gone that way, she thought.

Gil cleared his throat. "We cannot go on and we cannot cross the river," he said tiredly. "Therefore we go back the way we have come."

"Then go where, sir?" a Petrassi soldier asked.

"Elija?" Gil turned to the boy.

"There are other paths, plenty of them," Elija answered. "We thought this the best way but we were wrong. They shift with every rainstorm. We will have to try another way."

"We guessed this would happen," Indaro added, trying to sound positive, as if it were part of the plan. "That is why we gave ourselves so much time."

One by one the invaders turned and started back the way they had come. "Be careful," Gil ordered. "Watch your feet." There was a constant drip and drizzle of water on their heads from the unseen roof above them, and the churned mud underfoot was doubly treacherous going back. Gil knew there was always a temptation to hurry when retracing your steps, a need to chase time, and they could ill-afford to lose warriors before the battle even began.

There *was* still plenty of time. Yet Indaro was discouraged by the setback. She missed Doon, for her friend had been a constant in battle, and without her Indaro's left side felt strangely vulnerable, unarmoured. When they left Old Mountain they had ridden first to the high plain where Fell had left Doon's body. Together they had buried her in the hard ground, facing the sunrise, while Gil and his men watched. Indaro had spoken the familiar words, commending Doon to the Gods of Ice and Fire and privately, in her heart, to Aduara, goddess of the blood of women, whose worship they shared. As she walked through the sewers Indaro daydreamed that one day, when the war was over, she would ride, perhaps with Fell at her side, to the small farm in the southlands where Doon's mother might yet live, and tell her of the heroism of her daughter and the courage with which she gave her life for the City. She felt tears welling and she wiped her face.

She dropped back to speak to Stalker. The extra leagues they were walking would be a torture to him. She fell in beside him, noting he had taken out the stick he carried in his pack and was using it to support his right leg.

"We will be stopping soon," she told him, guessing. "I expect Gil will call a halt when we have returned to where we started."

"What do you want, woman," he replied irritably, glaring at the ground, "to send me back in the boats? Well I'll not go. I'd rather die in this arsehole of the City than be sent to safety like . . . a woman."

She grinned at him and eventually he smiled back, despite his anger, when he realised what he'd said.

"I was going to say," she told him, "that I'll strap your ankle again if you think it'd help."

"No thank you," he replied curtly. "I'll get Garret to do it. You've got all the mothering skills of a wolf monkey." He explained, "They eat their young when the going gets hard."

Indaro smiled. "Only the smallest and sweetest," she said.

They marched on companionably for a while. Indaro found she had become absurdly fond of the northlander, but she knew it might be as Fell said—he would have to be left in the lightless sewers if the worst came to the worst. For some reason she thought then of Broglanh, whose part in all this she didn't entirely understand, and she yearned for his easy confidence, his unquenchable good humour. Would even Broglanh lose his good spirits in the endless blackness of the Halls?

When finally they returned to the rotten bridge, and could see the distant daylight outside again, Gil called a halt and they rested on an outcrop of rock. The soldiers drank from their waterskins and kicked the sticky mud off their boots. Gil called Indaro and Elija to him.

"Which way now?" he asked.

Elija had brought the plans from his pack and was wrestling the large, flimsy sheets out of their waterproof packing.

"Here!" he said, pressing his finger on the paper. "This is another way— it leads to the Fallowly Dike, which goes under the palace."

"But this shows it goes underwater," Gil said, frowning.

"We could take it as far as we can—until we reach the flooding, then strike off to higher ground."

"Indaro?"

Indaro looked at the map. "It is better to go the way we are uncertain about than to follow a path we already know is flooded," she argued. "The Fallowly Dike is high, only just under the surface, high above all the floods. And it's been raining outside, remember, raining for three days now. We need to take the highest way to get there. I don't think this is it."

Gil looked at the boy. "Elija?"

He looked conflicted. "There are many ways to the dike, according to the plans. That way is very narrow," he said. "A narrow way is more likely to be flooded than a wide one. This way"—decisively he tapped again on a line on the map—"I'm sure I remember it."

Indaro was racked with uncertainty. She only had Elija's word that he knew a path through the sewers, and he was looking more unreliable by the moment. She took another long look at the map, trying to fix in her head the way to the Fallowly Dike. Her sense of direction had never yet played her false. She knew the dike was to the north-east of them, and if they kept on roughly in that direction they could not avoid striking it. She nodded reluctantly.

The way very quickly became grim, the tunnels narrow and steep. Gil still led the way, while Elija and his guards stayed in the middle of the army, and Indaro and Stalker brought up the rear. Water ran constantly by them, mostly fresh, Indaro noted, often half filling the tunnels they struggled through. The water was icy and they were soaked and freezing. The lanterns kept going out and were only relit with difficulty. Indaro found herself wishing for the reassurance of a flickering torch.

At the back of the slow-moving army Indaro and Stalker had long waits, sometimes in awkward places, while the rest of the soldiers ahead of them negotiated one obstacle after another. Word was sent down the line each time, but it was frustrating to wait in the drenching water, sometimes, it seemed, for an hour or more, while two hundred men made their way through a tiny crack in a tunnel wall or up a steep vertical drain. In her previous life underground, Indaro had mostly kept to the well-worn paths through the high Halls, walking with torch aloft and one hand on her sword, watching the rats and the Dwellers scurry fearfully out of her way. She had never had to endure this, burrowing like a mole in the semi-darkness, a blind mole in a waterlogged tunnel, with the great weight of the City bearing down on them.

She knew Stalker was finding it much harder than she, for he was not agile, and his broad shoulders barely fit into some of the narrow crevices they had to climb through. Each time they came to a new opening she measured it with her eyes, wondering if he would make it this time, or whether she would have to leave him in the dark.

At last, when Indaro was starting to believe she could tolerate no more, she squeezed through a long narrow tunnel and came out into an open space with a torrent of water running through it. She could feel by the air pressure that they were in a high, wide tunnel, and Indaro guessed it was the Fallowly Dike. All the soldiers were sitting resting on the sides of the dike, waiting for them patiently, and a ragged cheer went up as Stalker struggled out last.

Gil nodded a greeting to Indaro, then raised his voice above the roar of water. "We have made good time now. We will all eat and spend two hours resting, then move on. The way should be easier from here."

Elija wandered over to sit with Indaro, and greeted Stalker with a shy smile.

"Is this where you expected to be?" asked Stalker.

Elija frowned. "The maps don't show these narrow cracks and drains we've been through. But I think we're in the Fallowly Dike, so we're going in the right direction."

Indaro offered, "But I find it strange that such a major waterway, if this is it, is at such a low level. It had been raining for days when we entered the caves."

Elija nodded. "All the tunnels should be full. Yet we have not been once stopped by water."

He pulled out the maps again and spread them in the dim light. "If I'm right, then we are here," Elija said, jabbing his finger at the map. Indaro peered at where he was pointing. "Then we are near the palace. The dike doesn't go under the Keep, but very close to it."

Elija's face was pale grey, translucent as water. Indaro wondered how a boy so frail could have endured all he had. She felt afraid for him, just as she felt afraid for Stalker. A fine commander I make, she told herself, worrying about my men when my eyes should be on the mission—*my* mission, to rescue Fell and get us away safely. Then Elija and Stalker and Garret, and the hero Shuskara, all of them can find their own way home.

Home. When she thought of the word it no longer conjured visions of her father's house on the Salient. That was long ago lost to her. Home meant safety, an enduring safety where she would go to sleep each night without a sword within reach. And it meant Fell. In her heart of hearts she truly believed that she would first bring Fell to safety, then he would bring her safe home, wherever that was.

They set off again feeling a little refreshed, and with lighter hearts, knowing they were close to their goal.

But a while farther on Gil called a halt and raised his hand. He listened, cocking his head. The soldiers faltered to a halt and fell silent, trying to hear what Gil was detecting above the roar of the torrent. Indaro thought she could hear it too, a groaning sound like the timbers of a house in a gale. Cautiously Gil moved forward, Indaro at his side with lantern raised.

Then they all stopped. For a moment Indaro did not know what she was seeing, and when she did her heart leaped into her mouth.

The tunnel in front of them was blocked, almost completely, by a huge plug of debris which allowed only the narrow torrent to escape to one side. Indaro could see a massive piece of timber, an oak tree perhaps, wedged sideways in a narrow spot in the tunnel. Rubble had built up behind it—branches, scraps of wreckage, metal and wood, from houses, and pieces of bodies. Behind it the stream had been trapped and built up and now the whole tunnel reverberated with the groaning of the tortured mass of debris as it fought to hold back the weight of water. As they watched, horrified, the plug seemed to move. Indaro was sure she could see the tree shifting and she visualised it tearing free, hurtling towards her followed by a black wall of watery death.

"Back!" Gil ordered, and with a will the soldiers started running the way they had come. Indaro found it almost impossible to turn her back on the nightmare in front of them, as if by shifting her eyes away she would release the massive weight of water at their backs.

The army hurried, all of them panicked by the threat behind them, but no one cut and ran. Gil and Elija were conferring as they went, Elija's eyes darting to and fro, seeking a side exit from the dike. The groaning behind them seemed to intensify the farther away they went. Indaro tried to tell herself it was an echoing effect in the enclosing tunnel. But she feared they had only moments to find a way out before the flood was released and they were all swept away like bugs in a drainpipe.

*   *   *

Above ground it was nearing midday. Somewhere in the world, perhaps, the sun was shining, but above the City heavy thunderclouds smothered the daylight. It was raining all over the land. In the north, on the rocky coastline of the Little Sea, it rained on the encampments of two of the largest armies still in contention in this endless war—the City's Third Imperial and the Odrysian Wolves. The Day of Summoning would be the first day the two forces had not engaged in more than eighteen months. In the west it rained over the Salient, and the single boat whose crew waited patiently for any lost or injured soldiers returning from the caves. They would wait for another full day, then return with an empty boat to their home in Adrastto. In the south it rained on the Petrassi armies which held the City's southernmost forests and mountains, and the two dams which flooded ever fuller, high above the level of the City, now straining against their weakening walls. And far to the east it rained on the citadel at Old Mountain, empty again now except for the small brown-skinned women who danced joyfully in the downpour, celebrating their goddess who brought forth plenty from the land and washed the blood of men from the world.

By the time the afternoon came, a paler darkness had settled over the City.

In its thick light Emly ran along a wide storm drain. The grey water was above her ankles and she was conscious of the loud splashing of her thin leather boots as she ran. The soldiers chasing her were making ten times the noise she was, but there was still a ridiculous temptation to be quiet, to tiptoe. She slowed to a halt and, chest heaving, stopped and leaned back against the wet stone wall. As her panting slowed she held her breath and listened for her pursuers. Nothing was running down there except for water. She peered back along the endless tunnel. She carried no torch, but ornate metal grilles high in the ceiling let in the grimy daylight in regular splashy pools. She could see only the line of high stone arches fading into the distant dark. No one.

She craned her neck, looking up at the grille above her. The iron was wrought in an intricate pattern of flowers and beasts. Such beautiful decoration to cover a drain, she thought. She wondered if she was under the Red Palace. She was pleased her sense of direction in the tunnels had not fled over the years. Tantalising daylight filtered down towards her, a thick light filled with dust and grime. But there was no escape that way. The drain cover was far above her head.

She set off again, at a pace she thought the armoured soldiers would be unlikely to exceed. There were no forks in the tunnel, no side drains she could dive along to escape her pursuers. And, more worryingly, the drain was sloping inexorably downwards.

She thought back to the previous day. She had departed her new host's house with the early morn. She had left a note for him, but she still felt guilty for abusing his hospitality. She resolved to herself to return when this day was over and apologise. The librarian, with his painfully humped back, had seemed a kind man.

She had left behind her few belongings and dressed in warm trousers, cinched at the waist for they were far too big, and layers of shirts and woollens. It would be warmer underground, she knew, whatever the temperature up top.

In her sheltered life with Bartellus she had learned little about the City and had trouble finding her way to Gervain in the dawn light. When at last she arrived at the entrance to the culvert she remembered from so long ago she breathed a sigh of relief. Looking round to see no one was watching she ducked her head and entered. Down there she was the expert and she felt a rising confidence as she stepped back into her home territory for the last time.

She had been unlucky to meet a guard patrol dawdling along quietly, perhaps on their way back to barracks after a long shift. The six men had spotted her as she saw them and, with eager shouts, they had set off after her. She knew they were chasing her not because she was a conspirator, or a Dweller, but because she was a girl. Her plight would be vile if they caught her and she might not survive it.

The roof was getting lower and the tunnel darker. Em felt a rising panic. In total darkness she would be lost, in every sense of the word. She would flounder around until she drowned in a lightless cistern, or fell unseeing from a treacherous ledge, or was found by the soldiers crying in a corner, begging them to take her.

She saw a thin pool of light quivering on the wetness in her path, and gratefully stopped again. She looked up. In the ceiling she could make out the lower mouth of a high funnel. It was the size of a fat man. From it filtered a distant pearly light. She blinked and peered again, and thought she could see a sturdy bar across one side of the mouth, perhaps the bottom rung of a metal ladder. Emly quickly unclasped from her waist a thin rope, stolen from the librarian, then unsheathed her purloined knife and tied it to the end of the rope. She took a deep breath and calmed her body. Then she threw the knife up at the metal bar. It bounced off and clattered to the floor.

It was then she heard the sound she had dreaded: the distant grate of armoured boots on the stone of the tunnel, the grunt of soldiers still keen for the hunt.

She tossed the knife again. This time it didn't even reach the bar. She scooped it up and tried a third time. The knife fell over the bar and wedged in the gap between the bar and the wall of the chimney. Holding her breath she carefully pulled on it—and it came free, falling and striking her hard above her left eye. Forgetting caution, she dropped her head back and screamed, the eerie sound bouncing off the walls of the tunnel, rippling the black water at her feet, making waves in the dingy air that surrounded her.

Dashing away the blood trickling into her eye, she tried again, and again the knife wedged between the bar and the wall. Em took a calming breath and jerked the rope. This time the ripple dislodged the knife and it fell neatly behind the bar, straight into her waiting hand. She quickly untied it then grabbed the double length of rope. Her years of working with heavy pieces of glass had given strength to her arms and shoulders, and she pulled herself up with ease. She was right, it was an old ladder. In moments she was tucked inside the high funnel, clinging closely to the side, drawing up the rope.

And moments later the soldiers tramped by beneath her. Not one head was raised. Then they had passed and she heard their boots splashing into the distance.

Emly looked up. Now she had a choice. After hours in that tunnel, stuck like a rat in a pipe, she could choose. Climb back down and continue her underground search for the dungeons, hoping there were no other patrols. Or climb, and find her way through the palace. Despite her anxiety for Bartellus, she convinced herself the best way was up.

The high funnel was old and the walls uneven. There were hand and footholds, but they were crumbly and treacherous. It sloped a little, giving her some purchase, but was too wide. Climbing like a spider, arms and legs splayed awkwardly, she inched up the drain, heading for the distant light. Her legs and arms started trembling with the effort, but the funnel was getting narrower, making the climb easier.

At last she reached a junction of three ways. Bracing her legs against one side and her back against the other, she rested her trembling arms. Her eyes were gritty with tiredness, and she kept blinking away blood trickling from the wound on her forehead.

She could carry on going up, or take either of the side tunnels. None seemed lighter than the others. Water was running down all of them. Tentatively she cleaned the dirty fingers of one hand under the flow, then put her fingers to her mouth. Rainwater. She cupped her hand and drank.

In the end she chose the right-hand tunnel, because she had drunk water from it and felt she owed it her trust. It was as good a reason as any.

It became narrower very quickly and the going became more difficult. The flow of rainwater increased until she had to avert her head from the torrent for fear of being drowned. Her arms and legs shrieked with exhaustion as she levered her way up. Keep going, she kept telling herself, keep going. You must be near the top. The light was getting stronger.

Then it went out.

Her limbs froze and for a moment her brain shut down. She whimpered, and tears coursed down her face, drowned in the river of rainwater. Her arms and legs scrabbled frantically at the walls of the funnel and she struggled up a little farther without thinking, fuelled by fear and dread.

Above the constant sound of water in her ears she heard something she recognised: a gritty rumbling noise. Then the light came on again and she looked up. She had reached the top of the drain and above her was a plain metal grating, barely wider than her shoulders. And above it—daylight. The sound was of a cart rumbling away. It must have halted over the grille for a moment, blocking the light.

Inching her way up, arms above her head, feet and knees braced against the sides, Em stretched and touched the cold bars of the grille with the tips of her fingers. She pushed. It did not budge. She pulled herself up closer and pushed again—and the grating failed to move a fraction.

There was a new sound now from the world outside: thunder rolling over the City. Icy rain lashed down and gushed into the drain onto Emly's raised face. She spluttered and coughed and ducked her head to keep it clear, but it was hard to breathe.

She shoved her fingers through the thick bars of the grille and wiggled them frantically. "Help!" she screamed, careless now of capture. "Help me!"

Suddenly the grating was snatched away by an unseen force, and a hard hand reached down and gripped her wrist. She found herself being pulled out of the pipe like a cork from a bottle. She was set on her feet, blinking in the light, coughing up water.

"What were you doing down there, lad?" her rescuer asked jovially. He was a burly man, bearded and shaggy, but not dressed as a soldier. With her hair plastered close to her body, he thought she was a boy in the dull light.

"Hiding, sir. Hiding from my master," she blurted out, head down.

"Down there? Should have drowned, idiot boy. Who's your master?"

Emly thought frantically. "Blacksmith," she muttered, hoping it was a suitable answer.

It seemed to be the right thing to say, for the man grunted and said, "Old Oren. Mean bastard."

Then, quite kindly, he said, "Get along then. Can't escape him like that. No getting out of the palace now, lad. It's all locked down."

Em nodded gratefully and turned and ran off into the nearest patch of darkness. Her spirits soared. She was in the palace!

Chapter 38

Bartellus' stumpy fingers were so cold he was unable to feel the pin he was digging with. He stopped from time to time to bring it to his lips to ensure it was still there. The metal spike tasted of long-dead meat and Bart wondered again how many lives had ended in the cell.

After a long time he had made a big enough hole in the base of the door to get one index finger in. He pulled at the door and he thought he could detect a slight movement in the rotten wood. He started working on making the hole bigger. He dared not use the hand with the broken fingers, even though they no longer pained him. Time was when the bones would have started to heal by now, but that was long ago. He could not risk breaking them again—he must give them a day to mend. So he worked one-handed, awkwardly leaning on one elbow.

As ever his mind retreated to the past, to his glory days—the battles of Coulden Creek, of Petrassa Fields, when he had led armies of tens of thousands, Fell riding at his side, when the City's armies were invincible and Shuskara owned the world. When he had learned from Broglanh, just a few weeks before, that Fell was leading a mission to kill the emperor and that he had a part in it, he had exulted. Time, and the ravages of time on his body, had for eight years forced him to accept the role of Old Bart, the fond father, master only of his own household. To stand at the head of an army again, sword in hand, a whole man, was an ambition he had no longer even dared cherish.

He ignored his misgivings about the assassination plan. He believed in Fell and believed he could kill the emperor. If it could be done, Fell would do it. And the plan took advantage of the emperor's curiosity and pride. When Shuskara had known him, known him as a friend, the Immortal had been easily bored and would quickly fall in with any suggested entertainment. Confined now to the palace, an old sick man, it was said, he would be intrigued by Fell, with the thought that the man might be his son. He would not be able to resist meeting him, even though he would expect a ruse.

But the follow-through, two hundred men, unknown Blues, smuggled in through the Halls to take on the Thousand? The slim element of surprise could not weigh heavily enough to even those odds, thought the old general.

So, with the emperor dead, and probably Fell also, and the Thousand still in control of the palace, it would be up to him to turn two armies, the Second Adamantine and the Fourth Imperial, behind the new emperor. In Fell's plan this would be Marcellus. But Marcellus with the Thousand at his back would be no better than Araeon. Bart's private plan was that Marcellus should die in battle too and the throne be taken by Rafael. There was no love lost between Rafe and the leader of the Thousand, Boaz. So then there would be a three-way division of power—Rafe Vincerus as successor by right, Boaz and the Thousand, and Shuskara and the armies.

His whole body was icy and it was a long time before he realised that the water in the dungeon was stealthily rising. It was swirling around his buttocks and freezing his privates. His legs, cramped by sitting on the cold wet floor for so long, spasmed painfully. He dragged himself up on his feet, using the door as a support. He tried to quell the panic. Then he investigated the rest of the cell. Yes, he was right—the water was deeper, up to his knees, in the lowest part of the room. It had risen silently and he, old fool, had not noticed. He put his hand against the base of the door and found a slight current. The water was coming in under the door. He moaned. To the choices available to him, death by torture or death by starvation, had been added one more.

He reached down and pulled at the door, hoping to shift it, but it was immoveable. He banged on the door, yelling for help, but he had no reason to think anyone could hear him, or care if they did.

Calming himself, he wondered if this was a daily occurrence. Perhaps the dungeon flooded, as the City waters rose, in a rhythm dictated by some natural tide, which would soon ebb again. Had he been there for more than a day? He had no idea. Or perhaps the dungeons were allowed to flood from time to time, to clean them out. Then the flood would ebb soon.

The water had crept to his waist, and he tried to push aside his fear and think again of when he was free. He tried to recall the names of the generals of the two armies he was intended to lead. He had known the Adamantine leader for half his life. He was a short man, bulky, with a chin beard. His name was . . . Bart knew him as well as he knew any man. They had fought together, drank and whored, and played games of chance over thirty years. He had a wife he loathed and three daughters he adored. He once had a three-legged dog called Joker. But Bart could not bring to mind the man's name. The other general, of the Fourth Imperial, was . . . yes, Constant Kerr, a man he hardly knew, distantly related to Flavius, someone the emperor called friend, but of a new generation. Bart was encouraged by this small success of memory.

But his mind drifted and he started, inevitably, wondering about Emly, fearing she had been captured, fearing for her fate. The water climbed his chest unfelt, and he was startled when it crawled under his collar and trickled down his neck. He stood up straighter, as straight as an old soldier could stand. A dozen times already he had considered letting himself drown in the water, relaxing, lying back, letting the water flow into his mouth and chest. A swift death and fairly painless, he guessed.

But an old enduring stubbornness, the determination which, with courage and luck, had propelled him through the ranks to lead an army, kept him from that act of committal. He held his head high and breathed shallowly the thick air, and held on.

Nearly a thousand years before, the name of one man, a commoner, a foreigner and the son of a farmer, was as familiar to every child as that of the emperor himself. Lazarides the Lapith was a name which made children giggle, so they remembered it, even though they did not know what he was, which was an engineer. But everyone knew he was the most important man in the City, apart from the Immortal.

In those days, when the City was younger, and less ambitious, and thus had fewer enemies, the emperor turned his mind to strengthening the core of the City, and he ordered that a new network of drains and tunnels, for sewage and rainwater, be constructed on top of the collapsing wreckage of the old system, itself built more than six hundred years before. He commanded engineers, and architects and common builders, from within the walls and without, to compete for the prize role of City engineer. The previous holder of the title had been hanged, drawn and quartered for some real or imagined slight against the Immortal, yet there was still an eager contest to fill the hapless man's boots.

Lazarides the Lapith was a genius. He appeared at the emperor's court in the Red Palace one day as if from nowhere. He was young, not yet thirty, and no architect or engineer of the City admitted having heard his name before. Yet his knowledge of the City's structure was comprehensive, and his detailed plans for the proposed new system made other men's efforts look like the chaotic drawings of children.

And they were beautiful. Drawn on thick creamy paper with many-coloured inks, they were illustrated with hundreds of tiny, intricate pictures of weirs and junctions, cross sections of pipes and giant cisterns, as well as prancing dogs and hunting cats, and workmen and scholars and whores, sailors and even engineers, rioting around the margins. The emperor was charmed by the drawings, and gave Lazarides the post of City engineer on the strength of them alone. Yet the young man proved to be an architect of skill, and a mathematician, an astronomer and philosopher. And his name is still remembered, by some.

In those days there was plenty of empty land within the City—meadows and open parks and a few farms. Lazarides cleared them all to dig deep, wide pits in which he placed the bones and joints of his new system, the main tunnels like the Fallowly Dyke, and the huge and complex weirs like the Saduccuss Gate, which folk much later called the Eating Gate. Although over a millennium many of the tunnels and cisterns collapsed, worn by age and water and time, the Saduccuss Gate was such an engineering marvel that it survived, almost undamaged, until the present day, and only started to break down because the structure of half-yearly checks and repairs was abandoned in the last century, abandoned in favour of the pursuit of war.

The function of the Saduccuss Gate, and Bartellus would have known this if only he had recognised the name in his reading, was to chew up and filter out any large debris from the uppermost layer of the sewers, to stop it blocking or impeding the older and more vulnerable lower tunnels. When the first barrel of the gate broke and was swept away, now more than ten years before, it started a disaster that was inevitable and catastrophic. The lower tunnels started blocking up, then clearing, then blocking again, over and over as the years passed. More and more of them gave way under the weight of water, and the lower levels flooded every autumn and winter and became too treacherous for the Dwellers to enter, even in summer. And the water levels throughout the City started to rise.

Now the gate's condition was terminal, critical. More than half the barrels had been swept away and the remaining gaps had become blocked. As the persistent winter rains built up the pressure, the wooden piles and old stone started to shift, first a hair's-breadth, then a finger's-width at a time.

When the ancient gate finally gave way, no one remembered its name and no one marked its passing.

*   *   *

Far below the Eating Gate, some way to the west, Indaro and the army were racing away from a lesser threat. They ran along the Fallowly Dyke, fleeing the creaking dam, looking desperately for a way out.

One soldier stopped and raised his lantern. "Here!" he shouted, "This way!"

He had spotted a high narrow fault in the rock. In its shadow they could see what might be worn and ancient steps leading steeply upwards. The soldier plunged into the entrance. They could see his boots, climbing, then he disappeared. The rest of the army crowded round, glancing back, eager for a chance of safety.

Elija grabbed Gil by the arm. "No!" he told him. "This is the wrong way!"

"It goes up," Gil argued, "away from the flood."

"No!" Elija cried desperately. "I've seen this on the map. I know where it goes. It goes up for a while then down to the Whithergo. Look . . ."

He dragged the maps out of his pack again. The damp sheets were dirty now and they stuck together. Seconds passed as he tried to unstick them. The soldiers jostled impatiently.

"It goes up. That's good enough for me," shouted one and he climbed through the narrow opening.

"Stop!" ordered Gil as others pressed forward. "Elija? Are you sure?"

But the boy had snatched up the papers and was already running farther down the dike. Indaro looked at Gil, who nodded, then they both followed the boy, and the army streamed after them. The groaning and creaking behind them seemed louder. Indaro was sure the dam would burst at any moment.

"Here!" Elija cried, throwing himself on his belly to crawl through a low slit in the rock. "This is the way!"

Indaro looked doubtfully at the black opening. It was scarcely big enough for her to slither through. What about the men? What about Stalker? She tried to remember this part of the map. Was Elija right? But her memory let her down, betrayed by fear and the overwhelming demands of urgency. Trying not to think she threw herself down and wriggled into the hole after Elija.

It was hard to crawl forward with the lantern held in front of her, but she moved as quickly as she could, conscious of soldiers following. She kept seeing glimpses of Elija's boots ahead in the jerking lantern light and tried to keep up.

After a few paces the tunnel opened out a little and started going upwards. Indaro could get her feet under her and she moved faster. From time to time she felt something behind her tap her boots and knew she was closely followed. Half crawling, half wriggling was exhausting, and she was ever-fearful the light would go out. She thought she would go insane if she was left wriggling through the earth in the darkness, like a blind mole, under the weight of the City.

Eons passed, and every muscle ached and she thought she could go on no longer. Then she could feel moving air again and, crawling and stumbling, she fell out on her knees on the floor of another wide tunnel. She scrambled out of the way of the following soldier and got to her knees. Elija was standing staring up at a great stone bridge spanning the tunnel, crossing a wide torrent of water. The bridge was old, and designed to cross a river many times the span of the present one. The boy pointed, and she stood and they both held up their lights. In the dim glow they could just make out a wide stone staircase, leading upwards, on the far side of the bridge. For the first time in hours Indaro felt a surge of hope.

The first step of the bridge was too high to climb, so Indaro linked her hands and boosted Elija up. More soldiers were emerging from the narrow crack in the rock and without pause they started climbing the bridge, helping each other up the giant steps.

More than half the army was through, including Gil Rayado, when they all heard the sound they dreaded—a distant rumbling. It came closer then, even muffled by many layers of rock, the explosion when the flood dam gave way was earth-shaking. The warriors still emerging into the tunnel moved with death at their heels. A dozen more scrambled out and started frantically climbing the bridge.

Indaro and Elija had reached the top. Indaro guessed the river they were crossing must be connected higher up with the Fallowly Dike, for the water level below them started rising quickly, the spume on top swirling with unseen currents. She watched the crack in the rock far below. One more soldier squirmed out, then a jet of water exploded from the opening. One man was washed from the pipe like an insect, arms and legs moving, then there were only corpses, drowned in the flood.

Indaro shook her head in wonder. The last man out alive was Stalker. Other soldiers dragged the crippled man up onto the first step of the bridge.

Then they shouted in alarm when a high wave of water appeared in the light of their lanterns tearing down the tunnel towards them, hitting the bridge with a sound of thunder. Soldiers still on the lower steps were swept away. Others, including Stalker, hung on grimly to the stones of the bridge as the waters washed over them. Heart in mouth, Indaro watched the water rising. She wondered if they were safe, even at the top. But after a moment or two the level started to fall again, subsiding slowly, leaving half-drowned soldiers to climb wearily to the top.

Indaro climbed back to where Stalker sat on the edge of the bridge, staring at the churning waters below.

"There's a stone stairway next," she told him, sitting down. "We'll be climbing away from the water."

"Good," he replied, "I'm sick of being a worm in the earth."

Indaro wanted to tell him she was glad he had survived, but she could not find the words.

Gil's second had been counting heads. "We've lost 42," he reported grimly.

Stalker looked up. "Some of them lost their nerve," he offered, "ran back to follow their comrades up those steps."

Indaro shook her head. "It must have been hard, waiting for everyone else to go through," she said.

"Aye," Stalker agreed, "it's always the waiting that gets you."

Gil had consulted with his timekeeper. "We'll rest here for two hours. Eat if you can," he ordered his troops. "I'm sending scouts." He indicated the next staircase. "Volunteers?"

Indaro lay down on the ancient stone, noting the deep grooves worn in the surface along the length of the bridge. Grooves worn by what? Not cart wheels, for no horse could climb the stone steps. By water? Across the line of the river? Scarcely. She shrugged and dismissed the problem. Her spine fitted neatly into a groove, and she lay back and tried to make her sinews relax, to take advantage of the respite from running and crawling.

She stared up at the roof of the tunnel, dark and unseen. She had lain like this, in the breaks between battles, a thousand times before, but always she had watched the sky, wondered about the stars and the moon, soothed by their familiarity, their serene indifference. Here there were no stars, no moon. She tried to pretend they were up there, obscured only by cloud and not by many layers of rock and earth.

Why did the moon always chase away the stars? she had often wondered. When she was a child her tutors told her the moon was a god, or the carriage of a god, perhaps the symbol of a god. The stars, there was general agreement, were the souls of people who had died on earth. When the moon was at its biggest, then the stars fled the sky, through fear or respect. But little Indaro had watched the stars carefully, and she noticed the number never changed. Yet people died all the time—even a child knew that—so why did the number of souls in the sky not increase? This worried her, but nobody seemed to know the answer.

When Archange had rescued her, so many years ago, she had learned everything anew; and she had found that the stars were merely chips of rock thrown into the sky by the great explosions on earth. This made sense. But then why did the chips of rock disappear when the moon was full? A satisfactory answer to one problem merely raised another. It seemed to Indaro that this was the way with everything in life.

She stopped thinking about it and fell asleep.

Fell Aron Lee was walking towards her across a high room filled with light. Pale draperies swished in a slight breeze, and far away she could hear the buzzing of insects on a summer's afternoon. Fell was in dress armour of red leather embellished with gold, something she had never seen him wear before. He looked so young, his skin flushed with health, his stride full of energy. But as he came closer she could see his eyes were dull and old, and full of fear. She held out her arms to him. She wanted to soothe away the pains and the heartache, to make him whole again. She was the only one who could.

Fell was looking at her, but suddenly his gaze shifted to something beyond her, and the blood drained from his face like water from a bowl. He stopped.

She did not turn round, but stepped forward. "Look at me," she said, although she could not hear the words. "Look at me, not at him!"

But Fell's gaze was fixed. She took another step, although she knew it was the wrong thing to do. "Look at me, not at him!"

Tears of blood started to run from Fell's eyes, coursing down his face to drip onto the red leather. A gout of blood spat from his mouth and his whole body shook as if in fever.

Then his chest exploded.

Indaro awoke, as she always did from the same nightmare, with panic in her throat, her fingers clawing at the rock beneath her. Around her was darkness and silence, punctuated by the snores of sleeping soldiers and the roar of distant water. Elija, who was lying beside her, turned his head and gazed at her. "Just a nightmare," he said. She lay back down, and slept without dreams.

At first Bartellus feared he was imagining it when the flood started to recede. But after a while he could feel the current plucking at his clothes as the waters flooded out of the cell, leaving him frozen and wretched, but alive. He spoke words of gratitude to the Gods of Ice and Fire, who had allowed him to suffer great hardship but had always shown mercy. As soon as he felt able, he bent down and inserted three fingers in the hole he had made in the door. He wrenched at it, and was sure this time he felt it move. Squatting down painfully on his haunches, he got a firmer grip and tried again, pulling with all his strength, so that his knee flared in agony and coloured lights flashed and danced in front of his eyes. He groaned with the effort, and the door creaked in harmony—and the rotting wood gave way with a loud crack. The vertical plank tore off at knee-height. The gap was not big enough to scramble through, but now the old man could get a good purchase on the other planks. It took all his strength, and he tore his right hand on the jagged edges of the timber, but at last he made a hole in the door large enough to squeeze through.

Once outside the cell he stood in total darkness, water swishing around his ankles, trying to get his bearings. The corridor sloped upwards to the left, down to the right, water flowing speedily over stone. His reading in the Great Library had told him that the dungeons were built in the reign of the emperor Saduccuss the master builder, when the Red Palace had been erected around the old fort, the Keep. Even then the dungeons had been victim to flooding in bad weather, and he had read with amusement, at the time, an angry letter to the chief engineer from the general in charge of the palace guard complaining that in heavy rain water trickled in through all the new cells and flooded the guards' quarters, which were on a lower level. Although Bart's every instinct told him to go upwards, he trusted

what he had read and started off down, to his right and towards the entrance, he hoped. He sighed, marvelling that he could recall a scrap of obscure information, read years before, when he could no longer remember
an old friend's name.

He shuffled along, one hand on the wall beside him, the other stretched
out. His deprived senses yearned for the sight of a light, although he knew
that if guards came that way, to check on their charges, he would be lost. He
flexed his left hand. The fingers seemed to have healed, but he doubted his
ability to fight.

When he came to a downward step he stumbled and nearly fell, then he
went more cautiously, down low steps, into deeper and deeper water. He
started to fear there would be no way out, that the entrance would be too
deeply flooded, but water was running away all the time, and it seemed to
get no deeper. He reached flat stone again. Then he heard someone speaking,
so close by that he stopped, heart in mouth.

A sharp voice argued, "What do we care? They'll be dead soon anyway.
Drowning is a mercy, I reckon."

A lower voice grumbled, "I'm just saying."

"What were we supposed to do?" asked the first voice. "Risk drowning
to get them out? Not my job, sonny. We were lucky to get out ourselves."

The other voice mumbled something Bart could not hear, and he stood
still, wondering what to do. He heard the sound of metal on metal.

"Where you going? Don't be a fool. If they're dead we'll only have to drag
the corpses out. Leave it to the next shift."

The other apparently relented, for there was silence for a while, then Bart
smelled a wonderful scent, of tobacco. He edged forward until his eyes detected a dim light. He moved towards it, careful not to make splashing
sounds. At a corner he peered round. At a meeting point of three corridors
two guards were smoking pipes, seated at a table with their booted feet up
out of the shallow water. There was a loaf of bread on the table, and a jug.
Bart's stomach clenched at the sight of it.

The guards were not young men, but Bartellus could not hope to take
one of them on, let alone two. He contemplated luring one to him by making
a sound, but he could not be sure they wouldn't both come, and he had no
weapon. The guards had no blades he could see, but they were both armed
with cudgels lying to hand on the table.

As he debated, the guard facing him stood with a sigh and walked over to the wall and opened his trousers. Both now had their backs to him and Bartellus took his chance. Trying to hurry without sloshing water, he crept towards the seated guard. He was halfway there when the pissing man must have heard him, for he turned and yelled.

Bart threw himself at the table, making a grab for a cudgel, as the seated guard turned and stood in one movement. Bart crashed into him, his grasp missing the weapon, and they both fell to the flooded floor. Bart sat up and punched the man on the jaw with all his strength. The blow connected but it was weak and hardly shook him. He knelt up and grabbed his cudgel from the table and aimed it at Bart's head. Bart, helpless, put up one arm and flinched.

"Here! Stop!" the other guard said calmly, doing up his trousers. "We don't want him dead."

The guard on the floor argued as he stood up, rubbing his jaw. "I didn't see you rushing to rescue him from the flood."

"Dead and drowned is one thing," the first one said. "You can't argue with the will of the gods. But dead from a crushed skull is another."

"But he hit me," moaned the second guard.

"Poor old fart," the first one said. "Look at him. Shame we can't do him the favour. He should have drowned."

But Bartellus had stopped listening. There was a movement in the blackness behind the first guard. A slender boy had emerged from the dark and was creeping up on the man armed with a club or bat. The second man saw him. "Daric!" he yelled. The first turned his head, straight into a swinging blow from the length of wood. The strike was not strong but it was well-aimed, and the guard's nose exploded in blood, and he staggered. He lunged forward but the boy dodged back and, putting all his might into the blow, hit him again on the ear. The guard fell to the floor. His colleague moved to attack but Bartellus grabbed him by the arm and the neck, dragging him back. The guard tried to shake him off, cuffing him round the head, but Bart hung on and the boy joined him. Together they wrestled the guard to the floor and held him there, face down in the floodwater, until he stopped struggling. Then the boy jumped up again and returned to the first guard, who lay motionless, and gave him a few whacks on the head to be sure. Then he looked at Bart and smiled.

"Father!"

Bartellus blinked, fearing he had finally gone insane.

"Emly?" he whispered.

Chapter 39

It was not dark, but it was not light either. It was just grey, a crepuscular gloom lit by a sinister gleam from the wet walls of the pit.

The gulon was strong, far stronger than Riis. It had dragged him down countless steps, its long teeth sunk deep in his neck. Finally it had brought him to its lair, a foul place of death and terror. Then it had fed on him, lying across his body lapping his wounds as he lay helpless in the floodwater. He had passed out for a while and as he rose again to consciousness he opened his eyes and moaned.

Riis took a deep breath, rallying his remaining strength, and screamed with all his might. He screamed out the pain and the dread and horror—and the gulon moved away from him at last, sliding off his body and slinking to the other side of the cave.

Riis had lost a lot of blood, but he thought he could stand if only the beast stayed off him. He dragged one arm under him, trying to get up, then realised with horror that his wrist was manacled to the wall. Someone had chained him as he slept.

"Do not struggle. This is the place of your death, soldier," said a voice softly. Riis turned his head, crying out as the neck wounds parted and blood flowed again.

The emperor stood in the doorway of the lair. His white shirt was a beacon of light in the gloom. His fair beard was neatly trimmed. He smiled at Riis, though his black eyes were those of a dead man.

"Keep it off me," the soldier pleaded. He believed his mind would snap if the beast came for him again. He glanced at it fearfully. It had lain down in the water beside the corpse of an old man and was rubbing up against it like a cat.

"Deidoro," the emperor said, and the gulon turned and looked at him. It bared its long yellow fangs.

"It . . ." said Riis, anxious to please the Immortal, to keep the thing away. He swallowed. "It has a name?"

"We brought them with us to this land, many of them," the emperor said, smiling a little as if reminiscing with a friend. "They all died eventually, of course. They are not suited to the climate. But some had mated with dogs and foxes, so they still live in the back streets and sewers, changed, lessened."

Riis spat some foulness from his mouth. "And Deidoro?"

"Deidoro is special. He is one of the originals, or a reflection of one, which is really the same thing. He is the emperor's pet. See how devoted he is." He gestured, and Riis realised with disgust the body lying in floodwater was not a corpse but a living man, old beyond time, in filthy ragged robes. As he watched the man's bony hand moved on the gulon's fur, stroking it. Riis tried to blink the dirt from his eyes. The old man seemed to be tied to the wall of the lair with lengths of wet cloth.

For a moment his pain and dread receded a little as he thought, Who is the emperor here?

"But you are not interested in the gulons and their history," said the fair-haired man briskly. "First you will tell me everything you know about the branded men and their plotting, or I will call Deidoro back. We have plenty of time, Riis, and the gulon is still hungry."

The underground river flowing sluggishly beneath the bridge was starting to rise again, and Gil Rayado ordered the army to press on upwards.

The stone stairs were steep and ancient, worn smooth by the tread of a million feet and made more treacherous by rivulets of water gushing down. Indaro climbed quickly, watching her footing. There were more than two hundred steps and when they reached the top there was only one way to go, along a corridor and through a many-pillared hall. This was where the water was coming from, for the ceiling of the hall was gushing water through a hundred cracks and crevices. In parts it was jetting out as if under great pressure, and the entire ceiling seemed to sag towards them, many of the pillars cracking and breaking under the strain.

The soldiers traversed the hall quickly, glancing nervously at the ceiling. Indaro hurried through and caught up with Gil and Elija on the other side, at yet another stairway.

"There is water above us, water below," she said. "Water always flows downwards. How can it still be above?"

Elija shook his head. "My guess is that the entire substructure of the City is collapsing. When a gate falls, then water rushes out and downwards. But when a tunnel collapses, water is stored up above it until it finds another way out. I think the dam we saw, the one that broke, was not the only one. I think a higher dam collapsed first. Do you remember, before we heard it fall there was a distant roaring of water? I think a higher gate, a weir, gave way and its collapse caused the lower one to break too."

He frowned. "I don't know, but I think the higher levels in this part of the City have been flooded for some time, but now some of the water has been released to make its way down to the lower depths."

"Then perhaps the Hall of Watchers might be passable?" Indaro suggested hopefully. She was eager to see a part of the Halls she recognised.

"Perhaps," Elija repeated doubtfully.

"Are we under the Keep yet?" Gil asked him.

"I think so," Elija replied. "Or very near."

"Then we stick to our plan. There must be a way into the Keep from the Halls, even if it means climbing a sewage pipe. If we fail to find that way, then we might have to try the Hall of Watchers."

Stalker, who had joined them as they spoke, suddenly pulled a knife and flung it. It speared a rat running up the steps at their feet.

"Rats. I hate 'em," he commented, bending to drag out the knife, wiping it on the rodent's oily fur.

"Have you noticed," said Gil, "that there are more rats now? For half a day we have seen hardly any. Now they are everywhere. It is a sign that we are near our goal."

"Rats like to be near people," agreed Indaro, watching a dozen or more skittering up the stairs in front of them.

At Gil's orders the warriors started putting on breastplates and helms.

Archers unwrapped bowstrings from greased packages and strung their bows. Now the way upwards was clear, Elija was moved back to the centre of the army, and armed and armoured men stalked ahead, swords at the ready. At the top of the second staircase they entered a new maze.

At last they reached a door sunk deep in a mossy wall. Stout and riveted, it looked as though it had not opened in a hundred years. The iron handle had rusted away, and when Gil grasped the wooden nub sticking out of the hole where the handle had been, it too came away in his hand. He threw it down, and put his hand in the hole and pulled. The door scraped open. Beyond it was a guard room. It was small and square, with racks for weapons on two sides, iron shackles embedded in one wall, and it was furnished with a crumbling table and chairs. They crossed the room, moving quietly, to another door. This looked newer and recently used.

A feeling of misgiving rose in Indaro's breast. Was this the way into the Keep? After a miserable day of struggling through tunnels and floods, it seemed too easy. She drew her sword.

Gil put his hand on the handle of the inner door. There was silence in the room, as if all the soldiers were holding their breath.

Gil smiled grimly. "If there are enemy warriors on the other side, then it doesn't matter how much noise we make."

He eased the door open and peered, then he passed through and his troops followed. They found themselves in a corridor, high and long, but narrow. There was a stone wall on one side and a wooden one on the other. Single file they crept along. Light, hard and bright, gleamed from myriad cracks in the wooden wall. Indaro suddenly realised it was panelling; they were behind the panelling of a room. Like rats running behind the walls. Gil had come to the same realisation, and he stopped and signalled for total silence.

"Are we in the Keep?" he whispered.

Elija nodded confidently.

"This is what we came here for," Gil said to his troops. "By my estimate it is near to noon on the Day of Summoning. Take a few moments to make peace with your gods, for we will likely not survive this day." He looked around at them. "Remember what we are here for—to kill as many of the Thousand as possible and give Fell time. Your sacrifice will be unknown, tales will not be told of your courage. Hold on. Stay alive as long as you can. Kill them all."

"Let's get on with it, then," Stalker muttered.

Gil grinned at him, then raised the hilt of his sword and crashed it through the wooden panelling. Light splintered into the narrow space, then other men started ripping away the flimsy wall and they stepped blinking into a wide chamber bathed in light.

Indaro looked around. The room was empty of furnishing but was decorated with murals of blue sky and white clouds. Sunlight filtered in from high windows and Indaro's eyes drank it in—it was the first sunlight she had seen for weeks.

Gil paused, unsure which way to go, and he turned to Elija. But before he could say anything a City soldier came running into the room. He skidded to a halt at the sight of the armed invaders and opened his mouth to shout, but he was felled by arrows from several bows. The Petrassi archers cheered, exhilarated by the kill.

Then a second soldier arrived and let out a yell. "They're here! Here!" He was slain too, but they could hear the sound of running feet in the distance and within moments warriors started streaming into the chamber. Indaro saw the black and silver of the Thousand. And they were fresh and eager for blood.

"They're here!" she thought. They were expected. She heard an alarm gong begin its deep boom far away.

Indaro parried a sword-cut and returned it, her sword sliding off the warrior's breastplate. She was unbalanced and ducked away from the slashing blade. With an ear-shattering scream she rammed her sword into the man's groin where two pieces of armour met. The man went down, blood jetting, and Indaro stepped back, looking round for Elija. He was flat against the wall, alarm in his eyes, trying to make his way back the way they had come. Garret and the Petrassi soldier Nando were screening him from attack. As she watched Nando took a blade to the belly, and she leaped forward and slashed her sword at the attacker's neck. Her blade slid off armour, but the man was distracted and Garret rammed his knife into his face above the cheek-guard.

For a while the invaders held their own, but more defenders kept pouring into the room. Finally there were so many they were waiting two and three deep for a chance to get at the army. Gil went down, a slashing sword wound to the thigh. Indaro made her way through the melee to him. She knelt down.

"I've got to find Fell," she said.

"Take Elija," he gasped, blood gushing from his leg, "and Garret and Stalker, and try the Hall of Watchers. We'll keep them busy."

She nodded. She had no words for him, but clapped him on the shoulder then made her way back along the wall, behind the fighting. She told Elija and Garret to retreat and they obeyed, but when she ordered Stalker to follow he shook his head.

"You'll leave these brave men here to die?" he argued, skewering his man and pausing to draw breath.

Instantly fury rose in her breast. "I'm here for Fell, not for Gil Rayado!" she shouted above the noise of battle. She grabbed him by the front of his jerkin. "A handful of us can make no difference here. Our mission is to stay alive, until we have done what we are here for."

Stalker ducked under a blow to his head, and Indaro leaped to stab the attacker. Her sword slid off the breastplate, but she had winded him and as the man bent forward she held her sword two-handed and rammed it down above the breastplate, through his neck to his heart. She abandoned the blunted sword in his body and grabbed his. Then she turned to Stalker, who nodded.

"Aye," he conceded reluctantly, "but I was enjoying myself."

He limped after her as she ran along the wall and back out into the guard room.

"Elija, take us to the Hall of Watchers," she ordered, and the young man nodded, then set off at a run.

Dol Salida was not a religious man. This did not stop him praying to the soldiers' gods when he was in mortal danger, and when he was in the prison camp he took part in the religious rituals of other, more devout, men. But it was his belief that a person's lot in life was fixed, maybe from the moment of conception—and calling upon the gods for riches or for rescue could not change that. He thought they were either indifferent to the pleas of men, or non-existent, and it made no difference either way.

But when he was a new cavalryman, all of sixteen and eager to taste the dizzying pleasures of the world, he had attended the ritual of the goddess of summoning, Rharata, called the Radiant. He was invited there by a girl he had hoped to impress, and her family were devotees of the winter goddess. The Feast of Summoning celebrated the birth of Rharata in human form, on the first day of winter, when the Families were summoned to bring gifts to the divine child. Rather to his surprise Dol Salida found he enjoyed the ceremony of songs and dances, and the warmed spiced wines which accompanied it, and he had attended at each year's-end since, when he was able.

Since he had been at the Red Palace he had made a point of it, for the Day of Summoning was specially significant to the Families, and no one who cared for their good opinion, particularly that of the Vincerii, could afford to ignore it.

So Dol was limping towards Rharata's Tower in the west wing when he heard in the distance the deep boom of the gong which signalled alarm in the palace. Moments later a century of the Thousand raced by him, armour clattering, mailed boots striking sparks from the floor. He backed against a wall to let them pass, and called out, "What's happening?"

"Intruders!" someone shouted.

"Where?"

But they had gone, and Dol followed. He was pleased to find the information he had passed on had been correct. He wanted to see what would happen.

They were heading away from the west wing towards the centre of the palace, and Dol quickly lost them. Then he heard boots marching and he followed the sound down two levels before he saw another century he recognised as the Warhounds heading towards the Keep. It was commanded by Leona Farra Kerr, a boot-faced woman with ginger hair.

"Where are the intruders?" he asked, but she ignored him.

Dol could not keep up with the soldiers, but when they entered the doors of the Keep he was close behind. He had never been behind the green walls, but he did not hesitate to enter. He looked around in wonder. He had heard stories that the walls of the Keep were carved of gold and gems and the floors were made of deep crystal. Dol had never believed them. On the contrary, the Keep's reputation as a place of death and horror conjured in his mind an austere place of hard stone and cold metal. But he was walking through high halls and sumptuous rooms filled with rich furniture, carved woods and gold leaf, jewel-coloured draperies and muscled statuary.

More soldiers ran past him on the soft carpets, and he chased them down two more stairways. He could hear the clash and crash of arms and armour now. He wondered how deeply the Keep was built, and why it was not awash with floodwater.

Injured soldiers were carried past him, away from the battle, and he realised for the first time that it might be wise to be holding a weapon other than his old silver-topped stick. He came at last to a high doorway. Beyond it was a chamber with sky blue walls decorated with white clouds. Blue-skin soldiers were battling an overwhelming weight of the Thousand. As he watched, Dol wondered that so small an enemy force, perhaps fewer than fifty, could still be fighting. They had retreated to a corner, behind a wall of their dead and dying. The warriors of the Thousand were hampered by so many bodies, including their own, and it could, to Dol's veteran's eye, be a long and bloody task to winkle out the last of the enemy force.

Suddenly he was aware of a presence at his back, and he turned to see the Vincerii. He pressed against a wall and the two men passed without a glance. There was a faltering of the battle, then silence punctuated only by the sounds of warriors drawing breath and the moans of the dying. Dol saw some of the Thousand grin and relax, as if the battle was already over. A few sheathed their weapons.

Marcellus spoke with Leona, then looked around assessingly at the embattled Blues.

"Gil Rayado!" he said in his amiable way. "I hardly expected to see you here."

A tall, lean fighter, crippled by a deep sword-slash to one leg, stood and eyed him.

"Did you not, Marcellus?" he said pleasantly. "As I recall, the last time I saw you I said we would next meet in your City."

"If I remember correctly," Marcellus said courteously, "you said 'in the ruins of your City.'" He looked around him. "Of all the thousand halls in the Red Palace this is perhaps not one of the most magnificent. Its statuary was never very fine and has suffered from this day's work, and the murals are by journeymen. Yet I would not call it a ruin," he said with heavy humour.

Rayado replied, "Get on with it, man. I have come here to fight, not to hear you talk."

"You have come here to die," corrected Marcellus.

Rayado shrugged.

"And we are not fooled," Marcellus added, "by this diversion. Your assassin is already dead, or he wishes he were. Your men achieve nothing by dying here, and we do not wish to lose any more of our warriors. Put down your blade, Gil, and I promise you my soldiers will not touch any of your men."

"I don't believe you."

Marcellus smiled. "I am speaking the perfect truth. And I assure you that you yourself will die in this palace anyway."

Dol felt sympathy with the Blueskin leader. Given the choice of surrendering himself to probable torture and certain death, with the slim hope of saving his men's lives, or dying with them, Dol was not certain what he would do. If he elected to die with his troops it might appear that his fear of torture, which all men share, was stronger than his concern for their lives.

"Would you like to discuss it among yourselves?" Marcellus asked solicitously. "A vote perhaps? I believe that in your land many decisions are made by the will of the people." Dol could see the man was in high good spirits.

Rayado spoke to a warrior at his side, then he came forward, climbing awkwardly over the bodies of his own men and those of the Thousand.

"Who betrayed us?" he asked.

"It is called intelligence," Marcellus replied. "Something you clearly know nothing about."

"Then I have nothing more to say to you," Rayado said.

Marcellus clapped him on the back. "Now, we both know that's not true," he said cheerily. "By this day's end you will be babbling everything you know to anyone who will listen to you."

"I ask one thing of you, Marcellus."

"Name it."

"That I be allowed to meet the emperor."

"We can arrange that," Marcellus answered. "The Immortal will want to see you. He has had a busy day today, yet he is still eager for company." Then he ordered Leona and a small detachment to take the prisoner away.

Dol Salida wondered if Marcellus would be true to his word, but he never found out, for at that moment Rafe Vincerus noticed him hovering in the doorway. He nodded his head in acknowledgement of Dol's part in the day's business, then gestured to the doorway. Dol obediently turned from

the hall and limped away, back towards the west wing and the revels of
Rharata. He was quickly overtaken by warriors marching away from the
hall, so he guessed that, with their leader gone, the remaining Blues had
been quickly and efficiently despatched.

The water was rising faster than Indaro thought possible. She, with her
three companions, hurried along gloomy tunnels, ever east. Indaro was
starting to recognise places as they loomed out of the gloom—the corner of
a wall here, the top of a staircase there. But she was always past them and
moving on as her memory slowly caught up. She marvelled that Elija knew
so certainly where he was going.

Soon they were splashing through ankle-deep water again, and she
asked the boy, "Is the Hall of Watchers on this level?"

He shook his head. "One down." He glanced at her face, which must
have shown her concern, for he said, "But the water is rising unevenly, as it
did in the lower levels—we might still get there."

They came to a dry corridor lined with forgotten statues, glowering loft-
ily at them from high plinths. At the end was a staircase leading down. Elija
descended quickly, Indaro close behind, and they came to the bottom where
the water was waist-deep and visibly rising. Without hesitation Elija threw
himself in, and started half wading, half swimming along a dark tunnel.
Raising her light, Indaro could not see the end and she paused before following him, her heart in her mouth. After all they had been through she wanted
to die with her sword in her hand, not drowned like a rat in a pipe. The warriors looked at each other, but there was no choice—they had trusted Elija
this far.

The roof became lower and the floor dropped away and Indaro found
herself swimming. She was finding it hard to keep her light above the water,
and behind her lights went out as the others lost their grip. Elija had no light
and Indaro struggled to keep up with him so he could see where he was
going. He does not need to see, she thought, he is in thrall to this place.

At last the boy was forced to stop. They had come to a low arch which
dipped to meet the water and they could go no farther. Indaro felt panic rising in her chest. Her hands were shaking, from cold or fear. She held her

little lantern high, the only light left now. Stalker was still with them, she was amazed to see, his face gaunt and shadow-haunted.

Elija told the others, "We must swim under this arch. There is probably a tunnel beyond."

"Probably," Stalker echoed.

"The archway leads somewhere," Elija told them. "Keep feeling the roof and eventually we will come out into a higher place, a hall or a staircase. We will be without light, but I know the way now, even in the dark."

He spoke with such confidence that Indaro felt her nerves steadying. Then she remembered what he had told her back in the relative comfort of Old Mountain. "I do not know the Hall of Watchers. I have never been there." She shook her head, trying to dislodge the ominous memory.

The boy nodded to her, his eyes feverish, then he ducked under the black water and disappeared, leaving a few thick-skinned bubbles popping slowly on the surface. Indaro passed her light to Garret and, trying not to think, ducked her head and swam under the archway. It was icy cold. She felt rough ceiling above her and, with blind faith, she kicked out and followed Elija, hoping the tunnel was straight and there were no side ways to get lost in. She kicked and kicked, one hand out in front of her, one above. Once she felt something move under her searching hand and hoped it was Elija's fleeing foot. She remembered the last time she had blindly followed his boots, through a crack in the earth—that too was terrifying but at least there had been light and air. She could feel agony in the chest as she kept kicking forward, her head was bursting with pain, her limbs weakening, deprived of air for too long, the need to open her throat and let in the water too strong, the uncaring, peaceful, cold water . . .

She felt a hand grasp hers. She held on and kicked feebly one last time. Her head emerged into air and she breathed long and painfully, gasping and spluttering. Elija pulled on her arm. "Make way for the others!" he ordered.

She scrambled clumsily onto a low stone ledge. Then she turned and reached out. She found a flapping hand and Garret came flopping up beside her, gasping. One more to come. "Stalker?" she asked the darkness. There was no reply. They waited. After a silent count of a hundred, Indaro turned to Elija and ordered, "Lead on!"

As they shuffled through the utter blackness, hand in hand, the blind following a boy, Indaro felt a sob rise in her chest. Despite his injury, Stalker had followed her everywhere she had asked. She knew northlanders did not press their womenfolk to fight, and she suspected he despised women warriors, yet he had followed uncomplaining, fighting like a demon when asked to, burrowing in the earth like a worm, swimming to his death in a flooded drain under the City.

She felt Garret squeeze her hand. "Old Stalker, he was a one," he said. "I thought he'd be standing there at the end, when the rest of us were dead. Like Fell."

She had scarcely thought of Fell for hours, and it was typical that it would be Garret who brought him up. Her mission in this gods-forsaken place was to save Fell—but Garret was still expecting Fell to save them, as he always had. She coughed, then she could not stop coughing, feeling the sharp pain deep in her side. Am I injured? she thought. Impossible to tell through all her aches and pains. She remembered ducking a sword-slash during the ambush, and wondered if she had been cut. She put it out of her mind. It scarcely mattered as long as she kept moving.

In front of her Elija paused. Then he stepped forward more cautiously, letting go of her hand. She could tell from the air around her that they had come out into an open space, and guessed he feared falling down stairs or into an open drain. They could hear water gushing on all sides, and Indaro felt an urgent need to hurry. She would rather cut her own throat than swim blindly along another tunnel.

"Where are we?" she asked Elija, trying to sound calm.

But he made no reply and she could hear him shuffling forwards slowly, exploring. She let go of Garret's hand and worked her way to her left, placing her feet with care lest the ground disappear from under her. Her hand reached the reassurance of a rough wall, and she let her fingers graze along it. She felt a pillar standing proud of the wall and on it, at head height, a carved shape. Eagerly she ran her hands over it. She could feel the smooth head, protruding eyes and sharp beak of an eagle. Her heart beat faster. She measured a long pace along the wall and found another pillar, another stone bird. In her mind's eye she saw these creatures, and a dozen more like them, guarding a round chamber, brightly lit by torchlight. The watching birds.

Triumphantly she cried, "We're here! Elija, you found it. This is the Hall of Watchers!"

Chapter 40

The questioner in the pit now was a boy, a lad of perhaps fourteen, who perched on the stone steps at the edge of the lair, his booted feet above the foul water. He asked Riis about the enemy's plans and about Fell Aron Lee. Riis gabbled everything he could think of about the hostages, the trial, and the branding, as if his torrent of words could hold at bay the gulon which still crouched by the old man, watching him. He held back everything he knew about the invasion, and he buried deepest of all the name Shuskara.

Which way?" Elija asked, relief in his voice.

Indaro thought. There were two entrances to the Hall of Watchers and they must have stumbled on the one which led to the High Halls, through which she had once helped carry the old man Bartellus and Elija's sister. They must have walked straight through the gateway without being aware of it.

She reached out and found his sleeve in the dark. "This way," she said.

The other door was on the far side of the Hall, through a narrow gateway. She groped along, feeling each bird with surety of recognition. An owl, a seagull in flight, a songbird with its beak open. Along a corridor, then she came to the bottom of the winding stairs which she had once confidently run up and down a dozen times a day. Long ago.

Her eyes desperate for the smallest gleam of light she hurried up the steps, losing the others in her haste. Through another doorway, then up a wider, straight flight. Then she stopped, her elation under check. She waited for the others to catch up and heard their boots stepping much more cautiously on the wet stone steps.

"Elija?" she asked the dark.

"Here."

"In a moment we will be in the Library of Silence." If, she thought, they haven't sealed off the door against the rising water. "So you must stay to the rear. It might be that they are waiting for us."

She tried the handle. It moved grudgingly under pressure, but the door was warped and reluctant to move. She called Garret and together they forced it enough to slip through. Beyond was more darkness, more silence. She listened, every nerve jangling. All she could hear was a deep, damp quiet and the ever-present rush of distant water.

"Wait," she whispered.

She walked forward, hands out, and found she was between high shelves full of books. Yes, she remembered, the little door came out deep in the stacks, hidden in the farthest recesses of the library. She walked forward more confidently, then to her right where her groping hand came to a pillar, and at head-height a bracket with a torch. The torch felt damp, but she hoped it would light. She went back with it, feeling the squelch of waterlogged books under her boots.

"A light," she said. There was a long pause, and some rummaging, then she heard the scrape of a phosphorus stick Garret had somehow managed to keep dry. It sparked and flared, and she held the torch to it. For a worrying while it would not catch but then the torch blazed. The old familiar light dazzled them painfully but their spirits rose.

"Wait," Indaro said again, and this time she walked confidently through the library. Thoughts flashed into her mind of the last time she had been here, saying a bitter goodbye to Archange, and a time before, when she watched as a ragged little girl ate her first meal in weeks. She opened the main door and peered through, then thrust her torch out and glanced up and down the corridor. No one. She called softly to the others.

The marble and stone corridors of the Red Palace were lit only by high windows which grudgingly leaked in the sunlight, leaving the floors in gloom. Feeling like insects scuttling along the base of a wall, they made their way towards the Keep. Servants and guards passed them from time to time, but in the vastness of the palace it was easy to hide in side rooms and dark arches. Indaro kept listening at doors and opening them softly. Finally she beckoned the others in through a doorway. The chamber they found themselves in was rich and elegant, furnished with thick carpets and soft upholstery. The air was chilly and damp and it seemed abandoned.

"These are apartments for foreign visitors, I think," said Elija, looking round in wonder.

"We could hide out for a year without anyone finding us," commented Garret. "Why are we here?" he asked Indaro.

She rolled her shoulders and twisted her neck, trying to ease the tension. "If I am to die today," she explained, "I don't want to do it looking like a rat dipped in shit."

She tried the doors of the apartment and found the washroom. There was a deep sunken bath of some white stone and crystal basins, and she found embroidered drying cloths. In the corner was an ornate hand pump. Indaro smiled and closed the door against the men. She stripped off her clothes and investigated the wound in her side. It was still trickling blood, but not enough to matter. The edges of the wound were raw and inflamed and she washed it as best she could, then washed the rest of her body. She rinsed out all her filthy clothes, then wrung them out and put them back on with difficulty, flinching as the clammy fabric clung to her skin. Lastly she washed her hair and towelled it dry, then tied it back on her neck.

On a marble tabletop she found a round hand mirror of ivory and gold. She picked it up and stared at her reflection. She saw hot, feverish eyes, cheekbones like knives, and the pallor of the grave. She put the mirror down and washed her face again, rubbing at her skin, then looked in the mirror again. She had summoned an unhealthy flush to her cheeks. It was no improvement. I look like a three-day-dead corpse decorated for the funeral, she thought.

She ran her fingers over the back of the mirror, tracing the painted flowers and birds. She thought it was the prettiest thing she had ever seen. She went to shove it into her backpack, then thought a moment and sat down on the floor and turned the pack out. There was no food or water left. Her medical supplies, such as they were, had been ruined by water and muck. Likewise the grubby pieces of paper holding the addresses of dead soldiers' families, information she had carried with her over the years, hoping one day to bring long-delayed consolation to mothers and brothers. They were all illegible now. From the bottom of the pack she took a sharp knife in a leather sheath. She left the sodden pack leaking onto the fine carpet and returned to the main chamber.

Elija and Garret were stretched out on couches, staining them with the moisture draining from their filthy clothes. Elija seemed fast asleep. She wondered whether to leave him there, quietly walk away and leave him asleep. He could stay for a long time without being found, then perhaps slip unseen out of the palace once it returned to normality, if it ever did.

"They knew we were coming," said Garret. He offered her dried beef and she took some and chewed on it. She was well used to the taste, which was revolting, but she could feel new energy rallying. She ate some more and drank water from her waterskin. There seemed no point answering Garret. He was right.

"I wonder what old Brog's up to," Garret mused, out of the blue.

Indaro looked at him. "He's with Fell." She wondered sometimes if Garret paid any attention to what was going on around him. Perhaps he was the perfect warrior: she just had to tell him to fight and he fought, without hesitation, without question.

"That's what I mean," he replied.

Then she realised he was being subtle, in his own way, as if mentioning Fell's desperate mission might make her burst into tears. This cheered her and she grinned at him, then shook Elija awake.

"Our other mission is to help Fell and Broglanh," she said, "to kill the emperor and escape alive. If the Immortal knows why Fell is here, which he must by now . . ."

"Not necessarily," put in Elija. "Whoever warned the Thousand we were coming might not have known about Fell, or if he did he might have kept it to himself for his own reasons. Diverting part of the Thousand to chase us down works in our favour. It is what we are here for."

She shook her head, uncertain. "The emperor is not a fool. He must see that the arrival of this alleged son, on the same day as an attack on the palace, is not a coincidence."

"We don't know what the emperor is," mused Elija, and Indaro realised how right he was.

She nodded, trying to clarify her thoughts. She saw no point in mentioning that some of the warriors they had left behind, Petrassi and Odrysian, would have been captured and tortured, and might have given them away to the enemy. "Nothing has changed," she said, "we stick to the original plan. We will head for the Keep, to find Fell and Broglanh and perhaps the emperor. Weight of numbers can't help us there. Stealth and silence will be our friends."

Indaro looked at Elija. "It's your choice what you do. You are not a warrior."

"I was not a warrior when I decided to come on this mission. I cannot go back now." He glanced at the door through which they had come. "I would rather die than return to the sewers. Besides, the water is rising. That way will be barred to us. I'll stay with you. Who knows, maybe I will be of use before the end."

Indaro glanced at Garret, who nodded. Elija did not realise that by going with them he might be condemning them. They would protect him now, perhaps to the death, for he was one of their own. His face was pale, his eyes desperate. Indaro knew he had only undertaken this mission in the hope of finding Emly, and they seemed no closer to that.

She promised him, "We will find Emly, if she lives." They both knew she could make no such promise, but he smiled wanly and nodded.

"Let's go," she said. "You won't need that." She indicated Elija's backpack. He looked reluctant to leave it, but she said, "The maps are useless now. Do you have any food?" He shook his head.

"Come then."

It was noon on the Day of Summoning and they had little time left to find Fell.

The rituals of Summoning began with songs and dance, the children of the palace garbed in furs and hides to represent the wild creatures of the land—or those who lived there in times past, before the coming of the gods, Dol Salida could not remember which. His attention was distracted by thoughts of the battle. It was a long time since he had seen a true battle, not just a scrap outside a tavern or a scuffle between street traders and militia. It stirred memories, not pleasant ones. He had no wish to be a young man again, to pierce flesh and tear sinew, to bathe in the blood of his enemies. I am getting soft, he thought, for his sympathies had been with the invaders, fighting courageously to a certain death against overwhelming numbers.

Yet he was the author of it. Early that morning he had received a note from his patron, in their private code, telling him there was to be an attack on the palace. At first he had been baffled, asking himself why she would relay the information through him rather than alert the authorities. He had delayed a while before deciding whom to tell. The obvious choice would be Dashoul, charged with all palace security which did not involve the Thousand—the routines of guarding gates, patrolling walls and manning dungeons were all performed by the City's common soldiery. Recently their rotations had been stepped up. In past years the same regiment had performed these duties for months, sometimes years on end, rendering them stale and ineffectual. Now, particularly since the attack on the Little Opera House, the soldiers were freshly rotated in every few weeks, sometimes direct from the field of battle. Only the dungeons guards stayed the same, for the duty required knowing the complexities of the tunnels and that was something which could not be quickly learned.

Dol respected Dashoul, a lean and laconic northlander, bald and beaked like a vulture, and knew the man would give him credit for the vital information. But that was not the same as presenting that information personally. So he sought to speak to the Vincerii and was granted a hasty audience with Rafe early in the morning before the lord left his private quarters. Rafe and his wife Fiorentina dwelled in the north wing in high apartments facing the sea.

Dol Salida had stepped into a receiving room, which was light and warm and smelled sweetly of winter roses. Rafael was speaking to his wife, and Fiorentina sketched a small, familiar wave to Dol before leaving through a side door.

"I forget," said Rafe, pushing back his black hair, which was damp from the bath, "you know my wife."

It was said neutrally, but Dol felt compelled to explain, "We were childhood friends. I was much older, of course. I knew the lady Petalina better." He knew he was babbling.

"What information do you have, Dol Salida?" Rafe pulled on a black jacket and brushed the shoulders, giving the clear impression he was about to go somewhere and had little time. Good enough, thought Dol, I need only a moment.

"The enemy has discovered a way into the Keep through the sewers. It will be invaded today."

Rafe paused in his brushing. "How do you know this?"

"I have reliable sources. Sources I trust."

Rafe stared at him, and Dol found the pressure of the stare like a real force in his mind. He was overwhelmed with the urge to tell the lord everything of his clandestine work, the name of his patron, his suspicions about Old Bart.

Instead he spat out, "Sully. His name is Sully." The lie seemed to ease the pressure in his head. "An old soldier, who has many sources. I do not ask their names. If names are bandied about, information dries up."

"You trust this man?"

"I trust him not to give me information which is unreliable."

"You believe there will be an attack on the palace?"

"I *know* there will be."

"Through the sewers?"

Dol nodded.

"Then it will be your lucky day, for both you and this Sully will become rich men."

Dol smiled thinly. He had no interest in wealth. He had as much as he needed, to keep his unassuming house and to help his family through any troubles they might meet. His sole interest was the good of the City. Dol Salida felt annoyed that the man thought him motivated by greed or, at least, interested in reward for performing his duty.

Perhaps that was why he forgot to pass on one small but important piece of intelligence. In the last days he had come to believe that the armies' hero Shuskara, mysteriously escaped from the dungeons eight years before, was even now back to those dungeons again. And that the general was somehow involved in the planned invasion, was perhaps the instigator of it.

For his part, Rafael Vincerus was not in the business of volunteering information, for in his very long life he had learned that information is more precious than gold and diamonds. So he did not tell Dol Salida, why should he, that the emperor had agreed to an audience with a man who claimed to be Fell Aron Lee who, among other things, was once the right-hand man to that same general.

No man could become a master of the game of urquat without a strong streak of competitiveness. Dol Salida had arranged for Bart's arrest on the grounds that he was father to a truant soldier, but now he believed that his old urquat partner was another man entirely. Dol bore no hard feelings against Shuskara the soldier; whatever he had done to anger the emperor had been grave, but the general had been a loyal warrior of the City over several decades, the greatest soldier of his generation, and that could not be argued. No, Dol's grudge against the man, if grudge it could be called, was more personal—he resented the fact that Old Bart had deceived him for several years in his innocent guise as the glassmaker's fond father and a veteran of the common soldiery. Dol Salida considered himself a humble servant of the City, but in fact he was a proud man, and did not like to be taken for a fool.

So it was a mixture of curiosity and hurt pride which led Dol to keep the name of Shuskara unspoken, and instead to take it upon himself to commandeer a passing soldier and venture down into the palace dungeons to unmask the general himself.

E mly struggled forward, one arm around Bart, trying to keep her father upright, and one holding the torch. They were making sluggish progress and she was terrified that any moment soldiers would arrive to arrest them or to kill them.

Bartellus had his eyes closed and all his concentration seemed to be on putting one foot in front of the other. Em's eyes darted round, looking nervously for boltholes in case someone came. They were making their way along a featureless stone corridor, moving upwards. Em had found her way into the dungeons with ease, her astonishing memory for direction taking her there as surely as if she were following a map. But the water was rising and they could not go back that way. So now she was in unknown territory. She was sure they were going the right way for she could occasionally smell wafts of fresh air above the rank odour of the dungeons.

She was consumed with guilt, feeling everything that had happened to her father was her fault. She kept tracing the events backwards which led them here—the attack on the barn, the escape from the fire and the arrival of Evan, the torching of the House of Glass and poor Frayling's death, Archange, the merchant's son and the lost veil. Before that she was living a life of quiet bliss, of blissful ignorance, safe in the knowledge that Bartellus would protect her from whatever life would bring them. She never thought it would be she who was the protector, and now she felt quite inadequate and painfully vulnerable.

She had only a vague understanding of the events sweeping them along.

But she knew Bartellus should not be struggling, half dead, through tunnels under the City, but leading a rebellion against the emperor, with Evan and the hero Fell Aron Lee at his side.

For the first time ever she wished they were back in the Halls again, where she was the expert on survival and where she could protect him. Once they were out of these tunnels she would feel lost in the glare of daylight. She did not know where they were going to emerge, in the palace or out in the City. Either way, they had to find somewhere to hide.

Bartellus seemed to have gained some strength, and he stood straighter, leaned on her less. He struggled in her grip.

"I'm all right," he muttered. "Let me go, girl. Where are we?" he asked.

"I don't know," she confessed, "but I can smell fresh air. We must keep going this way."

"What day is it?"

Em thought, uncertain. The time she was running from the patrol seemed weeks ago. She must have been in the tunnels for less than a day, but it felt like a lifetime. "The Day of Summoning," she told him at last.

"Is it noon yet?"

"I don't know."

"We must get to the barracks of the Fourth Imperial," he said, looking around him as if the building might be within sight. "They will be inside the palace, on duty from noon. We must get there before they are deployed."

Em stared at him in amazement. All she could think to say was, "We'll never find it."

"Then we must try," he growled.

"We must *escape*," she told him urgently. "We must get away from here, hide!" She wanted to say, "You cannot lead an army. You can barely stand. They will laugh at you and kill you for your insolence." But she just repeated, "We must find the way out, then stay hidden until it is dark. Then perhaps we can go . . ."

"Go where, little soldier?" he asked her. His voice was hard, and in his face once again she saw a trace of a man leading warriors into battle.

"Whatever happens today," he told her, "I will not live to see the end of it. I know this in my bones. If Fell kills Araeon, then chaos will be unleashed on the City. It will need a strong man to lead, to bring the armies together to march in step. It might be Marcellus. It might Boaz, or one of the other generals—I do not know who they are these days. It might even be Fell, if he lives. But while it happens I will not shrink away. You stay here; it might be safest for you. You are skilled at hiding in the dark." It sounded like an insult. "But I will go to the Keep, and put myself in the hands of the gods."

"Well said, my friend," said a voice.

Emly stepped back in alarm as a young soldier, tall and muscular, and armed with a sharp sword, advanced on them out of a dark tunnel. The man who had spoken, who limped behind him leaning on a stick, was old and leathery, with a wide white moustache and deep-set eyes.

Bartellus sighed. "I did not expect to see you here, Dol Salida. Do you wish to kill me too?"

"I haven't yet decided," answered the man. "Although you seem to have earned many enemies for a glassmaker's harmless father. This is your daughter Emly? Why is she here?"

"She is a valiant child and tried to rescue me from torment in the dungeons."

"Valiant indeed," said Dol Salida approvingly.

"What are your intentions, Dol?"

"What are yours, Shuskara?"

"How long have you known who I am?"

"You fooled me well, old friend. I confess I am embarrassed, for information is my business, and I had no idea I was playing urquat each week with a traitor to the City."

"Treachery is in the eye of the beholder."

Dol Salida shook his head. "No, old friend, it is not. A man who conspires against the emperor is a traitor. It is really quite simple."

"The City is dying," the general said, "because evil holds sway. My first duty is to the City, not to the Immortal."

Dol Salida limped forward and asked, quite gently, "Are you sure you are not blinded by the need for vengeance? I understand that. You have been hard-used by the Immortal. But he is still emperor and will be obeyed. You are a traitor and all traitors must die."

He signalled to the young warrior, who lifted his sword.

"Please don't harm my daughter," Bart asked, despair in his voice.

Dol nodded. "I will see she is safe, general. This is not her battle."

"No," Emly breathed, readying herself to leap in front of the sword. In that moment Bart's life was more important than her own, for she could not imagine hers without him.

But she was stunned to see the young warrior reverse his weapon and present it to the old general, as he dropped to one knee on the muddy floor.

"Lord Shuskara," he said. "You have my blade and my life. Command me."

Chapter 41

"We need to go down another level," Elija said. According to the maps in his head there was only one entrance to the Keep. He had no doubt there were others, but they could not afford time trying to find them. He knew the entrance was in the west of the palace, marked on most maps as the Porphyry Gate. It had lodged in his mind because of the strange word, and he wondered what it meant.

He led Indaro and Garret along a wide corridor. They ran, for it was clearly a major route through the palace and they were likely to meet opposition at any moment. Elija spotted a staircase going down to his left, and he ran down it, the warriors at his heels. As they reached the bottom they heard marching feet and a platoon of soldiers came into sight. With a yell the leader drew his sword.

There was nowhere to go except back up. Indaro pushed Elija up in front of her then turned to face the soldiers, Garret beside her. There were twenty or more soldiers, but they could only get to the stairs two at a time. The first pair were on them, but Indaro and Garret had the advantage of height and desperation. They killed the first two without difficulty. Even Elija quickly realised these were not battle-hardened warriors, but youngsters of sixteen or seventeen, younger than him, recently pressed into the army. They wore clean red uniforms and their boots and weapons were shiny.

Stepping back up a step, Garret said, "New Wildcats."

Glancing nervously up the staircase, Elija thought, We can't be trapped here. He saw the leader speak to one of his soldiers, who ran off. Within moments it seemed they heard the deep sound of a gong echoing through the palace. Elija ran up the steps, back to the main corridor. He looked right and left. No one. But he knew that any time another platoon of soldiers would be on them.

On the stairs below Indaro slashed one youngster through the throat just as Garret disabled another with a blade to the groin.

"Now!" she yelled, and they turned and raced up the stairs. The soldiers had to clamber up over the bodies of their dead to follow, giving them valuable moments.

"This way!" Elija fled before them down the corridor, then through a connecting passageway and down another corridor. This ended in a doorway and they had no choice but to go through. They found themselves in a magnificent hall decorated with white stone statues, and full of books. There were three doors in the wall opposite. Elija hesitated. Which one? Maps teemed through his head, with mazes of tunnels and gates and stairs and halls and . . .

"Which way?" Indaro asked urgently. They could hear the sound of the gong and shouts and running feet.

But it was too late. One of the doors opposite flew open, and soldiers came crashing through. Elija glanced out of the door they had come through and saw more at their heels. He slammed the door shut. Then he backed into a corner. Indaro and Garret turned over a heavy wooden table, then retreated behind it.

The warriors, more of the Thousand, Elija saw with dismay, were waiting for orders. Their leader, a burly, red-faced man, commanded, "We want them alive. Marcellus' orders."

The soldiers came at them with respect, four at a time. One vaulted the table and was speared in mid-leap by Garret's sword. As Garret was at full stretch he was attacked from the side by a second soldier, who aimed for his exposed armpit. Garret swayed sideways and the weapon whispered by his body, then slammed into the horizontal table leg. Indaro parried a thrust to her neck then ducked a ferocious sweep to the head. She skewered the first attacker in the eye but was unbalanced and the second assailant, a big red-headed warrior, ran her through the hip. She fell to one knee, blood splashing down her leg.

These are no youngsters, Elija thought, they are warriors as skilful as Indaro and Garret, but fresher and more eager. We will not survive this time, he thought, backing behind his two friends. They will capture us and torture us. He found himself wishing he had stayed in the room they had rested in, as Indaro had suggested. He did not fear death, but he did fear torture.

Elija saw there was no chance the two could defend themselves for more than moments. He rushed forward. He had no skill with weapons, but he picked up a sword, fallen from a dead man's hand.

Indaro was on her feet again. It was as though the wound had given her extra strength and energy. She fought as if possessed, and when one man went down she screamed a battle cry which froze Elija's blood.

The only thing keeping them alive was the upended table. The commander of the warriors bellowed an impatient order to drag it away. As one soldier grabbed a wooden leg Elija slashed at the man's wrist with all his might, half severing the hand. A second stepped up to take his place, and Elija, encouraged, darted forward again. But his blade slid harmlessly off the man's armour. The warrior grabbed the boy by the throat and threw him angrily into the corner.

Elija hit the wall hard and felt an agonising pain. He stared down at his left arm in shock. The forearm was bent at an unnatural angle. For a moment he did not recognise it as his own limb. He groaned as the pain swelled and racked his body. He cradled the injured arm in his right hand and the agony increased. His vision blurred. He sank to the floor, too shocked to move.

Then there was a shouted order and the fighting died away. Elija looked up fearfully. Why are they stopping? Is it over? The warriors stepped aside for a man to enter the room. Elija saw he was dressed like a lord and was unarmed. He wondered if this was the emperor.

"The last of the traitors," the man said with satisfaction, smiling at them as if he was well pleased, and Elija found the pounding in his heart ease. The man's tone was reasonable. Traitors? he thought. Who are the traitors?

Indaro glanced at Elija. Her practised eye assessed the broken arm. He would not be able to go on, a frail boy like that. He had to make a sling—surely he knew this? Then she remembered this was the first time he had seen battle. He did not know about injuries. She would see to it later.

She felt very calm. The sword weighed heavy in her hand and she lowered it, noting Garret had put his down too. The warriors in black and silver were cleaning their weapons and sheathing them. Some helped injured comrades, others checked the dead. The battle was over. All that remained was the clearing-up.

The man in the centre of the room was looking at Garret. "What is your name, soldier?" he asked.

"Garret," he replied and the man's black eyes passed over him, uninterested.

Indaro felt she should do something, say something. There was a reason they were here, but she could not remember it.

"I am Indaro Kerr Guillaume," she managed, her voice rasping as if rusty from lack of use. "And you are?"

He raised his eyebrows. "Marcellus Vincerus," he said, and he added, "and you are Rubin's sister."

She nodded, her attempt at conversation at an end. She was pleased the man knew of Rubin. Perhaps he had met him. She felt calm now the battle was over, and grateful to the man for ending it. She could not remember why they had been fighting. Probably something pointless, she thought.

"So your father is responsible for this doomed venture," Marcellus said. "I thought he no longer had it in him."

Indaro frowned. "No," she said. He has it all wrong, she thought. Eager to set him straight, she was about to tell him about Mason and Gil Rayado, and about Fell and general Shuskara, when a soldier ran into the room.

"Lord!" Marcellus turned. Indaro blinked and rubbed her eyes. As if waking from a dream, she hefted her sword, moving sluggishly.

"The Immortal!" the soldier cried. "He is under attack. In the Hall of Emperors!"

Without hesitation the lord strode towards the door.

"Marcellus," asked the commander, "do you want these three questioned?"

Pausing, his lord said, "No. Just let them go."

And Marcellus left the room, his warriors at his heels. Indaro watched the door close, heard the latch snicker shut. In the silence she stared at Garret, baffled.

PART SEVEN

The Gulon Veil

Chapter 42

The last Petrassi army lay becalmed on the foothills of the great mountain range called the Wall of the Gods south of the City. Had its commanders wished to conceal the twenty thousand armed men they would have succeeded, for after half a year endured in one place, much of it under pouring rain, the army had blended into the landscape, the speckled greys and browns of men, their tents, horses and supplies indistinguishable from earth, brush and rock. Once these rolling hills had been thickly clothed with stands of oak and beech, but the City in its unceasing hunger had chewed up all the timber, leaving thick, near-impenetrable undergrowth in places, and elsewhere bald rock. A crimson eagle, soaring uncaring beneath the rain clouds, might not spot the army camped on the slopes. Although it would hear it, for twenty thousand men make a constant rumble of noise, even at night.

And it would certainly smell it. Between the front lines of the encamped army and the southern plain of the City lay thousands of rotting corpses, grave witness to the battles fought by the City to regain this crucial land from the Petrassi. The invaders had held on grimly, despite crippling losses, and the City army, frustrated and exhausted, was now retired behind its walls of stone.

It was well short of noon, the morning grey and rain-soaked as ever, and somewhere near the centre of the encampment a man sat in a tent writing by lantern light. Hayden Weaver, commander of the last great army to stand against the City, wrote a letter to his wife each day. Sometimes it was brief and hurried, a mere sentence indicating he was still alive. But often, as today, he had the leisure to tell dear Anna of the previous day's events, the gossip among his young officers, even the troop deployments, for he always ensured each day's letter was not despatched until the following morning; he would not want word of his death to be followed by a cheerful missive from him.

A fat drop of water fell on the thick writing paper and Hayden cursed. He took off his spectacles, looked up and cursed again. The material of the tent was so sturdy that a veritable lake of rain had built up on it, and the ceiling was sagging alarmingly in the middle. The general stood and grabbed his sword, sheathed and belted, and lunged at the bulging tent with the hilt-end, forcing the water up and out. He heard a volley of shouts and curses from outside and smiled to himself, his good humour restored. He sat down again and signed his name with a flourish, then held the letter up to the warmth of the lantern to dry.

His brother ducked in through the tent flap, grinning broadly.

"Well done," said Mason. "You drenched Pieter Arendt and his aides."

They smiled at each other. There was a long history of rivalry between the two families. "Man has too many aides," Hayden commented.

Mason coughed. "It's foul in here," he complained. "That lantern's smoking." Hayden only grunted, and Mason walked over to a side table and poured himself a glass of wine. He took a deep sip to moisten his throat then sat down in a folding canvas chair and stretched his legs out comfortably. He watched his brother fold and seal the letter.

Mason Weaver had waited until Gil Rayado had left Old Mountain with Fell and the others, then he had collected his small bag of possessions, mounted up and made his way west and south-west, alone, travelling at night through enemy territory, until he reached the Odrysian garrison at Mount Gargaron. There he had killed time for two interminable days while the commander had verified his credentials then sent him on, with good luck wishes, to the Petrassi army camped ten leagues to the south.

Now the day they had planned for for so long had arrived. The explosives were laid. Everyone had their orders. All they could do was wait. Mason settled more comfortably in his chair. He had waited forty years. He could wait a few hours longer.

His brother laid the letter on the table, patted it fondly, then gazed up at Mason. The two were not alike. Hayden, the elder, was tall and thin, stooped, with the demeanour of a scholar. It was Mason, stocky and heavy of shoulder, who looked like the old soldier, although he had not been one for a very long time.

"You never have any doubts, do you?" commented Hayden. It was not really a question.

"And you have nothing but," his brother replied.

"Only between you and me. Never for the men."

Mason nodded.

A soldier came in through the tent opening and shook himself like a dog. Hayden frowned as he was sprayed with raindrops.

"Sorry, sir," said the aide, although he did not look sorry. Perhaps he had been standing outside. "There's a rider coming from the north."

"Bring him in." The aide nodded and went back out into the rain.

"I am arguing," said Hayden as if there had been no interruption, "that Marcellus as emperor would almost certainly sue for peace. We have been told that from many sources, including Archange."

"*Almost certainly,*" Mason repeated. "How many thousands of lives, lives of our own people, rest on that 'almost certainly'? It is too late, brother. Cities have been destroyed, whole nations wiped out. Generations of our young men have been killed. The Petrassi live on the edge of extinction. Our friends the Odrysians are dwindling, dying, their womenfolk in hiding in foreign lands. I was at the Lion's Palace, remember. There are fewer than two hundred Tuomi still living." His voice was rough with emotion and he paused for a moment.

"I know Marcellus," he reminded his brother, more calmly, "and I do not think that is a judgement of him I would agree with."

Hayden, frowning, put his finger to his lips. Mason fell silent and they could both hear a louder silence from outside, of soldiers hushed to hear their argument. Then there was a flurry of movement and voices and the aide appeared again at the tent flap. He ushered in a young man in riding leathers and a waterproof cape. This rider was barely more than a child, slender and pale, his straw hair plastered to his head. Rain was still sheeting off him and he stared regretfully at the rough-planked floor where pools of water were gathering.

"Well?" Hayden asked.

The aide said, "He is Adelmus, a rider with the Odrysian scouts. I can vouch for his identity."

"Adelmus?"

"Sir," said the rider, still gazing at the floor. "The alarm gongs have started. In the Red Palace."

"How long ago?"

The scout seemed baffled by the question. Hayden wondered if this was the best the Odrysians had left.

"Before I left, sir."

Hayden suppressed his irritation. "Did you leave immediately?"

The boy nodded, sniffing and wiping his nose on his sleeve.

"And you rode post-haste?"

"Yes, sir."

"Thank you, Adelmus." To the aide he said, "See he has food and returns safely to his people. And Tyler."

"Sir?" The aide paused.

"Why has an Odrysian reached us with this news before one of our own?"

"I don't know, sir." Tyler seemed about to shrug, then stifled the gesture. "Perhaps our own scouts have been captured."

"Do we trust this boy? He seems simple."

This time Tyler did shrug. "He is who he says he is, sir. Perhaps the Odrysians choose their scouts for their speed in the saddle rather than their speed of thought."

Hayden grunted and glanced at Mason, who glanced at the timepiece on the desk and said, "It is still well before noon. We can afford to wait for confirmation."

The general shook his head. He stood and grabbed his sword-belt again. He slung it round his hips, then stepped out of the tent into the thick drizzle. Pieter Arendt and his brothers and aides and followers turned to watch him from under their rain shelter. He saw their heads come up and their shoulders straighten. The murmured buzz of conversation all around slowed and stopped as soldiers noticed him and realised it was time. Unit commanders appeared suddenly out of the greyness, watching him expectantly. Some held the reins of fresh horses, saddled and ready.

Hayden looked around. Weak sunlight shone through the rain clouds, the first they had seen for days. Was that a good omen? On a clear day they would have a view three ways, once one of the loveliest on earth: to the west across the sea, silver as slate in winter, dark like wine in the heat of summer; to the east across plains that had been rich with grasses and the horses which thrived on them; and northwards to the greatest city on earth. Hayden looked to the north. It was just possible to see the outline of the City. It lay on its desolate plain like a dried scab, the general thought.

"Tyler."

"Sir."

"Give the order to demolish the lower dam."

The aide nodded and moved off into the greyness. There was a long silence, men waited, horses neighed and shifted, snorting. Then a flare burst suddenly into the sky, climbing through the rain, spluttering and hissing. Its baleful yellow glow turned the warriors' upturned faces to death's-heads.

"Prepare to march," ordered the general.

F̲ell Aron Lee had been in the City for two long nights. He had entered with some difficulty. All the great gates were locked, bolted and barred in a surge of vigilance after the deaths in the Little Opera House. Traders, foreigners and even ordinary citizens had to wait, sometimes for days, before they were reluctantly let in, or out, by surly and suspicious guards. Fell had left Indaro and Gil and the others a league or so from the wall, and rode in alone. He was amazed to find a tent city had sprung up outside the gate. Many thousands were camped in the pouring rain waiting to get in. He had presented the special papers provided by Saroyan to the guards, who left him kicking his heels for hours under a leaking awning while they checked he was who he said he was, then let him through without apology.

He stayed at a small clean inn in Gervain, where he was a stranger. He kept to his room by day, sleeping away the hours, then walking the streets of the Paradise quarter at night, once unknowingly tracing Indaro's steps to the square in front of the white temple and its unparalleled view of the Shield.

At dawn on his second morning in the inn there was a light tap on his door.

"Yes?"

"Sami," said a low voice.

Fell flung open the door. He and Broglanh grinned at each other, uncertain what to say for there was so much to be said. Fell felt tension easing from his chest for the first time in days. With Evan Quin Broglanh at his side, his chances were increased manyfold.

He realised the soldier still thought of him as his commander, and thus it was Fell's place to ask the questions. "Did you know me when you joined the Wildcats?" he asked.

Broglanh grunted. "No, you bastard, you'd changed a lot. It was later. We were at Copperburn, remember, with those trees? I was on guard duty. You and the general, the one with the ears, you walked past me, ignored me of course, just a peasant, talking about the next day's action. I knew your voice. Then afterwards, next time we met, I could see Arish looking out of your eyes. It was creepy. Did you know me, just a grunt?"

"I saw your name on the roster of incomers." He felt a little sheepish. Why had he never spoken to him about their days as hostages together, after all they went through? Why did he not trust him with his new identity—Evan of all people?

"When did you take the name Broglanh?"

"I was adopted. I was ten."

"What happened to the others?"

"Parr and Ranul died," Broglanh said shortly. "Riis is our man in the palace. He commands a century of the Thousand." He shook his head, marvelling. "He has Marcellus' ear—or so he claims."

Fell looked sharply at him. "Does he indeed? Do you doubt him?"

"I don't doubt his bravery," Broglanh replied, "or his commitment."

"But?"

"But he resents his minor role. He's itching to be the hero."

"What *is* his role?"

"Misdirection. Diverting the Thousand. Keeping them busy, away from the emperor. If we fail, turning his Nighthawks against the emperor and killing him themselves."

"Hardly minor."

Broglanh sniffed. "He's jealous of you. Always was."

Fell was astonished. "Jealous of *me*?"

Broglanh grinned. "All of us, all the hostages, wanted to be like Arish, so damned confident, so good at everything. Ranul hated you for it, at least at first he did. Before the dogs. And Riis and Parr were always coming up with plans to undermine you, but you were always so pigging lucky too."

"And you?"

Broglanh shook his head. "I was just a brat. What was I, eight? You were my hero. Then you disappeared. We all thought you were dead in an alley somewhere." He frowned. "You should have told us."

"I couldn't. Shuskara took a great risk, taking me away, hiding who I was."

"He took a risk getting involved in our defence."

"He paid for that in the end. They killed his family. The Immortal never forgets an injury."

"Yes, well," said Broglanh grimly. "He's not the only one."

Not for the first time, Fell felt a flush of shame that so many years had passed while he abandoned his vow as a youngster. While Broglanh, the youngest of them, had never forgotten, but apparently nursed his anger and determination down the years.

"That's why you sent me away, with Indaro," his old friend said, "To take the chance. To kill the emperor then. But it was just another decoy."

Even that wasn't true. Fell had sent him away for sentimental reasons, because part of him still saw the man as a boy, to be protected as he wanted to protect Indaro. He asked, "What happened to you after Indaro left you with a broken arm?"

Broglanh shrugged as though it wasn't important, and grinned. "How is she?"

"The same." A shadow passed over Fell's heart as he thought of the dangers she would be facing.

As if he understood, Broglanh said, "She'll get through, her and Garret. She'll probably get to the emperor before we do. In fact," he said cheerfully, "bastard's probably dead already. And we can just go and get drunk."

Hours later Fell was sitting on a wooden bench in the courtyard of the Northmen, legs stretched out in front of him, crossed at the ankles, his arms folded. He yawned, then sighed. He and Broglanh had been waiting in the courtyard, inside the Gate of Peace, since sunup. They had run out of light conversation, but were both conscious of a metal grille, let into the white stone wall behind them, which stopped any discussion which might get them arrested and executed. There wasn't a lot to discuss—get as close to the emperor as possible and kill him with whatever came to hand. Not much of a plan. But good enough.

At the gates of the Red Palace their papers had been taken away and scrutinised and they had been searched for weapons. Fell had a slender stiletto sewn into his stiff leather jerkin, and a knife in his boot. They were ordered to shake out their boots, but the knife was pinned into a specially built recess in the leather and it stayed undiscovered. Broglanh had poison pellets, supplied by Gil's allies among the Buldekki tribesmen, concealed in the hem of his faded red jacket.

The tree-shaded courtyard was one of Fell's favourite parts of the City, with its white stone carvings of wolves and werewomen leaping along one wall. Broglanh had never been there before and he had gazed up at them incredulously. The women had fangs, and fur on their backs, and tails, but also creamy white breasts, and they bounded through a carved jungle towards the pack of snarling wolves, and it was unclear whether they would mate or kill.

Fell stood. He had spent the last many days, while not in the saddle, going through rigorous exercises aimed at keeping his body strong and his mind calm and focussed. Now he could feel his muscles stiffening as he sat. He swung his arms and paced the courtyard in the thick drizzle, resisting the temptation to run on the spot. He forced frustration and boredom from his mind, concentrating on relaxing the muscles of his shoulders and neck. He might get only one chance, and he had to be ready.

He saw Broglanh look up. A palace servant was crossing the courtyard. He beckoned to them. Broglanh stood, and they followed the man into the dark of the palace. He led them through a warren of corridors, and down two flights of stairs to where the halls were lit by torches and the air smelled damp and musty. Fell felt Broglanh glance at him, but he did not respond. His focus was taking in everything, the width of the corridor, the height of the torch-brackets, and whether the bald servant, dressed in white robes, was armed or not.

They came to a high wooden door, barred with iron. The servant opened it and walked in. The two warriors glanced at each other, then followed him, alert for confrontation. They found themselves in a square white room furnished with a desk and several wooden chairs. The desk was covered with papers. It was so clearly an office, part of the ponderous palace bureaucracy, that Fell smiled.

Another door opened and a tall man came in, a very tall man Fell recognised as Boaz, commander of the Thousand. Fell had marked him as the first person to kill after the Immortal, for he was the only serious opposition to the Vincerii as emperor. He was flanked by two soldiers with swords sheathed.

Boaz looked at them both, then nodded to Fell.

"Fell Aron Lee?"

"Yes, sir."

"Who is this?" he gestured to Broglanh.

"My aide, Garvy."

"You will not need an aide. He will be escorted out."

They had expected that, of course. Broglanh's brief was to linger in the palace for as long as possible, in the hope of being of help. Fell nodded curtly at him and Broglanh turned to go.

"A moment, soldier," said Boaz. "First take off your shirts, both of you."

Fell avoided looking at Broglanh. He shrugged off his jerkin and dropped it on the floor, then took off his shirt. Broglanh did the same. The servant who had brought them there peered closely at their chests and backs, searching the many injuries on their skin. He looked at Boaz and shook his head.

"You have many honourable scars," Boaz said, and Fell thought there was respect in his voice. He was a soldier himself, after all. They put their shirts on again, and Boaz nodded to the servant, who led Broglanh from the room.

"Our sources say you claim to be the son of the Immortal," Boaz commented. His eyes hardened.

"No, sir!" Fell contrived to look embarrassed, slipping into his old jerkin, feeling the solidity of the hidden knife. "I'm the son of the Lion of the East, at least that was what I was told. I don't speak of it, sir. Now I'm a loyal son of the City. I don't care about the past. But"—he lowered his eyes as if to hide shame, but really hiding the lack of it—"I was in my cups in an inn, after the defeat of the Maritime, I said I would go back to my real home as the City was doomed. I didn't mean it, sir, I was just mouthing off. I was asked if I remembered my father. I said not—I was born after the Immortal's attack on the Lion's Palace. Someone laughed and said I must be the Immortal's bastard." He shrugged. "It was just the ale talking, sir."

Boaz was staring at him, his face clean of emotion.

"And," Fell rattled on, "I forgot about it, but someone must have reported it to the palace . . ." He trailed off. "I make no claim, sir. Who my father was is not important. I'm loyal to the City. I believe I've proved that."

"Yet you changed your name, concealing from the City that the child Arish became Fell Aron Lee."

Hating himself, Fell said, "That was Shuskara's idea." In his head he vowed to make up the disloyalty to Shuskara if it was in his power. "He believed he was protecting me."

"Son of an enemy of the City. Friend of a traitor to the City," Boaz mused. "You cannot choose your sire, soldier, but you can choose your friends. You chose unwisely."

"Shuskara's treachery came many years after we parted."

"Do you have anything to prove you are Arish?"

Fell shook his head.

"No birthmarks? No mementoes of your dead mother?"

"I don't care about the past," Fell repeated.

Boaz considered. He was a dark-eyed, dark-complected cadaverous man, with deeply pockmarked skin and, Fell noticed, unusually long fingers, which were permanently clenched and twisted, as if by disease or torture. He was a legendary warrior, although he had not taken the field in thirty years.

"Your reputation precedes you," the general said, after a long moment. "Where do you wish to be assigned now the Maritime is no more?"

Fell was stumped. He had not given the matter a moment's thought, for he did not expect to survive.

"I go where I'm sent," he replied stolidly.

Led through a new maze of corridors, following Boaz and flanked by the two guards, Fell wondered at the general's motives. He was said to be fiercely loyal to the emperor, yet if the Immortal were dead, he would be one of the men best placed to be emperor. Mason's plan would make Marcellus emperor, yet the Vincerii were of a kind with their emperor, perhaps no better than him, perhaps worse. In all his conversations with Mason Fell had never teased out of the man what he thought the Serafim really were. At different times he had called them more than human, and inhuman. Once he had said they were demons. Then he would become impatient with the questioning and say brusquely that the Serafim would die by the sword like any men, like all men.

Fell felt a deep uncertainty about the plot he was involved in, but this was one thing he believed deep in his soul, that the emperor would die before this day was out. That was his first, his only, duty. If he succeeded there would be many decisions to be made—but not by him.

He thanked the gods that he and Broglanh had had their brands cut away and replaced with ugly scars imitating recent knife wounds. Mason had told him the palace authorities were aware of the branded men, but not of their significance. He wondered if Riis had had his disguised too, and hoped so.

They entered the green walls of the Keep then followed a wide corridor leading upwards in a steep slope. At the end was a huge door, gilded and painted in gold and crimson. It was guarded by two of the Thousand. This had to be an important place, thought Fell, for the Thousand were not given mere guard duty. He relaxed his shoulders, visualising the exact position of the small knife at his side, its heft and its feel in his palm.

"This is the Hall of Emperors," Boaz announced, stepping inside.

Fell looked around. They were in a vast chamber, built like a vertical cylinder, round and deep. They had entered near the top. A wide staircase, carpeted with red, lit by hundreds of torches, wound round the curved walls of the hall, descending slowly towards the floor, which was red and slick like fresh blood. There was an atmosphere of dread in the place which bore down on Fell like a stinking blanket, stifling thought. He shook his head to clear it and felt a headache spring up instantly. He breathed in cautiously and tasted foetid air, the air of a charnel house closed for centuries. His stomach roiled and he fought the urge to turn and leave the room.

Grim-faced warriors of the Thousand were stationed two steps apart all down the staircase, and Fell was almost relieved to see them. They were men like him, ordinary men with bones and muscles and blood, and if they could stand to be in this terrible place, then so could he.

When they reached the bottom of the stairway Fell realised the floor was not covered with blood—it was awash with water, less than ankle-deep, lying over red carpet. But the water looked oily and unwholesome, and Fell found himself reluctant to step into it. He did though, splashing a little, following Boaz to the centre of the high room.

"Wait here," the general said, and he crossed the flooded room and disappeared through a doorway. It was framed with a substance which glittered, reflecting light like crystal, and Fell saw Boaz's image doubled and redoubled countless times as he passed through.

Fell looked around him and smiled. There were more than two hundred warriors in the hall, all staring at him, but only two mattered, the pair behind him. He turned casually and grinned at them. They had their blades in hand, and were a sword's length away, but they would not stop him killing the emperor if the man came within six paces of him. His spirits rose and he allowed himself to consider the chances of fighting his way out.

A door creaked, and he looked at the crystal doorway but no one was there. His headache had swelled, and he concentrated on relaxing his neck and shoulders, focussing on the power in his legs, his arms. I will not need the knife, he thought. I will kill him with my bare hands. I will break his neck then, if I am still alive, snap his back—just to be sure.

A man strode out of the crystal doorway. He walked across the hall to within ten paces of Fell and stopped.

Fell's disappointment was crushing. The man was middle-aged, tall, fair and bearded, with the bland gaze of a man who has spent his life among books, or waiting to play the part of another. A blank slate. He smiled affably at Fell. Just one of the decoys.

Fell put his feelings aside. This is just one more obstacle to get through, he thought. You have passed some test set by Boaz. Now you must pass this one, and perhaps *then* you will get the chance to meet the true emperor.

"Lord," he said, bowing his head dutifully.

"We have met before, Arish," the man said, his voice light and colourless.

"When I was a child. Yes, lord," Fell replied. He thought, You had only one eye in those days, lord.

"Amazing what they can do with glass," the man told him. Neither eye looked to be made of glass. Both were black, and warm as a skull. One eyelid drooped slightly, as if the man were about to wink. Fell knew Mason had told him something about the eyes, but he could not remember what.

The feeling of dread and confusion wrapped him in stifling folds. Can he read my mind? he thought.

The man smiled. "No, I can't read your mind, Arish. But I remember you, a child of six or so. I showed you your father's severed head. It was green with rot by then, yet you were brave and did not cry. I remember that, though

I had just lost the eye and was in great pain. It was your mother who destroyed it, the eye. Did you know that?"

Fell was trying to think, but the pain in his head was agonising, and the man seemed so reasonable, so friendly in fact, that he was starting to believe he had made a terrible mistake coming here.

The man stepped forward, close to Fell. Through the pain and confusion Fell could smell the stink of him, like something long-dead, slowly rotting, and he saw the man's clothes were filthy, as if he had worn them all his life. A spasm of revulsion ran through him and his mind cleared a little. The creature was standing close to him. Fell knew that was important but he could not remember why. It took all his courage not to turn and run away.

The man said, "You are not my son, are you, Fell? We have always known that. You came here to kill me, like all the others.

"We know all your plans," he went on, after a pause. "Your friends betrayed you. And you will all die, die slowly. Because they will come to this room, one by one, all the little plotters. They will throw themselves at me and break, just as all these small nations, these insignificant cities threw themselves at the City and broke upon its walls."

He seemed to have grown taller, and Fell felt like the child Arish before him again. He lowered his head and raised his hands to his face, covering his eyes from the pain and bafflement, trying to hide. In the distance he heard the sound of a gong beating brassily, over and over, echoing the pulsing pain in his head. He pressed his right index finger into the depression in his skull where the lance had caught him so long ago. Sometimes this gave him respite from the pain. He pressed hard and felt his mind clearing a little.

Then he remembered why he was there. He looked up. The creature had turned his back and was striding back to the crystal doorway. Fell blinked hard, trying to force his way out of the miasma in his mind. He reached inside his jerkin, touching the smooth hilt of the dagger. His fingers were like thumbs. It would not come out. Then suddenly he pulled it clear and in one smooth movement, compelled by memory rather than skill, he threw the knife with all his strength and saw it thunk deep into the creature's back.

No one had stopped him. No one had moved. The emperor paused. He reached around, awkwardly crooking his elbow, and dragged the bloodstained knife from his lower ribs. He dropped it on the floor, and only then turned.

"Don't kill him. I want him alive and undamaged," he ordered his warriors.

Then he stepped from the room, and the soldiers seemed to breathe again. All around the walls they were stirring, as if from a dream of ice. Fell heard a whisper of metal on leather behind him, and he ran across the room and picked up the small knife, then turned to defend himself.

Chapter 43

The great wall of water from the broken dam roared down the hillsides, scouring the ground before it. Trees which had stood for longer than the ages of man were snapped off like twigs. The animals remaining in those parts, a few starving deer and scrawny foxes, ran before it but were overtaken, overwhelmed. Nothing was left in its wake but bare rock and dead earth.

The Adamantine Wall had stood facing south, a symbol of power and arrogance, for more than eight hundred years. It was built when the young City was at its zenith and was a trumpet-blast of defiance to the kingdoms of the southlands, themselves wealthy with trade and proud with armies. It replaced the older Sarantine Wall, four leagues to the north, and was more than forty spans tall in places, wider at the base than the top, and with deep towers every hundred paces. It was built of limestone blocks, cunningly shaped to fit together without mortar. It had just one set of double gates, and was considered impregnable, for in all its thousand years it had never been breached.

The soldiers on the ramparts that day were the last survivors of the 14th Celestine Infantry, called the Shovelheads. They had been on duty since daybreak, and were grumbling among themselves, as soldiers will. They complained about the poor food and the woeful lack of supplies, particularly armour and weapons. They resented manning a wall which clearly needed no one to guard it. They resented their commanders, the rain, the lazy pigging Sevens—the 7th Light Infantry, who had been due to replace them at noon but who unaccountably hadn't turned up, and the cancellation of their ale ration. Most of all they resented the Nighthawks, whose place they had taken only a handful of days before when the horse-shaggers had been undeservedly promoted to the Thousand.

They could not see the wall of water coming, for the grey cloud hung low over the City, and the rain cut visibility to a few paces. But they heard it, and one by one they fell silent. It sounded like thunder, but no thunder had ever grumbled on for so long. It sounded like the rumble of a cavalry charge, but even horsemen were not stupid enough to attack the City wall. When it finally broke through the cloud and mist before their eyes, they couldn't believe what they saw and many of them died in ignorance.

When the leading edge of the waters hit, travelling at twice the speed of a galloping horse, it was higher than the wall and everyone standing on the ramparts was wiped out in a heartbeat. The wall shifted, groaned, then crumbled in many places, although many of the towers defied that first blow.

The water, diminished but not halted by its attack on the Adamantine Wall, flowed on over and through the Sarantine Wall. It carried a lethal load of branches and other debris picked up on its way. Everyone in its path died. The houses and shacks of the poor in the quarters of Barenna and Burman South were swept away, and the people died, crushed by the weight of water or drowned. It dived downward wherever it could, flooding the sewers once again and destroying the final remnants of the ancient machinery there, drowning the last of the Dwellers, although there were few left to die. By the time it reached the Red Palace it was running out of power, and the guards there watched first with horror then relief as the wave lapped harmlessly against the wall beneath their feet.

When they heard the sound of thunder they thought it was a distant storm and did not realise the Blues had unleashed the second reservoir.

* * *

Fell spun on his heel and slashed the knife through the chin-piece of one soldier, slicing it on through the throat of another. Blood sprayed hotly over him. As the two warriors fell back he snatched one of their swords and revelled in the snarls of anger from their comrades. The Thousand were hampered by the command not to injure their prey, and he guessed their dread of their lord was so great they barely risked bruising him.

But he knew it could not last long—sheer weight of numbers would bear him down within moments.

He twisted, sliced and spun. He had to keep moving; he could not afford the luxury of a lunge, a thrust to groin or eye. He used the sword two-handed, keeping it always in motion, slashing, slicing, ripping.

"Stop him! Stop him now!" a voice commanded, and he grinned to himself. He revelled in their frustration. He could hear curses raining upon him as they tried to reach him without grossly harming him. In the distance he heard the sound of a gong. Two gongs now, beaten in an alternating faster rhythm. He wondered if he were the cause of it.

The hilt of a dagger glanced off his head and he stumbled. He could not fall. They would be on him in a heartbeat. He danced forward and sideways, slicing off half a hand, dodging back as the victim howled. He thanked the Gods of Ice and Fire that the Thousand kept their weapons so sharp.

"Kill him!" he heard someone shout in rage, and the deep voice countermanded, "You know your orders." Fell grinned in exultation. But then the same voice ordered, "Encircle him. Locked shields."

Surrounded and defended by the bodies of his enemy, he took the moment to snatch a shield from the floor and settle it on his arm. "Who's next?" he asked. He looked round, then deliberately stepped up onto two piled bodies. He heard growls of anger at the offense, but they had their orders and he could no longer hope to lure them into coming at him one at a time.

The warriors spread out evenly around him, locking their shields in a wall of metal. Inexorably they started moving in. He knew his brief run was over. They would bind him and take him through the crystal doorway to whatever hideous fate the emperor planned. But he could still kill the creature, given a moment's chance.

Suddenly there was a change in the air. Some of his attackers glanced up. Fell risked a look. At the top of the winding staircase the warriors of the

Thousand had turned towards a new enemy. He heard the crash and slide of weapons, saw the sparkling glitter of moving metal. Then he caught sight of a flash of red hair, flowing like water in torchlight. Indaro!

Balanced on the back of a dead man, he took a deep breath. "Wildcats to me!" he bellowed, and from above he heard her answering yell, then another. His heart soared.

Then the flailing body of a warrior came arcing down, thrown off the landing. Fully-armoured, he crashed in an explosion of sharp metal onto the soldiers around Fell. Several went down, and for a moment there was a gap in the ring of steel.

Fell leaped lightly across the bodies of the dead and injured, jumped down and raced for the crystal doorway, on the track of the emperor.

Indaro hacked and slashed grimly, pain and exhaustion overcoming any residual grace. She parried a lunge, her blade cleaving the man's neck, but a red-bearded soldier lashed out with his foot, spilling her to the floor. Desperately she rolled against another soldier's calves and he stumbled over her, in the path of a killing sword-thrust from the red-bearded man. She jumped up, snatching a second sword from the carpet, and despatched him with a blow to the neck.

Broglanh was battling wildly against two warriors. Indaro stepped in to aid him, crushing the windpipe of one man, who fell choking. Spinning on her heel she plunged one blade into an attacker's belly while blocking a slashing blow from another man. Broglanh despatched him with a disembowelling thrust.

The three of them had cleared the landing and were at the top of the stairs. Garret and Broglanh were starting to force their way down. They and the defenders could only stand two abreast and for a moment Indaro had nothing to do. She glanced down. It was a high, round hall, blood-red, and the winding stairs all the way round the chamber were full of soldiers. Far below, on the floor of the hall, another battle was going on. She looked down and blinked. Was that Fell in the centre of the battle?

Then she heard the cry that lifted her heart—Fell's familiar bellow, "Wildcats to me!"

Throwing her head back she screamed, "Wildcats!" Fell was still alive, and they were coming to save him. She heard her two friends reply and saw them attack with renewed vigour.

Desperate now to get back into the battle, Indaro picked up a fallen sword and sent it spinning over their heads into the ranks of the defenders. She heard a clang of metal on metal and a cry of pain, and a soldier toppled over the edge of the landing, plummeting down to the floor far below. She heard the crash of metal and shouts of anger. Elated, she smiled and picked up another sword. This time she aimed it and hit a soldier behind the two current defenders. He fell forward, knocking into the man in front of him, unfooting him, allowing Broglanh to slide his sword under the defender's chin-piece. He lurched forward and Broglanh put his boot on the man's shoulder and toppled him back into his comrades. Two of them fell, and for a moment the defenders were disorganised. Shoulder to shoulder Garret and Broglanh moved down several steps.

Indaro ran back across the landing to the doorway and looked up the corridor. No one was in sight. Leaning on them, she pushed the heavy doors closed. They groaned as if unused to the movement. There was no way to lock or bar them on the inside, so she dragged three enemy corpses against them, hoping that was enough to stop the doors. She hadn't the strength to do more.

She ran back to the staircase and looked down again at the scene on the floor below. Fell had disappeared now, and soldiers were streaming out through a doorway. Her mind screaming with frustration, with impatience to get back into the battle, she hurried down the stairs behind her two friends, who were fighting the fight of their lives. "Garret, step back, give me a chance," she shouted to him above the din. "I'll relieve you."

Garret gave no indication of having heard. She watched as he battled on, apparently tireless, invulnerable. He had been fighting, with only a scrap of food and little rest, all day yet he was uninjured. She found herself watching him in awe, mesmerised by the flashing blade, the graceful precise moves.

Then time seemed to slow. The air was bright with clarity, heavy with fate. She saw Garret's sword strike an enemy blade. A spark arced between them. Then Garret's blade snapped and Indaro saw one half fly up above their heads, tumbling through the air, unhurriedly, end over end. Garret, unbalanced, parried a second blow with the broken sword and tried to ram it home into the belly of his attacker. But the sword was too short and he had to stretch. Indaro watched as the other defender saw the chance and plunged his own blade under Garret's armpit. It sank deep into the chest, seeking the heart. Broglanh killed the man instantly but it was too late. Garret crumpled to the bloodstained carpet. Indaro stepped over his body and was back in the battle.

She could scarcely believe it, but this was the strangest day of Emly's eventful life so far and she was prepared to believe anything. Bartellus was growing visibly stronger.

On the verge of death when she discovered him, the old man had neither slept nor eaten, and had drunk only a little stale water, yet his back was straighter, his gait more determined. Although she still held on to his arm, she wondered which of them was supporting the other as they hurried through the dungeons.

It was the soldier, a Nighthawk he called himself, who had made the difference, she guessed. Bartellus seemed to respond to the company of warriors. The Nighthawk, whose name was Darius, said Riis had been arrested and taken to the Keep. At the news Bartellus looked grim.

"Do you know why?" he asked, but Darius shook his head. "We were told he was charged with treason. The Nighthawks didn't believe that and planned to rescue him before he was tortured. But then the limping one ordered me to accompany him to the dungeons. I went with him hoping to find Riis."

Now the warrior walked ahead of them, the tip of his sword at the neck of the old man with the stick. Their pace was slow, dictated by Dol Salida. Bartellus had refused to let Darius kill the old man, and Em could feel impatience fizzing from the soldier. He was tall and lean and his reddish hair was shorn close to his head. He wore black and silver armour which glistened in the torchlight. He reminded her a little of Evan. She wondered where her lover was and whether he too had been taken by the enemy.

They had emerged from the dungeons and were walking the corridors of the Red Palace. Em gazed around her in wonder. The place was flooded, water swished round their ankles, and they could hear sounds of thunder, which was not thunder for it seemed to come from within the walls, and distant screams and shouts and the crash of metal. The only people they saw were servants and the odd soldier, but they were all fleeing and had no interest in the trio. At one point they came to a part of the palace which had collapsed and they were forced to climb over broken walls and rubble. Sunlight shone down on them through a hole in the roof. The men looked around in amazement, not knowing what had caused the destruction.

Emly was walking in a dream-state, from tiredness and fear and disorientation. She had no idea where they were, or where they were going. When she saw the daylight she was amazed.

Bartellus called a halt and turned to her. "We are going to the Keep, Emly, if it still stands. Only death and blood await us there. We will find you a place of safety first."

"What about the Fourth Imperial?" she asked him, clinging to their old plan.

The general looked embarrassed. "It seems I haven't been keeping up with current events. The Fourth was disbanded two years ago." He smiled and she saw a glimpse of her father again, the man who had rescued her from the Halls.

"We will find somewhere safe for you," he repeated. "No one will pay attention to one girl in all this chaos."

"Look around you," she told him with a hint of impatience. "The palace is falling down. Nowhere is safe. I would rather be with you, Father."

He nodded abstractedly, the decision made, his mind already on other things. To Darius, who was waiting impatiently, he asked, "How far are we from the Keep? I cannot tell."

"Moments," said the warrior curtly.

"Keep well behind us," Bart told Em, "and if there is a battle run away. If we get separated, make your way back to the House of Glass."

She gazed at him fearfully. "The House of Glass burned down," she reminded him.

He shook his head, annoyed by his erratic memory. "To Meggy's house then. If it still stands."

"And if it does not?"

"Then I will find you."

But then it was too late for words, for they heard the sound of running, booted feet behind them. Bartellus and Darius raised their swords, but in moments they were overtaken by warriors in black and silver.

Chapter 44

When Hayden Weaver clambered over the rubble of the Adamantine Wall it had finally stopped raining and a watery sunlight shone on the ruins of the City, for the first time that winter. Hayden was not a superstitious man; he did not believe in signs and portents, but if he had been then he might have seen it as an omen.

It was hard to believe two great waves of water had passed over these streets only that morning. The surfaces of stone and wood and brick glistened in the sunlight and were clean, and clear of people, animals, debris. But the water had all gone, vanished into sewers and drains. When the wet roadways and avenues dried, perhaps in a few hours, it would be impossible to tell what catastrophe had happened here, to kill so many people and demolish so many of the buildings. Most of the corpses had been washed away, into canals and culverts perhaps, or they rested silently in the homes in which they had drowned. Or maybe, Hayden thought, the City was already empty, most of its people long-dead on battlefields, the rest, children and young mothers and old crones fled long since.

The floodwater had done most of its damage in the south of the City, between the two great walls and the Red Palace, some ten leagues distant. The palace itself, already fatally weakened by the collapse of the drainage system, or so the general's engineers advised, was expected to topple under the ferocity of the floods. But, squinting against the growing light, Hayden could see that it still stood, although some of its towers and minarets seemed to have vanished.

"Mason?" He looked around for his brother, who knew more about the City and its buildings than any man living.

"He headed for the palace," said Tyler.

"And you let him?" asked Hayden angrily.

"He is not under my command, lord," said the aide with his customary cool courtesy. "He was going alone. He would not wait. I sent a platoon of soldiers with him."

Hayden nodded. Mason had sped down from the camp with a troop of light cavalry, the Petrassi's crack troops, riding hard to be the first to breach the wall. Hayden had followed with the heavy cavalry, intent on building a bridgehead within the Sarantine Wall before the bulk of the infantry arrived. He was not surprised his brother had forged on toward the palace. It was not part of their plan but, as Tyler said, his brother did not answer to him. Hayden was only annoyed that he had not anticipated the move and stopped it.

Until this moment the brothers' plans had been the same—to execute the emperor with the connivance of disgruntled City warriors, and to deal a lethal blow by unleashing the dams. But they had long disagreed on how the story would be played out next. Mason wanted the City destroyed; he would be satisfied only if it were razed to the ground. He had personal reasons for that and Hayden respected them. But Hayden and Gil Rayado both believed the death of the emperor, and a massive show of force by the allies, would be sufficient to force the City to surrender. Marcellus was a reasonable man who, when he saw the City was at its enemies' mercy, would sue for peace. Hayden and Gil were the military leaders so ultimately Mason had to defer to them. But he wasn't happy about it. He wanted not only the emperor dead but the Vincerii too, and Hayden guessed where he had gone.

But he could not afford to think about Mason any longer, so he did not.

The first scouts were already returning with news of the amphitheatre which, in his forward planning, the general had designated his base of operations. The walls were largely unbreached, it was slowly draining of water, and it would be useable before nightfall. Hayden nodded. He turned and looked to his troops. Already several thousand were mustering in the large open place between the two walls. Rubble was being cleared and cavalry horses were being led in, single file, through a breach in the Adamantine Wall.

Tyler opened a folding table in front of the general and the familiar map of the City was rolled out. His senior men gathered round, jostling for space and Hayden took a quick headcount. All present that should be.

"This area," he said, pointing at the map, "is the part of the City we predicted would be hardest hit by the water. Barenna, Amphitheatre and part of Burman South. Pieter"—he gestured to Arendt—"take your horsemen and create a forward line on this boundary here"—he ran his finger along the line of buildings they had already discussed. "If the geography is radically different from what we predicted, take your own initiative. Kill any City soldiers you find within the perimeter."

"And civilians?"

"Let them leave the zone."

Hayden sent part of his heavy infantry behind Arendt's cavalry to secure the forward line. There the forces would stay until they received word from the palace—perhaps an offer of surrender.

His horse Rosteval had been brought up, and he mounted and rode slowly towards the flooded amphitheatre. He knew this part of the City as well as if he had lived there all his life, though he had never entered the walls before. The sunlight was getting stronger and steam was starting to rise from the glistening stone of roads and walls. All around him women and children were creeping from buildings, fleeing the advancing soldiers, or lying helpless in the sodden streets, injured and begging for aid. He realised why he had not seen them before, for they were plastered with mud and were the same colour as the stone around them. He saw a child, a girl, he thought, it was hard to tell, her legs crushed by a fallen wall, looking up at him pleadingly as he passed high above. He hardened his heart. This was not the first time he had watched the anguish of non-combatants. Innocents always suffer in war, and enough Petrassi women and children had died on the swords of the City's warriors. But even so this weapon they had used, the unleashing of two great reservoirs, was an atrocity which sat ill with him. It would help end the war, if Fell Aron Lee's mission was successful, and even if it was not, but it seemed a high price to pay. His brother had spent decades looking forward to stalking the ruins of the City, sword in hand, but he had a personal feud to fight. Hayden Weaver was just a soldier, and deep down he believed only other soldiers were fair targets in wartime.

He saw some City warriors gathered together to form a fighting unit. There were ten or so of them, an elite infantry troop by their uniforms, most of them carrying injuries. The Petrassi cavalry, fresh and full of the zest for battle, fell on them and wiped out all but two. The pair, one with a half-severed arm, retreated to the ruins of a demolished building, shouting curses upon the Blues who were responsible for such an evil crime. One of the men would be dead within the hour, thought the general, the other would be winkled out before nightfall. The flooded City would be full of such small dramas, such acts of valour. No matter the courage of the invaders, they would never be the heroes of this day.

In the amphitheatre too, when they got there, they found a company of heroes defending a stretch of its walls, soldiers, both men and women, and a few wrinkled old men who should have long ago been consigned to the earth. The general waited, talking quietly to his aide, until his men had killed them all, then he rode in. Rosteval, experienced old boy though he was, flinched a little as a muddy child rose suddenly in front of him from the rubble.

"Please lord, help my mother. She's hurt. Please help!"

Hayden stared down at him, his stony expression belying the surge of feeling in his breast. The boy was about eight, the same age as his own youngest, now safe with his mother. The general urged his mount on, but then turned in his saddle when he heard a commotion behind him. The boy had drawn a small knife and hacked at the chest of the horse following Rosteval. The animal, pained and startled, had reared and smashed the child in the face with its iron hoof. The boy lay motionless in the mud. The company rode sedately past him and down into the huge bowl of the amphitheatre.

By the time the sun grazed the western horizon the Petrassi camp was bustling, tents raised, latrines dug, rations distributed. Everything had gone like clockwork, and there were fewer casualties than the general had bargained for. They would wait for dawn now, wait to see if Fell had been successful. He would hope for news of Gil Rayado and his army, but he did not really expect to. Tomorrow, or perhaps the next day, all would become clear.

The sun vanished from the rain-washed sky, leaving the golden gleam of dusk, as Hayden Weaver sat in his tent with three of his commanders, and the ever-watchful Tyler. When all was dark Hayden stood, yawning, and dismissed them to their beds. He knew none would rest well, but all would get some sleep for they were soldiers and always slept when they could. The five men turned as a soldier came crashing through the tent entrance, almost stumbling to the floor in his haste.

"General sir, your brother is taken!"

The soldier was bloodstained and his face was grey and sweating. He could scarcely stand.

"Where?" Hayden asked. "Tell me."

Tyler thrust a chair at the soldier, Hayden nodded and the man sank into it, his legs giving way.

"There were ten of us. Yellowjackets. Your brother, sir . . ."

"Mason."

"Yes. He ran on ahead. We were trying to watch the terrain, but he seemed to forget us, so we just had to run after him. We were ordered to protect him." He avoided Hayden's eyes and the general guessed what he thought of that mission.

"What happened?"

"We were lucky at first. Or the Rats hadn't time to regroup. We only saw civilians, and most of them were dead or drowned. Then we came to the palace. It was on the other side of a lake and Mason stopped there, on the shore. There was a building in the middle. As we watched it the building, a round white thing, it just crumbled in front of our eyes and fell into the water. And then we could see the water was draining out of the lake, inching down so fast you could see it. The men didn't like that. It seemed like witchcraft. They didn't want to go on, but Mason set off round the shore. So we followed him."

"How was he captured?" Hayden asked impatiently.

"Three men came to meet us, walked out from the palace. A lord, unarmed, and two armed men."

"They defeated the ten of you?" asked Pieter Arendt. Hayden said nothing, but dread filled his heart.

The man shook his head and his face was puzzled. "The lord told us to put down our arms, and there was a buzzing in my ears and a pain in my head and I had to drop my blade. I had no choice. There was nothing I could do. It was sorcery, sir." He held his hands to his ears, remembering, and the general saw blood had flowed from them and was drying on his neck. "I blacked out. I don't know how long for. When I came round the others, my comrades, were all dead. And your brother, sir, was gone."

He gazed up at the general, puzzlement in his eyes. "*Was* it sorcery, sir?"

"It was not magic, soldier," Hayden replied. "The alchemists of the City have discovered an herb which, when burned, causes people to fall asleep. We must guard against it." It was a well-rehearsed lie, and the soldier seemed reassured. Hayden told him, "Now go, see to your wounds."

When the injured man had left Hayden stood in silence for a moment.
Arendt said, "Your orders, general."

The general stirred. "My orders stand. This changes nothing."

Arendt said, "We assume the man was allowed his life to bring you this news."

"Of course—but if Marcellus thinks it will provoke me, he is wrong."

There was nothing more to say and the commanders, all men grown old and weary in the service of Petrus, gratefully left the tent for their beds.

When only Tyler was left, the aide picked up his half-full wine glass and subsided into a chair.

"Do you want my opinion?"

"No, boy, but it has never stopped you before."

"I think the emperor is dead and that was Marcellus' last throw to save his own skin. He plans to ransom your brother for his life. And Mason walked into it."

When Hayden made no reply, the aide went on, "The City is collapsing, falling apart."

"We unleashed two lakes-full of water on it, remember?"

"But the emperor would not let the palace fall, if he still lived. He has the power to prevent it."

"What do you know of the emperor's powers, boy?" Hayden rounded on him.

"Only," Tyler replied, unmoved, "what I learned by listening in on the counsels of the rich and powerful."

Hayden shook his head. He said, "This makes no difference to our plans."

"Will you send a team after your brother?"

The general shook his head. "Mason's fate was sealed forty years ago. He is already dead, or dying. We will not see each other again."

He thought of his family, his wife and three boys, now living safely far in the west, guests of an old king who ruled a windswept isle coveted by no one. He had last seen Anna nine years before, and it was more than twenty since he had last walked the mountains of his native land. Petrus had been conquered, ravished, by the City a century before and Hayden and his brother were born and raised in the high, forbidding eyries of tribesmen who had no interest in who owned the nation of Petrus, only defending their own high passes and mountaintops with a ferocity which had convinced the City to leave them alone. Thirty, nearly forty years ago the City armies had started leaving the land, first leaving a strong military presence, then a string of garrisons, and finally quitting for good. The Petrassi, those few who remained, had to fight for their land all over again, were still fighting, with waves of invaders who swept down from the colder, grimmer countries of the far north, lured by Petrus' green plains and rich river valleys.

The general looked at young Tyler, slouched comfortably in a chair, the empty wine glass drooping from his fingers. He asked him something he had never asked before, for to even speak the words seemed like tempting fate.

"What will you do when our wars are over?"

The aide looked up, and Hayden realised he was no longer a young man, but middle-aged, with gaunt cheeks and clouded eyes.

"I will stay with you, general."

"And if I dismiss you?"

"I have nowhere else to go."

"Will you not return to Petrus?"

"I cannot return there for I have never set foot there. I have fought in more countries than I can remember, but not in Petrus. And I have no family that I know of. There will be no one to welcome me home, nor home to go to."

T he warriors of the Thousand looked identical in their black and silver armour. After a while Indaro started to believe she was killing the same soldier over and over again. When a woman leaped up the stairs to meet her, over the bodies of her friends, Indaro was almost relieved. The woman was tall, but she was still half a head shorter than her comrades. She had fierce blue eyes and a livid scar across one cheek.

"Woman," Broglanh muttered from her right, telling Indaro he'd noticed, though his eyes never moved from his own opponent, a black-bearded giant. Indaro knew what he was thinking. The woman soldier, with her shorter reach, would need to move closer to get to Indaro, and would be an easy target for Broglanh's sword if Blackbeard gave him a half a moment.

Indaro and Broglanh had the advantage in this battle in every way but one. They had the height, two or three stairs above the defenders, and they were not impeded by the dead bodies of their friends, or indeed by the live bodies of comrades pressing forward behind them. Indaro realised the defenders were losing their discipline in their eagerness to get at them.

Their problem was that they were both weary beyond reason, Indaro especially. Her mouth was filled with dust, her eyes with grit, and her body ached all over. She was finding it hard to keep her focus and had already suffered two more minor injuries to the arms as well as the wound in her side.

The woman warrior snarled and lanced her sword towards Indaro's neck. Indaro swayed, then took an extra step back as if unbalanced. The woman pressed forward and lunged at her belly, knee bent, arm extended. In the instant Broglanh swapped his sword to his left hand and thrust it under the woman's armour where it gaped at the back of her shoulder. At the same time Indaro stepped neatly behind Broglanh's stretched body and brought her own sword down two-handed on Blackbeard's helm. The big man sagged at the knees. Broglanh stepped back and, with a grunt of satisfaction, beheaded him. The armoured corpse toppled backwards, and Indaro kicked the injured woman down the stairs. She and Broglanh moved downwards two more steps. They glanced at each other. Indaro felt a surge of energy course through her.

Then, from behind, came the sound they had anticipated with dread: the pounding of a mailed fist on the great doors. Indaro knew the piled corpses would not keep them closed for more than a few moments.

"They're coming!" she said urgently to Broglanh.

"I hear them," he said, lashing his sword across an opponent's face.

She glanced over the edge of the staircase to her left. They were close enough to the floor now to jump without breaking their legs, but dozens of warriors down there were waiting for them, swords at the ready. She heard a ripple of excitement. The Thousand knew this fight was nearing an end.

"Whatever we're going to do, let's do it fast!" Broglanh muttered, parrying a lancing sword-thrust.

"When the doors open, we'll go back up. Try and fight our way out."

He looked grim, as well he might. If they turned and ran back up the stairs they would have a few seconds' head start on the warriors below them. If there were more than three or four at the doors they would be caught between the two groups and cut down like dogs. They heard the groan of the doors opening.

"Now!" she cried, and they both turned and leaped back up the staircase. They had fought their way halfway down and, as they raced up again, side by side, the soldiers of the Thousand shouted and cursed behind them.

It was as she feared; the great doors were half open and warriors in black and silver were pouring through. She and Broglanh were stuck in the middle, and death or capture was certain. Should they let themselves be taken?

"Broglanh!" she shouted and he stopped, close to the top of the stairs. If they threw themselves over now they would die from the fall and probably injure a few of the defenders. She opened her mouth to speak.

"Broglanh!" It was a deeper, male voice echoing her own cry. Broglanh stared upwards, amazed.

"Nighthawks! These two are friends. Defend them." The voice was that of an old man, but it was firm and authoritative. It was also familiar, Indaro thought.

Framed between the doors stood a shabby old man, dirty and unshaven and dressed like a beggar. Beside him was a slender child. Around them these new soldiers of the Thousand had stopped at his command. Indaro blinked. Nighthawks? she wondered.

The Nighthawk century, which had overtaken Bartellus and Em in the corridor outside, were heading for the Keep, seeking to rescue Riis. Darius quickly told them who Bartellus was. Then the young soldier turned to him.

"We are all with you, Lord Shuskara. We plan to save our leader, but if you order it, we will kill the emperor first."

A veteran, thin and grizzled, approached Bartellus hesitantly. There was the light of respect in his eyes that Bartellus had not seen for a decade. "My name is Chevia, general," he said. "We fought together at the last battle of Araz. I was with the Pigstickers, the Fourth, in the final valley."

The memory came back to Bart in a vivid flash. "I remember, Chevia," he said. "We holed up in that cave for three long days. We all thought our days were numbered then. How's the hand?"

"Good as new," said Chevia, grinning, showing a hand with just two fingers. He was clearly pleased to be remembered.

"Will you stand beside me this day, soldier? Whatever it brings?"

"Yes, lord." Chevia looked around. "We all will."

There were nods of agreement and a few shouts from among the Night-hawks. As Bartellus looked around them he saw many were men grown old in the service of the City. He felt his eyes prickle and he cursed himself. The last thing they needed now were an old man's tears. He searched for Emly and found her standing beside Darius looking lost.

"Warriors," he said, "this is my daughter Emly. You will guard her as if she were your daughter too, or your sister. Em, keep to the rear and warn us if more soldiers come."

She nodded and he saw the fear lift a little from her eyes for she now had a job to do.

"What's behind these doors, Darius?"

The warrior shook his head. "We are new to this, Shuskara. The Night-hawks have not been into the Keep."

"Dol Salida?" Bartellus had brought him along in the hope that he might aid them, but the urquat master shook his head. Bart had no idea if he was ignorant or just unhelpful.

Surprisingly, Chevia spoke up. "It is called the Hall of Emperors, gen-eral. It is the centre of the Keep. All corridors lead to it. It is a high round room with a winding stair round the walls. At the foot is a doorway made of crystal. It is said to be the entrance to the Immortal's own quarters."

"Good enough," said Bartellus, drawing his sword. "Open the doors."

Men sprang forward and pushed at the doors but found them blocked from the other side. One banged on the carved wood in frustration. More stepped forward to lean on the doors and slowly they groaned open, pushing aside three corpses piled behind. Bartellus stepped through. He was on a wide landing littered only with the dead and his spirits lifted as he realised that the emperor's defences had already been breached. Has Fell been here? he wondered. An enormous stairway spiralled down from his right, circling the great blood-coloured chamber. It too was littered with bodies garbed in black and silver. Halfway down the staircase two warriors were battling sol-diers of the Thousand, who were milling on the steps below them and crowded on the circular floor. As the general stepped forward the pair aban-doned their battle and turned and raced back up the stair. As they came close he saw one was a woman. The other was Evan Broglanh.

Elation rose in him.

"Broglanh!" he shouted, and the warrior halted, looking up at him with astonishment.

The general ordered his men, "Nighthawks. These two are friends. Defend them."

The two weary warriors escaped into the protection of the Nighthawks, who sprang forward willingly to oppose the chasing soldiers.

"Hold!" came a bellowed order from the floor of the hall and the defenders paused. The Nighthawks turned for orders to Bartellus, who nodded. As they watched, swords at the ready, a burly bearded warrior strode up the stairs towards them, stepping over and round the corpses of men and women.

"Where is Fell?" Bartellus asked Broglanh quietly as the warrior approached.

"He was alive when we last saw him. He went through that doorway down there"—he pointed—"hunting the emperor, we guess. We were trying to follow him, to back him up. But there were too many for us."

Bartellus smiled grimly, looking at the corpses piled up on the staircase and the floor below. "Yes," he said, "a very poor show, Evan."

The commander of the Thousand approached them, his dark brows drawn together, his face red.

"We have had enough bloodshed today," he said in a voice like waves dragging pebbles on the beach. "Warriors of the Thousand . . ."

Then, gazing at Bartellus, he stopped, shock and disbelief written on his face.

"Shuskara," he breathed. "Of all men . . ."

And the murmur went round the hall, the name Shuskara passed from mouth to mouth, the susurration echoing off the curved walls until the huge chamber seemed to resound with it. Bartellus let it linger.

Then, "Fortance," he responded, raising his voice so it reverberated off the walls. "It's been many years. Are those children of yours all grown?"

"All but two," Fortance said, sheathing his sword and climbing up to him, still frowning. "And all but two dead in the service of the City."

Bart bowed his head gravely. "We are here to end all that."

Fortance spat on the floor. "By killing my finest warriors, men and women who were once your comrades?" He gazed at Broglanh and his flame-haired companion with venom. For the first time Bartellus realised this was the woman Indaro, whom he'd last seen with Archange in the depths of the Halls. So you *are* the swordswoman you claimed to be, he thought. But even as he watched Indaro slumped to the floor, her head drooping. The general turned away, dismissing her from his mind.

"The City is dying, Fortance," he said. "The war must end. Only the death of the emperor can ensure that. Marcellus is an honourable man. We all know that. He will be a just emperor. He will end the war and save the City."

The old soldier said, "We are the emperor's bodyguard. We do not turn our backs on our duty. One old man with a grudge and a bunch of rebel horsemen will not change our minds. Your men"—he looked around at the Nighthawks contemptuously—"were recruited to defend the emperor too."

"These men," said Bart, "are the true defenders of the City. They are ready to fight for its future . . ."

"By siding with the enemy?" Fortance shouted, his face the colour of oxblood.

"Once the emperor is gone the Blues will withdraw . . ."

"You believe that, you old fool?" Fortance asked in amazement.

"They have no interest in taking the City or killing its people . . ."

"Then why have thousands of our people died today, drowned and washed into the sewers like rats?"

Bart was silent. He had no idea what the man was talking about, and his heart was filled with misgivings. But he kept his face unmoved, and Fortance went on. "And now a Blue army has breached the walls and attacked Barenna and Amphitheatre. And you say they mean us no harm? Have you lost your wits, Shuskara?"

Bartellus was baffled. Nothing in the plan Broglanh had outlined for him had included a mass invasion of the City. He started to wonder if he had indeed lost his mind. But he dragged his thoughts back to their present predicament, ruthlessly ignoring that which he could do nothing about. There were two hundred or more warriors waiting for them on the floor of the hall. He had fewer than a hundred. They could not fight their way through. The defenders could not fight their way out. All Bart and his warriors could do was keep them occupied, and give Fell more time.

He sighed. "Return to your troops, Fortance. We will die on different sides this day."

Chapter 45

Indaro suddenly realised she was sitting on the floor. Surrounded by soldiers who seemed to be on her side, her body had told her it was time to rest. The battle had not started. Bartellus must be reluctant to throw his few troops against a force twice their size, she thought. The grumpy old soldier from the Hall of Watchers, she thought. Who would have guessed I'd see him again?

With an effort she fumbled at the sword-wound in her hip and found it was leaking pale fluid. Its edges were red and angry so she pulled her tunic over it and put it from her mind. There was nothing useful she could do about it. There were other injuries, two gashes on her sword-arm and a shallow cut across the top of her chest. They were all bleeding freely and her clothes were saturated and sticky. When she'd had a rest she'd staunch the bleeding then go and find Fell. She closed her eyes and realised her head was pounding. Had she been hit on the head? Probably. Suddenly she jerked forward and vomited on the floor.

A hand held out a waterskin to her and she took it, gulping the warm water. It came straight back up again.

"Sorry," she muttered, "waste of water."

"Just sip it. It will sit better," the girl said.

Indaro looked up. She wondered who this child was. She was no warrior, obviously. She was tiny and pretty, with a heart-shaped face which was familiar. Indaro guessed she belonged to the palace, or to one of the warriors.

"I'm Emly," the girl whispered. "We met in the Halls. You gave me food."

Indaro racked her muddled brains. "I remember," she lied. "What are you doing here?"

"I am with Bartellus. And Evan."

"Evan Broglanh?" Indaro asked, totally confused now.

On cue, Broglanh crouched down beside her. Even in her feeble state Indaro recognised the adoring glance the girl gave the warrior. Ahh, she thought. Poor little girl.

Broglanh was unceremoniously rummaging through Indaro's clothing searching for wounds. He found the deep one in her hip and frowned, and leaned forward, sniffing it. They both knew it was bad. He cleaned it with water and peered at it again.

"Have you still got that pigging useless salve?"

She shook her head. "Everything we had washed away. We had a bit of trouble getting here," she added. "While you and Fell were strolling in the front door." Broglanh stuffed clean bandage into the wound on her chest then stood and took something from the hem of his stained and dirty jerkin.

"Here. Take this." He was holding out a round black pill covered with fluff.

"No," she said, grimacing. "What is it?"

"Poison pill."

She glared at him. "You want to poison me?"

"It's a Buldekki thing," he explained irritably. Broglanh hated explaining anything. "Two pills will kill you, but one will put you in a long sleep. You can lie down in one of the empty rooms. They're all abandoned. You'll wake up feeling better."

Or dead, she thought. She shook her head. "I have to find Fell. And there's a battle to fight."

"You can't even stand up. What are you going to do, bite their legs?"

"If I have to." She leaned her head back against the wall and gazed around. She looked at Bartellus then at the child and her memory took her back to the Hall of Watchers.

"Emly!" she whispered, suddenly remembering the little girl she'd clothed a hundred years before.

"Yes?" The girl bent towards her, thinking she wanted something.

Indaro wanted to show she remembered her, but she could think of nothing to say. She saw Broglanh and the child exchange glances. They thought she was losing it.

"Indaro." The space around her became crowded as Bartellus knelt down to speak to her. Broglanh pulled Emly away.

"Indaro, you are everything you said you were," the old man told her. "I regret my harsh words to you when last we met."

This sounded like a speech of farewell. Indaro had heard plenty of them before. Had given a few.

"I'm not dying," she said, though her head was muddled and she was having trouble holding on to consciousness. "I'll recover. I always recover."

"You did magnificently to get this far," Bartellus told her. He leaned forward urgently. "This way is barred to us. We need to get to the emperor by another route. Do you know the way?"

She shook her head, only taking in the first of his words. "I didn't get us this far," she argued. "It was the boy Elija."

She wanted to mention Fell, to tell the old man the warrior had been here and that they must follow him, but she couldn't speak. She closed her eyes and darkness claimed her.

Fell Aron Lee was chasing down a winding stone stairway, following the emperor, following the reek of him. The crumbling stair became narrow and low, but the walls were lit by an eerie luminescence the soldier had never seen before. It was pale green, the colour of a drowned corpse. Fell did not question it. It helped him, for he had no torch, and he did not wish to think what caused it. He ran on down until he felt he was in the deepest bowels of the City.

Why isn't this underwater, a part of his brain wondered. Far above there was water lying everywhere. Here it was mostly dry. But the rest of his brain didn't care. He knew the emperor was ahead—there was nowhere else he could have gone, no exits, no side tunnels. And eventually Fell would catch him, and this time he would make sure the creature was dead.

He was drowning.

He was falling through deep water, his body twisting in the strong currents. This is the way to die, he thought, not in the screaming agony of shattered bones, torture, gangrene. Just calm and peaceful, dropping away, giving up, letting go.

There seemed to be no bottom and as he fell the pressure on him increased, leaning on his chest like a drunken whore. He started to feel panic, and he moved his limbs, trying to escape the weight, to find that peaceful place again. His head began to ache and his lungs felt ready to burst. He was holding his breath. Why was he holding his breath?

He was drowning.

Fell surged up out of the water, frantically pushing a dead weight off his chest. He gulped in great draughts of air, then he was choking and spluttering, for the air was thick and noisome and tasted like spoiled meat. He coughed and spat in the water. He was sitting waist-deep in blackness. He felt stone underneath and slimy water around him, and the filthy taste of the air told him he was in a sewer. He scrambled up, trying to get as far from the foul water as possible.

He was mystified. *How did I get to this place?* He shook his head to clear it, but the thick miasma pressing down on him dulled his thoughts. He had been running down a long stone stair. It seemed to go on forever. He must have fallen, cracked his head, or been attacked. He could not remember. He bent down and groped in the water for his sword, and found it. Strength coursed through him.

His eyes were getting used to the dark and he could see the alien luminescence on the walls which had guided his way. He peered at it and put his hand to it gingerly but it was soft and disgusting and it moved under his palm like something alive. He snatched his hand away, shuddering, and looked around for the way out.

Something shifted stealthily nearby and he drew his sword on the instant, fear rising in his throat. Moving his head back and forth, seeking shapes in the gloom, he finally saw a deeper darkness in the grey around him. He blinked the grease from his eyes.

He drew in his breath as he saw a man, a creature, lying half in the water only a few paces from him. In the dim light it looked like an old man dressed in rags, with a long beard, and wispy hair plastered to his balding head. He seemed to be stuck to the wall behind him by thick ropes of slime which glistened like the walls. Fell felt his stomach revolting. The man lifted his hands to him in supplication and Fell took a step forward. The light thickened and now he could see the man was ancient, his face deeply lined and sagging like warm wax. The bands of thick mucus seemed to be extruding from his body, holding him to the walls and the stone floor beneath.

There was a separate, sticky movement in the darkness and Fell could make out a second shape clinging closely to the creature's side. It was a beast, a dog maybe, with big eyes and fangs which showed as it opened its mouth at Fell, hissing or snarling. The soldier saw it wore a thick collar which glistened in the dim light. It raised its head and licked the decaying face of its master. Then it turned and stared farther into the gloomy lair. Fell followed its gaze and saw another soldier, in the uniform of the Thousand, lying drowned in the water. The gods help him, he thought.

The old man made a wet, gargling sound and Fell realised it was trying to say his name. *Fell.*

"What do you want from me?" he asked, and he heard the terror sharpening his voice.

As the creature moved it made a sucking sound, as if something under the water was giving way. Fell stepped back, revolted.

Then "Help me," it said, quite distinctly.

Fell stood, hopelessly conflicted. He believed he should kill this thing and it was lying vulnerable before him. But he was overwhelmed with pity. Whatever it was it was in pain, or crippled in some way. He should step forward and pierce it through, release it from its misery, but he could not even do that. He recalled his dream, the weight on his chest and he wondered if the creature had been crawling on him as he lay unconscious and he shuddered, forcing down black bile.

He raised his sword.

"Fell," a new voice spoke clearly behind him, and it was like a cool breeze on a sweltering day.

"Araeon cannot harm you and you cannot harm him. Come."

He swung round. Marcellus Vincerus stood at his side, as if he had always been there. Fell saw he was unarmed. He was gazing at the creature with what might have been compassion. Then he said again, "Come this way." He showed the warrior his back and stepped through an archway in the darkness. And Fell sheathed his sword and followed him.

Fell trailed after Marcellus up a flight of winding stairs. Were these the same steps he came down? No, these were torchlit, wider and higher. They climbed, it seemed, for hours. Marcellus had no trouble climbing and he moved before Fell with all the strength of a much younger man. Fell was tired, and he found it hard to keep up and he wondered when the staircase would end. He realised he was hungry and tried to remember when he had last eaten.

Nevertheless he felt calm and at peace, a peace he had never felt in his life before. He knew now that Mason was right: Marcellus would be a good emperor; he would restore the City to its past grandeur. And the creature below, he was just a sad, demented old man who could no longer rule. He would die soon, or be killed. It would be a mercy. Fell considered going back down again and killing him, but he was drawn upwards by the charisma of Marcellus. Daylight started to filter in from somewhere above, and he could hear the distant sounds of battle. He thought fondly of Indaro and Broglanh and Garret and all the others who were fighting so valiantly. It would soon be over and then there would be peace.

As he stepped up and up towards the light, he thought he had never been so happy.

When at last they reached the top Fell saw it was morning. The sun was rising in grandeur into a sky of summer blue. He was on a high tower, square-sided and floored with old timber. The walls were crenellated with pale brick. In the centre of the wooden floor was a strange glass building. Fell walked over to it. He could see it had once been a pyramid, but much of the glass was broken, and that which remained was mossy and dark.

Fell peered inside and saw Marcellus already standing there, one hand on a metal device bolted to the floor. It was a tall shaft, tall as a man, with a metal tube attached to the top on a hinge. Fell had no idea what it was for. He stepped inside, his boot crunching on broken glass, and Marcellus glanced up.

"This is an observatory," he explained. "We would watch the stars from here."

"Why?"

"Did you never lie at night and watch the stars revolving above you and wonder about them?"

"I never wondered about them, for they never change and my wondering would achieve nothing."

Marcellus smiled. "How very pragmatic of you, Fell." He looked up. "Did you know that the moon is receding, getting smaller and more distant?"

Fell shrugged. He neither knew nor cared.

"When I first came here the moon dominated the sky. Now it is fleeing, heading for the dark and the cold."

He stepped out into daylight again and walked to the south side of the tower. Fell followed him and together they gazed down. Beyond the many towers and minarets of the palace they could see the City spread out before them. In the south much of it was destroyed, walls crumbled and buildings fallen. Fell could see no bodies from this height, but a thick glaze of mud lay over everything. He frowned, baffled but not perturbed. Something about this was not right, but he could not say what.

Marcellus was watching him. "Ah," he said, "you did not know of this. I am glad."

"What happened here, lord?"

"Your friends destroyed the high dams and flooded the City. Thousands died yesterday, drowned, and thousands more will die today of their injuries. The palace itself is collapsing from the lowest levels up."

He pointed. "Out there in the south is an army of twenty thousand Blues. They have breached the wall yet they are holding position, waiting for something. What are they waiting for, Fell?"

Fell shook his head. "I know nothing of this."

"What *do* you know?"

"My part was to kill the emperor," Fell told him, happy to be of help.

"Two assassins," said Marcellus, raising his brows. "Two invasions. Double redundancy."

He thought for a while, then said, "A two-pronged attack is a basic of battlefield strategy. You know that. More subtle, and far more difficult to execute is the three-fold attack. But I have never seen this four-fold strategy except on the urquat board. I guess the mastermind behind the plan is an urquat player." He seemed to be speaking to himself, but Fell nodded politely. "Not Hayden Weaver. He is a fine general. Only he has the authority to bring an army within reach of their hated enemy and to hold them there without attacking. Yet he is not a man of subtlety. Who is the source of this plan?"

Fell was grateful to have a question he could answer. "Mason," he said.

Marcellus shook his head. "I have already spoken to Mason Weaver. He is filled with bile and would have slaughtered every man in the City if he had half a chance. He knows more about this grand scheme than you do, yet he does not know whose idea it was to betray the diversionary army. That was the part of the scheme—such a ruthless part—which nearly caused the emperor's death."

He said, more sharply, "You have been played for a fool, soldier. All of you—Mason, Gil Rayado, your friend Indaro."

Fell didn't care. His role here was ended, and he could tell the lord nothing of any use. He felt calm and at peace.

As they watched together a thin minaret, an elaborately carved spike of green and red marble, leaned drunkenly to one side before falling through a roof below in a crash of stone and tile.

"The foundations of the palace have been compromised," Marcellus explained as the noise drifted away. "The structures which kept the river water and the sewers flowing have been left to rot. My fault. Our fault. Lack of focus. Centuries of decadence. And now the water from the dams is delivering the final blow. The palace will not be habitable for much longer."

He turned to look at the corner of the tower. Fell followed his gaze and saw the shape of a man huddled in the corner. It was Mason. He had last seen him at Old Mountain only days before. Fell was interested but not surprised. Nothing was surprising on this day of days.

They walked over. Mason was gravely wounded but he still lived. His eyes had been put out and blood was leaking from his lids and from his ears and nose. Fell could see the lifeblood pumping weakly from his side, where a slender knife was embedded. One blood-covered hand groped blindly for the blade.

Marcellus knelt, taking the searching hand and guiding it away. "Don't," he said gently. "Don't pull it out." As he gazed at his enemy, Fell saw only compassion in his eyes.

Mason, his face contorted in agony, muttered, "My death is inevitable, Marcellus. I would rather die without a piece of metal lodged under my ribs. Do you really need to prolong this?"

"Mason," said Fell.

The injured man groaned at the sound of his voice. "Fell?" he whispered. "He has you too? Then I am dead already, Marcellus. You have won, as always."

"First," said Fell, crouching down, "tell me the truth." The thrall that held him was waning. His mind started to clear. "You have lied to us from the first, Mason. You owe me the truth, now you are dying and I am soon to die."

Marcellus watched them silently.

"You wanted the emperor dead, as did I," Fell said to the dying man. "You wanted the City destroyed, washed away. That I understand. Your people are dying because of the war. And the City was dying too, although I know that gave you pleasure. But why fool us with the elaborate plan? Did Gil Rayado know? And Saroyan? Did you send them both to their deaths as a diversion?"

"You've seen the powers of these creatures, these Serafim," Mason whispered. "If all the armies of the City and its enemies turned against them, we still could not be sure of killing them. This was our last throw, Fell. If this failed we had nothing left. We had to use everything in our arsenal." He muttered, "Have some perspective."

Marcellus sat back on his haunches. "You have failed," he told Mason. "The City will survive," he said. "The greater part of it is untouched. The palaces on the Shield will ride out the storm. The last Families will be watching with interest. Araeon had many enemies among them, but none would move against him. He was their brother. Now they will rally and sally out and descend on your armies. There will be more death and more suffering, but the City will survive. It always has."

"You were ready to destroy the whole City in the hope of killing one man?" Fell asked Mason. "You would tear down a house to kill a single rat?"

"Petty selfish people," Marcellus said, standing and gazing at the sky. "You never see beyond your own small needs and passions."

"My sister," Marcellus said, turning to Fell. "Whom you call Archange."

Fell frowned. He remembered the tall woman who had defended the hostages in the trial so many years ago. Indaro danced across his thoughts again. She knew Archange, had worked with her. What has she got to do with this? he wondered.

"Mason once loved my sister," explained Marcellus. "And she loved him, in her way. He was a young soldier then, of the Petrassi nobility. They were not our enemies in those days. She married him, against our entreaties."

"They were determined to have me killed," said Mason weakly. "They call us primitives."

Marcellus looked at him sadly. "If we had wanted you dead, you would have died then. It would have been better if you had. For the City and all its enemies. It was one of many mistakes we made.

"He was exiled from the City, and from Petrus too. He could not sell his sword in any land in his own name. He lost his woman, his family, and his name. He has spent forty years plotting his revenge for this slight."

Mason bared his teeth. "The taste is sweet on my tongue," he said.

"He loved a goddess," Marcellus said to Fell as if it explained everything. "It is a dreadful fate. He could never recover from that."

"She loved me," whispered Mason, his voice failing. Fell's practised eye saw he had only moments to live.

Marcellus sighed. "We all loved you," he replied. "You blame us, but everything we did was out of love."

Mason seemed to rally a little and blood dripped from his mouth. "Our lands are barren and the fields reek with the smell of corpses. A million men and a generation of young women have died under the swords of our enemy. The City is populated only by children and crones, and old maimed men living lives of misery. Is this how the gods show their love?"

Marcellus gazed off into the distance, apparently adrift in his own thoughts, and he did not answer. For a long time the only sound was of Mason's weak, whistling breath. Then it stopped. Marcellus knelt and felt for the beat at the base of the man's throat. "He is dead," he said.

Chapter 46

Em had been sitting on the floor holding the dying woman's hand. The gesture meant more to her, she guessed, than it did to Indaro, who seemed unaware of her presence. The hand was lifeless and cold, although from time to time the girl could detect a low, slow beat of life force deep beneath the skin. Emly felt numb, exhausted beyond movement. All her hope, her ambition, had been to free her sick father from the dungeon. Now that man had changed beyond recognition. Dead-eyed, she'd watched him move with a purpose, striding back and forth on the wide landing, survey-ing the activities of the enemy warriors below, consulting with his troops, giving orders. He was garbed in armour, a breastplate and sword-belt. She did not know him any more. Evan stayed at his side, his eyes on the general, listening, advising. He had not glanced at her. She felt adrift and alone.

But then Bartellus had crouched down to speak to Indaro, glancing at Em with a small smile which warmed her heart a little. And Indaro said the one word which brought Emly's soul back to life.

"Elija."

"Elija was with you?" Bartellus asked, surprised, and Indaro nodded. "Broglanh, did you know this?" he asked the soldier. Evan shook his head.

"Where is he?" Emly asked her urgently. "Is he alive?"

"Injured," Indaro muttered. She gestured at the doors behind them. "Back there."

She seemed to be losing consciousness again. The girl resisted the im-pulse to shake her. "Where? Was he badly hurt?" she asked.

"Broken arm," the woman told her, her eyes closed.

"Where? Where is he?" Em asked her. Then, "Please, Indaro."

The woman frowned. There was a long, frustrating pause, and she opened her eyes, her eyes like flowers. "Back there," she repeated, with cer-tainty although her voice was weak. "Up the sloping corridor. Up the stone stairs. Keep the green wall on your left . . . I mean, the right. Take the first, no . . . the second, on the right. The corridor has a white marble floor and a blue ceiling. The room," she hesitated, remembering, "the room is on the right, carved doors, near a fountain with dolphins. I told him to hide."

Em jumped up, her lethargy blown away like smoke in a breeze. "I'll find him," she told her father. She snatched up a half-empty waterskin lying on the floor then looked around for something to defend herself with.

Bartellus took her by the arm and she thought he was going to stop her, but all he said was, "I can send no one with you."

"I'll be better on my own," she reassured him, although it was not true. Evan handed her a long-bladed knife and she stuck it in the waist of her trousers, scarcely noticing him now. She took a deep breath.

"Be quick," her father said. "The palace is collapsing. If you find him come back here if you can. The Keep is the oldest part of the building. It might be the safest."

Em looked down at the hundreds of armoured warriors, and she thought the Hall of Emperors was the most perilous place she had ever been in, but she merely nodded, thinking only of her brother. If she discovered him and he was still alive, then she would decide what to do.

Bart clasped her to him for a moment. "Good luck, little soldier," he whispered, then he let her go and turned back to his troops.

Em ran up the corridor, glad to be doing something. Immediately she saw the stone stairs winding upwards. She ran up them, her hand on the knife in her waistband. At the top she followed the hallway, keeping the green marble wall to her right, as instructed. It was a long corridor, curving round. She crept along nervously, her eyes darting about, fearing more soldiers. She saw no one, although she could hear the distant sounds of battle, cries and shouts.

She paused, listening. Something was coming. Something terrifying. She felt her limbs suddenly start to shake and her heart start panicking in her breast. She looked around but there was nowhere to hide, only blank walls stretching away in each direction. She moaned and her legs started to give way.

A young man, tall and fair, dressed in green, appeared around the curve of the corridor. He was younger than she and he looked, if anything, more scared. Em felt her fear drift away. Was this boy frightened of the unnamed thing too? She walked towards him and they passed each other, each sticking to one side of the corridor, eyeing each other uncertainly. Em considered speaking but the young man said nothing, only watched her as she passed. His eyes were dark as pitch, she saw. Then she was past and she hurried on.

She passed one corridor on her right, and took the second. She found herself not in a corridor with a blue ceiling, but facing a pile of debris where part of the building had collapsed. It had happened recently, for dust hung thickly in the air and it was hard to see past it. Emly could see the light of day streaming in above. She picked her way over the stones and masonry, peering ahead, trying to see if she could get past the heaped debris. Something moved under her foot and she stopped, listening to the sound of shifting stone and sifting dust. The air cleared a little and ahead of her she could see a gaping hole where the falling roof stones had shattered the floor and fallen right through. She crept up to it, placing her feet with care. Peering over the lip of the hole she could see that several floors beneath her had given way. Water, black and threatening, roiled far beneath.

She looked ahead. On the other side of the fall the corridor continued, and she could see the blue ceiling Indaro had spoken of. She had to go this way. There was a broken ledge clinging precariously to the wall. She could walk along it. It was quite wide. But as she made her decision a drunken pillar on the far side of the hole tottered and collapsed, bringing down with it more of the ceiling. She crouched, covering her head, fearing the rest of the roof would give way, and she heard the crash and splash as it plummeted into the water.

As the dust subsided she stood and stepped forward, placing her feet carefully. She edged her way along the ledge, testing each footfall, finding small handholds in the stone wall beside her, hardly daring to breathe. She took one quick glance down into the hole, glimpsing pale bodies in the water. On firmer ground again she moved more quickly, finally leaping from the ledge onto the marble floor of the corridor.

She hurried on, assessing each door she passed. Many were carved. She looked for the dry fountain Indaro had mentioned, but could not see it. She wondered if it was destroyed in the roof fall. Then she spotted it. She had been expecting a large fountain such as in a public square. But, of course, this was a small drinking fountain set in the wall, with three stone dolphins leaping over it. She looked around eagerly. There were several carved doors nearby. She ran to the first, pushing the doors, hearing the grate of dust and grit as they opened and peering around them.

"Elija," she whispered. Then louder, "Elija!"

It was a bedchamber, furniture covered with ghostly white cloths, dust lying thickly on the floor. Her voice echoed emptily. No one had entered there in years. She ran to the next room, then the next. She looked back along the corridor. The water fountain was nearly out of sight. What had Indaro said? The room was on the right? Which right? Her right? Em ran back to the fountain, then to a pair of carved doors set deep in a dark recess. She pushed them open. They moved silently.

Inside was a scene of frozen carnage and for a moment her heart seemed to judder to a halt. Bodies of armed men were strewn on the floor and on the bloodflecked furniture. The odours of blood and excrement were pungent in the air. Em put her hand to her mouth. She guessed she had found the right place, but could anyone still be alive in here?

"Elija?" she whispered.

There was a groan from her left, and she flinched as she saw an armoured arm move. Her breathing shallow, she forced her legs to take her to him and she found a dying warrior, half his head hacked away but still alive, still moving. She backed away, then dragged her eyes from the suffering man.

"Elija!" she called.

Desperately her eyes searched the room. Most of the bodies were at one end. In that corner was an upturned table. She crept over to it, nervously stepping round corpses, unwilling to climb over them for fear that one might come alive and grab her.

She peered over the edge of the table. In the corner was the figure of a man, unarmoured, tall yet thin and frail, lying with one arm held in the other hand. His dark head was sunk on his breast. He did not look like a soldier. Was he dead or asleep? She edged round the table. She knelt down and peered at the smudged, dirty face. She saw nothing in it she recognised. She sighed and stood, looking around her, uncertain where to go next.

At the sound the man moved, as if shifting in his sleep. He clutched his arm and moaned quietly. Em's heart leaped.

"Elija?" she asked hesitantly.

She touched his good shoulder. "Elija?"

His eyes opened and there was a flash of fear in his face as he looked up at her, and in that moment she knew him. Joy flooded her and she knelt beside him, trying to take him in her arms, to hold him close to her, to comfort him.

"Emly?"

He looked up at her, disbelief in his eyes. Then hesitant recognition became certainty, and her brother burst into tears.

The battlefield seemed to go on forever. It was old, ancient, its thousands upon thousands of corpses just dry husks, dusty with age, their torment muted and softened by ages, by the wind and rain. There were no colours, for their blood had long-since dried and blown away. Even the insects, the beetles and flies and their maggots, had taken their fill and departed. Centuries before.

The only sounds were the warm wind from the south soughing through a jutting ribcage, flapping an odd scrap of dried cloth, sifting sand sibilantly across corroding metal plate.

And footsteps, gritty on the parched ground.

Her boots had been old when she first set out. They wouldn't last her much longer. She watched, head bowed, as each one came into view, then slipped away, left, right, left, right. Each toe had once boasted an embossed figure—a snake and a scorpion. Where had they gone? Then she remembered these weren't her boots; they had belonged to some nameless woman, her carcase ripped by the weapons of men and then used by wild creatures for food and shelter. Only her boots remained intact, their surface scoured by sand. Indaro had wrestled them off, then knocked them out, treading on the huge centipede that wriggled from one of them. They fitted fairly well. She had walked a long way in them.

She was aware that someone was walking beside her. She feared it was Maccus Odarin and she turned her head away for she did not want to see him stumbling along on the rotten leg, did not want to see him die again.

"Where are we going?" her companion asked cheerfully.

With relief she realised it wasn't Maccus, and she looked round.

"Where are we going?" Rubin asked. His hair was longer than she remembered and she was shocked to see there were grey streaks in the red. How old was he, eighteen, twenty? She was troubled that she couldn't remember her brother's age, couldn't even remember if he was older or younger than her.

Now it was her father, Reeve, walking beside her. He was saying, "Vincerus, Sarkoy, Broglanh, Gaeta, Khan, and Kerr. Remember these names. They are your past and your future. They are your enemies."

She had heard these words often as a child.

"They all fear Sarkoy and Vincerus," her father went on, staring down, watching puffs of dust spurt up from the soil. "But only the Gaetas know the true power of the veil."

She woke with a start. The dream took a while to drift away, then she realised she should probably get up. But time passed, and still she found she was slumped on the floor. She pulled herself up to sit straighter against the wall. The wound in her side had stopped hurting. That's either a very good or a very bad sign, she thought.

The battle had started again. She could hear the clash of swords and shields, the agonising grunts of pain, shouts of encouragement, exultation and horror. She could smell fresh blood, and it was no longer hers. Men were milling around on the landing in front of her. She watched legs passing back and forth—legs clad in metal greaves and armoured kilts, legs in leather trousers, some in cotton or linen, some naked and hairy. She found herself counting them automatically, then stopped. It was not her job to count the toll. She wondered that there were no women among the warriors. She was the only one, it seemed. Then she remembered the Nighthawks were previously a cavalry unit. The City had few women riders. They weren't considered skilful enough to ride and fight at the same time. Only skilful enough to be butchered in the infantry lines.

She rubbed dirt from her eyes. Legs clad in silk, dark green silk were walking towards her. The silk shimmered in the hectic torchlight, and she wanted to reach out and feel the weight of it, touch the sheen of something other than filthy cotton and wool.

The green-clad figure crouched down to speak to her and she recognised the youngster she had rescued from the wreckage of the emperor's carriage. He was pale and fair. His eyebrows were gracefully arched above dark eyes. One eyelid seemed to droop a little, giving him a lazy air. He was unarmed. He was no more than sixteen.

"Do you know who I am?" he asked her.

"I helped you from the Immortal's carriage," she replied, drawing back against the wall. The eyes were black and hot as pitch.

"Did you know who I was then?"

"No," she answered, rendered stiff by his sinister proximity. She no longer had a weapon with her. And she noticed for the first time that she stank like a week-old corpse. She looked around but the milling soldiers seemed oblivious to the newcomer.

He nodded. "Nevertheless, your intention was noble. So I will not kill you today.

"You are injured," he noted. "Are you dying?"

"No."

"No," he agreed, "you are probably not. You are Indaro Kerr Guillaume, and I really ought to kill you." He seemed undecided.

Indaro's eyes flickered across the floor seeking a weapon. There was a discarded shield an arm's-length away. She could defend herself with it, kill him with it. He looked so delicate, his arms and legs thin and bony. But somehow she could not move, and he stood and walked away. She wanted to cry out a warning, but no one would hear her in the racket of battle. And he was just a boy. So she watched him gliding across the floor, weaving his way among the armed men, unnoticed by the warriors, as if invisible. He disappeared down the stairs.

Bartellus stood watching the battle from his vantage point on the high landing. The Nighthawks were attacking the Thousand with renewed fury. They were ferocious fighters, only recently returned from three years in the field, he'd been told. Bart remembered riding with the First Adamantine decades before . . .

"General," Broglanh urged, "let me get in there." It was not the first time he'd asked. He was crackling with energy, and Bart knew it was physically painful for the warrior to be doing nothing while men were fighting and dying paces away.

"I need you with me," he grunted. He glanced at the warrior. "That's an order."

It was ironic. Evan Broglanh knew better than anyone that he was just a tired old man, the rags of the prisoner still sticking out from under his shiny armour. Broglanh had spent the last few weeks protecting him, dragging him from one unsafe place to another, cajoling him when he was desolate, forcing him to eat sometimes. He had been bodyguard, nursemaid and son to him. Now he was dutiful lieutenant and they both knew he would not shatter the fragile illusion of Shuskara's authority by going against his orders. So Broglanh waited at his side, and fumed.

Bart watched the crystal doorway far below. It was hours now since Fell had disappeared. There was no reason to think he was still alive. There was no reason to think he wasn't. All the general could do was to keep the Thousand occupied. He did the sums over and over in his head. Three centuries of the bodyguard were out of the City, thanks to Saroyan's last act. Indaro had estimated that Gil Rayado's army had disabled the better part of a century. There must be two hundred or more dead in this chamber. Some would have been lost in the flooding and the palace collapse. Whichever way you looked at it they were running out of men. So far none of the common soldiery had been drafted in to take them on. Why not? Did the emperor and the brothers not trust them? Bart had no idea.

A wave of weariness passed through him. He wanted very much to sit down. But he forced his knees to lock and his back to straighten and he looked on grimly as brave men died. The Nighthawks had battled their way down the staircase back to the point where Broglanh and Indaro had been when he first saw them. For the loss of forty or so of their number. Suddenly Bart was overwhelmed with the desire to wade down in among them and add his blade to the battle. He had done all he could do. It would be an honourable end. He hefted his sword and opened his mouth to speak to Broglanh.

Then a cry came from the doors behind him, where injured men were stationed to watch the corridor.

"They're coming, general!"

He swung round, old blood surging, as fresh warriors appeared. Broglanh leaped joyfully to the attack. Bartellus shouted an order and half the Nighthawks on the stairs turned and raced back up. As he waded into the fray Bartellus saw even Indaro had levered herself painfully from the floor.

One of the newcomers broke through the first defence and launched himself at the general. Bart raised his heavy sword and parried the blow, feeling the jolt through his body, stumbling back under its power. As he fell to one knee the attacker raised his sword for a killing blow and Bart, with an agonised grunt, thrust his blade up under the man's breastplate. The warrior fell and Bart climbed to his feet and hacked at the man's throat until he was dead.

He looked round. The position was hopeless. The warriors on the floor below, hearted by the reinforcements, were forcing their way back up the stairs and the Nighthawks seemed to have lost the power to stop them. On the landing more armoured men were trying to get in and the weary defenders were barely holding the line.

Then there was a shouted order, repeated, echoing round the walls of the circular chamber, and suddenly their opponents backed off. The new warriors started retreating again, in good order, through the great doors. None of the exhausted defenders had the energy or the will to follow them. Bart looked to Broglanh, who stood, sword dripping gore, looking baffled. He returned the look, eyebrows raised. *What new ploy is this?* his gaze asked. The warriors of the Thousand pulled the high doors closed behind them and they heard the hollow grinding of some mechanism as they were locked.

Bartellus looked down. The Thousand were streaming away through the crystal doorway, leaving a floor covered with corpses and blood. The surviving Nighthawks looked bewildered as they watched the backs of the disappearing warriors.

"Why are they leaving?" he asked Broglanh, but the warrior was already racing down the staircase. Fell, the general thought.

But then Broglanh slowed and stopped. Bartellus saw his eyes were on the crystal doorway where a lone man had appeared, dark-haired and slender, in the livery of the Thousand. He stepped forward gracefully, looking around with interest. He gazed up to the high landing, straight into the general's eyes.

Only then did Bart recognise Rafe Vincerus, and horror froze his soul. All hope drained from him, replaced by black despair. How had he ever thought he could beat these people?

A low buzzing started in his ears, and swiftly a sharp pain started up at the base of his skull. Now he knew why all the warriors had been ordered away. Rafe planned to kill everyone in the chamber. Forcing his feet to move, he tottered to the edge of the landing. He opened his mouth but something like an incoherent squawk came out.

"Shuskara!" Rafe cried.

He must have been surprised, caught off-guard, for the pain receded and Bart managed to speak a word. "Coward!"

Then he cried, "You lower yourself by using your evil magics on fine warriors, Rafe."

Rafe raised his voice. "So, Shuskara, you have finally emerged from your burrow. We guessed we would see you before the end. Marcellus predicted this day's work was down to you."

"Face me like a man, Rafe, not some cheap conjuror."

"Gladly, traitor!" Rafe bent and grabbed a sword from a dead man's grip, then he ran across the chamber floor and leaped up the stairs, bounding lightly over the black and silver corpses, past his injured warriors and those of the enemy. He had the strength and agility of a man of twenty summers and Bart knew he could not stand against him for more than moments. Despite this the old man's heart swelled with determination. If he could give his troops a reprieve from this demon's spells then perhaps . . . Perhaps what, Bart? he thought. In his heart he knew that for him there was no good ending to this day.

Rafe reached the wide landing and paused, addressing his opponent formally with his sword. Then he lunged, his blade aimed at Bart's belly. Bartellus swayed awkwardly and the tip of the sword veered off his leather belt. He brought his blade down on Rafe's neck. But he was far too slow. The warrior parried the blow easily then slashed at Bart's legs. Bartellus felt a searing agony and he almost toppled backwards. He stumbled back a pace. He felt sweat break out all over and his heart raced. Stay upright, he ordered his body. If you fall you are dead. Rafe grinned and slashed the air with the borrowed sword, then came on. Bart knew he was being toyed with. He snatched up an abandoned shield and settled it on his arm.

Rafe shook his head. "You should have stayed in your mouse-hole, old fool."

Bartellus' blade flicked out and caught him on the side of the head. It was a shallow cut but Rafe was annoyed. His face hardened and he attacked in earnest. Bart parried and blocked with desperation and was forced towards the edge of the landing. He stepped back clumsily, staggering above the high drop. His body was failing him, but his mind still worked. He allowed his head to droop. Rafe pressed forward. Bart stumbled towards him. As he had expected Rafe sent a lightning thrust to his belly. Bartellus stepped into it. Ignoring the explosion of agony he slammed his own blade under Rafe's chin, seeking the throat. The warrior's eyes widened with shock and he fell, blood gushing from his neck.

Bartellus stood for a moment, clutching his stomach where blood poured in a mortal stream. The chamber was deathly quiet. His heartbeat and his harsh breathing were the only sounds he could hear. Bart had all the time in the world. He thought of Emly and hoped she had found her brother. And his mind went back to the garden, to the two boys waving in the sunlight.

Then he toppled backwards off the staircase and plummeted to the stone floor far below.

Chapter 47

Indaro stepped up. Rafe Vincerus was not dead, though blood gushed from his throat, and he crouched on the landing holding his hand to his neck seeking to stem the flow. As the woman moved forward a pace he looked up at her and she averted her gaze. *Don't let them look into your eyes,* Mason had told them. Yet it seemed not to help, for her mind felt sluggish, her legs encased in iron.

He was only seven paces away, and Indaro stared at her feet, willing them to move forward. One pace. Two. She risked a look. He had not moved and the blood was still gushing from his neck. He *must* be weakening. She prayed to Aduara that this man, this piece of meat, would spill all his blood as tribute to the goddess. Her head felt stuffed and full; her grip on consciousness was failing. Three paces. Four. She raised her sword.

She cast another glance at her enemy. Incredibly, he was standing now, his own sword-hand raised.

She thought of Stalker and Garret, and all the men and women who had died this day on both sides of the battle. She thought of Bartellus, lying broken on the hall floor. And she thought of Fell. I will not be beaten by this thing, she thought.

She raised her sword in her right hand and Rafe batted it easily aside, and she plunged the knife in her left hand through his eye and into his brain.

On the highest tower high above her Fell and Marcellus turned away from Mason's body and walked to the east of the battlements. Fell turned his face up to the sunlight, feeling its cleansing warmth. His mind was clear. Marcellus' hold over him was gone. They stood together like old friends.

Fell needed to understand. "Who is the man I met in the Hall of Emperors?" he asked.

"That is Araeon, whom you call the Immortal, the emperor."

"Then what was the creature in the dark?"

"Also the emperor."

"He can change his appearance?"

Marcellus shook his head. "You make it sound like a magicker's sleight of hand. He does not put on a false beard. But he can appear different to others' eyes."

"Can you?"

"No, it is Araeon's attribute. And he can create other . . . forms of himself. We all can. Although it takes a great deal of strength and Araeon's has been waning for a long time."

"You *all* can? Who are you all?"

"We are called the Serafim. We came to the City many centuries ago, Araeon and I, and Archange. And many others."

Fell thought about it. Then he said, "Indaro told me she saw the emperor's carriage destroyed by one of the Blues' sorcerous explosions. Yet he lived. Can he be killed?" he asked simply.

"We are not immortal, despite the title. We have blood flowing through us, as you do. We can die, as you can."

"Then . . ."

"The man in the carriage, and the one you saw in the Hall of Emperors, was a reflection. A real and solid reflection, one which lives and breathes, but one which would die if Araeon no longer lived."

Fell had a vision of the emperor in his dark lair, hideously birthing creatures like himself. He shuddered and bile rose in his throat. He vomited on the floor, then wiped his mouth. Afterwards he felt calmer. It was some relief that after all the years of war the floodgates of his feelings had given way. There had been times over the years when he had longed to recover his powers of disgust.

Marcellus was watching him. "It repels you," he commented.

"Of course." Fell asked, "What will happen now?" He gestured. "To the City."

"Your small army has been trapped in the Hall of Emperors. They will be despatched. The Red Palace will be uninhabitable for a long time. So we will retreat to the Shield, to our palace there, the Serafia. Then we will wait to see what Hayden Weaver does. We have plenty of time. We can wait him out. Or we will ally with the remaining Serafim and force him out."

"Remaining Serafim?"

"We have taken on the burden of ruling for too long. It is time for others to take our place."

"Others like you?" Fell said with distaste.

Marcellus chuckled. "Do not judge us, Fell. *You* are not like us, for you are not of the City, but we are not so different from your friends and comrades. We have bred with them for many centuries. Our life force runs strongly in most of the City's people. In fact, we are more like them than *you* are.

"Do you know why the Blues hate us so?" he asked.

Fell grinned sardonically. "Because we destroyed their cities, killed their people and made a desert of their lands?"

"Because we are not like them. People fear those who are different. If you sever the arm of a Blue he stops fighting, and if he is not treated quickly, he dies. It takes more than that to kill a warrior of the City. You must have noticed, in your years as a warrior, how easily the Blueskins die. They are frail creatures, particularly under torture."

"I am one of those frail creatures."

"And you will live, if you survive this day, until you are eighty or so. The people of the City live much longer than that."

"How long?"

Marcellus paused as if to collect his thoughts. "Your friend Shuskara. How old is he?"

Is, Fell thought. Then it is true, Shuskara still lives. He felt determination kindle in his breast again. He said, "I don't know. Seventy?"

"He is over two hundred," Marcellus told him.

Fell shook his head but he could no longer summon the disbelief he once felt.

"And Indaro Kerr Guillaume?" Marcellus said.

"What about her?" Fell asked sharply. "Are you telling me she's three hundred years old?"

Marcellus smiled. "No, she is what she appears to be—a woman in her thirties. I met her when she was a child, so I know.

"Do you not find it remarkable that she has survived years of battle when all around her have died? She recovers from wounds that would kill strong men."

"I have survived longer," Fell replied. "And, as you say, I am not of the City."

"Yes, but you are a commander."

"I lead my troops into battle." He felt he was being judged.

"I am not questioning your courage, Fell. But you are not a common soldier. You are a legend among your warriors. They rally to you, and they love you. And they help keep you safe."

Fell thought of a soldier running up to him with a breastplate, another throwing him a sword in the heat of battle. He admitted to himself it was true.

"What are you saying? That Indaro is one of you, a Serafim?"

"No, I am saying she benefits from the blood of the Families that flows in her veins, as do most of the City's people. Her mother was an offshoot of the Kerr Family which spawned Flavius Randell Kerr, your late unlamented general. Her father Reeve, a Guillaume, is much older than Shuskara. If Indaro survives this day she could live a very long life. She is hard to kill."

"She is a rare woman," Fell said.

"Ah, I see you are fond of her. I would say that these days she is unique."

"She has a brother."

"*Had* a brother. Rubin is dead."

Fell had guessed it, but Marcellus stated it as a fact.

"Do you know everything that happens in the City?" he asked.

"Far from it. For example, I don't know the significance of the branded men. I was hoping you'd tell me."

Fell wondered, Is there any reason not to, now, at the end of all things?

Marcellus said, "Ranul the messenger bore an *S*-shaped brand. As did your friend Riis. I suspect you once had one too."

"Riis is dead?"

"Yes."

"We were hostages together as boys," Fell explained. "Riis and I, and Ranul. And others. The emperor ordered our friend killed, burned alive, in public. His name was Sami."

Marcellus looked at him in wonder. "I never cease to be amazed at the strangeness of you primitives. You and Mason, holding on to rancour over all these years, conspiring to bring down a great City because of personal grudges."

"I was a child," Fell explained. He thought about it and said, "He laughed to see a boy die in agony. Such a creature should not be allowed to live, emperor or beggar."

"Did others in the crowd laugh?"

"Yes. It was an entertainment. That's why they were there."

Then he said, "Tell me about Ranul. How did he die?"

"He tried to kill the emperor and came very close. It was eight years ago. He chose the guise of a Panjali messenger. They are a tribe who live in the arid plains in the far north-east of Odrysia. They keep to the old ways which includes a rigid caste system. Their messengers are holy men, raised from birth to undertake a sacred mission in times of great danger, when the tribe is in peril of its existence. They cannot read or write. Or speak—their tongues are cut out when they reach puberty. Traditionally, the messenger's head is shaved for his mission, a message is tattooed on the scalp and the hair allowed to grow back before the man is sent to a foreign court. The foreign leader then has the head shaved again to reveal the message."

"Ranul chose to have his tongue cut out?" Fell thought about the fat bully he had known, and the depths of hatred and determination which had made him follow such a path.

"It was the authentic touch which brought him into the emperor's presence. He was almost successful."

Fell asked, "How did he die?"

"I don't know. I was not there. He was cunning and he fought bravely, I'm told. But he was gravely injured. He managed to steal a priceless artefact of the Serafim and threatened to destroy it. Araeon allowed him to escape into the sewers with it rather than risk its destruction."

"What was it, this artefact?"

"The Gulon Veil." Seeing Fell's baffled look, Marcellus added, "Seemingly a woman's trifle. In fact an object of great power. Its loss caused Araeon irreparable injury."

"How did Ranul know of it?"

Marcellus' face clouded. "He had inside help."

Fell shook his head. "You value a piece of cloth so highly, yet each year you throw thousands of men and women into an unwinnable battle for an impossible aim. Yet you call *us* strange creatures."

"We are all complex," Marcellus told him with a trace of pride. "Mason said Araeon is evil. He is not, although many of the things he has done were evil. But he is also capable of great kindness, and compassion and, yes, regret. As am I."

"What do you regret, lord?"

Marcellus gazed inward. "Killing the only person who ever loved me completely.

"Mason's words reminded me," he explained, "of something I had long ago forgotten. It was love that kept us here in the City with those who considered us gods. Yet I chose to kill my love to save my own life. Until this hour I had mourned her, and regretted her death, but I saw it as an unfortunate necessity. Now I wonder what my love was worth if I could discard it so easily."

Fell felt cold loathing course through him. Here we are, he thought, standing above a ruined City, and the First Lord is mourning lost love, rather than grieving for all the innocents, men and women and children, and the loyal warriors who had died that day.

"Mason told me he wanted you to succeed Araeon," he said. "He told me you would be a good emperor as emperors go."

Marcellus stared at the floor. Then he shook his head. "He lied," he said. "Mason had many talents, and one of them was his skill at reading men. In you he saw a warrior who believed in the concept of the honourable soldier. Your personal need for vengeance was not enough for you. So he gave you a higher purpose—kill the emperor and replace him with an honourable soldier in his stead."

Marcellus stood silently, head lowered, shoulders slumped. Then he looked up, a hard decision made.

"Is that your only regret?" Fell asked formally. "The death of one woman?"

"It is."

Fell raised his sword and formally Marcellus answered. The two men circled. The duel began with a blistering series of thrusts, parries and ripostes. Fell knew within moments he was outclassed but he remained serene—sure in the knowledge that, no matter what, his blade would find its home in the body of the man he faced. Back and forth across the roof the two warriors fought, their blades flickering in the sunlight. Three times Marcellus' blade nicked Fell's skin, twice on the upper arm, once on the cheek. A trickle of blood dripped to his chin. Marcellus was the better sword master by far, but Fell was fast and agile and his opponent could find no opening for the killing thrust.

"You are a fine swordsman," commented Marcellus pleasantly. A flicker of doubt disturbed Fell's serenity. Could this creature be killed? But he pushed it away and it dropped into the recesses of his mind. His whole existence had been a preparation for this moment, and he allowed a lifetime of training and a thousand battles to do their work.

Marcellus launched another attack. Fell blocked the blade, rolled his wrist and lanced the tip deep into his opponent's right shoulder, slicing through muscle and ligament. The sword fell from his nerveless limb but with uncanny speed Marcellus' left hand caught it before it hit the ground.

Without missing a beat he attacked again. Fell parried then spun away, seeking space and balance. Marcellus followed. His blade lunged towards Fell's throat. He parried it then blocked another cut. Off-balance, he went down on one knee. He dived to his right, rolled and came up just as Marcellus swung his blade in a murderous arc. Two-handed, Fell brought his sword sharply up and sliced through the fingers of Marcellus' left hand. Marcellus cried out and dropped his sword, falling to his knees.

Fell stepped back, breathing heavily, sweat dripping off his face and arms.

Marcellus groped for the blade with his disabled hand, but he could not pick it up. He raised his black gaze to Fell. Fell saw no regret there, no remorse. He spun his blade and threw it with all his might into Marcellus' chest. It pierced deeply and stuck here, quivering. Marcellus groaned in anguish but did not fall. Fell walked over to him, and picked up the other sword.

Marcellus struggled to speak. He threw back his head and roared like a bull in anguish. The sound seemed to rise through his chest from the centre of his heart. He drew a long, gurgling breath. His face was purple but suddenly the colour drained away like water down a pipe. He became still. Fell wondered if he was dead. He bent his head close in. A sound came from Marcellus' lips, and he strained to hear.

Marcellus whispered, "All gods die hard."

Fell nodded. He straightened, swung his blade and sliced off his head. "Not hard enough," he said.

Deep in the bowels of the palace beneath them, in a place beyond torment and horror, Riis still lived.

He should have drowned. He lay submerged but somehow had fallen with his head rammed against a crumbling piece of stone. He moaned as he realised he was alive. His body was in agony, his mind teetering on the brink of sanity.

He could see nothing, but his ears detected a movement nearby and he flinched. The slosh of water was accompanied by a faint hissing sound. Riis tried to move, to pull away, but he was too badly hurt. He lay there in terror, helpless, waiting for the gulon.

A touch as light as a feather on his naked knee and, despite his injuries, he jerked in panic, trying to pull his leg away. His eyes were adapting and by the weak light of the lair he could see the shape close to him, sidling forward up his helpless body. Its breath hissed and he could feel its greasy pelt slithering on his skin. He forced one hand to move and flailed at the beast with it. He felt teeth graze his arm, then a sharp nip as it bit him. Compared with the pain in the rest of his body it was nothing, yet the bite focussed his thoughts and fired his determination. His one good hand grabbed for the beast's snout but it bit him on the arm then retreated out of range. He kicked out at it but missed, and nearly passed out again as pure agony surged through his body. With a colossal effort he dragged himself up a little against the wall, his body screaming, his senses fading. He tried to breathe deeply, to gather his strength.

Time passed and he dozed, woke in a panic of fear, then drifted again. The pain was cradling him like a friend. He knew he was dying and he felt at peace.

Fell bent and picked up the severed head, then flung it with all his strength out over the battlements. Superstitious perhaps, but he wanted to ensure Marcellus Vincerus was truly dead. He looked at the torso. The blade had sliced between the pale bones in the neck. Blood had gushed briefly. It looked like the corpse of any decapitated warrior Fell had seen, and he had seen many.

He looked over to Mason's body, small and hunched, a pile of rags. After all the lies, Fell felt nothing for him except indifference.

He turned his face to the sun. He still had his last task to do, his only task. He would descend again to the lair and slay the emperor. And any reflection of him he could find. Then he would join Indaro, if she lived, and leave this accursed City for good.

He made his way to the stairwell. He recalled that as he climbed it in the thrall of Marcellus it rose directly from the depths of the palace to this eyrie, no side-tunnels, no diversions. But when he went down he quickly came to a point where the stairs divided. He took the right, then right again when he had to choose. He came to a level corridor, which then started to rise, so he doubled back, but soon he was lost in a maze, ankle-deep in water again.

At last his grateful eyes detected a faint gleam of light. He stumbled towards it, sloshing through the water. The torchlight grew stronger and with a surge of relief he found he had made it back to the crystal doorway. Beyond was the Hall of Emperors and, perhaps, Indaro. He slowed and listened. There were no sounds of battle. Were they all dead? He stepped through the doorway.

The chamber was a charnel house. Hundreds of bodies lay piled on the circular floor and on the winding stairway. There were groans and cries from wounded men and women. A few exhausted warriors, dead-eyed, wandered among them despatching the gravely injured. All seemed to be wearing the uniform of the Thousand. Fell could make no sense of it. He saw a glint of coppery hair among the corpses and his heart lurched. He knelt and turned the body over but found it was a woman of middle years, with more grey than red in her hair. Her throat was slashed, her face serene.

He stood and looked around the chamber. He spotted Broglanh sitting on the stairs, his head in his hands.

Then he saw her. She had already seen him and was making her way painfully down the staircase, leaning on the wall, her eyes fixed to him. One hand clutched her belly, the other listlessly held a blade which trailed and bumped on the carpeted stairs. She was thin and pale as a wraith, drenched in blood, and her legs seemed barely to hold her up. There was a hectic light in her eyes as she held him with her gaze.

He sheathed his sword and walked towards her. They met in the centre of the great hall, surrounded by the dead. Her violet eyes were locked on him as if fixing him to her forever.

"They were waiting for us," she said calmly. "Someone told them we were coming."

"You were a diversion," he pointed out. "There's no point creating a diversion if no one knows about it."

She smiled.

"You've got blood on your teeth," he said.

Behind her a young man appeared, walking towards them. Fell watched him over Indaro's shoulder. He was scarcely more than a boy and was dressed in green silk, a stark contrast with the blood-spattered soldiers. The warriors had all stopped what they were doing to watch him pick his way around the corpses. They seemed frozen in place, unbreathing.

The boy kept glancing at Fell, a hesitant smile on his face, as if he knew him, as if he had something to say. He was very close before Fell realised he had eyes of the darkest pitch. One eyelid drooped slightly, as if he were about to wink. Fell tried for his sword, but his hand seemed to push through treacle. He opened his mouth to warn Indaro but had no words. She had her back to the boy and was only starting to realise something was wrong. Fell stared at the creature in despair, unable to drag his eyes away.

Indaro's gaze cleared as she saw the thing reflected in Fell's gaze. The hand that was limply holding the sword came up. She spun the blade to reverse it and, her eyes still fixed to Fell's, she rammed the sword backwards with all her remaining strength into the creature's chest.

When the beast came for him Riis was ready. He knew what to do. He felt a sliding weight on his chest and long teeth at his throat and he jerked back his head and grabbed the thing by the neck with his one good hand. His fingers met the wide gold collar protecting the animal's throat. He pushed down panic and shifted his grip, allowing the beast to stretch across him. As he felt its teeth slide into his neck he squeezed with all his remaining strength. The beast thrashed around, then its teeth let go.

It was hissing like a snake, its breath foul in his face. He felt its claws raking his chest and legs as it tried to get away. He gritted his teeth and squeezed ever tighter. He visualised his hand gripped around the beast's neck, even after his death. There was a cracking of bone, then he felt something give. He held on. The beast convulsed, and sighed deep in its chest. Then its body stopped moving. Riis waited, forcing himself to hold his grip. But the thing was dead.

Indaro's blade moved very slowly, inching towards the Immortal's breast. Araeon looked down, watching its progress with interest. Many people had tried to slide smooth metal into his body over the centuries. His reflexes were failing now, he recognised that, but they were still a thousand times faster than those of the primitives in the chamber. The blade was heading accurately for the descending aorta—remarkable considering the woman warrior was aiming by watching his reflection in Fell's eyes. Reflection, he thought. Ironic. Araeon decided he would step to one side, wrest the sword from her grasp and cut her head off, in front of her lover.

With part of his mind, the part which, despite everything, remained logical and disinterested, he wondered if Marcellus had been right, that he had lost all human compassion. He was a little sorry Marcellus was dead; he had been a good friend, a valuable member of the Serafim team. But the day had been fast approaching when Araeon would have had to kill him himself. And the Bitch too. Then he could step up the war and the City would prevail. He would return to the Serafia. It could be defended. It would be his base of operations, as in the old days. And the Bitch's get would be a comfort to him in his old age.

He felt the blade touch his chest.

Suddenly the disintegrating structure of his mind was pierced by a scream of terror. Deidoro! The gulon! He felt the last torment of his reflection as it gasped, a hand tight around its throat, throttling it, stopping its breath.

And in that fraction of a heartbeat Indaro's sword drove through the emperor's chest, through the great blood vessel and it burst asunder.

*   *   *

Riis fell back. He could feel clean blood pouring from his neck, washing away the pain, the horror.

He was riding a great white horse across a grassy plain towards distant mountains. The sky was ice blue and the air crystal with morning dew. He was heading for home, where his parents and his brother were waiting.

Riis smiled.

Indaro did not dare to turn. Her wild gaze was still fixed on Fell's face.

"Is he dead? Is he dead?"

Fell nodded, and she looked round.

The body lay on its back, the sword sticking up from its chest, green limbs splayed. Fell watched, half expecting it to reshape itself into the figure of a middle-aged emperor, or the demented creature from the pit of slime. But it didn't. It remained the body of a young man, with fair wispy hair which floated in the water. It looked so harmless.

Indaro's legs buckled and he caught her as she fell. He grasped her to him tightly.

"I love you," he whispered.

Chapter 48

Quintos, sergeant of the guards on the Paradise Gate, lifted his leather eyepatch and gingerly rubbed the empty socket. The vacant eye itched in the dry summer and ached all the year round. Quintos splashed his face with water drawn from the gate's cistern and the cool water felt good on the creased and puckered scar tissue.

He'd lost the eye in a scrap with the Blues in some gods-forsaken valley

deep in the Mountains of the Moon over two years before. It was Quintos'
own fault. They were winning the skirmish, the diminishing troop of Blueskins retreating before them. The enemy were far outnumbered and, Quintos had to admit, still game, but they were giving way pace by pace, death by
death. His friend and comrade Kallin Blackbeard had surged ahead and was
swinging his old broadsword, slicing throats and chests and a few backs.
Quintos had stepped in too close, leaning forward to thrust his sword into
the vitals of an injured Blue. Kallin swung back and in the moment the tip
of his sword pricked Quintos' eye neatly like piercing a pickled egg. The
surgeon had tried to save it but in days it had started to rot, then there was
no choice but to rip it out.

In the retreat back to the City he'd broken his leg in several places falling
down a rocky cliff he'd missed in the dark and that had healed badly.

His general Marcus Rae Khan had come to speak to him after that. The
lord had told Quintos he was out of the war. Only Marcus himself could say
those words and he'd accept them. The general understood fighting as well
as any common soldier and he understood the pride of the fighting man.
Marcus pledged he would find him an honoured place in service of the City
and he was as good as his word. Now Quintos guarded a gate which guarded
the City, and he could hope for no more honourable task than that.

Quintos limped back up the steps beside the great wooden gates onto the
top of the wall. It was silent up there—the unnatural silence of noise interrupted, he thought. The pause between battles.

When they heard the City had been invaded the rest of the guards had
taken arms and eagerly set off for the war in the south. Quintos hadn't
blamed them, or tried to stop them but he had stayed at his post. The great
gates were closed, barred and bolted and the army of refugees outside who
had been trying to get in all season had evaporated like dew in the night. The
Paradise quarter had been emptying since the summer, homes abandoned,
streets drifting with rubbish. But no one had tried to leave via the gate.
Quintos had not seen a soul all day.

He turned his back on the empty plain in front of the gate and surveyed
the City. His eye detected movement and he shifted his head, trying to find
perspective. A hooded man was leading a horse across a distant square in
the direction of the gate. He disappeared into the jumble of buildings and
Quintos sat down to wait for him to emerge again. The man and horse were

in no hurry and it was a while before they appeared from an alley nearby. The man was cloaked and booted, ready for a journey. Deserter, thought Quintos, and he went down to meet them.

Up close he could see the bay stallion was a fine animal, strong and well-fed although it was caked in drying mud as if it had swum across a river. The man's boots and legs were muddy too, although the cloak was new and stank of money and power. Quintos' heart hardened and he laid his hand to his blade.

Then the man threw his hood back. "Do you know me, soldier?"

It was all Quintos could do not to fall to his knees.

"Yes, lord," he breathed.

The man looked around at the silent streets, the empty wall.

"You are alone here?"

Something in his tone broke through the awe which was holding Quintos.

"Yes, lord." Then, thinking the lord might think his friends deserters, he added, "They went to fight the invaders. We were told the walls in the south were breached."

"Yet you chose to stay."

Feeling bound to explain, the soldier said, "General Marcus gave me this duty and I will do it until he or the emperor himself tells me otherwise."

Then, embarrassed by his words, he compounded it by blurting, "Are you leaving the City, lord?"

The man looked at him with pitch-black eyes. "What is your name, soldier?"

"Quintos, lord. They call me Leathereye."

"Of course they do. Will you open the gate for me, Quintos?"

The soldier ran to oblige. He checked carefully through the spyhole before pulling back the two wrist-thick lower bolts. Then, using all his strength, he lifted the great bar. It was hard for one man, but he managed it and the bar thudded back into its socket. Warm damp air gasped in from the plain, with the smell of iron and dirt on its breath. Panting a little, Quintos stood aside.

As the horseman walked through the gateway, holding the reins of his obedient mount, he paused close to Quintos. The soldier felt the power rolling off him like ocean breakers.

He asked, "Did you see anyone leave the City today, Quintos?"

"No, lord, not a soul."

The Keep collapsed with infinite slowness. Far underground, chambers unseen for hundreds of years crumbled and disintegrated. Statues carved by artists who had died a millennium before turned their blind eyes for the last time on the blackness and dissolved, condensed and flattened as the deepest strata of the City, forgotten by time, becoming one with the rocky earth. The machines of men which held the destructive floodwaters from the Keep stuttered and stopped at last. Water started seeping in through the darkest recesses of the ancient building, oozing through cracks and crannies, mounting the deepest staircases, pouring through doorways and long-abandoned corridors.

When the level started to rise in the Hall of Emperors the surviving warriors picked up Shuskara's dying body and carried him out to a rose-haunted courtyard. In a place of white pillars he was laid on a bier facing east and there they came, one by one, to say their farewells. Fell and Broglanh, and the new leader of the Nighthawks, Darius, stood at his head. Elija and Emly sat at his feet. Still shaken by the terrors of the day, Indaro lay nursing her wounds on a stone couch cushioned with winter roses.

And it was there, for the last time, that Archange came to meet the old general.

She laid a hand on his arm and he opened his eyes. There was a beat before he recognised her, then he smiled.

"I will not bandy words with you today, lady," he said.

She said nothing for a while, listening to the lifeblood slowing in his veins. Then she told him, "I cannot save you this time, Shuskara. You are too badly injured."

She looked up sternly as Emly sobbed. "Do not be sad, girl. Yesterday your father was a condemned criminal facing torment and a lonely death. Today he is the hero of the City, once again the triumphant Shuskara. His name will live forever and men will speak it with pride. Any warrior would consider that worth dying for."

"I did nothing," the general whispered. "Indaro is the hero. She battled impossible odds and she killed a man who couldn't be killed."

Archange turned to the woman warrior but her face was stone.

"Yes. Indaro," she said. "Because I believe you were a pawn in this day's work I will be merciful. I will forget I have seen you here today. But when the sun sets you will be branded a criminal and hunted down by all the forces of the City, and any who shelter you will put themselves in peril."

There were angry shouts from the other warriors but Indaro just nodded. "I will not return to my father's house. Do not seek me there."

"That would be wise."

Fell was heartsick. "Are we all to be treated like criminals?" he demanded.

Archange turned her gaze on him and he saw the depth of ages in her black eyes and his anger faded. You could be no more angry with these people than with thunder and lightning. Yet so many had died, and he was tormented by the fear that perhaps Marcellus was the best of them.

"I have been, among many other things," she told him, "an historian. And it is the task of the historian to discriminate between the traitors and the loyalists, the invaders and the liberators, the freedom fighters and the terrorists. And to place the blame. The Immortal has been assassinated. Indaro killed him. Where else would the blame lie?"

"She was part of an army. It could just as well have been me that delivered the deathblow," Fell argued.

"But it was not," she answered. "When you had the chance you felt compassion."

"I killed Marcellus," he told her.

She stared at him for a heartbeat and he wondered if this was news to her. "Do you really think you could have killed him if he had not chosen it?" Archange asked him.

She turned from Fell and placed her hand on Shuskara's heart. There was a long moment, then she said formally, "A hero of the City has died today." Emly gave a little cry and wept.

Archange looked around them as the assembled soldiers bowed their heads. "The historian also decides who was the hero, who the villain. Shuskara will be long remembered when the Vincerus name is dust."

"Forgive me, lady." The old man in the corner was leaning heavily on a stick. Fell had never seen him before. "The woman skewered a boy, barely more than a child. Was that the emperor?"

Archange looked around her, frowning, and Darius swiftly brought a chair. She seated herself beside the general's body, arranging her skirts around her.

"Where I come from, Dol Salida," she said, "it is possible to create life and place it in bodies of flesh and make them live. We call these creations reflections. Their life is dependent on their creator. Araeon—the emperor— created many of these, several hundred I would guess over the years. Most were replicas of himself, but some were unlike him, some not even human. Araeon could also, with the same . . . magics . . . create different appearances for himself. In recent years the boy in green was one he often returned to."

She sighed. "He was a giant among us, the oldest of us, our hero and our father. But even the strongest weaken in the end."

She was silent for a while and Fell wondered if that was all the explanation they would be given, but she went on, "And Marcellus was one of the youngest, a genius in his way, an orphan. He was lonely, I believe, even among such a close-knit group as we once were. He created only one reflection in his long life. A brother."

"Rafe?" the old man said, "What happened to him?"

She told him, "A reflection cannot exist without its original. Rafe died when Marcellus did."

Suddenly Fell realised he could not wait to be away from this place, this palace with its evil eternal creatures living together for centuries, self-involved, incestuous, infecting the entire City with their poisonous blood. He looked at Indaro, who was still frowning at Archange's words. We will leave here, he thought, and we will never return.

Archange had fallen silent, and was fingering the silvery veil around her throat.

For the first time the child Emly spoke up. "My veil," she said. Fell thought her voice was creaky, as if rusty and unused. "How did you come by it?"

Archange looked down. The tiny metal and glass beasts adorning the hem shone in the sunlight.

"It is mine," she told the girl. "It was always mine."

She slipped the veil from her shoulders and, with a sweeping gesture, laid it on the ground in front of them, so they could all see the circular parade of animals. Fell crouched down to look at it. It seemed to be made of thousands of the thinnest threads of silver. In the centre a stitchwork gulon sat with its brush tucked neatly round its paws.

"It was lost for years and has been hard-used," Archange told the girl. "Where did *you* come by it?"

Emly dipped her head, self-conscious now all were watching her. "In the Halls. Father found it on a corpse."

"A corpse with tattoos on his head?" Emly nodded. Archange frowned. "Then Bartellus had it with him when we first met in the Halls?"

"Yes."

The old woman smiled ruefully and shook her head. "Many deaths could have been prevented had I known that at the time," she said. "It is the most valuable artefact in the world," she told them all. "It is also the oldest. Only the eternal mountains are older. And I sometimes think it has a mind of its own."

"Is it magic?" Emly asked.

"In your terms I suppose it is. Its threads were once part of a shell, like a butterfly's chrysalis, within which the reflections were born. But the chrysalis was destroyed, smashed to smithereens, five hundred years ago. It took us a very long time to find a way of reconstructing the threads and weaving them together again. It has never worked properly since, but it will." She smiled at Em. Standing, she rearranged it around her shoulders.

As if on cue soldiers of the Thousand marched in. The black-bearded leader glanced around the assembled warriors and his gaze rested for a moment on Fell and Indaro. Then he spoke quietly to Archange.

"I am to speak to my counsellors," she told them. "We have much to discuss."

"What happens now, lady?" Fell asked her. "Will you surrender the City?"

She seemed reluctant to answer, and he said, "Marcellus claimed the last of the Serafim will ride down from the Shield and continue the battle."

She was fiddling with the veil like a finicky old lady. "Do not question me, Fell," she said mildly.

He allowed anger to sound in his voice. "We fought this battle so the war would end," he said. "We will not see that betrayed."

"Who do you think you are talking to!" she asked him. Suddenly she had grown taller, and her eyes flashed with a black power which rocked him back on his heels. The air in the courtyard crackled as though struck by lightning and he was blinded by the glare.

"How dare you speak of betrayal! You are traitors and are only alive this moment on my whim," she cried.

When he looked again he saw all the roses round the courtyard had blackened and charred. A cold wind whipped through the white pillars and the flowers fell to dust. He heard a child's sob of fear, then a moan and he looked to Indaro. He saw her wounds had opened again and rushed to her side.

Archange had seated herself once more and she looked as he had seen her before, a handsome old woman in pale blue robes.

"You have won today's battle," she said quietly. "Araeon and Marcellus are both dead. I am no soldier and I do not wish to prolong the slaughter. The Serafim will not ride out. I will see to that. But the City will not surrender to its enemies."

"You will not fight but you will not surrender," Fell commented evenly.

"I will follow the example of women throughout history and bend, like a reed, with the winds of history," she said.

Liar, Fell thought. You will ruthlessly force others to do your will, just as you have always done.

"A thousand thousand years ago," Archange said, her voice so quiet it barely stirred the air, "in a place called Cumae there was a woman renowned as a seeress, a sybil. Her fame came to the attention of the gods who, then as now, were jealous and could be whimsical and cunning and cruel within one action. The sun god appeared to the woman on the beach at sunrise. He spoke respectfully and told her her wisdom had impressed him and he offered to grant her a wish. She bent and scooped up a handful of sand, and asked the god to grant her as many years as were grains in her grasp. He agreed, proving, at least to his own satisfaction, that she was not as wise as she thought, for she did not ask for eternal youth, and was condemned to grow older and more crabbed and pained as the centuries marched on."

Fell wondered if this was a plea for understanding. But, as with Marcellus at the end, he felt only dislike for the woman.

Archange stood and turned to the girl. "Come with me, Emly. I will see your brother gets the aid he needs. Dol Salida, you have my thanks for this day's work. Now I have another task for you."

She swept from the room, soldiers clattering after her, and finally the only ones left with the old man's body were Fell, Indaro and Broglanh.

Fell said, "I wonder if Shuskara would be happy to know he died as part of that woman's game," he said.

Broglanh said cheerfully, "We're soldiers—we're always pieces in someone's game. But we are alive and the emperor is dead. That was the plan. The plan succeeded. Today was a good day."

He looked at Indaro and his smile faded. "Where will you go, Red?"

"I don't know."

"You need medical care."

She shook her head wearily. "There's no time. I must be far from the City by dawn."

Fell took her hand. It was so small, the skin rough and calloused under the blood and dirt. He raised it to his mouth and kissed it. "We will both be gone by dawn," he said.

The inside of the jolting carriage was splashed with colour, soft blues and greens and pinks all over the walls and ceiling. Emly had spent so long in the dark she had forgotten such colours existed. Beside her a painted horse trotted across a cornfield under a sunset sky. The girl traced the animal's outline, feeling the tiny brushstrokes of the jaunty tail under her fingertip.

Glancing at the old woman, who seemed to be asleep, she kicked off her boots and pulled her feet up on the carriage seat. The soft material, like rabbit's fur, was delicious on her bare skin.

Elija was lying on the opposite seat. He was dead to the world, in a deep, healing lorassium sleep. His arm had been set and splinted by a kind, grave man who told her it would knit well, for he was young.

Then Archange had come to her again and asked the question for the third time. *Will you let me take care of you, Emly?* Gratefully, this time she said yes. Her father was dead and she was a young woman in a ruined city full of soldiers. And she had her brother to think of. She thought longingly of Evan, but a wide streak of practicality told her she could not rely on the warrior as a protector. She would accept Archange's help and be grateful for it.

So now they were riding through the city in a carriage drawn by six horses, with outriders before and behind. They were heading east, towards the great mountain called the Shield of Freedom. Em stuck her head out of the window. This part of the City had not been damaged by the floods, and people were hurrying by with piles of possessions on their backs, or on donkeys, or on old carts. Many of them looked up at the imperial carriage with dead, or envious, eyes. She guessed they were leaving the invaded City, for they all seemed to be moving with a purpose, but some were going one way, some another; there seemed no rhyme or reason.

She looked up. On the steep slopes of the Shield the afternoon sunlight lit the palaces dotted among swathes of dark forest. She could make out a winding white road, ever rising, which would appear for a while then plunge back into the trees. Emly wondered if they were travelling up there. She hoped so. She craned her neck but could not see the top of the mountain. Is there a palace right at the top? she thought. Is that where Archange lives?

She considered if she could get word to Evan, but he had been close to Archange's side since they left the Red Palace, so she guessed he probably knew where she was. There was to be a hero's funeral for Bartellus in two days' time, and Evan Broglanh would certainly be there.

Em became aware of the thunder of hooves, growing louder. She peered out. The men and horses, a small army it seemed, were armoured in grey and she realised, her chest tightening, that these were the enemy. She retreated into the carriage and looked anxiously to Archange. The old woman seemed to be sleeping peacefully, her head supported on a soft cushion in the corner of the carriage. But without opening her eyes she said, "Don't be afraid. They won't harm you."

Then she roused herself and sat up, patting down a stray hair, rearranging the neck of her gown.

Reassured, Emly gazed out again and saw a rider had detached himself from the body of the army and was speaking with the leader of Archange's guard. The old woman waited impatiently for a few moments, then she leaned across Em and called sharply, "General!"

The men turned towards her and she cried, "Let him through, you fools!"

The rider was garbed in dark travel-stained clothes, a uniform of some sort, Emly thought, with an insignia on his breast. He was old, with long unkempt grey hair, and he looked as though he had not slept for a week. He appeared to be unarmed.

"Greetings, lady," he said, coming up to the carriage door. He opened it but stood outside in the dust. His voice was rough as though he had been inhaling sand, but he did not sound like a foreigner to Em's ears.

"Hayden," Archange replied. She reached forward a skinny hand and he touched her pale fingers with his dirty stubby ones.

"I regret to tell you your brother is dead," she told him briskly, sounding anything but regretful.

"I feared so," he said calmly, but Em thought she saw a light go out in his gaze. "How did he die?"

"Marcellus killed him."

The soldier nodded. "Appropriate," he said. "Marcellus is also dead, I'm told."

"He killed himself."

The soldier frowned. "Marcellus is the last person I would expect to take his own life."

She shrugged. "You did not know him well. I spoke to the soldier who was with him. It is clear to me that he chose to die."

The man said nothing, and after a moment Archange went on, "In a thousand years one can accumulate a lot of deeds one is not proud of. I think the burden of these weighed heavily on his soul. He had lived too long. I don't think he planned it. I think it was a sudden impulse, a whim in the heat of battle."

The windows of the carriage darkened as two enemy soldiers came up to Hayden. One spoke to him briefly while the other handed him a leather cup. He gave quiet orders, then rinsed his mouth out and spat on the ground.

"This changes nothing, Archange," he told her. "Our pact still stands. I will start to withdraw my army tomorrow."

"'Start to'?" she repeated. "You invaded the City in a matter of hours. You will leave as quickly."

"I do not wish to stay in this charnel house, believe me. But we have far to travel and many wounded to consider."

"We have discussed this. We will keep your wounded safe if you leave your medics to care for them and for our own injured."

"I trust your word, lady. But I cannot trust your armies."

"Yet you must. As I must trust yours. There have been tales of rapine and looting," she said.

"And those men have been executed. They were all mercenaries. Our forthcoming war is a holy one. We will start it as we mean to proceed, with honour and justice."

Archange sighed and glanced at the two youngsters. The rider looked at Em and Elija as though seeing them for the first time. "Who are these?"

"They are young relatives I am seeing to safety. Then I shall meet Marcus."

"I have been promised his army."

"And you will have it." She sat forward. "Hayden. You have liberated our City. The people of the City will now help you free your own lands. You have my word. But with Araeon and Marcellus and Rafael all dead I have much to do. It will take a while for my own people to fill their places. We will meet at sunset, as we agreed. I will have Marcus with me." She sat back and smoothed down her dress. "And his army."

"Who will be your first counsellor?"

"A man called Dol Salida. He is an old soldier, like you, and a man of subtlety and intelligence. You will like him and you will be able to do business with him."

"And Araeon's generals? Will you retain any?"

"A few. Those promoted by Marcellus. Most are dead. And those that survived largely did so by running away. They were buffoons and are best forgotten. I have my own men." She glanced at Em, who was taking in every word. "We will discuss this later."

He nodded and made to leave, then he turned back and said, "It is good to see you again, Archange."

She smiled. "And you, old friend," she said.

There was silence in the carriage as they listened to the Blues riding away.

Em sorted through everything that had been said. "Who is Marcus?" she asked finally.

"Marcus Rae Khan is a general and one of us, a Serafim."

Em thought of what had been said about generals, and she asked shyly, "Will Evan be made a general?"

Archange snorted. "No, girl, he is far too valuable to me to waste."

She smiled and said, "You will find men talk a great deal about honour and loyalty, whether they are soldiers or merchants or lovers or thieves. Be careful. If a man speaks to you of his honour remember he is speaking from the most selfish part of his heart. Did Evan Broglanh use such words to bring you to his bed?"

Em bowed her head a little and thought before she spoke, as she had seen Archange do. Then she asked, "Does that mean you do not trust your friend Hayden?"

Archange smiled thinly. "I trust him to do what is in his best interests, which today are in line with mine."

She turned and punched the cushion behind her head and leaned back into it. "Now, be silent, girl. I have much to do today and I am no longer young." She closed her eyes firmly.

Em settled herself back and picked up the box lying on the seat beside her. Archange had entrusted it to her. It was carved of shining white wood, a thing of beauty. She held it on her lap and undid the tiny gold bolt. Inside the Gulon Veil shimmered as if alive. It was neatly folded to fit the box and two of its tiny figurines lay on top. They were the golden wyvern, made for Em by the goldsmith in Parting Street, and the glass rabbit Frayling had created. She stroked the little rabbit and tears welled in her eyes as she thought of Frayling.

"Emly."

She looked up. Elija's eyes were open and he was looking at her. Instantly she was on her knees beside him, holding his good hand in both of hers.

"Where are we?" His brow furrowed as he gazed around the moving carriage. "Where are we going?"

"We're safe," she assured him. "Safe," she repeated. "The empress is going to take care of us."

He nodded, but she was sure he did not understand. His eyes closed and he drifted back to sleep. She sat holding his hand for a while, then her head drooped against his chest and Emly slept too.

Epilogue

They fled the City. They fled all cities. They crossed land and sea, moving lightly, keeping to the less-travelled roads, always racing from the past.

The days were short when they reached the shore of a rocky island in the misty north, where summers were cool, winters bitter, and where the wind howled across the bleak flats all year round. The people of the island were wild and quiet, and they answered to no city or government, for the only powers they recognised were their harsh gods and the winter storms. They gazed sideways at the penniless newcomers, with their scars and their haunted eyes, but they left them alone. No one knew where they came from. No one cared.

The man and woman found a house in the lee of the small graveyard, its mossy grey stones tilted by the winds. They saw the irony in it, but it was a quiet place, even for this island, and they were both comfortable with the dead.

They never spoke about the past, and they were afraid to wish for the future. They spoke little together, and when they did it was of the movements of the weather, the changes of the sea. They were proud of their first crops, green seedlings pushing through the dark unforgiving soil, and the small fishing boat they built together on that first winter.

It was spring when she fell sick, but it was only when her stomach became round and hard that they realised, with awe, that she was carrying a child. They had never thought it possible, with her wounds. It was a hard labour, but when the child slipped out, thin and bony as a leveret, and he saw it was a girl Fell wept for the first time since he was a child. The girl had her father's sky blue eyes and black hair, and her mother's temperament. She grew thin and strong on the harsh land and, as the years passed, she nursed their souls and healed their wounds . . .